FROM THE PAGES OF
THE HOUSE OF THE DEAD AND
POOR FOLK

In the remote parts of Siberia in the midst of steppes, mountains, or impassable forests, there are scattered here and there wretched little wooden towns of one, or at the most two, thousand inhabitants, with two churches, one in the town and one in the cemetery—more like fair-sized villages in the neighbourhood of Moscow than towns.

(from *The House of the Dead*, page 7)

Our prison stood at the edge of the fortress grounds, close to the fortress wall. One would sometimes, through a chink in the fence, take a peep into God's world to try and see something; but one could see only a strip of the sky and the high earthen wall overgrown with coarse weeds, and on the wall sentries pacing up and down day and night.

(from *The House of the Dead*, page 12)

I realized that besides the loss of freedom, besides the forced labour, there is another torture in prison life, almost more terrible than any other—that is, compulsory life in common. Life in common is to be found of course in other places, but there are men in prison whom not everyone would care to associate with and I am certain that every convict felt this torture, though of course in most cases unconsciously.

(from *The House of the Dead*, pages 26–27)

Life in prison was so dreary, a convict is a creature by nature so eager for freedom, and from his social position so careless and reckless, that to "have his fling for all he is worth," to spend all his fortune carousing with noise and music and so to forget his depression, if only for the moment, naturally attracts him.

(from *The House of the Dead*, page 43)

The prison authorities are sometimes surprised that after leading a quiet, exemplary life for some years, and even being made a foreman for his model behaviour, a convict with no apparent reason suddenly breaks out, as though he were possessed by a devil, plays pranks, drinks, makes an uproar and sometimes positively ventures on serious crimes—such as open disrespect to a superior officer, or even commits murder or rape. They look at him and marvel. And all the while possibly the cause of this sudden outbreak, in the man from whom one would least have expected it, is simply the poignant hysterical craving for self-expression, the unconscious yearning for himself, the desire to assert himself, to assert his crushed personality, a desire which suddenly takes possession of him and reaches the pitch of fury, of spite, of mental aberration, of fits and nervous convulsions.

(from *The House of the Dead*, pages 83–84)

The other day the editor of the notes from "The House of the Dead" received information from Siberia that the criminal really was innocent and had suffered ten years in penal servitude for nothing.

(from *The House of the Dead*, page 255)

His name is Gorshkov—such a grey little man; he goes about in such greasy, such threadbare clothes that it is sad to see him; ever so much worse than mine. He is a pitiful, decrepit figure (we sometimes meet in the passage); his knees shake, his hands shake, his head shakes, from some illness I suppose, poor fellow.

(from *Poor Folk*, page 318)

The whole family lives in one room, only divided by a screen for decency. There was a little coffin standing in the room already—a simple little coffin, but rather pretty; they bought it ready-made; the boy was nine years old, he was a promising boy, they say.

(from *Poor Folk*, page 352)

Why does it happen that a good man is left forlorn and forsaken, while happiness seems thrust upon another?

(from *Poor Folk*, page 396)

What good are frills and flounces? Why, it is nonsense, Varinka! Here it is a question of a man's life: and you know a frill's a rag; it's a rag, Varinka, a frill is; why, I shall buy you frills myself, that's all the reward I get; I shall buy them for you, my darling, I know a shop, that's all the reward you let me hope for, my cherub, Varinka.

(from *Poor Folk*, page 423)

THE HOUSE OF
THE DEAD
AND
POOR FOLK

Fyodor Dostoevsky

Translated by Constance Garnett

With an Introduction by Joseph Frank
Notes by Elina Yuffa

George Stade
Consulting Editorial Director

BARNES & NOBLE CLASSICS
NEW YORK

BARNES & NOBLE CLASSICS
NEW YORK

Published by Barnes & Noble Books
122 Fifth Avenue
New York, NY 10011

www.barnesandnoble.com/classics

Poor Folk was first published in 1846 as *Bednyye lyudi*. *The House of the Dead* was first published in 1861 as *Zapiski iz myortvogo doma*. Constance Garnett's translation of *The House of the Dead* first appeared in 1915; her translation of *Poor Folk* appeared in the collection *The Gambler and Other Stories* in 1917.

Published in 2004 by Barnes & Noble Classics with new Introduction, Notes, Biography, Chronology, Inspired By, Comments & Questions, and For Further Reading.

Introduction
Copyright © 2004 by Joseph Frank.

Note on Fyodor Dostoevsky; The World of Fyodor Dostoevsky, *The House of the Dead* and *Poor Folk*; Notes; Inspired by *The House of the Dead*; Comments & Questions; and For Further Reading
Copyright © 2004 by Barnes & Noble, Inc.

"The Peasant Marey" is from Fyodor Dostoevsky's *A Writer's Diary*, Vol. 1, 1873–1876, translated by Kenneth Lantz (Evanston, IL: Northwestern University Press). Copyright © 1994 by Northwestern University Press. Reprinted by permission of the publisher.

The House of the Dead and Poor Folk
ISBN 978-1-59308-194-2
LC Control Number 2003116509

Produced and published in conjunction with:
Fine Creative Media, Inc.
322 Eighth Avenue
New York, NY 10001

Michael J. Fine, President and Publisher

Printed in the United States of America

QM

9   11   13   15   17   16   14   12   10

FYODOR DOSTOEVSKY

Fyodor Mikhailovitch Dostoevsky was born in Moscow on October 30, 1821. His mother died when he was fifteen, and his father, a strict but conscientious former army surgeon, sent him and his older brother, Mikhail, to preparatory school in St. Petersburg. Fyodor continued his education at the St. Petersburg Academy of Military Engineers and graduated as a lieutenant in 1843. After serving as a military engineer for a short time, and inheriting some money from his father's estate, he retired from the army and decided instead to devote himself to writing.

Dostoevsky won immediate recognition with the 1846 publication of his first work of fiction, a short novel titled *Poor Folk*. The important Russian critic Vissarion Grigorievitch Belinsky praised his work and introduced him into the literary circles of St. Petersburg. Over the next few years Dostoevsky published several stories, including "The Double" and "White Nights." He also became involved with a progressive group known as the Petrashevsky Circle, headed by the charismatic utopian socialist Mikhail Petrashevsky. In 1849 Czar Nicholas I ordered the arrest of all the members of the group, including Dostoevsky. He was kept in solitary confinement for eight months while the charges against him were investigated and then, along with other members of Petrashevsky's group, was sentenced to death by firing squad. At the last minute Nicholas commuted the sentence to penal servitude in Siberia for four years, and then service in the Russian Army—but only at the last minute. This near-execution haunts much of Dostoevsky's subsequent writing.

The ten years Dostoevsky spent in prison and then in exile in Siberia had a profound effect on him. By the time he returned to St. Petersburg in 1859, he had rejected his radical ideas and acquired a new respect for the religious ideas and ideals of the Russian people. He had never been an atheist, but his Christianity was now closer to the Orthodox faith. While in exile he had also married.

Dostoevsky quickly resumed his literary career in St. Petersburg. He and his brother Mikhail founded two journals, *Vremya* (1861–1863) and *Epokha* (1864–1865). Dostoevsky published many of his well-known post-Siberian works in these journals, including *The House of the Dead*, an account of his prison experiences, and the dark, complex novella "Notes from Underground."

The next several years of Dostoevsky's life were marked by the deaths of his wife, Maria, and his brother Mikhail. He began to gamble compulsively on his trips abroad, and he suffered from bouts of epilepsy. In 1866, while dictating his novel *The Gambler* to meet a deadline, he met a young stenographer, Anna Snitkina, and the two married a year later. Over the next fifteen years Dostoevsky produced his finest works, including the novels *Crime and Punishment* (1866), *The Idiot* (1868), *The Possessed* (1871–1872), and *The Brothers Karamazov* (1879–1880). His novels are complex psychological studies that examine man's struggle with such elemental issues as good and evil, life and death, belief and reason. Fyodor Mikailovitch Dostoevsky died from a lung hemorrhage on January 28, 1881, in St. Petersburg at the age of fifty-nine.

TABLE OF CONTENTS

THE WORLD OF FYODOR DOSTOEVSKY, THE HOUSE OF THE DEAD AND POOR FOLK

1821   Fyodor Mikhailovitch Dostoevsky is born on October 30 in Moscow. The second of seven children, he grows up in a middle-class household run by his father, a former army surgeon and strict family man.

1833   Aleksandr Pushkin's novel in verse *Eugene Onegin* is published.

1837   Fyodor's mother dies. He and his older brother Mikhail are sent to a preparatory school in St. Petersburg.

1838   Dostoevsky begins his tenure at the St. Petersburg Academy of Military Engineers, where he studies until 1843. He becomes acquainted with the works of such writers as Byron, Corneille, Dickens, Goethe, Gogol, Homer, Hugo, Pushkin, Racine, Rousseau, Shakespeare, and Schiller.

1839   Dostoevsky's father is, according to rumor, murdered on his country estate, presumably by his own serfs.

1842   Part 1 of Nikolay Gogol's novel *Dead Souls* is published.

1843   Dostoevsky graduates from the Academy as a lieutenant, but instead of pursuing a career in the army, resolves to dedicate his life to writing.

1844   His first published work appears, a Russian translation of Honoré de Balzac's 1833 novel *Eugénie Grandet*. Dostoevsky begins work on his first novel, *Poor Folk*.

1845   On the basis of *Poor Folk*, Dostoevsky wins the friendship and acclaim of Russia's premier literary critic, Vissarion Grigorievitch Belinsky, later author of the scathingly critical "Letter to Gogol" (1847).

1846   *Poor Folk* and "The Double" are published. "The Double" is the first work in which Dostoevsky writes about the psychology of the split self. Dostoevsky meets the utopian socialist M. V. Butashevitch-Petrashevsky.

1847   Dostoevsky publishes numerous short stories, including "A Weak Heart," "Polzunkov," and "The Landlady."

1848   He publishes the short story "White Nights." The *Communist Manifesto*, by Karl Marx and Friedrich Engels, is published. Revolutions break out in France, Germany, Hungary, Italy, and Poland.

1849   Dostoevsky is arrested for his participation in the socialist Petrashevsky Circle. He first spends eight months in solitary confinement and is then condemned to death by firing-squad. Czar Nicholas I commutes his sentence to penal servitude in Siberia, but orders this to be announced only at the last minute.

1850   Dostoevsky begins his four-year internment at Omsk prison in western Siberia. While imprisoned he abandons the radical ideas of his youth and becomes more deeply religious; his only book in prison is a copy of the Bible.

1852   Part 2 of Gogol's *Dead Souls* is published.

1853   The Crimean War breaks out, the cause being a dispute between Russia and France over the Palestinian holy places.

1854   Still exiled in Siberia, Dostoevsky begins four years of compulsory military service.

1857   He marries the widow Maria Dmitrievna Isaeva.

1859   Dostoevsky and Maria are allowed to return to St. Petersburg.

1861   He and his brother Mikhail establish *Vremya* (Time); the journal publishes Dostoevsky's *The House of the Dead*, a work based on his experiences in Siberia.

1862   Dostoevsky travels to England, France, Germany, Italy, and Switzerland, a trip that engenders in him an anti-European outlook. He gambles heavily at resorts abroad, losing money.

1863   Dostoevsky makes a second trip to Europe and arranges to meet Apollinaria Suslova in Paris; he had published a story by her in *Vremya* the previous year. The two have an affair.

1863   The progressive Nikolay Chernyshevsky publishes the utopian novel *What Is to Be Done?*, which Dostoevsky will react against a year later in "Notes from Underground." *Vremya* is banned for printing an article mistakenly thought to support the Polish rebellion.

1864   Dostoevsky and his brother Mikhail establish *Epokha* (Epoch), the short-lived successor to *Vremya*; the journal publishes "Notes from Underground," the first of Dostoevsky's masterworks. Dostoevsky's wife, Maria, dies from tuberculosis. His brother Mikhail dies three months later.

1865   Burdened with debt, Dostoevsky embarks on another failed gambling spree in Europe. He proposes to Apollinaria Suslova without success.

1866   *Crime and Punishment* starts serial publication at the beginning of the year. Dostoevsky interrupts the writing in October in order to work on *The Gambler*, forced to meet the contract deadline for that book in order to retain the rights to his published works, including *Crime and Punishment*. He dictates *The Gambler* to a stenographer, Anna Grigorievna Snitkina, over the course of a month. He and Anna, who is twenty-five years his junior, become romantically involved.

1867   Dostoevsky marries Anna Snitkina, one of the most fortunate events of his life. To escape debtor's prison, the two live abroad for the next four years, in Geneva, Florence, Vienna, Prague, and finally Dresden. Dostoevsky's epilepsy worsens. He begins work on his novel *The Idiot*, in which the protagonist is an epileptic. The first three of what will be six volumes of Leo Tolstoy's *War and Peace* appear in print in December, bound in yellow covers.

1868   *The Idiot* is published in installments this year and the next. The fourth volume of *War and Peace* appears in March.

1869   The final volumes of *War and Peace* are published: the fifth in February and the sixth in December.

1871   Dostoevsky and his wife return to St. Petersburg. Serialization of his novel *The Possessed* begins.

1873   Dostoevsky becomes editor of the conservative weekly *Grazhdanin* (The Citizen); "A Writer's Diary" becomes a regular and popular feature of the weekly.

1875   Tolstoy begins publishing *Anna Karenina*.

1876   *A Writer's Diary* is published as a monojournal—that is, written and edited entirely by Dostoevsky; in it he publishes "The Meek One."

1877   "The Dream of a Ridiculous Man" is published in *A Writer's Diary*.

1879   *A Writer's Diary* ceases, and serialization begins in another journal of *The Brothers Karamazov*, widely considered Dostoevsky's greatest novel.

1880 Six months before his death, Dostoevsky delivers his famous speech on Pushkin at the dedication of the Pushkin memorial in Moscow.

1881 Dostoevsky dies from a lung hemorrhage on January 28 in St. Petersburg. His epitaph, also the epigraph to *The Brothers Karamazov*, is from the Bible (John 12:24); it reads, "Verily, verily, I say unto you, Except a corn of wheat fall into the ground and die, it abideth alone: but if it die, it bringeth forth much fruit" (King James Version).

1886 The German philosopher Friedrich Nietzsche publishes *Beyond Good and Evil*, which was greatly influenced by *The Possessed*.

1912 Constance Garnett begins her translations of the works of Dostoevsky, introducing his writings to the English-reading world.

INTRODUCTION

If one were asked to select two books of Dostoevsky that represent the variety and range of his literary talent, no better choice could be made than the ones published in this volume. Dostoevsky is best known for his larger and later novels, such as *Crime and Punishment* and *The Devils* (also translated as *The Possessed*), and an influential critical tradition views him primarily as the unsurpassed chronicler of the moral-psychological dilemmas of the alienated, refractory urban intelligentsia. This aspect of his work has had the greatest influence on later writers, particularly as he became more widely read outside of Russia; but it represents much too limited a perspective on the full scope of his creations.

To be sure, there are elements of the later Dostoevsky in *Poor Folk*, with its vivid depiction of the St. Petersburg background and its first embryonic sketch of educated types; but its main character is not a member of the intelligentsia at all and anything but rebellious. He is a humble, socially and emotionally downtrodden clerk in the vast Russian bureaucracy of St. Petersburg, frightened to death at his temerity in questioning, even in thought, the supreme virtues of the God-ordained order in which he lives.

The House of the Dead, on the other hand, stands alone in the Dostoevsky corpus as an unprecedented depiction, the first in Russian literature, of the prison gulags of the vast czarist empire. Dostoevsky's initial readers were shocked by the conditions of life he described, but we have since learned from Solzhenitsyn that these gulags were relatively humane compared to their successors under the Bolsheviks. The book also contains a gallery of Russian peasant types and sketches of Russian peasant life that equal those of Turgenev and Tolstoy, both of whom admired the book (Tolstoy thought it the best work Dostoevsky had ever written). Such peasant types are depicted only fleetingly in the major novels; but they were by no means, as we see here, outside Dostoevsky's creative purview.

These two books are thus miles apart in theme and artistic treatment. The first initiates Dostoevsky's exploration of guilt-ridden characters; the second demonstrates his ability as an objective reporter and observer of a new social milieu. But there is one thing they have in common: Both opened the path to fame (if not to fortune) for their author. Poor Folk brought him to the forefront of the Russian literary scene at the age of twenty-four, and for a brief period he was, quite literally, the talk of the town.

Dostoevsky began The House of the Dead when he was thirty-nine, having returned to Russia after serving a prison sentence in Siberia and being absent from the literary scene for ten years. His first creations at this time, the novellas Uncle's Dream and The Friend of the Family, were received quite tepidly, and it was generally felt that his talent had not survived his exile. His prison memoirs, however, convinced even his detractors that they had been mistaken. These memoirs created a sensation by opening up a hitherto concealed world for the Russian reader; and the outcast criminal inhabitants of this hidden universe, generally looked down upon as little better than subhuman, were treated by Dostoevsky with respect and even occasionally with sympathy. He made no effort to conceal their sometimes horrendous crimes; but he saw them as sentient human beings whose behavior deserved to be understood if not pardoned.

2

Poor Folk is Dostoevsky's first novel, and the story of its creation, as well as its reception, has become famous in the annals of Russian literature. Both Dostoevsky and his older brother, Mikhail, had made up their minds as adolescents to follow a literary career. Both, however, obeyed the wishes of their father to study to become military engineers, and Dostoevsky was still taking advanced courses, though living independently, in the years just preceding his literary debut. Even before leaving home for their studies, he and Mikhail had steeped themselves in the literature of their time. Indeed, the admiration of the youthful Fyodor for Pushkin was so great that, on hearing of the poet's death in a duel (in 1837), he told his family that if he had not already been wearing mourning for his mother, he would have done so in memory of Pushkin. One of the very last speeches he made in his life was a panegyric of Pushkin as equal, if not superior, to the greatest writers of European literature.

Dostoevsky came to maturity during a transition period in Russian culture, a moment when it was evolving from the metaphysical-spiritual influence of German Romanticism toward the more down-to-earth social thematics of the French. His letters to Mikhail are thus filled with references to writers of both types. E. T. A. Hoffmann enjoyed a tremendous vogue at this time in Russia, and in 1838 Fyodor writes that he had read "all of Hoffmann in Russian and German." He continued to admire this Romantic fabulist; in 1861 he wrote an article declaring him superior to Edgar Allan Poe. But he was enthusiastically proclaiming simultaneously that "Balzac is great. His characters are the creations of universal mind!" (letter of August 9, 1838). Dostoevsky's first publication, as a matter of fact, was a translation of Balzac's *Eugénie Grandet*, undertaken at the end of 1843 to supplement his income.

No French writer was more important for Dostoevsky than Victor Hugo, who, as the poet wrote of himself, "pleaded for those who are the lowest and the most miserable." In a letter of 1840 Dostoevsky declared Hugo's Christian social Romanticism to be as momentous for the modern world as Homer had been for the ancient; and Hugo's social-Christian radicalism left a permanent imprint on his own ideological views. One of Hugo's works, *Le dernier jour d'un condamné* (*The Last Day of a Condemned Man*), is the diary of someone awaiting execution for an unspecified crime—an intensely moving, and still very relevant, anguished outcry against capital punishment. Dostoevsky knew it by heart; and when he believed he was going to be executed himself, phrases from it came to his mind. Traces of its effect can also be found throughout his novels.

In the early 1840s, the most prestigious literary genre was still that of Romantic tragedy, with Russians like Pushkin (*Boris Godunov*) following in the footsteps of Shakespeare, Schiller, and Hugo. It is thus no surprise to learn that Dostoevsky's first try at literary composition should have been in this genre. In 1841 he read to friends parts of two dramas, *Mary Stuart* and *Boris Godunov*, which, alas, have not survived. But the titles are enough to show the range of his literary ambition, which did not hesitate to measure itself against the greatest. Romantic drama, however, was already losing its appeal for the younger generation, and Dostoevsky's own evolution followed the literary trend.

The new vogue turned to the social thematics of French Romanticism, as well as to the prose forms that were being developed, such as the so-called "physiological sketch," to portray the feel and texture of ordinary life. One of the dominating figures of Russian literature, the impassioned and fiery critic Vissarion Belinsky, had become converted to French Utopian Socialism in 1841, and immediately began to urge Russian writers to follow the French example. Gogol's *Dead Souls* had been published in 1842, and his *Petersburg Tales*, including "The Overcoat," in 1843. Belinsky interpreted Gogol very freely as having pioneered the down-to-earth and socially conscious depiction of Russian life that he wished to encourage; and in 1843—as Dr. Riesenkampf, with whom Dostoevsky shared a flat, tells us in his memoirs—Dostoevsky "was particularly fond of reading Gogol and loved to declaim pages of *Dead Souls* by heart."

Dostoevsky did not immediately surrender the idea of writing for the stage, but his references at this time to a work called *The Jew Yankel* (from a character in Gogol's novel *Taras Bulba*) indicate a shift to a less elevated subject. Whether such a work was ever written remains in doubt; but in the early fall of 1844 he tells Mikhail he is working on "a rather original novel" which he hopes will bring in 400 rubles. This is the first reference to *Poor Folk*; Dostoevsky planned to send the manuscript to Belinsky's journal *Notes of the Fatherland*, but it reached its destination by a much more original route.

3

Dostoevsky was then sharing a flat with D. V. Grigorovich, himself a burgeoning writer, and read him the completed work. Grigorovich was so impressed that he took the manuscript to N. A. Nekrasov, destined to become a famous poet and already an active literary editor. Both were so overcome that they rushed to Dostoevsky's apartment at four in the morning—it was a Petersburg "white night"—to congratulate him on his accomplishment. Both were among a group of young writers who, clustered around Belinsky, were known as his *pléiade*; and Nekrasov took the manuscript to Belinsky the next day. Belinsky's reaction is best described in the words of P. V. Annenkov, an important critic and cultural commentator, who visited him two days later. "You see this manuscript?" he said. "I haven't been able to tear myself away from it for almost two days now. It's a novel by a beginner, a new talent . . . but his novel reveals such secrets of life and character in Russia as no one before even dreamed of . . . —it's the first attempt at a social novel we've had" (P. V. Annenkov, *The Extraordinary Decade*, translated by Irwin R. Titunik, Ann Arbor: University of Michigan Press, 1968, p. 150).

Belinsky's enthusiasm is quite understandable because, as Dostoevsky wrote to Mikhail shortly after joining the *pléiade* himself, he "seriously sees in me *a public proof* and justification of his opinions" (letter of October 8, 1845). The critic had called for the Russians to follow the French lead, and lower-class Russian life had now begun to be depicted in all its varieties (a famous sketch of Grigorovich, used by Dostoevsky in *Poor Folk*, was devoted to organ-grinders). But emphasis was placed on the description of externals, on photographic accuracy (the sketches were also called "daguerreotypes," and were accompanied by illustrations), rather than on imaginative penetration and inner identification with the people involved. Also, even when an author collected his sketches in a volume, they were not united by any sort of narrative continuity. Dostoevsky created the first Russian social novel by fusing such physiological sketches into a story about two lonely souls struggling to keep afloat in the sea of St. Petersburg life.

Dostoevsky is once supposed to have said (though the source has never been located) that all of Russian literature emerged from Gogol's "The Overcoat." Whether or not he ever uttered such a thought, there is no doubt that the dictum applies to *Poor Folk*. Indeed, the reference to Gogol illustrates a more important general point. There has been a strong tendency, especially in Western criticism, to focus on Dostoevsky's quite sensational biography in seeking to explore the sources of his work. But such sources are as much literary and social-cultural as purely personal, and whatever happened in his life was invariably assimilated and interpreted in terms of such a larger context. To understand his work, it is thus necessary to keep this larger ideological context constantly in mind.

In *Poor Folk*, we find the influences not only of Gogol but also of Nikolay Karamzin, the title of whose story "Poor Liza" is immediately evoked. Both works depict the sad fate of the lower classes (in "Poor Liza" a peasant flower-girl is seduced and abandoned by a noble lover), but Dostoevsky's tone is far grittier than Karamzin's idyllic-sentimental treatment. Parodies are also included in *Poor Folk* of Romantic historical novels, and reference is made to the latest vogue for "physiological sketches." Of most importance is the relation of *Poor Folk* to two stories, Pushkin's "The Stationmaster" and Gogol's "The Overcoat," both of which are read by Dostoevsky's main character, Makar Dyevushkin. The first, like "Poor Liza," again dwells on the misfortunes of the humble and the defenseless when confronted with their betters, and Makar sees his own sad fate prefigured in that of the hapless stationmaster. Gogol's story, however, drives him into a rage; and a good way to approach *Poor Folk* is to examine the reason for his indignation.

"The Overcoat" is very far from embodying the plea for social justice that Belinsky was now advocating, though it does contain one passage in which such an appeal is made. But the story is as much a caricature of the main figure, who bears the implicitly scatological name of Akaky Akakievich, as it is a call for a more benevolent attitude toward those of his inferior status. Gogol's story takes its place in a long line of stories in which such characters, lower-level copyists and clerks in the St. Petersburg bureaucracy, were the butt of comic anecdotes; and his own treatment is no different. Akaky is a human cipher, perfectly happy to grind away at his routine task and incapable of assuming any other; the narrator views him with the same relentless mockery that Akaky experiences at the hands of his office-mates. But at one point a younger clerk rebukes the others for mercilessly tormenting their helpless victim, and reminds them that he is, after all, "their brother." Akaky's life is temporarily enriched when he acquires a new overcoat (hence the title), which becomes for him the equivalent of a loved object. A few days later it is stolen as he is walking home during the night. Unceremoniously evicted when he shows up at the home of an official of his district to appeal for aid, he dies shortly afterward.

4

Dostoevsky's *Poor Folk* turns this story inside out, as it were, by adopting the form of the sentimental epistolary novel. His two main characters write letters to each other, and we thus become aware of everything through their reactions and responses rather than through the supercilious remarks of a narrator. Makar Dyevushkin is a middle-aged copying clerk like Akaky, and his correspondent is Varvara Dobroselov, a young girl barely out of her teens. The two are related in some distant fashion, and Makar is trying to protect her from the wiles of a procuress who, in the guise of a friend of the family, has already succeeded in selling her once to a wealthy libertine. Dyevushkin is timidly in love with Varvara himself, but the difference in their ages, if nothing else, makes any such relation impossible; what she feels for him is friendly affection and gratitude, nothing more.

Both are tender, lonely, fragile souls, whose solicitude for each other brings a ray of warmth into their otherwise bleak lives; but their innocent little idyll is soon ended by the pressure of the sordid forces against which they struggle. Dyevushkin reduces himself to abject poverty for the sake of Varvara, and he suffers agonies of humiliation, which he tries to conceal, as he sinks lower and lower in the social scale. Finally, Varvara's violator shows up again and churlishly offers her marriage—not out of remorse or even desire but because he wishes to engender an heir to disinherit a nephew. The hopelessness of her position, and the chance to reestablish her social situation, compel Varvara to accept a loveless union with a callous mate and a harsh life in the Russian provinces.

This simple story line is surrounded with a number of accessories that enlarge it into a true social novel. Inserted among the earlier letters is Varvara's diary, which introduces the classic contrast between the happiness and innocence of rustic childhood and the dangers and corruptions of the city. In these pages we catch a glimpse of a succession of penniless girls who have suffered the same fate as Varvara, or who, under the guise of beneficence, are being prepared for it by the sinister procuress Anna Fyodorovna. The same insert-diary also contains a portrait of the gravely ill tubercular young student Pokrovsky, a devotee of Pushkin, who is Dostoevsky's first delineation of the new young intellectual, a *raznochinets* (meaning he has no official rank or status), eventually to evolve into Raskolnikov in *Crime and Punishment*. As Varvara's informal tutor and intellectual mentor, Pokrovsky stirs her first romantic feelings. He is the illegitimate son of Bykov, the same landowner who raped Varvara, by another of Anna Fyodorovna's "protégées"; the latter was then married off to a drunken ex-clerk who gave the young man his name.

The relation of the pseudo-father, old Pokrovsky, to his educated son, whose cultural attainments he admires to the point of idolatry, symbolizes as well the aspirations of Makar Dyevushkin himself to rise to a higher social-cultural status than the one in which he is placed. The funeral of young Pokrovsky, with the older one running after the carriage in a pouring rain as books fall out of his pockets, rivals Dickens in its tragicomic pathos. Belinsky remarked that it was impossible not to laugh at old Pokrovsky; "but if he does not touch you deeply at the same time you are laughing . . . do not speak of this to anyone, so that some Pokrovsky, a buffoon and a drunkard, will not have to blush for you as a human being." Another narrative line involves the Gorshkov family, who have come from the provinces so that the father, an ex-clerk, may clear himself of a charge; they live in such heartrending poverty that even the impoverished Dyevushkin cannot resist giving them twenty kopecks to buy some food.

These narrative strands interweave to build up an image of the unavailing struggle to keep afloat humanly in the face of crushing circumstances. Everywhere is poverty and humiliation, the exploitation of the weak and the helpless by the rich, powerful, and unscrupulous—all this in the midst of crowded St. Petersburg slum life, with its nauseating odors and debris-littered dwellings. Describing his own quarters, Dyevushkin writes: "On every landing there are boxes, broken chairs and cupboards, rags hung out, windows broken, tubs stand about full of all sorts of dirt and litter, eggshells and the refuse of fish; there is a horrid smell . . . in fact it is not nice" (p. 317). Dostoevsky's use of anticlimax here conveys the slightly risible (but nonetheless touching and moving) quality of Dyevushkin as a person. Yet amidst all this squalor, there are treasures of emotive responsiveness and moral sensitivity that appear in the most unlikely figures—unlikely, at least, from the point of view of previous Russian literature.

Poor Folk combines these local-color aspects of the physiological sketches with a new and unerring insight into the tortures of the humiliated sensibility. "Poor people are touchy—that's in the nature of things," Dyevushkin explains to Varvara. "I felt that even in the past. The poor man is exacting; he takes a different view of God's world, and looks askance at every passer-by and turns a troubled gaze about him and looks to every word, wondering whether people are not talking about him, whether they are saying that he is so ugly, speculating about what he would feel exactly," and so on. (p. 374). This "different view of God's world," the world as seen from below rather than above, constitutes the major innovation of Dostoevsky vis-à-vis

Gogol. The situations and the psychology of *Poor Folk* thus speak for themselves against class pride and class prejudice; but the book also contains a much more outspoken protest, even though cast in terms of an easily comprehended "allegory."

5

Makar Dyevushkin is by no means an uncomplicated character, and he undergoes a distinct evolution. In his early letters, he accepts his lowly place in life without a murmur of protest, even taking pride in performing his unassuming task as conscientiously as he can. He is perfectly content to live in the world as he finds it, although he refuses to accept the lowly image of himself that he knows exists in the eyes of his social superiors. But this unquestioned acceptance of the rightness and justness of the social order as it exists is severely shaken by his inability to protect and provide for Varvara.

At the very lowest point of Dyevushkin's misery—when he is being hounded by his landlady, insulted by the boardinghouse slaveys, and tormented by his ragged appearance—he loses heart entirely and takes to drink. But this is also the moment when a faint spark of rebellion flares even in his docile breast. Walking along one of the fashionable St. Petersburg streets just after leaving the dreary slums in which he lives, he suddenly begins to wonder why he and Varvara should be condemned to poverty and misery. And he guiltily finds himself protesting ("I know . . . that it's wrong to think that, that it is free-thinking") against a world in which some people are just born to wealth, "while another begins life in the orphan asylum . . . . And you know it often happens that Ivan the fool is favoured by fortune" (p. 396). Such notions are an attack on the entire structure of his own hierarchical society; and he goes even further by proclaiming the distinctly Utopian Socialist idea that the humblest worker is more worthy of respect, because he is more useful, than any wealthy, idle social parasite.

Dyevushkin's timid revolt against social injustice is embodied in his vision of an apartment house, on whose ground floor lives a poor shoemaker, whose only concern is the "boots" that he makes to feed his family. "His children are crying and his wife is hungry"; why should he not think only of "boots?" But elsewhere in the same building there is "a wealthy man in his gilded apartments," and he also thinks of "boots, that is, boots in a different manner, in a different sense, but still boots." Why is there not someone to tell him to stop "thinking of nothing but yourself, living for nothing but yourself. . . . Look about you, can't you see some object more noble to worry about than your boots?" (p. 400). Such a plea for the wealthy to concern themselves with the plight of the less fortunate, as Dostoevsky formulates it, obviously has Christian overtones; and if we are to define Dostoevsky's political beliefs at all in this period, it would be as a Christian Socialist.

The same motif is dramatized in another scene, but given more than a material significance, when Dyevushkin is summoned to appear before his civil service superior because of some minor error. His terror and tatterdemalion garments so move the kindhearted General that he gives Dyevushkin a hundred rubles. Refusing to allow the grateful clerk to kiss his hand, he gives him an egalitarian handshake instead; and this respect for his human dignity takes on more importance for Dyevushkin than the money. "I swear that however cast down I was and afflicted in the bitterest days of our misfortunes, . . . I swear that the hundred rubles is not as much to me as that his Excellency deigned to shake hands with me, a straw, a worthless drunkard!" (pp. 405–406). This tension between the psychological and spiritual on the one hand, and the economic and material on the other, will run through all of Dostoevsky's later work and eventually receive its unsurpassed expression in "The Legend of the Grand Inquisitor" (in *The Brothers Karamazov*).

Another motif timidly broached in *Poor Folk*, and which also anticipates the later Dostoevsky, occurs as Varvara is preparing to leave after her marriage. She has placed her fate, she says, in God's "holy, inscrutable power," and Dyevushkin can only agree. "Of course, everything is according to God's will; that is so, that certainly must be so—that is, it certainly must be God's will in this; and the providence of the Heavenly Creator is blessed, of course, and inscrutable. . . . only Varinka, how can it be so soon? . . . I shall be left alone" (pp. 415–416). Dyevushkin's despairingly stumbling efforts to reconcile a belief in God's wisdom and goodness with the tragedy of his own life, and implicitly of human life in general, clearly foreshadow the anguished reflections of many other Dostoevsky characters assailed by the same conundrum.

6

The French Utopian Socialists who influenced Dostoevsky, and particularly those of the Christian variety, were not advocates of violence or revolution; they believed it possible to change the world by demonstrating the benefits of their precepts. One may well wonder, therefore, why Dostoevsky and all the other members of the discussion group to which he belonged (the Petrashevsky Circle) were arrested in the spring of 1849. One reason is that the wave of revolution that swept through Europe in 1848 had frightened Czar Nicholas I. Although the Petrashevtsi as a whole were guilty of nothing more than talk that might be considered subversive, and which they had carried on undisturbed for several years, this was enough now for the Czar to order them hauled in. It was once generally accepted in Dostoevsky scholarship that, like most of the others, he had been an innocent victim of a despotic tyrant; and various theories have been offered as to why, in later life, he seemed to have accepted his condemnation with relative equanimity.

In fact, however, as we now know, he was far from being as innocent as was long believed. The Petrashevsky Circle as a whole never made any attempt to conceal their meetings or discussions; but Dostoevsky belonged to a small secret group within the larger circle whose aim was to foment a revolution against serfdom. The seven members of this small group managed to conceal its existence from the commission of army officers appointed to investigate the activities of the circle as a whole. But why should a Christian Socialist like Dostoevsky have participated in such a conspiracy?

The answer is probably that he hated serfdom with every bone in his body, and his seething revulsion against it was openly expressed the few times that he spoke at the larger group gatherings. Also, he may well have believed (though this is only inferential) that his father had been murdered by the serfs on their country property. This may help to explain why he agreed to become a member of this activist subgroup, and even acted as a recruiting agent. A friend he visited recalled Dostoevsky (in a document first published in 1922) sitting in his nightshirt "like a dying Socrates" unsuccessfully trying to persuade him to join. Dostoevsky thus lived all his life with the knowledge that he had once himself been a secret revolutionary conspirator, and his masterful depiction of the psychology of such characters can be attributed to this personal experience.

After his arrest, he was held in solitary confinement for a year and a half, questioned repeatedly (his caste status as a Russian nobleman precluded any physical mistreatment) and finally forced to undergo the ordeal of a mock execution. He believed for about a half hour that he had been sentenced to be shot, but then learned his true sentence—four years in a labor camp, and then service in the Russian Army. This mock execution was one of the most crucial experiences of his life; it was then, standing in the shadow of death, that the religious question so timidly adumbrated in *Poor Folk* began to take on the supreme importance it assumed in his later works. It also conditioned him to open his eyes and his sensibility to the manner in which the Christian ethos had penetrated—or so he came to believe—to the depths of the personality even of the most ignorant and illiterate Russian peasant-convicts among whom he was now condemned to live.

Dostoevsky served out his prison term, began life in relative freedom as a private in the Army, and then, with the help of influential friends in St. Petersburg, was promoted to officer—which gave him the privilege of resigning and resuming his literary career. He produced two novellas, as already mentioned, while still in Siberia, but his major work of this time, *The House of the Dead*, was written after his return. Dostoevsky had thought of such a work earlier, and mentions it in a letter in 1859 to his brother Mikhail while still on the way back to the capital. "These *Notes from the House of the Dead*," he tells him, "have now taken shape in my mind. . . . My figure will disappear. These are the notes of an unknown; but I guarantee their interest. There will be the serious and the gloomy and the humorous and peasant conversation with a particular convict coloring . . . recorded by me *on the spot* [Dostoevsky had kept a notebook in the camp] and the depiction of characters *unheard of* previously in literature . . . and finally, the most important, my name." So that while Dostoevsky himself will presumably disappear (he becomes only the editor of a manuscript left by a minor official who murdered his wife), in fact everyone will be aware that the editor is talking about himself. Indeed, there are several indications in the text that, unlike the peasant-convicts accused of common-law offenses, the author has been sent to Siberia for a political crime and not for murder.

Dostoevsky and Mikhail were planning to bring out a new journal *Vremya* (Time) in 1860, a period of relative liberalization of the press. Most of the book was published there in monthly installments, and it contributed greatly to the success of the magazine. The first several chapters, however, were published in another, rather obscure periodical. Dostoevsky was worried that his aim of opening the gates of the prison-camp world to public inspection would never pass the censorship; and he decided to allow another editor to explore the lay of the land.

His first installment was published without a hitch, but the second ran into trouble—of a kind that often turns the history of czarist censorship into a black comedy. Far from objecting, as might have been expected, that the portrayal of prison conditions was too harsh to be permitted, the censors feared that peasants might be tempted to commit crimes just to enjoy the amenities of prison life that Dostoevsky portrayed. This objection was overcome by the consideration that the largely illiterate peasants were hardly likely to read the book; and Dostoevsky also wrote a supplement, not included in the final text, explaining that, even if one lived in paradise, "the moral torture" of loss of freedom would make camp life ultimately unbearable.

7

The House of the Dead appears, on the surface, to be an extremely simple book. It contains the memoirs of Dostoevsky's years in the prison camp, and for the readers of his time it brought to public scrutiny a whole world hitherto concealed from their gaze. Here was a gallery of peasant-criminals, most of whom had committed at least one murder, and about whom nobody else had ever written with such intimate knowledge. The aim of the work was to reveal their lives and their psychology, depicted, so far as possible, from their own point of view. Dostoevsky was in a unique position to accomplish this task because his sentence had placed him, unlike other members of his class, on the same social level as the peasant-convicts (actually on an inferior level, since they were better able to perform the physical tasks assigned). They thus behaved with him unrestrainedly, as would not have been possible in nonprison conditions, where the class distinction would have governed their conduct and their words.

For the first time the Russian reader was presented with a peasant world possessing its own norms and values, which Dostoevsky depicts primarily through sketches of the utterances, actions, and behavior of its inhabitants. The book unleashed a huge debate in the Russian press about the conditions it described, and some of the senselessly cruel regulations it brought to light were angrily challenged. Dostoevsky also stressed that there were different motivations for a crime such as murder (sometimes it was sordid, sometimes self-defense), even though all murders were inexplicably punished with the same sentence; and such considerations led to widespread discussion of Russian legal anomalies. What predominated in the reaction to the book was a recognition of the author's "humanism." Dostoevsky, it was felt, had succeeded in "redeeming" a whole class of criminals and outcasts (not all, to be sure, but the vast majority) and, as it were, returning them to the human fold. No attempt was made to lessen their misdeeds, or to sentimentalize over their fate. But instead of being seen as aberrant monsters, they were shown rather as human beings whose often desperate crimes could be understood as responses to difficult and tormenting situations.

For present-day readers, the impact of Dostoevsky's book in its own time is of less interest than what it reveals about the author himself. As we have said, he made superficial efforts to conceal his own presence by inventing a fictitious narrator, and his focus is on the world he is portraying rather than directly on himself. But in *A Writer's Diary* (Vol. 1, 1873–1876; see "For Further Reading"), Dostoevsky spoke of these years as having brought about "the regeneration of my convictions"—that is, the convictions he had held before his arrest and imprisonment. These were now abandoned—though the process was by no means instantaneous—and replaced by those to which he remained faithful for the remainder of his life. Without approaching this change of heart and mind directly, *The House of the Dead* can nonetheless, if read with sufficient care, help us to understand the transformation brought about by his prison years in Dostoevsky's ideas and values.

One such transformation involved the relation between the upper, educated class and the people. We now know he had believed in the possibility of fomenting a revolution among the peasantry—a revolution led and guided by upper-class superiors like himself. No such hope could continue to exist, however, after the events portrayed in part II, chapter VII, "The Complaint." Here Dostoevsky describes how he attempted to join a protest organized by the peasant-convicts against the miserable rations they were being fed; but they forcibly led him away to the kitchen where the nonpeasant convicts, and others who had refused to join the strike, were gathered. "I had never before been so insulted in the prison," he writes, even though he depicts his daily humiliation on other grounds, "and this time I felt it very bitterly" (p. 265). The quotidian offenses to his dignity were only incidental and personal; but here his rejection cut to the core of what had been a deeply held conviction.

When he questioned a friendly prisoner about this incident, asking why he and other "noblemen" had not been able to join in with them "as comrades," the peasant-convict replied in perplexity: "But . . . but how can you be our comrades?" (p. 270). The gap between the peasants and the noblemen was so great, not only in status but in mentality, that "in spite of the fact that [the ex-nobles] are deprived of all the rights of their rank . . . [the others] never consider them their comrades. This is not the result of conscious prejudice but comes about of itself, quite sincerely and unconsciously" (p. 32). The very notion of them acting together thus proved to be completely delusory; and never afterward would Dostoevsky believe that the Russian peasantry would respond to any call of revolution issuing from the intelligentsia. Indeed, such calls were often uttered in a vocabulary whose terms the peasants could not even understand; and he would continue to maintain that the greatest social problem of Russia, whatever the economic or political situation, was to bridge the yawning gap of incomprehension between the peasantry and the educated class.

Also, Dostoevsky's view of the peasantry itself underwent an extremely significant evolution. A work like Poor Folk, with its sympathy and pity for the lower classes (even if not the peasantry) would indicate that Dostoevsky shared the Christian Socialist view of their moral superiority to their betters. In a letter to his brother Mikhail, written just before departing for exile, he remarked that he was not being sent to a jungle but would be with other beings like himself, perhaps even better than himself. Nothing was more shocking and upsetting for him than to find, in the prison camp, a world that could only be labeled as one of moral horror. The peasant-convicts stole from each other incessantly, and Dostoevsky was not spared; every form of vice was available, including female and male prostitution; drunken quarrels were a daily occurrence, and cruel beatings among the convicts themselves were frequent. Dostoevsky's image of this world is painted in appalling colors. "Noise, uproar, laughter, swearing, the clank of chains, smoke and grime, shaven heads, branded faces, ragged clothes, everything defiled and degraded" (p. 14). Dostoevsky sometimes fled to the hospital, even though not ill and despite the risk of infection, where friendly doctors allowed him to stay. "I was constantly going to the hospital . . . to get away from the prison. It was unbearable there, more unbearable than [the hospital], morally more unbearable" (p. 214).

Nonetheless, after a certain amount of time, Dostoevsky's revulsion against the prisoners and their world began to be altered by other impressions. For one thing, the more he learned about the circumstances in which many of their crimes had been committed, the more he could see that they were often a response to unbearable oppression or mistreatment. Moreover, what impressed him very deeply was that, whatever their crimes, the peasants unconditionally accepted the traditional Christian morality that condemned their behavior. Indeed, it was only because this morality exercised its effect that the pandemonium of the ordinary prison environment was occasionally replaced, even if only momentarily, by a less revolting atmosphere.

At Christmas, for example, gifts for the prisoners were sent by the lower classes of the town, and these were divided evenly by the convicts themselves with no quarreling at all. The effect of the holy day was enough to stem the incessant thievery and brutal brawling. At Easter the convicts were relieved of work and went to church two or three times a day. They "prayed very earnestly and every one of them brought his poor farthing to the church every time to buy a candle, or to put it in the collection. . . . When with the chalice in his hands the priest read the words, '. . . accept me, O Lord, even as the thief,' almost all of them bowed down to the ground with a clanking of chains, apparently applying the words literally to themselves" (p. 230). However much they may have violated Christ's commandments, their reverence for them did not diminish, and these continued to remain the standard by which they judged their own behavior. One of Dostoevsky's most fervent convictions was that—unlike, as he believed, the European proletariat—the Russian people would never attempt to justify, or refuse to acknowledge, their violations of the moral law.

What occurred to Dostoevsky at this time is best depicted in a sketch, "The Peasant Marey" (see page 425), that curiously enough he wrote several years later (see *A Writer's Diary*, Vol. 1, 1873–1876). Here he returns to reminisce about his prison years, and though the sketch is not included in his memoirs it symbolically condenses the lengthier internal development that occurred during this time. It is placed in Easter week, when the convicts, after their brief moment of piety, had returned to their usual rowdiness and unruliness. "Disgraceful, hideous songs; card games in little nooks under the bunks; a few convicts, already beaten half to death; . . . knives had already been drawn a few times" (p. 425). To escape this repulsive spectacle, Dostoevsky walks outside and meets an educated Polish convict, also a political prisoner, who says to him in French: "I hate these bandits." The Pole obviously intuited that Dostoevsky was harboring much the same revulsion against his barbarous fellow-countrymen.

Dostoevsky then returns to his bunk bed and recalls an episode from his childhood. Walking alone in a forest, where his mother had warned him that wolves might be wandering, he thought he heard a cry that a wolf was roaming in the vicinity. Frightened, he ran to one of his father's serf-peasants named Marey, plowing in a field. The gray-haired Marey assured the terrified child that no cry had been uttered and, calming him with the tenderness of "a mother," blessed him with the sign of the Cross and sent him home. This spontaneous kindness on the part of an enserfed peasant with every reason to abhor his master and his master's family suddenly resurfaces in Dostoevsky's memory, transforming his entire attitude to the peasant-world around him as he ponders its meaning. "I suddenly felt I could regard these unfortunates in an entirely different way and that suddenly, through some sort of miracle, the former hatred and anger in my heart had vanished. . . . This disgraced peasant, with shaven head and brands on his cheek, drunk and roaring out his hoarse, drunken song—why he might also be that very same Marey; I cannot peer into his heart, after all" (p. 430). Dostoevsky was thus capable of acknowledging the abhorrent aspects of peasant behavior, but also of seeking for—and finding, as he persuaded himself—the redeeming Christian features lying concealed beneath the repellent surface.

At the very same time that the peasant-convicts were thus meta-morphosing into "Marey," Dostoevsky could not find a single re-deeming feature in an upper-class convict named Aristov, referred to in this translation as "A." He had been sent to prison for having falsely denounced others to the authorities as political subversives in exchange for payment to finance a life of debauchery. In prison, he served as a spy on his fellow inmates for the sadistic major in charge of the camp. He was clever, good-looking, well educated, and for Dostoevsky "the most revolting example of the depths to which a man can sink and degenerate, and the extent to which he can destroy all moral feeling in himself without difficulty or repentance"(p. 78). Far better the instinctive Christianity of the peasants, whatever their crimes, than Aristov's self-satisfied and gloating pleasure in his own ignominy! In *Crime and Punishment*, the name of Aristov is first given to the character who became Svidrigailov; and Dostoevsky's later decla-ration that, morally speaking, the people had nothing to learn from the educated class, may well be traced to such a recollection.

8

There can be no doubt that one aspect of Dostoevsky's "regeneration of his convictions" referred to this change in his former condescend-ingly upper-class attitude toward the peasantry. But there is another, much deeper feature of this "regeneration" that can be detected in *The House of the Dead*, and which involves his own most fundamental re-ligious idea-feelings. It was long thought that Dostoevsky became converted to atheism in the 1840s and, under the stress of his mock execution and the ordeal of the prison camp, returned to a belief in God and to fidelity to God's anointed, the Czar. Matters are not so simple, however, and there is no evidence that he ever lost his faith in the existence of God and the divinity of Christ, though he was thor-oughly familiar with all the arguments being made against them by such thinkers as Ludwig Feuerbach and D. F. Strauss. But he remained a Christian Socialist, whose ideal was to embody the law of love preached by a divine Christ into the daily life of his own society.

However, the ordeal of the mock execution had brought him face to face with eternity, and observations in the prison camp had also revealed to him the power of the irrational in the human psyche. The convicts sometimes acted in the most irrational and even self-destructive ways simply to give themselves a sense of freedom; and they were often sustained by the most delusory hopes about the betterment of their conditions. Without such hope, indeed, Dostoevsky concluded that they would have gone berserk (some of them did).

Such observations are not specifically applied to religion, but there is one striking passage in the book which, if extended a bit, gives us a revelatory glimpse into the transformation of Dostoevsky's own faith as a result of his prison years. Noting that the prisoners resented the forced labor they were required to perform, he yet remarks that it was not intolerable because it made sense and could be seen to serve a useful purpose. But what if they were required to perform perfectly useless tasks? What if they "had to pour water from one vessel into another and back, over and over again, to pound sand, to move a heap of earth from one place to another and back again—I believe the convict would hang himself in a few days or would commit a thousand crimes, preferring rather to die than endure such humiliation, shame and torture" (p. 26). (Nothing of this sort, to be sure, happened in Dostoevsky's camp; but his conclusion can be supported by evidence gathered from Nazi work camps during World War II.)

What does this have to do, it may be asked, with the question of religious faith? The answer is that, if we transpose the terms of this passage slightly, its religious-metaphysical implications become self-evident. Not to believe in God and immortality, for the Dostoevsky who emerged from the prison camp, is to be condemned to live in an ultimately senseless universe—analogous to that of the prisoners performing a useless task. The result, as he said himself, was that either a thousand crimes would be committed to escape such humiliating degradation, or those condemned to such a fate would destroy themselves.

The characters in his great novels (all written after *The House of the Dead*), who have lost or renounced their faith, consequently behave in this fashion—they commit crimes or take their own lives. And while their motives are more complicated than in Dostoevsky's thought-experiment, the psychological root of their behavior is much the same—the Christian moral laws of their universe have become senseless for them, and they have become monsters in their misery. The world of the post-Siberian Dostoevsky is thus no longer limited to applying the Christian law of love to earthly life, or rather, this problem is now broadened and enriched by an excruciatingly heightened awareness of the importance of its linkage with the ultimate religious and supernatural sources of the Christian faith.

9

The House of the Dead is thus a superb job of reportage, opening up a whole new world for the Russian reader, as well as providing a penetrating glimpse into Dostoevsky's inner development. As a work, however, it seems at first sight to be more or less a collection of scenes and sketches, fascinating in their own right but given unity only by a common location. In fact, though, the book is very carefully constructed to correspond indirectly, by the manner in which its material is organized and arranged, with the inner process of Dostoevsky's encounter with, and assimilation of, this strange new world.

In part I, the first six chapters depict his disorienting perceptions and the initial shock of contact ("First Impressions"), which then move on to the depiction of individual characters (Petrov, Isay Fomitch, and Baklushin). In part II the chapters are held together externally ("The Hospital") or by loose general groupings ("Prison Animals" and "Comrades"). The narrator, whose surprised and startled reactions were quite prominent earlier, fades into the background as he merges into the everyday life of the community.

Dostoevsky's handling of time is particularly subtle, and it anticipates the experiments of our own day in correlating the shape of the narrative to accord with subjective experience. Time literally comes to a stop in the early chapters as the narrator concentrates on the novelty of the unfamiliar environment into which he has been thrown. More than a hundred pages are devoted to his first month; but the years then pass by unobtrusively as he becomes accustomed to camp routine, though time comes into prominence thematically as the end of his sentence nears. (The narrator received a ten-year sentence, but Dostoevsky had only been given four.)

The House of the Dead is nominally a memoir, but it can be better described as a semi-fictional autobiography. As such it takes its place with two other works written about the same time, Turgenev's Notes of a Hunter (1852) and Tolstoy's Sevastopol Sketches (1855–1856). Dostoevsky could well have been inspired by their example in the sketch-form that he created for the account of his prison-camp years. All three works in fact share the same overriding theme—the encounter of a member of the upper, educated class with the Russian people—and each author treats it in his own distinctive way.

Turgenev stresses the spiritual beauty and richness of Russian peasant life, the poetry of its customs and superstitions, and by so doing makes the serf status of the peasants and the casual cruelty of their treatment all the more unforgivable. Tolstoy discovers the Russian peasantry amidst the besieged bastions of Sevastopol, and is astonished by the calm tranquillity of their unassuming heroism—so different from the vanity occupying the consciousness of their upper-class officers, dreaming of decorations and promotions. Only Dostoevsky, however, depicts the Russian people in *revolt* against their enslaved condition, implacably hating the nobles who have oppressed them and ready to use their knives and axes to strike back when mistreatment becomes unendurable.

At the very end of the book, just before his own fetters were struck off and he was once again a free man, Dostoevsky sets down a statement about the convicts that has led to some misunderstanding. "After all," he wrote, "one must tell the whole truth; these men were exceptional men. Perhaps they were the most gifted, the strongest of our people. But their mighty energies were vainly wasted, wasted abnormally, unjustly, hopelessly." Dostoevsky here is obviously protesting against serfdom and the whole complex of Russian social customs that treated the peasant as an inferior species; those who refused to accept such injustice and revolted against it could well be seen as the "strongest" of the people, whose "mighty energies" had been perverted.

However, among the notes left by Nietzsche and later published in *The Will to Power*, the philosopher wondered whether one of his subconscious (*unwillkürlich*) aims was not "to return a good conscience to an evil human being . . . and the evil human being precisely insofar as he is the strongest human being. Here one should bring in the judgment of Dostoevsky about the criminals in the prison camp" (book 2, note 233). For Nietzsche, presumably, Dostoevsky's peasant-convicts were "evil human beings," whose "strength" derived from having overcome the inhibitions of customary moral constraints.

Nothing, however, could have been farther from Dostoevsky's own point of view. Indeed, perhaps the most important conviction he had acquired as a result of his prison camp ordeal was that, even in their worst excesses, the Russian people had never abandoned the moral law proclaimed by Christ.

Joseph Frank is Professor Emeritus of Comparative Literature at Princeton University and Professor Emeritus of Comparative Literature and Slavic Languages and Literature at Stanford University. He is the author of a five-volume study of Dostoevsky's life and work. The first four volumes received the National Book Critics Circle Award for Biography, two Christian Gauss Awards, two James Russell Lowell Awards of the Modern Language Association, a Los Angeles Times Book Prize, and other honors. Frank is also the author of Through the Russian Prism: Essays on Literature and Culture, The Widening Gyre, and The Idea of Spatial Form.

THE HOUSE OF THE DEAD

CONTENTS

PART I

INTRODUCTION

IN THE REMOTE PARTS of Siberia in the midst of steppes, mountains, or impassable forests, there are scattered here and there wretched little wooden towns of one, or at the most two, thousand inhabitants, with two churches, one in the town and one in the cemetery—more like fair-sized villages in the neighbourhood of Moscow than towns. They are usually well provided with police officers, superintendents and minor officials of all sorts. A post in Siberia is usually a snug berth in spite of the cold. The inhabitants are simple folk and not of liberal views; everything goes on according to the old-fashioned, solid, time-honoured traditions. The officials, who may fairly be said to be the aristocracy of Siberia, are either born and bred in Siberia, or men who have come from Russia, usually from Petersburg or Moscow, attracted by the extra pay, the double travelling expenses and alluring hopes for the future. Those of them who are clever at solving the problem of existence almost always remain in Siberia, and eagerly take root there. Later on they bring forth sweet and abundant fruit. But others of more levity and no capacity for solving the problems of existence soon weary of Siberia, and wonder regretfully why they came. They wait with impatience for the end of their three years' term of office, and instantly, on the expiration of it, petition to be transferred and return home abusing Siberia and sneering at it. They are wrong: not only from the official standpoint but from many others, one may find a blissful existence in Siberia. The climate is excellent; there are many extremely wealthy and hospitable merchants; many exceedingly well-to-do natives. Young ladies bloom like roses, and are moral to the last extreme. The wild game-birds fly about the streets and positively thrust themselves upon the sportsman. The amount of champagne consumed is supernatural. The caviare is marvellous. In some parts the crops often yield fifteenfold. In fact it is a blessed land. One need only know how to reap the benefits of it. In Siberia people do know.

In one of these lively, self-satisfied little towns with most charming

inhabitants, the memory of whom is imprinted for ever on my heart,
I met Alexandr Petrovitch Goryanchikov, a man who had been a gentleman and landowner born in Russia, had afterwards become a convict
in the second division for the murder of his wife, and on the expiration
of his ten years' sentence was spending the rest of his life humbly and
quietly as a settler in the town. Although he was officially described as
an inhabitant of a neighbouring village, he did actually live in the town
as he was able to earn some sort of a living there by giving lessons to
children. In Siberian towns one often meets teachers who have been
convicts; they are not looked down upon. They are principally employed in teaching French, of which in the remote parts of Siberia the
inhabitants could have no notion but for them, though the language is
so indispensable for success in life. The first time I met Alexandr Petrovitch was in the house of Ivan Ivanitch Gvozdikov, an old-fashioned
and hospitable official who had gained honours in the service and had
five very promising daughters of various ages. Alexandr Petrovitch gave
them lessons four times a week for thirty kopecks a lesson. His appearance interested me. He was an exceedingly pale, thin man, small and
frail-looking, who could hardly be called old—about five-and-thirty.
He was always very neatly dressed in European style. If one talked
to him he looked at one very fixedly and intently, listened with strict
courtesy to every word one uttered, as though reflecting upon it, as
though one had asked him a riddle or were trying to worm out a secret,
and in the end answered clearly and briefly, but so weighing every
word that it made one feel ill at ease, and one was relieved at last when
the conversation dropped. I questioned Ivan Ivanitch about him at the
time and learnt that Goryanchikov was a man of irreproachably moral
life, and that otherwise Ivan Ivanitch would not have engaged him for
his daughters; but that he was dreadfully unsociable and avoided everyone, that he was extremely learned, read a great deal but spoke very little, and in fact it was rather difficult to talk to him; that some people
declared that he was positively mad, though they considered that this
was not a failing of much importance; that many of the most respected
persons in the town were ready to be kind to Alexandr Petrovitch in all
sorts of ways; that he might be of use, indeed, writing petitions and so
forth. It was supposed that he must have decent relations in Russia,
possibly people of good position, but it was known that from the time
of his conviction he had resolutely cut off all communication with

them—in fact he was his own enemy. Moreover, everyone in the town knew his story, knew that he had killed his wife in the first year of his marriage, had killed her from jealousy, and had surrendered himself to justice (which had done much to mitigate his sentence). Such crimes are always looked upon as misfortunes, and pitied accordingly. But in spite of all this the queer fellow persisted in holding himself aloof from everyone, and only came among people to give his lessons.

I paid no particular attention to him at first but, I can't tell why, he gradually began to interest me. There was something enigmatic about him. It was utterly impossible to talk freely with him. He always answered my questions, of course, and with an air, indeed, of considering it a sacred obligation to do so; but after his answers I somehow felt it awkward to ask him anything more; and there was a look of suffering and exhaustion on his face afterwards. I remember one fine summer evening, as I was walking home with him from Ivan Ivanitch's, it occurred to me suddenly to invite him in for a minute to smoke a cigarette. I can't describe the look of horror that came into his face; he was utterly disconcerted, began muttering incoherent words, and, suddenly looking angrily at me, rushed away in the opposite direction. I was positively astounded. From that time he looked at me with a sort of alarm whenever we met. But I did not give in: something attracted me to him, and a month later for no particular reason I went to Goryanchikov's myself. No doubt I acted stupidly and tactlessly. He lodged in the very outskirts of the town in the house of an old woman of the working class, who had a daughter in consumption, and this daughter had an illegitimate child, a pretty, merry little girl of ten. Alexandr Petrovitch was sitting beside this child teaching her to read at the moment when I went in. Seeing me, he was as confused as though he had been caught in a crime. He was utterly disconcerted, jumped up from his chair and gazed open-eyed at me. At last we sat down; he watched every look in my face intently, as though he suspected in each one of them some peculiar mysterious significance. I guessed that he was suspicious to the point of insanity. He looked at me with hatred, almost as though asking me: how soon are you going? I began talking about our town and the news of the day; it appeared that he did not know the most ordinary news of the town known to everyone, and what is more, did not care to. Then I began talking of the country and its needs; he heard me in silence and looked me in the face so strangely that at last I felt ashamed of what I was saying. I almost succeeded in tempting him, however, with new books and reviews; they had just come by post, they were in my hands and I offered to lend them, uncut. He glanced eagerly at them but at once changed his mind and declined my offer, alleging that he had no time for reading. At last I took leave of him, and as I went out I felt as though an insufferable weight were taken off my heart. I felt ashamed, and it seemed horribly stupid to pester a man who made it his great aim to shrink as far as possible out of sight of everyone. But the thing was done. I remember that I noticed scarcely a single book in his room, and so it was not true that he read a great deal as people said. Yet passing by his windows once or twice, very late at night, I noticed a light in them. What was he doing, sitting up till daybreak? Could he have been writing? And if so, what?

Owing to circumstances I left the town for three months. Returning home in the winter, I learnt that Alexandr Petrovitch had died in the autumn, in solitude, without even sending for the doctor. He was already almost forgotten in the town. His lodgings were empty. I immediately made the acquaintance of his landlady, intending to find out from her what had occupied her lodger, and whether he had written anything. For twenty kopecks she brought me quite a hamper of manuscript left by her late lodger. The old woman confessed that she had already torn up two exercise books. She was a grim and taciturn old woman from whom it was difficult to extract anything much. She could tell me nothing very new of her lodger. According to her, he scarcely ever did anything, and for months together did not open a book or take up a pen; but he would walk up and down the room all night, brooding, and would sometimes talk to himself; that he was very fond of her little grandchild, Katya, and was very kind to her, especially since he had heard that her name was Katya, and that on St. Katherine's day he always had a requiem service sung for someone. He could not endure visitors; he never went out except to give his lessons; he looked askance even at an old woman like her when she went in once a week to tidy up his room a bit, and scarcely ever said a word to her all those three years. I asked Katya whether she remembered her teacher. She looked at me without speaking, turned to the wall and began to cry. So this man was able to make someone, at least, love him.

I carried off his papers and spent a whole day looking through them. Three-fourths of these papers were trifling, insignificant scraps, or exercises written by his pupils. But among them was one rather thick volume of finely written manuscript, unfinished, perhaps thrown aside and forgotten by the writer. It was a disconnected description of the ten years spent by Alexandr Petrovitch in penal servitude. In parts this account broke off and was interspersed by passages from another story, some strange and terrible reminiscences, jotted down irregularly, spasmodically, as though by some overpowering impulse. I read these fragments over several times, and was almost convinced that they were written in a state of insanity. But his reminiscences of penal servitude— "Scenes from the House of the Dead" as he calls them himself somewhere in his manuscript—seemed to me not devoid of interest. I was carried away by this absolutely new, till then unknown, world, by the strangeness of some facts, and by some special observations on these lost creatures, and I read some of it with curiosity. I may, of course, be mistaken. To begin with I am picking out two or three chapters as an experiment—the public may judge of them.

CHAPTER I

THE HOUSE OF THE DEAD

Our prison stood at the edge of the fortress grounds, close to the fortress wall. One would sometimes, through a chink in the fence, take a peep into God's world to try and see something; but one could see only a strip of the sky and the high earthen wall overgrown with coarse weeds, and on the wall sentries pacing up and down day and night. And then one would think that there are long years before one, and that one will go on coming to peep through the chink in the same way, and will see the same wall, the same sentries and the same little strip of sky, not the sky that stood over the prison, but a free, far-away sky. Imagine a large courtyard, two hundred paces long and a hundred and fifty wide, in the form of an irregular hexagon, all shut in by a paling, that is, a fence of high posts stuck deeply into the earth, touching one another, strengthened by crossway planks and pointed at the top; this was the outer fence of the prison. On one side of the fence there is a strong gate, always closed, always, day and night, guarded by sentries; it is opened on occasion to let us out to work. Outside that gate is the world of light and freedom, where men live like the rest of mankind. But those living on this side of the fence picture that world as some unattainable fairyland. Here there is a world apart, unlike everything else, with laws of its own, its own dress, its own manners and customs, and here is the house of the living dead—life as nowhere else and a people apart. It is this corner apart that I am going to describe.

When you come into the enclosure you see several buildings within it. On both sides of the large inner court run two long log-houses of one storey. These are the prison barracks. Here the convicts live, distributed in divisions. Then at the further end of the enclosure another similar log-house: this is the kitchen, divided in two for the use of two messes. Beyond it another building, where are the cellars, the storehouses and stables, all under one roof. The middle of the courtyard is empty and forms a fairly large level square. Here the convicts fall in, here they are mustered, and their names are called over in the morning, at midday, and in the evening, and on occasion several times a day as well—if the sentries are suspicious and not very clever at counting. A fairly wide space is left all round between the buildings and the fence. Here behind the buildings prisoners of an unsociable and gloomy disposition like to walk in their spare time, to think their own thoughts, hidden from all eyes. Meeting them as they walked there, I used to like looking into their grim, branded faces, and guessing what they were thinking about. There was a prisoner whose favourite occupation in his spare time was counting the posts in the fence. There were fifteen hundred of them, and he had counted and noted them all. Every post stood for a day with him: he marked off one post every day, and in that way could see at a glance from the number of posts uncounted how many days he had left in prison before his term was out. He was genuinely glad every time one side of the hexagon was finished. He had many years yet to wait, but one had time in prison to learn patience. I once saw a convict who had been twenty years in prison and was being released take leave of his fellow prisoners. There were men who remembered his first coming into the prison, when he was young, careless, heedless of his crime and his punishment. He went out a grey-headed, elderly man, with a sad sullen face. He walked in silence through our six barrack-rooms. As he entered each room he prayed to the ikons, and then bowing low to his fellow prisoners he asked them not to remember evil against him. I remember too how a prisoner who had been a well-to-do peasant in Siberia was one evening summoned to the gate. Six months, before, he had heard that his former wife had married again, and he was terribly downcast about it. Now she herself had come to the prison, asked for him, and given him alms. They talked for a couple of minutes, both shed tears and parted for ever. I saw his face when he returned to the barracks. . . . Yes, in that place one might learn to be patient.

When it got dark we used all to be taken to the barracks, and to be locked up for the night. I always felt depressed at coming into our barrack-room from outside. It was a long, low-pitched, stuffy room, dimly lighted by tallow candles, full of a heavy stifling smell. I don't understand now how I lived through ten years in it. I had three planks on the wooden platform; that was all I had to myself. On this wooden platform thirty men slept side by side in our room alone. In the winter we were locked up early; it was fully four hours before everyone was asleep. And before that—noise, uproar, laughter, swearing, the clank of chains, smoke and grime, shaven heads, branded faces, ragged clothes, everything defiled and degraded. What cannot man live through! Man is a creature that can get accustomed to anything, and I think that is the best definition of him.

There were two hundred and fifty of us in the prison, and the number scarcely varied. Some came, others completed their sentence and went away, others died. And there were some of all sorts. I imagine every province, every region of Russia had some representative there. There were some aliens, and there were some prisoners even from the mountains of Caucasus. They were all divided according to the degree of their criminality, and consequently according to the number of years they had to serve. I believe there was no sort of crime that had not sent some prisoner there. The bulk of the prison population were exiled convicts or *sylno-katorzhny* of the civilian division (the *silno-katorzhny*, or heavily punished convicts, as the prisoners naïvely mispronounced it).

These were criminals entirely deprived of all rights of property, fragments cut off from society, with branded faces to bear witness for ever that they were outcasts. They were sentenced to hard labour for terms varying from eight to twelve years, and afterwards they were sent to live as settlers in some Siberian village. There were prisoners of the military division, too, who were not deprived of rights, as is usual in Russian disciplinary battalions. They were sentenced for brief terms; at the expiration of their sentence they were sent back whence they had come, to serve in the Siberian line regiments. Many of them returned almost at once to the prison for some second serious offence, this time not for a short term, but for twenty years: this division was called the "lifers." But even these "lifers" were not deprived of all rights. Finally there was one more, fairly numerous, special division of the most terrible criminals, principally soldiers. It was called "the special section." Criminals were sent to it from all parts of Russia. They considered themselves in for life, and did not know the length of their sentence. According to law they had to perform double or treble tasks. They were kept in the prison until some works involving very severe hard labour were opened in Siberia. "You are in for a term, but we go onwards into servitude," they used to say to other prisoners. I have heard that this class has since been abolished. The civilian division, too, has been removed from our prison also, and a single disciplinary battalion of convicts has been formed. Of course, the officials in control of the prison were all changed at the same time. So I am describing the past, things long bygone.

It was long ago; it all seems like a dream to me now. I remember how I entered the prison. It was in the evening, in January. It was already dark, the men were returning from their work, and they were getting ready for the roll-call. A non-commissioned officer with moustaches at last opened for me the door of this strange house in which I was to spend so many years, and to endure sensations of which I could never have formed the faintest idea if I had not experienced them. I could never have imagined, for instance, how terrible and agonizing it would be never once for a single minute to be alone for the ten years of my imprisonment. At work to be always with a guard, at home with two hundred fellow prisoners; not once, not once alone! Yet this was not the worst I had to get used to!

There were here men who were murderers by mischance and men who were murderers by trade, brigands and brigand chiefs. There were simple thieves, and tramps who were pickpockets or burglars.

There were people about whom it was difficult to guess why they had come. Yet each had his own story, confused and oppressive as the heaviness that follows a day's drinking. As a rule they spoke little of their past, they did not like talking about it and evidently tried not to think of bygone days. I knew some among them, even murderers, so gay, so heedless of everything that one might bet with certainty that their consciences never reproached them. But there were gloomy faces, too, men who were almost always silent. As a rule it was rare for anyone to talk of his life, and curiosity was not the fashion; it was somehow not the custom and not correct. Only on rare occasions, from want of something better to do, some prisoner would grow talkative, and another would listen coldly and gloomily. No one could astonish anyone here. "We are men who can read," they would often say with strange satisfaction. I remember how a robber began once when he was drunk (it was sometimes possible to get drunk in prison) telling how he had murdered a boy of five, how he had enticed him at first with a toy, led him away to an empty shed, and there had murdered him. The whole roomful of men, who had till then been laughing at his jokes, cried out like one man, and the brigand was forced to be silent; it was not from indignation they cried out, but simply because there is no need to talk *about that*, because talking *about that* is not the correct thing. I may mention in parenthesis that they were "men who could read," and not in the slang, but in the literal sense. Probably more than half of them actually could read and write. In what other place in which Russian peasants are gathered together in numbers can you find two hundred and fifty men, half of whom can read and write? I have heard since that someone deduces from such facts that education is detrimental to the people. That is a mistake; there are quite other causes at work here, though it must be admitted that education develops self-reliance in the people. But this is far from being a defect.

The divisions were distinguished from one another by their dress: some had half their jackets brown and half grey, and the same with their trousers—one leg dark brown and one grey. One day when we were at work a girl who was selling rolls looked at me intently for some time and then suddenly burst out laughing. "Ugh, how horrid," she cried, "they had not enough grey cloth and they had not enough black!" There were others whose jackets were all grey, and only the sleeves were blackish-brown. Our heads were shaved in different ways too: some had half the head shaved lengthways and others transversely.

At the first glance one could discover one conspicuous trait, common to all this strange family; even the most prominent and original personalities, who unconsciously dominated the others, tried to adopt the common tone of the prison. Speaking generally, I may say that, with the exception of a few indefatigably cheerful fellows who were consequently regarded with contempt by everyone, they were all sullen, envious, dreadfully vain, boastful people, prone to take offence and great sticklers for good form. Not to be surprised at anything was regarded as the greatest merit. They were all mad on keeping up to their standard of good form. But often the most aggressive conceit was followed in a flash by the most cringing feebleness. There were some genuinely strong characters; they were simple and unaffected. But strange to say, among these really strong people there were some who were vain to the most exaggerated degree, to a morbid point. As a rule vanity and regard for appearances were most conspicuous. The majority of them were corrupt and horribly depraved. Slander and backbiting went on incessantly; it was hell, outer darkness. But no one dared to rebel against the self-imposed rules and the accepted customs of the prison; all submitted to them. There were exceptional characters who found it hard and difficult to submit, but still they did submit. Some who came to the prison were men who had lost their heads, had become too reckless when at liberty, so that at last they committed their crimes as it were irresponsibly, as it were without an object, as it were in delirium, in intoxication, often from vanity excited to the highest pitch. But they were quickly suppressed, though some had been the terror of whole villages and towns before they came to prison. Looking about him, the new-comer soon realized that he had come to the wrong place, that there was no one he could impress here, and he gradually submitted and fell in with the general tone. This general tone was apparent externally in a certain peculiar personal dignity of which almost every inmate of the prison was acutely conscious. It was as though the status of a convict, of a condemned prisoner, was a sort of rank, and an honourable one too. There was no sign of shame or repentance! Yet there was an external, as it were official, resignation, a sort of philosophic calm. "We are a lost lot," they used to say; "since we didn't know how to get on in freedom now we must walk the Green Street, and count the ranks." "Since we disobeyed our fathers and mothers, now we must obey the drum tap." "We wouldn't embroider with gold, so now we break stones on the road." Such things were often said by way of moral reflections and proverbial sayings, but never seriously. They were all words. I doubt whether one of the convicts ever inwardly admitted his lawlessness. If anyone, not a prisoner, were to try reproaching the criminal for his crime, upbraiding him (though it is not the Russian way to reproach a criminal), an endless stream of oaths would follow. And what masters of abuse they were! They swore elaborately, artistically. Abuse was carried to a science with them; they tried to score not so much by insulting words as by insulting meaning, spirit, ideas—and that is subtler and more malignant. This science was developed to a higher point by their incessant quarrels. All these people were kept at work by force, consequently they were idle, consequently they were demoralized; if they had not been depraved beforehand, they became so in prison. They had all been brought together here apart from their own will; they were all strangers to one another.

"The devil must have worn out three pairs of shoes before he brought us all here," they used to say of themselves, and so backbiting, intrigues, womanish slander, envy, quarrelling, hatred were always conspicuous in this hellish life. No old women could be such old women as some of these cut-throats. I repeat, there were strong characters even among them, men who had been accustomed all their lives to go ahead and to dominate, hardy and fearless. These men were instinctively respected; yet though they for their part were often very jealous over their prestige, as a rule they tried not to oppress the others, did not pick quarrels over trifles, behaved with exceptional dignity, were reasonable and almost always obeyed the authorities—not from any principle of obedience, nor from a sense of duty, but as though it were a sort of contract with the authorities for the mutual advantage of both. On the other hand they were treated with consideration.

I remember how one of these convicts, a fearless and determined man, well known to the authorities for his brutal propensities, was once summoned to be punished for some offence. It was a summer day and not in working hours. The officer who was immediately responsible for the management of the prison came himself to the guard-house, which was close to our gate, to be present at the punishment. This major was, so to speak, a fateful being for the prisoners; he had reduced them to trembling before him. He was insanely severe, "flew at people," as the convicts said. What they feared most in him was his penetrating lynx-like eyes, from which nothing could be concealed. He seemed to see without looking. As soon as he came into the prison he knew what was being done at the furthest end of it. The prisoners used to call him "eight eyes." His system was a mistaken one. By his ferocious, spiteful actions he only exasperated people who were already exasperated, and if he had not been under the governor of the prison, a generous and sensible man who sometimes moderated his savage outbursts, his rule might have led to great trouble. I can't understand how it was he did not come to a bad end; he retired and is alive and well, though he was brought to trial for his misdeeds.

The convict turned pale when his name was called. As a rule he lay down to be flogged resolutely and without a word, endured his punishment in silence and got up again quite lively, looking calmly and philosophically at the mishap that had befallen him. He was always, however, handled with caution. But this time he thought himself for some reason in the right. He turned pale and managed, unseen by the guard, to slip into his sleeve a sharp English knife. Knives and all sharp instruments were sternly forbidden in prison. Searches were made frequently and unexpectedly, and they were no joking matter for the penalties were severe; but as it is difficult to find what a thief particularly means to hide, and as knives and instruments were always indispensable in the prison, in spite of searches they were always there. And if they were taken away, new ones were immediately obtained. All the convicts rushed to the fence and looked through the crevices with beating hearts. They all knew that this time Petrov did not mean to lie down to be flogged, and that it would be the end of the major. But at the critical moment our major got into his droshki and drove away, leaving the execution of the punishment to another officer. "God himself delivered him!" the convicts said afterwards. As for Petrov, he bore his punishment quite calmly. His wrath passed off with the departure of the major. The convict is obedient and submissive up to a certain point; but there is a limit which must not be overstepped. By the way, nothing can be more curious than these strange outbreaks of impatience and revolt. Often a man is patient for several years, is resigned, endures most cruel punishment, and suddenly breaks out over some little thing, some trifle, a mere nothing. From a certain point of view he might be called mad, and people do call him so in fact.

I have said already that in the course of several years I never saw one sign of repentance among these people, not a trace of despondent brooding over their crime, and that the majority of them inwardly considered themselves absolutely in the right. This is a fact. No doubt vanity, bad example, brag, false shame are responsible for a great deal of this. On the other side, who can say that he has sounded the depths of these lost hearts, and has read what is hidden from all the world in them? Yet surely it would have been possible during all those years to have noticed, to have detected something, to have caught some glimpse which would have borne witness to some inner anguish and suffering in those hearts. But it was not there, it certainly was not there. No, it seems crime cannot be interpreted from preconceived conventional points of view, and the philosophy of it is a little more difficult than is supposed. Of course, prisons and penal servitude do not reform the criminal; they only punish him and protect society from further attacks on its security. In the criminal, prison and the severest hard labour only develop hatred, lust for forbidden pleasures, and a fearful levity. But I am firmly convinced that the belauded system of solitary confinement attains only false, deceptive, external results. It drains the man's vital sap, enervates his soul, cows and enfeebles it, and then holds up the morally withered mummy, half imbecile, as a model of penitence and reformation. Of course, the criminal who revolts against society hates it, and almost always considers himself in the right and society in the wrong. Moreover, he has already endured punishment at its hands, and for that reason almost considers himself purged and quits with society. There are points of view, in fact, from which one is almost brought to justify the criminal. But in spite of all possible points of view everyone will admit that there are crimes which always and everywhere from the beginning of the world, under all legal systems, have unhesitatingly been considered crimes, and will be considered so as long as man remains human. Only in prison have I heard stories of the most terrible, the most unnatural actions, of the most monstrous murders told with the most spontaneous, childishly merry laughter.

I am particularly unable to forget one parricide. He was of the upper class and in the service, and had been something like a prodigal son. He was thoroughly dissipated in his behaviour, and made debts everywhere. His father, an old man of sixty, tried to influence and restrain him; but the father had a house, a small estate, and, it was suspected, money, and the son killed the father through greed for his inheritance. The crime was only discovered a month later. The murderer himself gave information to the police that his father had disappeared, he knew not where. He spent all that month in the most profligate way. At last in his absence the police found the body. There was running right across the yard a ditch covered with planks for carrying off refuse water. The body was lying in this ditch. It was dressed and tidy, the grey head which had been cut off had been put on the body, and under the head the murderer laid a pillow. He did not confess, was deprived of his rank and rights, and sent to penal servitude for twenty years. All the time I spent with him, he was in the liveliest, merriest spirits. He was an unaccountable, feather-brained fellow, irresponsible in the highest degree, though by no means stupid. I never noticed any special cruelty in him. The convicts despised him—not on account of his crime, which was never mentioned, but for his foolishness, for his not knowing how to behave. In conversation he sometimes referred to his father. Once talking to me about the healthy constitution hereditary in their family, he added: "My parent, for instance, never complained of any illness right up to the end." Such savage insensibility seems impossible. It is phenomenal; it is not a case of simple crime, but of some constitutional defect, some mental and bodily monstrosity not yet understood by science. Of course I did not believe this criminal's story. But people who came from the same town and must have known every detail of his history told me about the whole case. The facts were so clear that it was impossible not to believe in them.

The convicts heard him cry out one night in his sleep, "Hold him, hold him! Chop off his head, his head, his head!"

Almost all the convicts raved and talked in their sleep. Oaths, thieves' slang, knives, axes were what came most frequently to their tongues in their sleep. "We are a beaten lot," they used to say; "our guts have been knocked out, that's why we shout at night."

Forced and penal labour was not an occupation, but a compulsory task: the convict completed his task or worked the allotted hours and returned to the prison. The work was looked upon with hatred. If it were not for his own private work to which he was devoted with his whole mind, his whole interest, a man could not live in prison. And, indeed, how else could all that mass of men, who had had experiences, lived keenly and desired to live, who had been forcibly brought together here, forcibly torn away from society and normal existence, be expected to live a normal and regular life here of their own free will? Idleness alone would have developed in the convict here criminal propensities of which he had no idea before. Without labour, without lawful normal property man cannot live; he becomes depraved, and is transformed into a beast. And so, in obedience to a natural craving and a sort of sense of self-preservation, everyone in the prison had his special craft and pursuit. The long summer day was almost filled up with the compulsory work; there was hardly time in the brief night for sleep. But in the winter the convict had by regulation to be locked up in prison as soon as it got dark. What could he do in the long dull hours of the winter evenings? And so in spite of prohibition almost every prison ward was transformed into a huge workshop. Work, occupation, were not formally forbidden; but it was strictly forbidden to have in one's possession in prison any tools, and without these work was impossible. But they worked by stealth, and I fancy that in some cases the authorities shut their eyes to it. Many convicts came to the prison knowing nothing, but they learnt from others, and afterwards went back into the world skilled workmen. There were cobblers there, shoemakers, tailors, cabinet-makers, locksmiths, woodcarvers and gilders. There was one Jew, Isay Bumshtein, a jeweller and pawnbroker. They all worked and earned something. They got orders for work from the town. Money is coined liberty, and so it is ten times dearer to the man who is deprived of freedom. If money is mingling in his pocket, he is half consoled, even though he cannot spend it. But money can always and everywhere be spent, and, moreover, forbidden fruit is sweetest of all. Even vodka could be got in prison. Pipes were strictly forbidden, but everyone smoked them. Money and tobacco saved them from scurvy and other diseases. Work saved them from crime; without work the convicts would have devoured one another like spiders in a glass jar. In spite of this, both work and money were forbidden. From time to time a sudden search was made at night and all forbidden articles were carried off, and however carefully money was hidden, it was sometimes found by the searchers. This was partly why it was not saved but was quickly spent on drink; that was how vodka came to be brought into prison. After every search the guilty, in addition to losing their property, were severely punished. But after every search all they had lost was immediately replaced, new articles were promptly procured, and everything went on as before. The authorities knew this and the convicts did not grumble at the punishments, though such a life was like living on Vesuvius.

Those who did not know a craft carried on some other sort of trade. Some ways of doing so were rather original. Some, for instance, were only occupied in buying and retailing, and they sometimes sold things which it would never occur to anyone outside the walls of the prison to buy or sell, or, indeed, to consider as things at all. But the prisoners were very poor and had great commercial ability. The poorest rag had its price and was turned to account. They were so poor that money had quite a different value in prison. A great and complicated piece of work was paid for in farthings. Some practised moneylending with success. Convicts who had been extravagant or unlucky carried their last possessions to the moneylender and got from him a few copper coins at a fearful rate of interest. If the articles were not redeemed at the time fixed, they were sold without delay or remorse; the moneylending flourished to such an extent that even prison property liable to inspection was accepted as a pledge; for instance, the prison clothes, boots, and so on—things which were essential for every convict at every moment. But such transactions sometimes took a different though not altogether unexpected turn: the pawner after receiving the money would sometimes, without further talk, go straight to the senior sergeant in command, and inform him of the pawning of prison property, and it would be immediately taken back from the pawnbroker without even a report on the subject to the higher authorities. It is a curious fact that sometimes this was not followed by a quarrel: the moneylender returned what was required in sullen silence, and seemed even to expect what had happened. Perhaps he could not help admitting that in the pawner's place he would have done the same. And so even if he sometimes swore afterwards, it would be without malice, simply to appease his conscience.

Generally speaking, they stole from one another dreadfully. Almost everyone had a box of his own, with a lock on it to keep his prison belongings in. This was allowed; but boxes were no security. One may imagine that there were skilful thieves among them. A convict who was sincerely attached to me (this is no exaggeration) stole from me a Bible, the only book which one was allowed to have in the prison; he confessed it to me himself the same day, not from repentance, but feeling sorry for me because I spent such a long time looking for it.

There were convicts who traded in vodka and soon grew rich. Of this trade I will speak more in detail later: it was rather remarkable. There were many convicts who were in prison for smuggling, and so it was scarcely to be wondered at that vodka was brought into the prison in spite of guards and supervision. Smuggling, by the way, is a crime of a peculiar character. Would it be believed, for instance, that gain is only a secondary consideration with some smugglers, and is never in the foreground of their minds? Yet there are cases of this kind. A smuggler works from inclination, from passion. He is on one side an artist. He risks everything, runs terrible dangers; he is cunning, invents dodges, and gets out of scrapes, and sometimes acts with a sort of inspiration. It is a passion as strong as gambling. I knew a convict in the prison, of colossal proportions physically, but so quiet, gentle and meek that it was impossible to imagine how he had got into prison. He was so mild and easy to get on with that all the while he was in prison he never quarrelled with anyone. But he was a smuggler who came from the western frontier, and, of course, he could not resist smuggling vodka into the prison. How often he was punished for doing this, and how he dreaded the lash! And for bringing in the vodka he was paid the merest trifle. No one made money out of it but the dealer. The queer fellow loved art for art's sake. He was as lachrymose as a woman, and how often after being punished he swore and vowed not to smuggle. He manfully controlled himself sometimes for a whole month, but yet in the end he broke down. . . . Thanks to men like him, there was no stint of vodka in the prison.

Finally there was another source of income for the convicts, which, though it did not enrich them, was constant and very welcome. This was charity. The higher classes in Russia have no idea how deeply our merchants, tradespeople and peasants concern themselves about "the unfortunates." Almsgiving is almost continual, usually in the form of bread, fancy loaves and rolls, far more rarely in money. But for these gifts, in many places prisoners, especially those who are awaiting trial and are much worse treated than convicts, would fare badly. The alms are divided with religious exactitude among the convicts. If there is not enough for all, the loaves are cut up equally, sometimes even into six portions, and every prisoner invariably receives his piece.

I remember the first time I received money alms. It was soon after my arrival in the prison. I was returning from my morning work alone with the guard. There came to meet me a mother and her child, a little girl of ten, pretty as an angel. I had seen them once already, the mother was the widow of a soldier. Her husband, a young soldier, had died in hospital in the convict ward while awaiting his trial, at the time when I, too, was lying ill there. The mother and daughter came to say good-bye to him; both cried terribly. Seeing me the little girl flushed and whispered something to her mother. The latter at once stopped short, found a farthing in her bag and gave it to the child. The latter flew running after me. "There, poor man, take a farthing, for Christ's sake!"[1] she cried, overtaking me and thrusting the coin into my hand. I took her farthing, and the girl returned to her mother quite satisfied. I treasured that farthing for a long time.

CHAPTER II

FIRST IMPRESSIONS (1)

THE FIRST MONTH AND all the early days of my prison life rise vividly before my imagination now. My other prison years flit far more dimly through my memory. Some seem to have sunk completely into the background, to have melted together, leaving only one collective impression—oppressive, monotonous, suffocating.

But all I went through during my first days in Siberia is as vivid to me now as though it had happened yesterday. And this is bound to be so.

I remember clearly that from the first step what struck me most in this life was that I found in it nothing striking, nothing exceptional or, rather, nothing unexpected. It seemed as though I had had glimpses of it in my imagination when, on my way to Siberia, I tried to conjecture what lay in store for me. But soon I began to find a mass of the strangest surprises, the most monstrous facts awaiting me at every step. And it was only later, after I had been some time in the prison, that I realized fully the exceptional, the surprising nature of such an existence, and I marvelled at it more and more. I must confess that this wonder did not leave me throughout the long years of my imprisonment; I never could get used to it.

My first impression on entering the prison was most revolting, and yet strange to say it seemed to me that life in prison was much easier than on the journey I had fancied it would be. Though the prisoners wore fetters, they walked freely about the prison, swore, sang songs, did work on their own account, smoked, even drank vodka (though very few of them) and at night some of them played cards. The labour, for instance, seemed to me by no means so hard, so *penal*, and only long afterwards I realized that the hardness, the penal character of the work lay not so much in its being difficult and uninterrupted as in its being *compulsory*, obligatory, enforced. The peasant in freedom works, I dare say, incomparably harder, sometimes even all night, especially in the summer; but he is working for himself, he is working with a rational object, and it makes it much easier for him than for the convict working at forced labour which is completely useless to himself. The idea has occurred to me that if one wanted to crush, to annihilate a man utterly, to inflict on him the most terrible of punishments so that the most ferocious murderer would shudder at it and dread it beforehand, one need only give him work of an absolutely, completely useless and irrational character. Though the hard labour now enforced is uninteresting and wearisome for the prisoner, yet in itself as work it is rational; the convict makes bricks, digs, does plastering, building; there is sense and meaning in such work. The convict worker sometimes even grows keen over it, tries to work more skilfully, faster, better. But if he had to pour water from one vessel into another and back, over and over again, to pound sand, to move a heap of earth from one place to another and back again—I believe the convict would hang himself in a few days or would commit a thousand crimes, preferring rather to die than endure such humiliation, shame and torture. Of course such a punishment would become a torture, a form of vengeance, and would be senseless, as it would achieve no rational object. But as something of such torture, senselessness, humiliation and shame is an inevitable element in all forced labour, penal labour is incomparably more painful than any free labour—just because it is forced.

I entered the prison in winter, however, in December, and had as yet no conception of the summer work, which was five times as hard. In winter compulsory work was generally scarce in our prison. The convicts used to go to the River Irtish to break up old government barges, to work in the workshops, to shovel away snow-drifts from government buildings, to bake and pound alabaster and so on. The winter day was short, the work was soon over and all of us returned early to the prison, where there was scarcely anything for us to do, if one did not happen to have work of one's own. But only a third of the prisoners, perhaps, were occupied in work of their own. The others were simply idle, wandered aimlessly all over the prison, swore at one another, got up intrigues and rows, got drunk if they could scrape up a little money, at night staked their last shirt at cards, and all this from boredom, from idleness, from having nothing to do. Later on I realized that besides the loss of freedom, besides the forced labour, there

is another torture in prison life, almost more terrible than any other—
that is, *compulsory life in common*. Life in common is to be found of course
in other places, but there are men in prison whom not everyone
would care to associate with and I am certain that every convict felt
this torture, though of course in most cases unconsciously.

The food too seemed to me fairly sufficient. The convicts used to
declare that it was not so good in disciplinary battalions in European
Russia. That I cannot undertake to pronounce upon: I have not been in
them. Moreover, many of the convicts were able to have food of their
own. Beef cost a halfpenny a pound, in summer three farthings. But
only those who always had money used to buy food for themselves;
the majority of the convicts ate only what was provided. But when the
convicts praised the prison fare they referred only to the bread and
they blessed the fact that it was given us all together and was not
served out in rations. The latter system horrified them; had the bread
been served out by weight, a third of the people would have been
hungry; but served in common there was plenty for everyone. Our
bread was particularly nice and was celebrated throughout the town. It
was ascribed to the successful construction of the prison oven. But the
cabbage soup was very unattractive. It was cooked in a common caul-
dron, was slightly thickened with grain and, particularly on working
days, was thin and watery. I was horrified at the immense number of
cockroaches in it. The convicts took absolutely no notice of them.

The first three days I did not go to work; it was the custom with
every prisoner on arrival to give him a rest after the journey. But I had
to go out next day to have my fetters changed. My fetters were not
the right pattern, they were made of rings, "tinklers," as the convicts
called them. They were worn outside the clothes. The regulation
prison fetters that did not prevent the prisoner from working were
not made of rings, but of four iron rods almost as thick as a finger,
joined together by three rings. They had to be put on under the
trousers. A strap was fastened to the middle ring and this strap was
fastened to the prisoner's belt which he wore next to his shirt.

I remember my first morning in the prison. In the guardhouse at
the prison gates the drum beat for daybreak and ten minutes later the
sergeant on duty began unlocking the prison wards. We began to
wake up. By the dim light of a tallow candle the prisoners got up
from their sleeping platform, shivering with cold. Most of them were

silent and sleepily sullen. They yawned, stretched and wrinkled up
their branded foreheads. Some were crossing themselves, others had
already begun to quarrel. The stuffiness was awful. The fresh winter
air rushed in at the door as soon as it was opened and floated in
clouds of steam through the barracks. The prisoners crowded round
the buckets of water; in turns they took the dipper, filled their mouths
with water and washed their hands and faces from their mouths. Water
was brought in overnight by the *parashnik* or slop-pail man. In every
room there was by regulation a prisoner elected by the others to do
the work of the room. He was called the *parashnik* and did not go out
to work. His duty was to keep the room clean, to wash and scrub the
platform beds and the floor, to bring in and remove the night pail
and to bring in two buckets of fresh water—in the morning for
washing and in the daytime for drinking. They began quarrelling at
once over the dipper; there was only one for all of us.

"Where are you shoving, you roach-head!" grumbled a tall surly
convict, lean and swarthy with strange protuberances on his shaven
head, as he pushed another, a stout, squat fellow with a merry, ruddy
face. "Stay there!"

"What are you shouting for? Folks pay for their stay, you know!
You get along yourself! There he stands like a monument. There isn't
any *fortikultiapnost* about him, brothers!"

This invented word produced a certain sensation. Many of them
laughed. That was all the cheery fat man wanted. He evidently played
the part of a gratuitous jester in the room. The tall convict looked at
him with the deepest contempt.

"You great sow!" he said as though to himself. "He's grown fat on
the prison bread. Glad he'll give us a litter of twelve sucking pigs by
Christmas."

The fat man got angry at last.

"But what sort of queer bird are you?" he cried, suddenly turning
crimson.

"Just so, a bird."

"What sort?"

"That sort."

"What sort's that sort?"

"Why, that sort, that's all."

"But what sort?"

They fixed their eyes on each other. The fat man waited for an answer and clenched his fists as though he meant to fall to fighting at once. I really thought there would be a fight. All this was new to me and I looked on with curiosity. But afterwards I found out that such scenes were extremely harmless; that they were played by way of a farce for the general entertainment and hardly ever ended in fights. It was all a fairly typical specimen of prison manners.

The tall convict stood calm and majestic. He felt that they were looking at him and waiting to see whether he would discredit himself by his answer or not; that he must keep up his reputation and show that he really was a bird and what sort of bird he was. He looked with inexpressible contempt at his opponent, trying to insult him to the utmost by looking down upon him as it were over his shoulder, as though he were examining him like an insect, and slowly and distinctly he brought out:

"Cocky-locky!"

Meaning that that was the bird he was. A loud roar of laughter greeted the convict's readiness.

"You are a rascal not a cocky-locky!" roared the fat man, feeling he had been done at every point and flying into a violent rage.

But as soon as the quarrel became serious the combatants were at once pulled up.

"What are you shouting about!" the whole room roared at them.

"You'd better fight than split your throats!" someone called from a corner.

"Likely they'd fight!" sounded in reply. "We are a bold, saucy lot; when we are seven against one we are not frightened."

"They are both fine fellows! One was sent here for a pound of bread, and the other is a plate-licking jade; he guzzled a country woman's junket, that's what he got the knout for!"

"Come, come, come, shut up!" cried the veteran soldier who had to be in the room to keep order and so slept on a special bedstead in the corner.

"Water, lads! Old Petrovitch has waked up. Good morning, old veteran Petrovitch, dear brother!"

"Brother . . . brother indeed! I never drank a rouble with you and I am brother, am I!" grumbled the old soldier putting his arms into the sleeves of his overcoat.

They were making ready for inspection; it began to get light; a dense, closely packed crowd had gathered in the kitchen. The convicts in their sheepskins and particoloured caps were crowding round the bread which one of the cooks was cutting up for them. The cooks were chosen by the prisoners, two for each kitchen. They kept the knife, one only for each kitchen, to cut up the bread and meat.

In every corner and all about the tables there were convicts with their caps and sheepskins on, their belts fastened, ready to go out to work at once. Before some of them stood wooden cups of kvas. They crumbled the bread into the kvas and sipped that. The noise and uproar were insufferable; but some were talking quietly and sensibly in the corners.

"A good breakfast to old man Antonitch, good morning!" said a young convict sitting down by a frowning and toothless prisoner.

"Well, good morning, if you mean it," said the other, not raising his eyes and trying to munch the bread with his toothless gums.

"I thought you were dead, Antonitch, I really did."

"No, you may die first, I'll come later."

I sat down beside them. Two steady-looking convicts were talking on my right, evidently trying to keep up their dignity with one another.

"They won't steal from me, no fear," said one. "There's more chance of my stealing something from them."

"I am a prickly customer too."

"Are you though? You are a jail-bird like everyone else; there's no other name for us. . . . She'll strip you and not say thank you. That's where my money went, brother. She came herself the other day. Where could I go with her? I began asking to go to Fedka-Hangman's, he's got a house at the end of the town, he bought it from the Jew, Scabby-Solomon, the fellow who hanged himself afterwards."

"I know. He used to sell vodka here three years ago and was nick-named Grishka Black Pot-house. I know."

"No, you don't know. That was another fellow, Black Pot-house."

"Another! You know a fat lot. I'll bring you ever so many witnesses."

"You'll bring witnesses! Where do you come from and who am I?"

"Who are you? Why, I used to beat you and I don't boast of it and you ask who are you!"

"You used to beat me! Why, the man's not born who'll beat me, and the man who did is underground."

"You Bender pest!"

"Siberian plague take you!"

"And I hope a Turkish sabre will have something to say to you!"

A storm of abuse followed.

"Come, come! They are at it again!" people shouted round them. "They couldn't live in freedom; they may be glad they've bread to eat here. . . ."

They quieted them down at once. Swearing, "wagging your tongue" is allowed. It is to some extent an entertainment for all. But they don't always let it come to a fight, and it is only rarely, in exceptional cases, that enemies fight. Fights are reported to the major; investigations follow, the major himself comes—in short, everyone has to suffer for it, and so fights are not allowed. And indeed the combatants swear at one another rather for entertainment, for the exercise of their linguistic powers. Often they deceive themselves, they begin very hot and exasperated. One fancies they will fall on one another in a minute; not a bit of it: they go on to a certain point and then separate at once. All this surprised me immensely at first. I have intentionally quoted here a typical specimen of convict conversation. I could not imagine at first how they could abuse one another for pleasure, find in it amusement, pleasant exercise, enjoyment. But one must not forget their vanity. A connoisseur in abuse was respected. He was almost applauded like an actor.

The evening before, I had noticed that they looked askance at me.

I had caught several dark looks already. On the other hand some of the convicts hung about me suspecting I had brought money with me. They began making up to me at once, began showing me how to wear my new fetters, got me—for money of course—a box with a lock on it, for me to put away the prison belongings already served out to me, as well as some underclothes I brought with me into the prison. Next day they stole it from me and sold it for drink. One of them became most devoted to me later on, though he never gave up robbing me at every convenient opportunity. He did this without the slightest embarrassment, almost unconsciously, as though fulfilling a duty, and it was impossible to be angry with him.

Among other things, they told me that I ought to have tea of my own, that it would be a good thing for me to have a teapot too, and meanwhile they got me one on hire, and recommended a cook, saying that for thirty kopecks a month he would cook me anything I liked if I cared to eat apart and buy my own provisions. . . . They borrowed money from me of course, and every one of them came to borrow from me three times the first day.

As a rule, convicts who have been gentlemen are looked at with hostility and dislike.

In spite of the fact that they are deprived of all the rights of their rank and are put on exactly the same level as the other prisoners, the convicts never consider them their comrades. This is not the result of conscious prejudice but comes about of itself, quite sincerely and unconsciously. They genuinely looked upon us as gentlemen, though they liked to taunt us with our downfall.

"No, now it's time to pull up! In Moscow, Pyotr drove like a lord, but now Pyotr sits and twists a cord," and similar pleasantries were frequent.

They looked with enjoyment at our sufferings, which we tried to conceal from them. We used to have a particularly bad time at work because we had not as much strength as they had and could not do our full share in helping them. Nothing is harder than to win people's confidence (especially such people's) and to gain their love.

There were several men belonging to the upper classes in the prison. To begin with there were five or six Poles. I will speak of them separately later on. The convicts particularly disliked the Poles, even more than those who had been Russian gentlemen. The Poles (I am speaking only of the political prisoners) were elaborately, offensively polite and exceedingly uncommunicative with them. They never could conceal from the convicts their aversion for them, and the latter saw it very clearly and paid the Poles back in the same coin.

I spent nearly two years in the prison before I could succeed in gaining the goodwill of some of the convicts. But in the end most of them grew fond of me and recognized me as a "good" man.

There were four other Russians of the upper class besides me. One was a mean abject little creature, terribly depraved, a spy and informer by vocation. I had heard about him before I came to the prison, and broke off all relations with him after the first few days. Another was the parricide of whom I have spoken already. The third was Akim

Akimitch; I have rarely met such a queer fellow as this Akim Akimitch. I have still a vivid recollection of him. He was tall, lean, dull-
witted, awfully illiterate, very prosy and as precise as a German. The
convicts used to laugh at him, but some of them were positively
afraid to have anything to do with him, owing to his fault-finding,
his exactingness and his readiness to take offence. He got on to familiar terms with them from the first, he quarrelled and even fought with
them. He was phenomenally honest. If he noticed any injustice he always interfered, though it might have nothing to do with him. He was
naïve in the extreme; when he quarrelled with the convicts he sometimes reproached them with being thieves and seriously exhorted
them not to steal. He had been a lieutenant in the Caucasus. We were
friendly from the first day, and he immediately told me about his
case. He began as a cadet in an infantry regiment in the Caucasus,
plodded on steadily for a long time, was promoted to be an officer at
last, and was sent as senior in command to a fortress. One of the allied chieftains burnt his fortress and made a night assault upon it.
This was unsuccessful. Akim Akimitch was wily and gave no sign of
knowing who had done it. The attack was attributed to the hostile
tribes, and a month later Akim Akimitch invited the chieftain to visit
him in a friendly way. The latter came, suspecting nothing. Akim Akimitch drew up his company, proved the chieftain's guilt and upbraided
him before them all, pointing out to him that it was shameful to burn
fortresses. He discoursed to him in great detail on the way allied chiefs
should behave in the future, and, in conclusion, shot him and at once
sent in a full report of the proceedings to the authorities. For all this he
was court-martialled and condemned to death, but the sentence was
commuted and he was sent to Siberia to penal servitude in the second
division for twelve years. He fully recognized that he had acted irregularly. He told me he knew it even before he shot the chieftain, he
knew that an ally ought to be legally tried; but, although he knew this,
he seemed unable to see his guilt in its true light.

"Why, upon my word! Hadn't he burnt my fortress? Was I to say
thank you to him for it?" he said to me in reply to my objections.

But, although the convicts laughed at Akim Akimitch's foolishness,
they respected him for his preciseness and practical ability.

There was no handicraft which Akim Akimitch did not understand.
He was a cabinet-maker, a cobbler, a shoemaker, a painter, a gilder,

a locksmith, and he had learnt all this in the prison. He was self-taught in everything; he would take one look at a thing and do it. He used to make all sorts of little boxes, baskets, lanterns, children's toys, and sold them in the town. In that way he made a little money and he immediately spent it on extra underclothes, on a softer pillow or a folding mattress. He was in the same room as I was, and was very helpful to me during my first days in prison.

When they went out from prison to work the convicts used to be drawn up in two rows before the guard-house; in front of them and behind them the soldiers were drawn up, with loaded muskets. An officer of the Engineers, the foreman and several engineers of the lower rank, who used to superintend our work, came out. The foreman grouped the convicts and sent them to work in parties where they were needed.

I went with the others to the engineers' workshop. It was a low-pitched stone building standing in a large courtyard which was heaped up with all sorts of materials; there was a smithy, a locksmith's shop, a carpenter's, a painter's and so on. Akim Akimitch used to come here and work at painting; he boiled the oil, mixed the colours and stained tables and other furniture to look like walnut.

While I was waiting for my fetters to be changed, I was talking to Akim Akimitch about my first impressions in prison.

"Yes, they are not fond of gentlemen," he observed, "especially politicals; they are ready to devour them; no wonder. To begin with, you are a different sort of people, unlike them; besides, they've all been serfs or soldiers. Judge for yourself whether they would be likely to be fond of you. It's a hard life here, I can tell you. And in the Russian disciplinary battalions it's worse still. Some of these fellows come from them and they are never tired of praising our prison, they say it's like coming from hell to paradise. It's not the work that's the trouble. There in the first division they say the authorities are not all military, anyhow they behave very differently from here. There they say the convicts can have little homes of their own. I haven't been there, but that's what they say. They don't have their heads shaved, they don't wear a uniform, though it's a good thing they do wear a uniform and have their heads shaved here; it's more orderly, anyway, and it's pleasanter to the eye. Only they don't like it. And look what a mixed rabble they are! One will be a Kantonist,[2] another will be a Circassian, a third an Old

Believer, a fourth will be an orthodox peasant who has left a wife and dear little children behind in Russia, the fifth will be a Jew, the sixth a gipsy, and the seventh God knows who; and they've all got to live together, they've all got to get on together somehow, eat out of the same bowl, sleep on the same bed. And no sort of freedom. If you want an extra crust you must eat it on the sly; every farthing you've to hide in your boots, and nothing before you but prison and more prison. . . . You can't help all sorts of nonsense coming into your head."

But I knew that already. I particularly wanted to question him about our major. Akim Akimitch made no secret of things and I remember my impression was not altogether agreeable.

But I had to live for two years under his rule. All that Akim Akimitch told me about him turned out to be perfectly true, with the only difference that the impression made by the reality is always stronger than that made by description. The man was terrible, just because being such a man he had almost unlimited power over two hundred souls. In himself he was simply a spiteful and ill-regulated man, nothing more; he looked on the convicts as his natural enemies and that was his first and great mistake. He really had some ability, but everything, even what was good in him, came out in a distorted form. Unrestrained and ill-tempered, he would sometimes burst into the prison even at night, and if he noticed that a convict was sleeping on his left side or on his back he would have him punished next day: "You've to sleep on your right side, as I've ordered you." In the prison he was hated and feared like the plague. His face was purplish crimson and ferocious. Everyone knew that he was completely in the hands of his orderly, Fedka. What he loved most in the world was his poodle, Trezorka, and he almost went mad with grief when Trezorka fell ill. They say he sobbed over him as though it had been his own son; he drove away one veterinary surgeon and, after his usual fashion, almost beat him. Hearing from Fedka that one of the convicts in the prison was a self-taught "vet" who was very successful in curing animals, he called him in at once.

"Help me! I'll load you with gold, cure Trezorka!" he shouted to the convict.

The man was a Siberian peasant, crafty, clever, really a very skilful vet, though a peasant in every sense of the word.

"I looked at Trezorka," he told the convicts afterwards, long after his visit to the major, however, when the whole story was forgotten.

"I looked—the dog was lying on a white cushion on the sofa and I saw it was inflammation, that it ought to be bled and the dog would get well, yes indeed! And I thinks to myself—what if I don't cure it, what if it dies? 'No, your honour,' said I, 'you called me in too late; if it had been yesterday or the day before, I could have cured the dog, but now I can't.'"

So Trezorka died.

I was told in detail of an attempt to kill the major. There was a convict in the prison who had been there several years and was distinguished for his mild behaviour. It was observed, too, that he hardly ever spoke to anyone. He was looked upon as a bit queer in the religious way. He could read and write and during the last year he was continually reading the Bible, he read it day and night. When everyone was asleep he would get up at midnight, light a church wax candle, climb on to the stove, open the book and read till morning. One day he went up and told the sergeant that he would not go to work. It was reported to the major; he flew into a rage, and rushed into the prison at once himself. The convict threw himself upon him with a brick he had got ready beforehand, but missed his aim. He was seized, tried and punished. It all happened very quickly. Three days later he died in the hospital. As he lay dying he said that he meant no harm to anyone, but was only seeking suffering. He did not, however, belong to any dissenting sect. In the prison he was remembered with respect.

At last my fetters were changed. Meanwhile several girls selling rolls had come into the workshop. Some of them were quite little girls. They used to come with the rolls till they were grown up; their mothers baked them and they brought them for sale. When they were grown up they still came, but not to sell bread; this was almost always the case. There were some who were not little girls. The rolls cost a halfpenny and almost all the convicts bought them.

I noticed one of the convicts, a grey-headed but ruddy cabinet-maker, smiling and flirting with the baker girls. Just before they came in he had tied a red handkerchief round his neck. A fat peasant woman whose face was covered with pock-marks put her tray on his bench. Conversation began between them.

"Why didn't you turn up yesterday?" said the convict with a self-satisfied smile.

"Upon my word I did, but not a sign to be seen of you," answered the lively woman.

"I was wanted, or you may be sure I'd have been there . . . The day before yesterday all your lot came to see me."

"Who did?"

"Maryashka came, Havroshka came, Tchekunda came, Twopenny-halfpenny came."

"What does it mean?" I asked Akim Akimitch. "Is it possible?"

"It does happen," he answered, dropping his eyes discreetly, for he was an extremely chaste man.

It certainly did happen, but very rarely, and in spite of immense difficulties. On the whole, men were much more keen on drinking, for instance, than on that sort of thing, in spite of its being naturally difficult for them to live in the way they were forced to do. Women were difficult to get hold of. The time and place had to be found, arrangements had to be made, meetings had to be fixed, seclusion had to be sought, which was particularly difficult, the guards had to be won over, which was still more difficult, and altogether a sum of money—immense, relatively speaking—had to be spent. Yet I happened sometimes, later on, to be a witness of amatory scenes. I remember one day in the summer we were three of us in a shed on the bank of the Irtish, heating some sort of kiln; the guards were good-natured fellows. At last two "frillies," as the convicts called them, made their appearance.

"Well, where have you been so long? I bet you've been at the Zvyerkovs," was how they were greeted by the convict whom they had come to see and who had been expecting them a long time.

"I've been so long? Why, I haven't been there longer than a magpie on a pole," the girl answered gaily.

She was the dirtiest girl imaginable. She was the one called Tchekunda. With her came Twopenny-halfpenny. The latter was beyond all description.

"I've not seen you for a long time, either," the gallant went on, addressing Twopenny-halfpenny; "how is it you seem to be thinner?"

"Maybe. I used to be ever so fat, but now one would think I'd swallowed a needle."

"Always being with the soldiers, eh?"

"No, that's a lie that spiteful tongues have told you; though what of it? Though I'm thin as any rake, the soldier-lads I'll ne'er forsake!"

"You chuck them and love us; we've got cash. . . ."

To complete the picture, imagine this gallant with a shaven head, in parti-coloured clothes, guarded and in fetters.

I took leave of Akim Akimitch, and hearing that I might go back to the prison, I went back escorted by a guard. The convicts were already coming home. The men on piece-work are the first to return. The only way of making a convict work hard is to put him on piece-work. Sometimes huge tasks are set them, but they always do the work twice as quickly as when they are working by the day. When he finishes his task the convict goes home without hindrance and no one prevents his doing so.

They don't dine all together, but as they come in, just as it happens; indeed, there would not have been room for them all at once in the kitchen. I tried the soup, but not being used to it I could not eat it, and I made myself some tea. We sat down at the end of the table. With me was a comrade of the same social class as myself.

Convicts kept going and coming. There was plenty of room however; they were not yet all in. A group of five men sat down together at the big table. The cook poured them out two bowls of soup and put on the table a whole dish of fried fish. They were keeping some sort of fête and eating their own food. They cast unfriendly glances in our direction. One of the Poles came in and sat down beside us.

"I've not been at home, but I know all the news," a tall convict shouted aloud as he walked into the kitchen and looked round at everyone present.

He was a thin, muscular man of fifty. There was something sly, and at the same time merry, about his face. What was particularly striking about him was his thick, protruding lower lip; it gave a peculiarly comic look to his face.

"Well, have you had a good night? Why don't you say good morning? Hullo, my Kursk friends!" he added, sitting down beside the group who were eating their own food. "A good appetite to you! Give a welcome to a friend."

"We are not Kursk men, brother."

"Tambov, then?"

"But we are not from Tambov either. You'll get nothing from us, brother. You go and ask a rich peasant."

"I've colliwobbles and rumble-tumbles in my belly to-day. And where is he living, your rich peasant?"

"Why, Gazin yonder is a rich peasant, you go to him."

"Gazin's having a spree to-day, lads, he is drinking; he is drinking all his money."

"He's worth a good twenty roubles," observed another. "It's a good business, lads, selling vodka."

"Well, won't you welcome a friend? I must have a sup of regulation fare, then."

"You go and ask for some tea. The gentlemen there have got some."

"Gentlemen? There are no gentlemen here. They are the same as we are now," a convict sitting in the corner brought out gloomily. He had not said a word till then.

"I should like some tea, but I am ashamed to ask; we have our pride!" observed the convict with the protruding lip, looking good-naturedly at us.

"I'll give you some, if you like," I said, inviting the convict to have tea; "would you like some?"

"Like it? To be sure I'd like it."

He came up to the table.

"At home he ate broth out of a shoe, but here he's learnt to like tea; and wants to drink it like the gentry," the gloomy convict pronounced.

"Why, does no one drink tea here?" I asked him. But he did not deign to answer me.

"Here they are bringing rolls. Mayn't we have a roll, too?"

Rolls were brought in. A young convict brought in a whole bundle and was selling them in the prison. The baker girl used to give him one roll out of every ten he sold; he was reckoning on that tenth roll.

"Rolls, rolls!" he cried, entering the kitchen. "Moscow rolls, all hot! I'd eat them myself, but I haven't the money. Come, lads, the last roll is left; surely someone, for his mother's sake?"

This appeal to filial affection amused everyone and several rolls were bought.

"I say, lads," he announced, "Gazin will get into trouble, the way he's carrying on! Upon my word, he has pitched on a time to drink! Ten to one, Eight-Eyes will be round."

"They'll hide him. Why, is he very drunk?"

"Rather! He is wild, he is pestering everyone."

"Oh, it will end in a fight, then. . . ."

"Of whom are they talking?" I asked the Pole, who had sat down beside me.

"It's Gazin, a convict. He does a trade in vodka here. When he's saved up money enough, he spends it in drink. He is spiteful and cruel; when he is sober he is quiet, though; when he is drunk it all comes out; he flies at people with a knife. Then they have to restrain him."

"How do they restrain him?"

"A dozen convicts fall upon him and begin beating him horribly until he loses consciousness, they beat him till he is half dead. Then they lay him on the bed and cover him with a sheepskin."

"But they may kill him!"

"Anyone else would have been killed by now, but not he. He is awfully strong, stronger than anyone in the prison and of the healthiest constitution. Next day he is perfectly well."

"Tell me, please," I went on questioning the Pole; "here they are eating their own food while I drink my tea. And yet they look as though they were envious of the tea. What does it mean?"

"It's not because of the tea," answered the Pole. "They are ill-disposed to you because you are a gentleman and not like them. Many of them would like to pick a quarrel with you. They would dearly like to insult you, to humiliate you. You will meet with a lot of unpleasantness here. We have an awfully hard time. It's harder for us than for any of them. One needs to be philosophical to get used to it. You will meet unpleasantness and abuse again and again for having your own food and tea, though very many of them here frequently have their own food, and some have tea every day. They may, but you mustn't."

He got up and went away from the table; a few minutes later his words came true.

CHAPTER III

FIRST IMPRESSIONS (2)

M——y (THE POLE WHO had been talking to me) had scarcely gone out when Gazin rolled into the kitchen, hopelessly drunk.

This convict, drunk in broad daylight, on a working day when all were bound to be out at work, under the rule of a stern officer who might come into the prison at any moment, under the control of the sergeant who never left the prison, with guards and sentries about—in short, in the midst of severity and discipline—threw into confusion all the ideas I had begun to form of prison life. And it was a long time before I could explain to myself all the facts which were so puzzling to me during my early days in prison.

I have mentioned already that the convicts always had private work of their own and that such work was a natural craving in prison life; that, apart from this craving, the prisoner is passionately fond of money, and prizes it above everything, almost as much as freedom, and that he is comforted if he has it jingling in his pocket. On the other hand, he becomes dejected, sad, uneasy and out of spirits when he has none, and then he is ready to steal or do anything to get it. But, though money was so precious in prison, it never stayed long with the lucky man who had it. To begin with, it was difficult to keep it from being stolen or taken away. If the major discovered it in the course of a sudden search, he promptly confiscated it. Possibly he spent it on improving the prison fare; anyway, it was taken to him. But much more frequently it was stolen; there was no one who could be relied upon. Later on, we discovered a way of keeping money quite securely: it was put into the keeping of an Old Believer who came to us from the Starodubovsky settlements.

He was a little grey-headed man of sixty. He made a vivid impression on me from the first minute. He was so unlike the other convicts, there was something so calm and gentle in his expression that I remember I looked with a peculiar pleasure at his serene, candid eyes,

which were surrounded with tiny wrinkles like rays. I often talked to
him and I have rarely met a more kindly, warm-hearted creature in my
life. He had been sent there for a very serious offence. Among the Starodubovsky Old Believers, some converts to the Orthodox Church were
made. The government gave them great encouragement and began to
make great efforts for the conversion of the others. The old man resolved with other fanatics to stand up for the faith, as he expressed it.
An orthodox church was being built and they burnt it down. As one of
the instigators, the old man was sent to penal servitude. He had been
a well-to-do tradesman and left a wife and children behind him, but
he went with a brave heart into exile, for in his blindness he considered it "martyrdom for the faith." After spending some time with him,
one could not help asking oneself how this meek old man, as gentle as
a child, could have been a rebel. Several times I talked to him of "the
faith"; he would never yield an inch in his convictions, but there was
no trace of anger or of hatred in his replies. And yet he had destroyed
a church and did not deny doing it. It seemed that from his convictions he must have considered his action and his suffering for it a
glorious achievement. But, however closely I watched him and studied him, I never detected the faintest sign of pride or vanity in him.
There were other Old Believers in the prison, mostly Siberians. They
were very well-educated people, shrewd peasants, great students of
the Bible who quibbled over every letter, and great dialecticians in
their own way; they were a crafty, conceited, aggressive and extremely
intolerant set. The old man was absolutely different. Though perhaps
better read than they, he avoided argument. He was of a very communicative disposition. He was merry, often laughing, not with the coarse
cynical laugh of the other convicts, but with a gentle candid laugh, in
which there was a great deal of childlike simplicity that seemed peculiarly in keeping with his grey hair. I may be mistaken, but I fancy that
one can know a man from his laugh, and if you like a man's laugh before you know anything of him, you may confidently say that he is a
good man. Though the old man had gained the respect of all throughout the prison, he was not in the least conceited about it. The convicts used to call him grandfather, and they never insulted him. I
could partly imagine the sort of influence he must have had on his
fellow believers. But in spite of the unmistakable courage with which
he endured his punishment, there was also a deep inconsolable

melancholy in his heart, which he tried to conceal from all. I lived in the same room with him. One night I woke up at three o'clock and heard the sound of quiet, restrained weeping. The old man was sitting on the stove (the same stove on which the Bible reader who threw the brick at the major used to pray at night). He was saying his prayers over his manuscript book. He was weeping and I could hear him saying from time to time, "Lord, do not forsake me! Lord, give me strength! My little ones, my darling little ones, I shall never see you again!" I can't describe how sad it made me.

It was to this old man that almost all the convicts began by degrees to give their money, for him to take care of it. Almost all the prisoners were thieves, but suddenly for some reason the belief gained ground that the old man could not steal. They knew that he hid the money given into his keeping in some place so secret that no one could find it. In the end he explained his secret to me and some of the Poles. On one of the posts of the fence there was a twig apparently adhering firmly on the trunk. But it could be taken out, and there was a deep hollow in the wood. Here "grandfather" used to hide the money and then insert the twig again so that no one could ever find anything.

But I am wandering from my story. I was just saying why money never stayed long in a convict's pocket. Apart from the difficulty of keeping it, life in prison was so dreary, a convict is a creature by nature so eager for freedom, and from his social position so careless and reckless, that to "have his fling for all he is worth," to spend all his fortune carousing with noise and music and so to forget his depression, if only for the moment, naturally attracts him. It was strange to see how some of them would work unceasingly, sometimes for several months, simply to spend all their earnings in one day, leaving nothing, and then to drudge away for months again, till the next outbreak. Many of them were very fond of getting new clothes, which were never of the regulation pattern: black trousers unlike the uniform, tunics, coats. Cotton shirts and belts studded with metal discs were also in great demand. They dressed up on holidays, and then always paraded through all the prison wards to show themselves to all the world. Their pleasure in fine clothes was quite childish, and in many things the convicts were perfect children. It is true that all these fine things soon vanished from the owner's possession—sometimes they pawned or sold them for next to nothing the same evening. The

outbreak of drinking developed gradually, however. It was put off as
a rule till a holiday or till a nameday: on his nameday the convict set
a candle before the ikon and said his prayers as soon as he got up;
then he dressed in his best and ordered a dinner. He bought beef and
fish, Siberian patties were made; he would eat like an ox, almost always alone, rarely inviting his comrades to share his meal. Then
vodka was brought out; the hero of the day would get drunk as a lord
and always walked all over the prison, reeling and staggering, trying
to show to everyone that he was drunk, that he was "jolly" and so deserving of general respect. Everywhere among the Russian people a
certain sympathy is felt for a drunken man; in prison he was positively treated with respect. There were certain aristocratic customs
connected with prison revelry. The carousing convict always hired
music. There was a little Pole in prison, a runaway soldier, a nasty little fellow who played the fiddle and had an instrument—his one
possession in the world. He had no sort of trade, and his only way of
earning money was by playing lively dances for convicts who were
having a spree. His duty was to follow his drunken employer from
room to room and to play the fiddle with all his might. Often his face
betrayed boredom and dejection. But the shout of "Play on, you're
paid to do it!" made him go on scraping away. The convict can always
feel confident when he begins drinking that, if he gets too drunk, he
will certainly be looked after, will be put in bed in time and hidden
away if the authorities turn up, and all this will be quite disinterested.
The sergeant and the veteran guards, who lived in the prison to keep
discipline, could have their minds at rest too: the drunken convict
could not create any disorder. All the prisoners in the room looked after him, and if he were noisy or unmanageable they would quickly
restrain him and even tie him up. And so the inferior prison officials
winked at drunkenness and were unwilling to notice it. They knew
very well that if vodka were not allowed it would make things worse.
But how was vodka obtained?

It was bought in the prison itself from the so-called "publicans."
There were several of them, and they carried on their trade successfully
and unintermittently, though the number of those who drank and
"made merry" was small, for merry-making costs money and the convicts' money is hardly earned. The "publicans'" operations were begun,
managed and carried on in a very original way. Suppose a convict

knows no trade and is not willing to exert himself (there were men like this), but is keen on getting money and of an impatient disposition, in a hurry to make his pile. If he has a little money to start with, he makes up his mind to trade in vodka: it's a bold and risky enterprise involving considerable danger. He may have to pay for it with a flogging, and lose his stock and his capital all at once. But the "publican" takes the risk. He begins with a small sum, and so at first he smuggles the vodka into the prison himself, and, of course, disposes of it to great advantage. He repeats the experiment a second and a third time, and if he does not get caught he quickly sells his stock and only then builds up a real trade on a large scale: he becomes an entrepreneur, a capitalist, employs agents and assistants, runs far less risk and makes more and more money. His subordinates risk themselves for him.

There are always in the prison lots of men who have wasted all they have on cards or drink, wretched ragged creatures who have no trade but have a certain pluck and daring. The only asset such a man has left is his back; it may still be of some use to him and so the spendthrift profligate decides to turn it to profit. He goes to the "publican" and offers his services for smuggling vodka; a well-to-do "publican" has several such working for him. Somewhere outside the prison there is some person—a soldier, a workman, sometimes even a woman—who for a comparatively large commission buys vodka at a tavern with the "publican's" money and conceals it in some out-of-the-way place where the convicts go to work. Almost always the intermediary tests the quality of the vodka to begin with, and ruthlessly fills up the measure with water; the "publican" may take it or leave it—a convict is not in a position to make his own terms. He must be thankful that he has got the vodka, however poor the quality, and has not lost his money altogether. The "publican" introduces his agents to the intermediary beforehand, and then they go to the latter carrying with them the guts of a bullock, which have been washed and then filled with water to keep them supple and fit to hold vodka. When he has filled the guts with vodka the convict winds them round himself where they will be least conspicuous. I need not say that this calls forth all the ingenuity, all the thievish cunning of the smuggler. His honour is to some extent involved: he has to deceive both the guards and the sentries. He does deceive them: the guard, often a raw recruit, is never a match for a clever thief. Of course the guard is the subject of special study beforehand; besides, the time and place where he is working is all carefully considered, too, by the smuggler. The convict may be building a stove; he climbs on to the stove; who can tell what he is doing there? A guard cannot be expected to climb after him. On his way to the prison he takes some money in his hand, fifteen or twenty silver kopecks, in case of need, and waits for the corporal at the gate. The corporal examines every convict returning from work, and feels him over before opening the prison door to him. The man smuggling in vodka usually reckons on the corporal's scrupling to handle him too minutely in some parts. But sometimes the wily corporal does not stand on ceremony and discovers the vodka. Then there is only one thing left to do: the smuggler, unseen by the guard, silently slips into the corporal's hand the coin he has been keeping concealed in his own. It sometimes happens that, thanks to this manœuvre, he gets successfully into the prison with the vodka. But sometimes this method does not answer, and then he has to pay with his last asset, his back. It is reported to the major, the asset is flogged, and cruelly flogged, the vodka is confiscated and the agent takes it all on himself without giving away his employer, and, be it noted, not because he scorns to tell tales, but simply because it does not pay him to do so. He would be flogged anyway; his only consolation would be that the other man would be flogged too. But he will need his employer again, though in accordance with custom and previous agreement the smuggler gets nothing from his employer to compensate him for the flogging. As for telling tales in general, it is very common. In prison the man who turns traitor is not exposed to humiliation; indignation against him is unthinkable. He is not shunned, the others make friends with him; in fact, if you were to try and point out the loathsomeness of treachery, you would not be understood. The convict with whom I had broken off all relations, a mean and depraved creature who had been a gentleman, was friendly with the major's orderly, Fedka, and served him as a spy, while the latter reported all he heard about the convicts to the major. Every one of us knew this, yet no one ever dreamed of punishing the scoundrel or even reproaching him for it.

But I am wandering from my subject. It happens, of course, that vodka is smuggled in successfully. Then the "publican" takes the guts, pays for them, and begins to count the cost. It turns out when he reckons it that the stuff has cost him a great deal, and so to increase his profit he dilutes the vodka once more, adding almost an equal bulk of water, and then he is ready for his customers. On the first holiday, sometimes even on a working day, the customer turns up: this is a convict who has been working like an ox for some months, and has saved up his money in order to spend it all on drink on some day fixed beforehand. Long before it arrives, this day has been the object of the poor toiler's dreams at night and happy day-dreams over his work, and its fascination has kept up his spirits through the weary routine of prison life. At last the happy day dawns in the east; his money has been saved, not taken away, not stolen, and he brings it to the publican. To begin with, the latter gives him the vodka as pure as possible, that is, only twice diluted; but as the bottle gets emptier he invariably fills it up again with water. A cup of vodka costs five or six times as much as in a tavern. You can imagine how many cups of such vodka must be drunk, and what they will have cost before the point of intoxication is reached. But from having lost the habit of drinking, and having abstained from it so long, the convict readily gets drunk and he usually goes on drinking till he has spent all his money. Then he brings out all his new clothes; the publican is a pawnbroker as well. He first gets hold of the newly acquired personal possessions, then the old things and finally the prison clothes. When he has drunk up everything to the last rag, the drunken convict lies down to sleep, and next day, waking up with the inevitable splitting headache, he vainly entreats the publican to give him just a sip of vodka as a pick-me-up. Mournfully he endures his sad plight and the same day sets to work again, and works again for several months unceasingly, dreaming of the happy day of debauch lost and gone for ever, and by degrees beginning to take heart again and look forward to another similar day, still far away, but sure to come sometime in its turn.

As for the publican, after making a huge sum of money—some dozens of roubles—he gets the vodka ready for the last time, adding no water to it for he means it for himself—he has done enough of trading, it is time for him to enjoy himself too! Then begins an orgy of drinking, eating and music. With such means at his disposal he even softens the hearts of the inferior prison officials. The debauch sometimes lasts several days. All the vodka he has prepared is soon drunk, of course; then the prodigal resorts to the other publicans, who are on

the look-out for him, and drinks until he has spent every farthing!
However carefully the convicts guard their drunken fellow, he is sometimes seen by a higher official, by the major or the officer on duty. He
is taken to the guard-house, stripped of his money if he has it on him
and finally flogged. He shakes himself, goes back into the prison, and
a few days later takes up his trade in vodka again. Some of the festive
characters, the rich ones of course, have dreams of the fair sex, too;
for a big bribe to the guard escorting them, they can sometimes be
taken in secret to some place in town instead of to work. There in
some out-of-the-way little house at the furthest end of the town
there is a feast on a huge scale, and really large sums of money are
squandered. Even a convict is not despised if he has money. A guard
is picked out beforehand who knows his way about. Such guards are
usually future candidates for prison themselves. But anything can be
done for money, and such expeditions almost always remain a secret.
I must add that they are a very rare occurrence; so much money is
needed and devotees of the fair sex have recourse to other methods
which are quite free from danger.

Before I had been many days in prison my curiosity was particularly aroused by a young convict, a very pretty lad. He was called
Sirotkin. He was rather an enigmatic creature in many ways. What
struck me first of all was his beautiful face; he was not more than
three-and-twenty. He was in the "special division," that is, of criminals with a life sentence, which means that he was considered one of
the worst of the military convicts. Mild and gentle, he talked little and
rarely laughed. He had blue eyes, regular features, a clear-skinned
delicate face and fair hair. He was such a pretty fellow that even his
half-shaven head hardly disfigured him. He knew no sort of trade but
he often had money, though not much at a time. One could see that he
was lazy, and he was untidy in his dress. But occasionally someone
would give him something nice to wear, even sometimes a red shirt,
and Sirotkin was obviously pleased at his new clothes and walked
about the prison to show himself. He did not drink nor play cards, and
hardly ever quarrelled with anyone. He used to walk behind the
prison with his hands in his pockets, quiet and dreamy. What he
could be dreaming about it was difficult to guess. If one called to him
sometimes from curiosity, asked him some question, he answered at
once and even respectfully, not like a convict, though always briefly

and uncommunicatively; and he looked at one like a child of ten years old. When he had any money he did not buy himself something necessary, did not get his coat mended, did not order new boots, but bought rolls or gingerbread and ate them like a child of seven. "Ah, you Sirotkin,"* the convicts would say to him sometimes, "you are an orphan all forlorn!" Out of working hours he used to wander about the prison barracks; almost everyone else would be at work, only he had nothing to do. If anything was said to him, usually a taunt (he and the others in his division were often made fun of), he would turn round and go off to another room without saying a word; sometimes he blushed crimson if he were much ridiculed. I often wondered how this peaceable, simple-hearted creature had come into prison. Once I was in the convicts' ward in the hospital. Sirotkin too was ill, and was in the bed next to mine; one evening we fell into talk. Somehow he got warmed up, and incidentally told me how he had been taken for a soldier, how his mother cried seeing him off, and how wretched he was as a recruit. He added that he could not endure the life of a recruit, because everyone there was so cross and stern, and the officers were almost always displeased with him.

"How did it end?" I asked. "What brought you here? And in the special division too. . . . Ah, Sirotkin, Sirotkin!"

"Why, I was only a year in the battalion, Alexandr Petrovitch, and I came here because I killed my commanding officer."

"I'd heard it, Sirotkin, but I can't believe it. How could you kill anyone?"

"It happened so, Alexandr Petrovitch. I was awfully miserable."

"But how do the other recruits manage? Of course it's hard at first, but they get used to it and in the end they become fine soldiers. Your mother must have spoiled you; she fed you on milk and goodies till you were eighteen."

"My mother was very fond of me, it's true. She took to her bed when I went for a recruit and I've heard she never got up from it. . . . Life was very bitter to me at last when I was a recruit. The officer did not like me, he was always punishing me—and what for? I gave way to everyone, was punctual in everything, did not touch vodka, did not

---

*In Russian *Sirota* (Garnett's note).

pick up any habits; it's a bad business, you know, Alexandr Petrovitch, when one picks up habits. Such cruel-heartedness everywhere, no chance to have a good cry. Sometimes you'd get behind a corner and cry there. Well, I was once on sentry duty. It was at night; I was put as sentry by the gun-rack. It was windy; it was autumn, and pitch-dark. And I felt so sick, so sick. I stood my gun on the ground, I twisted off the bayonet and put it on one side; slipped off my right boot, put the barrel to my breast, leant against it and with my big toe pulled the trigger. It missed fire. I looked at the gun, cleaned the touch-hole, poured some fresh powder into it, struck the flint and put the gun to my breast again. And would you believe it? The powder flashed but the gun did not go off again. I wondered what was the meaning of it. I took my boot and put it on, fixed on the bayonet and walked to and fro, saying nothing. It was then I made up my mind to do what I did: I did not care where I went if I could get away from there. Half an hour later, the officer rode up; he was making the chief round of inspection. He went straight for me: "Is that the way to stand on sentry duty?" I took my gun in my hand and stuck the bayonet into him up to the hilt. I've come four thousand miles and I am here with a life sentence. . . ."

He was not lying. And for what other crime could he have been given a life sentence? Ordinary crimes are punished far more leniently. But Sirotkin was the only good-looking one of these "lifers." As for the others in the same case, of whom there were about fifteen among us, it was strange to look at them: there were only two or three tolerable faces among them; the others were all such hideous creatures, filthy-looking, with long ears. Some of them were grey-headed men. If possible, I will describe all this group more exactly later on. Sirotkin was often friendly with Gazin, the convict whom I mentioned at the beginning of the chapter, describing how he staggered into the kitchen drunk and how he upset my preconceived ideas of prison life.

This Gazin was a horrible creature. He made a terrible and painful impression on everyone. It always seemed to me that there could not be a more ferocious monster than he was. I have seen at Tobolsk, Kamenev, a robber famous for his crimes; later on I saw Sokolov, a runaway soldier who was being tried for terrible murders he had committed. But neither of them made such a repulsive impression on me as Gazin. I sometimes felt as though I were looking at a huge gigantic spider of the size of a man. He was a Tatar, terribly strong, stronger than anyone in the prison, of more than average height, of Herculean proportions, with a hideous, disproportionately huge head; he walked with a slouch and looked sullenly from under his brows. There were strange rumours about him in the prison; it was known that he had been a soldier, but the convicts said among themselves, I do not know with what truth, that he was an escaped convict from Nertchinsk, that he had been sent more than once to Siberia and had escaped more than once, had more than once changed his name, and had at last been sent to our prison with a life sentence. It was said, too, that he had been fond of murdering small children simply for pleasure: he would lure the child to some convenient spot, begin by terrifying and tormenting it, and after enjoying to the full the shuddering terror of the poor little victim, he would kill it with a knife slowly, with deliberation and enjoyment. All this perhaps was invented in consequence of the feeling of oppression Gazin aroused in everyone; but all these stories were in keeping with him, and harmonized with his appearance. Yet at ordinary times, when he was not drunk, his behaviour in prison was very orderly. He was always quiet, did not quarrel with anyone, and avoided quarrels, but, as it seemed, from contempt for the others, as though he considered himself superior to all the rest; he spoke very little, and was, as it were, intentionally reserved. All his movements were calm, deliberate, self-confident. One could see from his eyes that he was very intelligent and exceedingly cunning; but there was always something of supercilious derision and cruelty in his face and smile. He traded in vodka, and was one of the richest vodka dealers in the prison. But about twice in the year he would get drunk himself, and then all the brutality of his nature came out. As he gradually got drunk, he began at first attacking people with gibes, the most spiteful, calculated, as it seemed, long-premeditated taunts; finally, when he was quite drunk he passed into a stage of blind fury, snatched up a knife and rushed at people. The convicts knowing his terrible strength ran and hid themselves: he fell upon anyone he met. But they soon found means to get control of him. A dozen men, inmates of the same prison ward as Gazin, would suddenly rush at him all at once and begin beating him. Nothing crueller could be imagined: they beat him on the chest, on the heart, on the pit of the stomach, on the belly; they beat him hard and beat him a long time; they only desisted when he lost consciousness and lay like a corpse. They could not have brought themselves to beat any other convict like that: to beat like that meant killing any other man, but not Gazin. Then they wrapped his unconscious body in a sheepskin and carried it to the bed. "He'll sleep it off." And he did in fact get up next morning almost uninjured and went to work, silent and sullen. Every time Gazin got drunk everyone in the prison knew that the day would certainly end in a beating for him. And he knew this himself and yet he got drunk. So it went on for several years; at last it was noticed that Gazin was beginning to break up. He began to complain of pains of all sorts, grew noticeably weaker and was more and more often in the hospital. "He is breaking up!" the convicts said among themselves.

He came into the kitchen, followed by the nasty little Pole with the fiddle, who was generally hired by the "festive convicts" to enhance their jollity, and he stood still in the middle of the room, silently and attentively scanning all present. All were silent. At last seeing me and my companion, he looked at us spitefully and derisively, smiled self-complacently, seemed to think of something, and staggering heavily came towards our table.

"Where did you get the money for this little treat may I inquire?" he began (he spoke Russian).

I exchanged silent glances with my companion, realizing that the best thing was to hold our tongues and not to answer him. At the first contradiction he would have flown into a fury.

"So you've money, have you?" He went on questioning us. "So you've a lot of money, eh? Have you come to prison to drink tea? You've come to drink tea, have you? Speak, damn you!"

But seeing that we had made up our minds to be silent and to take no notice of him, he turned crimson and shook with rage. Near him in the corner stood a big tray which was used for the slices of bread cut for the dinner or supper of the convicts. It was large enough to hold the bread for half the prison; at the moment it was empty. He picked it up with both hands and raised it above us. In another moment he would have smashed our heads. A murder, or an attempt at murder, threatened the whole prison with extremely unpleasant consequences: it would be followed by inquiries, searches and greater severity, and so the convicts did their utmost not to let things come to such an extremity. And yet in spite of that, on this occasion all kept quiet and waited. Not one word in our defence! Not one shout at Gazin, so intense was their hatred of us! They were apparently pleased at our dangerous position. But the incident passed off without harm: just as he was about to bring down the tray someone shouted from the passage:

"Gazin! Vodka's stolen!" He let the tray fall crashing on the floor and rushed like mad out of the kitchen.

"Well, God saved them!" the convicts said among themselves.

And they repeated it long after. I could not find out afterwards whether the news of the theft of the vodka was true or invented on the spur of the moment to save us.

In the evening, after dusk, before the prison was locked up, I walked round the fence and an overwhelming sadness came upon me. I never experienced such sadness again in all my prison life. The first day of confinement, whether it be in prison, in the fortress, or in Siberia, is hard to bear. . . But I remember what absorbed me more than anything was one thought, which haunted me persistently all the time I was in prison, a difficulty that cannot be fully solved—I cannot solve it even now: the inequality of punishment for the same crime. It is true that crimes cannot be compared even approximately. For instance, two men may commit murders; all the circumstances of each case are weighed; and in both cases almost the same punishment is given. Yet look at the difference between the crimes. One may have committed a murder for nothing, for an onion; he murdered a peasant on the high road who turned out to have nothing but an onion. "See, father, you sent me to get booty. Here I've murdered a peasant and all I've found is an onion." "Fool! An onion means a farthing! A hundred murders and a hundred onions and you've got a rouble!" (a prison legend). Another murders a sensual tyrant in defence of the honour of his betrothed, his sister, or his child. Another is a fugitive, hemmed in by a regiment of trackers, who commits a murder in defence of his freedom, his life, often dying of hunger; and another murders little children for the pleasure of killing, of feeling their warm blood on his hands, of enjoying their terror, and their last dove-like flutter under the knife. Yet all of these are sent to the same penal servitude.

It is true that there are variations in the length of the sentence. But these variations are comparatively few, and the variations in the same sort of crime are infinitely numerous. There are as many shades of difference as there are characters. But let us admit that it is impossible to get over this inequality, that it is in its own way an insoluble problem, like squaring the circle.

Apart from this, let us look at another inequality, at the difference in the effect of a punishment. One man will pine, waste away like a candle in prison, while another had no notion till he came to prison that such a jolly existence, such a pleasant club of spirited companions was to be found in the world. Yes, there are some in prison like that. Or take the case of an educated man with an awakened conscience, intelligence, heart. The mere ache of his own heart will kill him by its torments sooner than any punishment. He condemns himself for his crime more unsparingly, more relentlessly than the most rigorous law. And beside him is another who has never once all the time he has been in prison thought of the murder he has committed. He positively considers he has done right. And there are men who commit crimes on purpose to be sent to penal servitude, in order to escape from a far more penal life of labour outside. There he lived in the deepest degradation, never had enough to eat and worked from morning to night for his exploiter; in prison the work is lighter than at home, there is bread in plenty and of better quality than he has ever seen before; and on holidays there is beef; then there are alms and there is a chance of earning something. And the company? It consists of shrewd crafty fellows who know everything; and he looks on his companions with respectful astonishment; he has never seen anyone like them before; he looks upon them as the very highest society in the world. Is the punishment equally felt in these two cases? But why trouble oneself with unanswerable questions! The drum beats, it is time to be back in our wards.

CHAPTER IV

FIRST IMPRESSIONS (3)

THE LAST ROLL-CALL BEGAN. After this call-over the prison wards are locked up, each with its own lock, and the convicts remain shut up till daybreak.

The roll was called by a sergeant and two soldiers. For this purpose the convicts were sometimes drawn up in ranks in the yard, and the officer on duty was present. But more frequently the ceremony was conducted in a more homely fashion. The roll was called indoors. This is how it was on that occasion. The men on duty made many mistakes, were wrong in their reckoning, went away and came back again. At last the poor fellows brought their sum out right and locked our prison room. In it there were as many as thirty convicts, rather closely packed on the bed. It was too early to go to sleep. Obviously, everyone needed something to do.

The only representative of authority in the room was the veteran soldier whom I have mentioned already. There was also in each room a head convict who was appointed by the major himself, on the grounds of good behaviour, of course. It often happened that these head convicts were involved in some serious mischief; then they were flogged, at once degraded and replaced by others. In our room the head convict was Akim Akimitch, who to my surprise not infrequently shouted at other convicts. They usually responded with jeers. The veteran was wiser, he never interfered in any way, and, if he ever did open his lips, it was no more than a matter of form to satisfy his conscience. He sat in silence on his bedstead sewing a boot. The convicts took hardly any notice of him.

On that first day of my prison life I made one observation, and found as time went on that it was correct. All who are not convicts, whoever they are, from those who have the most contact with them such as guards, soldiers on duty, down to all who have ever had any connexion with prison life, have an exaggerated idea of convicts. It is

55

as though they were every minute in uneasy expectation of the convicts suddenly flying at them with a knife. But what is most remarkable, the convicts were themselves aware that they were feared, and it gave them a certain conceit. And yet the very best man to look after convicts is one who is not afraid of them. And, indeed, in spite of his conceit the convict likes it much better when one trusts him. One may even win his affection by doing so. It happened, though very rarely during my life in prison, that some superior officer came into the prison without a guard. It was worth seeing how it impressed the convicts, and impressed them in the most favourable way. Such a fearless visitor always aroused their respect, and if any harm had been possible, it would not have been so in his presence. The dread inspired by convicts is found everywhere where there are prisoners, and I really do not know to what exactly it is due. It has, of course, some foundation, even in the external appearance of the convict, who is, after all, an acknowledged malefactor; besides, everyone who comes near the prison feels that all this mass of people has been brought together not of their own will, and that, whatever measures are taken, a live man cannot be made into a corpse; he will remain with his feelings, his thirst for revenge and life, his passions and the craving to satisfy them. At the same time I am convinced that there is no need to fear convicts. A man does not so quickly or so easily fly at another with a knife. In fact, if there may be danger, if there is sometimes trouble, the rarity of such instances shows how trifling the risk is. I am speaking, of course, only of convicted prisoners, many of whom are glad to have reached the prison at last (a new life is sometimes such a good thing!) and are consequently disposed to live quietly and peaceably. Moreover, the others will not let those who are really troublesome do mischief. Every convict, however bold and insolent he may be, is afraid of everything in prison. But a convict awaiting punishment is a different matter. He is certainly capable of falling on any outsider, apropos of nothing, simply because he will have to face a flogging next day, and if he does anything to bring about another trial his punishment will be delayed. Here there is an object, a motive for the attack; it is "to change his luck" at any cost and as quickly as possible. I know one strange psychological instance of the kind.

In the military division in our prison there was a convict who had

been a soldier, and had been sentenced for two years without depri-
vation of rights, an awful braggart and a conspicuous coward. As a
rule boastfulness and cowardice are rarely found in a Russian soldier.
Our soldiers always seem so busy that if they wanted to show off they
would not have time. But if one is a braggart he is almost always an
idler and a coward. Dutov (that was the convict's name) served out
his sentence at last and returned to his line regiment. But as all, like
him, sent to prison for correction are finally corrupted there, it usually happens that after they have been not more than two or three
weeks in freedom, they are arrested again and come back to the
prison, this time not for two or three years, but as a "lifer" for fifteen
or twenty years; and so it happened with him. Three weeks after leaving the prison, Dutov stole something, breaking a lock to do so, and
was insolent and unruly as well. He was tried and sentenced to a severe punishment. Reduced to the utmost terror by the punishment
awaiting him, being a most pitiful coward, he fell, knife in hand,
upon an officer who went into the convicts' room, the day before he
would have had to "walk the Green Street." Of course, he was well
aware that by such an act he greatly increased his sentence and his
term of penal servitude, but all he was reckoning on was putting off
the terrible moment of punishment for a few days, even for a few
hours! He was such a coward that he did not even wound the officer,
but only attacked him as a matter of form, that there might appear to
be a new crime for which he would be tried again.

The minute before punishment is certainly terrible for the condemned man, and in the course of several years it was my lot to see a
good number of men on the eve of this fatal day. I usually came across
these condemned prisoners in the convict ward of the hospital when
I lay there ill, which happened pretty often. It is well known to all the
convicts throughout Russia that the people most compassionate to
them are doctors. They never make any distinction between convicts
and other people, as almost all outsiders do, except, perhaps, the peasants. The latter never reproach the convict with his crime, however terrible it may have been, and forgive him everything on account of the
punishment he has endured and his general misery. Significantly the
peasants all over Russia speak of crime as a misfortune, and of criminals as the unfortunate. It is a definition of deep import, and it is the
more significant because it is unconscious, instinctive. The doctors

are truly a refuge for the convicts in many cases, especially for those awaiting punishment, who are kept far more severely than the ordinary prisoners. The convict awaiting punishment, who has reckoned the probable date of the awful ordeal, often gets into hospital, trying to ward off the terrible moment, even by a little. When he is taking his discharge from the hospital, knowing almost for certain that the fatal hour will be next day, he is nearly always in a state of violent agitation. Some try from vanity to conceal their feelings, but their awkward show of swagger does not deceive their companions. Everyone understands how it is, but is silent from humane feeling.

I knew a convict, a young man who had been a soldier, condemned for murder to the maximum number of strokes. He was so panic-stricken that on the eve of the punishment he drank off a jug of vodka, in which he had previously soaked snuff. Vodka, by the way, is always taken just before the flogging. It is smuggled in long before the day, and a high price is paid for it. The convict would rather go without every necessity for six months than fail to have the money for a bottle of vodka to be drunk a quarter of an hour before the flogging. There is a general belief among the convicts that a drunken man feels the lash or the sticks less acutely. But I am wandering from my story. The poor fellow after drinking his jug of vodka was at once taken ill in earnest; he began vomiting blood and he was carried to the hospital almost unconscious. The vomiting so affected his chest that in a few days he showed unmistakable signs of consumption, of which he died six months later. The doctors who treated him for tuberculosis did not know how it had been caused.

But, speaking of the cowardice so often found in the convict before punishment, I ought to add that some, on the contrary, astonish the observer by their extraordinary fearlessness. I remember some examples of courage which approached insensibility, and such examples were not so very rare. I particularly remember my meeting with a terrible criminal. One summer day a rumour spread in the hospital wards that a famous robber, a runaway soldier called Orlov, would be punished that evening, and would be afterwards brought to the ward. While the convict patients were expecting Orlov to be brought in, they asserted that he would be punished cruelly. They were all in some excitement, and I must confess that I, too, awaited the famous robber's arrival with extreme curiosity. I had heard marvellous stories about him long before. He was a criminal such as there are few, who had murdered old people and children in cold blood—a man of a terrible strength of will and proud consciousness of his strength. He had confessed to many murders, and was sentenced to be beaten with sticks.

It was evening before he was brought. It was dark and the candles had been lighted in the ward. Orlov was almost unconscious, horribly pale, with thick, dishevelled pitch-black hair. His back was swollen and red and blue. The convicts were waiting on him all night, constantly bringing him water, turning him over, giving him medicines, as though they were looking after a brother or a benefactor. Next day he regained consciousness completely, and walked twice up and down the ward! It amazed me: he had come into the hospital so very weak and exhausted. He had received at one time half of the whole number of blows to which he was sentenced. The doctor had only stopped the punishment when he saw that its continuance would inevitably cause his death. Moreover, Orlov was small and weakly built and exhausted by long imprisonment before his trial. Anyone who has met prisoners awaiting their trial probably remembers long after their thin, pale, worn-out faces, their feverish looks. But, in spite of that, Orlov was recovering quickly. Evidently the energy of his spirit assisted nature. He was certainly not an ordinary man. I was moved by curiosity to make a closer acquaintance with him, and for a week I studied him. I can confidently say that I have never in my life met a man of such strength, of so iron a will as he. I had already seen at Tobolsk a celebrity of the same kind, formerly a brigand chief. He was a wild beast in the fullest sense of the word, and when you stood near him you felt instinctively that there was a terrible creature beside you, even before you knew his name. But in that case what horrified me was the spiritual deadness of the man. The flesh had so completely got the upper hand of all spiritual characteristics that at the first glance you could see from his face that nothing was left but a fierce lust of physical gratification—sensuality, gluttony. I am convinced that Korenev—that was the brigand's name—would have been in a panic and trembling with fear before a flogging, although he could cut a man's throat without turning a hair.

Orlov was a complete contrast to him. His was unmistakably the case of a complete triumph over the flesh. It was evident that the

man's power of control was unlimited, that he despised every sort of
punishment and torture, and was afraid of nothing in the world. We
saw in him nothing but unbounded energy, a thirst for action, a thirst
for vengeance, an eagerness to attain the object he had set before him.
Among other things I was struck by his strange haughtiness. He
looked down on everything with incredible disdain, though he made
no sort of effort to maintain this lofty attitude—it was somehow natural. I imagine there was no creature in the world who could have
worked upon him simply by authority. He looked upon everything
with surprising calmness, as though there were nothing in the universe that could astonish him, and though he quite saw that the other
convicts looked on him with respect, he did not pose to them in the
least. Yet vanity and self-assertion are characteristic of almost all convicts without exception. He was very intelligent and somehow
strangely open, though by no means talkative. To my questions he
answered frankly that he was only waiting to recover in order to get
through the remainder of his punishment as quickly as possible,
that he had been afraid beforehand that he would not survive it;
"but now," he added, winking at me, "it's as good as over. I shall walk
through the remainder of the blows and set off at once with the party
to Nerchinsk, and on the way I'll escape. I shall certainly escape! If
only my back would make haste and heal!" And all those five days he
was eagerly awaiting the moment when he could be discharged, and
in the meantime was often laughing and merry. I tried to talk to him
of his adventures. He frowned a little at such questions, but always answered openly. When he realized that I was trying to get at his conscience and to discover some sign of penitence in him, he glanced at
me with great contempt and haughtiness, as though I had suddenly in
his eyes become a foolish little boy, with whom it was impossible to
discuss things as you would with a grown-up person. There was even
a sort of pity for me to be seen in his face. A minute later he burst out
laughing at me, a perfectly open-hearted laugh free from any hint of
irony, and I am sure that, recalling my words when he was alone, he
laughed again to himself, many times over perhaps. At last he got his
discharge from hospital with his back hardly healed. I was discharged
at the same time, and it happened that we came out of the hospital together, I going to the prison and he to the guard-house near the
prison where he had been detained before. As he said good-bye, he

shook hands with me, and that was a sign of great confidence on his part. I believe he did it because he was much pleased with himself, and glad that the moment had come. He could not really help despising me, and must have looked upon me as a weak, pitiful, submissive creature, inferior to him in every respect. Next day he was led out for the second half of his punishment.

When our prison room was shut it suddenly assumed a special aspect—the aspect of a real dwelling-place, of a home. It was only now that I could see the prisoners, my comrades, quite at home. In the daytime the sergeants, the guards and officials in general could make their appearance at any moment in the prison, and so all the inmates behaved somewhat differently, as though they were not quite at ease, as though they were continually expecting something with some anxiety. But as soon as the room was shut up they all quietly settled down in their places, and almost every one of them took up some handicraft. The room was suddenly lighted up. Every one had his candle and his candlestick, generally made of wood. One worked at a boot, another sewed some garment. The foul atmosphere of the room grew worse from hour to hour. A group of festive souls squatted on their heels round a rug in a corner to a game of cards. In almost every prison room there was a convict who kept a threadbare rug a yard wide, a candle and an incredibly dirty, greasy pack of cards, and all this together was called the *maidan*. The owner of these articles let them to the players for fifteen kopecks a night; that was his trade. The players usually played "Three Leaves," "Hillock," and such games. They always played for money. Each player heaped a pile of copper coins before him—all he had in his pocket—and only got up when he had lost every farthing or stripped his companions. The game went on till late in the night, sometimes lasting till daybreak, till the moment when the door was opened. In our room, as in all the other rooms of the prison, there were always a certain number of destitute convicts, who had lost all their money at cards or on vodka or who were simply beggars by nature. I say "by nature" and I lay special stress on this expression. Indeed, everywhere in Russia, in all surroundings and under all conditions, there always are and will be certain strange individuals, humble and not infrequently by no means lazy, whose destiny is to be destitute for ever. They are always without family ties and always slovenly, they always look cowed and depressed about something, and are always at the beck and call of someone, usually a dissipatey fellow, or one who has suddenly grown rich and risen. And position of respect or anything calling for initiative is a burden and affliction to them. It seems as though they had been born on the understanding that they should begin nothing of themselves and only wait on others, that they should do not what they like, should dance while others pipe; their vocation is only to carry out the will of others. And what is more, no circumstance, no change of luck can enrich them. They are always beggars. I have noticed that such individuals are to be found not only among the peasants, but in every class of society, in every party, in every association, and on the staff of every magazine. It is the same in every room, in every prison, and, as soon as a game of cards is got up, such a beggar always turns up to wait on the party. And, indeed, no card party can get on without an attendant. He was usually hired by all the players in common for five kopecks the night, and his chief duty was to stand all night on guard. As a rule he used to freeze six or seven hours together in the passage in the dark, in thirty degrees of frost, listening to every knock, every clang, every step in the yard. But sometimes the major or the officers on duty visited the prison rather late at night, came in quietly and discovered the men at play and at work, and the extra candles, which could indeed be seen from the yard. Anyway, when the key was grating in the lock of the door that led from the passage to the yard, it was too late to hide what they were doing, put out the lights and go to bed. But as the attendant on duty caught it severely from the card players afterwards, cases of such neglect were extremely rare. Five kopecks, of course, is a ridiculously small sum, even for prison, but I was always struck in prison by the harshness and mercilessness of employers, in this and also in other cases. "You've had your money, so do your work!" was an argument that would bear no objection. For the trifle he had paid the employer would take all he could take—take, if he could, more than was his due, and he considered that he was conferring a favour on the other into the bargain. The convict who is drunk and making merry, flinging his money right and left, always beats down his attendant, and I have noticed it not only in one prison, not only in one group of players.

I have mentioned already that almost all in the room had settled down to some sort of work: except the card players there were not more than five people quite idle; they immediately went to bed. My place on the bed was next to the door. On the other side of the bed, his head nearly touching mine, lay Akim Akimitch. Till ten or eleven he worked, making some sort of coloured Chinese lantern, which had been ordered in the town for a fairly good price. He made lanterns in a masterly way, and worked methodically, without stopping; when he had finished his work he put it away tidily, spread out his little mattress, said his prayers, and conscientiously went to bed. Conscientiousness and orderliness he carried apparently to the point of trivial pedantry; evidently he must have considered himself an exceedingly clever person, as is usually the case with limited and dull-witted people. I did not like him from the first day, though I remember I thought a great deal about him that first day, and what surprised me most was that such a man should have got into prison instead of making his way in the world. Later on, I shall have to speak more than once of Akim Akimitch.

But I will briefly describe all the inmates of our room. I had many years to spend in it, and these were all my future comrades and associates. It may well be understood that I looked at them with eager curiosity. Next to me on the left were a group of mountaineers from the Caucasus, who had been sent here to various term of imprisonment, chiefly for robbery. There were two Lezghis, one Tchetchenian and three Daghestan Tatars. The Tchetchenian was a gloomy and morose person; he hardly spoke to anyone, and was always looking about him from under his brows with hatred and a venomous, malignantly sneering smile. One of the Lezghis was an old man with a long, thin, hooked nose, a regular brigand in appearance. But the second, Nurra, made upon me from the first day a most charming and delightful impression. He was a man still young, of medium height, of Herculean build, with the face of a Finnish woman, quite flaxen hair, light blue eyes, and a snub nose. He had bandy legs from having spent all his previous life on horseback. His whole body was covered with scars, bayonet and bullet wounds. In the Caucasus he had belonged to an allied tribe, but was always riding over on the sly to the hostile mountaineers, and making raids with them on the Russians. Everyone in prison liked him. He was always good-humoured and cordial to everyone, he worked without grumbling and was calm and serene, though he often looked with anger at the filth and loathsomeness of prison life, and was furiously indignant at all the thieving, cheating, and drunkenness, in fact, at everything that was dishonest; but he never picked a quarrel, he merely turned away with indignation. He had never during his prison life stolen anything himself, or been guilty of any bad action. He was exceedingly devout, he religiously repeated his prayers; during the fasts before the Mohammedan holy days he fasted fanatically, and spent whole nights over his prayers. Everyone liked him and believed in his honesty. "Nurra's a lion," the convicts used to say, and the name "lion" had stuck to him. He was firmly persuaded that on the expiration of his sentence he would be sent home to the Caucasus, and only lived on the hope of it. I believe he would have died had he been deprived of it. I got a vivid impression of him on my first day in prison. It was impossible to overlook his good sympathetic face among the surly, ill-humoured and sneering faces of the other convicts. Within my first half-hour in the prison he slapped me on the shoulder as he passed by me, and laughed good-naturedly in my face. I could not make out at first what this meant. He spoke Russian very badly. Soon afterwards, he came up to me again, and smiling gave me another friendly pat on the shoulder. He did it again and again, and so it went on for three days. It meant, as I guessed and found out later, that he was sorry for me, that he felt how hard it was for me to get used to prison, that he wanted to show his goodwill to me, to cheer me up and assure me of his protection. Kind, simple-hearted Nurra!

The Daghestan Tatars were three in number and they were all brothers. Two of them were middle-aged men, but the third, Aley, was not more than two-and-twenty and looked even younger. His place on the bed was next to me. His handsome, open, intelligent, and at the same time good-naturedly simple face won my heart from the first minute. I was so thankful that fate had sent me him as a neighbour rather than any other. His whole soul was apparent in his handsome, one might even say beautiful, face. His smile was so confiding, so childishly trustful, his big black eyes were so soft, so caressing, that I always found a particular pleasure in looking at him, even a consolation in my misery and depression. I am not exaggerating. When he was in his native place one of his elder brothers—he had five of them, two of the others had been sent to some sort of penal factory—ordered him to take his sabre, to get on his horse and to go with them on some sort of expedition. The respect due to an elder brother is so great among the mountaineers that the boy did not dare ask, did not even dream of asking, where they were going, and the others did not think it necessary to inform him. They were going out on a pillaging expedition, to waylay and rob a rich Armenian merchant on the road. And so indeed they did: they killed the escort, murdered the Armenian and carried off his goods. But the affair was discovered; all the six were caught, tried, convicted, punished, and sent to penal servitude in Siberia. The only mercy shown by the court to Aley was that he received a shorter sentence: he had been sent to Siberia for four years. His brothers were very fond of him, and their affection was more like a father's than a brother's. He was their comfort in exile, and sullen and gloomy as they usually were, they always smiled when they looked at him, and when they spoke to him (though they spoke to him very little, as though they still thought of him as a boy with whom it was useless to talk of serious things) their surly faces relaxed, and I guessed that they spoke to him of something humorous, almost childish; at least they always looked at one another and smiled good-humouredly after listening to his answer. He hardly dared to address them, so deep was his respect for them. It was hard to imagine how this boy was able during his prison life to preserve such a gentle heart, to develop such strict honesty, such warm feelings and charming manners, and to escape growing coarse and depraved. But his was a strong and steadfast nature in spite of all its apparent softness. As time went on I got to know him well. He was pure as a chaste girl, and any ugly, cynical, dirty, unjust or violent action in the prison brought a glow of indignation into his beautiful eyes, making them still more beautiful. But he avoided all strife and wrangling, though he was not one of those men who allow themselves to be insulted with impunity and knew how to stand up for himself. But he never had quarrels with anyone, everyone liked him and was friendly to him. At first he was simply courteous to me. By degrees I began talking to him; in a few months he had learned to speak Russian very well, which his brothers never succeeded in doing all the time they were in Siberia. He seemed to me a boy of marked intelligence and peculiar modesty and delicacy, who had in fact reflected a good deal. I may as well say at once that I consider Aley far from being an ordinary person, and I look back upon my meeting with him as one of the happiest meetings in my life. There are natures so innately good, so richly endowed by God, that the very idea of their ever deteriorating seems impossible. One is always at ease about them. I am at ease about Aley to this day. Where is he now?

One night, when I had been some time in prison, I was lying on the bed musing; Aley, always occupied and industrious, happened to be doing nothing at the moment, though it was early to go to bed. But it was their Mussulman holiday, and they were not working. He was lying down with his hands clasped behind his head, pondering on something, too. All at once he asked me:

"Are you very sad just now?" I looked at him with curiosity and it seemed strange to me to hear this rapid direct question from Aley, always so delicate, so considerate, so full of the wisdom of the heart. But looking more intently I saw in his face such sadness, such distress at some memory, that I felt at once that his own heart was heavy at that moment and I told him so. He sighed and smiled mournfully. I loved his smile, which was always warm and tender. Besides, when he smiled he showed two rows of pearly teeth which the greatest beauty in the world might have envied.

"Ah, Aley, no doubt you are thinking how they are keeping this holiday at home in Daghestan? It must be nice there."

"Yes," he answered enthusiastically, and his eyes shone. "But how do you know I am thinking about it?"

"How can I help knowing! It's better there than here, isn't it?"

"Oh, why do you say that! . . ."

"What flowers there must be there now, what a paradise!"

"O-oh, better not talk of it."

He was deeply stirred.

"Listen, Aley, had you a sister?"

"Yes, but why?"

"She must be a beauty if she is like you."

"Like me! She is such a beauty, there is no one in Daghestan handsomer. Ah, she is a beauty, my sister! You've never seen anyone like her. My mother was beautiful too."

"Was your mother fond of you?"

"Ah! What are you saying! She must have died of grieving over me by now. I was her favourite son. She loved me more than my sister, more than anyone. . . . She came to me in my dreams last night and cried over me."

He sank into silence and said nothing more that evening. But from that time forward he sought every opportunity to talk to me, though the respect which he for some reason felt for me always prevented him from speaking first. But he was greatly delighted whenever I addressed him. I questioned him about the Caucasus, about his former life. His brothers did not hinder his talking to me, in fact they seemed to like it. Seeing that I was getting fonder and fonder of Aley, they, too, became much more cordial to me.

Aley helped me at work, did his utmost to be of service to me in the prison, and I could see that he was delighted when he could do anything to please me or make my life easier, and in his efforts to please me there was not a trace of anything cringing or self-seeking, nothing but a warm, friendly feeling for me which he no longer concealed. He had, moreover, a good deal of mechanical ability: he learnt to make underclothes fairly well, and to make boots and later on, as far as he could, to do carpentering. His brothers praised him and were proud of him.

"Listen, Aley," I said to him one day, "why don't you learn to read and write Russian? It would be a great advantage to you in Siberia later on, you know."

"I should like to very much. But of whom can I learn?"

"Lots of men here can read and write! But if you like, I'll teach you."

"Oh, please do!" And he positively sat up on the bed and clasped his hands, looking at me imploringly.

We set to work the next evening. I had the Russian translation of the New Testament, a book not prohibited in prison. With this book alone and no alphabet, Aley learnt in a few weeks to read excellently. In three months he had completely mastered the language of the book. He learnt eagerly, with enthusiasm.

One day we read together the whole of the Sermon on the Mount. I noticed that he seemed to read parts of it aloud with special feeling.

I asked him if he liked what he had read.

He glanced at me quickly and the colour came into his face.

"Oh, yes," he answered. "Yes. Jesus is a holy prophet. Jesus speaks God's words. How good it is!"

"What do you like best of all?"

"Where He says 'forgive, love, don't hurt others, love even your enemies.' Ah, how well He speaks!"

He turned to his brothers who were listening to our conversation, and began warmly saying something to them. They talked earnestly for a long time together, and nodded their heads approvingly. Then with a dignified and gracious, that is, a typically Mussulman, smile (which I love so much, and love especially for its dignity) they turned to me and repeated that Jesus was a prophet of God, and that He worked great marvels; that He had made a bird out of clay, had breathed on it and it had flown away . . . and that that was written in their books. They were convinced that in saying this they were giving me great pleasure by praising Jesus, and Aley was perfectly happy that his brothers had deigned and desired to give me this pleasure.

The writing lessons, too, were very successful. Aley procured paper (he would not let me buy it with my money), pens and ink, and in about two months he had learnt to write an excellent hand. This actually impressed his brothers. Their pride and satisfaction knew no bounds. They did not know how to show their gratitude to me. If they happened to be working near me, they were continually helping me, and looked on it as a happiness to be able to. I need hardly say the same of Aley. He loved me perhaps as much as he loved his brothers. I shall never forget how he left the prison. He drew me away behind the prison, flung himself on my neck and cried. He had never before kissed me or shed tears. "You've done so much for me, so much for me," he said, "that my father and my mother could not have done more: you have made a man of me. God will repay you and I shall never forget you. . . ."

Where is he now, my good, dear, dear Aley?

Besides the Circassians there was a group of Poles in our room, and they made a family apart, and had hardly anything to do with the other convicts. I have mentioned already that their exclusiveness and their hatred of the Russian prisoners made them hated by everyone. There were six of them; they were men broken and made morbid by suffering. Some of them were educated men; I will speak of them more fully afterwards. During my later years in prison I used sometimes to get books from them. The first book I read made a great, strange and peculiar impression upon me. I will speak of these impressions more particularly later; they were most interesting to me, and I am sure that to many people they would be utterly unintelligible. Some things one cannot judge without experience. One thing

I can say, that moral privation is harder to bear than any physical agonies. When a peasant goes to prison he finds there the company of his
equals, perhaps even of his superiors. He has lost a great deal, of
course—home, family, everything, but his environment is the same.
The educated man condemned to the same punishment often loses
infinitely more. He must overcome all his cravings, all his habits, live
under conditions that are insufficient for him; must learn to breathe a
different air. . . . He is a fish out of water. . . . And often a punishment supposed to be equal in law is ten times as cruel for him. This is
the truth, even if we consider only the material habits which have to
be sacrificed.

But the Poles formed a group apart. There were six of them and
they kept together. The only other person they liked in our room was
a Jew, and him they liked perhaps simply because he amused them.
He was liked indeed by the other convicts too, though every one
without exception laughed at him. He was the only Jew among us,
and I can't think of him even now without laughing. Every time I
looked at him I could not help recalling Gogol's Jew Yankel in "Taras
Bulba,"[3] who when he undressed at night and prepared to get into the
cupboard where he slept with his wife, looked exactly like a chicken.
Isay Fomitch, our Jew, was the very image of a plucked chicken. He
was a man about fifty, short and weakly built, cunning and at the same
time decidedly stupid. He was impudent and conceited, and at the
same time awfully cowardly. He was covered all over with wrinkles,
and on his forehead and each cheek bore the marks of having been
branded on the scaffold. I could never understand how he had survived sixty lashes. He had been sent here charged with murder. He
had hidden away a receipt which his friends had procured from a
doctor immediately after his punishment. It was the receipt for an
ointment supposed to remove all traces of branding in a fortnight. He
dare not make use of this ointment in the prison, and was awaiting
the end of his twelve years' term of imprisonment, after which he
fully intended to take advantage of the receipt when he could live as
a settler. "Else I shall never be able to get married," he said to me
once, "and I certainly want to be married." We were great friends;
he was always in excellent spirits; he had not a bad time in prison. He
was a jeweller by trade, always had more than enough work from the
town, in which there was no jeweller, and so escaped hard labour. Of

course he was a pawnbroker at the same time, and supplied the whole prison with money at a percentage and on security. He had come to the prison before me, and one of the Poles gave me a minute description of his arrival. It is a most amusing story which I will tell later on; I shall speak of Isay Fomitch more than once again.

Among the other prisoners in our room were four Old Believers, elderly men and great Bible readers, one of whom was the old fellow from the Starodubovsky settlement. Then there were two or three Little Russians, gloomy fellows; a young convict of three-and-twenty with a lean little face and a sharp little nose, who had already committed eight murders; a group of false coiners one of whom kept all the room amused; and finally several gloomy and sullen individuals, shaven and hideous, taciturn and envious, who looked with hatred about them and meant to look like that, to scowl, to be silent and full of hatred for long years to come, the whole term of their imprisonment. Of all this I had only a glimpse on that first desolate evening of my new life, a glimpse in the midst of smoke and filth, of oaths and indescribable obscenity, of foul air, of clanking fetters, of curses and shameless laughter. I lay down on the bare boards of the bed, and putting my clothes under my head (I had not a pillow yet), covered myself with my sheepskin; but for a long while I could not get to sleep, though I was utterly worn out and shattered by all the monstrous, unexpected impressions of that first day. But my new life was only just beginning. There was much awaiting me in the future of which I had never dreamed, of which I had no foreboding.

CHAPTER V

THE FIRST MONTH (1)

THREE DAYS AFTER MY arrival in prison I was ordered to go out to work. That first day of work is very distinct in my memory, though nothing very unusual happened to me in the course of it, except in so far as my position was in itself unusual. But it was still one of my first impressions, and I still looked eagerly at everything. I had spent those three days in the greatest depression. "This is the end of my wanderings: I am in prison!" I was continually repeating to myself. "This is to be my haven for many long years, my niche which I enter with such a mistrustful, such a painful sensation. . . . And who knows? Maybe when I come to leave it many years hence I may regret it!" I added, not without an element of that malignant pleasure which at times is almost a craving to tear open one's wound on purpose, as though one desired to revel in one's pain, as though the consciousness of one's misery was an actual enjoyment. The idea of ever regretting this hole struck me with horror: I felt even then how monstrously a man may get used to things. But that was all in the future, and meantime everything about me was hostile and—terrible, for though not everything was really so, it seemed so to me. The savage curiosity with which my new comrades, the convicts, stared at me, the extra surliness of their behaviour towards the new member of their community, who had been a "gentleman." A surliness which sometimes reached the point of active hatred—all this so tortured me that I was eager to begin work, so as to find out and test all my sufferings as soon as possible, to begin living like all the rest, so as to get into the same rut with all the others without delay. Of course there was a great deal I did not notice then; I had no suspicion of things that were going on in front of me. I did not divine the presence of consolation in the midst of all that was hostile. Yet the few kind and friendly faces I had come across in the course of those three days helped to give me courage.

The kindest and friendliest of all was Akim Akimitch. And among the faces of other convicts that were sullen and full of hatred, I could not help noticing some kind and good-natured ones. "There are bad people everywhere, and good ones among the bad," I hastened to console myself by reflecting: "and who knows? These people are perhaps by no means so much worse than the *remainder* who have *remained* outside the prison." Even as I thought this, I shook my head at the idea, and yet, my God, if I had only known at the time how true that thought was!

Here, for instance, was a man whom I only came to understand fully in the course of many many years, and yet he was with me and continually near me almost all the time I was in prison. This was the convict Sushilov. As soon as I begin to speak of prisoners being no worse than other men, I involuntarily recall him. He used to wait on me. I had another attendant too. From the very beginning Akim Akimitch recommended me one of the convicts called Osip, telling me that for thirty kopecks a month he would cook my food for me every day, if I so disliked the prison fare, and had the money to get food for myself. Osip was one of the four cooks elected by the convicts for our two kitchens. They were, however, quite free to accept or refuse the appointment and could throw it up at any moment. The cooks did not go out to work, and their duties were confined to baking bread and preparing soup. They were not called "povars" (i.e. male cooks) but "stryapki" (i.e. female cooks), not as a sign of contempt for them—for sensible, and as far as might be, honest convicts were chosen for the kitchen—but just as an amiable pleasantry which our cooks did not resent in the slightest. Osip was, as a rule, elected, and for several years in succession he was almost always cook, and only threw up the job occasionally for a time, when he was overcome with violent melancholy and a craving for smuggling in vodka. He was a man of rare honesty and gentleness, though he was in prison for smuggling. He was the tall, sturdy smuggler I have mentioned already. He was afraid of everything, especially of a flogging, was friendly to everyone, very meek and mild. He never quarrelled, yet he had such a passion for smuggling that he could not resist bringing in vodka in spite of his cowardice. Like the other cooks he carried on a trade in vodka, though, of course, not on the same scale as Gazin, for instance, because he had not the courage to risk much. I always got on capitally with Osip. As for providing one's food, the cost was trifling. I am not far wrong if I say that I hardly spent more than a rouble a month on my board, always excluding bread, which was part of the prison fare, and occasionally soup, which I took if I were very hungry in spite of the disgust it inspired, though that, too, passed off almost completely in time. Usually I bought a pound of beef a day. And in winter a pound cost a halfpenny. One of the old veterans, of whom there was one in each room to keep order, used to go to the market to buy beef. These veterans voluntarily undertook to go to market every day to buy things for the prisoners and charged the merest trifle, next to nothing, for doing so. They did this for the sake of their own peace and comfort, for they could hardly have existed in the prison if they had refused. In this way they brought in tobacco, tea in bricks, beef, fancy bread and so on, everything in fact but vodka. They were not asked to bring in vodka, though they were sometimes regaled with it.

For years together Osip roasted me a piece of beef, always the same cut. But how it was roasted is another question, and indeed is not what mattered. It is a remarkable fact that for several years I hardly exchanged two words with Osip. Several times I tried to talk to him, but he was incapable of keeping up a conversation; he would smile or answer "yes" or "no," and that was all. It was strange to see this Hercules who was like a child of seven.

Another convict who helped me was Sushilov. I did not ask for his services nor seek them. He found me out and placed himself at my disposal of his own accord; I don't remember when or how it happened. He did my washing. There was a large hole for emptying the water at the back of the prison, made on purpose. The washing troughs stood above this hole and the convicts' clothes were washed there. Sushilov invented a thousand different little duties to please me: he got my tea ready, ran all sorts of errands, took my jacket to be mended, greased my boots four times a month; all this he did eagerly, fussily, as though no one knew what duties he was overwhelmed with; in fact he completely threw in his lot with mine, and took all my business on himself. He would never say, for instance, "You have so many shirts, your jacket is torn," and so on, but always "*We* have so many shirts now, *our* jacket is torn." He watched me to forestall every want, and seemed to make it the chief object of his life. He had no trade, and I think he earned nothing except from me. I paid him what I could, that is in halfpence, and he was always meekly satisfied. He could not help serving some-one, and pitched upon me, I fancy, as being more considerate than oth-ers and more honest in paying. He was one of those men who could never grow rich and get on, and who undertook to act as sentry for card players, standing all night in the freezing cold passage, listening to every sound in the yard, on the alert for the major. They charged five farthings for spending almost the whole night in this way, while if they blundered they lost everything and had to pay for it with a beating. I have mentioned them already. It is the leading characteristic of such men to efface their personality always, everywhere, and before almost everyone, and to play not even a secondary, but a tertiary part in every-thing done in common. All this is innate in them.

Sushilov was a very pitiful fellow, utterly spiritless and humbled, hopelessly down-trodden, though no one used to ill-treat him, but he was down-trodden by nature. I always for some reason felt sorry for him. I could not look at him without feeling so, but why I was sorry for him I could not have said myself. I could not talk to him ei-ther; he, too, was no good at conversation, and it was evidently a great labour to him. He only recovered his spirits when I ended the conversation by giving him something to do, asking him to go some-where or to run some errand. I was convinced at last that I was be-stowing a pleasure upon him by doing so. He was neither tall nor short, neither good-looking nor ugly, neither stupid nor clever, some-what pockmarked and rather light-haired. One could never say any-thing quite definite about him. Only one other point: he belonged, I believe, as far as I could guess, to the same section as Sirotkin and be-longed to it simply through his submissiveness and spiritlessness. The convicts sometimes jeered at him, chiefly because he had *exchanged* on the way to Siberia, and had exchanged for the sake of a red shirt and a rouble. It was because of the smallness of the price for which he had sold himself that the convicts jeered at him. To exchange meant to change names, and consequently sentences, with someone else. Strange as it seems, this was actually done, and in my day the practice flourished among convicts on the road to Siberia, was consecrated by tradition and defined by certain formalities. At first I could not be-lieve it, but I was convinced at last by seeing it with my own eyes.

This is how it is done. A party of convicts is being taken to Siberia.

There are some of all sorts, going to penal servitude, to penal factories, or to a settlement; they travel together. Somewhere on the road, in the province of Perm for instance, some convict wants to exchange with another. Some Mihailov, for instance, a convict sentenced for murder or some other serious crime, feels the prospect of many years' penal servitude unattractive. Let us suppose he is a crafty fellow who has knocked about and knows what he is doing. So he tries to find someone of the same party who is rather simple, rather down-trodden and submissive, and whose sentence is comparatively light, exile to a settlement or to a few years in a penal factory, or even to penal servitude, but for a short period. At last he finds a Sushilov. Sushilov is a serf who is simply being sent out to a settlement. He has marched fifteen hundred miles without a farthing in his pocket—for Sushilov, of course, never could have a farthing—exhausted, weary, tasting nothing but the prison food, without even a chance morsel of anything good, wearing the prison clothes, and waiting upon everyone for a pitiful copper. Mihailov accosts Sushilov, gets to know him, even makes friends with him, and at last at some *étape** gives him vodka. Finally he suggests to him, would not he like to exchange? He says his name is Mihailov, and tells him this and that, says he is going to prison, that is, not to prison but to a "special division." Though it is prison it is "special," therefore rather better. Lots of people, even in the government in Petersburg for instance, never heard of the "special division" all the time it existed. It was a special, peculiar little class in one of the remote parts of Siberia, and there were so few in it, in my time not more than seventy, that it was not easy to get to hear of it. I met people afterwards who had served in Siberia and knew it well, who yet heard for the first time of the "special division" from me. In the Legal Code there are six lines about it: "There shall be instituted in such and such a prison a special division for the worst criminals until the opening of works involving harder labour in Siberia." Even the convicts of this division did not know whether it was a permanent or a temporary institution. No time limit was mentioned, all that was said was "until the opening of works involving harder labour," so it was meant for convicts who were in for life.

It is no wonder that Sushilov and the rest of his party knew nothing

---

*Stage; point in time (French).

about it, even including Mihailov, who could only form an idea of the "special division" from the gravity of his crime, for which he had already received three or four thousand blows. He might well conclude they were not sending him to anything very nice. Sushilov was on his way to a settlement; could anything be better? "Wouldn't you like to exchange?" Sushilov, a simple-hearted soul, a little tipsy and overwhelmed with gratitude to Mihailov for being kind to him, does not venture to refuse. Besides, he has heard already from the others that exchanges are possible, that other people have exchanged, so that there is nothing exceptional or unheard of about it. They come to an agreement. The shameless Mihailov, taking advantage of Sushilov's extraordinary simplicity, buys his name for a red shirt and a silver rouble, which he gives him on the spot before witnesses. Next day Sushilov is no longer drunk; but he is given drink again; besides, it is a mean thing to go back on a bargain; the rouble he has taken has gone on drink, and the red shirt quickly follows it. If he won't keep his bargain he must give back the money. And where is Sushilov to get a whole silver rouble? And if he does not repay it the gang will make him; that's a point they are strict about. Besides, if he has made a promise he must keep it—the gang will insist on that too; or else they will devour him. They will beat him, perhaps, or simply kill him; in any case, they will threaten to.

Indeed, if the gang were once to be indulgent in such a matter, the practice of changing names would be at an end. If it were possible to go back on a promise and break a bargain after taking money, who would ever keep it afterwards? This, in fact, is a question that concerns the gang, concerns all, and therefore the gang is very stern about it. At last Sushilov sees that there is no begging off it and makes up his mind to agree without protest. It is announced to the whole gang; and other people are bribed with drink and money, if necessary. It is just the same to them, of course, whether Mihailov or Sushilov goes to the devil, but vodka has been drunk, they have been treated, so they hold their tongues. At the next *étape* the roll is called; when Mihailov's name is called, Sushilov answers "here," when Sushilov's is called, Mihailov shouts "here" and they go on their way. Nothing more is said about it. At Tobolsk the convicts are sorted: Mihailov is sent to a settlement and Sushilov is conducted with extra guards to the "special division." Protest later is impossible; and after all, how could he prove it? How many years would an inquiry into such a case take? Might he not come in for something else? Where are his witnesses? If he had them they would deny it. So the upshot of it is that for a red shirt and a rouble Sushilov is sent to the "special division."

The convicts laughed at Sushilov not because he had exchanged (though they feel contempt for all who exchange a lighter sentence for a heavier one, as they do for all fools who have been duped) but because he had done it for a red shirt and a rouble—too trivial a price. Convicts usually receive large sums, relatively speaking, for exchanging. They sometimes charge dozens of roubles. But Sushilov was so submissive, such a nonentity, so paltry in the eyes of all that he was not even worth laughing at.

I got on very well with Sushilov for several years. By degrees he became extremely devoted to me. I could not help noticing it, so that I became quite attached to him too. But one day he did not do something I had asked him, though I had just given him some money and—I can never forgive myself for it—I had the cruelty to say to him, "Well, Sushilov, you take the money but you don't do your work." He said nothing, ran to do the job, but became suddenly depressed. Two days passed. I thought to myself, "Surely it can't be on account of what I said?" I knew that one of the convicts called Anton Vassilyev was worrying him very persistently about a trifling debt. "Probably he has no money and is afraid to ask me!" On the third day I said to him: "Sushilov, I think you wanted to ask me for the money to pay Anton Vassilyev? Take it." I was sitting on the bed at the time; Sushilov was standing before me. He seemed greatly impressed at my offering him the money, at my thinking of his difficult position of my own accord, especially as he had, in his own opinion, been paid too much by me of late, so that he had not dared to hope I would give him more. He looked at the money, then at me, suddenly turned away and went out. All this surprised me very much. I followed him and found him behind the prison. He was standing facing the fence with his head bent down and his elbow leaning on the fence.

"Sushilov, what is it?" I asked him. He did not look at me, and I noticed to my great amazement that he was on the point of tears.

"Alexandr Petrovitch, you think . . ." he began in a breaking voice, trying to look away, "that I . . . do for you . . . for money . . . but I . . . e—ech!"

Then he turned to the fence again, even striking his forehead against it—and broke into sobs! It was the first time I had seen a man crying in prison. With great effort I comforted him, and though after that he began to serve me and look after me more zealously than ever—if possible— yet from certain hardly perceptible signs I perceived that his heart could never forgive me that reproach; and yet other people laughed at him, nagged at him on every occasion, and sometimes abused him violently— and he was on amiable and even friendly terms with them, and never took offence. Yes, indeed, it is very hard to understand a man, even after long years!

That is why I could not see the prisoners at first as they really were, and as they seemed to me later. That is why I said that, though I looked at everything with eager and concentrated attention, I could not discern a great deal that was just before my eyes. It was natural that I was struck at first by the most remarkable and prominent facts, but even these I probably saw incorrectly, and all that was left by them was an oppressive, hopelessly melancholy sensation, which was greatly confirmed by my meeting with A., a convict who had reached the prison not long before me, and who made a particularly painful impression upon me during the first days I was in prison. I knew, however, before I reached the prison, that I should meet A. there. He poisoned that first terrible time for me and increased my mental suf- ferings. I cannot avoid speaking about him.

He was the most revolting example of the depths to which a man can sink and degenerate, and the extent to which he can destroy all moral feeling in himself without difficulty or repentance. A. was that young man of good family of whom I have mentioned already that he reported to the major everything that took place in the prison, and was friendly with his orderly Fedka. Here is a brief account of his story. After quarrelling with his Moscow relations, who were horri- fied by his vicious conduct, he arrived in Petersburg without finish- ing his studies, and to get money he gave information to the police in a very base way, that is, sold the lives of a dozen men for the imme- diate gratification of his insatiable lust for the coarsest and most depraved pleasures. Lured by the temptations of Petersburg and its taverns, he became so addicted to his vices that, though he was by no means a fool, he ventured on a mad and senseless enterprise: he was soon detected. In his information to the police he had implicated innocent people, and deceived others, and it was for this he was sent for ten years to Siberia to our prison. He was still quite young, life was only beginning for him. One would have thought such a terrible change in his fate must have made a great impression on his nature, would have called forth all his powers of resistance, and have caused a complete transformation in him. But he accepted his new life without the slightest perturbation, without the slightest aversion, indeed; he was not morally revolted by it, nor frightened by anything except the necessity of working, and the loss of the taverns and other attractions of Petersburg. It actually seemed to him that his position as a convict set him free to commit even more scoundrelly and revolting actions. "If one is a convict, one may as well be one; if one is a convict, one may do nasty things and it's no shame to." That was literally his opinion. I think of this disgusting creature as a phenomenon. I spent several years among murderers, profligates and thorough-going scoundrels, but I can positively say that I never in my life met such an utter moral downfall, such complete depravity and such insolent baseness as in A. There was amongst us a parricide, of good family; I have mentioned him already, but I became convinced from many traits and incidents that even he was incomparably nobler and more humane than A. All the while I was in prison A. seemed to me a lump of flesh with teeth and a stomach and an insatiable thirst for the most sensual and brutish pleasures. And to satisfy the most trifling and capricious of his desires he was capable of the most cold-blooded murder, in fact of anything, if only the crime could be concealed. I am not exaggerating; I got to know A. well. He was an example of what a man can come to when the physical side is unrestrained by any inner standard, any principle. And how revolting it was to me to look on his everlasting mocking smile! He was a monster; a moral Quasimodo.[4] Add to that, that he was cunning and clever, good-looking, even rather well-educated and had abilities. Yes, such a man is a worse plague in society than fire, flood and famine! I have said already that there was such general depravity in prison that spying and treachery flourished, and the convicts were not angry at it. On the contrary they were all very friendly with A., and behaved far more amiably to him than to us. The favour in which he stood with our drunken major gave him importance and weight among them. Meanwhile he made the major believe that he could paint portraits (he had

made the convicts believe that he had been a lieutenant in the Guards)
and the major insisted on A.'s being sent to work in his house, to
paint the major's portrait, of course. Here he made friends with the
major's orderly, Fedka, who had an extraordinary influence over his
master, and consequently over everything and everybody in the
prison. A. played the spy amongst us to meet the major's requirements, and when the latter hit A. in the face in his fits of drunkenness
he used to abuse him as being a spy and a traitor. It happened sometimes, pretty often in fact, that the major would sit down and command A. to go on with his portrait immediately after beating him.
Our major seemed really to believe that A. was a remarkable artist, almost on a level with Brüllov,[5] of whom even he had heard. At the
same time he felt himself quite entitled to slap him in the face, feeling probably that, though he was a great artist, he was now a convict,
and had he been ten times Brüllov the major was still his superior,
and therefore could do what he liked with him. Among other things
he made A. take off his boots for him and empty his slops, and yet for
a long time he could not get over the idea that A. was a great artist.
The portrait lingered on endlessly, almost for a year. At last the major
realized that he was being duped, and becoming convinced that the
portrait never would be finished, but on the contrary became less and
less like him every day, he flew into a rage, gave the artist a thrashing
and sent him to hard labour in the prison as a punishment. A. evidently regretted this, and felt bitterly the loss of his idle days, his tit-
bits from the major's table, the company of his friend Fedka and all
the enjoyments that Fedka and he contrived for themselves in the major's kitchen. At any rate after getting rid of A., the major gave up persecuting M., a convict whom A. was always slandering to the major.

At the time of A.'s arrival M. was the only "political" in the prison.
He was very miserable, had nothing in common with the other convicts, looked upon them with horror and loathing, failed to observe
what might have reconciled him to them, and did not get on with
them. They repaid him with the same hatred. The position of people
like M. in prison is awful as a rule. M. knew nothing of the crime that
had brought A. to prison. On the contrary, seeing the sort of man he
had to do with, A. at once assured him that he was being punished
for the very opposite of treachery, almost the same thing in fact as the
charge for which M. was suffering. The latter was greatly delighted at

having a comrade, a friend. He waited upon him, comforted him in the first days of prison, imagining that he must be in great distress, gave him his last penny, fed him, and shared the most necessary things with him. But A. conceived a hatred for him at once, just because he was a fine man, just because he looked with horror on anything mean, because he was utterly unlike himself; and all that M. told A. about the major and the prison A. hastened at the first opportunity to report to the major. The major took an intense dislike to M. in consequence and persecuted him. Had it not been for the governor of the prison, it would have ended in a tragedy. A. was not in the least disconcerted when M. found out later on how base he had been; on the contrary he liked meeting him and looked at him ironically. It evidently gave him gratification. M. himself pointed this out to me several times. This abject creature afterwards ran away from the prison, with another convict and a guard, but that escape I will describe later. At first he made up to me, thinking I had heard nothing of his story. I repeat, he poisoned my first days in prison and made them even more miserable. I was terrified at the awful baseness and degradation into which I had been cast and in the midst of which I found myself. I imagined that everything here was as base and as degraded. But I was mistaken, I judged of all by A.

I spent those three days wandering miserably about the prison and lying on the bed. I gave the stuff that was served out to me to a trustworthy convict recommended to me by Akim Akimitch, and asked him to make it into shirts, for payment, of course (a few halfpence a shirt). I provided myself at Akim Akimitch's urgent advice with a folding mattress made of felt encased in linen, but as thin as a pancake, and also got a pillow stuffed with wool, terribly hard till one was used to it. Akim Akimitch was quite in a bustle arranging all these things for me, and helped to get them himself. With his own hands he made me a quilt out of rags of old cloth cut out of discarded jackets and trousers which I bought from other convicts. The prison clothes become the property of the prisoner when they are worn out; they are at once sold on the spot in the prison, and however ancient a garment might be, there was always a hope of getting something for it. I was much surprised at first by all this. It was practically my first contact with men of the peasant class. I had suddenly become a man of the same humble class, a convict like the rest. Their habits, ideas, opinions, customs became, as it were, also mine, externally, legally anyway, though I did not share them really. I was surprised and confused, as though I had heard nothing of all this and had not suspected its existence. Yet I had heard of it and knew of it. But the reality makes quite a different impression from what one hears and knows. I could, for instance, never have suspected that such things, such old rags could be looked upon as objects of value. Yet it was of these rags I made myself a quilt! It was hard to imagine such cloth as was served out for the convict's clothing. It looked like thick cloth such as is used in the army, but after very little wearing it became like a sieve and tore shockingly. Cloth garments were, however, only expected to last a year. Yet it was hard to make them do service for so long. The convict has to work, to carry heavy weights; his clothes quickly wear out and go into holes. The sheepskin coats are supposed to last three years, and they were used for that time as coats by day and both underblanket and covering at night. But a sheepskin coat is strong, though it was not unusual to see a convict at the end of the third year in a sheepskin patched with plain hempen cloth. Yet even very shabby ones were sold for as much as forty kopecks at the end of the three years. Some in better preservation even fetched as much as sixty or seventy, and that was a large sum in prison.

Money, as I have mentioned already, was of vast and overwhelming importance in prison. One may say for a positive fact that the sufferings of a convict who had money, however little, were not a tenth of what were endured by one who had none, though the latter, too, had everything provided by government, and so, as the prison authorities argue, could have no need of money. I repeat again, if the prisoners had been deprived of all possibility of having money of their own, they would either have gone out of their minds, or have died off like flies (in spite of being provided with everything), or would have resorted to incredible violence—some from misery, others in order to be put to death and end it all as soon as possible, or anyway "to change their luck" (the technical expression). If after earning his money with cruel effort, or making use of extraordinary cunning, often in conjunction with theft and cheating, the convict wastes what he has earned so carelessly, with such childish senselessness, it does not prove that he does not appreciate it, though it might seem so at the first glance. The convict is morbidly, insanely greedy of money, and if he throws it away like so much rubbish, he throws it away on what he considers of even more value. What is more precious than money for the convict? Freedom or some sort of dream of freedom. The prisoner is a great dreamer. I shall have something to say of this later, but, while we are on the subject, would it be believed that I have known convicts sentenced for twenty years who, speaking to me, have quite calmly used such phrases as "you wait a bit; when, please God, my term is up, then I'll . . ." The word convict means nothing else but a man with no will of his own, and in spending money he is showing a will of his own. In spite of brands, fetters and the hateful prison fence which shuts him off from God's world and cages him in like a wild beast, he is able to obtain vodka, an article prohibited under terrible penalties, to get at women, even sometimes (though not always) to bribe the veterans and even the sergeants, who will wink at his breaches of law and discipline. He can play the swaggering bully over them into the bargain, and the convict is awfully fond of bullying, that is, pretending to his companions and even persuading himself, if only for a time, that he has infinitely more power and freedom than is supposed. He can in fact carouse and make an uproar, crush and insult others and prove to them that he can do all this, that it is all in his own hands, that is, he can persuade himself of what is utterly out of the question for the poor fellow. That, by the way, is perhaps why one detects in all convicts, even when sober, a propensity to swagger, to boastfulness, to a comic and very naïve though fantastic glorification of their personality. Moreover all this disorderliness has its special risk, so it all has a semblance of life, and at least a far-off semblance of freedom. And what will one not give for freedom? What millionaire would not give all his millions for one breath of air if his neck were in the noose?

The prison authorities are sometimes surprised that after leading a quiet, exemplary life for some years, and even being made a foreman for his model behaviour, a convict with no apparent reason suddenly breaks out, as though he were possessed by a devil, plays pranks, drinks, makes an uproar and sometimes positively ventures on serious crimes—such as open disrespect to a superior officer, or even commits murder or rape. They look at him and marvel. And all the while possibly the cause of this sudden outbreak, in the man from whom one would least have expected it, is simply the poignant hysterical craving for self-expression, the unconscious yearning for himself, the desire to assert himself, to assert his crushed personality, a desire which suddenly takes possession of him and reaches the pitch of fury, of spite, of mental aberration, of fits and nervous convulsions. So perhaps a man buried alive and awakening in his coffin might beat upon its lid and struggle to fling it off, though of course reason might convince him that all his efforts would be useless; but the trouble is that it is not a question of reason, it is a question of nerves. We must take into consideration also that almost every expression of personality on the part of a convict is looked upon as a crime, and so it makes no difference whether it is a small offence or a great one. If he is to drink he may as well do it thoroughly, if he is to venture on anything he may as well venture on everything, even on a murder. And the only effort is to begin: as he goes on, the man gets intoxicated and there is no holding him back. And so it would be better in every way not to drive him to that point. It would make things easier for everyone.

Yes; but how is it to be done?

CHAPTER VI

THE FIRST MONTH (2)

I HAD A LITTLE money when I entered the prison; I carried only very little on me for fear it should be taken away, but as a last resource I had several roubles hidden in the binding of a New Testament, a book which one is allowed to have in prison. This book, together with the money hidden in the binding, was given me in Tobolsk by men who were exiles too, who could reckon their years of banishment by decades, and had long been accustomed to look at every "unfortunate" as a brother. There are in Siberia, and practically always have been, some people who seem to make it the object of their lives to look after the "unfortunate," to show pure and disinterested sympathy and compassion for them, as though they were their own children. I must briefly mention here one encounter I had.

In the town where our prison was there lived a lady, a widow called Nastasya Ivanoyna. Of course none of us could make her acquaintance while we were in prison. She seemed to devote her life to the relief of convicts, but was especially active in helping us. Whether it was that she had had some similar trouble in her family, or that someone particularly near and dear to her had suffered for a similar* offence, anyway she seemed to consider it a particular happiness to do all that she could for us. She could not do much, of course; she was poor. But we in prison felt that out there, beyond the prison walls, we had a devoted friend. She often sent us news, of which we were in great need. When I left prison and was on my way to another town, I went to see her and made her acquaintance. She lived on the outskirts of the town in the house of a near relation. She was neither old nor young, neither good-looking nor plain; it was impossible to tell even whether she were intelligent or educated. All that one could see in her was an infinite kindliness, an irresistible desire to please one, to comfort one, to do something nice

---

*That is, political (Garnett's note).

for one. All that could be read in her kind gentle eyes. Together with a comrade who had been in prison with me I spent almost a whole evening in her company. She was eager to anticipate our wishes, laughed when we laughed, was in haste to agree with anything we said and was all anxiety to regale us with all she had to offer. Tea was served with savouries and sweetmeats, and it seemed that if she had had thousands she would have been delighted, simply because she could do more for us and for our comrades in prison. When we said goodbye she brought out a cigarette-case as a keepsake for each of us. She had made these cigarette-cases of cardboard for us (and how they were put together!) and had covered them with coloured paper such as is used for covering arithmetic books for children in schools (and possibly some such school book had been sacrificed for the covering). Both the cigarette-cases were adorned with an edging of gilt paper, which she had bought, perhaps, expressly for them. "I see you smoke cigarettes, so perhaps it may be of use to you," she said, as it were apologizing timidly for her present. . . . Some people maintain (I have heard it and read it) that the purest love for one's neighbour is at the same time the greatest egoism.[6] What egoism there could be in this case, I can't understand.

Though I had not much money when I came into prison, I could not be seriously vexed with those of the convicts who, in my very first hours in prison, after deceiving me once, came a second, a third, and even a fifth time to borrow from me. But I will candidly confess one thing: it did annoy me that all these people with their naïve cunning must, as I thought, be laughing at me and thinking of me as a simpleton and a fool just because I gave them money the fifth time of asking. They must have thought that I was taken in by their wiles and cunning, while, if I had refused them and driven them away, I am convinced they would have respected me a great deal more. But annoying as it was, I could not refuse. I was annoyed because I was seriously and anxiously considering during those first days what sort of position I could make for myself in the prison, or rather on what sort of footing I ought to be with them. I felt and thoroughly realized that the surroundings were completely new to me, that I was quite in the dark and could not go on living so for several years. I had to prepare myself. I made up my mind, of course, that above all I must act straightforwardly, in accordance with my inner feelings and conscience. But I knew, too, that that was a mere aphorism, and that the most unexpected difficulties lay before me in practice.

And so, in spite of all the petty details of settling into the prison which I have mentioned already, and into which I was led chiefly by Akim Akimitch, and, although they served as some distraction, I was more and more tormented by a terrible devouring melancholy. "A dead house," I thought to myself sometimes, standing on the steps of the prison at twilight and looking at the convicts who had come back from work, and were idly loafing about the prison yard and moving from the prison to the kitchen and back again. I looked intently at them and tried to conjecture from their faces and movements what sort of men they were, and what were their characters. They sauntered about before me with scowling brows or overjubilant faces (these two ex- tremes are most frequently met with, and are almost typical of prison life), swearing or simply talking together, or walking alone with quiet even steps, seemingly lost in thought, some with a weary, apathetic air, others (even here!) with a look of conceited superiority, with caps on one side, their coats flung over their shoulders, with a sly insolent stare and an impudent jeer. "This is my sphere, my world, now," I thought, "with which I must live now whether I will or not." I tried to find out about them by questioning Akim Akimitch, with whom I liked to have tea, so as not to be alone. By the way, tea was almost all I could take at first. Tea Akim Akimitch did not decline, and used himself to prepare our absurd, home-made little tin samovar, which was lent me by M. Akim Akimitch usually drank one glass (he had glasses, too), drank it silently and sedately, returning it to me, thanked me and at once began working at my quilt. But what I wanted to find out he could not tell me. He could not in fact understand why I was interested in the char- acters of the convicts surrounding us, and listened to me with a sort of sly smile which I very well remember. Yes, evidently I must find out by experience and not ask questions, I thought.

On the fourth day, early in the morning, all the convicts were drawn up in two rows at the prison gates before the guard-house, just as they had been that time when I was being refettered. Soldiers with loaded rifles and fixed bayonets stood opposite them, in front and behind. A soldier has the right to fire at a convict if the latter attempts to escape; at the same time he would have to answer for firing except in extreme necessity; the same rule applies in case of open mutiny among the con- victs. But who would dream of attempting to escape openly? An officer of engineers, a foreman and also the non-commissioned officers and soldiers who superintend the works were present. The roll was called; those of the convicts who worked in the tailoring room set off first of all; the engineering officers had nothing to do with them; they worked only for the prison and made all the prison clothes. Then the contingent for the workshops started, followed by those who did unskilled work, of whom there were about twenty. I set off with them.

On the frozen river behind the fortress were two government barges which were of no more use and had to be pulled to pieces, so that the timber might not be wasted, though I fancy all the old material was worth very little, practically nothing. Firewood was sold for next to nothing in the town, and there were forests all round. They put us on this job chiefly to keep us occupied, and the convicts themselves quite understood that. They always worked listlessly and apathetically at such tasks, and it was quite different when the work was valuable in itself and worth doing, especially when they could succeed in getting a fixed task. Then they seemed, as it were, inspirited, and although they got no advantage from it, I have seen them exert themselves to the utmost to finish the work as quickly and as well as possible; their vanity indeed was somehow involved in it. But with work such as we had that day, done more as a matter of form than because it was needed, it was difficult to obtain a fixed task and we had to work till the drum sounded the recall home at eleven o'clock in the morning.

The day was warm and misty; the snow was almost thawing. All our group set off to the river-bank beyond the fortress with a faint jingling of chains, which gave a thin, sharp metallic clank at every step, though they were hidden under our clothes. Two or three men went into the house where the tools were kept to get the implements we needed. I walked with the rest and felt a little more cheerful: I was in haste to see and find out what sort of work it was. What was this hard labour? And how should I work for the first time in my life?

I remember it all to the smallest detail. On the road we met a workman of some sort with a beard; he stopped and put his hand in his pocket. A convict immediately came forward out of our group, took off his cap, took the alms—five kopecks—and quickly rejoined the others. The workman crossed himself and went on his way. The five kopecks were spent that morning on rolls, which were divided equally among the party.

Some of our gang were, as usual, sullen and taciturn, others indifferent and listless, others chattered idly together. One was for some reason extraordinarily pleased and happy, he sang and almost danced on the way, jingling his fetters at every caper. It was the same short, thick-set convict who on my first morning in prison had quarrelled with another while they were washing because the latter had foolishly ventured to declare that he was a "cocky-locky." This merry fellow was called Skuratov. At last he began singing a jaunty song of which I remember the refrain:

> I was away when they married me
> I was away at the mill.

All that was lacking was a balalaika.

His extraordinary cheerfulness, of course, at once aroused indignation in some of our party; it was almost taken as an insult.

"He is setting up a howl!" a convict said reproachfully, though it was no concern of his.

"The wolf has only one note and that you've cribbed, you Tula fellow!" observed another of the gloomy ones, with a Little Russian accent.

"I may be a Tula man," Skuratov retorted promptly, "but you choke yourselves with dumplings in Poltava."

"Lie away! What do you eat? Used to ladle out cabbage soup with a shoe."

"And now it might be the devil feeding us with cannon balls," added a third.

"I know I am a pampered fellow, mates," Skuratov answered with a faint sigh, as though regretting he had been pampered and addressing himself to all in general and to no one in particular, "from my earliest childhood bred up—(that is, brought up, he intentionally distorted his words)—on prunes and fancy bread; my brothers have a shop of their own in Moscow to this day, they sell fiddlesticks in No Man's street, very rich shopkeepers they are."

"And did you keep shop too?"

"I, too, carried on in various qualities. It was then, mates, I got my first two hundred . . ."

"You don't mean roubles?" broke in one inquisitive listener, positively starting at the mention of so much money.

"No, my dear soul, not roubles—sticks. Luka, hey, Luka!"

"To some I am Luka but to you I am Luka Kuzmitch," a thin little sharp-nosed convict answered reluctantly.

"Well, Luka Kuzmitch then, hang you, so be it."

"To some people I am Luka Kuzmitch, but you should call me uncle."

"Well, hang you then, uncle, you are not worth talking to! But there was a good thing I wanted to say. That's how it happened, mates, I did not make much in Moscow; they gave me fifteen lashes as a parting present and sent me packing. So then I . . . ."

"But why were you sent packing?" inquired one who had been carefully following the speaker.

"Why, it's against the rules to go into quarantine and to drink tin-tacks and to play the jingle-jangle. So I hadn't time to get rich in Moscow, mates, not worth talking about. And I did so, so, so want to get rich. I'd a yearning I cannot describe."

Many of his listeners laughed. Skuratov was evidently one of those volunteer entertainers, or rather buffoons, who seemed to make it their duty to amuse their gloomy companions, and who got nothing but abuse for their trouble. He belonged to a peculiar and noteworthy type, of which I may have more to say hereafter.

"Why, you might be hunted like sable now," observed Luka Kuzmitch. "Your clothes alone would be worth a hundred roubles."

Skuratov had on the most ancient threadbare sheepskin, on which patches were conspicuous everywhere. He looked it up and down attentively, though unconcernedly.

"It's my head that's priceless, mates, my brain," he answered. "When I said good-bye to Moscow it was my one comfort that I took my head with me. Farewell, Moscow, thanks for your bastings, thanks for your warmings, you gave me some fine dressings! And my sheepskin is not worth looking at, my good soul. . . ."

"I suppose your head is, then?"

"Even his head is not his own but a charity gift," Luka put in again. "It was given him at Tyumen for Christ's sake, as he marched by with a gang."

"I say, Skuratov, had you any trade?"

"Trade, indeed! he used to lead puppydogs about and steal their tit-bits, that was all his trade," observed one of the gloomy convicts.

"I really did try my hand at cobbling boots," answered Skuratov, not observing this biting criticism. "I only cobbled one pair."

"Well, were they bought?"

"Yes, a fellow did turn up; I suppose he had not feared God or honoured his father and mother, and so the Lord punished him and he bought them."

All Skuratov's audience went off into peals of laughter.

"And I did once work here," Skuratov went on with extreme nonchalance. "I put new uppers on to Lieutenant Pomortzev's boots."

"Well, was he satisfied?"

"No, mates, he wasn't. He gave me oaths enough to last me a lifetime, and a dig in the back with his knee too. He was in an awful taking. Ah, my life has deceived me, the jade's deceived me!"

> And not many minutes later
> Akulina's husband came . . .

he unexpectedly carolled again, and began pattering a dance step with his feet.

"Ech, the graceless fellow," the Little Russian who was walking beside me observed with a side glance of spiteful contempt at Skuratov.

"A useless fellow," observed another in a serious and final tone.

I could not understand why they were angry with Skuratov, and why, indeed, all the merry ones seemed to be held in some contempt, as I had noticed already during those first days. I put down the anger of the Little Russian and of the others to personal causes. But it was not a case of personal dislike; they were angry at the absence of reserve in Skuratov, at the lack of the stern assumption of personal dignity about which all the prisoners were pedantically particular; in fact, at his being a "useless fellow", to use their own expression. Yet they were not angry with all the merry ones, and did not treat all as they did Skuratov and those like him. It depended on what people would put up with: a good-natured and unpretentious man was at once exposed to insult. I was struck by this fact indeed. But there were some among the cheerful spirits who knew how to take their own part and liked doing so, and they exacted respect. In this very group there was one of these prickly characters; he was a tall good-looking fellow with a large wart on his cheek and a very comic expression, though his face was rather handsome and intelligent. He was in reality a light-hearted and very charming fellow, though I only found out that side of him later on. They used to call him "the pioneer" because at one time he had served in the Pioneers; now he was in the "special division." I shall have a great deal to say of him later.

Not all of the "serious-minded," however, were so outspoken as the indignant Little Russian. There were some men in the prison who aimed at superiority, at knowing all sorts of things, at showing resourcefulness, character and intelligence. Many of these really were men of intelligence and character, and did actually attain what they aimed at, that is, a leading position and a considerable moral influence over their companions. These clever fellows were often at daggers drawn with one another, and every one of them had many enemies. They looked down upon other convicts with dignity and condescension, they picked no unnecessary quarrels, were in favour with the authorities, and took the lead at work. Not one of them would have found fault with anyone for a song, for instance; they would not have stooped to such trifles. These men were very polite to me all the time I was in prison, but they were not very talkative, also apparently from a sense of dignity. I shall have to speak more in detail of them also.

We reached the river-bank. The old barge which we had to break up was frozen into the ice below us. On the further side of the river the steppes stretched blue into the distance; it was a gloomy and desert view. I expected that everyone would rush at the work, but they had no idea of doing so. Some sat down on the logs that lay about on the bank; almost all of them brought out of their boots bags of local tobacco which was sold at three farthings a pound in the market, and short willow pipes of home manufacture. They lighted their pipes; the soldiers formed a cordon round us and proceeded to guard us with a bored expression.

"Whose notion was it to break up this barge?" one observed as it were to himself, not addressing anyone. "Are they in want of chips?"

"He wasn't afraid of our anger, whoever it was," observed another.

"Where are those peasants trudging to?" the first asked after a pause, not noticing of course the answer to his first question, and pointing to a group of peasants who were making their way in Indian file over untrodden snow in the distance. Everyone turned lazily in that direction and to while away the time began mocking at them. One of the peasants, the last of the file, walked very absurdly, stretching out his arms and swinging his head on one side with a long peasant's cap on it. His whole figure stood out clearly and distinctly against the white snow.

"Look how brother Peter has rigged himself out!" observed one, mimicking the peasant accent.

It is remarkable that the convicts rather looked down on peasants, though half of them were of the peasant class.

"The last one, mates, walks as though he was sowing radishes."

"He is a slow-witted fellow, he has a lot of money," observed a third.

They all laughed, but lazily too, as it were reluctantly. Meantime a baker woman had come, a brisk lively woman.

They bought rolls of her for the five kopecks that had been given us and divided them in equal shares on the spot.

The young man who sold rolls in prison took two dozen and began a lively altercation, trying to get her to give him three rolls instead of the usual two as his commission. But the baker woman would not consent.

"Well, and won't you give me something else?"

"What else?"

"What the mice don't eat."

"A plague take you," shrieked the woman and laughed.

At last the sergeant who superintended the work came up with a stick in his hand.

"Hey, there, what are you sitting there for? Get to work!"

"Set us a task, Ivan Matveitch," said one of the "leaders" slowly getting up from his place.

"Why didn't you ask for it at the start? Break up the barge, that's your task."

At last they got up desultorily and slouched to the river. Some of them immediately took up the part of foreman, in words, anyway. It appeared that the barge was not to be broken up anyhow, but the timber was to be kept as whole as possible, especially the crossway beams which were fixed to the bottom of the barge by wooden bolts along their whole length.

"We ought first of all to get out this beam. Set to this, lads," observed one of the convicts who had not spoken before, a quiet and unassuming fellow, not one of the leading or ruling spirits; and stooping down he got hold of a thick beam, waiting for the others to help him. But nobody did help him.

"Get it up, no fear! You won't get it up and if your grandfather the bear came along, he wouldn't," muttered someone between his teeth.

"Well then, brothers, how are we to begin? I don't know . . ." said the puzzled man who had put himself forward, letting go the beam and getting on to his feet again.

"Work your hardest you'll never be done . . . why put yourself forward?"

"He could not feed three hens without making a mistake, and now he is to be first . . . The fidget!"

"I didn't mean anything, mates . . ." the disconcerted youth tried to explain.

"Do you want me to keep covers over you all? Or to keep you in pickle through the winter?" shouted the sergeant again, looking in perplexity at the crowd of twenty convicts who stood not knowing how to set to work. "Begin! Make haste!"

"You can't do things quicker than you can, Ivan Matveitch."

"Why, but you are doing nothing! Hey, Savelyev!, Talky Petrovitch ought to be your name! I ask you, why are you standing there, rolling your eyes? Set to work."

"But what can I do alone?"

"Set us a task, Ivan Matveitch."

"You've been told you won't have a task. Break up the barge and go home. Get to work!"

They did set to work at last, but listlessly, unwillingly, incompetently. It was quite provoking to see a sturdy crowd of stalwart workmen who seemed utterly at a loss how to set to work. As soon as they began to take out the first and smallest beam, it appeared that it was breaking, "breaking of itself," as was reported to the overseer by way of apology; so it seemed they could not begin that way but must try somehow else. There followed a lengthy discussion among the convicts what other way to try, what was to be done? By degrees it came, of course, to abuse and threatened to go further. . . . The sergeant shouted again and waved his stick, but the beam broke again. It appeared finally that axes were not enough, and other tools were needed. Two fellows were dispatched with a convoy to the fortress to fetch them, and meantime the others very serenely sat down on the barge, pulled out their pipes and began smoking again.

The sergeant gave it up as a bad job at last.

"Well, you'll never make work look silly! Ach, what a set, what a set!" he muttered angrily, and with a wave of his hand he set off for the fortress, swinging his stick.

An hour later the foreman came. After listening calmly to the convicts he announced that the task he set them was to get out four more beams without breaking them, and in addition he marked out a considerable portion of the barge to be taken to pieces, telling them that when it was done they could go home. The task was a large one, but, heavens! how they set to! There was no trace of laziness, no trace of incompetence. The axes rang; they began unscrewing the wooden bolts. Others thrust thick posts underneath and, pressing on them with twenty hands, levered up the beams, which to my astonishment came up now whole and uninjured. The work went like wild fire. Everyone seemed wonderfully intelligent all of a sudden. There was not a word wasted, not an oath was heard, everyone seemed to know what to say, what to do, where to stand, what advice to give. Just half an hour before the drum beat, the last of the task was finished, and the convicts went home tired but quite contented, though they had only saved half an hour of their working day. But as far as I was concerned I noticed one thing; wherever I turned to help them during the work, everywhere I was superfluous, everywhere I was in the way, everywhere I was pushed aside almost with abuse.

The lowest ragamuffin, himself a wretched workman, who did not dare to raise his voice among the other convicts who were sharper and cleverer than he, thought himself entitled to shout at me on the pretext that I hindered him if I stood beside him. At last one of the smarter ones said to me plainly and coarsely:

"Where are you shoving? Get away! Why do you poke yourself where you are not wanted?"

"Your game's up!" another chimed in at once.

"You'd better take a jug and go round asking for halfpence to build a fine house and waste upon snuff, but there's nothing for you to do here."

I had to stand apart, and to stand apart when all are working makes one feel ashamed. But when it happened that I did walk away and stood at the end of the barge they shouted at once:

"Fine workmen they've given us; what can one get done with them? You can get nothing done."

All this, of course, was done on purpose, for it amused everyone. They must have a gibe at one who has been a "fine gentleman," and, of course, they were glad to have the chance.

It may well be understood now why, as I have said already, my first question on entering the prison was how I should behave, what attitude I should take up before these people. I had a foreboding that I should often come into collision with them like this. But in spite of all difficulties I made up my mind not to change my plan of action which I had partly thought out during those days; I knew it was right. I had made up my mind to behave as simply and independently as possible, not to make any special effort to get on intimate terms with them, but not to repel them if they desired to be friendly themselves; not to be afraid of their menaces and their hatred, and as far as possible to affect not to notice, not to approach them on certain points and not to encourage some of their habits and customs—not to seek in fact to be regarded quite as a comrade by them. I guessed at the first glance that they would be the first to despise me if I did. According to their ideas, however (I learned this for certain later on), I ought even to keep up and respect my class superiority before them, that is, to study my comfort, to give myself airs, to scorn them, to turn up my nose at everything; to play the fine gentleman in fact. That was what they understood by being a gentleman. They would, of course, have abused me for doing so, but yet they would privately have respected me for it. To play such a part was not in my line; I was never a gentleman according to their notions; but, on the other hand, I vowed to make no concession derogatory to my education and my way of thinking. If I had begun to try and win their goodwill by making up to them, agreeing with them, being familiar with them and had gone in for their various "qualities," they would have at once supposed that I did it out of fear and cowardice and would have treated me with contempt. A. was not a fair example: he used to visit the major and they were afraid of him themselves. On the other side, I did not want to shut myself off from them by cold and unapproachable politeness, as the Poles did. I saw clearly that they despised me now for wanting to work with them, without seeking my own ease or giving myself airs of superiority over them. And although I felt sure that they would have to change their opinion of me later, yet the thought that they had, as it were, the right to despise me, because they imagined I was trying to make up to them at work—this thought was very bitter to me.

When I returned to the prison in the evening after the day's work, worn out and exhausted, I was again overcome by terrible misery. "How many thousands of such days lie before me," I thought, "all the same, all exactly alike!" As it grew dusk I sauntered up and down behind the prison by the fence, silent and alone, and suddenly I saw our Sharik running towards me. Sharik was the dog that belonged to our prison, just as there are dogs belonging to companies, batteries and squadrons. He had lived from time immemorial in the prison, he belonged to no one in particular, considering everyone his master, and he lived on scraps from the kitchen. He was a rather large mongrel, black with white spots, not very old, with intelligent eyes and a bushy tail. No one ever stroked him, no one took any notice of him. From the first day I stroked him and fed him with bread out of my hands. While I stroked him, he stood quietly, looking affectionately at me and gently wagging his tail as a sign of pleasure. Now after not seeing me for so long—me, the only person who had for years thought of caressing him—he ran about looking for me amongst all of them, and finding me behind the prison, ran to meet me, whining with delight. I don't know what came over me but I fell to kissing him, I put my arms round his head; he put his forepaws on my shoulders and began licking my face. "So this is the friend fate has sent me," I thought, and every time I came back from work during that first hard and gloomy period, first of all, before I went anywhere else, I hurried behind the prison with Sharik leaping before me and whining with joy, held his head in my arms and kissed him again and again, and a sweet and at the same time poignantly bitter feeling wrung my heart. And I remember it was positively pleasant to me to think, as though priding myself on my suffering, that there was only one creature in the world who loved me, who was devoted to me, who was my friend, my one friend—my faithful dog Sharik.

CHAPTER VII

NEW ACQUAINTANCES. PETROV

BUT TIME PASSED AND little by little I got used to it. Every day I was less and less bewildered by the daily events of my new life. My eyes grew, as it were, accustomed to incidents, surroundings, men. To be reconciled to this life was impossible, but it was high time to accept it as an accomplished fact. Any perplexities that still remained in my mind I concealed within myself as completely as possible. I no longer wandered about the prison like one distraught, and no longer showed my misery. The savagely inquisitive eyes of the convicts were not so often fixed on me, they did not watch me with such an assumption of insolence. They had grown used to me too, apparently, and I was very glad of it. I walked about prison as though I were at home, knew my place on the common bed and seemed to have grown used to things which I should have thought I could never in my life have grown used to.

Regularly once a week I went to have half my head shaved. Every Saturday in our free time we were called out in turn from the prison to the guard-house (if we did not go we had to get shaved on our own account) and there the barbers of the battalion rubbed our heads with cold lather and mercilessly scraped them with blunt razors; it makes me shiver even now when I recall that torture. But the remedy was soon found: Akim Akimitch pointed out to me a convict in the military division who for a kopeck would shave with his own razor anyone who liked. That was his trade. Many of the convicts went to him to escape the prison barbers, though they were by no means a sensitive lot. Our convict barber was called the major, why I don't know, and in what way he suggested the major I can't say. As I write I recall this major, a tall, lean, taciturn fellow, rather stupid, always absorbed in his occupation, never without a strop on which he was day and night sharpening his incredibly worn out razor. He was apparently concentrated on this pursuit, which he evidently looked upon as his vocation in life. He was really extremely happy when the razor was in good condition and someone came to be shaved; his lather was warm, his hand was light, the shaving was like velvet. He evidently enjoyed his art and was proud of it, and he carelessly took the kopeck he had earned as though he did the work for art's sake and not for profit.

A. caught it on one occasion from our major when, telling him tales about the prisoners, he incautiously spoke of our barber as the major. The real major flew into a rage and was extremely offended. "Do you know, you rascal, what is meant by a major?" he shouted, foaming at the mouth, and falling upon A. in his usual fashion. "Do you understand what is meant by a major? And here you dare to call a scoundrelly convict major before me, in my presence!" No one but A. could have got on with such a man.

From the very first day of my life in prison, I began to dream of freedom. To calculate in a thousand different ways when my days in prison would be over became my favourite occupation. It was always in my mind, and I am sure that it is the same with everyone who is deprived of freedom for a fixed period. I don't know whether the other convicts thought and calculated as I did, but the amazing audacity of their hopes impressed me from the beginning. The hopes of a prisoner deprived of freedom are utterly different from those of a man living a natural life. A free man hopes, of course (for a change of luck, for instance, or the success of an undertaking), but he lives, he acts, he is caught up in the world of life. It is very different with the prisoner. There is life for him too, granted—prison life—but whatever the convict may be and whatever may be the term of his sentence, he is instinctively unable to accept his lot as something positive, final, as part of real life. Every convict feels that he is, so to speak, *not at home*, but on a visit. He looks at twenty years as though they were two, and is fully convinced that when he leaves prison at fifty-five he will be as full of life and energy as he is now at thirty-five. "I've still life before me," he thinks and resolutely drives away all doubts and other vexatious ideas. Even those in the "special division" who had been sentenced for life sometimes reckoned on orders suddenly coming from Petersburg: "to send them to the mines at Nerchinsk and to limit their sentence." Then it would be all right: to begin with, it is almost six months' journey to Nerchinsk, and how much pleasanter the journey would be than being in prison! And afterwards the term in Nerchinsk would be over and then. . . . And sometimes even grey-headed men reckoned like this.

At Tobolsk I have seen convicts chained to the wall. The man is kept on a chain seven feet long; he has a bedstead by him. He is chained like this for some exceptionally terrible crime committed in Siberia. They are kept like that for five years, for ten years. They are generally brigands. I only saw one among them who looked as if he had belonged to the upper classes; he had been in the government service somewhere. He spoke submissively with a lisp; his smile was mawkishly sweet. He showed us his chain, showed how he could most comfortably lie on the bed. He must have been a choice specimen! As a rule they all behave quietly and seem contented, yet every one of them is intensely anxious for the end of his sentence. Why, one wonders? I will tell you why: he will get out of the stifling dank room with its low vaulted roof of brick, and will walk in the prison yard . . . and that is all. He will never be allowed out of the prison. He knows those who have been in chains are always kept in prison and fettered to the day of their death. He knows that and yet he is desperately eager for the end of his time on the chain. But for that longing how could he remain five or six years on the chain without dying or going out of his mind? Some of them would not endure it at all.

I felt that work might be the saving of me, might strengthen my physical frame and my health. Continual mental anxiety, nervous irritation, the foul air of the prison might well be my destruction. Being constantly in the open air, working every day till I was tired, learning to carry heavy weights—at any rate I shall save myself, I thought, I shall make myself strong, I shall leave the prison healthy, vigorous, hearty and not old. I was not mistaken: the work and exercise were very good for me. I looked with horror at one of my companions, a man of my own class: he was wasting like a candle in prison. He entered it at the same time as I did, young, handsome and vigorous, and he left it half-shattered, grey-headed, gasping for breath and unable to walk. No, I thought, looking at him; I want to live and will live. But at first I got into hot water among the convicts for my fondness for work, and for a long time they assailed me with gibes and contempt. But I took no notice of anyone and set off cheerfully, for instance, to the baking and pounding of alabaster—one of the first things I learnt to do. That was easy work.

The officials who supervised our work were ready, as far as possible, to be lenient in allotting work to prisoners belonging to the upper classes, which was by no means an undue indulgence but simple justice. It would be strange to expect from a man of half the strength and no experience of manual labour the same amount of work as the ordinary workman had by regulation to get through. But this "indulgence" was not always shown, and it was as it were surreptitious; a strict watch was kept from outside to check it. Very often we had to go to heavy work, and then, of course, it was twice as hard for the upper-class convicts as for the rest.

Three or four men were usually sent to the alabaster, old or weak by preference, and we, of course, came under that heading; but besides these a real workman who understood the work was always told off for the job. The same workman went regularly for some years to this task, a dark, lean, oldish man called Almazov, grim, unsociable and peevish. He had a profound contempt for us. But he was so taciturn that he was even lazy about grumbling at us.

The shed in which the alabaster was baked and pounded stood also on the steep, desolate river-bank. In winter, especially in dull weather, it was dreary to look over the river and at the far-away bank the other side. There was something poignant and heart-rending in this wild desolate landscape. But it was almost more painful when the sun shone brightly on the immense white expanse of snow. One longed to fly away into that expanse which stretched from the other side of the river, an untrodden plain for twelve hundred miles to the south. Almazov usually set to work in grim silence; we were ashamed, as it were, that we could not be any real help to him, and he managed alone and asked no help from us, on purpose, it seemed, to make us conscious of our short-comings and remorseful for our uselessness. And yet all he had to do was to heat the oven for baking in it the alabaster, which we used to fetch for him. Next day, when the alabaster was thoroughly baked, the task of unloading it from the oven began. Each of us took a heavy mallet, filled himself a special box of alabaster and set to work to pound it. This was delightful work. The brittle alabaster was quickly transformed to white shining powder, it crumbled so well and so easily. We swung our heavy mallets and made such a din that we enjoyed it ourselves. We were tired at the end and at the same time we felt better; our cheeks were flushed, our blood circulated more quickly. At this point even Almazov began to look at us with indulgence, as people look at small children; he smoked his pipe condescendingly, though he could not help grumbling when he had to speak. But he was like that with everyone, though I believe he was a good-natured man at bottom.

Another task to which I was sent was to turn the lathe in the workshop. It was a big heavy wheel. It needed a good deal of effort to move it, especially when the turner (one of the regimental workmen) was shaping some piece of furniture for the use of an official, such as a banister or a big table leg for which a big log was required. In such cases it was beyond one man's strength to turn the wheel and generally two of us were sent—myself and another "gentleman" whom I will call B. For several years whenever anything had to be turned this task fell to our share. B. was a frail, weakly young fellow who suffered with his lungs. He had entered the prison a year before my arrival together with two others, his comrades—one an old man who spent all his time, day and night, saying his prayers (for which he was greatly respected by the convicts) and died before I left prison, and the other quite a young lad, fresh, rosy, strong and full of spirit, who had carried B. for more than five hundred miles on the journey when the latter was too exhausted to walk. The affection between them was worth seeing. B. was a man of very good education, generous feelings and a lofty character which had been embittered and made irritable by illness. We used to manage the wheel together and the work interested us both. It was first-rate exercise for me.

I was particularly fond, too, of shovelling away the snow. This had to be done as a rule after snowstorms, which were pretty frequent in winter. After a snowstorm lasting twenty-four hours, some houses would be snowed up to the middle of the windows and others would be almost buried. Then as soon as the storm was over and the sun came out, we were driven out in big gangs, sometimes the whole lot of us, to shovel away the snowdrifts from the government buildings. Everyone was given a spade, a task was set for all together, and sometimes such a task that it was a wonder they could get through it, and all set to work with a will. The soft new snow, a little frozen at the top, was easily lifted in huge spadefulls and was scattered about, turning to fine glistening powder in the air. The spade cut readily into the white mass sparkling in the sunshine. The convicts were almost always merry over this job. The fresh winter air and the exercise warmed them up. Everyone grew more cheerful; there were sounds of laughter, shouts, jests. They began snowballing each other, not without protest, of course, from the serious ones, who were indignant at the laughter and merriment; and the general excitement usually ended in swearing.

Little by little, I began to enlarge my circle of acquaintance. Though, indeed, I did not think of making acquaintances myself; I was still restless, gloomy and mistrustful. My acquaintanceships arose of themselves. One of the first to visit me was a convict called Petrov. I say visit me and I lay special emphasis on the word; Petrov was in the "special division," and lived in the part of the prison furthest from me. There could apparently be no connection between us, and we certainly had and could have nothing in common. And yet in those early days Petrov seemed to feel it his duty to come to our room to see me almost every day, or to stop me when I was walking in our leisure hour behind the prison as much out of sight as I could. At first I disliked this. But he somehow succeeded in making his visits a positive diversion to me, though he was by no means a particularly sociable or talkative man. He was a short, strongly built man, agile and restless, pale with high cheek-bones and fearless eyes, with a rather pleasant face, fine white close-set teeth, and an everlasting plug of tobacco between them and his lower lip. This habit of holding tobacco in the mouth was common among the convicts. He seemed younger than his age. He was forty and looked no more than thirty. He always talked to me without a trace of constraint, and treated me exactly as his equal, that is, behaved with perfect good-breeding and delicacy. If he noticed, for instance, that I was anxious to be alone, he would leave me in two or three minutes after a few words of conversation, and he always thanked me for attending to him, a courtesy which he never showed, of course, to anyone else in prison. It is curious that such relations continued between us for several years and never became more intimate, though he really was attached to me. I cannot to this day make up my mind what he wanted of me, why he came to me every day. Though he did happen to steal from me later on, he stole, as it were, *by accident*; he scarcely ever asked me for money, so he did not come for the sake of money or with any interested motive.

I don't know why, but I always felt as though he were not living in prison with me, but somewhere far away in another house in the town, and that he only visited the prison in passing, to hear the news, to see me, to see how we were all getting on. He was always in a hurry, as though he had left someone waiting for him, or some job unfinished. And yet he did not seem flustered. The look in his eyes, too, was rather strange: intent, with a shade of boldness and mockery. Yet he looked, as it were, into the distance, as though beyond the things that met his eyes he were trying to make out something else, far away. This gave him an absent-minded look. I sometimes purposely watched where Petrov went when he left me. Where was someone waiting for him? But he would hurry away from me to a prison ward or a kitchen, would sit down there beside some convicts, listen attentively to their conversation and sometimes take part in it himself, even speaking with heat; then he would suddenly break off and relapse into silence. But whether he were talking or sitting silent, it always appeared that he did so for a moment in passing, that he had something else to do and was expected elsewhere. The strangest thing was that he never had anything to do: he led a life of absolute leisure (except for the regulation work, of course). He knew no sort of trade and he scarcely ever had any money. But he did not grieve much over the lack of it. And what did he talk to me about? His conversation was as strange as himself. He would see, for instance, that I was walking alone behind the prison and would turn abruptly in my direction. He always walked quickly and turned abruptly.

He walked up, yet it seemed he must have been running.

"Good morning."

"Good morning."

"I am not interrupting you?"

"No."

"I wanted to ask you about Napoleon. He is a relation of the one who was here in 1812, isn't he?"[7] (Petrov was a kantonist and could read and write.)

"Yes."

"He is some sort of president, they say, isn't he?"

He always asked rapid, abrupt questions, as though he were in a hurry to learn something. It seemed as though he were investigating some matter of great importance which would not admit of any delay.

I explained how he was a president and added that he might soon be an emperor.

"How is that?"

I explained that too, as far as I could. Petrov listened attentively, understanding perfectly and reflecting rapidly, even turning his ear towards me.

"H'm . . . I wanted to ask you, Alexandr Petrovitch: is it true, as they say, that there are monkeys with arms down to their heels and as big as a tall man?"

"Yes, there are."

"What are they like?"

That, too, I explained as far as I was able.

"And where do they live?"

"In hot countries. There are some in the island of Sumatra."

"That's in America, isn't it? Don't they say that the people in those parts walk on their heads?"

"Not on their heads. You mean the Antipodes."

I explained what America was like and what was meant by the Antipodes. He listened as attentively as though he had come simply to hear about the Antipodes.

"A-ah! Last year I read about the Countess La Vallière. Arefyev got the book from the adjutant's. Is it true or is it just invented? It's written by Dumas."[8]

"It's invented, of course."

"Well, good-bye. Thank you."

And Petrov vanished, and we rarely talked except in this style.

I began inquiring about him. M. positively warned me when he heard of the acquaintance. He told me that many of the convicts had inspired him with horror, especially at first, in his early days in prison; but not one of them, not even Gazin, had made such a terrible impression on him as this Petrov.

"He is the most determined, the most fearless of all the convicts," said M. "He is capable of anything; he would stick at nothing if the fancy took him. He would murder you if it happened to strike him; he would murder you in a minute without flinching or giving it a thought afterwards. I believe he is not quite in his right mind."

This view interested me very much. But M. could give me no reason for thinking so. And strange to say, I knew Petrov for several years afterwards and talked to him almost every day, he was genuinely attached to me all that time (though I am absolutely unable to say why) and all those years he behaved well in prison and did nothing horrible, yet every time I looked at him and talked to him I felt sure that M. was right, and that Petrov really was a most determined and fearless man who recognized no restraint of any sort. Why I felt this I can't explain either.

I may mention, however, that this Petrov was the convict who had intended on being led out to be flogged to murder the major, when the latter was saved only "by a miracle" as the convicts said, through driving away just before. It had happened once, before he came to prison, that he had been struck by the colonel at drill. Probably he had been struck many times before, but this time he could not put up with it and he stabbed his colonel openly, in broad daylight, in the face of the regiment. But I don't know all the details of this story; he never told it me. No doubt these were only outbursts when the man's character showed itself fully all at once. But they were very rare in him. He really was sensible and even peaceable. Passions were latent in him, and hot, violent passions, too; but the burning embers were always covered with a layer of ashes and smouldered quietly. I never saw the faintest trace of vanity or boastfulness in him, as in others. He rarely quarrelled; on the other hand he was not particularly friendly with anyone, except perhaps with Sirotkin, and then only when the latter was of use to him. Once, however, I saw him seriously angry. Something was not given him, something which was properly his share. A convict in the civilian division called Vassily Antonov was quarrelling with him. He was a tall, powerful athlete, spiteful, quarrelsome, malicious and very far from being a coward. They had been shouting at each other for a long time and I thought that the matter would at most end in a blow or two, for at times, though rarely, Petrov swore and fought like the meanest convict. But this time it was not so: Petrov suddenly blanched, his lips suddenly quivered and turned blue; he began breathing hard. He got up from his place and slowly, very slowly with his bare noiseless steps (in summer he was very fond of going barefoot) he approached Antonov. There was a sudden silence in the noisy shouting crowd; one could have heard a fly. Everyone waited to see what would happen. Antonov leapt up as he approached, looking aghast . . . I could not bear the sight of it and left the room. I expected to hear the shriek of a murdered man before I had time to get down the steps. But this time, too, it ended in nothing: before Petrov had time to reach him, Antonov hastily and in silence flung him the object about which they were disputing, which was some old rag they used to put round their legs. Of course, two or three minutes later, Antonov swore at him a little to satisfy his conscience and keep up appearances by showing that he was not quite cowed. But Petrov took no notice of his abuse, did not even answer it; it was not a question of abuse, the point had been won in his favour; he was very well pleased and took his rag. A quarter of an hour later, he was sauntering about the prison as usual with an air of complete unconcern, and seemed to be looking round to find people talking about something interesting, that he might poke his nose in and listen. Everything seemed to interest him, yet it somehow happened that he remained indifferent to most things and simply wandered aimlessly about the prison, drawn first one way and then another. One might have compared him with a workman, a stalwart workman who could send the work flying but was for a while without a job, and meantime sat playing with little children. I could not understand either why he remained in prison, why he did not run away. He would not have hesitated to run away if he had felt any strong inclination to do so. Men like Petrov are only ruled by reason till they have some strong desire. Then there is no obstacle on earth that can hinder them. And I am sure he would have escaped cleverly, that he would have outwitted everyone, that he could have stayed for a week without bread, somewhere in the forest or in the reeds of the river. But he evidently had not reached that point yet and did not fully desire it. I never noticed in him any great power of reflection or any marked common sense. These people are born with one fixed idea which unconsciously moves them hither and thither; so they shift from one thing to another all their lives, till they find a work after their own hearts. Then they are ready to risk anything. I wondered sometimes how it was that a man who had murdered his officer for a blow could lie down under a flogging with such resignation. He was sometimes flogged when he was caught smuggling in vodka. Like all convicts without a trade he sometimes undertook to bring in vodka. But he lay down to be flogged, as it were with his own consent, that is, as though acknowledging that he deserved it; except for that, nothing

would have induced him to lie down, he would have been killed first.
I wondered at him, too, when he stole from me in spite of his unmistakable devotion. This seemed to come upon him, as it were, in
streaks. It was he who stole my Bible when I asked him to carry
it from one place to another. He had only a few steps to go, but he
succeeded in finding a purchaser on the way, sold it, and spent the
proceeds on drink. Evidently he wanted very much to drink, and anything that he wanted very much he *had* to do. That is the sort of man
who will murder a man for sixpence to get a bottle of vodka, though
another time he would let a man pass with ten thousand pounds on
him. In the evening he told me of the theft himself without the
slightest embarrassment or regret, quite indifferently, as though it
were a most ordinary incident. I tried to give him a good scolding;
besides, I was sorry to lose my Bible. He listened without irritation,
very meekly, in fact; agreed that the Bible was a very useful book, sincerely regretted that I no longer possessed it, but expressed no regret
at having stolen it; he looked at me with such complacency that I at
once gave up scolding him. He accepted my scolding, probably reflecting that it was inevitable that one should be sworn at for such
doings, and better I should relieve my feelings and console myself by
swearing: but that it was all really nonsense, such nonsense that a serious person would be ashamed to talk about it. It seemed to me that
he looked upon me as a sort of child, almost a baby, who did not
understand the simplest things in the world. If I began, for instance,
on any subject not a learned or bookish one, he would answer
me, indeed, but apparently only from politeness, confining himself
to the briefest reply. I often wondered what the book knowledge
about which he usually questioned me meant to him. I sometimes
happened to look sideways at him during our conversations to see
whether he were laughing at me. But no; usually he was listening
seriously and even with some attention, though often so little that I
felt annoyed. He asked exact and definite questions, but showed no
great surprise at the information he got from me, and received it
indeed rather absent-mindedly. I fancied, too, that he had made up
his mind once for all, without bothering his head about it, that it
was no use talking to me as one would to other people, that apart
from talking of books I understood nothing and was incapable of
understanding anything, so there was no need to worry me.

I am sure that he had a real affection for me, and that struck me very much. Whether he considered me undeveloped, not fully a man, or felt for me that special sort of compassion that every strong creature instinctively feels for someone weaker, recognizing me as such— I don't know. And although all that did not prevent him from robbing me, I am sure he felt sorry for me as he did it. "Ech!" he may have thought as he laid hands on my property, "what a man, he can't even defend his own property!" But I fancy that was what he liked me for. He said to me himself one day, as it were casually, that I was "a man with too good a heart" and "so simple, so simple, that it makes one feel sorry for you. Only don't take it amiss, Alexandr Petrovitch," he added a minute later, "I spoke without thinking, from my heart."

It sometimes happens that such people come conspicuously to the front and take a prominent position at the moment of some violent mass movement or revolution, and in that way achieve all at once their full possibilities. They are not men of words and cannot be the instigators or the chief leaders of a movement; but they are its most vigorous agents and the first to act. They begin simply, with no special flourish, but they are the first to surmount the worst obstacles, facing every danger without reflection, without fear—and all rush after, blindly following them to the last wall, where they often lay down their lives. I do not believe that Petrov has come to a good end; he would make short work of everything all at once, and, if he has not perished yet, it is simply that the moment has not come. Who knows, though? Maybe he will live till his hair is grey and will die peaceably of old age, wandering aimlessly to and fro. But I believe M. was right when he said that Petrov was the most determined man in all the prison.

CHAPTER VIII

DETERMINED CHARACTERS. LUTCHKA

IT IS DIFFICULT TO talk about "determined" characters; in prison as everywhere else they are few in number. A man may look terrible; if one considers what is said of him one keeps out of his way. An instinctive feeling made me shun such people at first. Afterwards I changed my views in many respects, even about the most terrible murderers. Some who had never murdered anyone were more terrible than others who had been convicted of six murders. There was an element of something so strange in some crimes that one could not form even a rudimentary conception of them. I say this because among the peasantry murders are sometimes committed for most astounding reasons. The following type of murderer, for instance, is to be met with, and not uncommonly indeed. He lives quietly and peaceably and puts up with a hard life. He may be a peasant, a house-serf, a soldier or a workman. Suddenly something in him seems to snap; his patience gives way and he sticks a knife into his enemy and oppressor. Then the strangeness begins: the man gets out of all bounds for a time. The first man he murdered was his oppressor, his enemy; that is criminal but comprehensible; in that case there was a motive. But later on he murders not enemies but anyone he comes upon, murders for amusement, for an insulting word, for a look, to make a round number or simply "out of my way, don't cross my path, I am coming!" The man is, as it were, drunk, in delirium. It is as though, having once overstepped the sacred limit, he begins to revel in the fact that nothing is sacred to him; as though he had an itching to defy all law and authority at once, and to enjoy the most unbridled and unbounded liberty, to enjoy the thrill of horror which he cannot help feeling at himself. He knows, too, that a terrible punishment is awaiting him. All this perhaps is akin to the sensation with which a man gazes down from a high tower into the depths below his feet till at last it would be a relief to throw himself headlong—anything to put

110

an end to it quickly. And this happens even to the most peaceable and till then inconspicuous people. Some of these people positively play a part to themselves in this delirium. The more down-trodden such a man has been before, the more he itches now to cut a dash, to strike terror into people. He enjoys their terror and likes even the repulsion he arouses in others. He assumes a sort of *desperateness*, and a desperate character sometimes looks forward to speedy punishment, looks forward to being *settled*, because he finds it burdensome at last to keep up his assumed recklessness. It is curious that in most cases all this state of mind, this whole pose persists up to the moment of the scaffold, and then it is cut short once for all; as though its duration were prescribed and defined beforehand. At the end of it, the man suddenly gives in, retires into the background and becomes as limp as a rag. He whimpers on the scaffold and begs forgiveness of the crowd. He comes to prison and he is such a drivelling, snivelling fellow that one wonders whether he can be the man who has murdered five or six people.

Some, of course, are not soon subdued even in prison. They still preserve a certain bravado, a certain boastfulness which seems to say "I am not what you take me for; I am in for six souls!" But yet he, too, ends by being subdued. Only at times he amuses himself by recalling his reckless exploits, the festive time he once had when he was a "desperate character," and if he can only find a simple-hearted listener there is nothing he loves better than to give himself airs and boast with befitting dignity, describing his feats, though he is careful not to betray the pleasure this gives him. "See the sort of man I was," he seems to say.

And with what subtlety this pose is maintained, how lazily casual the story sometimes is! What studied nonchalance is apparent in the tone, in every word! Where do such people pick it up?

Once in those early days I spent a long evening lying idle and depressed on the plank bed and listened to such a story, and in my inexperience took the storyteller to be a colossal, hideous criminal of an incredible strength of will, while I was inclined to take Petrov lightly. The subject of the narrative was how the speaker, Luka Kuzmitch, for no motive but his own amusement had laid out a major. This Luka Kuzmitch was the little, thin, sharp-nosed young convict in our room, a Little Russian by birth, whom I have mentioned already. He was really

a Great Russian, but had been born in the south; I believe he was a
house-serf. There was really something pert and aggressive about him,
"though the bird is small its claw is sharp." But convicts instinctively
see through a man. They had very little respect for him, or as the convicts say, "little respect to him." He was fearfully vain. He was sitting
that evening on the platform bed, sewing a shirt. Sewing undergarments was his trade. Beside him was sitting a convict called Kobylin, a
tall, stalwart lad, stupid and dull-witted but good-natured and friendly,
who slept next to him on the bed. As they were neighbours, Lutchka
frequently quarrelled with him and generally treated him superciliously, ironically and despotically, of which Kobylin in his simplicity
was not fully conscious. He was knitting a woollen stocking listening
indifferently to Lutchka. The latter was telling his story rather loudly
and distinctly. He wanted everyone to hear, though he tried to pretend
that he was telling no one but Kobylin.

"Well, brother, they sent me from our parts," he began, sticking in
his needle, "to Tch—v for being a tramp."

"When was that, long ago?" asked Kobylin.

"It will be a year ago when the peas come in. Well, when we came
to K. they put me in prison there for a little time. In prison with me
there were a dozen fellows, all Little Russians, tall, healthy, and as
strong as bulls. But they were such quiet chaps; the food was bad; the
major did as he liked with them. I hadn't been there two days before
I saw they were a cowardly lot. 'Why do you knuckle under to a fool
like that?' says I.

"'You go and talk to him yourself!' they said, and they fairly
laughed at me. I didn't say anything. One of those Little Russians was
particularly funny, lads," he added suddenly, abandoning Kobylin and
addressing the company generally. "He used to tell us how he was
tried and what he said in court, and kept crying as he told us; he had
a wife and children left behind, he told us. And he was a big, stout,
grey-headed old fellow. 'I says to him: nay!' he told us. And he, the devil's son, kept on writing and writing. 'Well,' says I to myself, 'may you
choke. I'd be pleased to see it.' And he kept on writing and writing and
at last he'd written something and it was my ruin! Give me some
thread, Vassya, the damned stuff is rotten."

"It's from the market," said Vassya, giving him some thread.

"Ours in the tailoring shop is better. The other day we sent our veteran for some and I don't know what wretched woman he buys it from," Lutchka went on, threading his needle by the light.

"A crony of his no doubt."

"No doubt."

"Well, but what about the major?" asked Kobylin, who had been quite forgotten.

This was all Lutchka wanted. But he did not go on with his story at once; apparently he did not deign to notice Kobylin. He calmly pulled out his thread, calmly and lazily drew up his legs under him and at last began to speak.

"I worked up my Little Russians at last and they asked for the major. And I borrowed a knife from my neighbour that morning; I took it and hid it to be ready for anything. The major flew into a rage and he drove up. 'Come,' said I, 'don't funk it, you chaps.' But their hearts failed them, they were all of a tremble! The major ran in, drunk. 'Who is here? What's here? I am Tsar, I am God, too.' As he said that I stepped forward," Lutchka proceeded, "my knife in my sleeve.

" 'No,' said I, 'your honour,' and little by little I got closer. 'No, how can it be, your honour,' said I, 'that you are our Tsar and God too?'

" 'Ah, that's you, that's you,' shouted the major. 'You mutinous fellow!'

" 'No,' I said, and I got closer and closer. 'No,' I said, 'your honour, as may be well known to yourself, our God the Almighty and All Present is the only One. And there is only one Tsar set over us by God himself. He, your honour, is called a monarch,' says I. 'And you,' says I, 'your honour, are only a major, our commander by the grace of the Tsar and your merits,' says I. 'What, what, what, what!' he fairly cackled; he choked and couldn't speak. He was awfully astonished. 'Why, this,' says I, and I just pounced on him and plunged the whole knife into his stomach. It did the trick. He rolled over and did not move except for his legs kicking. I threw down the knife. 'Look, you fellows, pick him up now!' says I."

Here I must make a digression. Unhappily such phrases as "I am your Tsar, I am your God, too," and many similar expressions were not uncommonly used in old days by many commanding officers. It must be admitted, however, that there are not many such officers left; perhaps they are extinct altogether. I may note that the officers who liked to use and prided themselves on using such expressions were mostly those who had risen from the lower ranks. Their promotion turns everything topsy-turvy in them, including their brains. After groaning under the yoke for years and passing through every subordinate grade, they suddenly see themselves officers, gentlemen in command, and in the first intoxication of their position their inexperience leads them to an exaggerated idea of their power and importance; only in relation to their subordinates, of course. To their superior officers they show the same servility as ever, though it is utterly unnecessary and even revolting to many people. Some of these servile fellows hasten with peculiar zest to declare to their superior officers that they come from the lower ranks, though they are officers, and that "they never forget their place." But with the common soldiers they are absolutely autocratic. Now, of course, there are scarcely any of these men left, and I doubt if anyone could be found to shout, "I am your Tsar, I am your God." But in spite of that, I may remark that nothing irritates convicts, and indeed all people of the poorer class, so much as such utterances on the part of their officers. This insolence of self-glorification, this exaggerated idea of being able to do anything with impunity, inspires hatred in the most submissive of men and drives them out of all patience. Fortunately this sort of behaviour, now almost a thing of the past, was always severely repressed by the authorities even in old days. I know several instances of it.

And, indeed, people in a humble position generally are irritated by any supercilious carelessness, any sign of contempt shown them. Some people think that if convicts are well fed and well kept and all the requirements of the law are satisfied, that is all that is necessary. This is an error, too. Everyone, whoever he may be and however down-trodden he may be, demands—though perhaps instinctively, perhaps unconsciously—respect for his dignity as a human being. The convict knows himself that he is a convict, an outcast, and knows his place before his commanding officer; but by no branding, by no fetters will you make him forget that he is a human being. And as he really is a human being he ought to be treated humanely. My God, yes! Humane treatment may humanize even one in whom the image of God has long been obscured. These "unfortunates" need even more humane treatment than others. It is their salvation and their joy. I have met some good-hearted, high-minded officers. I have seen the influence they exerted on these degraded creatures. A few kind words from them meant almost a moral resurrection for the convicts. They were as pleased as children and as children began to love them. I must mention another strange thing: the convicts themselves do not like to be treated too familiarly and *too* softly by their officers. They want to respect those in authority over them, and too much softness makes them cease to respect them. The convicts like their commanding officer to have decorations, too, they like him to be presentable, they like him to be in favour with some higher authority, they like him to be strict and important and just, and they like him to keep up his dignity. The convicts prefer such an officer: they feel that he keeps up his own dignity and does not insult them, and so they feel everything is right and as it should be.

     *   *   *   *   *   *

"You must have caught it hot for that?" Kobylin observed calmly.

"H'm! Hot, my boy, yes—it was hot certainly. Aley, pass the scissors! Why is it they are not playing cards to-day, lads?"

"They've drunk up all their money," observed Vassya. "If they hadn't they'd have been playing."

"If! They'll give you a hundred roubles for an 'if' in Moscow," observed Lutchka.

"And how much did you get altogether, Lutchka?" Kobylin began again.

"They gave me a hundred and five, my dear chap. And, you know, they almost killed me, mates," Lutchka declared, abandoning Kobylin again. "They drove me out in full dress to be flogged. Till then I'd never tasted the lash. There were immense crowds, the whole town ran out: a robber was to be flogged, a murderer, to be sure. You can't think what fools the people are, there's no telling you. The hangman stripped me, made me lie down and shouted, 'Look out, I'll sting you.' I wondered what was coming. At the first lash I wanted to shout, I opened my mouth but there was no shout in me. My voice failed me. When the second lash came, you may not believe it, I did not hear them count *two*. And when I came to I heard them call 'seventeen.' Four times, lad, they took me off the donkey, and gave me half an hour's rest and poured water over me. I looked at them all with my eyes starting out of my head and thought 'I shall die on the spot. . . .'"

"And you didn't die?" Kobylin asked naïvely.

Lutchka scanned him with a glance of immense contempt; there was a sound of laughter.

"He is a regular block!"

"He is not quite right in the top storey," observed Lutchka, as though regretting he had deigned to converse with such a man.

"He is a natural," Vassya summed up conclusively.

Though Lutchka had murdered six people no one was ever afraid of him in the prison, yet perhaps it was his cherished desire to be considered a terrible man.

CHAPTER IX

ISAY FOMITCH—THE BATH-HOUSE— BAKLUSHIN'S STORY

CHRISTMAS WAS APPROACHING. THE convicts looked forward to it with a sort of solemnity, and looking at them, I too began to expect something unusual. Four days before Christmas Day they took us to the bath-house. In my time, especially in the early years, the convicts were rarely taken to the bath-house. All were pleased and began to get ready. It was arranged to go after dinner, and that afternoon there was no work. The one who was most pleased and excited in our room was Isay Fomitch Bumshtein, a Jewish convict whom I have mentioned in the fourth chapter of my story. He liked to steam himself into a state of stupefaction, of unconsciousness; and whenever going over old memories I recall our prison baths (which deserve to be remembered), the blissful countenance of that prison comrade, whom I shall never forget, takes a foremost place in the picture. Heavens, how killingly funny he was! I have already said something about his appearance: he was a thin, feeble, puny man of fifty, with a wrinkled white body like a chicken's and on his cheeks and forehead awful scars left from being branded. His face wore a continual expression of imperturbable self-complacency and even blissfulness. Apparently he felt no regret at being in prison. As he was a jeweller and there were no jewellers in the town, he worked continually at nothing but his own trade for the gentry and officials of the town. He received some payment for his work. He wanted for nothing, was even rich, but he saved money and used to lend it out at interest to all the convicts. He had a samovar of his own, a good mattress, cups, and a whole dining outfit. The Jews in the town did not refuse him their acquaintance and patronage. On Saturdays he used to go with an escort to the synagogue in the town (which is sanctioned by law). He was in clover, in fact. At the same time he was impatiently awaiting the end of his twelve years' sentence "to get married." He was a most comical mixture of naïveté, stupidity, craft, impudence, good-nature, timidity,

117

boastfulness and insolence. It surprised me that the convicts never
jeered at him, though they sometimes made a joke at his expense.
Isay Fomitch was evidently a continual source of entertainment and
amusement to all. "He is our only one, don't hurt Isay Fomitch," was
what they felt, and although Isay Fomitch saw his position he was obviously proud of being so important and that greatly amused the convicts. His arrival in the prison was fearfully funny (it happened before
my time, but I was told of it). One day, in the leisure hour towards
evening, a rumour suddenly spread through the prison that a Jew had
been brought, and was being shaved in the guard-room and that he
would come in directly. There was not a single Jew in the prison at the
time. The convicts waited with impatience and surrounded him at
once when he came in at the gate. The sergeant led him to the civilian
room and showed him his place on the common bed. Isay Fomitch
carried in his arms a sack containing his own belongings, together
with the regulation articles which had been given to him. He laid
down the sack, climbed on to the bed and sat down, tucking his feet
under him, not daring to raise his eyes. There were sounds of laughter and prison jokes alluding to his Jewish origin. Suddenly a young
convict made his way through the crowd carrying in his hand his
very old, dirty, tattered summer trousers, together with the regulation leg-wrappers. He sat down beside Isay Fomitch and slapped him
on the shoulder.

"I say, my dear friend, I've been looking out for you these last six
years. Look here, how much will you give?"

And he spread the rags out before him.

Isay Fomitch, who had been too timid to utter a word and so cowed
at his first entrance that he had not dared to raise his eyes in the crowd
of mocking, disfigured and terrible faces which hemmed him in, was
cheered at once at the sight of the proffered pledge, and began briskly
turning over the rags. He even held them up to the light. Everyone
waited to hear what he would say.

"Well, you won't give me a silver rouble, I suppose? It's worth it,
you know," said the would-be borrower, winking at Isay Fomitch.

"A silver rouble, no, but seven kopecks maybe."

And those were the first words uttered by Isay Fomitch in prison.
Everyone roared with laughter.

"Seven! Well, give me seven, then; it's a bit of luck for you. Mind you take care of the pledge; it's as much as your life's worth if you lose it."

"With three kopecks interest makes ten," the Jew went on jerkily in a shaking voice, putting his hand in his pocket for the money and looking timidly at the convicts. He was fearfully scared, and at the same time he wanted to do business.

"Three kopecks a year interest, I suppose?"

"No, not a year, a month."

"You are a tight customer, Jew! What's your name?"

"Isay Fomitch."

"Well, Isay Fomitch, you'll get on finely here! Good-bye." Isay Fomitch examined the pledge once more, folded it up carefully and put it in his sack in the midst of the still laughing convicts.

Everyone really seemed to like him and no one was rude to him, though almost all owed him money. He was himself as free from malice as a hen, and, seeing the general goodwill with which he was regarded, he even swaggered a little, but with such simple-hearted absurdity that he was forgiven at once. Lutchka, who had known many Jews in his day, often teased him and not out of ill-feeling, but simply for diversion, just as one teases dogs, parrots, or any sort of trained animal. Isay Fomitch saw that clearly, was not in the least offended and answered him back adroitly.

"Hey, Jew, I'll give you a dressing!"

"You give me one blow and I'll give you ten," Isay Fomitch would respond gallantly.

"You damned scab!"

"I don't care if I am."

"You itching Jew!"

"I don't care if I am. I may itch, but I am rich; I've money."

"You sold Christ."

"I don't care if I did."

"That's right, Isay Fomitch, bravo! Don't touch him, he's the only one we've got," the convicts would shout, laughing.

"Aie, Jew, you'll get the whip, you'll be sent to Siberia."

"Why, I am in Siberia now."

"Well, you'll go further."

"And is the Lord God there, too?"

"Well, I suppose he is."

"Well, I don't mind, then. If the Lord God is there and there's money, I shall be all right everywhere."

"Bravo, Isay Fomitch, you are a fine chap, no mistake!" the convicts shouted round him, and though Isay Fomitch saw they were laughing at him, he was not cast down.

The general approval afforded him unmistakable pleasure and he began carolling a shrill little chant "la-la-la-la-la" all over the prison, an absurd and ridiculous tune without words, the only tune he hummed all the years he was in prison. Afterwards, when he got to know me better, he protested on oath to me that that was the very song and the very tune that the six hundred thousand Jews, big and little, had sung as they crossed the Red Sea, and that it is ordained for every Jew to sing that song at the moment of triumph and victory over his enemies.

Every Friday evening convicts came to our ward from other parts of the prison on purpose to see Isay Fomitch celebrate his Sabbath. Isay Fomitch was so naïvely vain and boastful that this general interest gave him pleasure, too. With pedantic and studied gravity he covered his little table in the corner, opened his book, lighted two candles and muttering some mysterious words began putting on his vestment. It was a parti-coloured shawl of woollen material which he kept carefully in his box. He tied phylacteries on both hands and tied some sort of wooden ark by means of a bandage on his head, right over his forehead, so that it looked like a ridiculous horn sprouting out of his forehead. Then the prayer began. He repeated it in a chant, uttered cries, spat on the floor, and turned round, making wild and absurd gesticulations. All this, of course, was part of the ceremony and there was nothing absurd or strange about it, but what was absurd was that Isay Fomitch seemed purposely to be playing a part before us, and made a show of his ritual. Suddenly he would hide his head in his hands and recite with sobs. The sobs grew louder and in a state of exhaustion and almost howling he would let his head crowned with the ark drop on the book; but suddenly, in the middle of the most violent sobbing he would begin to laugh and chant in a voice broken with feeling and solemnity, and weak with bliss. "Isn't he going it!" the convicts commented. I once asked Isay Fomitch what was the meaning of the sobs and then the sudden solemn transition to happiness and bliss. Isay Fomitch particularly liked such questions from me. He at once explained to me that the weeping and sobbing were aroused at the thought of the loss of Jerusalem, and that the ritual prescribed sobbing as violently as possible and beating the breast at the thought. But at the moment of the loudest sobbing, he, Isay Fomitch, was *suddenly*, as it were accidentally (the suddenness was also prescribed by the ritual), to remember that there is a prophecy of the return of the Jews to Jerusalem. Then he must at once burst into joy, song, and laughter, and must repeat his prayers in such a way that his voice itself should express as much happiness as possible and his face should express all the solemnity and dignity of which it was capable. This sudden transition and the obligation to make it were a source of extreme pleasure to Isay Fomitch: he saw in it a very subtle *künst-stück*, and boastfully told me of this difficult rule. Once when the prayer was in full swing the major came into the ward accompanied by the officer on duty and the sentries. All the convicts drew themselves up by the bed; Isay Fomitch alone began shouting and carrying on more than ever. He knew that the prayer was not prohibited, it was impossible to interrupt it, and, of course, there was no risk in his shouting before the major. But he particularly enjoyed making a display before the major and showing off before us. The major went up within a step of him. Isay Fomitch turned with his back to his table and waving his hands began chanting his solemn prophecy right in the major's face. As it was prescribed for him to express extreme happiness and dignity in his face at that moment, he did so immediately, screwing up his eyes in a peculiar way, laughing and nodding his head at the major. The major was surprised but finally went off into a guffaw, called him a fool to his face and walked away; and Isay Fomitch vociferated louder than ever. An hour later, when he was having supper, I asked him, "And what if the major in his foolishness had flown into a rage?"

"What major?"

"What major! Why, didn't you see him?"

"No."

"Why, he stood not a yard away from you, just facing you."

But Isay Fomitch began earnestly assuring me that he had not seen the major and that at the time, during the prayer, he was usually in such a state of ecstasy that he saw nothing and heard nothing of what was going on around him.

I can see Isay Fomitch before me now as he used to wander about the prison on Saturdays with nothing to do, making tremendous efforts to do nothing at all, as prescribed by the law of the Sabbath. What incredible anecdotes he used to tell me every time he came back from the synagogue! What prodigious news and rumours from Petersburg he used to bring me, assuring me that he had got them from his fellow Jews, and that they had them first-hand.

But I have said too much of Isay Fomitch.

There were only two public baths in the town. One of these, which was kept by a Jew, consisted of separate bathrooms, for each of which a fee of fifty kopecks was charged. It was an establishment for people of the higher class. The other bath-house was intended for the working class; it was dilapidated, dirty and small, and it was to this house that we convicts were taken. It was frosty and sunny, and the convicts were delighted at the very fact of getting out of the fortress grounds and looking at the town. The jokes and laughter never flagged all the way. A whole platoon of soldiers with loaded rifles accompanied us, to the admiration of the whole town. In the bath-house we were immediately divided into two relays: the second relay had to wait in the cold ante-room while the first were washing themselves. This division was necessary, because the bath-house was so small. But the space was so limited that it was difficult to imagine how even half of our number could find room. Yet Petrov did not desert me; he skipped up of his own accord to help, and even offered to wash me. Another convict who offered me his services was Baklushin, a prisoner in the "special division" who was nicknamed "the pioneer," and to whom I have referred already as one of the liveliest and most charming of the convicts, as indeed he was. I was already slightly acquainted with him. Petrov even helped me to undress, for, not being used to it, I was slow undressing, and it was cold in the ante-room, almost as cold as in the open air.

It is, by the way, very difficult for a convict to undress till he has quite mastered the art. To begin with, one has to learn how to unlace quickly the bands under the ankle irons. These bands are made of leather, are eight inches in length and are put on over the undergarment, just under the ring that goes round the ankle. A pair of these bands costs no less than sixty kopecks and yet every convict procures them, at his own expense, of course, for it is impossible to walk without them. The ring does not fit tightly on the leg, one can put one's finger in between, so that the iron strikes against the flesh and rubs it, and without the leather a convict would rub his leg into a sore in a day. But to get off the bands is not difficult. It is more difficult to learn how to get off one's underlinen from under the fetters. It is quite a special art. Drawing off the undergarments from the left leg, for instance, one has first to pull it down between the ring and the leg, then freeing one's foot one has to draw the linen up again between the leg and the ring; then the whole of the left leg of the garment has to be slipped through the ring on the right ankle, and pulled back again. One has to go through the same business when one puts on clean linen. It is hard for a novice even to guess how it can be done; I was first taught how to do it at Tobolsk by a convict called Korenev, who had been the chief of a band of robbers and had been for five years chained to the wall. But the convicts get used to it, and go through the operation without the slightest difficulty.

I gave Petrov a few kopecks to get me soap and a handful of tow; soap was, indeed, served out to the convicts, a piece each, the size of a halfpenny and as thick as the slices of cheese served at the beginning of supper among middle-class people. Soap was sold in the ante-room as well as hot spiced mead, rolls and hot water. By contract with the keeper of the bath-house, each convict was allowed only one bucketful of hot water; everyone who wanted to wash himself cleaner could get for a half-penny another bucketful, which was passed from the ante-room into the bathroom through a little window made on purpose. When he had undressed me, Petrov took me by the arm, noticing that it was very difficult for me to walk in fetters.

"You must pull them higher, on to your calves," he kept repeating, supporting me as though he were my nurse, "and now be careful, here's a step."

I felt a little ashamed, indeed; I wanted to assure Petrov that I could walk alone, but he would not have believed it. He treated me exactly like a child not able to manage alone, whom everyone ought to help. Petrov was far from being a servant, he was pre-eminently not a servant; if I had offended him, he would have known how to deal with me. I had not promised him payment for his services, and he did not ask for it himself. What induced him, then, to look after me in this way?

When we opened the door into the bathroom itself, I thought we were entering hell. Imagine a room twelve paces long and the same in breadth, in which perhaps as many as a hundred and certainly as many as eighty were packed at once, for the whole party were divided into only two relays, and we were close on two hundred; steam blinding one's eyes; filth and grime; such a crowd that there was not room to put one's foot down. I was frightened and tried to step back, but Petrov at once encouraged me. With extreme difficulty we somehow forced our way to the benches round the wall, stepping over the heads of those who were sitting on the floor, asking them to duck to let us get by. But every place on the benches was taken. Petrov informed me that one had to buy a place and at once entered into negotiations with a convict sitting near the window. For a kopeck the latter gave up his place, receiving the money at once from Petrov, who had the coin ready in his fist, having providently brought it with him into the bathroom. The convict I had ousted at once ducked under the bench just under my place, where it was dark and filthy, and the dirty slime lay two inches thick. But even the space under the benches was all filled; there, too, the place was alive with human beings. There was not a spot on the floor as big as the palm of your hand where there was not a convict squatting, splashing from his bucket. Others stood up among them and holding their buckets in their hands washed themselves standing; the dirty water trickled off them on to the shaven heads of the convicts sitting below them. On the top shelf and on all the steps leading up to it men were crouched, huddled together washing themselves. But they did not wash themselves much. Men of the peasant class don't wash much with soap and hot water; they only steam themselves terribly and then douche themselves with cold water—that is their whole idea of a bath. Fifty birches were rising and falling rhythmically on the shelves; they all thrashed themselves into a state of stupefaction. More steam was raised every moment. It was not heat; it was hell. All were shouting and vociferating to the accompaniment of a hundred chains clanking on the floor . . . Some of them, wanting to pass, got entangled in other men's chains and caught in their owns chains the heads of those below them; they fell down, swore, and dragged those they caught after them. Liquid filth ran in all directions. Everyone seemed in a sort of intoxicated, over-excited condition; there were shrieks and cries. By the window of the ante-room from which the water was handed out there was swearing, crowding, and a regular scuffle.

The fresh hot water was spilt over the heads of those who were sitting on the floor before it reached its destination. Now and then the moustached face of a soldier with a gun in his hand peeped in at the window or the half-open door to see whether there were anything wrong. The shaven heads and crimson steaming bodies of the convicts seemed more hideous than ever. As a rule the steaming backs of the convicts show distinctly the scars of the blows or lashes they have received in the past, so that all those backs looked now as though freshly wounded. The scars were horrible! A shiver ran down me at the sight of them. They pour more boiling water on the hot bricks and clouds of thick, hot steam fill the whole bath-house; they all laugh and shout. Through the cloud of steam one gets glimpses of scarred backs, shaven heads, bent arms and legs; and to complete the picture Isay Fomitch is shouting with laughter on the very top shelf. He is steaming himself into a state of unconsciousness, but no degree of heat seems to satisfy him; for a kopeck he has hired a man to beat him, but the latter is exhausted at last, flings down his birch and runs off to douche himself with cold water. Isay Fomitch is not discouraged and hires another and a third; he is resolved on such an occasion to disregard expense and hires even a fifth man to wield the birch. "He knows how to steam himself, bravo, Isay Fomitch!" the convicts shout to him from below. Isay Fomitch, for his part, feels that at the moment he is superior to everyone and has outdone them all; he is triumphant, and in a shrill crazy voice screams out his tune "la-la-la-la-la," which rises above all the other voices. It occurred to me that if one day we should all be in hell together it would be very much like this place. I could not help expressing this thought to Petrov; he merely looked round and said nothing.

I wanted to buy him, too, a place beside me, but he sat down at my feet and declared that he was very comfortable. Meantime Baklushin was buying us water and brought it as we wanted it. Petrov declared that he would wash me from head to foot, "so that you will be all nice and clean," and he urged me to be steamed. This I did not venture on. Petrov soaped me all over. "And now I'll wash your little feet," he added in conclusion. I wanted to reply that I could wash them myself, but I did not contradict him and gave myself into his hands completely. There was not the faintest note of servility about the expression "little feet"; it was simply that Petrov could not call my feet simply feet, probably because other real people had feet, while mine were "little feet."

After having washed me he led me back to the ante-room with the same ceremonies, that is, giving me the same support and warnings at every step, as though I were made of china. Then he helped me to put on my linen, and only when he had quite finished with me he rushed back to the bathroom to steam himself.

When we got home I offered him a glass of tea. Tea he did not refuse; he emptied the glass and thanked me. I thought I would be lavish and treat him to a glass of vodka. This was forthcoming in our ward. Petrov was extremely pleased; he drank it, cleared his throat and observing that I had quite revived him, hurried off to the kitchen as though there were something there that could not be settled without him. His place was taken by another visitor, Baklushin "the pioneer," whom I had invited to have tea with me before we left the bath-house.

I don't know a more charming character than Baklushin's. It was true that he would not knuckle under to anyone; indeed, he often quarrelled, he did not like people to meddle with his affairs—in short, he knew how to take his own part. But he never quarrelled for long, and I believe we all liked him. Wherever he went everyone met him with pleasure. He was known even in the town as the most amusing fellow in the world who was always in high spirits. He was a tall fellow of thirty with a good-natured and spirited countenance, rather good-looking, though he had a wart on his face. He could contort his features in a killing way, mimicking anyone he came across, so that no one near him could help laughing. He, too, belonged to the class of comic men, but he would not be set upon by those who despised and detested laughter, so they never abused him for being a "foolish and useless" person. He was full of fire and life. He made my acquaintance during my first days and told me that he was a kantonist and had afterwards served in the pioneers, and had even been noticed and favoured by some great personages, a fact which he still remembered with great pride. He began at once questioning me about Petersburg. He even used to read. When he came to have tea with me he at once entertained the whole ward by describing what a dressing down Lieutenant S. had given the major that morning, and sitting down beside me, he told me with a look of pleasure, that the theatricals would probably come off. They were getting up theatricals in the prison for Christmas. Actors had been discovered, and scenery was being got ready by degrees. Some people in the town had promised to lend dresses for the actors, even for the female characters; they positively hoped by the assistance of an orderly to obtain an officer's uniform with epaulettes. If only the major did not take it into his head to forbid it, as he did last year. But last Christmas he had been in a bad temper: he had lost at cards somewhere, and, besides, there had been mischief in the prison, so he had forbidden it out of spite; but now perhaps he would not want to hinder it. In short, Baklushin was excited. It was evident that he was one of the most active in getting up the performance, and I inwardly resolved on the spot that I would certainly be present. Baklushin's simple-hearted delight that everything was going well with the theatricals pleased me. Little by little, we got into talk. Among other things he told me that he had not always served in Petersburg; that he had been guilty of some misdemeanour there and had been transferred to R., though as a sergeant in a garrison regiment.

"It was from there I was sent here," observed Baklushin.

"But what for?" I asked.

"What for? What do you think it was for, Alexandr Petrovitch? Because I fell in love."

"Oh, well, they don't send people here for that yet," I retorted laughing.

"It is true," Baklushin added, "it's true that through that I shot a German there with my pistol. But was the German worth sending me here for, tell me that!"

"But how was it? Tell me, it's interesting."

"It's a very funny story, Alexandr Petrovitch."

"So much the better. Tell me."

"Shall I? Well, listen, then."

I heard a strange, though not altogether amusing, story of a murder.

"This is how it was," Baklushin began. "When I was sent to R. I saw it was a fine big town, only there were a lot of Germans in it. Well, of course, I was a young man then; I stood well with the officers; I used to pass the time walking about with my cap on one side, winking at the German girls. And one little German girl, Luise, took my fancy. They were both laundresses, only doing the finest work, she and her aunt.

Her aunt was a stuck-up old thing and they were well off. I used to walk up and down outside their windows at first, and then I got to be real friends with her. Luise spoke Russian well, too, she only lisped a little, as it were—she was such a darling, I never met one like her . . . I was for being too free at first, but she said to me, 'No, you mustn't, Sasha, for I want to keep all my innocence to make you a good wife,' and she'd only caress me and laugh like a bell . . . and she was such a clean little thing, I never saw anyone like her. She suggested our getting married herself. Now, could I help marrying her, tell me that? So I made up my mind to go to the lieutenant-colonel for permission. . . . One day I noticed Luise did not turn up at our meeting-place, and again a second time she didn't come, and again a third. I sent a letter; no answer. What is it? I wondered. If she had been deceiving me she would have contrived somehow, have answered the letter, and have come to meet me. But she did not know how to tell a lie, so she simply cut it off. It's her aunt, I thought. I didn't dare go to the aunt's; though she knew it, we always met on the quiet. I went about as though I were crazy; I wrote her a last letter and said, 'If you don't come I shall come to your aunt's myself.' She was frightened and came. She cried; she told me that a German called Schultz, a distant relation, a watch-maker, well-off and elderly, had expressed a desire to marry her—'to make me happy,' he says, and not to be left without a wife in his old age; and he loves me, he says, and he's had the idea in his mind for a long time, but he kept putting it off and saying nothing. 'You see, Sasha,' she said, 'he's rich and it's a fortunate thing for me; surely you don't want to deprive me of my good fortune?' I looked at her—she was crying and hugging me. . . . 'Ech,' I thought, 'she is talking sense! What's the use of marrying a soldier, even though I am a sergeant?' 'Well, Luise,' said I, 'good-bye, God be with you. I've no business to hinder your happiness. Tell me, is he good-looking?' 'No,' she said, 'he is an old man, with a long nose,' and she laughed herself. I left her. 'Well,' I thought, 'it was not fated to be!' The next morning I walked by his shop; she had told me the street. I looked in at the window: there was a German sitting there mending a watch, a man of forty-five with a hooked nose and goggle eyes, wearing a tail-coat and a high stand-up collar, such a solemn-looking fellow. I fairly cursed; I should like to have broken his window on the spot . . . but there, I thought, it's no good touching him, it's no good crying over spilt milk! I went home to the barracks at dusk, lay down on my bed and would you believe it, Alexandr Petro-vitch, I burst out crying. . . .

"Well, that day passed, and another and a third. I did not see Luise. And meantime I heard from a friend (she was an old lady, another laundress whom Luise sometimes went to see) that the German knew of our love, and that was why he made up his mind to propose at once, or else he would have waited another two or three years. He had made Luise promise, it seemed, that she would not see me again; and that so far he was, it seems, rather churlish with both of them, Luise and her aunt; as though he might change his mind and had not quite decided even now. She told me, too, that the day after tomor-row, Sunday, he had invited them both to have coffee with him in the morning and that there would be another relation there, an old man who had been a merchant but was very poor now and served as a caretaker in a basement. When I knew that maybe on Sunday every-thing would be settled, I was seized with such fury that I did not know what I was doing. And all that day and all the next I could do nothing but think of it. I felt I could eat that German.

"On Sunday morning I did not know what I would do, but when the mass was over I jumped up, put on my overcoat and set off to the German's. I thought I would find them all there. And why I went to the German's, and what I meant to say, I did not know myself. But I put a pistol in my pocket to be ready for anything. I had a wretched little pis-tol with an old-fashioned trigger; I used to fire it as a boy. It wasn't fit to be used. But I put a bullet in it: I thought 'if they try turning me out and being rude I'll pull out the pistol and frighten them all.' I got there, there was no one in the shop, they were all sitting in the backroom. And not a soul but themselves, no servant. He had only one, a German cook. I walked through the shop and saw the door was shut, but it was an old door, fastening with a hook. My heart beat; I stood still and lis-tened: they were talking German. I kicked the door with all my might and it opened. I saw the table was laid. On the table there was a big coffee-pot and the coffee was boiling on a spirit lamp. There were bis-cuits; on another tray a decanter of vodka, herring and sausage, and an-other bottle with wine of some sort. Luise and her aunt were sitting on the sofa dressed in their best; on a chair opposite them the German, her suitor, with his hair combed, in a tail-coat and a stand-up collar stick-ing out in front. And in another chair at the side sat another German, a fat grey-headed old man who did not say a word. When I went in Luise turned white. The aunt started up but sat down again, and the German frowned, looking so cross, and got up to meet me.

" 'What do you want?' said he. I was a bit abashed, but I was in such a rage.

" 'What do I want! Why, you might welcome a visitor and give him a drink. I've come to see you.'

"The German thought a minute and said, 'Sit you.'

"I sat down. 'Well, give me some vodka,' I said.

" 'Here's some vodka,' he said, 'drink it, pray.'

" 'Give me some good vodka,' said I. I was in an awful rage, you know.

" 'It is good vodka.'

"I felt insulted that he treated me as though I were of no account, and above all with Luise looking on. I drank it off and said:

" 'What do you want to be rude for, German? You must make friends with me. I've come to you as a friend.'

" 'I cannot with you be friend,' said he, 'you are a simple soldier.'

"Then I flew into a fury.

" 'Ah, you scarecrow,' I said, 'you sausage-eater! But you know that from this moment I can do anything I like with you? Would you like me to shoot you with my pistol?'

"I pulled out my pistol, stood before him and put the muzzle straight at his head. The women sat more dead than alive, afraid to stir; the old man was trembling like a leaf, he turned pale and didn't say a word.

"The German was surprised, but he pulled himself together.

" 'I do not fear you,' said he, 'and I beg you as an honourable man to drop your joke at once and I do not fear you.'

" 'That's a lie,' said I, 'you do!'

"Why, he did not dare to move his head away, he just sat there.

" 'No,' said he, 'you that will never dare.'

" 'Why don't I dare?' said I.

" 'Because,' said he, 'that is you strictly forbidden and for that they will you strictly punish.'

"The devil only knows what that fool of a German was after. If he hadn't egged me on he'd have been living to this day. It all came from our disputing.

" 'So I daren't, you think?'

" 'No.'

" 'I daren't?'

" 'To treat me so you will never dare.'

" 'Well, there then, sausage!' I went bang and he rolled off his chair. The women screamed.

"I put the pistol in my pocket and made off, and as I was going into the fortress I threw the pistol into the nettles at the gate.

"I went home, lay down on my bed and thought: 'They'll come and take me directly.' One hour passed and then another—they did not take me. And when it got dark, such misery came over me; I went out; I wanted to see Luise, whatever happened. I went by the watchmaker's shop. There was a crowd there and police. I went to my old friend: 'Fetch Luise!' said I. I waited a little, and then I saw Luise running up. She threw herself on my neck and cried. 'It's all my fault,' said she, 'for listening to my aunt.' She told me that her aunt had gone straight home after what happened that morning and was so frightened that she was taken ill, and said nothing. 'She's told no one herself and she's forbidden me to,' says she. 'She is afraid and feels "let them do what they like." No one saw us this morning,' said Luise. He had sent his servant away too, for he was afraid of her. She would have scratched his eyes out if she had known that he meant to get married. There were none of the workmen in the house either, he had sent them all out. He prepared the coffee himself and got lunch ready. And the relation had been silent all his life, he never used to say anything, and when it had all happened that morning he picked up his hat and was the first to go. 'And no doubt he will go on being silent,' said Luise. So it was. For a fortnight no one came to take me and no one had any suspicion of me. That fortnight, though you mayn't believe it, Alexandr Petrovitch, was the happiest time in my life. Every day I met Luise. And how tender, how tender she grew to me! She would cry and say, 'I'll follow you wherever they send you, I'll leave everything for you!' It was almost more than I could bear, she wrung my heart so. Well, and in a fortnight they took me. The old man and the aunt came to an understanding and gave information against me. . . ."

"But excuse me," I interrupted, "for that they could not have given you more than ten or twelve years at the utmost in the civil division, but you are in the special division. How can that be?"

"Oh, that is a different matter," said Baklushin. "When I was brought to the court the captain swore at me with nasty words before the court. I couldn't control myself and said to him, 'What are you swearing for? Don't you see you are in a court of justice, you scoundrel!' Well, that gave a new turn to things; they tried me again and for everything together they condemned me to four thousand blows and sent me here in the special division. And when they brought me out for punishment, they brought out the captain too: me to walk down the 'green street,' and him to be deprived of his rank and sent to serve as a soldier in the Caucasus. Good-bye, Alexandr Petrovitch. Come and see our performance."

CHAPTER X

CHRISTMAS

AT LAST THE HOLIDAYS came. The convicts did hardly any work on Christmas Eve. Some went to the sewing-rooms and workshops; the others were sent to their different tasks, but for the most part, singly or in groups, came back to prison immediately afterwards and they all remained indoors after dinner. Indeed the majority had left the prison in the morning more on their own business than for the regulation work: some to arrange about bringing in and ordering vodka; others to see friends, male and female, or to collect any little sums owing to them for work done in the past. Baklushin and others who were taking part in the theatricals went to see certain acquaintances, principally among the officers' servants, and to obtain necessary costumes. Some went about with an anxious and responsible air, simply because others looked responsible, and though many of them had no grounds for expecting money, they, too, looked as though they were reckoning on getting it. In short everyone was looking forward to the next day in expectation of a change, of something unusual. In the evening the veterans in charge who had been marketing for the convicts brought in eatables of all sorts: beef, sucking-pigs, even geese. Many of the convicts, even the humblest and most careful who used to save up their farthings from one year's end to another, felt obliged to be lavish for such an occasion and to celebrate befittingly the end of the fast. The next day was a real holiday, guaranteed to them by law and not to be taken from them. On that day the convict could not be set to work and there were only three such days in the year.

And who knows what memories must have been stirred in the hearts of these outcasts at the coming of such a day! The great festivals of the Church make a vivid impression on the minds of peasants from childhood upwards. They are the days of rest from their hard toil, the days of family gatherings. In prison they must have been remembered with grief and heartache. Respect for the solemn day had

passed indeed into a custom strictly observed among the convicts;
very few caroused, all were serious and seemed preoccupied, though
many of them had really nothing to do. But whether they drank or
did nothing, they tried to keep up a certain dignity. . . . It seemed as
though laughter were prohibited. In fact they showed a tendency to
be over-particular and irritably intolerant, and if anyone jarred on the
prevailing mood, even by accident, the convicts set on him with out-
cries and abuse and were angry with him, as though he had shown
disrespect to the holiday itself. This state of mind in the convicts was
remarkable and positively touching. Apart from their innate reverence
for the great day, the convicts felt unconsciously that by the obser-
vance of Christmas they were, as it were, in touch with the whole of
the world, that they were not altogether outcasts and lost men, not altogether cut off; that it was the same in prison as amongst other people. They felt that; it was evident and easy to understand.

Akim Akimitch too made great preparations for the holiday. He
had no home memories, for he had grown up an orphan among
strangers, and had faced the hardships of military service before he
was sixteen; he had nothing very joyful to remember in his life, for
he had always lived regularly and monotonously, afraid of stepping
one hair's-breadth out of the prescribed path; he was not particularly
religious either, for propriety seemed to have swallowed up in him all
other human qualities and attributes, all passions and desires, bad and
good alike. And so he was preparing for the festival without anxiety or
excitement, untroubled by painful and quite useless reminiscences,
but with a quiet, methodical propriety which was just sufficient for
the fulfilment of his duties and of the ritual that has been prescribed
once and for all. As a rule he did not care for much reflection. The inner meaning of things never troubled his mind, but rules that had
once been laid down for him he followed with religious exactitude.
If it had been made the rule to do exactly the opposite, he would
have done that to-morrow with the same docility and scrupulous-
ness. Once only in his life he had tried to act on his own judgment,
and that had brought him to prison. The lesson had not been thrown
away on him. And though destiny withheld from him for ever all understanding of how he had been to blame, he had deduced a solitary
principle from his misadventure—never to use his own judgment
again under any circumstances, for sense "was not his strong-point,"

as the convicts used to say. In his blind devotion to established ritual, he looked with a sort of anticipatory reverence even upon the festal sucking-pig, which he himself stuffed with kasha and roasted (for he knew how to cook), as though regarding it not as an ordinary pig which could be bought and roasted any day, but as a special, holiday pig. Perhaps he had been used from childhood to see a sucking-pig on the table at Christmas, and had deduced from it that a sucking-pig was indispensable on the occasion; and I am sure that if he had once missed tasting sucking-pig on Christmas Day he would for the rest of his life have felt a conscience-prick at having neglected his duty.

Until Christmas Day he remained in his old jacket and trousers, which were quite threadbare though neatly darned. It appeared now that he had been carefully keeping away in his box the new suit given to him four months ago and had refrained from touching it, with the delectable idea of putting it on for the first time on Christmas Day. And so he did. On Christmas Eve he got out his new suit, unfolded it, examined it, brushed it, blew on it and tried it on. The suit seemed a good fit; everything was as it should be, buttoning tightly to the collar; the high collar stood up as stiff as cardboard under his chin; at the waist it fitted closely, almost like a uniform. Akim Akimitch positively grinned with delight, and not without a certain swagger he turned before the tiny looking-glass, round which at some leisure moment he had pasted a border of gold paper. Only one hook on the collar seemed not quite in the right place. Noticing it Akim Akimitch made up his mind to alter it; he moved it, tried the coat on again and then it was perfectly right; then he folded it up as before and put it away in his box again, with his mind at rest. His head was satisfactorily shaven; but examining himself carefully in the looking-glass he noticed that his head did not seem perfectly smooth—there was a scarcely visible growth of hair and he went at once to "the major" to be properly shaven according to regulation. And although Akim Akimitch was not to be inspected next day, he was shaven simply for conscience' sake, that he might leave no duty unperformed before Christmas. A reverence for epaulettes, buttons and details of uniform had from childhood been indelibly impressed upon his mind and upon his heart, as a duty that could not be questioned and as the highest form of the beautiful that could be attained by a decent man.

After this, as the senior convict in the ward, he gave orders for hay to be brought in, and carefully superintended the laying of it on the floor. The same thing was done in the other wards. I don't know why, but hay was always laid on the floor at Christmas time. Then having finished his labours Akim Akimitch said his prayers, lay down on his bed and at once fell into a sweet sleep like a baby's, to wake up as early as possible next morning. All the convicts did the same, however. In all the wards they went to bed much earlier than usual. Their usual evening pursuits were laid aside, there was no thought of cards. All was expectation of the coming day.

At last it came. Quite early, before daybreak, as soon as the morning drum had sounded, the wards were unlocked and the sergeant on duty who came in to count over the prisoners gave them Christmas greetings, and was greeted by them in the same way, with warmth and cordiality. After hastily saying their prayers Akim Akimitch and many of the others who had geese or sucking-pigs in the kitchen hurried off to see what was being done with them, how the roasting was getting on, where they had been put and so on. From the little prison windows blocked up with snow and ice, we could see through the darkness in both kitchens bright fires that had been kindled before daybreak, glowing in all the six ovens. Convicts were already flitting across the courtyard with their sheepskins properly put on or flung across their shoulders, all rushing to the kitchen. Some, though very few, had already been to the "publicans." They were the most impatient. On the whole, all behaved decorously, peaceably, and with an exceptional seemliness. One heard nothing of the usual swearing and quarrelling. Everyone realized that it was a great day and a holy festival. Some went into other wards to greet special friends. One saw signs of something like friendship. I may mention in parenthesis that there was scarcely a trace of friendly feeling among the convicts—I don't mean general friendliness, that was quite out of the question, I mean the personal affection of one convict for another. There was scarcely a trace of such a feeling among us, and it is a remarkable fact: it is so different in the world at large. All of us, as a rule, with very rare exceptions, were rough and cold in our behaviour to one another, and this was, as it were, the accepted attitude adopted once for all.

I, too, went out of the ward. It was just beginning to get light. The stars were growing dim and a faint frosty haze was rising. The smoke was puffing in clouds from the kitchen chimneys. Some of the convicts I came upon in the yard met me with ready and friendly Christmas greetings. I thanked them, and greeted them in the same way. Some of them had never said a word to me till that day.

At the kitchen door I was overtaken by a convict from the military division with his sheepskin thrown over his shoulders. He had caught sight of me in the middle of the yard and shouted after me, "Alexandr Petrovitch, Alexandr Petrovitch!" He was running towards the kitchen in a hurry. I stopped and waited for him. He was a young lad with a round face and a gentle expression; very taciturn with everyone; he had not spoken a word to me or taken any notice of me since I entered the prison; I did not even know his name. He ran up to me out of breath and stood facing me, gazing at me with a blank but at the same time blissful smile.

"What is it?" I asked wondering, seeing that he was standing and gazing at me with open eyes, was smiling but not saying a word.

"Why, it's Christmas," he muttered, and realizing that he could say nothing more, he left me and rushed into the kitchen.

I may mention here that we had never had anything to do with one another and scarcely spoke from that time till I left the prison.

In the kitchen round the glowing ovens there was great crowding and bustling, quite a crush. Everyone was looking after his property; the cooks were beginning to prepare the prison dinner, which was earlier that day. No one had yet begun eating, though some of them wanted to; but they had a regard for decorum in the presence of the others. They were waiting for the priest, and the fast was only to be broken after his visit. Meanwhile, before it was fully daylight, we heard the corporal at the prison gate calling the cooks. He shouted almost every minute and went on for nearly two hours. The cooks were wanted to receive the offerings, which were brought into the prison from all parts of the town. An immense quantity of provisions was brought, such as rolls, cheesecakes, pastries, scones, pancakes and similar good things. I believe there was not a housewife of the middle or lower class in the town who did not send something of her baking by way of Christmas greeting to the "unfortunate" and captives. There were rich offerings—large quantities of fancy bread made of the finest flour. There were very humble offerings too—such as a farthing roll and a couple of rye cakes with a smear of sour cream on them: these were the gifts of the poor to the poor, and all they had to give. All were accepted with equal gratitude without distinction of gifts and givers. The convicts took off their caps as they received them, bowed, gave their Christmas greetings and took the offerings into the kitchen. When the offerings were piled up in heaps, the senior convicts were sent for, and they divided all equally among the wards. There was no scolding or quarrelling; it was honestly and equitably done. The share that was brought to our ward was divided among us by Akim Akimitch with the help of another convict. They divided it with their own hands, and with their own hands gave each convict his share. There was not the slightest protest, not the slightest jealousy; all were satisfied; there could be no suspicion of an offering being concealed or unfairly divided.

Having seen to his cooking, Akim Akimitch proceeded to array himself. He dressed himself with all due decorum and solemnity, not leaving one hook unfastened, and as soon as he was dressed he began saying his real prayers. He spent a good time over them. A good many of the convicts, chiefly the elder ones, were already standing saying their prayers. The younger ones did not pray much: the most they did even on a holiday was to cross themselves when they got up. When his prayers were over, Akim Akimitch came up to me and with a certain solemnity offered me his Christmas greeting. I at once invited him to join me at tea and he invited me to share his sucking-pig. Soon after, Petrov, too, ran up to greet me. He seemed to have been drinking already and, though he ran up out of breath, he did not say much; he only stood a little while before me as though expecting something, and soon went off into the kitchen again. Meanwhile in the military ward they were preparing for the priest. That ward was arranged differently from the others; the plank bed ran along the walls instead of being in the middle of the room as in all the other wards, so that it was the only room in the prison which had a clear space in the middle. It probably was so arranged in order that when necessary the convicts could be all gathered together there. In the middle of the room they put a table, covered it with a clean towel, and on it set the ikon and lighted the lamp before us. At last the priest came with the cross and the holy water. After repeating prayers and singing before the ikon, he stood facing the convicts and all of them with genuine reverence came forward to kiss the cross. Then the priest walked through all the wards and sprinkled them with holy water. In the kitchen he praised our prison bread, which was famous throughout the town, and the convicts at once wanted to send him two new freshly baked loaves; a veteran was at once dispatched to take them. They followed the cross out with the same reverence with which they had welcomed it and then almost immediately the governor and the major arrived. The governor was liked and even respected among us. He walked through all the wards, escorted by the major; he gave them all Christmas greetings, went into the kitchen and tried the prison soup. The soup was excellent: nearly a pound of beef for each prisoner had been put into it in honour of the occasion. There was boiled millet, too, and butter was liberally allowed. When he had seen the governor off, the major gave orders that they should begin dinner. The convicts tried to avoid his eye. We did not like the spiteful way in which he glanced to right and to left from behind his spectacles, trying even to-day to find something amiss, someone to blame.

We began dinner. Akim Akimitch's sucking-pig was superbly cooked. I don't know how to explain it, but immediately after the major had gone, within five minutes of his departure, an extraordinary number of people were drunk, and yet only five minutes before they had all been almost sober. One suddenly saw flushed and beaming faces and balalaikas were brought out. The little Pole with a fiddle was already at the heels of a reveller who had engaged him for the whole day; he was scraping away merry jig tunes. The talk began to grow louder and more drunken. But they got through dinner without much disturbance. Everyone had had enough. Many of the older and more sedate at once lay down to sleep. Akim Akimitch did the same, apparently feeling that on a great holiday one must sleep after dinner. The old dissenter from Starodubov had a brief nap and then clambered on the stove, opened his book and prayed almost uninterruptedly till the dead of night. It was painful to him to see the "shamefulness," as he said, of the convicts' carousing. All the Circassians settled themselves on the steps and gazed at the drunken crowd with curiosity and a certain disgust. I came across Nurra: "Bad, bad!" he said, shaking his head with pious indignation, "Ough, it's bad! Allah will be angry!" Isay Fomitch lighted his candle with an obstinate and supercilious air and set to work, evidently wanting to show that the holiday meant nothing to him. Here and there, card parties were made up. The players were not afraid of the veterans, though they put men on the look-out for the sergeant, who for his part was anxious not to see anything. The officer on duty peeped into the prison three times during the day. But the drunken men were hidden and the cards were slipped away when he appeared, and he, too, seemed to have made up his mind not to notice minor offences. Drunkenness was looked on as a minor offence that day. Little by little, the convicts grew noisier. Quarrels began. Yet the majority were still sober and there were plenty to look after those who were not. But those who were drinking drank a vast amount. Gazin was triumphant. He swaggered up and down near his place on the bed, under which he had boldly stored away the vodka, hidden till that day under the snow behind the barracks, and he chuckled slyly as he looked at the customers coming to him. He was sober himself; he had not drunk a drop. He meant to carouse when the holidays were over, when he would have emptied the convicts' pockets. There was singing in all the wards. But drunkenness was passing into stupefaction and the singing was on the verge of tears. Many of the prisoners walked to and fro with their balalaikas, their sheepskins over their shoulders, twanging the strings with a jaunty air. In the special division they even got up a chorus of eight voices. They sang capitally to the accompaniment of balalaikas and guitars. Few of the songs were genuine peasant songs. I only remember one and it was sung with spirit:

> I, the young woman,
> Went at eve to the feast.

And I heard a variation of that song which I had never heard before. Several verses were added at the end:

> I, the young woman,
> Have tidied my house;
> The spoons are rubbed,
> The boards are scrubbed,
> The soup's in the pot,
> The peas are hot.

For the most part they sang what are called in Russia "prison" songs, all well-known ones. One of them, "In times gone by," was a comic song, describing how a man had enjoyed himself in the past and lived like a gentleman at large, but now was shut up in prison. It described how he had "flavoured blancmange with champagne" in old days and now:

> Cabbage and water they give me to eat,
> And I gobble it up as though it were sweet.

A popular favourite was the hackneyed song:

> As a boy I lived in freedom,
>   Had my capital as well.
> But the boy soon lost his money,
>   Straightway into bondage fell.

and so on. There were mournful songs too. One was a purely convict song, a familiar one too, I believe:

> Now the dawn in heaven is gleaming,
> Heard is the awakening drum.
> Doors will open to the jailer,
> The recording clerk will come.
> We behind these walls are hidden,
> None can see us, none can hear.
> But the Lord of Heaven is with us,
> Even here we need not fear. . . .

Another was even more depressing but sung to a fine tune and probably composed by a convict. The words were mawkish and somewhat illiterate. I remember a few lines of it:

> Never more shall I behold
> The country of my birth.
> In suffering, guiltless, I'm condemned
> To pass my life on earth.
> The owl upon the roof will call

And grief my heart will tear,
His voice will echo in the woods,
And I shall not be there.

This song was often sung amongst us, not in chorus, but as a solo. Someone would go out on to the steps, sit down, ponder a little with his cheek on his hand and begin singing it in a high falsetto. It made one's heart ache to hear it. There were some good voices among us.

Meanwhile it was beginning to get dark. Sadness, despondency and stupefaction were painfully evident through the drunkenness and merry-making. The man who had been laughing an hour before was sobbing, hopelessly drunk. Others had had a couple of fights by now. Others, pale and hardly able to stand, lounged about the wards picking quarrels with everyone. Men whose liquor never made them quarrelsome were vainly looking for friends to whom they could open their hearts and pour out their drunken sorrows. All these poor people wanted to enjoy themselves, wanted to spend the great holiday merrily, and, good God! how dreary, how miserable the day was for almost all of us. Everyone seemed disappointed. Petrov came to see me twice again. He had drunk very little all day and was almost sober. But up to the last hour he seemed to be still expecting that something must be going to happen, something extraordinary, festive and amusing. Though he said nothing about it, one could see this in his eyes. He kept flitting from ward to ward without wearying. But nothing special happened or was to be met with, except drunkenness, drunken, senseless oaths and men stupefied with drink. Sirotkin, too, wandered through the wards, well washed and looking pretty in a new red shirt; he, too, seemed quietly and naïvely expectant of something. By degrees it became unbearable and disgusting in the wards. No doubt there was a great deal that was laughable, but I felt sad and sorry for them all, I felt dreary and stifled among them.

Here were two convicts disputing which should treat the other. Evidently they had been wrangling for a long time and this was not their first quarrel. One in particular seemed to have an old grudge against the other. He was complaining and speaking thickly, was struggling to prove that the other had been unfair to him: some sheepskin coat had been sold, a sum of money had been made away with somehow, a year before at carnival. There was something else besides. . . . He was a tall muscular fellow of peaceable disposition and by no means a fool. When he was drunk he was disposed to make friends with anyone and to open his heart to him. He even swore at his opponent and got up a grievance against him in order to be reconciled and more friendly afterwards. The other, a short, thick-set, stubby man, with a round face, was a sharp and wily fellow. He had drunk more than his companion, perhaps, but was only slightly drunk. He was a man of character and was reputed to be well off, but it was for some reason to his interest just now not to irritate his expansive friend, and he led him up to the vodka dealer; while the friend kept repeating that he should and must treat him "if only you are an honest man."

The "publican," with a shade of respect for the short man and a shade of contempt for his expansive companion, because the latter was being treated and not drinking at his own expense, brought out some vodka and poured out a cupful.

"No, Styopka, you owe it me," said the expansive friend, seeing he had gained his point, "for it's what you owe me."

"I am not going to waste my breath on you!" answered Styopka.

"No, Styopka, that's a lie," protested the other, taking the cup from the "publican," "for you owe me money, you've no conscience! Why, your very eyes are not your own but borrowed. You are a scoundrel, Styopka, that's what you are; that's the only word for you!"

"What are you whining about?—you've spilt your vodka. One stands you treat, so you might as well drink," cried the publican to the expansive friend, "You can't keep us standing here till to-morrow!"

"But I am going to drink it—what are you shouting about! A merry Christmas to you, Stepan Dorofeitch!" cup in hand he turned politely, and made a slight bow to Styopka whom half a minute before he had called a scoundrel. "Good health to you for a hundred years, not reckoning what you've lived already!" He emptied his cup, cleared his throat and wiped his mouth. "I could carry a lot of vodka in my day, lads," he observed with grave dignity, addressing the world in general and no one in particular, "but now it seems age is coming upon me. Thank you, Stepan Dorofeitch."

"Not at all."

"But I shall always tell you of it, Styopka, and besides your behaving like a regular scoundrel to me, I tell you . . ."

"And I've something to tell you, you drunken lout," Styopka broke in, losing all patience. "Listen and mark my words. Look here: we'll halve the world between us—you take one half, and I'll take the other. You go your way and don't let me meet you again. I am sick of you."

"Then you won't pay me the money?"

"What money, you drunken fool?"

"Ah, in the next world you'll be wanting to pay it, but I won't take it. We work hard for our money, with sweat on our brows and blisters on our hands. You'll suffer for my five kopecks in the other world."

"Oh, go to the devil!"

"Don't drive me, I am not in harness yet."

"Go on, go on!"

"Scoundrel!"

"You jail-bird!"

And abuse followed again, more violent than before.

Here two friends were sitting apart on the bed. One of them, a tall, thick-set, fleshy fellow with a red face, who looked like a regular butcher, was almost crying, for he was very much touched. The other was a frail-looking, thin, skinny little man, with a long nose which always looked moist and little piggy eyes which were fixed on the ground. He was a polished and cultivated individual; he had been a clerk and treated his friend a little superciliously, which the other secretly resented. They had been drinking together all day.

"He's taken a liberty!" cried the fleshy friend, shaking the clerk's head violently with his left arm, which he had round him. By "taking a liberty" he meant that he had hit him. The stout one, who had been a sergeant, was secretly envious of his emaciated friend and so they were trying to outdo one another in the choiceness of their language.

"And I tell you that you are wrong too . . ." the clerk began dogmatically, resolutely refusing to look at his opponent and staring at the floor with a dignified air.

"He's taken a liberty, do you hear!" the first man broke in, shaking his friend more violently than ever. "You are the only friend I have in the world, do you hear? And that's why I tell you and no one else, he's taken a liberty!"

"And I tell you again, such a feeble justification, my friend, is only a discredit to you," said the clerk in a high-pitched, bland voice.

"You'd better admit, my friend, that all this drunken business is due to your own incontinence."

The stout convict staggered back a little, looked blankly with his drunken eyes at the self-satisfied clerk and suddenly and quite unexpectedly drove his huge fist with all his might into his friend's little face. That was the end of a whole day's friendship. His dear friend was sent flying senseless under the bed. . . .

A friend of mine from the special division, a clever good-humoured fellow of boundless good-nature and extraordinarily simple appearance, who was fond of a joke but quite without malice, came into our ward. This was the man who on my first day in prison had been at dinner in the kitchen, asking where the rich peasant lived and declaring that he had pride, and who had drunk tea with me. He was a man of forty, with an extraordinarily thick lower lip and a large fleshy nose covered with pimples. He was holding a balalaika and carelessly twanging the strings. A diminutive convict with a very large head was following him about as though he were on a string. I had scarcely seen him before, and indeed no one ever noticed him. He was a queer fellow, mistrustful, always silent and serious; he used to work in the sewing-room, and evidently tried to live a life apart and to avoid having anything to do with the rest. Now, being drunk, he followed Varlamov about like a shadow. He followed him about in great excitement, waving his arms in the air, bringing his fist down on the wall and on the bed, and almost shedding tears. Varlamov seemed to be paying no attention to him, as though he were not beside him. It is worth remarking that these men had had scarcely anything to do with one another before; they had nothing in common in their pursuits or their characters. They belonged to different divisions and lived in different wards. The little convict's name was Bulkin.

Varlamov grinned on seeing me. I was sitting on my bed by the stove. He stood at a little distance facing me, pondered a moment, gave a lurch, and coming up to me with unsteady steps, he flung himself into a swaggering attitude and lightly touching the strings, chanted in measured tones with a faint tap of his boot:

> Round face! fair face!
> Like a tomtit in the meadow
> Hear my darling's voice!

> When she wears a dress of satin
> With some most becoming trimming,
> Oh, she does look nice!

This song seemed the last straw for Bulkin; he gesticulated, and addressing the company in general he shouted:

"He keeps telling lies, lads, he keeps telling lies! Not a word of truth in it, it is all a lie!"

"Respects to old Alexandr Petrovitch!" said Varlamov. He peeped into my face with a sly laugh, and was on the point of kissing me. He was very drunk. The expression "old" So-and-so is used among the people all over Siberia even in addressing a lad of twenty. The word "old" suggests respect, veneration, something flattering, in fact.

"Well, Varlamov, how are you getting on?"

"Oh, I am jogging along. If one's glad it's Christmas, one gets drunk early; you must excuse me!" Varlamov talked in rather a drawl.

"That's all lying, all lying again!" shouted Bulkin, thumping on the bed in a sort of despair. But Varlamov seemed determined to take no notice of him, and there was something very comic about it, because Bulkin had attached himself to Varlamov from early morning for no reason whatever, simply because Varlamov kept "lying," as he somehow imagined. He followed him about like a shadow, found fault with every word he said, wrung his hands, banged them against the walls and the bed till they almost bled, and was distressed, evidently distressed, by the conviction that Varlamov "was lying." If he had had any hair on his head, I believe he would have pulled it out in his mortification. It was as though he felt responsible for Varlamov's conduct, as though all Varlamov's failings were on his conscience. But what made it comic was that Varlamov never even looked at him.

"He keeps lying, nothing but lying and lying! There's not a word of sense in all he says!" shouted Bulkin.

"But what's that to you?" responded the convicts laughing.

"I beg to inform you, Alexandr Petrovitch, that I was very handsome and that the wenches were awfully fond of me . . ." Varlamov began suddenly, apropos of nothing.

"He's lying! He's lying again!" Bulkin broke in with a squeal. The convicts laughed.

"And didn't I swell it among them! I'd a red shirt and velveteen breeches; I lay at my ease like that Count Bottle, that is, as drunk as a Swede; anything I liked in fact!"

"That's a lie!" Bulkin protested stoutly.

"And in those days I had a stone house of two storeys that had been my father's. In two years I got through the two storeys, I'd nothing but the gate left and no gate posts. Well, money is like pigeons that come and go."

"That's a lie," Bulkin repeated more stoutly than ever.

"So the other day I sent my parents a tearful letter; I thought maybe they'd send me something. For I've been told I went against my parents. I was disrespectful to them! It's seven years since I sent it to them."

"And haven't you had an answer?" I asked laughing.

"No, I haven't," he answered, suddenly laughing too, bringing his nose nearer and nearer to my face. "And I've a sweetheart here, Alexandr Petrovitch . . ."

"Have you? A sweetheart?"

"Onufriev said the other day: 'My girl may be pock-marked and plain, but look what a lot of clothes she's got; and yours may be pretty, but she is a beggar and goes about with a sack on her back.' "

"And is it true?"

"It's true she is a beggar!" he answered, and he went off into a noiseless laugh; there was laughter among the other convicts too. Everyone knew indeed that he had picked up with a beggar girl and had only given her ten kopecks in the course of six months.

"Well, what of it?" I asked, wanting to get rid of him at last.

He paused, looked at me feelingly and pronounced tenderly:

"Why, things being so, won't you be kind enough to stand me a glass? I've been drinking tea all day, Alexandr Petrovitch," he added with feeling, accepting the money I gave him, "I've been swilling tea till I am short of breath, and it's gurgling in my belly like water in a bottle."

When he was taking the money Bulkin's mental agitation reached its utmost limits. He gesticulated like a man in despair, almost crying.

"Good people!" he shouted, addressing the whole ward in his frenzy. "Look at him! He keeps lying! Whatever he says, it's nothing but lies, lies and lies!"

"But what is it to you," cried the convicts, wondering at his fury, "you ridiculous fellow?"

"I won't let him tell lies!" cried Bulkin with flashing eyes, bringing his fist down on the bed with all his might. "I don't want him to tell lies!"

Everyone laughed. Varlamov took the money, bowed to me and, grimacing, hurried out of the ward, to the publican, of course. And then he seemed for the first time to become aware of Bulkin.

"Well, come along!" he said to him, stopping in the doorway, as though he were of some use to him. "You walking-stick!" he added as he contemptuously made way for the mortified Bulkin to pass out before him, and began twanging the balalaika again.

But why describe this Bedlam! The oppressive day came to an end at last. The convicts fell heavily asleep on the plank bed. They talked and muttered in their sleep that night even more than usual. Here and there they were still sitting over cards. The holiday, so long looked forward to, was over. Tomorrow the daily round, to-morrow work again.

CHAPTER XI

THE THEATRICALS

ON THE THIRD DAY in Christmas week we had the first performance of our theatricals. A great deal of trouble had no doubt been spent on getting them up, but the actors had undertaken it all so that the rest of us had no idea how things were going, what was being done. We did not even know for certain what was to be performed. The actors had done their best during those three days to get hold of costumes when they went out to work. When Baklushin met me he did nothing but snap his fingers with glee. Even the major seemed to be in a decent mood, though we really were not sure whether he knew of the theatricals. If he did know, would he give his formal sanction or only make up his mind to say nothing, winking at the convicts' project, insisting of course that everything should be as orderly as possible? I imagine he knew about the theatricals and could not but have known of them, but did not want to interfere, realizing that he might make things worse by prohibiting them: the convicts would begin to be disorderly and drunken, so that it would really be much better for them to have something to occupy them. I assume that this was the major's line of argument, simply because it is most natural, sensible and correct. It may even be said if the convicts had not got up theatricals or some such entertainment for the holidays, the authorities ought to have thought of it themselves. But as our major's mind did not work like the minds of the rest of mankind but in quite the opposite way, it may very well be that I am quite in error in supposing that he knew of the theatricals and allowed them. A man like the major must always be oppressing someone, taking something away, depriving men of some right—making trouble somewhere, in fact. He was known all over the town for it. What did it matter to him if restrictions might lead to disturbances in prison? There were penalties for such disturbances (such is the reasoning of men like our major) and severity and strict adherence to the letter of the law is all that the scoundrelly convicts need. These obtuse ministers of the law absolutely fail to understand and are incapable of understanding that the strict adherence to the letter of it, without using their reason, without understanding the spirit of it, leads straight to disturbance, and has never led to anything else. "It is the law, there's nothing more to be said," they say, and they are genuinely astonished that they should be expected to show common sense and a clear head as well. This seems particularly unnecessary to many of them, a revolting superfluity, a restriction and a piece of intolerance.

But however that may have been, the senior sergeant did not oppose the convicts, and that was all they cared about. I can say with certainty that the theatricals and the gratitude felt for their being permitted were the reason why there was not one serious disturbance in the prison during the holidays: not one violent quarrel, not one case of theft. I myself witnessed the convicts themselves trying to repress the riotous or quarrelsome, simply on the ground that the theatricals might be prohibited. The sergeant exacted a promise from the convicts that everything should be orderly and that they would behave themselves. They agreed joyfully, and kept their promise faithfully; they were much flattered at their words being trusted. It must be added, however, that it cost the authorities nothing to allow the theatricals, they had not to contribute. No space had to be set apart for the theatre—the stage could be rigged up and taken to pieces again in a quarter of an hour. The performance lasted for an hour and a half, and if the order had suddenly come from headquarters to stop the performance, it could all have been put away in a trice. The costumes were hidden in the convicts' boxes. But before I describe how the theatricals were arranged and what the costumes were like, I must describe the programme, that is, what it was proposed to perform.

There was no written programme. But on the second and third performances a programme in the handwriting of Baklushin made its appearance for the benefit of the officers and of distinguished visitors generally who had honoured our theatricals by being present at the first performance. The officer of the guard usually came, and on one occasion the commanding officer of the guards came himself. The officer of the engineers came, too, on one evening, and it was for visitors like these the programme was prepared. It was assumed that the fame of the prison theatricals would spread far and wide in the fortress and would even reach the town, especially as there was no theatre in the town. There was a rumour that one performance had been got up by a society of amateurs, but that was all. The convicts were like children, delighted at the smallest success, vain over it indeed. "Who knows," they thought and said among themselves, "perhaps even the highest authorities will hear about it, they'll come and have a look; then they'll see what the convicts are made of. It's not a simple soldiers' performance with dummy figures, floating boats, and dancing bears and goats. We have actors, real actors, they act high-class comedies, there's no theatre like it even in the town. General Abrosimov had a performance, they say, and is going to have another, but I dare say he'll only beat us in the dresses. As for the *conversations*, who knows whether they'll be as good! It will reach the governor's ears, maybe, and—you never can tell!—he may take it into his head to have a look at it himself. There's no theatre in the town. . . ." In fact the prisoners' imagination was so worked up during the holidays, especially after the first success, that they were ready to fancy they might receive rewards or have their term of imprisonment shortened, though at the same time they were almost at once ready to laugh very good-naturedly at their own expense. They were children, in fact, perfect children, though some of these children were over forty.

But though there was no regular programme I already knew in outline what the performance would consist of. The first piece was called "Filatka and Miroshka, or The Rivals." Baklushin had boasted to me a week beforehand that the part of Filatka which he was undertaking would be acted in a style such as had never been seen even in the Petersburg theatres. He strolled about the wards bragging without shame or scruple, though with perfect good-nature; and now and then he would suddenly go through a bit of "theatrical business," a bit of his part, that is, and they all would laugh, regardless of whether the performance was amusing; though even then, it must be admitted, the convicts knew how to restrain themselves and keep up their dignity. The only convicts who were enraptured by Baklushin's pranks and his stories of what was coming were either quite young people, greenhorns, deficient in reserve, or else the more important among the convicts whose prestige was firmly established, so that they had no reason to be afraid of giving vent to their feelings of any sort,

however simple (that is, however unseemly, according to prison notions) they might be. The others listened to the gossip and rumours
in silence; they did not, it is true, contradict or disapprove, but they
did their utmost to take up an indifferent and even to some extent supercilious attitude to the theatricals. Only during the last days just
before the performance everyone began to feel inquisitive. What was
coming? How would our men do? What was the major saying? Would
it be as successful as it was last year? and so on.

Baklushin assured me that the actors had been splendidly chosen,
every one "to fit his part"; that there would even be a curtain, that
Filatka's betrothed was to be acted by Sirotkin "and you will see
what he is like in woman's dress," he added, screwing up his eyes
and clicking with his tongue. The benevolent lady was to wear a
mantle and a dress with a flounce, and to carry a parasol in her hand.
The benevolent gentleman was to come on in an officer's coat with
epaulettes, and was to carry a cane in his hand. There was to be a
second piece with a highly dramatic ending called "Kedril the Glutton." The title aroused my curiosity, but in spite of all my inquiries I
could learn nothing about this piece beforehand. I only learnt that
they had not taken the play out of a book, but from a "written
copy"; that they got the play from a retired sergeant living in the
town who had probably once taken part in a performance of it
himself in some soldiers' entertainment. In our remote towns and
provinces there are such plays which no one seems to know anything about, and which have perhaps never been printed, but seem
to have appeared of themselves, and so have become an indispensable part of every "people's theatre." It would be a very, very good
thing if some investigator would make a fresh and more careful
study of the people's drama, which really does exist, and is perhaps
by no means valueless. I refuse to believe that all I saw on our prison
stage was invented by the convicts themselves. There must be a con-
tinuous tradition, established customs and conceptions handed down
from generation to generation and consecrated by time. They must
be looked for among soldiers, among factory hands, in factory
towns, and even among the working classes in some poor obscure
little towns. They are preserved, too, in villages and provincial towns
among the servants of the richer country gentry. I imagine indeed
that many old-fashioned plays have been circulated in written copies

all over Russia by house-serfs. Many of the old-fashioned landowners and Moscow gentlemen had their own dramatic companies, made up of serf actors. And these theatres laid the foundations of the national dramatic art of which there are unmistakable signs. As for "Kedril the Glutton," I was able to learn nothing about it beforehand, except that evil spirits appear on the stage and carry Kedril off to hell. But what does the name Kedril mean, why is it Kedril and not Kiril? Whether it is a Russian story or of foreign origin I could not find out. It was announced that finally there would be a "pantomime to the accompaniment of music." All this of course was very interesting. The actors were fifteen in number—all smart, spirited fellows. They bestirred themselves, rehearsed—sometimes behind the prison—held their tongues and kept things secret. In fact they meant to surprise us with something extraordinary and unexpected.

On working days the prison was locked up early, as soon as night came on. Christmas week was an exception: they did not lock up till the evening tattoo. This concession was made expressly for the sake of the theatre. Almost every afternoon during Christmas week they sent a messenger from the prison to the officer of the watch with a humble request "to allow the theatricals and leave the wards unlocked a little longer," adding that this had been allowed the day before and there had been no disorder. The officer of the watch reasoned that "there really had been no disorder the day before, and if they gave their word that there would be none to-day, it meant that they would see to that themselves and that made things safer than anything. Besides, if the theatricals were not allowed, maybe (there's no knowing with a lot of criminals!) they might get up some mischief through spite and get the watch into trouble." Another point was that it was tedious to serve on the watch, and here was a play, not simply got up by the soldiers, but by the convicts, and convicts are an interesting lot; it would be amusing to see it. The officers of the watch always had the privilege of looking on.

If his superior officer came along he would ask, "Where is the officer of the watch?" "He is in the prison counting over the convicts and locking the wards"—a straightforward answer and a sufficient explanation. And so every evening through the Christmas holidays the officers of the watch allowed the performance, and did not lock the wards till the evening tattoo. The convicts knew beforehand that there would be no hindrance from the officers of the watch, and they had no anxiety on that ground.

About seven o'clock Petrov came to fetch me and we went to the performance together. Almost all the inmates of our ward went to the performance except the Old Believer and the Poles. It was only on the very last performance, on the fourth of January, that the Poles made up their minds to be present, and only then after many assurances that it was nice and amusing, and that there was no risk about it. The disdain of the Poles did not irritate the convicts in the very least, and they were welcomed on the fourth of January quite politely. They were even shown into the best places. As for the Circassians and still more Isay Fomitch, the performance was to them a real enjoyment. Isay Fomitch paid three kopecks every time, and on the last performance put ten kopecks in the plate and there was a look of bliss on his face. The actors decided to collect from the audience what they were willing to give for the expenses of the theatre and for their own "fortifying." Petrov assured me that I should be put into one of the best seats, however crowded the theatre might be, on the ground that being richer than most of them I should probably subscribe more liberally and also that I knew more about acting. And so it was. But I will first describe the room and the arrangement of the theatre.

The military ward in which our stage was arranged was fifteen paces long. From the yard one mounted some steps into the passage leading to the ward. This long ward, as I have mentioned already, was different from the others: the bed platform ran round the walls so that the middle of the room was free. The half of the room nearest to the steps was given up to the spectators and the other half which communicated with another ward was marked off for the stage. What struck me first of all was the curtain. It stretched for ten feet across the room. To have a curtain was such a luxury that it was certainly something to marvel at. What is more, it was painted in oil colours with a design of trees, arbours, lakes and stars. It was made of pieces of linen, old and new, such as they were able to collect among the convicts, old leg wrappers and shirts sewn together after a fashion into one large strip, and where the linen fell short the gap was filled simply with paper which had been begged, sheet by sheet, from various offices and departments. Our painters, amongst whom the "Brüllov" of the prison, A., was conspicuous, had made it their work to decorate and paint it. The effect was surprising. Such a refinement delighted even the most morose and fastidious of the convicts, who, when it came to the performance, were without exception as childish in their admiration as the most enthusiastic and impatient. All were very much pleased and even boastful in their pleasure.

The stage was lighted by means of a few tallow candles which were cut into pieces. In front of the curtain stood two benches brought from the kitchen, and in front of the benches were three or four chairs from the sergeant's room. The chairs were intended for any officers that might come in, the benches for the sergeants and the engineering clerks, foremen and other persons in official positions, though not officers, in case any such looked in on the performance. And as a fact, spectators from outside were present at every performance; there were more on some evenings than on others, but at the last performance there was not a vacant seat on the benches. In the back of the room were the convicts themselves, standing, and in spite of the suffocating, steamy heat of the room wearing their coats or sheepskins and carrying their caps in their hands, out of respect for their visitors. Of course the space allotted to the convicts was too small. And not only were people literally sitting on others, especially in the back rows, but the beds too were filled up, as well as the spaces to right and left of the curtain, and there were even some ardent spectators who always went round behind the scenes, and looked at the performance from the other ward at the back. The crush in the first part of the ward was incredible, and might even be compared to the crush and crowding I had lately seen at the bath-house. The door into the passage was open and the passage, where the temperature was 20° below zero, was also thronged with people. Petrov and I were at once allowed to go to the front, almost up to the benches, where we could see much better than from the back. They looked upon me as to some extent a theatre-goer, a connoisseur, who had frequented performances very different from this; they had seen Baklushin consulting me all this time and treating me with respect; so on this occasion I had the honour of a front place. The convicts were no doubt extremely vain and frivolous, but it was all on the surface. The convicts could laugh at me, seeing that I was a poor hand at their work. Almazov could look with contempt upon us "gentlemen" and pride himself on knowing how to burn alabaster. But, mixed with their persecution and

ridicule, there was another element: we had once been gentlemen;
we belonged to the same class as their former masters, of whom they
could have no pleasant memories. But now at the theatricals they
made way for me. They recognized that in this I was a better critic,
that I had seen and knew more than they. Even those who liked me
least were (I know for a fact) anxious now for my approval of their
theatricals, and without the slightest servility they let me have the
best place. I see that now, recalling my impressions at the time. It
seemed to me at the time—I remember—that in their correct esti-
mate of themselves there was no servility, but a sense of their own
dignity. The highest and most striking characteristic of our people is
just their sense of justice and their eagerness for it. There is no trace
in the common people of the desire to be cock of the walk on all occasions and at all costs, whether they deserve to be or not. One has
but to take off the outer superimposed husk and to look at the kernel
more closely, more attentively and without prejudice, and some of us
will see things in the people that we should never have expected.
There is not much our wise men could teach them. On the contrary,
I think it is the wise men who ought to learn from the people.

Before we started, Petrov told me naïvely that I should have a front
place partly because I should subscribe more. There was no fixed price
of admission: everyone gave what he could or what he wished. When
the plate was taken round almost everyone put something in it, even if
it were only a halfpenny. But if I were given a front place partly on account of money, on the supposition that I should give more than others, what a sense of their own dignity there was in that again! "You are
richer than I am, so you can stand in front, and though we are all
equal, you'll give more; and so a spectator like you is more pleasing to
the actors. You must have the first place, for we are all here not thinking of the money, but showing our respect, so we ought to sort ourselves of our own accord." How much fine and genuine pride there is
in this! It is a respect not for money, but respect for oneself. As a rule
there was not much respect for money, for wealth, in the prison, especially if one looks at convicts without distinction, as a gang, in the
mass. I can't remember one of them seriously demeaning himself for
the sake of money. There were men who were always begging, who
begged even of me. But this was rather mischief, roguery, than the real
thing; there was too much humour and naïveté in it. I don't know

whether I express myself so as to be understood. But I am forgetting the theatricals. To return.

Till the curtain was raised, the whole room was a strange and animated picture. To begin with, masses of spectators crowded, squeezed tightly, packed on all sides, waiting with patient and blissful faces for the performance to begin. In the back rows men were clambering on one another. Many of them had brought blocks of wood from the kitchen; fixing the thick block of wood against the wall, a man would climb on to it, leaning with both hands on the shoulders of someone in front of him, and would stand like that without changing his attitude for the whole two hours, perfectly satisfied with himself and his position. Others got their feet on the lower step of the stove and stayed so all the time, leaning on men in front of them. This was quite in the hindmost rows, next to the wall. At the sides, too, men were standing on the bed in dense masses above the musicians. This was a good place. Five people had clambered on to the stove itself and, lying on it, looked down from it. They must have been blissful. The window-sills on the opposite wall were also crowded with people who had come in late or failed to get a good place. Everyone behaved quietly and decorously. Everyone wished to show himself in the best light before the gentry and the officers. All faces expressed a simple-hearted expectation. Every face was red and bathed in sweat from the closeness and heat. A strange light of childlike joy, of pure, sweet pleasure, was shining on these lined and branded brows and cheeks, on those faces usually so morose and gloomy, in those eyes which sometimes gleamed with such terrible fire. They were all bare-headed, and all the heads were shaven on the right side.

Suddenly sounds of bustle and hurrying were heard on the stage. In a minute the curtain would rise. Then the band struck up. This band deserves special mention. Eight musicians were installed on the bed on one side; two violins (one from the prison and one borrowed from someone in the fortress, but both the fiddlers were convicts), three balalaikas, all home-made, two guitars and a tambourine instead of a double-bass. The violins simply scraped and squealed, the guitars were wretched, but the balalaikas were wonderful. The speed with which they twanged the strings with their fingers was a positive feat of agility. They played dance tunes. At the liveliest part of the tunes, the balalaika-players would tap the case of the instruments with their knuckles; the tone, the taste, the execution, the handling of the instrument and the characteristic rendering of the tune, all was individual, original and typical of the convicts. One of the guitarists, too, played his instrument splendidly. This was the gentleman who had murdered his father. As for the tambourine, it was simply marvellous. The player whirled it round on his finger and drew his thumb across the surface; now we heard rapid, resonant, monotonous taps; then suddenly this loud distinct sound seemed to be broken into a shower of innumerable jangling and whispering notes. Two accordions also appeared on the scene. Upon my word I had had no idea till then what could be done with simple peasant instruments: the blending and harmony of sounds, above all, the spirit, the character of the conception and rendering of the tune in its very essence were simply amazing. For the first time I realized fully all the reckless dash and gaiety of the gay dashing Russian dance songs.

At last the curtain rose. There was a general stir, everyone shifted from one leg to the other, those at the back stood on tiptoe, someone fell off his block of wood, everyone without exception opened his mouth and stared, and absolute silence reigned. . . . The performance began.

Near me was standing Aley in a group consisting of his brothers and all the other Circassians. They were all intensely delighted with the performance, and came every evening afterwards. All Mohammedans, Tatars and others, as I have noticed more than once, are passionately fond of spectacles of all sorts. Next to them Isay Fomitch had tucked himself in. From the moment the curtain rose, he seemed to be all ears and eyes, and simple-hearted, greedy expectations of delights and marvels. It would have been pitiful indeed if he had been disappointed. Aley's charming face beamed with such pure childlike joy that I must confess I felt very happy in looking at him, and I remember that at every amusing and clever sally on the part of the actors, when there was a general burst of laughter, I could not help turning to Aley and glancing at his face. He did not see me—he had no attention to spare for me! On the left side quite near me stood an old convict who was always scowling, discontented and grumbling. He, too, noticed Aley, and I saw him more than once turn with a half-smile towards him: he was so charming! "Aley Semyonitch" he called him, I don't know why.

They began with "Filatka and Miroshka." Filatka acted by Baklushin was really splendid. He played his part with amazing precision. One could see that he had thought out every phrase, every movement. Into the slightest word or gesture he knew how to put value and significance in perfect harmony with the character he was acting. And to this conscientious effort and study must be added an inimitable gaiety, simplicity and naturalness. If you had seen Baklushin, you would certainly have agreed that he was a born actor of real talent. I had seen Filatka more than once at theatres in Moscow and Petersburg, and I can say positively that the city actors were inferior to Baklushin in the part of Filatka. By comparison with him they were too much of *paysans*, and not real Russian peasants. They were too anxious to mimic the Russian peasant. Baklushin was stirred, too, by emulation. Everyone knew that in the second play the part of Kedril would be taken by the convict Potseykin, who was for some reason considered by all a more talented actor than Baklushin, and at this Baklushin was as chagrined as a child. How often he had come to me during those last few days to give vent to his feelings! Two hours before the performance he was in a perfect fever. When they laughed and shouted to him from the crowd: "Bravo, Baklushin! First-rate!", his whole face beamed with pleasure, there was a light of real inspiration in his eyes. The scene of his kissing Miroshka, when Filatka shouts to him beforehand "Wipe your nose!" and wipes his own, was killingly funny. Everyone was rocking with laughter. But what interested me more than all was the audience; they were all completely carried away. They gave themselves up to their pleasure without reserve. Shouts of approbation sounded more and more frequently. One would nudge his neighbour and hurriedly whisper his impressions, without caring or even noticing who was beside him. Another would turn ecstatically to the audience at an amusing passage, hurriedly look at everyone, wave his hand as though calling on everyone to laugh and immediately turn greedily round to the stage again. Another one simply clicked with his fingers and his tongue, and could not stand still, but being unable to move from his place, kept shifting from one leg to the other. By the end of the performance the general gaiety had reached its height. I am not exaggerating anything. Imagine prison, fetters, bondage, the vista of melancholy years ahead, the life of days as monotonous as the drip of water on a dull autumn day, and suddenly all these oppressed and outcast are allowed for one short hour to relax, to rejoice, to forget the weary dream, to create a complete theatre, and to create it to the pride and astonishment of the whole town—to show "what fellows we convicts are!" Of course everything interested them, the dresses, for example; they were awfully curious for instance to see a fellow like Vanka Otpety or Netsvetaev or Baklushin in a different dress from that in which they had seen them every day for so many years. "Why, he is a convict, a convict the same as ever, with the fetters jingling on him, and there he is in a frock-coat, with a round hat on, in a cloak—like an ordinary person! He's got on moustaches and a wig.! Here he's brought a red handkerchief out of his pocket, he is fanning himself with it, he is acting a gentleman—for all the world as though he were a gentleman!" And all were in raptures. "The benevolent country gentleman" came on in an adjutant's uniform, a very old one, it's true, in epaulettes and a cap with a cockade, and made an extraordinary sensation. There were two competitors for the part, and, would you believe it, they quarrelled like little children as to which should play it: both were eager to appear in an adjutant's uniform with shoulder knots. The other actors parted them, and by a majority of votes gave the part to Netsvetaev, not because he was better-looking and more presentable than the other and so looked more like a gentleman, but because Netsvetaev assured them that he would come on with a cane and would wave it about and draw patterns on the ground with it like a real gentleman and tiptop swell, which Vanka Otpety could not do, for he had never seen any real gentlemen. And, indeed, when Netsvetaev came on the stage with his lady, he kept on rapidly drawing patterns on the floor with a thin reedy cane which he had picked up somewhere, no doubt considering this a sign of the highest breeding, foppishness and fashion. Probably at some time in his childhood, as a barefoot servant boy, he had happened to see a finely-dressed gentleman with a cane and been fascinated by his dexterity with it, and the impression had remained printed indelibly on his memory, so that now at thirty he remembered it exactly as it was, for the enchantment and delectation of the whole prison. Netsvetaev was so absorbed in his occupation that he looked at no one; he even spoke without raising his eyes, he simply watched the tip of his cane. "The benevolent country lady," too, was a remarkable conception in its way: she came on in a shabby old muslin dress which looked no better than a rag, with her neck and arms bare, and her face horribly rouged and powdered, with a cotton nightcap tied under her chin, carrying a parasol in one hand and in the other a painted paper fan with which she continually fanned herself. A roar of laughter greeted this lady's appearance; the lady herself could not refrain from laughing several times. A convict called Ivanov took the part. Sirotkin dressed up as a girl looked very charming. The verses, too, went off very well. In fact, the play gave complete satisfaction to all. There was no criticism, and indeed there could not be.

The orchestra played the song, "My porch, my new porch," by way of overture, and the curtain rose again. The second piece was "Kedril," a play somewhat in the style of Don Juan; at least the master and servant are both carried off to hell by devils at the end. They acted all they had, but it was obviously a fragment, of which the beginning and the end were lost. There was no meaning or consistency in it. The action takes place in Russia, at an inn. The innkeeper brings a gentleman in an overcoat and a battered round hat into the room. He is followed by his servant Kedril carrying a trunk and a fowl wrapped up in a piece of blue paper. Kedril wears a sheepskin and a footman's cap. It is he who is the glutton. He was acted by Baklushin's rival, Potseykin. His master was acted by Ivanov, who had been the benevolent lady in the first piece. The innkeeper, Netsvetaev, warns them that the room is haunted by devils and then goes away. The gentleman, gloomy and preoccupied, mutters that he knew that long ago and tells Kedril to unpack his things and prepare the supper. Kedril is a coward and a glutton. Hearing about the devils, he turns pale and trembles like a leaf. He would run away, but is afraid of his master. And, what's more, he is hungry. He is greedy, stupid, cunning in his own way, and cowardly; he deceives his master at every step and at the same time is afraid of him. He is a striking type, which obscurely and remotely suggests the character of Leporello. It was really remarkably rendered. Potseykin had unmistakable talent, and in my opinion was even a better actor than Baklushin. Of course, when I met Baklushin next day, I did not express my opinion quite frankly; I should have wounded him too much. The convict who acted the master acted pretty well, too. He talked the most fearful nonsense; but his delivery was good and spirited, and his gestures were appropriate. While Kedril was busy with the trunk, the master paced up and down the stage lost in thought, and announced aloud that that evening he had reached the end of his travels. Kedril listened inquisitively, made grimaces, spoke

aside, and made the audience laugh at every word. He had no pity for
his master, but he had heard of the devils; he wants to know what
that meant and so he begins to talk and ask questions. His master at
last informs him that in some difficulty in the past he had invoked the
aid of hell; the devils had helped him and had extricated him; but that
to-day the hour had come, and that perhaps that evening the devils
would arrive according to their compact to carry off his soul. Kedril
begins to be panic-stricken. But the gentleman keeps up his spirits
and tells him to prepare the supper. Kedril brightens up, brings out
the fowl, brings out some wine and now and then pulls a bit off the
fowl and tastes it. The audience laughs. Then the door creaks, the
wind rattles the shutters; Kedril shudders and hastily, almost unconsciously, stuffs into his mouth a piece of chicken too huge for him to
swallow. Laughter again. "Is it ready?" asks the gentleman striding
about the room. "Directly, sir . . . I am getting it ready," says Kedril.
He seats himself at the table and calmly proceeds to make away with
his master's supper. The audience is evidently delighted at the smart-
ness and cunning of the servant and at the master's being made a fool
of. It must be admitted that Potseykin really deserved the applause he
got. The words "Directly, sir, I am getting it ready," he pronounced
superbly. Sitting at the table, he began eating greedily, starting at every
step his master took, for fear the latter should notice what he was
about; as soon as the master turned round he hid under the table,
pulling the chicken after him. At last he had taken off the edge of his
appetite; the time came to think of his master. "Kedril, how long will
you be?" cries the master. "Ready," Kedril replies briskly, suddenly realizing that there is hardly anything left for his master. There is nothing but one drumstick left on the plate. The gentleman, gloomy and
preoccupied, sits down to the table noticing nothing, and Kedril
stands behind his chair holding a napkin. Every word, every gesture,
every grimace of Kedril's, when, turning to the audience, he winked
at his simpleton of a master, was greeted by the spectators with irresistible peals of laughter. But as the master begins to eat, the devils appear. At this point the play became quite incomprehensible, and the
devils' entrance was really too grotesque; a door opened in the wing
and something in white appeared having a lantern with a candle in it
instead of a head; another phantom, also with a lantern on his head,
held a scythe. Why the lanterns, why the scythe, why the devils in

white? No one could make out. Though, indeed, no one thought of it. It was evidently as it should be. The gentleman turns pretty pluckily to the devils and shouts to them that he is ready for them to take him. But Kedril is as frightened as a hare; he creeps under the table, but for all his fright does not forget to take the bottle with him. The devils vanish for a minute; Kedril creeps out from under the table. But as soon as the master attacks the chicken once more, three devils burst into the room again, seize the master from behind, and carry him off to the lower regions. "Kedril, save me!" shouts his master, but Kedril has no attention to spare. This time he has carried off the bottle, a plate, and even the loaf under the table. Here he is now, alone; there are no devils, no master either. Kedril creeps out, looks about him and his face lights up with a smile. He winks slyly, sits down in his master's place, and nodding to the audience says in a half-whisper, "Well, now I am alone . . . without a master!" Everyone roars at his being without a master, and then he adds in a half-whisper, turning confidentially to the audience and winking more and more merrily, "The devils have got my master!"

The rapture of the audience was beyond all bounds! Apart from the master's being taken by the devils, this was said in such a way, with such slyness, such an ironically triumphant grimace, that it was impossible not to applaud. But Kedril's luck did not last long. He had hardly taken the bottle, filled his glass and raised it to his lips when the devils suddenly come back, steal up on tiptoe behind him, and seize him under the arms. Kedril screams at the top of his voice; he is so frightened he dare not look round. He cannot defend himself either; he has the bottle in one hand and the glass in the other, and cannot bring himself to part with either. For half a minute he sits, his mouth wide open with fright, staring at the audience with such a killing expression of cowardly terror that he might have sat for a picture. At last he is lifted up and carried away; still holding the bottle, he kicks and screams and screams. His screams are still heard from behind the scenes. But the curtain drops and everyone laughs, everyone is delighted . . . the orchestra strikes up the Kamarinsky.

They begin quietly, hardly audibly, but the melody grows stronger and stronger, the time more rapid; now and then comes the jaunty note of a flip on the case of the instrument. It is the Kamarinsky in all its glory, and indeed it would have been nice if Glinka could by chance have heard it in the prison. The pantomime begins to the music, which is kept up all through. The scene is the interior of a cottage. On the stage are a miller and his wife. The miller in one corner is mending some harness; in the other corner his wife is spinning flax. The wife was played by Sirotkin, the miller by Netsvetaev.

I may observe that our scenery was very poor. Both in this play and in the others we rather supplied the scene from our imagination than saw it in reality. By way of a background there was a rug or a horse-cloth of some sort; on one side a wretched sort of screen. On the left side there was nothing at all, so that we could see the bed, but the audience was not critical and was ready to supply all deficiences by their imagination, and indeed, convicts are very good at doing so. "If you are told it's a garden, you've got to look on it as a garden, if it's a room it's a room, if it's a cottage it's a cottage—it doesn't matter, and there is no need to make a fuss about it."

Sirotkin was very charming in the dress of a young woman. Several compliments were paid him in undertones among the audience. The miller finishes his work, takes up his hat, takes up his whip, goes up to his wife and explains to her by signs that he must go out, but that if his wife admits anyone in his absence then . . . and he indicates the whip. The wife listens and nods. Probably she is well acquainted with that whip: the hussy amuses herself when her husband is away. The husband goes off. As soon as he has gone, the wife shakes her fist after him. Then there is a knock: the door opens and another miller appears, a neighbour, a peasant with a beard, wearing a full coat. He has a present for her, a red kerchief. The woman laughs, but as soon as the neighbour tries to embrace her, there is another knock. Where can he hide? She hurriedly hides him under the table and sits down to her distaff again. Another admirer makes his appearance: an army clerk, in military dress. So far the pantomime had gone admirably, the gestures were perfectly appropriate. One could not help wondering as one looked at these impromptu actors; one could not help thinking how much power and talent in Russia are sometimes wasted in servitude and poverty. But the convict who acted the clerk had probably at some time been on some private or provincial stage, and he imagined that our performers, one and all, had no notion of acting and did not move on the stage as they ought to. And he paced the stage as we are told the classic heroes used to in the past: he would take one long stride, and before moving the other leg, stop short, throw his head and his whole body back, look haughtily around him and take another stride. If such deportment is absurd in the classical drama, in an army clerk in a comic scene it is even more ridiculous. But our audience thought that probably it was as it ought to be and took for granted the long strides of the lanky clerk without criticising them. The clerk had hardly reached the middle of the stage before another knock was heard: the woman was in a flutter again. Where was she to put the clerk? Into a chest which stood conveniently open. The clerk creeps into the chest and she shuts the lid on him. This time it is a different sort of visitor, a lover, too, but of a special kind. It is a Brahmin, and even dressed as one. There is an overwhelming burst of laughter from the audience. The Brahmin was acted by the convict Koshkin, and acted beautifully. He looked like a Brahmin. In pantomime he suggests the intensity of his feelings. He raises his hands to heaven, then lays them on his heart; but he has hardly begun to be sentimental when there is a loud knock at the door. From the sound one can tell it is the master of the house. The frightened wife is beside herself, the Brahmin rushes about like one possessed and implores her to conceal him. She hurriedly puts him behind the cupboard and, forgetting to open the door, rushes back to her work and goes on spinning, heedless of her husband's knocking. In her alarm she twiddles in her fingers an imaginary thread and turns an imaginary distaff, while the real one lies on the floor. Sirotkin acted her terror very cleverly and successfully. But the husband breaks open the door with his foot, and whip in hand approaches his wife. He has been on the watch and has seen it all, and he plainly shows her on his fingers that she has three men hidden and then he looks for the stowaways. The one he finds first is the neighbour, and cuffing him he leads him out of the room. The terrified clerk wanting to escape puts his head out from under the lid and so betrays himself. The husband thrashes him with the whip, and this time the amorous clerk skips about in anything but a classic style. The Brahmin is left; the husband is a long while looking for him. He finds him in the corner behind the cupboard, bows to him politely and drags him by the beard into the middle of the stage. The Brahmin tries to defend himself, shouts "Accursed man, accursed man!" (the only words uttered in the pantomime), but the husband takes no notice and deals with him after his own fashion. The wife, seeing that her turn is coming next, flings down the flax and the distaff and runs out of the room; the spinning-bench tips over on the floor, the convicts laugh. Aley tugs at my arm without looking at me, and shouts to me, "Look! The Brahmin, the Brahmin!" laughing so that he can hardly stand. The curtain falls. A second scene follows.

But there is no need to describe them all. There were two or three more. They were all amusing and inimitably comic. If the convicts did not positively invent them, each of them put something of his own into them. Almost every one of the actors improvised something, so that the following evenings the same parts acted by the same actors were somewhat different. The last pantomime of a fantastic character concluded with a ballet. It was a funeral. The Brahmin with numerous attendants repeated various spells over the coffin, but nothing was of use. At last the strains of the "Setting Sun" are heard, the corpse comes to life and all begin to dance with joy. The Brahmin dances with the re-suscitated corpse and dances in a peculiar Brahminical fashion. And so the theatricals were over till the next evening. The convicts dispersed merry and satisfied; they praised the actors, they thanked the sergeant. There were no sounds of quarrelling. Everyone was unusually con-tented, even as it were happy, and fell asleep not as on other nights, but almost with a tranquil spirit—and why, one wonders? And yet it is not a fancy of my imagination. It's the truth, the reality. These poor people were only allowed to do as they liked, ever so little, to be merry like human beings, to spend one short hour not as though in prison—and they were morally transformed, if only for a few minutes. . . .

Now it is the middle of the night. I start and wake up. The old man is still praying on the stove, and will pray there till dawn. Aley is sleeping quietly beside me. I remember that he was still laughing and talking to his brothers about the theatricals as he fell asleep, and un-consciously I look closer into his peaceful childlike face. Little by lit-tle, I recall everything: the previous day, the holidays, the whole of that month . . . I lift up my head in terror and look round at my sleeping companions by the dim flickering light of the prison candle. I look at their poor faces, at their poor beds, at the hopeless poverty and destitution—I gaze at it—as though I wanted to convince myself that it is really true, and not the continuation of a hideous dream.

But it is true: I hear a moan, someone drops his arm heavily and there is the clank of chains. Another starts in his sleep and begins to speak, while the old man on the stove prays for all "good Christians," and I hear the even cadence of his soft prolonged, "Lord Jesus Christ, have mercy upon us."

"After all, I am not here for ever, only for a few years," I think, and I lay my head on the pillow again.

PART II

CHAPTER I

THE HOSPITAL (1)

SOON AFTER THE HOLIDAYS I was taken ill and went into our military hospital. It stood apart, half a mile from the fortress. It was a long one-storey building painted yellow. In the summer when the buildings were done up, an immense quantity of yellow ochre was spent on it. Round the huge courtyard of the hospital were grouped the offices, the doctors' houses and other buildings. The principal building consisted only of wards for the patients. There were a number of wards, but only two for the convicts, and these were always very crowded, especially in the summer, so that the beds had often to be moved close together. Our wards were full of all sorts of "unfortunate people." Our convicts, soldiers of all sorts awaiting trial, men who had been sentenced and men who were awaiting sentence, and men who were on their way to other prisons, all came here. There were some, too, from the disciplinary battalion—a strange institution to which soldiers who had been guilty of some offence or were not trustworthy were sent for reformation, and from which two or more years later they usually came out scoundrels such as are rarely to be met with. Convicts who were taken ill in our prison usually informed the sergeant of their condition in the morning. Their names were at once entered in the book, and with this book the invalid was sent to the battalion infirmary under escort. There the doctor made a preliminary examination of all the invalids from the various military divisions in the fortress, and any who were found to be really ill were admitted to the hospital. My name was entered in the book, and between one and two, when all the prisoners had gone out to work after dinner, I went to the hospital. The sick convict usually took with him all the money he could collect, some bread—for he could not expect to get rations at the hospital that day—a tiny pipe and a pouch of tobacco with a flint for lighting it. The latter articles he kept carefully hidden in his boots. I entered the precincts of the hospital, feeling some curiosity about this novel aspect of our prison life.

It was a warm, dull, depressing day, one of those days when an institution such as a hospital assumes a peculiarly callous, dejected and sour appearance. I went with the escort into the waiting-room, where there were two copper baths. There were two patients with their escort in the room already, not convicts, but men awaiting their trial. A hospital assistant came in, scanned us indolently with an air of authority, and still more indolently went to inform the doctor on duty. The latter soon made his appearance. He examined us, treated us very kindly, and gave each of us a medical chart with our name on it. The further description of the illness, the medicines and diet prescribed, were left for the doctor who was in charge of the convict wards. I had heard before that the convicts were never tired of praising the doctors. "They are like fathers to us," they said in answer to my inquiries when I was going to the hospital. Meanwhile, we had changed our clothes. The clothes we had come in were taken from us and we were dressed up in hospital underlinen and provided with long stockings, slippers, night-caps and thick cloth dressing-gowns of dark brown colour, lined with something that might have been coarse linen or might have been sticking-plaster. In fact, the dressing-gown was filthy to the last degree, but I only fully realized this later. Then they took us to the convict wards, which were at the end of a very long, clean and lofty corridor. The appearance of cleanliness everywhere was very satisfactory; everything that caught the eye was shining—though perhaps this may have seemed so to me by contrast with the prison. The two prisoners awaiting trial went into the ward on the left, while I went to the right. At the door, which fastened with an iron bolt, stood a sentry with a gun; beside him stood a sub-sentry to relieve him. The junior sergeant (of the hospital guard) gave orders I should be admitted, and I found myself in a long, narrow room, along two walls of which were rows of beds, about twenty-two altogether, of which three or four were unoccupied. The bedsteads were wooden and painted green, of the kind only too familiar to all of us in Russia, the sort of bedstead which by some fatality is never free from bugs. I was put in the corner on the side where there were windows.

As I have said before, there were some convicts from our prison here. Some of these knew me already, or at least had seen me. But the majority were prisoners awaiting trial or from the disciplinary battalions. There were only a few who were too ill to get up. The others suffering from slight ailments, or convalescent, were either sitting on their beds or walking up and down the ward, where there was space enough for exercise between the two rows of beds. There was a suffocating hospital smell in the ward. The air was tainted with unpleasant effluvia of different sorts, as well as with the smell of drugs, although the fire was kept almost all day long in the stove in the corner. My bed had a striped quilt over it. I took it off. Under it was a cloth blanket lined with linen, and coarse sheets and pillow-cases of very doubtful cleanliness. Beside the bed stood a small table with a jug and a tin cup. All this was tidily covered with a little towel put ready for me. Underneath the table was a shelf on which patients kept a jug of kvas, or any such thing, and those who drank tea, a teapot; but very few of them did drink tea. The pipes and tobacco pouches which almost all the patients, even the consumptive ones, possessed were hidden under the mattresses. The doctor and the other attendants scarcely ever examined the beds, and even if they did find a man smoking, they pretended not to notice it. But the convicts were almost always on their guard, and went to the stove to smoke. It was only at night that they sometimes smoked in bed; but no one ever went through the wards at night, except perhaps the officer of the hospital guard.

I had never been a patient in a hospital till then, so everything surrounding me was perfectly new to me. I noticed that I excited some curiosity. They had already heard about me, and stared at me without ceremony, and even with a shade of superciliousness, as a new boy is looked at at school, or a petitioner is looked at in a government office. On the right of me lay a clerk awaiting his punishment, the illegitimate son of a captain. He was being tried for making counterfeit coin, and he had been for a year in the hospital apparently not ill in any way, though he assured the doctors that he had aneurism of the heart. He had attained his object and escaped penal servitude and corporal punishment. A year later he was sent to T——k to be kept at a hospital. He was a broad, sturdily built fellow of eight-and-twenty, a great rogue with a good knowledge of the law, very sharp, extremely self-confident, and free and easy in his behaviour. He was morbidly vain, had persuaded himself in earnest that he was the most truthful and honourable of men and, what is more, had done nothing wrong, and he clung to this conviction to the end. He spoke to me first; he

began questioning me with curiosity, and described to me in some
detail the external routine of the hospital. First of all, of course, he told
me that he was the son of a captain. He was very anxious to make
himself out a nobleman, or at least "of good family."

The next one who approached me was a patient from the disciplinary battalion, and he began to assure me that he knew many of the
"gentleman" exiles, mentioning them by their names. He was a grey-
headed soldier; one could see from his face that he was romancing.
His name was Tchekunov. He was evidently trying to make up to me,
probably suspecting I had money. Noticing that I had a parcel containing tea and sugar, he at once proffered his services in getting a
teapot and making tea. M. had promised to send me a teapot next day
from prison by one of the convicts who came to the hospital to work.
But Tchekunov managed all right. He got hold of an iron pot and
even a cup, boiled the water, made the tea, in fact waited on me with
extraordinary zeal, which at once called forth some malignant jeers at
his expense from a patient lying opposite me. This was a man called
Ustyantsev, a soldier under sentence, who from fear of corporal punishment had drunk a jug of vodka after steeping snuff in it, and had
brought on consumption by so doing; I have mentioned him already.
Till that moment he had been lying silent, breathing painfully, looking at me intently and earnestly and watching Tchekunov with indignation. His extraordinarily bitter intensity gave a comic flavour to his
indignation. At last he could stand it no longer:

"Ugh, the flunky! He's found a master!" he said gasping, his voice
broken with emotion. He was within a few days of his death.

Tchekunov turned to him indignantly.

"Who's the flunkey?" he brought out, looking contemptuously at
Ustyantsev.

"You are a flunkey!" the other replied in a self-confident tone, as
though he had a full right to call Tchekunov over the coals, and in fact
had been appointed to that duty.

"Me a flunkey?"

"That's what you are. Do you hear, good people, he doesn't believe
it! He is surprised!"

"What is it to you? You see the gentleman is helpless. He is not
used to being without a servant! Why shouldn't I wait on him, you
shaggy-faced fool?"

"Who's shaggy-faced?"

"You are shaggy-faced."

"Me shaggy-faced?"

"Yes, you are!"

"And are you a beauty? You've a face like a crow's egg . . . if I am shaggy-faced."

"Shaggy-faced is what you are! Here God has stricken him, he might lie still and die quietly. No, he must poke his nose in! Why, what are you meddling for?"

"Why! Well, I'd rather bow down to a boot than to a dog. My father didn't knuckle under to anybody and he told me not to. I . . . I . . ."

He would have gone on but he had a terrible fit of coughing that lasted for some minutes, spitting blood. Soon the cold sweat of exhaustion came out on his narrow forehead. His cough interrupted him, or he would have gone on talking; one could see from his eyes how he was longing to go on scolding; but he simply waved his hand helplessly, so that in the end Tchekunov forgot about him.

I felt that the consumptive's indignation was directed rather at me than at Tchekunov. No one would have been angry with the latter, or have looked on him with particular contempt, for his eagerness to wait upon me and so earn a few pence. Everyone realized that he did this simply for gain. Peasants are by no means fastidious on that score, and very well understand the distinction. What Ustyantsev disliked was myself, he disliked my tea, and that even in fetters I was like "a master," and seemed as though I could not get on without a servant, though I had not asked for a servant and did not desire one. I did, as a fact, always prefer to do everything for myself, and indeed I particularly wanted not even to look like a spoiled idle person, or to give myself the airs of a gentleman. I must admit while we are on the subject that my vanity was to some extent concerned in the matter. But—I really don't know how it always came to pass—I never could get away from all sorts of helpers and servants who fastened themselves upon me, and in the end took complete possession of me, so that it was really they who were my masters and I who was their servant, though it certainly did appear as though I were a regular "gentleman," as though I gave myself airs, and could not get on without servants. This annoyed me very much, of course. But Ustyantsev was a consumptive and an irritable man. The other patients preserved an air of indifference, in which there was a shade of disdain. I remember they were all absorbed in something particular: from their conversation I learnt that a convict who was then being punished with the sticks was to be brought to us in the evening. The patients were expecting him with some interest. They said, however, that his punishment was a light one—only five hundred blows.

By degrees I took in my surroundings. As far as I could see, those who were really ill were suffering from scurvy and affections of the eye—diseases frequent in that region. There were several such in the ward. Of the others who were really ill, some had fever, skin diseases or consumption. This was not like other wards—here patients of all kinds were collected together, even those suffering from venereal diseases. I speak of "those who were really ill," because there were some here who had come without any disease, "to have a rest." The doctors readily admitted such sham invalids from sympathy, especially when there were many beds empty. Detention in the guard-houses and prisons seemed so disagreeable, compared with the hospital, that many convicts were glad to come to the hospital in spite of the bad air and the locked ward. There were indeed some people, especially from the disciplinary battalion, who were fond of lying in bed and of hospital life in general. I looked at my new companions with interest, but I remember my curiosity was especially aroused by one from our prison, a man who was dying, also consumptive, and also at the last gasp. He was in the bed next but one beyond Ustyantsev, and so almost opposite me. His name was Mihailov; a fortnight before I had seen him in the prison. He had been ill a long while and ought to have been in the doctor's hands long before; but with obstinate and quite unnecessary patience he had controlled himself, and gone on, and only at Christmas he had come into the hospital to die three weeks later of galloping consumption; it was like a fire consuming him. I was struck this time by the awful change in his face, which was one of the first I noticed when I entered the prison; it somehow caught my eye then. Near him was a soldier of the disciplinary battalion, an old man of filthy and revolting habits. . . . However, I cannot go over all the patients. I have mentioned this old man now simply because he made some impression on me at the time, and in the course of one minute gave me a full idea of some peculiarities of the convict ward. This old fellow, I remember, had a very heavy cold at the time. He was constantly sneezing, and went on sneezing for the whole of the following week, even in his sleep, in fits of five or six sneezes at a time, regularly repeating each time, "Oh Lord, what an affliction." At that minute he was sitting on the bed greedily stuffing his nose with snuff from a paper parcel, so that his sneezes might be more violent and complete. He sneezed into a checked cotton handkerchief of his own, that had been washed a hundred times and was faded to the last extreme; and as he sneezed he wrinkled up his nose in a peculiar way into tiny innumerable creases, and showed the relics of ancient blackened teeth between his red dribbling jaws. Then at once he opened his handkerchief, scrutinized the phlegm in it, and immediately smeared it on his brown hospital dressing-gown, so that the handkerchief remained comparatively clean. He did this the whole week. This persistent miserly care of his own handkerchief at the sacrifice of the hospital dressing-gown aroused no sort of protest from the other patients, though one of them would have to wear that dressing-gown after him. But our peasants are not squeamish and are strangely lacking in fastidiousness. I winced at that moment and I could not help at once beginning to examine with disgust and curiosity the dressing-gown I had just put on. Then I realized that it had been attracting my attention for a long time by its strong smell; by now it had become warm on me and smelt more and more strongly of medicines, plasters, and, as I thought, of something decomposing, which was not to be wondered at, since it had been for immemorial years on the backs of patients. Possibly the linen lining may have been washed sometimes; but I am not sure of that. At the present, anyway, it was saturated with all sorts of unpleasant discharges, lotions, matter from broken blisters, and so on. Moreover, convicts who had just received corporal punishment were constantly coming into the convict wards with wounded backs. Compresses were applied and then the dressing-gown being put on straight over the wet shirt could not possibly escape getting messed, and everything that dropped on it remained.

And the whole time I was in prison, that is, several years, I used to put on the dressing-gown with fear and mistrust whenever I had to be in hospital (and I was there pretty often). I particularly disliked the huge and remarkably fat lice I sometimes came across in those dressing-gowns. The convicts enjoyed killing them, so that when one was squashed under the convict's thick, clumsy nail, one could see from the hunter's face the satisfaction it gave him. We particularly disliked bugs, too, and sometimes the whole ward joined in their destruction on a long dreary winter evening. And though, apart from the bad smell, everything on the surface was as clean as possible in the ward, they were far from being fastidious over the cleanliness of the inside, so to speak. The patients were accustomed to it and even accepted it as natural. And indeed the very arrangements of the hospital were not conducive to cleanliness. But I will talk of these arrangements later.

As soon as Tchekunov had made my tea (made, I may mention in parenthesis, with the water in the ward which was brought up only once in the twenty-four hours, and was quickly tainted in the foul atmosphere), the door was opened with some noise and the soldier who had just been punished was led in under a double escort. This was the first time I saw a man after corporal punishment. Afterwards they came in often, some so seriously injured that they had to be carried in, and this was always a source of great interest to the patients, who usually received them with an exaggeratedly severe expression and a sort of almost affected seriousness. However, their reception depended to some extent on the gravity of their crime, and consequently on the number of strokes they had received. Those who had been very badly beaten and were reputed to be great criminals enjoyed greater respect and greater consideration than a runaway recruit, like the one who was brought in now, for instance. But in neither case were there any remarks expressive of special compassion or irritation. In silence they helped the victim and waited upon him, especially if he could not do without assistance. The hospital attendants knew that they were leaving the patient in skilful and experienced hands. The necessary nursing usually took the form of constantly changing the sheet or shirt, which was soaked in cold water and applied to the torn flesh of the back, especially if the patient were too weak to look after himself. Another necessary operation was the skilful extraction of splinters, which were often left in the wounds from broken sticks, and this was usually very painful to the patient. But I was always struck by the extraordinary stoicism with which the victims bore their sufferings. I have seen many of them, sometimes terribly beaten, and hardly one of them uttered a groan! Only their faces

changed and turned white, their eyes glowed, they looked preoccupied and uneasy, their lips quivered, so that the poor fellows often bit
them till they almost bled.

The soldier who had come in was a strongly built, muscular lad of
twenty-three, with a handsome face, tall, well-made and dark-skinned.
His back had been rather badly beaten. The upper part of his body
was stripped to below the waist; on his shoulders was laid a wet
sheet, which made him shiver all over, as though he were in a fever,
and for an hour and a half he walked up and down the ward. I looked
into his face: it seemed to me he was thinking of nothing at that moment; he looked strangely and wildly around with wandering eyes,
which it was evidently an effort for him to fix on anything. It seemed
to me that he looked intently at my tea. The tea was hot and steaming;
the poor fellow was chilled and his teeth were chattering. I offered
him a drink. He turned to me mutely and abruptly, took the cup,
drank it off standing and without putting in sugar, in great haste,
seemingly purposely to avoid looking at me. When he had emptied
it, he put back the cup without a word, and without even a nod to me
began pacing up and down the ward again. He was beyond words or
nods! As for the convicts, they all for some reason avoided speaking to
him; on the contrary, though they helped him at first, they seemed to
try expressly to take no further notice of him afterwards, perhaps
feeling it best to leave him alone as much as possible, and not to
bother him with questions or "sympathy," and he seemed perfectly
satisfied to be left alone.

Meanwhile it got dark and the night-lamp was lighted. Some,
though very few, of the convicts had, it appeared, candlesticks of their
own. At last, after the doctor's evening visit, the sergeant of the guard
came in, counted over the patients and the ward was locked. A tub
was first brought in, and I learnt with surprise that it was kept in the
ward all night, for though there was accommodation only two steps
away in the corridor, it was against the rules for the convicts to leave
the ward on any pretext at night, and even during the day they were
only allowed to be absent for a moment. The convict wards were not
like the ordinary ones, and the convict had to bear his punishment
even in illness. Who had first made this rule I do not know; I only
know that there was no reason for it, and the utter uselessness of such
formalism was nowhere more apparent than in this case. The doctors

were certainly not responsible for the rule. I repeat, the convicts could not say enough in praise of their doctors, they looked on them as fathers and respected them. Everyone was treated with kindness and heard a friendly word from the doctor, and the convicts, cast off by all men, appreciated it, for they saw the genuineness and sincerity of these friendly words and this kindness. It might have been different: no one would have called the doctors to account if they had behaved differently, that is, more roughly and inhumanely; so they were kind from real humanity. And of course they knew that a sick man, even though he were a convict, needed fresh air as much as any other patient, even of the highest rank. Patients in the other wards, those who were convalescent, I mean, could walk freely about the corridors, take plenty of exercise, and breathe fresher air than that of the ward, which was always tainted and inevitably charged with stifling fumes. It is both terrible and disgusting to me now to realize how foul the tainted atmosphere of our ward must have been at night after the tub had been brought into the heated room, where there were patients suffering from dysentery and such complaints. When I said just now that the convict had to bear his punishment even though he were sick, I did not and I do not, of course, suppose that such a rule was made simply as a form of punishment. Of course, that would be senseless calumny on my part. It is useless to punish a sick man. And, since that is so, it follows that probably some stern, inevitable necessity had forced the authorities to a measure so pernicious in its effects. What necessity? But what is so vexatious is that it is impossible to find any explanation of this measure, and many others so incomprehensible that one cannot even conjecture an explanation of them. How explain such useless cruelty? On the theory that the convict will purposely sham illness to get into the hospital, will deceive the doctors, and if allowed to leave the ward at night will escape under cover of darkness? It is impossible to treat such a notion seriously. Where could he escape? How could he escape? In what clothes could he escape? By day they are allowed to leave the room one at a time, and it might be the same at night. At the door stands a sentinel with a loaded gun, and although the lavatory is only two steps from the door, the convict is always accompanied by a guard, and the one double window in it is covered by a grating. To get out of the window it would be necessary to break the grating and the double frame. Who would allow this? Even supposing anything so absurd as that he could first kill the guard without making a noise or letting him cry out, he would still have to break the window frame and the grating. Note that close beside the sentry sleep the ward attendants, and that ten paces away stands another armed sentinel at the door of another convict ward with another guard and other attendants beside him. And where can a man run in the winter in stockings and slippers, in a hospital dressing-gown and a nightcap? And since this is so, since there is so little danger (that is, really, none at all) why a rule so burdensome to the patients, perhaps in the last days of their lives, sick men who need fresh air even more than the healthy? What is it for? I could never understand it.

But since we have once begun asking why, I cannot pass over another point which for many years stood out as the most perplexing fact, for which I could never find a solution. I must say a few words about this before I go on with my description. I am thinking of the fetters, which are never removed from a convict, whatever illness he may be suffering from. Even consumptives have died before my eyes with their fetters on. Yet everyone was accustomed to it, everyone regarded it as an established fact that could not be altered. I doubt whether anybody even thought about it, since during the years I was there it never struck one of the doctors even to petition the authorities that a patient seriously ill, especially in consumption, might have his fetters removed. The fetters were in themselves not a very great weight. They weighed from eight to twelve pounds. It is not too great a burden for a healthy man to carry ten pounds. I was told, however, that after several years the convict's legs begin to waste from wearing fetters. I do not know whether it is true, though there is some probability of it. Even a small weight, a weight of no more than ten pounds, makes the limb abnormally heavy, and may have some injurious action after a length of time. But admitting that it is not too much for a healthy man, is it the same for a sick man? And even supposing it is not too much for an ordinary patient, is it not very different for the dangerously ill, for consumptives whose arms and legs waste away in any case, so that a straw's weight is too heavy for them? And, indeed, if the doctors succeeded in freeing only the consumptives, that would be in itself a really great and good action. Someone will say perhaps that the convict is a wicked man and does not deserve kindness; but surely there is no need to double the sufferings of one who is already stricken by the hand of God! And one cannot believe that this is done simply for the sake of punishment. Even by law the consumptive is exempt from corporal punishment. Consequently we must look upon the retention of fetters as a mysterious and important measure of precaution. But what the reason for it is I cannot imagine. There can really be no fear that the consumptive will escape. Who would dream of such a thing, especially in the advanced stages of the disease? To sham consumption and to deceive the doctors in order to escape is impossible. It is not a disease that can be simulated; it is unmistakable. And by the way, are convicts put into fetters merely to prevent them escaping, or to make it more difficult for them to do so? Certainly not. Fetters are simply a form of degradation, a disgrace, and a physical and moral burden. That at least is what they are meant to be. They could never hinder anyone from running away. The least skilful, the least expert convict can quickly and easily file them off or can smash the rivet with a stone. The fetters are no obstacle at all; and if that is so, if they are put on the condemned convict simply as a punishment, I ask again: is it right to punish a dying man in this way?

And now as I write this, I vividly recall the death of the consumptive patient, Mihailov, whose bed was nearly opposite mine, not far from Ustyantsev's. He died, I remember, four days after I came in. Possibly I have mentioned the case of the consumptives through unconsciously recalling the impressions and ideas which came into my mind at the sight of that death. I knew little of Mihailov himself, however. He was quite young, not more than five-and-twenty, tall, thin, and of extremely attractive appearance. He was in the "special division," and was strangely silent, always gently and quietly melancholy, as though he were "drying up" in prison, as the convicts said of him. He left a pleasant memory among them. I only remember that he had fine eyes, and I really do not know why he comes back to my mind so distinctly. He died at three o'clock in the afternoon on a bright frosty day. I remember the glowing slanting rays of the sun pierced through the green frozen panes of our windows. The sunshine was streaming full on the dying man. He was unconscious, and lay for several hours in the death agony. From early morning he had scarcely recognized those who went up to him. The patients would have liked to do something for him, seeing his distress; his breathing was deep, painful and raucous; his chest heaved as though he could not get air. He flung off his quilt and his clothes, and began at last to tear off his shirt; even that seemed a weight to him. The other patients went to his help and took off his shirt. It was terrible to see that long, long body, the arms and legs wasted to the bone, the sunken belly, the strained chest, the ribs standing out like a skeleton's. Nothing remained on his body but a wooden cross and a little bag with a relic in it, and his fetters which might, it seemed, have slipped off his wasted legs. Half an hour before his death the whole ward was hushed, we began to talk almost in whispers. Everyone moved about noiselessly. The patients did not talk much, and then of other things; they only looked now and then at the dying man, who was gasping more and more terribly. At last, with a straying and uncertain hand, he fumbled at the cross on his chest and began pulling it off, as though even that were a weight that worried and oppressed him. The patients removed the cross, too. Ten minutes later he died. They knocked at the door for the sentry and told him. An attendant came in, looked blankly at the dead man, and went to fetch a medical assistant. The medical assistant, a good-natured young fellow somewhat excessively occupied with his personal appearance, which was prepossessing however, soon came in, went up to the dead man with rapid steps that sounded noisy in the silent ward, and with a particularly unconcerned air, which he seemed to have assumed for the occasion, took his wrist, felt his pulse and went away with a wave of his hand. Word was sent to the sergeant in charge: the criminal was an important one and could not be certified as dead without special ceremony. While we were waiting for the sergeant, one of the convicts suggested in a low voice that it might be as well to close the dead man's eyes. Another man listened attentively, without a word went up to the dead man and closed his eyes. Seeing the cross lying on the pillow, he picked it up, looked at it, and put it round Mihailov's neck again; then he crossed himself. Meanwhile the dead face was growing rigid; the sunlight was flickering on it; the mouth was half open; two rows of white young teeth glistened between the thin parched lips.

At last the sergeant on duty came in, in a helmet and with a sabre, followed by two guards. He went up, moving more slowly as he got nearer, looking in perplexity at the hushed convicts who were gazing grimly at him from all sides. When he was a little way off, he stood stock-still, as though he were scared. The sight of the naked and wasted body with nothing on but the fetters impressed him, and he suddenly unbuckled his sword-belt, took off his helmet, which he was not required to do, and solemnly crossed himself. He was a grim-looking, grey-headed man who had seen many years of service. I remember that at that moment Tchekunov, also a grey-headed man, was standing near. He stared the whole time mutely and intently into the sergeant's face, and with strange attention watched every movement he made. But their eyes met and something made Tchekunov's lower lip quiver; he twisted it into a grin and, nodding rapidly, as it were involuntarily, towards the dead man, he said to the sergeant:

"He too had a mother!" and he walked away. I remember those words stabbed me to the heart. What made him say them, what made him think of them? They began lifting the dead body: they lifted the bed as well; the straw rustled, the chains clanked loudly on the floor in the silent ward . . . they were picked up. The body was carried out. Suddenly everyone began talking aloud. We could hear the sergeant in the corridor sending someone for the smith. The fetters were to be removed from the dead man. . . .

But I am digressing.

CHAPTER II

THE HOSPITAL (2)

THE DOCTORS WENT THEIR rounds in the morning; between ten and eleven they made their appearance in our ward all together, with the chief doctor at their head, and an hour and a half before that our special ward doctor used to visit the ward. At that time our ward doctor was a friendly young man and a thoroughly good doctor. The convicts were very fond of him and only found one fault in him: that he was "too soft." He was in fact not very ready of speech and seemed ill at ease with us, he would almost blush and change the diet at the first request of the patient, and I believe he would even have prescribed the medicines to suit their fancy if they had asked him. But he was a splendid young man.

It may be said that many doctors in Russia enjoy the love and respect of the peasants, and, as far as I have observed, that is perfectly true. I know that my words will seem paradoxical when one considers the distrust of medicine and of foreign drugs universally felt by the common people in Russia. A peasant will, in fact, even in severe illness, go on for years consulting a wise woman, or taking his home-made remedies (which are by no means to be despised), rather than go to a doctor, or into a hospital. There is one important element in this feeling which has nothing to do with medicine, that is, the general distrust felt by the peasants for everything which is stamped with the hall-mark of government; moreover, the people are frightened and prejudiced against hospitals by all sorts of horrible tales and gossip, often absurd but sometimes not without a foundation of fact. But what they fear most is the German routine of the hospital, the presence of strangers about them all the time they are ill, the strict rules in regard to diet, the tales of the rigorous severity of the attendants and doctors and of the cutting open and dissection of the dead and so on. Besides, the people argue that they will be treated by "the gentry," for doctors are after all "gentlemen." But all these terrors disappear

185

very quickly when they come into closer contact with the doctors
(generally speaking, not without exceptions, of course) which I think
is greatly to the credit of our doctors, who are for the most part
young men. The majority of them know how to gain the respect and
even the love of the people. Anyway, I am writing of what I have myself seen and experienced many times and in many places, and I have
no reason to think that things are different in other places. Here and
there, of course, there are doctors who take bribes, make a great
profit out of their hospitals and neglect their patients almost completely, till they forget all they have learnt. Such men are still to be
found, but I am speaking of the majority or rather of the tendency,
the spirit which animates the medical profession in our day. Whatever
one may say in defence of these renegades, these wolves in the fold,
however one may ascribe their shortcomings, for instance, to the
"environment" of which they too are the victims, they will always be
greatly to blame, especially if they also show a lack of humanity. Humanity, kindness, brotherly sympathy are sometimes of more use to
the patients than any medicines. It is high time we gave up apathetic
complaints of being corrupted by our environment. It is true no
doubt that it does destroy a great deal in us, but not everything, and
often a crafty and knowing rogue, especially if he is an eloquent
speaker or writer, will cover up not simply weakness but often real
baseness, justifying it by the influence of his "environment."

But again I have wandered from my subject; I merely meant to say
that the mistrust and hostility of the peasants are directed rather
against medical administration than against the doctors themselves.
When the peasant finds out what they are really like, he quickly loses
many of his prejudices. The general arrangements of our hospitals are
still in many respects out of harmony with the national spirit, their
routine is still antagonistic to the people's habits, and not calculated
to win their full confidence and respect. So at least it seems to me
from some of my personal experiences.

Our ward doctor usually stopped before every patient, examined
and questioned him gravely and with the greatest attention, and prescribed his medicine and his diet. Sometimes he noticed that there
was nothing the matter with the patient, but as the convict had come
for a rest from work, or to lie on a mattress instead of bare boards,
and in a warm room instead of in the damp lock-up, where huge

masses of pale and wasted prisoners were kept awaiting their trial (prisoners awaiting trial are almost always, all over Russia, pale and wasted—a sure sign that they are generally physically and spiritually worse off than convicted prisoners), our ward doctor calmly entered them as suffering from "febris catarrhalis"* and sometimes let them stay even for a week. We all used to laugh over this "febris catarrhalis." We knew very well that this was, by a tacit understanding between the doctor and the patient, accepted as the formula for malingering or "handy shooting pains," which was the convicts' translation of "febris catarrhalis." Sometimes a patient abused the doctor's soft-heartedness and stayed on till he was forcibly turned out. Then you should have seen our ward doctor: he seemed shy, he seemed ashamed to say straight out to the patient that he must get well and make haste to ask for his discharge, though he had full right to discharge him by writing on his chart "sanat est"† without any talk or cajoling. At first he gave him a hint, afterwards he tried as it were to persuade him: "Isn't your time up? You are almost well, you know; the ward is crowded," and so on and so on, till the patient himself began to feel ashamed, and at last asked for his discharge of his own accord. The chief doctor, though he was a humane and honest man (the convicts were very fond of him, too), was far sterner and more determined than the ward doctor; he could even show a grim severity on occasion, and he was particularly respected among us for it. He made his appearance followed by the whole staff, and also examined each patient separately, staying longer with those who were seriously ill, and he always managed to say a kind, encouraging word to them, often full of true feeling. Altogether he made a very good impression. Convicts who came in with a "handy shooting pain" he never rejected nor turned out, but if the patient were too persistent, he simply discharged him: "Well, brother, you've been here long enough, you've had a rest, you can go, you mustn't outstay your welcome." Those who persisted in remaining were either lazy convicts who shirked work, especially in the summer when the hours were long, or prisoners who were awaiting corporal punishment. I remember special

---

*Influenza, flu (Latin).
†Healthy (Latin).

severity, even cruelty, being used in one such case to induce the convict to take his discharge. He came with an eye affection; his eyes
were red and he complained of an acute shooting pain in them. He
was treated with blisters, leeches, drops of some corrosive fluid, but
the malady remained, the eyes were no better. Little by little, the doctors guessed that it was a sham: there was a continual slight inflammation which grew neither worse nor better, it was always in
the same condition. The case was suspicious. The convicts had long
known that he was shamming and deceiving people, though he did
not confess it himself. He was a young fellow, rather good-looking,
indeed, though he made an unpleasant impression on all of them: reserved, suspicious, frowning, he talked to no one, had a menacing
look, held aloof from everyone as though he were suspicious. I remember it even occurred to some people that he might do something violent. He had been a soldier, had been found out in thieving
on a large scale, and was sentenced to a thousand strokes and a convict battalion. To defer the moment of punishment, as I have mentioned before, convicts sometimes resorted to terrible expedients: by
stabbing one of the officials or a fellow convict they would get a new
trial, and their punishment would be deferred for some two months
and their aim would be attained. It was nothing to them that the punishment when it did come, two months later, would be twice or three
times as severe; all they cared about was deferring the awful moment
if only for a few days at any cost—so extreme is sometimes the pros-
tration of spirit of these poor creatures.

Some of the convicts whispered among themselves that we ought to
be on our guard against this man—he might murder someone in the
night. However, it was only talk, no special precautions were taken,
even by those who slept next to him. It was seen, however, that he
rubbed his eyes at night with plaster taken from the wall as well as
with something else, that they might be red in the morning. At last
the head doctor threatened him with a seton. In obstinate eye affections
of long duration when every medical expedient has been tried, to
preserve the sight, the doctors have recourse to a violent and painful
remedy; they apply a seton to the patient as they would to a horse.

But even then the poor fellow would not consent to recover. He
was too obstinate or perhaps too cowardly. A seton perhaps was not
so bad as the punishment with sticks, but it was very painful too. The

patient's skin, as much as one can grip in the hand, is pinched up behind the neck and all of it stabbed through with a knife which produces a long and wide wound all over the back of the neck. Through this wound they thrust a linen tape, rather wide—a finger's breadth. Then every day at a fixed hour they pull this tape in the wound so that it is opened again, that it may be continually separating and not healing. Yet for several days the poor fellow obstinately endured this torture, which was accompanied with horrible suffering, and only at last consented to take his discharge. His eyes became perfectly well in a single day, and as soon as his neck was healed he went to the lock-up to receive next day the punishment of a thousand strokes with sticks.

Of course the minute before punishment is awful; so awful that I am wrong in calling the terror of it cowardice and weakness of spirit. It must be awful when men are ready to endure twice or thrice the punishment, if only they can avoid facing it at once. I have mentioned, however, that there were some who asked for their discharge before their backs were quite healed after the first beating, in order to endure the remainder of their punishment and have their sentence over; and detention in the lock-up awaiting punishment was without doubt incomparably worse for all than life in prison. But apart from the difference in temperaments, years of being accustomed to blows and punishments play a great part in the fortitude and fearlessness of some. Men who have been frequently flogged seem to harden their hearts and their backs; at last they look upon the punishment sceptically, almost as a trifling inconvenience and lose all fear of it. Speaking generally, this is true. One of our convicts in the special divisions, a Kalmuck, who had been christened Alexandr or "Alexandra" as they used to call him in the prison, a queer fellow, sly, fearless and at the same time very good-natured, told me how he got through his four thousand "sticks." He told me about it, laughing and joking, but swore in earnest that if he had not from childhood—his earliest, tenderest childhood—always been under the lash, so that his back had literally never been free from scars all the while he lived with his horde, he never could have endured the punishment. He seemed to bless his education under the lash.

"I was beaten for everything, Alexandr Petrovitch!" he told me one evening, sitting on my bed, before the candles were lighted, "for everything and nothing, whatever happened, I was beaten for fifteen years on end, as far back as I can remember, several times every day; anyone beat me who liked, so that in the end I got quite used to it."

How he came to be a soldier I don't know; I don't remember, though perhaps he told me; he was an inveterate runaway and tramp. I only remember his account of how horribly frightened he was when he was condemned to four thousand "sticks" for killing his superior officer.

"I knew I should be severely punished and that perhaps I shouldn't come out alive, and though I was used to the lash, four thousand strokes is no joke; besides, all the officers were furious with me! I knew, I knew for certain that I shouldn't get through it, that I couldn't stand it; I shouldn't come out alive. First I tried getting christened; I thought maybe they'd forgive me, and though the fellows told me it would be no use, I shouldn't be pardoned, I thought I'd try it. Anyway, they'd have more feeling for a Christian after all. Well, they christened me and at the holy christening called me Alexandr; but the sticks remained, they did not take one off; I thought it was too bad. I said to myself: 'Wait a bit, I'll be a match for you all.' And would you believe it, Alexandr Petrovitch, I was a match for them! I was awfully good at pretending to be dead, that is, not being quite dead, but just on the point of expiring. I was brought out for punishment; I was led through the ranks for the first thousand; it burnt me; I shouted. I was led back for the second thousand; well, thought I, my end is come, they've beaten all sense out of me; my legs were giving way, I fell on the ground; my eyes looked lifeless, my face was blue, I stopped breathing and there was foam on my mouth. The doctor came up. 'He'll die directly,' said he. They carried me to the hospital and I revived at once. Then they led me out twice again and they were angry with me too, awfully angry, and I cheated them twice again; the second time I looked like dead after one thousand; and when it came to the fourth thousand every blow was like a knife in my heart, every blow was as good as three, it hurt so! They were savage with me. That niggardly last thousand—damn it—was as bad as all the three thousand together and had I not died before the very end (there were only two hundred left) they would have beaten me to death. But I took my own part; I deceived them again and shammed death. Again

they were taken in and how could they help being? The doctor believed I was dead. So they beat me for the last two hundred with all
the fury they could, they beat me so that it was worse than two thousand, but yet they didn't kill me, no fear! And why didn't they kill me?
Why, just because I've grown up from childhood under the lash. That's
why I am alive to this day. Ach, I have been beaten in my day!" he
added at the end of the story in a sort of mournful reverie, as though
trying to recall and reckon how many times he had been beaten. "But
no," he added, after a minute's silence. "There's no counting the beatings I've had! How could I? They're beyond reckoning." He glanced at
me and laughed, but so good-naturedly that I could not help smiling
in response. "Do you know, Alexandr Petrovitch, that whenever I
dream at night now, I always dream that I am being beaten? I never
have any other dreams." He certainly often cried out at night and so
loudly that the other convicts waked him up at once by prodding him,
and saying, "What are you shouting for, you devil!" He was a short
sturdy fellow of forty-five, good-humoured and restless; he got on
well with everyone and though he was very fond of stealing, and often got a beating among us for that, after all everyone stole and everyone was beaten for it.

I will add one other point. I was always amazed at the extraordinary good-nature, the absence of vindictiveness, with which all these
victims talked of how they had been beaten, and of the men who had
beaten them. Often there was not the slightest trace of spite or hatred
in their story, which gripped my heart at once, and made it throb violently. Yet they would tell the story and laugh like children.

M., for instance, described his punishment to me. He was not of
the privileged class and received five hundred strokes. I heard of this
from the others and asked him myself whether it were true, and how
it happened. He answered with a certain brevity, as though with an
inward pang; he seemed to avoid looking at me and his face flushed;
half a minute later he did look at me; there was a gleam of hatred in
his eyes, and his lips were quivering with indignation. I felt that he
could never forget that page in his past.

But almost all our convicts (I will not guarantee that there were no
exceptions) took quite a different view of it. It cannot be, I sometimes thought, that they consider themselves guilty and deserving of
punishment, especially when they have committed an offence, not

against one of their own class, but against someone in authority. The majority of them did not blame themselves at all. I have said already that I saw no signs of remorse even when the crime was against one of their class; as for crimes against officers in control of them, they did not count them at all. It sometimes seemed to me that for the latter class of crimes they had a peculiar, so to speak, practical, or rather matter-of-fact, point of view. They put it down to fate, to the inevitability of the act, and this was not done deliberately but was an unconscious attitude, a kind of creed. Though the convict is almost always disposed to consider himself justified in any crime against officers, so much so that there is no question about it in his mind, yet in practice he recognizes that the authorities take a very different view of his crime, and that therefore he must be punished, and then they are quits. It is a mutual struggle. The criminal knows and never doubts that he will be acquitted by the verdict of his own class, who will never, he knows, entirely condemn him (and for the most part will fully acquit him), so long as his offence has not been against his equals, his brothers, his fellow peasants. His conscience is clear, and with that he is strong and not morally disturbed, and that is the chief thing. He feels, as it were, that he has something to rest upon, and so he feels no hatred, but takes what has happened to him as something inevitable which has not begun with him and will not end with him, but will go on for long ages as part of a passive but stubborn and old-established feud. No soldier hates the individual Turk he is fighting with; yet the Turk stabs him, hacks at him, shoots him.

Yet not all the stories I heard, however, showed the same coolness and indifference. They talked of Lieutenant Zherebyatnikov, for instance, with a certain shade of indignation, though even in this case the feeling was not very strong. I made the acquaintance of this Lieutenant Zherebyatnikov when I was first in hospital—from the convicts' stories about him, I mean. Afterwards I met him in the flesh when he was on duty at the prison. He was a tall man about thirty, big and fat, with red puffy cheeks, white teeth and with a loud laugh like Nozdryov's.[9] One could see from his face that he was a man who never thought about anything. He was particularly fond of flogging and punishing with "sticks" when it was his duty to superintend. I hasten to add that I looked upon Lieutenant Zherebyatnikov at the time as a monster, and that was how he was regarded by the convicts themselves. There were, in the past, in that recent past, of course, of which "the tradition is still fresh though it is hard to believe in it,"[10] other officers who were eager to do their duty conscientiously and zealously. But as a rule they did their work in all simplicity of heart without relishing it. Zherebyatnikov had something of the pleasure of an epicure in administering punishment. He was passionately fond of the art of punishing, and he loved it as an art. He enjoyed it and like the worn-out aristocratic debauchees of the Roman Empire, he invented all sorts of subtleties, all sorts of unnatural tricks to excite and agreeably thrill his crass soul.

The convict is led out for punishment; Zherebyatnikov is the officer in command; the mere sight of the long ranks of men drawn up with thick sticks in their hands inspires him. He walks round the ranks complacently, and repeats emphatically that every man is to do his duty thoroughly, conscientiously, or else. . . . But the soldiers don't need to be told what that or else means. Then the criminal is brought out, and if he knows nothing of Zherebyatnikov, if he has not heard all about him, this would be the sort of trick the lieutenant would play on him—one of hundreds, of course; the lieutenant was inexhaustible in inventing them. At the moment when the convict is stripped and his hands are tied to the butt-ends of guns by which the sergeants afterwards drag him down the "Green Street," it is the regular thing for him to beg in a plaintive, tearful voice, entreating the commanding officer to make his punishment easier and not to increase it by unnecessary severity. "Your honour," cries the poor wretch, "have mercy on me, be a father to me; I'll pray for your honour all my life; don't destroy me, have pity on me!"

That was just what Zherebyatnikov wanted; he would pause, and would begin talking to the victim with a sentimental air.

"But what am I to do, my friend?" he would begin. "It's not I am punishing you, it's the law!"

"Your honour, it's all in your hands, have pity on me!"

"Do you suppose I don't feel for you? Do you suppose it's a pleasure to me to see you beaten? I am a man too. Am I a man or not, do you suppose?"

"For sure, your honour, we all know you are our father, we are your children. Be a father to me!" cries the convict, beginning to hope.

"But judge for yourself, my friend—you've got sense; I know that as a fellow creature I ought to be merciful and indulgent even to a sinner like you."

"It's the holy truth you are speaking, your honour."

"Yes, to be merciful however sinful you may be. But it's not my doing, it's the law! Think of that! I have my duty to God and to my country; I shall be taking a great sin upon myself if I soften the law, think of that!"

"Your honour!"

"But there! So be it, for your sake! I know I am doing wrong, but so be it. . . . I will have mercy on you this time. I'll let you off easy. But what if I am doing you harm? If I have mercy on you this once and let you off easily, and you'll reckon on it being the same next time and commit a crime again, what then? It will be on my conscience."

"Your honour! I'd not let friend or foe! As before the throne of the Heavenly Father . . ."

"All right, all right! But do you swear to behave yourself for the future?"

"Strike me dead, may I never in the world to come . . ."

"Don't swear, it's a sin. I'll believe your word. Do you give me your word?"

"Your honour!!!"

"Well, I tell you, I'll spare you simply for your orphan's tears. You are an orphan, aren't you?"

"Yes, your honour, alone in the world, neither father nor mother . . ."

"Well, for the sake of your orphan's tears; but mind you, it's the last time. . . . Take him," he adds in such a soft-hearted way that the convict does not know how to pray devoutly enough for such a benefactor.

But the fearful procession begins; he is led along; the drum begins to boom; the sticks begin flying.

"Give it him!" Zherebyatnikov bawls at the top of his voice. "Whack him! Flay him, flay him! Scorch him! Lay it on, lay it on! Hit him harder, the orphan, harder, the rascal! Touch him up, touch him up!"

And the soldiers hit as hard as they can, the poor wretch begins to scream and there are flashes before his eyes, while Zherebyatnikov runs after him along the line in peals of laughter, holding his sides, and hardly able to stand, so that one felt sorry for the dear man at last.

He is delighted and amused and only from time to time there is a pause in his loud hearty roars of laughter, and one hears again:

"Flay him, flay him! Scorch him, the rascal, scorch him, the orphan! . . ."

Or he would invent another variation. The convict brought out to punishment begins to entreat him again. This time Zherebyatnikov does not grimace or play a part with him, but goes in for frankness:

"I tell you what, my good fellow," he says, "I shall punish you properly, for you deserve it. But I tell you what I'll do for you: I won't tie you to the guns. You shall go alone, but in a new way. Run as fast as you can along the line! Every stick will hit you just the same, but it will sooner be over; what do you think? Would you like to try?"

The convict listens with perplexity and mistrust and hesitates. "Who knows," he thinks to himself, "maybe it will be easier. I'll run as hard as I can and the pain will not last a quarter so long and perhaps not all the sticks will hit me."

"Very well, your honour, I agree."

"Well, I agree too, then. Cut along! Mind now, look sharp!" he shouts to the soldiers, though he knows beforehand that not one stick will miss the guilty back; the soldier knows very well what would be in store for him if he missed.

The convict runs with all his might along the "Green Street," but of course he doesn't get beyond the fifteenth soldier: the sticks fall upon his back like lightning, like the tattoo on a drum, and the poor wretch drops with a scream, as though he had been cut down or struck by a bullet.

"No, your honour, better the regular way," he says, getting up slowly from the ground, pale and frightened.

And Zherebyatnikov, who knows the trick beforehand and how it ends, roars with laughter. But there is no describing all his diversions or all that was said about him.

Stories of somewhat different tone and spirit were told of Lieutenant Smekalov, who was commanding officer of our prison before our major was appointed. Though the convicts talked somewhat unconcernedly and without special anger of Zherebyatnikov, yet they did not admire his exploits, they did not speak well of him and were evidently disgusted by him. Indeed, they seemed to look down upon him with contempt. But Lieutenant Smekalov was remembered among

us with enjoyment and delight. He had no particular liking for punishment. There was nothing of the Zherebyatnikov element in him.
But he was by no means opposed to the lash; yet the fact is that even
his floggings were remembered among the convicts with love and
satisfaction—so successful was the man in pleasing them! And how?
How did he gain such popularity? It is true that the convicts, like all
the Russian people, perhaps, are ready to forget any tortures for the
sake of a kind word; I mention it as a fact without qualifying it in one
way or another. It was not difficult to please these people and to be
popular among them. But Lieutenant Smekalov had won a peculiar
popularity, so that even the way he used to administer punishment
was remembered almost with tenderness. "We had no need of a father," the convicts would say, and they would sigh, comparing their
recollections of their old commanding officer, Smekalov, with the
present major. "He was a jolly good fellow!"

He was a simple-hearted man, good-natured, perhaps, in his own
way. But sometimes it happens that there is a man in authority who
has not only good-nature but a generous spirit, and yet everyone dislikes him and sometimes they simply laugh at him. Smekalov knew
how to behave so that they looked upon him as one of themselves,
and this is a great art, or more accurately an innate faculty, which
even those who possess it never think about. Strange to say, some
men of this sort are not good-natured at all, yet they sometimes gain
great popularity. They don't despise, they don't scorn the people under their control—in that, I think, lies the explanation. There is no
sign of the fine gentleman, no trace of class superiority about them,
there is a peculiar whiff of the peasant inborn in them; and, my
word! what a keen scent the people have for it! What will they not
give for it? They are ready to prefer the sternest man to the most merciful, if the former has a smack of their own homespun flavour. And
what if the same man is really good-natured, too, even though in a
peculiar way of his own? Then he is beyond all price.

Lieutenant Smekalov, as I have said already, sometimes punished
severely, but he knew how to do it so that, far from being resented,
his jokes on the occasion were, even in my day when it was all long
past, remembered with enjoyment and laughter. He had not many such
jokes, however: he was lacking in artistic fancy. In fact, he really had
one solitary joke which was his mainstay for nearly a year; perhaps its

charm lay in its uniqueness. There was much simplicity in it. The guilty convict would be brought in to be flogged. Smekalov comes in with a laugh and a joke, he asks the culprit some irrelevant questions about his personal life in the prison not with any sort of object, not to make up to him, but simply *because he really wants to know*. The birch-rods are brought and a chair for Smekalov. He sits down and even lights his pipe; he had a very long pipe. The convict begins to entreat him. . . . "No, brother, lie down . . . it's no use," says Smekalov. The convict sighs and lies down. "Come, my dear fellow, do you know this prayer by heart?"

"To be sure, your honour, we are Christians, we learnt it from childhood."

"Well then, repeat it."

And the convict knows what to say and knows beforehand what will happen when he says it, because this trick has been repeated thirty times already with others. And Smekalov himself knows that the convict knows it, knows that even the soldiers who stand with lifted rods over the prostrate victim have heard of this joke long ago and yet he repeats it again—it has taken such a hold on him once for all, perhaps from the vanity of an author, just because it is his own composition. The convict begins to repeat the prayer, the soldiers wait with their rods while Smekalov bends forward, raises his hand, leaves off smoking, and waits for the familiar word. After the first lines of the well-known prayer, the convict at last comes to the words, "Thy Kingdom come." That's all he is waiting for. "Stay," cries the inspired lieutenant and instantly turning with an ecstatic gesture to a soldier he cries, "Now give him some."

And he explodes with laughter. The soldiers standing round grin too, the man who thrashes grins, even the man who is being thrashed almost grins, although at the word of command, "Now give him some," the rod whistles in the air to cut a minute later like a razor through his guilty flesh. And Smekalov is delighted, delighted just because he has had such a happy thought, and has himself found the word to rhyme with "come."

And Smekalov goes away perfectly satisfied with himself and, indeed, the man who has been flogged goes away almost satisfied with himself and with Smekalov, and half an hour later he will be telling the story in the prison of how the joke that had been repeated thirty times before had now been repeated for the thirty-first time. "He is a jolly good fellow! He loves a joke!"

There was even a flavour of maudlin sentimentality about some reminiscences of the good-natured lieutenant.

"Sometimes one would go by, brothers," a convict would tell us, his face all smiles at the recollection, "and he'd be sitting in the window in his dressing-gown, drinking his tea and smoking his pipe. I'd take off my cap. 'Where are you off to, Aksyonov?' he'd say. 'Why, to work, Mihail Vassilitch, first thing I must go to the work-room.' He'd laugh to himself. He was a jolly good fellow! Jolly is the only word!"

"We shall never see his like again," one of his listeners would add.

CHAPTER III

THE HOSPITAL* (3)

I HAVE SPOKEN ABOUT corporal punishment and the various officers who had to perform this interesting duty, because it was only when I went into the hospital that I formed an idea from actual acquaintance of these matters, of which, till then, I had only known by hearsay. From all the battalions, disciplinary and otherwise, stationed in our town and in the whole surrounding district, all who had received the punishment of the "sticks" were brought into our two wards. In those early days when I still looked so eagerly at everything about me, all these strange proceedings, all these victims who had been punished or were preparing for punishment, naturally made a very strong impression on me. I was excited, overwhelmed and terrified. I remember that at the same time I began suddenly and impatiently going into all the details of these new facts, listening to the talk and tales of the other convicts on this subject. I asked them questions, tried to arrive at conclusions. I had a great desire to know among other things all about the various grades of sentences and punishments, the varying severity of the different forms of punishments, the attitude of the convicts themselves. I tried to picture to myself the psychological condition of men going to punishment. I have mentioned already that it is unusual for anyone to be unconcerned before punishment, even those who have been severely punished and on more than one occasion. The condemned are overcome by an acute purely physical terror, involuntary and irresistible, which masters the man's whole moral being. Even during my later years in prison, I could not help watching with interest the prisoners who, after being in hospital till the wounds left by the first half of their punishment were healed, were leaving to endure next day the second half of their sentence.

---

*All that I am writing here about corporal punishment was true in my time. Now I am told that all this is changed and still changing (Dostoevsky's note).

This division of the punishment into two parts is always done by the decision of the doctor who is present at the punishment. If the number of strokes to be inflicted is too great for the prisoner to endure all at once, the sentence is inflicted in two or even three parts, according to the decision of the doctor at the actual time, as to whether the prisoner can safely go on walking through the ranks or whether doing so will endanger his life. As a rule five hundred, a thousand, or even fifteen hundred blows are endured at one time; but if the sentence is one of two or three thousand blows, the punishment has to be divided into two or even into three parts. Men leaving hospital for the second half of their punishment, after their wounded backs were healed, were usually gloomy, sullen and disinclined to talk on the day of their discharge and the day before. There was noticeable in them a certain dullness of intelligence, a sort of unnatural preoccupation. A man in this position does not readily enter into conversation, and is for the most part silent; what is interesting is that the convicts themselves never talk to him, and do not attempt to speak of what is in store for him. There is no unnecessary talk, nor attempt at consolation; they even try to pay no attention to him. Of course this is better for the victim.

There are exceptions: Orlov, for instance, whose story I have told already. After the first half of his punishment was over, the only thing that vexed him was that his back was so long healing, that he could not take his discharge sooner. He wanted to get the second half of his punishment over as soon as possible and to be sent off to his place of exile, hoping to escape on the road. But this man was kept up by the object he had in view, and God knows what was in his mind. His was a vital and passionate nature. He was much pleased and in a state of great excitement, though he controlled his feelings: for, before receiving the first part of his punishment, he had thought that they would not let him off alive, and that he would die under the sticks. Even while he was on his trial various rumours had reached him of what the authorities meant to do, and he prepared himself then to die. But, having got through the first half of the sentence, his spirits revived. He was brought into the hospital half dead: I had never seen such wounds; but he came in with joy in his heart, with the hope that he would outlive it, that the rumours were false. Having once come out alive from the sticks, he began now, after his long imprisonment, to dream of the open road, of escape, freedom, the plain and the forest. Two days after his discharge he died in the same hospital and in the same bed, after the second half of his punishment. But I have spoken of this already.

Yet the very prisoners whose days and nights were so gloomy beforehand endured the punishment itself with manly fortitude, even the most faint-hearted of them. I rarely heard a groan even on the first night of their arrival, and even from the most cruelly punished; the people as a rule know how to bear pain. I asked many questions about the pain. I wanted to find out definitely how bad the pain was, with what it might be compared. I really do not know what induced me to do this. I only remember one thing, that it was not from idle curiosity. I repeat that I was shaken and distressed. But I could not get a satisfactory answer from anyone I asked. It burns, scorches like fire—was all I could find out, and that was the one answer given by all. During those early days, as I got to know M. better, I asked him. "It hurts dreadfully," he said, "and the sensation is burning like fire; as though your back were being roasted before the hottest fire." In fact everyone said the same thing. But I remember that I made at the time one strange observation, for the accuracy of which I do not vouch, though the unanimous verdict of the prisoners on the subject strongly confirms it: that is that the birch, if many strokes are inflicted, is the worst of all punishments in use in Russia. At first sight it might seem that this was absurd and impossible. Yet five hundred, even four hundred, strokes may kill a man, and more than five hundred strokes are almost certain to. Even the man of the strongest endurance cannot survive a thousand. Yet five hundred blows with "sticks" can be endured without the slightest danger to life. Even men of not very strong constitution can endure the punishment of a thousand "sticks" without danger. Even two thousand will hardly kill a man of medium strength and healthy constitution. The convicts all said that the birch was worse than the "sticks." "The birch smarts more," they told me, "it's more agony." There is no doubt the birch is more agonizing than the sticks. It is more irritating, it acts more acutely on the nerves, excites them violently, and strains them beyond endurance. I do not know how it is now, but in the recent past there were gentlemen who derived from the power of flogging their victims something that suggests the Marquis de Sade and the Marquise de Brinvilliers.[11] I imagine there is something in this sensation which sends a thrill at once sweet and painful to the hearts of these gentlemen. There are people who are like tigers thirsting for blood. Anyone who has once experienced this power, this unlimited mastery of the body, blood and soul of a fellow man made of the same clay as himself, a brother in the law of Christ— anyone who has experienced the power and full licence to inflict the greatest humiliation upon another creature made in the image of God will unconsciously lose the mastery of his own sensations. Tyranny is a habit; it may develop, and it does develop at last, into a disease. I maintain that the very best of men may be coarsened and hardened into a brute by habit. Blood and power intoxicate; coarseness and depravity are developed; the mind and the heart are tolerant of the most abnormal things, till at last they come to relish them. The man and the citizen is lost for ever in the tyrant, and the return to human dignity, to repentance and regeneration becomes almost impossible. Moreover, the example, the possibility of such despotism, has a perverting influence on the whole of society: such power is a temptation. Society, which looks indifferently on such a phenomenon, is already contaminated to its very foundations. In short, the right of corporal punishment given to one man over another is one of the sores of social life, one of the strongest forces destructive of every germ, every effort in society towards civic feeling, and a sufficient cause for its inevitable dissolution.

The professional torturer is an object of disgust to society, but a gentleman torturer is far from being so. It is only lately that an opposite idea has been expressed, and that only in books and abstractly. Even those who express it have not all been able to extinguish in themselves the lust of power. Every manufacturer, every capitalist, must feel an agreeable thrill in the thought that his workman, with all his family, is sometimes entirely dependent on him. This is undoubtedly true: a generation does not so quickly get over what has come to it as a legacy from the past; a man does not so easily renounce what is in his blood, what he has, so to speak, sucked in with his mother's milk. Such rapid transformations do not occur. To acknowledge one's fault and the sins of one's fathers is little, very little; one must uproot the habit of them completely, and that is not so quickly done.

I have spoken of the torturer. The characteristics of the torturer exist in embryo in almost every man of to-day. But the brutal qualities do not develop equally. If they develop so as to overpower all the man's other qualities, he becomes, of course, a hideous and terrible figure. Torturers are of two kinds: some act of their own free will, others involuntarily, of necessity. The voluntary torturer is, of course, more degraded in every respect than the other, though the latter is so despised by the people, inspiring horror, loathing, an unaccountable, even mysterious, terror. Why this almost superstitious horror for one torturer and such an indifferent, almost approving, attitude to the other?

There are instances that are strange in the extreme. I have known people good-natured, even honest, and even respected by society who yet could not with equanimity let a man go until he screamed out under the lash, till he prayed and implored for mercy. It was the duty of men under punishment to cry out and pray for mercy. That was the accepted thing: it was looked upon as necessary and proper, and when, on one occasion, the victim would not scream, the officer, whom I knew personally and who might perhaps have been regarded in other relations as a good-natured man, took it as a personal insult. He had meant at first to let him off easily, but not hearing the usual "your honour, father, have mercy, I'll pray to God for you all my life" and the rest of it, he was furious, and gave the man fifty lashes extra, trying to wring cries and supplications out of him—and he attained his end. "It couldn't be helped, the man was rude," he said to me quite seriously.

As for the actual executioner who is not a free agent but acts under compulsion, he is as everyone knows a condemned convict who escapes his sentence by turning executioner. At first he learns his calling from another executioner, and when he is expert, he is attached permanently to the prison, where he lives apart in a special room, keeping house for himself, though he is almost always guarded. Of course, a live man is not a machine; although the executioner beats as a duty, he sometimes grows keen on his work, but, though the beating may be some satisfaction to himself, he scarcely ever feels personal hatred for his victim. His dexterity, his knowledge of his art and his desire to show off before his fellow convicts and the public stimulate his vanity. He exerts himself for art's sake. Besides, he knows very well that he is an outcast, that he is met and followed everywhere by superstitious terror, and there is no saying that this may not have an influence on him, may not accentuate ferocity and brutal tendencies in him. Even children know that he "has disowned father and mother." Strange to say, though, of the executioners I have seen, all have been men of some education, men of sense and intelligence who had an extraordinary vanity, even pride. Whether this pride has been developed in them in reaction against the general contempt felt for them, or whether it has been increased by the consciousness of the terror they inspire in their victim and the feeling of mastery over him, I do not know. Possibly the very ceremony and theatrical surroundings with which they make their appearance on the scaffold before the public help to develop a certain haughtiness in them. I remember that I had once for some time opportunities of frequently meeting an executioner and closely observing him. He was a thin, muscular man of forty, of medium stature with a rather pleasant, intelligent face and a curly head. He was always extraordinarily calm and dignified, behaved like a gentleman, always answered briefly, sensibly and even affably; but there was a haughtiness in his affability, as though he felt superior to me. The officers on duty often addressed him before me, and they positively showed him a sort of respect. He was conscious of this and before the officers he redoubled his politeness, frigidity and sense of personal dignity. The more friendly the officer was to him, the more unbending he became, and though he never departed from his refined courtesy, I am sure that he felt himself at the moment infinitely superior to the officer who was addressing him. One could see this from his face. Sometimes on hot summer days he would be sent under guard with a long thin pole to kill dogs in the town. There were an immense number of these dogs, who belonged to no one and multiplied with extraordinary rapidity. In hot weather they became dangerous, and by order of the authorities the executioner was sent to destroy them. But even this degrading duty evidently did not in the least detract from his dignity. It was worth seeing the majesty with which he paced up and down the town, accompanied by the weary guard, scaring the women and children by his very appearance, and how calmly and even superciliously he looked at all who met him.

The executioners have a very good time of it, though. They have plenty of money, they are very well fed, and have vodka to drink. They get money from bribes. The civilian prisoner who is condemned to corporal punishment always makes the executioner a preliminary present of something, even if it is his last penny. But from some rich prisoners the executioner demands a sum suitable to the victim's supposed means; they will exact as much as thirty roubles, sometimes even more. They bargain dreadfully with very rich prisoners. But the executioner cannot punish a man very lightly; he would answer for it with his own back. For a certain sum, however, he will promise the victim not to chastise him very severely. The condemned men almost always agree to his terms, for if they don't he really will punish them savagely, and it lies almost entirely in his hands. It sometimes happens that he demands a considerable ransom from a very poor prisoner; the relations come, bargain and bow down to him, and woe betide them if they do not satisfy him. In such cases the superstitious terror he inspires is a great help to him. What wild stories are told of executioners! The convicts themselves assured me that an executioner can kill a man at one blow. But when has there been an instance of this? However, it may be so. Of this they spoke with absolute confidence. The executioner assured me himself that he could do so. They told me, too, that he could aim a swinging blow at the convict's back, yet so that not the slightest bruise would follow and the convict would feel no pain. But of all these tricks and subtleties too many stories have been told already.

But even if the executioner is bribed to let the victim off easily, he gives the first blow with all his might. That is the invariable habit. He softens the later blows, especially if he has received his payment. But whether he has been bought off or not, the first blow is his own affair. I really do not know why this is their custom—whether to prepare the victim for the later blows, on the theory that after a very bad one the slighter ones will seem less painful, or whether simply to show off his power to the victim, to strike terror into him, to crush him at once, that he may realize the sort of man he has to deal with, to display himself, in fact. In any case, the executioner is in a state of excitement before he begins his work; he feels his power, he is conscious of mastery; at that moment he is an actor; the public gazes at him with wonder and alarm, and there is no doubt that he enjoys shouting to his victim at the first stroke, "Ready now, I'll scorch you"—the fatal and habitual phrase on these occasions. It is hard to imagine how far a man's nature may be distorted!

During those early days in the hospital, I listened with interest to all these convict stories. It was very dull for us all, lying in bed. One day was so much like another! In the morning we were entertained by the visit of the doctors, and soon after that, dinner. Eating, of course, was a great recreation in the monotony of our existence. The rations were various, as prescribed for the different patients. Some of them only had soup with some cereal in it, others only had porridge, others were restricted to semolina pudding, for which there were always many candidates. The convicts had grown nice from lying in bed so long and were fond of dainties. The convalescent received a slice of boiled beef, "bull" as they called it. Those who had scurvy were the best fed of all—they got beef with onion, horseradish and such things, and sometimes a glass of vodka. The bread, too, differed according to the patient's complaint; some was black, while some was nearly white and was well baked. This formality and exactitude in prescribing their diet only served to amuse the patients. Of course some patients did not care to eat at all. But those who had an appetite ate whatever they liked. Some exchanged their rations, so that the diet appropriate for one complaint was eaten by a patient suffering from something quite different. Others who were prescribed a lowering diet bought the beef or the diet prescribed for the scurvy, drank kvas or the hospital beer, buying it from those to whom it was prescribed. Some individuals even consumed the rations of two. The plates of food were sold and resold for money. A helping of beef was priced rather high; it cost five farthings. If there was none to sell in our ward, we used to send the attendant to the other convict ward, and if we could not get it there, we would send to the soldiers' or "free" ward, as it was called. Patients who wanted to sell it could always be found. They were left with nothing but bread, but they made money. Poverty, of course, was universal, but those who had money sent to market for rolls and even sweet things. Our attendants carried out all these commissions quite disinterestedly.

After dinner was the dreariest time; some of us, bored with nothing to do, fell asleep, while some were gossiping, others were quarrelling, others were telling stories. If no fresh patients were brought in, it was even duller. A new arrival almost always made some sensation, especially if no one knew him. The patients scrutinized him, tried to find out who and what he was, where he came from and what brought him there. They were particularly interested in those who were being forwarded to other prisons. These always had something to tell, though not as a rule about their personal life; if they did not speak of that of their own accord, they were never questioned about it, but were only asked where had they come from? With whom? What sort of a journey they had? Where they were going? and so on. Some were at once reminded by their account of something in their own past, and told of different journeys, parties and the officers in charge of them.

Prisoners who had suffered the punishment of the "sticks" were brought in about that time also, towards evening, that is. Their arrival always made rather a sensation as I have mentioned already, but they did not come every day, and on the days when there were none of them we felt dreary; all the patients seemed fearfully bored with one another and they even began to quarrel. We were glad to see even the lunatics, who were brought in to be kept under observation. The trick of pretending to be mad to escape corporal punishment was frequently adopted by convicts. Some were quickly detected, or rather they changed their tactics, and the convict who had been playing antics for two or three days would suddenly, apropos of nothing, behave sensibly, calm down and begin gloomily asking to be discharged. Neither the convicts nor the doctors reproached such a man, or tried to put him to shame by reminding him of the farce he had been playing. They discharged him without a word and let him go. Two or three days' later he was brought back after punishment. Such cases were, however, rare on the whole.

But the real madmen who were brought for observation were a perfect curse for the whole ward. Some of the lunatics who were lively, in high spirits, who shouted, danced and sang were at first welcomed by the convicts almost with enthusiasm. "Here's fun!" they would say, watching the antics of some new arrival. But I found it horribly painful and depressing to see these luckless creatures. I could never look at madmen without feeling troubled.

But the continual capers and uneasy antics of the madman who was welcomed with laughter on his arrival soon sickened us all, and in a day or two exhausted our patience. One of them was kept in our ward for three weeks, till we all felt like running away. To make matters worse, another lunatic was brought in at that very time, who made a great impression upon me. This happened during my third year in the prison. During my first year, or rather my first months, in prison, in the spring I went to a brickyard a mile and a half away to carry bricks for a gang of convicts who worked as stove builders. They had to mend the kilns in readiness for making bricks in the summer. That morning M. and B. introduced me to the overseer of the brick-yard, a sergeant called Ostrozhsky. He was a Pole, a tall thin old man of sixty, of extremely dignified and even stately appearance. He had been in the army for many years, and though he was a peasant by birth and had come to Siberia as a simple soldier after 1830, yet M. and B. loved and respected him. He was always reading the Catholic Bible. I con-versed with him and he talked with much friendliness and sense, de-scribed things interestingly, and looked good-natured and honest. I did not see him again for two years; I only heard that he had got into trouble about something; and suddenly he was brought into our ward as a lunatic. He came in shrieking and laughing, and began dancing about the ward with most unseemly and indecent actions. The con-victs were in ecstacies, but I felt very sad. Three days later we did not know what to do with him; he quarrelled, fought, squealed, sang songs even at night, and was continually doing such disgusting things that all began to feel quite sick. He was afraid of no one. They put him in a strait waistcoat, but that only made things worse for us, though without it he had been picking quarrels and fighting with almost everyone. Sometimes during those three weeks the whole ward rose as one man and begged the senior doctor to transfer our precious visitor to the other convict ward. There a day or two later they begged that he should be transferred back. And, as there were two restless and quar-relsome lunatics in the hospital at once, the two convict wards had them turn and turn about and they were one as bad as the other. We all breathed more freely when at last they were taken away.

I remember another strange madman. There was brought in one summer day a healthy and very clumsy-looking man of forty-five, with a face horridly disfigured by smallpox, with little red eyes buried in fat, and a very gloomy and sullen expression. They put him next to me. He turned out to be a very quiet fellow, he spoke to no one, but sat as though he were thinking about something. It began to get dark and suddenly he turned to me. He began telling me without the slightest preface, but as though he were telling me a great secret, that he was in a few days to have received two thousand "sticks," but that now it would not come off because the daughter of Colonel G. had taken up his case. I looked at him in perplexity and answered that I should not

have thought that the colonel's daughter could have done anything in
such a case. I had no suspicions at the time; he had been brought in
not as a lunatic but as an ordinary patient. I asked him what was the
matter with him. He answered that he did not know, that he had been
brought here for some reason, that he was quite well, but that the
colonel's daughter was in love with him; that a fortnight ago she had
happened to drive past the lock-up at the moment when he was
looking out of the grated window. She had fallen in love with him as
soon as she saw him. Since then, on various pretexts she had been
three times in the lock-up; the first time she came with her father
to see her brother, who was then an officer on duty there; another
time she came with her mother to give them alms, and as she passed
him she whispered that she loved him and would save him. It was
amazing with what exact details he told me all this nonsense, which,
of course, was all the creation of his poor sick brain. He believed devoutly that he would escape corporal punishment. He spoke calmly
and confidently of this young lady's passionate love for him, and although the whole story was so absurd, it was uncanny to hear such a
romantic tale of a love-sick maiden from a man nearly fifty of such a
dejected, woebegone and hideous appearance. It is strange what the
fear of punishment had done to that timid soul. Perhaps he had really
seen someone from the window, and the insanity, begotten of terror
and growing upon him every hour, had at once found its outlet and
taken shape. This luckless soldier, who had very likely never given a
thought to young ladies in his life before, suddenly imagined a whole
romance, instinctively catching at this straw. I listened without an-
swering and told the other convicts about it. But when the others
showed their curiosity he preserved a chaste silence.

Next day the doctor questioned him at length, and as he said that
he was not ill in any way, and as on examination this seemed to be
true, he was discharged. But we only learnt that they had put *sanat* on
his case-sheet after the doctors had left the ward, so that it was impossible to tell them what was the matter with him. And indeed we
hardly realized ourselves at the time what was really the matter. It was
all the fault of the officers who had sent him to the hospital without
explaining why they had sent him. There must have been some over-
sight. And perhaps those responsible may not have been at all sure
that he was mad, and had acted on vague rumours in sending him to

the hospital to be watched. However that may have been, the poor
fellow was taken out two days later to be punished. The unexpected-
ness of his fate seems to have been a great shock to him; he did not
believe in it till the last minute, and when he was led between the
ranks he screamed for help. When he was brought back to the hospital afterwards, he was taken to the other convict ward, as there was
no bed empty in ours. But I inquired about him and learnt that for
eight days he did not say a word to anyone, that he was crushed and
terribly depressed. He was transferred elsewhere, I believe, when his
back was healed. I never heard anything more of him, anyway.

As for the general treatment and the drugs, so far as I could see,
the patients who were only slightly ill scarcely followed the prescrip-
tions or took their medicines at all. But all who were seriously ill, all
who were really ill, in fact, were very fond of being doctored, and
took their mixtures and powders punctually, but what they liked best
of all were external remedies. Cuppings, leeches, poultices and
blood-letting—the remedies which our peasants are so fond of and
put such faith in—were accepted by the patients readily, even with
relish. I was interested by one strange circumstance. The very men
who were so patient in enduring agonizing pain from the sticks and
the birch often complained, writhed and even groaned when they
were cupped. Whether they had grown soft through illness or were
simply showing off, I really do not know. It is true our cuppings were
of a peculiar sort. The assistant had at some remote period lost, or
spoilt, the instrument with which the skin was pierced, or perhaps it
was worn out, so that he was obliged to make the necessary incisions
with a lancet. About twelve such incisions are made for every cupping; with the proper instrument it does not hurt. Twelve little pricks
are made instantaneously and the pain is scarcely felt. But when the
incisions are made by the lancet it is a very different matter: the
lancet cuts comparatively slowly, the pain is felt, and as for ten cuppings, for example, a hundred and twenty of such cuts had to be
made, the whole operation was rather unpleasant. I have tried it; but
though it was painful and annoying, still it was not so bad that one
couldn't help moaning over it. It was positively absurd sometimes to
see a tall sturdy fellow wriggling and beginning to whine. Perhaps
one may compare it with the way a man, who is firm and even self-
possessed in a matter of importance, will sometimes be moody and

fanciful at home when he has nothing to do, will refuse to eat what is given to him, scold and find fault, so that nothing is to his taste, everyone annoys him, everyone is rude to him, everyone worries him—will, in short, "wax fat and wanton," as is sometimes said of such gentlemen, though they are met even among the peasantry, and, living altogether as we did, we saw too many of them in our prison. Such a weakling would often be chaffed by the other convicts in the ward, and sometimes even abused by them. Then he would subside, as though he had only been waiting for a scolding to be quiet. Ustyantsev particularly disliked this complaining and never lost an opportunity for abusing the grumbler. He seized every chance of finding fault with anyone, indeed. It was an enjoyment, a necessity for him, due partly to his illness no doubt, but partly also to the dullness of his mind. He would first stare at the offender intently and earnestly and then begin to lecture him in a voice of calm conviction. He meddled in everything, as though he had been appointed to watch over the discipline and the general morality of the ward.

"He has a finger in every pie," the convicts would say, laughing. But they were not hard on him and avoided quarrelling with him; they only laughed at him sometimes.

"What a lot of talk!" they would say. "More than three wagon loads."

"A lot of talk? We don't take off our caps to a fool, we all know. Why does he cry out over a lancet prick? You must take the crust with the crumb, put up with it."

"But what business is it of yours?"

"No, lads," interrupted one of our convicts, "the cupping is nothing, I've tried it; but there's no pain worse than having your ear pulled for too long."

Everyone laughed.

"Why, have you had yours pulled?"

"Don't you believe it, then? Of course I have."

"That's why your ears stick out so."

The convict in question, whose name was Shapkin, actually had very long prominent ears. He had been a tramp, was still young, and was a quiet and sensible fellow who always spoke with a sort of serious concealed humour, which gave a very comical effect to some of his stories.

"But why should I suppose you'd had your ears pulled? And how was I to imagine it, you thickhead?" Ustyantsev put in his spoke again, addressing Shapkin with indignation, though the latter had not spoken to him but to the company in general. Shapkin did not even look at him.

"And who was it pulled your ear?" asked someone.

"Who? Why, the police captain, to be sure. That was in my tramping days, mates. We reached K. and there were two of us, me and another tramp, Efim, who had no surname. On the way we had picked up a little something at a peasant's at Tolmina. That's a village. Well, we got to the town and looked about to see if we could pick up something here and make off. In the country you are free to go north and south and west and east, but in the town you are never at ease, we know. Well, first of all we went to a tavern. We looked about us. A fellow came up to us, a regular beggar, with holes in his elbows, but not dressed like a peasant. We talked of one thing and another.

" 'And allow me to ask, have you got papers* with you or not?'

" 'No,' we said, 'we haven't.'

" 'Oh!' says he, 'I haven't either. I have two other good friends here,' says he, 'who are in General Cuckoo's service too.† Here we've been going it a little and meanwhile we've not earned a penny. So I make bold to ask you to stand us a pint.'

" 'With the greatest of pleasure,' say we. So we drank. And they put us up to a job that is in our own line, housebreaking. There was a house at the end of the town and a rich man lived there, with lots of property; so we decided to call on him at night. But we were caught, all the five of us, that night in his house. We were taken to the police station and then straight to the police captain's. 'I'll question them myself,' says he. He came in with a pipe, a cup of tea was brought in after him. He was a hearty-looking fellow, with whiskers. He sat down. Three others were brought in besides ourselves, tramps too. A tramp's a funny chap, you know, brothers: he never remembers anything; you might break a post on his head, you won't make him remember; he knows nothing. The police captain turned straight to me.

---

*Passports are meant (Dostoevsky's note).

†That is, living in the woods. He means that they too were tramps (Dostoevsky's note).

'Who are you?' he growled out at me with a voice that came out of his boots. Well, of course, I said what we all do: 'I don't remember anything, your honour, I've forgotten.'

" 'Wait a bit, I shall have something more to say to you, I know your face,' says he, staring, all eyes, at me. But I had never seen him before. Then to the next: 'Who are you?'

" 'Cut-and-run, your honour.'

" 'Is that your name?'

" 'Yes, your honour.'

" 'All right, you're Cut-and-run; and you?' he turns to the third.

" 'And I follow him, your honour.'

" 'But what's your name?'

" 'That's my name, your honour: I follow him.'

" 'But who has given you that name, you rascal?'

" 'Good people, your honour. There are good people in the world, your honour, we all know.'

" 'And who are these good people?'

" 'I've rather forgotten, your honour, you must graciously forgive me.'

" 'You've forgotten them all?'

" 'Yes, all, your honour.'

" 'But you must have had a father and mother? You must remember them, anyway?'

" 'It must be supposed I had them, your honour, but I've rather forgotten them too; perhaps I did have them, your honour.'

" 'But where have you lived till now?'

" 'In the woods, your honour.'

" 'Always in the woods?'

" 'Always.'

" 'And what about the winter?'

" 'I haven't seen the winter, your honour.'

" 'And you, what's your name?'

" 'Hatchet, your honour.'

" 'And you?'

" 'Quick-sharpener, your honour.'

" 'And you?'

" 'Sharpener—for sure, your honour.'

" 'You none of you remember anything?'

" 'None of us, your honour.'

"He stands and laughs and they look at him and laugh. But another time he might give you one in the jaw, it's all luck. And they were such a fat sturdy lot. 'Take them to prison,' says he, 'I'll talk to them later, but you stay here,' says he to me. 'Come this way, sit down.' I look—there's a table, paper and pen. What is he up to now? thinks I. 'Sit down on the chair,' says he, 'take the pen, write,' and he took hold of my ear and pulled it. I looked at him as the devil looked at the priest: 'I can't, your honour,' says I. 'Write!' says he. 'Have mercy, your honour!' 'Write,' says he, 'write as best you can.' And he kept pulling and pulling my ear and suddenly gave it a twist. Well, I tell you, lads, I'd rather have had three hundred lashes. There were stars before my eyes! 'You write, and that's all about it.' "

"Why, was he crazy or what?"

"No, he wasn't crazy. But not long before a clerk at. T. had played a fine prank: he nabbed the government money and made off with it, and he had ears that stuck out too. Well, they sent word of it in all directions and I seemed like the description. So he was trying whether I knew how to write and how I wrote."

"What a position, lad! And did it hurt?"

"I tell you it did."

There was a general burst of laughter.

"Well, and did you write?"

"Why, how could I write? I began moving the pen and I moved it about over the paper; he gave it up. He gave me a dozen swipes in the face and then let me go, to prison too, of course."

"And do you know how to write?"

"I did once, but since folks began writing with pens I lost the art."

Well, it was in tales like these or rather in chatter like this that our weary hours were spent. Good God, how wearisome it was! The days were long, stifling, exactly like one another. If one had only a book! And yet I was constantly going to the hospital, especially at first, sometimes because I was ill and sometimes simply for a rest, to get away from the prison. It was unbearable there, more unbearable than here, morally more unbearable. The hatred, enmity, quarrelling, envy, the continual attacks on us "the gentlemen," the spiteful, menacing faces! Here in the hospital all were more on an equal footing and lived more amicably. The saddest time of the whole day was the beginning of the evening when the candles were lit and night was coming on. They settled down to sleep early. The dim night-lamp gleamed, a spot of brightness in the distance near the door, while at our end it was half dark. The air grew close and fetid. Some patient unable to sleep would get up and sit for a couple of hours on his bed, his head bent forward in his nightcap, as though pondering something. One looks at him for an hour to pass the time and wonders what he is thinking about, or one begins to dream and think of the past, while fancy draws pictures in vivid colours with wide horizons. One recalls details which one would not remember at another time, and which one would not feel as one does then. And one speculates on the future, how one will get out of prison. Where will one go? When will that be? Whether one will return to one's native place? One muses and muses, and hope begins to stir in one's heart. . . . At other times one simply begins counting one, two, three, and so on, to put oneself to sleep. I have sometimes counted to three thousand and not slept. Someone would stir. Ustyantsev would cough his sickly consumptive cough and then groan feebly, and every time would add, "Lord, I have sinned!" And it is strange to hear this sick, broken, moaning voice in the complete stillness. In another corner there are others awake, talking together from their beds. One begins to tell something of his past, some event long gone by, of his tramping, of his children, of his wife, of the old days. You feel from the very sound of the far-away whisper that all he is telling is long over and can never return, and that he, the speaker, has cut off all connexion with it. The other listens. One can hear nothing but a soft measured whisper, like water trickling far away. I remember one long winter night I heard a story. It seemed to me at first like a nightmare, as though I had been lying in fever and had dreamed it all in delirium.

CHAPTER IV

AKULKA'S HUSBAND

(A STORY)

IT WAS RATHER LATE at night, about twelve o'clock. I had fallen asleep but soon woke up. The tiny dim light of the night-lamp glimmered faintly in the ward. . . . Almost all were asleep. Even Ustyantsev was asleep, and in the stillness one could hear how painfully he breathed and the husky wheezing in his throat at every gasp. Far away in the passage there suddenly sounded the heavy footsteps of the sentry coming to relieve the watch. There was a clang of a gun against the floor. The ward door was opened: the corporal, stepping in cautiously, counted over the patients. A minute later the ward was shut up, a new sentry was put on duty, the watchman moved away, and again the same stillness. Only then I noticed that on the left at a little distance from me there were two patients awake, who seemed to be whispering together. It used to happen in the ward sometimes that two men would lie side by side for days and months without speaking, and suddenly would begin talking, excited by the stillness of the night, and one would reveal his whole past to the other.

They had evidently been talking for a long time already. I missed the beginning and even now I could not make it all out; but by degrees I grew used to it and began to understand it all. I could not get to sleep; what could I do but listen? One was speaking with heat, half reclining on the bed, with his head raised, and craning his neck towards his companion. He was obviously roused and excited; he wanted to tell his story. His listener was sitting sullen and quite unconcerned in his bed, occasionally growling in answer or in token of sympathy with the speaker, more as it seemed out of politeness than from real feeling, and at every moment stuffing his nose with snuff. He was a soldier called Tcherevin from the disciplinary battalion, a man of fifty, a sullen pedant, a cold formalist and a conceited fool. The speaker, whose name was Shishkov, was a young fellow under thirty, a convict in the civil division in our prison, who worked in the tailor's workshop. So far, I had taken very little notice of him, and I was not drawn to see more of him during the remainder of my time in prison. He was a shallow, whimsical fellow; sometimes he would be silent, sullen and rude and not say a word for weeks together. Sometimes he would suddenly get mixed up in some affair, would begin talking scandal, would get excited over trifles and flit from one ward to another repeating gossip, talking endlessly, frantic with excitement. He would be beaten and relapse into silence again. He was a cowardly, mawkish youth. Everyone seemed to treat him with contempt. He was short and thin, his eyes were restless and sometimes had a blank dreamy look. At times he would tell a story; he would begin hotly, with excitement, gesticulating with his hands, and suddenly he would break off or pass to another subject, carried away by fresh ideas and forgetting what he had begun about. He was often quarrelling, and whenever he quarrelled would reproach his opponent for some wrong he had done him, would speak with feeling and almost with tears. . . . He played fairly well on the balalaika and was fond of playing it. On holidays he even danced, and danced well when they made him. He could very easily be made to do anything. It was not that he was specially docile but he was fond of making friends and was ready to do anything to please.

For a long time I could not grasp what he was talking about. I fancy, too, that at first he was constantly straying away from his subject into other things. He noticed perhaps that Tcherevin took scarcely any interest in his story, but he seemed anxious to convince himself that his listener was all attention, and perhaps it would have hurt him very much if he had been convinced of the contrary.

". . . He would go out into the market," he went on. "Everyone would bow to him. They felt he was a rich man; that's the only word for it."

"He had some trade, you say?"

"Yes, he had. They were poor folks there, regular beggars. The women used to carry water from the river ever so far up the steep bank to water their vegetables; they wore themselves out and did not get cabbage enough for soup in the autumn. It was poverty. Well, he rented a big piece of land, kept three labourers to work it; besides he had his own beehives and sold honey, and cattle too in our parts, you know; he was highly respected. He was pretty old, seventy if he was a day, his old bones were heavy, his hair was grey, he was a great big fellow. He would go into the market-place in a fox-skin coat and all did him honour. They felt what he was, you see! 'Good morning, Ankudim Trofimitch, sir.' 'Good day to you,' he'd say. He wasn't too proud to speak to anyone, you know. 'Long life to you, Ankudim Trofimitch!' 'And how's your luck?' he'd ask. 'Our luck's as right as soot is white; how are you doing, sir?' 'I am doing as well as my sins will let me, I am jogging along.' 'Good health to you, Ankudim Trofimitch!' He wasn't too proud for anyone, but if he spoke, every word he said was worth a rouble. He was a Bible reader, an educated man, always reading something religious. He'd set his old woman before him: 'Now wife, listen and mark!' and he'd begin expounding to her. And the old woman was not so very old, she was his second wife, he married her for the sake of children, you know, he had none from the first. But by the second, Marya Stepanovna, he had two sons not grown up. He was sixty when the youngest, Vasya, was born, and his daughter, Akulka, the eldest of the lot, was eighteen."

"Was that your wife?"

"Wait a bit. First there was the upset with Filka Morozov. 'You give me my share,' says Filka to Ankudim, 'give me my four hundred roubles—am I your servant? I won't be in business with you and I don't want your Akulka. I am going to have my fling. Now my father and mother are dead, so I shall drink up my money and then hire myself out, that is, go for a soldier, and in ten years I'll come back here as a field-marshal.' Ankudim gave him the money and settled up with him for good—for his father and the old man had set up business together. 'You are a lost man,' says he, 'Whether I am a lost man or not, you, grey-beard, you'd teach one to sup milk with an awl. You'd save off every penny, you'd rake over rubbish to make porridge. I'd like to spit on it all. Save every pin and the devil you win. I've a will of my own,' says he. 'And I am not taking your Akulka, anyway. I've slept with her as it is,' says he. 'What!' says Ankudim, 'do you dare shame the honest daughter of an honest father? When have you slept with her, you adder's fat? You pike's blood!' And he was all of a tremble, so Filka told me.

" 'I'll take good care,' says he, 'that your Akulka won't get any husband now, let alone me; no one will have her, even Mikita Grigoritch won't take her, for now she is disgraced. I've been carrying on with her ever since autumn. I wouldn't consent for a hundred crabs now. You can try giving me a hundred crabs, I won't consent. . . .'

"And didn't he run a fine rig among us, the lad! He kept the country in an uproar and the town was ringing with his noise. He got together a crew of companions, heaps of money; he was carousing for three months, he spent everything. 'When I've got through all the money,' he used to say, 'I'll sell the house, sell everything, and then I'll either sell myself for a soldier or go on the tramp.' He'd be drunk from morning till night, he drove about with bells and a pair of horses. And the way the wenches ran after him was tremendous. He used to play the *torba* finely."

"Then he'd been carrying on with Akulka before?"

"Stop, wait a bit. I'd buried my father just then too, and my mother used to make cakes, she worked for Ankudim, and that was how we lived. We had a hard time of it. We used to rent a bit of ground beyond the wood and we sowed it with corn, but we lost everything after father died, for I went on the spree too, my lad. I used to get money out of my mother by beating her."

"That's not the right thing, to beat your mother. It's a great sin."

"I used to be drunk from morning till night, my lad. Our house was all right, though it was tumbledown, it was our own, but it was empty as a drum. We used to sit hungry, we had hardly a morsel from one week's end to another. My mother used to keep on nagging at me; but what did I care? I was always with Filka Morozov in those days. I never left him from morning till night. 'Play on the guitar and dance,' he'd say to me, 'and I'll lie down and fling money at you, for I'm an extremely wealthy man!' And what wouldn't he do! But he wouldn't take stolen goods. 'I'm not a thief,' he says, 'I'm an honest man. But let's go and smear Akulka's gate with pitch, for I don't want Akulka to marry Mikita Grigoritch. I care more for that than for jelly.' The old man had been meaning to marry Akulka to Mikita Grigoritch for some time past. Mikita, too, was an old fellow in spectacles and a widower with a business. When he heard the stories about Akulka he drew back: 'That would be a great disgrace to me, Ankudim Trofimitch,' says he, 'and I don't want to get married in my old age.' So we smeared Akulka's gate. And they thrashed her, thrashed her for it at home. . . . Marya Stepanovna cried, 'I'll wipe her off the face of the earth!' 'In ancient years,' says the old man, 'in the time of the worthy patriarchs, I should have chopped her to pieces at the stake, but nowadays it's all darkness and rottenness.' Sometimes the neighbours all along the street would hear Akulka howling—they beat her from morning till night. Filka would shout for the whole market-place to hear: 'Akulka's a fine wench to drink with,' says he, 'You walk in fine array, who's your lover, pray! I've made them feel it,' says he, 'they won't forget it.'

"About that time I met Akulka one day carrying the pails and I shouted at her, 'Good morning, Akulina Kudimovna. Greetings to your grace! You walk in the fine array. Where do you get it, pray? Come, who's your lover, say!' That was all I said. But how she did look at me. She had such big eyes and she had grown as thin as a stick. And as she looked at me her mother thought she was laughing with me and shouted from the gateway, 'What are you gaping at, shameless hussy?' and she gave her another beating that day. Sometimes she'd beat her for an hour together. 'I'll do for her,' says she, 'for she is no daughter of mine now.'"

"Then she was a loose wench?"

"You listen, old man. While I was always drinking with Filka, my mother comes up to me one day—I was lying down. 'Why are you lying there, you rascal?' says she. 'You are a blackguard,' says she. She swore at me in fact. 'You get married,' says she. 'You marry Akulka. They'll be glad to marry her now even to you, they'd give you three hundred roubles in money alone.' 'But she is disgraced in the eyes of all the world,' says I. "You are a fool,' says she, 'the wedding ring covers all, it will be all the better for you if she feels her guilt all her life. And their money will set us on our feet again. I've talked it over with Marya Stepanovna already. She is very ready to listen.' 'Twenty roubles down on the table and I'll marry her,' says I. And would you believe it, right up to the day of the wedding I was drunk. And Filka Morozov was threatening me, too: 'I'll break all your ribs, Akulka's husband,' says he, 'and I'll sleep with your wife every night if I please.' 'You lie, you dog's flesh,' says I. And then he put me to shame before all the street. I ran home: 'I won't be married,' says I, 'if they don't lay down another fifty roubles on the spot.'"

"But did they agree to her marrying you?"

"Me? Why not? We were respectable people. My father was only ruined at the end by a fire; till then we'd been better off than they.

Ankudim says, 'You are as poor as a rat,' says he. 'There's been a lot of pitch smeared on your gate,' I answered. 'There's no need for you to cry us down,' says he. 'You don't know that she has disgraced herself, but there's no stopping people's mouths. Here's the ikon and here's the door,' says he. 'You needn't take her. Only pay back the money you've had.' Then I talked it over with Filka and I sent Mitri Bikov to tell him I'd dishonour him now over all the world; and right up to the wedding, lad, I was dead drunk. I was only just sober for the wedding. When we were driven home from the wedding and sat down, Mitrofan Stepanovitch, my uncle, said, 'Though it's done in dishonour, it's just as binding,' says he, 'the thing's done and finished.' Old Ankudim was drunk too and he cried, he sat there and the tears ran down his beard. And I tell you what I did, my lad: I'd put a whip in my pocket, I got it ready before the wedding. I'd made up my mind to have a bit of fun with Akulka, to teach her what it meant to get married by a dirty trick and that folks might know I wasn't being fooled over the marriage.

"Quite right too! To make her feel it for the future . . ."

"No, old chap, you hold your tongue. In our part of the country they take us straight after the wedding to a room apart while the others drink outside. So they left Akulka and me inside. She sits there so white, not a drop of blood in her face. She was scared, to be sure. Her hair, too, was as white as flax, her eyes were large and she was always quiet, you heard nothing of her, she was like a dumb thing in the house. A strange girl altogether. And can you believe it, brother, I got that whip ready and laid it beside me by the bed, but it turned out she had not wronged me at all, my lad!"

"You don't say so!"

"Not at all. She was quite innocent. And what had she had to go through all that torment for? Why had Filka Morozov put her to shame before all the world?"

"Yes . . ."

"I knelt down before her then, on the spot, and clasped my hands. 'Akulina Kudimovna,' says I, 'forgive me, fool as I am, for thinking ill of you too. Forgive a scoundrel like me,' says I. She sat before me on the bed looking at me, put both hands on my shoulders while her tears were flowing. She was crying and laughing. . . . Then I went out to all of them. 'Well,' says I, 'if I meet Filka Morozov now he is a dead man!' As for the old people, they did not know which saint to pray to. The mother almost fell at her feet, howling. And the old fellow said, 'Had we known this, we wouldn't have found a husband like this for you, our beloved daughter.'

"When we went to church the first Sunday, I in my astrakhan cap, coat of fine cloth and velveteen breeches, and she in her new hareskin coat with a silk kerchief on her head, we looked a well-matched pair: didn't we walk along! People were admiring us. I needn't speak for myself, and though I can't praise Akulina up above the rest, I can't say she was worse: and she'd have held her own with any dozen."

"That's all right, then."

"Come, listen. The day after the wedding, though I was drunk, I got away from my visitors and I escaped and ran away. 'Bring me that wretch Filka Morozov,' says I, 'bring him here, the scoundrel!' I shouted all over the market. Well, I was drunk too: I was beyond the Vlasovs' when they caught me, and three men brought me home by force. And the talk was all over the town. The wenches in the market-place were talking to each other: 'Girls, darlings, have you heard? Akulka is proved innocent.'

"Not long after, Filka says to me before folks, 'Sell your wife and you can drink. Yashka the soldier got married just for that,' says he. 'He didn't sleep with his wife, but he was drunk for three years.' I said to him, 'You are a scoundrel.' 'And you,' says he, 'a fool. Why, you weren't sober when you were married,' says he, 'how could you tell about it when you were drunk?' I came home and shouted, 'You married me when I was drunk,' said I. My mother began scolding me. 'Your ears are stopped with gold, mother. Give me Akulka.' Well, I began beating her. I beat her, my lad, beat her for two hours, till I couldn't stand up. She didn't get up from her bed for three weeks."

"To be sure," observed Tcherevin phlegmatically, "if you don't beat them, they'll . . . But did you catch her with a lover?"

"Catch her? No, I didn't," Shishkov observed, after a pause, and, as it were, with an effort. "But I felt awfully insulted. People teased me so and Filka led the way. 'You've a wife for show,' says he, 'for folks to look at.' Filka invited us with others, and this was the greeting he gave me: 'His wife is a tender-hearted soul,' says he, 'honourable and polite, who knows how to behave, nice in every way—that's what he thinks now. But you've forgotten, lad, how you smeared her gate with pitch yourself!' I sat drunk and then he seized me by the hair suddenly and holding me by the hair he shoved me down. 'Dance,' says he, 'Akulka's husband! I'll hold you by your hair and you dance to amuse me!' 'You are a scoundrel,' I shouted. And he says to me, 'I shall come to you with companions and thrash Akulka, your wife, before you, as much as I like.' Then I, would you believe it, was afraid to go out of the house for a whole month. I was afraid he'd come and disgrace me. And just for that I began beating her. . . ."

"But what did you beat her for? You can tie a man's hands but you can't stop his tongue. You shouldn't beat your wife too much. Show her, give her a lesson, and then be kind to her. That's what she is for."

Shishkov was silent for some time.

"It was insulting," he began again. "Besides, I got into the habit of it: some days I'd beat her from morning till night; everything she did was wrong. If I didn't beat her, I felt bored. She would sit without saying a word, looking out of the window and crying. . . . She was always crying, I'd feel sorry for her, but I'd beat her. My mother was always swearing at me about her: 'You are a scoundrel,' she'd say, 'you're a jail-bird!' 'I'll kill her,' I cried, 'and don't let anyone dare to speak to me; for they married me by a trick.' At first old Ankudim stood up for her; he'd come himself: 'You are no one of much account,' says he, 'I'll find a law for you.' But he gave it up. Marya Stepanovna humbled herself completely. One day she came and prayed me tearfully, 'I've come to entreat you, Ivan Semyonovitch, it's a small matter, but a great favour. Bid me hope again,' she bowed down, 'soften your heart, forgive her. Evil folk slandered our daughter. You know yourself she was innocent when you married her.' And she bowed down to my feet and cried. But I lorded it over her. 'I won't hear you now! I shall do just what I like to you all now, for I am no longer master of myself. Filka Morozov is my mate and my best friend. . . .'"

"So you were drinking together again then?"

"Nothing like it! There was no approaching him. He was quite mad with drink. He'd spent all he had and hired himself out to a store-keeper to replace his eldest son, and in our part of the country when a man sells himself for a soldier, up to the very day he is taken away everything in the house has to give way to him, and he is master over all. He gets the sum in full when he goes and till that time he lives in the house; he sometimes stays there for six months and the way he'll go on, it's a disgrace to a decent house. 'I am going for a soldier in place of your son,' the fellow would say, 'so I am your benefactor, so you must all respect me, or I'll refuse.' So Filka was having a rare time at the shopkeeper's, sleeping with the daughter, pulling the father's beard every day after dinner, and doing just as he liked. He had a bath every day and insisted on using vodka for water, and the women carrying him to the bath-house in their arms. When he came back from a walk he would stand in the middle of the street and say, 'I won't go in at the gate, pull down the fence,' so they had to pull down the fence in another place beside the gate for him to go through. At last his time was up, they got him sober and took him off. The people came out in crowds into the street saying, 'Filka Morozov's being taken for a soldier!' He bowed in all directions. Just then Akulka came out of the kitchen garden. When Filka saw her just at our gate, 'Stop,' he cried, and leapt out of the cart and bowed down before her. 'You are my soul,' he said, 'my darling, I've loved you for two years, and now they are taking me for a soldier with music. Forgive me,' said he, 'honest daughter of an honest father, for I've been a scoundrel to you and it's all been my fault!' And he bowed down to the ground again. Akulka stood, seeming scared at first, then she made him a low bow and said, 'You forgive me too, good youth, I have no thought of any evil you have done.' I followed her into the hut. 'What did you say to him, dog's flesh?' And you may not believe me but she looked at me: 'Why, I love him now more than all the world,' said she."

"You don't say so!"

"I did not say one word to her all that day . . . only in the evening. 'Akulka, I shall kill you now,' says I. All night I could not sleep; I went into the passage to get some kvas to drink, and the sun was beginning to rise. I went back into the room. 'Akulka,' said I, 'get ready to go out to the field.' I had been meaning to go before and mother knew we were going. 'That's right,' said she. 'It's harvest-time now and I hear the labourer's been laid up with his stomach for the last three days.' I got the cart out without saying a word. As you go out of our town there's a pine forest that stretches for ten miles, and beyond the forest was the land we rented. When we had gone two miles I stopped the horse. 'Get out, Akulina,' said I, 'your end has come.' She looked at me, she was scared; she stood up before me, she did not speak. 'I am sick of you,' says I, 'say your prayers!' And then I snatched her by the hair; she had two thick long plaits. I twisted them round my hand and held her tight from behind between my knees. I drew out my knife, I pulled her head back and I slid the knife along her throat. She screamed, the blood spurted out, I threw down the knife, flung my arms round her, lay down on the ground, embraced her and screamed over her, yelling; she screamed and I screamed; she was fluttering all over, struggling to get out of my arms, and the blood was simply streaming, simply streaming on to my face and on to my hands. I left her, a panic came over me, and I left the horse and set off running, and ran home along the backs of the houses and straight to the bath-house. We had an old bath-house we didn't use: I squeezed myself into a corner under the steps and there I sat. And there I sat till nightfall."

"And Akulka?"

"She must have got up, too, after I had gone and walked homewards too. They found her a hundred paces from the place."

"Then you hadn't killed her?"

"Yes. . . ." Shishkov paused for a moment.

"There's a vein, you know," observed Tcherevin, "if you don't cut through that vein straightaway a man will go on struggling and won't die, however much blood is lost."

"But she did die. They found her dead in the evening. They informed the police, began searching for me, and found me at nightfall in the bath-house! . . . And here I've been close upon four years," he added, after a pause.

"H'm . . . to be sure, if you don't beat them there will be trouble," Tcherevin observed coolly and methodically, pulling out his tobacco-pouch again. He began taking long sniffs at intervals. "Then again you seem to have been a regular fool, young fellow, too. I caught my wife with a lover once. So I called her into the barn; I folded the bridle in two. 'To whom do you swear to be true? To whom do you swear to be true?' says I. And I did give her a beating with that bridle, I beat her for an hour and a half. 'I'll wash your feet and drink the water,' she cried at last. Ovdotya was her name."

CHAPTER V

SUMMER TIME

BUT NOW IT IS the beginning of April, and Easter is drawing near. Little by little the summer work begins. Every day the sun is warmer and more brilliant; the air is fragrant with spring and has a disquieting influence on the nerves. The coming of spring agitates even the man in fetters, arouses even in him vague desires, cravings and a yearning melancholy. I think one pines for liberty more in the bright sunshine than in dull winter or autumn days, and that may be noticed in all prisoners. Although they seem glad of the fine days, yet at the same time their impatience and restlessness is intensified. In fact I have noticed that quarrels in prison become more frequent in the spring. Noise, shouting and uproar are heard more often, rows are more common; yet sometimes at work one suddenly notices dreamy eyes fixed on the blue distance, where far away beyond the Irtish stretch the free Kirghiz steppes, a boundless plain for a thousand miles. One hears a man heave a deep sigh from a full heart, as though he yearned to breathe that far-away free air and to ease with it his stifled and fettered soul. "Ech-ma!" the convict exclaims at last, and suddenly, as though shaking off dreams and brooding, he sullenly and impatiently snatches up the spade or the bricks he has to move from place to place. A minute later he has forgotten his sudden feeling and begun laughing or swearing according to his disposition. Or he suddenly sets to his task, if he has one, with extraordinary and quite superfluous zeal, and begins working with all his might, as though trying to stifle in himself something which is cramping and oppressing him within. They are all vigorous, men for the most part in the flower of their age and their strength. . . . Fetters are hard to bear at this season! I am not poetizing and am convinced of the truth of what I say. Apart from the fact that in the warmth, in the brilliant sunshine, when, in all your soul, in all your being, you feel nature with infinite force springing into life again around you, prison doors, guards and bondage are harder to bear than ever—apart from that, with the coming of spring and the return of the lark, tramping begins all over Siberia and Russia; God's people escape from prison and take refuge in the forests. After stifling dungeons, law courts, fetters and beatings, they wander at their own free will wherever they please, wherever it seems fair and free to them; they eat and drink what they find, what God sends them, and at night they fall asleep peacefully under God's eye in the forest, or the fields, troubling little for the future, and free from the sadness of prison, like the birds of the forest, with none to say goodnight to but the stars. There is no denying that one may have to face hardship, hunger and exhaustion "in the service of General Cuckoo." One may have to go for days together without bread; one must keep in hiding, out of sight of everyone; one may be driven to steal, to rob and sometimes even to murder. "A convict free is like a baby, what he wants he takes," is what they say in Siberia of the convict settlers. This saying applies in full force and even with some additions to the tramp. It is rare for a tramp not to be a robber and he is always a thief, more from necessity than from vocation, of course.

There are inveterate tramps. Some, after their imprisonment is over, run away from settlements. One would have thought that a man would be satisfied in the settlement and free from anxiety, but no, something lures him, beckons him away. Life in the forest, a life poor and terrible, but free and adventurous, has a fascination, a mysterious charm for those who have once known it, and one may sometimes see a sedate precise man, who was promising to become a capable farmer and a good settled inhabitant, run away to the forest. Sometimes a man will marry and have children, live for five years in one place, and suddenly one fine day disappear somewhere, leaving his wife, his children and the whole parish in amazement. A wanderer of this kind was pointed out to me in prison. He had never committed any special crime, at least I never heard anything of the kind spoken of, but he was always running away, he had been running away all his life. He had been on the southern frontier of Russia beyond the Danube, and in the Kirghiz steppes, and in Eastern Siberia and in the Caucasus—he had been everywhere. Who knows, perhaps in other circumstances, with his passion for travelling he might have been another Robinson Crusoe.[12] But I was told all this about him by other people; he spoke very little in prison himself and then only of necessity. He was a little peasant of fifty, extremely meek, with an extremely calm and even vacant face, calm to the point of idiocy. In the summer he was fond of sitting in the sun, always humming some song to himself, but so quietly that five steps away he was inaudible. His features were somehow wooden; he ate little and chiefly bread; he never bought a roll or a glass of vodka and I doubt whether he ever had any money or knew how to count. He was perfectly unconcerned about everything. He sometimes fed the prison dogs with his own hands and no one else ever did. Indeed, Russians in general are not given to feeding dogs. They said he had been married, twice indeed; it was said that he had children somewhere. . . . How he got into prison I have no idea. The convicts all expected him to give us the slip too, but either the time had not come or he was too old for it, for he went on living amongst us, calmly contemplating the strange environment in which he found himself. However, there was no reckoning on him, though one would have thought that he had nothing to run away for, that he would gain nothing by it.

Yet, on the whole, the life of a tramp in the forest is paradise compared with prison. That is easy to understand and indeed there can be no comparison. Though it's a hard life, it is freedom. That is why every convict in Russia, whatever prison he may be in, grows restless in the spring with the first kindly rays of sunshine. Though by no means everyone intends to run away; one may say with certainty, indeed, that owing to the difficulty of escape and the penalties attaching to it, not more than one in a hundred ventures upon it; yet the other ninety-nine dream at least of how they might escape and where they would escape to and comfort their hearts with the very desire, with the very imagination of its being possible. Some recall how they have run away in the past. . . . I am speaking now only of those who are serving their sentence. But of course those who are awaiting sentence take the risks of flight far more frequently than other prisoners. Convicts condemned for a term run away only at the beginning of their imprisonment, if at all. When a convict has been two or three years in prison, those years begin to have a value in his mind and by degrees he makes up his mind that he would rather finish his term in the legal way and become a settler than run such risks, and take the chances of ruin if he fails. And failure is so possible. Scarcely one in ten succeeds in changing his luck. Another class of convicts, who more frequently take the hazards of flight, consists of those who are condemned to very long terms. Fifteen or twenty years seem an eternity, and a man condemned for such lengthy periods is always ready to dream of changing his luck, even if he has passed ten years in prison.

The branding does something to prevent prisoners attempting flight.

To *change one's luck* is a technical expression, so much so that even in cross-examination a prisoner caught trying to escape will answer that he wanted to change his luck. This rather bookish expression is exactly what is meant. Every fugitive looks forward, not exactly to complete freedom—he knows that is almost impossible—but either to getting into another institution or being sent as a settler, or being tried again for a fresh offence committed when he was tramping; in fact he does not care what becomes of him, so long as he is not sent back to the old place he is sick of, his former prison. If these fugitives do not, in the course of the summer, succeed in finding some exceptional place in which to spend the winter, if for instance they do not chance upon someone willing for interested motives to shelter a fugitive, if they do not, sometimes by means of murder, obtain a passport of some sort with which they can live anywhere they like, they are all either caught by the police or go in autumn of their own accord in crowds into the towns and the prisons and remain there for the winter, not, of course, without hopes of escaping again in the summer.

Spring had an influence on me too. I remember how eagerly I sometimes peeped through the chinks in the fence and how long I used to stand with my head against the fence looking obstinately and insatiably at the greenness of the grass on our prison rampart and the deeper and deeper blue of the sky in the distance. My restlessness and depression grew stronger every day, and the prison became more and more hateful to me. The dislike with which as a "gentleman" I was continually regarded by the convicts during my first few years became intolerable, poisoning my whole life. During those first few years I often used to go into the hospital, though I had no illness, simply to avoid being in prison, simply to escape from this obstinate, irreconcilable hatred. "You have beaks of iron, you've pecked us to death," the convicts used to say to us, and how I used to envy the peasants who were brought to the prison! They were looked upon as comrades by everyone at once. And so the spring, the phantom of freedom, the general rejoicing of nature affected me with melancholy and nervous restlessness. At the end of Lent, I think in the sixth week, I took the sacrament. All the prisoners had been at the beginning of Lent divided by the senior sergeant into seven relays, one to take the sacrament during each week of the fast. Each of the relays consisted of about thirty men. I very much liked the week of the preparation for the sacrament. We were relieved of work. We went to the church, which was not far from the prison, twice or three times a day. It was long since I had been to church. The Lenten service so familiar to me from far-away days of childhood in my father's house, the solemn prayers, the prostrations—all this stirred in my heart the far, far-away past, bringing back the days of my childhood, and I remember how pleasant it was walking over the frozen ground in the early morning to the house of God, escorted by guards with loaded guns. The guards did not, however, go into the church. We stood all together in a group close to the church door, so far back that we could only hear the loud-voiced deacon and from time to time catch a glimpse of the black cope and the bald head of the priest through the crowd. I remembered how sometimes standing in church as a child I looked at the peasants crowding near the entrance and slavishly parting to make way for a thickly epauletted officer, a stout gentleman, or an over-dressed but pious lady, who invariably made for the best places and were ready to quarrel over them. I used to fancy then that at the church door they did not pray as we did, that they prayed humbly, zealously, abasing themselves and fully conscious of their humble state.

Now I, too, had to stand in the background, and not only in the background; we were fettered and branded as felons; everyone avoided us, everyone seemed to be even afraid of us, alms were always given to us, and I remember that this was positively pleasing to me in a way; there was a special subtlety in this strange pleasure. "So be it," I thought. The convicts prayed very earnestly and every one of them brought his poor farthing to the church every time to buy a candle, or to put in the collection. "I, too, am a man," he thought, and felt perhaps as he gave it, "in God's eyes we are all equal. . . ." We took the sacrament at the early mass. When with the chalice in his hands the priest read the words, ". . . accept me, O Lord, even as the thief," almost all of them bowed down to the ground with a clanking of chains, apparently applying the words literally to themselves.

And now Easter had come. We received from the authorities an egg each and a piece of white bread made with milk and eggs. Loads of offerings for the prisoners were brought from the town again. Again there was a visit from the priest with a cross, again a visit of the authorities, again a cabbage soup with plenty of meat in it, again drinking and desultory idleness—exactly as at Christmas, except that now one could walk about the prison yard and warm oneself in the sun. There was more light, more space than in the winter, but yet it was more melancholy. The long endless summer day seemed particularly unbearable in the holidays. On ordinary days, at least, it was shortened by work.

The summer tasks turned out to be far harder than our work in winter. All were chiefly employed upon building. The convicts dug out the earth, laid the bricks; some were employed as carpenters, locksmiths or painters in doing up the government buildings. Others went to the brickyard to make bricks. This was considered the hardest work of all. The brickyard was two or three miles from the fortress. At six o'clock, every summer morning, a whole party of convicts, some fifty in number, set off for the brickyard. For this work they chose unskilled labourers, that is, men who had no special craft or trade. They took bread with them, for, as the place was so far off, it was waste of time going six miles home to dinner and back, so they had dinner on their return in the evening. The tasks were set for the whole day and we could only just get through them by working all day long. To begin with, one had to dig and carry the clay, to fetch water, to pound the clay in a pit, and finally to make a great number of bricks out of it— I believe it was two hundred, or perhaps even two hundred and fifty, a day. I only went twice to the brickyard. The brickyard men returned in the evening, worn out and exhausted, and all the summer they were continually throwing it up against the others, declaring that they were doing the hardest work. That seemed to be their consolation. Yet some of them were very ready to go to the brickyard: in the first place, it was outside the town, it was a free open space on the banks of the Irtish. It was a relief to look about one, anyway—to see something not the regulation prison surroundings! One could smoke freely and even lie down for half an hour with great satisfaction.

I used to go as before to pound alabaster, or to the workshop, or I was employed to carry bricks on the building. I once had to carry bricks a distance of about a hundred and sixty yards, from the bank of the Irtish to the barracks that were being built on the other side of the fortress rampart, and I had to go on doing this every day for two months. I positively liked the work, though the cord in which I had to carry the bricks always cut my shoulder. But I liked to feel that I was obviously gaining muscular strength through the work. At first I could only carry eight bricks and each brick weighed nearly eleven pounds. But I got up to twelve and even fifteen bricks later on, and that was a great joy to me. In prison physical strength is no less necessary than moral strength to enable one to endure the hardships of that accursed manner of life.

And I wanted to go on living when I got out of prison.

I liked carrying bricks not only because it strengthened my muscles but also because the work took me to the bank of the Irtish. I speak of the river-bank so often because it was only from there one had a view of God's world, of the pure clear distance, of the free solitary steppes, the emptiness of which made a strange impression on me. It was only on the bank of the Irtish that one could stand with one's back to the fortress and not see it. All our other tasks were done either in the fortress or close by it. From the very first days I hated that fortress, some of the buildings particularly. The major's house seemed to me a damnable, loathsome place, and I always looked at it with hatred every time I passed by. On the river-bank one might forget oneself: one would look at that boundless solitary vista as a prisoner looks out to freedom from his window. Everything there was sweet and precious in my eyes, the hot brilliant sun in the fathomless blue sky and the far-away song of the Kirghiz floating from the further bank. One gazes into the distance and makes out at last the poor smoke-blackened tent of some Kirghiz. One discerns the smoke rising from the tent, the Kirghiz woman busy with her two sheep. It is all poor and barbarous, but it is free. One descries a bird in the limpid blue air and for a long time one watches its flight: now it darts over the water, now it vanishes in the blue depths, now it reappears again, a speck flitting in the distance. . . . Even the poor sickly flower which I found early in spring in a crevice of the rocky bank drew my attention almost painfully.

The misery of all that first year in prison was intolerable, and it had an irritating, bitter effect on me. During that first year I failed to notice many things in my misery. I shut my eyes and did not want to look. Among my spiteful and hostile companions in prison, I did not observe the good ones—the men who were capable of thought and feeling in spite of their repellent outer husk. In the midst of ill-natured sayings, I sometimes failed to notice kind and friendly words, which were the more precious because they were uttered with no interested motives, and often came straight from a heart which had suffered and endured more than mine. But why enlarge on this? I was very glad to get thoroughly tired: I might go to sleep when I got home. For the nights were an agony in the summer, almost worse than in the winter. The evenings, it is true, were sometimes very nice. The sun, which had been on the prison yard all day, set at last. Then followed the cool freshness of evening and then the comparatively cold night of the steppes. The convicts wandered in groups about the yard, waiting to be locked in. The chief mass, it is true, were crowding into the kitchen. There some burning question of the hour was always being agitated; they argued about this and that, sometimes discussed some rumour, often absurd, though it aroused extraordinary interest in these men cut off from the outer world; a report came for instance that our major was being turned out. Convicts are as credulous as children; they know themselves that the story is ridiculous, that it has been brought by a notorious gossip, an "absurd person"—the convict Kvasov whom it had long been an accepted rule not to believe, and who could never open his mouth without telling a lie; yet everyone pounced on his story, talked it over and discussed it, amusing themselves and ending by being angry with themselves and ashamed of themselves for having believed Kvasov.

"Why, who's going to send him away?" shouted one. "No fear, his neck is thick, he can hold his own."

"But there are others over him, surely!" protested another, an eager and intelligent fellow who had seen something of life, but was the most argumentative man in the world.

"One raven won't pick out another's eyes!" a third, a grey-headed old man who was finishing his soup in the corner in solitude, muttered sullenly as though to himself.

"I suppose his superior officers will come to ask you whether they're to sack him?" a fourth added casually, strumming lightly on the balalaika.

"And why not?" answered the second furiously. "All the poor people could petition for it, you must all come forward if they begin questioning. To be sure, with us it's all outcry, but when it comes to deeds we back out."

"What would you have?" said the balalaika player. "That's what prison's for!"

"The other day," the excited speaker went on, not heeding him, "there was some flour left. We scraped together what little there was and were sending it to be sold. But no, he heard of it; our foreman let him know; it was taken away; he wanted to make something out of it, to be sure. Was that fair now?"

"But who is it you want to complain to?"

"Who? Why, the inspector that's coming."

"What inspector?"

"That's true, lads, that an inspector's coming," said a lively young fellow of some education who had been a clerk and was reading "The Duchess la Vallière," or something of the kind. He was always merry and amusing, but he was was respected for having a certain knowledge of life and of the world. Taking no notice of the general interest aroused by the news that an inspector was coming, he went straight up to one of the cooks and asked for some liver. Our cooks often used to sell such things. They would, for instance, buy a large piece of liver at their own expense, cook it, and sell it in small pieces to the convicts.

"One ha'p'orth or two ha'p'orths?" asked the cook.

"Cut me two ha'p'orths; let folks envy me," answered the convict. "There's a general, lads—a general coming from Petersburg; he'll inspect all Siberia. That's true. They said so at the commander's."

This news produced an extraordinary sensation. For a quarter of an hour there was a stream of questions: who was it, what general, what was his rank, was he superior to the generals here? Convicts are awfully fond of discussing rank, officials, which of them takes precedence, which can lord it over the other, and which has to give way; they even quarrel and dispute and almost fight over the generals. One wonders what difference it can make to them. But a minute knowledge of generals and the authorities altogether is the criterion of a man's knowledge, discrimination and previous importance in the world. Talk about the higher authorities is generally considered the most refined and important conversation in prison.

"Then it turns out to be true, lads, that they are coming to sack the major," observes Kvasov, a little red-faced man, excitable and remarkably muddle-headed. He had been the first to bring the news about the major.

"He'll bribe them," the grim, grey-headed convict, who had by now finished his soup, brought out jerkily.

"To be sure he will," said another. "He's grabbed money enough! He had a battalion before he came to us. The other day he was wanting to marry the head priest's daughter."

"But he didn't—they showed him the door, he was too poor. He's not much of a match! When he gets up from a chair he takes all he's got with him. He lost all his money gambling at Easter. Fedka said so."

"Yes; the lad's not one to spend, but he gets through cash no end."

"Ah, brother, I was married, too. It's no use for a man to be married; when you are married the night's too short," remarked Skuratov, putting his word in.

"Oh, indeed! It was you we were talking about, of course," observed the free-and-easy youth who had been a clerk. "But you are a silly fool, Kvasov, let me tell you. Do you suppose the major could bribe a general like that, and that such a general would come all the way from Petersburg to inspect the major? You are a fool, my lad, let me tell you."

"Why, because he's a general won't he take it?" someone in the crowd observed sceptically.

"Of course he won't; if he does, he'll take a jolly big one."

"To be sure, he will; to match his rank."

"A general will always take bribes," Kvasov observed with decision.

"You've tried it on, I suppose?" said Baklushin, suddenly coming in and speaking contemptuously. "I don't believe you've ever seen a general."

"I have, though!"

"You are lying!"

"Liar yourself!"

"Lads, if he has seen one, let him tell us all directly what general he knows. Come, speak away—for I know all the generals."

"I've seen General Ziebert," Kvasov answered with strange hesitation.

"Ziebert? There isn't such a general. He looked at your back, I suppose, your Ziebert, when he was a lieutenant-colonel maybe, and you fancied in your fright he was a general!"

"No, listen to me!" cried Skuratov, "for I am a married man. There really was such a general at Moscow, Ziebert, of German family, though he was a Russian. He used to confess to a Russian priest every year, at the fast of the Assumption, and he was always drinking water, lads, like a duck. Every day he'd drink forty glasses of Moscow river water. They said that he took it for some disease, his valet told me so himself."

"He bred carp in his belly, I bet, with all that water," observed the convict with the balalaika.

"Come, do shut up! We are talking business and they . . . What is this inspector, brothers?" a fussy old convict called Martinov, who had been a hussar, anxiously inquired.

"What nonsense people talk!" observed a sceptic. "Where do they get it from and how do they fit it in? And it's all nonsense!"

"No, it's not nonsense," Kulikov, who had hitherto been majestically silent, observed dogmatically. He was a man of some consequence, about fifty, with an exceptionally prepossessing countenance and disdainfully dignified manners. He was aware of the fact, and was proud of it. He was a veterinary surgeon, partly of gipsy descent, who used to earn money by doctoring horses in the town, and sold vodka in prison. He was a clever fellow and had seen a good deal. He dropped his words as though he were bestowing roubles.

"That's the truth, lads," he went on calmly. "I heard it last week. There's a general coming, a very important one; he'll inspect the whole of Siberia. We all know he will be bribed, too, but not by our old Eight-eyes; he wouldn't dare to come near him. There are generals and generals, brothers. There are some of all sorts. Only I tell you, our major will stay where he is, anyway. That's a sure thing. We can't speak, and none of the officers will speak against one of their own lot. The inspector will look into the prison and then he'll go away and report that he found everything all right. . . ."

"That's right, lads, but the major's in a funk: he's drunk from morning till night."

"But in the evening he drives a different sort of cart. Fedka was saying so."

"You'll never wash a black dog white. It's not the first time he's been drunk, is it?"

"I say, what if the general really does nothing? It is high time they took notice of their goings on!" the convicts said to each other in excitement.

The news about the inspector was all over the prison in a moment; men wandered about the yard impatiently, repeating the news to one another, though some were purposely silent and maintained an indifferent air, evidently trying to increase their importance by so doing. Others remained genuinely unconcerned. Convicts with balalaikas were sitting on the barrack steps. Some went on gossiping. Others struck up songs, but all were in a state of great excitement that evening.

Between nine and ten we were all counted over, driven into the barracks and locked up for the night. The nights were short, we were waked between four and five, and we were never all asleep before eleven. There was always noise and talking till that hour and sometimes, as in winter, there were card parties. It became insufferably hot and stifling in the night. Though there were wafts of the cool night air from the open window, the convicts tossed about on their beds all night as though in delirium. The fleas swarmed in myriads. There were fleas in the winter, too, and in considerable numbers, but from the beginning of spring they swarmed in multitudes. Though I had been told of it before, I could not believe in the reality till I experienced it. And as the summer advanced, they grew more and more ferocious. It is true that one can get used to fleas—I have learnt this by experience; but still one has a bad time of it. They torment one so much that one lies at last as though in a fever, feeling that one is not asleep but in delirium. When at last, towards morning, the fleas desist, and as it were subside, and when one really drops into a sweet sleep in the cool of dawn, the pitiless tattoo of the drum booms out at the prison gate and the morning watch begins. Rolled up in your sheepskin you hear with a curse the loud, distinct sounds, as it were counting them, while through your sleep there creeps into your mind the insufferable thought that it will be the same tomorrow and the day after tomor-row, and for years together, right on to the day of freedom. But when, one wonders, will that freedom be, and where is it? Mean-while, one must wake up; the daily movement and bustle begins . . . men dress and hurry out to work. It is true one can sleep for an hour at midday.

The story of the inspector was true. The rumour received more and more confirmation each day, and at last we all knew for a fact that an important general was coming from Petersburg to inspect the whole of Siberia, that he had already arrived, that he was by now at Tobolsk. Every day fresh reports reached the prison. News came, too, from the town. We heard that everyone was frightened and fluttered, and trying to show things the best side up. It was said that the higher officers were preparing receptions, balls, festivities. The convicts were sent out in parties to level the road to the fortress, to remove hillocks, to paint the fences and posts, to repair the stucco, to whitewash; in fact, they tried all in a minute to set right everything that had to be shown.

The convicts understood all this very well, and talked with more and more heat and defiance among themselves. Their fancy took im-mense flights. They even prepared to make a complaint when the gen-eral should inquire whether they were satisfied. Meanwhile they quarrelled and abused each other.

The major was in great excitement. He used to visit the prison more frequently, he shouted at people, and fell upon them, sent pris-oners to the guard-house more frequently and was more zealous about cleanliness and decency. It was just at that time, as luck would have it, that a little incident took place which did not, however, as might have been expected, disturb the major at all, but on the con-trary gave him positive satisfaction. A convict stuck an awl into an-other's chest, just over the heart.

The convict who committed this crime was called Lomov; the man who was wounded was called Gavrilka among us; he was an inveter-ate tramp. I don't know if he had any other name; among us he was called Gavrilka.

Lomov had been a prosperous peasant from the K. district of T. province. All the Lomovs lived together in one family, the old father with his brother and three sons. They were well-to-do peasants. It was rumoured all over the province that they were worth as much as a hundred thousand roubles. They tilled the land, tanned skins, traded, but did more in the way of moneylending, sheltering tramps, receiving stolen goods, and such pursuits. Half the peasants in the district were in their debt and in bondage to them. They were reputed to be shrewd and crafty peasants, but at last they became puffed up with pride, especially when one important person in the district took to putting up at their house when he travelled, saw the old father and took to him for his quick-wittedness and practical ability. They began to think they could do what they liked, and ran greater and greater risks in illegal undertakings of all sorts. Everyone was complaining of them, everyone was wishing the earth would swallow them up; but they held their heads higher and higher. They cared nothing for police captains and excise officials. At last they came to grief and were ruined, but not for any wrongdoing, not for their secret crimes, but for something of which they were not guilty. They had a big outlying farm some seven miles from the village. Once they had living there in the autumn six Kirghiz, who had worked for them as bondsmen under a contract for many years. One night all these Kirghiz labourers were murdered. An inquiry was made. It lasted a long while. Many other misdeeds were discovered in the course of the inquiry. The Lomovs were accused of murdering their labourers. They told the tale themselves, and everyone in the prison knew about it; it was suspected that they owed a great deal to their labourers, and as they were greedy and miserly in spite of their wealth, they had murdered the Kirghiz to escape paying them the arrears of their wages. During the trial and legal proceedings they lost all their property. The old father died. The sons were scattered. One of the sons and his uncle were sent to our prison for twelve years. And after all they were completely innocent as far as the death of the Kirghiz was concerned. There afterwards turned up in our prison a notorious rogue and tramp called Gavrilka, a brisk and lively fellow, who was responsible for the crime. I did not hear, however, whether he admitted it himself, but the whole prison was convinced that he had a share in the murder. Gavrilka had had dealings with the Lomovs when he had been a tramp. He had come to the prison for a short term as a deserter from the army and a tramp. He had murdered the Kirghiz with the help of three other tramps; they had hoped to plunder the farm and carry off a lot of booty.

The Lomovs were not liked among us; why, I don't know. One of them, the nephew, was a fine fellow, clever and easy to get on with; but his uncle, who stuck the awl into Gavrilka, was a stupid and quarrelsome man. He had quarrelled with many of the prisoners before and had been often soundly beaten. Gavrilka everyone liked for his cheerful and easy temper. Though the Lomovs knew that he was the criminal and that they were suffering for his crime, they did not quarrel with him, although they were never friendly with him; and he took no notice of them either. And suddenly a quarrel broke out between Gavrilka and the uncle Lomov over a most disgusting girl. Gavrilka began boasting of her favours; Lomov was jealous, and one fine day he stabbed him with the awl.

Though the Lomovs had been ruined by their trial, yet they lived in comfort in prison. They evidently had money. They had a samovar, drank tea. Our major knew of it and hated the two Lomovs intensely. Everyone could see that he was always finding fault with them and trying to get them into trouble. The Lomovs put this down to the major's desire to get a bribe out of them. But they never offered him a bribe.

Of course, if Lomov had driven the awl a very little further in, he would have killed Gavrilka. But the assault ended in nothing worse than a scratch. It was reported to the major. I remember how he pranced in, out of breath, and obviously delighted. He treated Gavrilka with wonderful gentleness, quite as if he had been his own son.

"Well, my boy, can you walk to the hospital or not? No, you'd better drive. Get the horse out at once!" he shouted in excited haste to the sergeant.

"But I don't feel anything, your honour. He only gave me a little prick, your honour."

"You don't know, you don't know, my dear boy; we shall see . . . It's a dangerous place; it all depends on the place; he struck you just over the heart, the ruffian! And you, you," he roared, addressing Lomov, "now I'll make you smart! . . . To the guard-house!"

And he certainly did make him smart. Lomov was tried and, though the wound turned out to be the slightest of pricks, the intent was unmistakable. The criminal's term of imprisonment was increased and he was given a thousand strokes. The major was thoroughly satisfied.

At last the inspector arrived. The day after he arrived in the town he visited our prison. It was on a holiday. For some days before everything in the prison had been scrubbed, polished, cleaned. The prisoners were freshly shaven. Their clothes were white and clean. In the summer the regulation dress for the prisoners was white linen jacket and trousers. Every one of them had a black circle about four inches in diameter sown on the back of his jacket. A whole hour was spent in drilling the convicts to answer properly if the great man should greet them. There were rehearsals. The major bustled about like one possessed. An hour before the general's appearance the convicts were all standing in their places like posts with their arms held stiffly to their sides. At last, at one o'clock, the general arrived. He was a general of great consequence, of such consequence that I believe all official hearts must have throbbed all over Western Siberia at his arrival. He walked in sternly and majestically, followed by a great suite of the local authorities in attendance on him, several generals and colonels among them. There was one civilian, a tall and handsome gentleman in a swallow-tail coat and low shoes, who had come from Petersburg, too, and who behaved with extreme freedom and independence. The general frequently turned to him and with marked courtesy. This interested the convicts immensely—a civilian and treated with such esteem and by such a general, too! Later on they found out his surname and who he was, but there were numbers of theories. Our major, wearing a tight uniform with an orange-coloured collar, with his bloodshot eyes and crimson pimply face, did not, I fancy, make a particularly agreeable impression on the general. As a sign of special respect to the distinguished visitor, he had taken off his spectacles. He stood at a little distance, stiffly erect, and his whole figure seemed feverishly anticipating the moment when he might be wanted to fly to carry out his excellency's wishes. But he was not wanted. The general walked through the prison-ward in silence, he glanced into the kitchen; I believe he tried the soup. I was pointed out to him, they told him my story, and that I was of the educated class.

"Ah!" answered the general. "And how is he behaving himself now?"

"So far, satisfactorily, your excellency," they answered him.

The general nodded, and two minutes later he went out of the prison. The convicts were, of course, dazzled and bewildered, but yet they remained in some perplexity. Complaints against the major were, of course, out of the question. And the major was perfectly certain of that beforehand.

CHAPTER VI

PRISON ANIMALS

THE PURCHASE OF SORREL, an event which took place shortly afterwards in the prison, occupied and entertained the prisoners far more agreeably than the grand visit. We kept a horse in the prison for bringing water, carrying away refuse and such things. A convict was told off to look after it. He used to drive it, too, accompanied, of course, by a guard. There was a great deal of work for our horse, both in the morning and in the evening. The former Sorrel had been in our service for a long time. It was a good horse, but worn out. One fine morning, just before St. Peter's Day, this old Sorrel fell down after bringing in the barrel of water for the evening, and died within a few minutes. They were sorry for him; they all collected around him, discussing and disputing. The old cavalrymen, the gipsies, and the veterinary surgeons among us showered great erudition as regards horses on the occasion and even came to abusing one another, but they did not get old Sorrel on to his legs again. He lay dead with distended belly, which they all seemed to feel bound to poke at with their fingers. The major was informed of this act of God, and he at once decided that a new horse should be bought. On the morning of St. Peter's Day after mass, when we were all assembled together, horses for sale were led in. It was a matter of course that the convicts themselves should make the selection. There were some genuine connoisseurs in horse-flesh amongst us, and to deceive two hundred and fifty men who were specialists on the subject would be difficult. Kirghiz nomads, horse-dealers, gipsies, and townspeople turned up with horses. The convicts awaited with impatience the arrival of each fresh horse. They were as happy as children. What flattered them most of all was that they were buying a horse as though for themselves, as though they were really paying for it out of their own money, and had a full right to buy it like free men. Three horses were led in and taken away before they settled upon the fourth. The dealers who came in looked about them with some astonishment and even timidity and glanced round from time to time at the guards who led them in. A rabble of two hundred of these fellows, shaven, branded and fettered, at home in their own prison nest, the threshold of which no one ever crosses, inspired a certain sort of respect. Our fellows invented all sorts of subtleties by way of testing each horse that was brought; they looked it over and felt it in every part, and what is more, with an air as businesslike, as serious and important as though the welfare of the prison depended upon it. The Circassians even took a gallop on the horse. Their eyes glowed and they gabbled in their incomprehensible dialect, showing their white teeth and nodding with their swarthy, hook-nosed faces. Some of the Russians kept their whole attention riveted upon the Circassians' discussion, gazing into their eyes as though they would jump into them. Not understanding their language, they tried to guess from the expression of their eyes whether they had decided that the horse would do or not, and such strained attention might well seem strange to a spectator. One wonders why a convict should be so deeply concerned in the matter—and a convict so insignificant, humble and down-trodden that he would not have dared to lift up his voice before some of his own comrades—as though he had been buying a horse for himself, as though it made any difference to him what sort of horse were bought. Besides the Circassians, the former horse-dealers and gipsies were the most conspicuous; they were allowed the first word, there was even something like a chivalrous duel between two convicts in particular—Kulikov, who had been a gipsy horse-stealer and horse-dealer, and a self-taught vet, a shrewd Siberian peasant who had lately come to the prison and had already succeeded in carrying off all Kulikov's practice in the town. Our prison vets were greatly esteemed in the town, and not only the shopkeepers and merchants, but even the higher gentry applied to the prison when their horses fell ill, in spite of the fact that there were several regular veterinary surgeons in the town. Kulikov had had no rival until Yolkin, the Siberian peasant, had appeared upon the scene; he had a large practice and was, of course, paid for his services. He was a terrible gipsy and charlatan, and knew much less than he pretended. As far as money went he was an aristocrat among us and by his experience, intelligence, audacity and determination he had long won the involuntary respect of all the convicts in the prison. He was listened to and obeyed among us. But he talked little; he spoke as though he were making one a present of his words, and only opened his lips on the most important occasions. He was a regular fop, but he had a great deal of genuine energy. He was no longer young, but very handsome and very clever. He behaved to us convicts of the upper class with a sort of refined courtesy, and at the same time with extraordinary dignity. I believe that if he had been dressed-up and introduced into some club in Moscow or Petersburg as a count he would have been quite at home even there, would have played whist, would have talked well, speaking little but with weight, and that perhaps it would not have been detected all the evening that he was not a count but a tramp. I am speaking seriously; he was so clever, resourceful and quick-witted, moreover he had excellent manners and a good deal of style. He must have had many experiences of different kinds in his life. But his past was wrapped in the mists of obscurity. He was in the special division. But after the arrival of Yolkin, who, though he was a peasant, was a very crafty man of fifty, a dissenter, Kulikov's fame as a vet began to decline. In two months' time Yolkin had carried off almost the whole of his practice in the town; he cured, and it seemed quite easily, horses that Kulikov had given up as hopeless. Yolkin even cured some that the town veterinary surgeons had looked upon as incurable.

This peasant had been brought to prison with some others for false coining. What had induced him at his age to mix himself up in such doings! He used to tell us, laughing at himself, that by melting down three real gold coins they could only turn out one counterfeit one. Kulikov was rather mortified at Yolkin's veterinary successes and indeed his glory began to wane among the convicts. He kept a mistress in the town, wore a velveteen coat, had a silver ring on his finger, wore an earring, and boots of his own with decorated tops. Now, from want of money, he was forced to begin trading in vodka. Therefore everyone expected that the enemies would be sure to have a fight over the purchase of the new Sorrel; the convicts awaited it with curiosity. Each of them had his followers; the leading spirits on both sides were already getting excited and were gradually beginning to fall foul of one another. Yolkin had already pursed up his crafty face in a most sarcastic smile. But it turned out that they were mistaken. Kulikov did not attempt to be abusive, but he behaved in a masterly way. He began by giving way and even listening with attention to his rival's criticism, but, catching up one of his sayings, he observed modestly and emphatically that he was mistaken, and before Yolkin could recover and correct himself, he proved to him that he was in error on this point and on that. In fact Yolkin was routed quite unexpectedly and skilfully, and though he still carried the day, Kulikov's followers were satisfied.

"No, lads, you don't beat him easily; he can take his own part, rather!" said some.

"Yolkin knows more!" observed others, but they observed it rather deprecatingly. Both parties spoke suddenly in very conciliatory tones.

"It's not that he knows more, simply he has a lighter hand. And as for treating cattle, Kulikov is equal to anything there!"

"That he is, lad!"

"That he is."

Our new Sorrel was at last chosen and bought. It was a capital horse, young, strong and good-looking, with an extremely pleasant, good-humoured expression. It was, of course, irreproachable in all other respects. The convicts began haggling. The dealers asked thirty roubles, our fellows offered twenty-five. The bargaining was hot and lengthy. They kept adding and subtracting. At last they were amused at it themselves.

"Are you going to take the money out of your own purse? What are you bargaining about?" said some.

"Do you want to spare the government?" cried others.

"But, after all, lads, after all, it's sort of common money."

"Common money! Well, to be sure, there's no need to sow fools like us, we spring up of ourselves."

At last the bargain was clinched for twenty-eight roubles. The major was informed and the purchase was completed. Of course they brought out bread and salt and led the new Sorrel into the prison with all due ceremony. I don't think there was a convict who did not, on this occasion, pat the horse on the neck or stroke its nose. On the same day Sorrel was harnessed to bring in the water, and everyone looked with curiosity to see the new Sorrel drawing his barrel. Our water-carrier, Roman, looked at the new horse with extraordinary self-satisfaction. He was a peasant of fifty, of a silent and stolid character. And all Russian coachmen are of a very sedate and even taciturn character, as though it were really the case that constant association with horses gave a man a special sedateness and even dignity. Roman was quiet, friendly to everyone, not talkative; he used to take pinches from a horn of tobacco and had always from time immemorial looked after the prison Sorrels. The one that had just been bought was the third of that name. The convicts were all convinced that a horse of sorrel colour was suited to the prison, that it would be, so to speak, better for the house. Roman, too, maintained this idea. Nothing would have induced them to buy a piebald horse, for instance. The task of water-carrier was, by some special privilege, always reserved for Roman, and none of us would ever have dreamt of disputing his right. When the last Sorrel died, it never occurred to anyone, even the major, to blame Roman; it was God's will, that was all about it, and Roman was a good driver.

Soon the new Sorrel became the favourite of the prison. Though the convicts are a rough set of men, they often went up to stroke him. It sometimes happened that Roman, returning from the river with the water, got down to close the gate which the sergeant had opened for him, and Sorrel would stand still in the yard with the barrel, waiting for him, and looking towards him out of the corner of his eyes. "Go on alone," Roman would shout to him, and Sorrel would immediately go on alone, right up to the kitchen door, where he would stop, waiting for the cooks and the slop-pail men to come with their buckets for the water. "Clever Sorrel," the prisoners shouted to him; "he's brought the water alone! He does as he is told!"

"There, upon my word! Only a beast, but he understands!" "He is a capital fellow, Sorrel!"

Sorrel snorts and shakes his head as though he really did understand and is pleased at the praise. And someone is sure to bring him bread and salt at this point. Sorrel eats it and nods his head again as though to say: "I know you, I know you! I am a nice horse and you are a good man."

I used to like taking bread to Sorrel. It was pleasant to look into his handsome face and to feel on the palm of one's hand his soft warm lips quickly picking up the offering.

Our prisoners in general would readily have been fond of animals, and if they had been allowed, they would gladly have reared all sorts of domestic birds and animals in prison. And could anything be more calculated to soften and elevate the harsh and savage character of the convicts than such occupation? But this was not allowed. It was forbidden by the regulations, and there was no place suitable for it.

Yet it happened that there were several animals in prison during my time there. Besides Sorrel, we had dogs, geese, the goat Vaska and, for some time, there was an eagle.

We had as a permanent prison dog, as I mentioned already, Sharik, a clever, good-natured animal with whom I was always on friendly terms. But as among the peasants everywhere the dog is always looked upon as an unclean animal whom one should scarcely notice, hardly anyone paid any attention to Sharik. The dog was simply there, slept in the yard, lived on the scraps from the kitchen, and no one took any particular interest in him; it knew everyone, however, and looked upon everyone in prison as its master. When the prisoners came in from work, as soon as the shout "Corporals!" was heard at the guard-house, the dog ran to the gates with a friendly greeting for every group, wagging his tail and looking affectionately in the face of every convict as he came in, hoping for some sort of caress. But for many years he did not succeed in winning a caress from anyone except me, and so he loved me more than all.

I don't remember how it was that another dog, Byelka, came among us. The third, Kultyapka, I introduced myself, bringing him in as a puppy from where we were working. Byelka was a strange creature. He had once been run over by a cart and his spine was curved inwards, so that when he ran it looked like two white animals running, grown together. He was mangy too, and had discharging eyes; his tail, which was always between his legs, was mangy and patchy, almost without hair. A victim of destiny, he had evidently made up his mind to accept his lot without repining. He never barked or growled at anyone, as though he had not courage to. He lived for the most part behind the prison barracks in the hope of picking up food; if he saw any of us he would immediately, while we were some paces away, turn over on his back as a sign of humility, as much as to say, "Do with me what you will, you see I have no thought of resistance." And every convict before whom he rolled over would give him a kick with his boot, as though he felt it incumbent on him to do so. "Ah, the nasty brute," the convicts would say. But Byelka did not even dare to squeal, and if the pain was too much for him would give a muffled plaintive whine. He would roll over in the same way before Sharik or any other dog when anything called him outside the prison walls. He used to turn over and lie humbly on his back when some big long-eared dog rushed at him growling and barking. But dogs like humility and submissiveness in their fellows. The savage dog was at once softened and stood with some hesitation over the submissive creature lying before him with his legs in the air, and slowly, with great curiosity, he would begin sniffing him all over. What could the trembling Byelka have been thinking all this time? What if he bites me, the ruffian? was probably what was in his mind. But after sniffing him over attentively, the dog would leave him at last, finding nothing particularly interesting about him. Byelka would at once leap up and again hobble after the long string of dogs who were following some charming bitch, and though he knew for a certainty that he would never be on speaking terms with the charmer, still he hobbled after in the distance and it was a comfort to him in his trouble. He had apparently ceased to consider the point of honour; having lost all hope of a career in the future, he lived only for daily bread, and was fully aware of the fact. I once tried to caress him; it was something so new and unexpected for him that he suddenly collapsed on all fours on the ground trembling all over and beginning to whine aloud with emotion. I often patted him from compassion. After that he could not meet me without whining. As soon as he saw me in the distance, he would begin whining tearfully and hysterically. He ended by being killed by dogs on the rampart outside the prison.

Kultyapka was a dog of quite a different character. Why I brought him from the workshop into the prison when he was still a blind puppy, I don't know. I liked feeding him and bringing him up. Sharik at once took Kultyapka under his wing and used to sleep with him. When Kultyapka began to grow up, Sharik would let him bite his ears, pull his coat and play with him, as grown-up dogs usually play with puppies. Strange to say, Kultyapka hardly grew at all in height, but only in length and breadth. His coat was shaggy and of a light mouse colour; one ear hung down and one stood up. He was of a fervent and enthusiastic disposition like every puppy, who will as a rule squeal and bark with delight at seeing his master, dart up to lick his face and be ready to give the rein to all his other emotions, feeling that the proprieties are not to be considered and that all that matters is to show his enthusiasm. Wherever I might be, if I called "Kultyapka!" he would appear at once round some corner as though he had sprung out of the earth, and would fly to me with squealing rapture, turning somersaults and rolling over like a ball as he came. I was awfully fond of this little monster. It seemed as though fate had nothing in store for him but joy and prosperity. But one fine day a convict called Neustroev, who made women's shoes and tanned skins, happened to take special notice of him. An idea seemed to strike him. He called Kultyapka to him, felt his coat and rolled him on his back in a friendly way. Kultyapka, suspecting nothing, squealed with delight. But next morning he disappeared. I looked for him for a long time; he had utterly vanished. And only a fortnight later all was explained. Neustroev had taken a particular fancy to Kultyapka's coat. He skinned him, tanned the skin and lined with it the warm velvet boots which had been bespoken by the auditor's wife. He showed me the boots when they were finished. The dog-skin lining looked wonderfully well. Poor Kultyapka!

Many prisoners tanned skins, and they often brought into the prison dogs with good coats, who instantly disappeared. Some of these dogs were stolen, some even bought. I remember once seeing two convicts behind the kitchen consulting together and very busy about something. One of them held by a string a magnificent big black dog evidently of an expensive breed. Some rascal of a servant had brought it from his master's and sold it for about sixpence to our shoemakers. The convicts were just going to hang it. This was a thing very easily done; they would strip off the skin and flung the dead body into the big deep cesspool in the furthest corner of the prison yard, which stank horribly in the hottest days of summer. It was rarely cleaned out. The poor dog seemed to understand the fate in store for it. It glanced at each of the three of us in turn with searching and uneasy eyes and from time to time ventured to wag its drooping bushy tail, as though trying to soften us by this sign of its trust. I made haste to move away, and they no doubt finished the job to their satisfaction.

It was by chance that we came to keep geese. Who first introduced them and to whom they really belonged I don't know, but for some time they were a source of great diversion to the convicts and even became familiar objects in the town. They were hatched in the prison and were kept in the kitchen. When all the goslings were full grown, they all used to follow the convicts to work in a flock. As soon as the drum sounded and the prisoners began to move towards the gates, our geese would run after us, cackling, fluttering their wings one after another leaping over the high sill of the gate, and would unhesitatingly turn towards the right wing and there draw up and wait till the convicts were ready to start. They always attached themselves to the largest party, and while the convicts were at work they would graze close by. As soon as the party began to move off again towards the prison, the geese started too. It was reported in the fortress how the geese followed the convicts to work. "Hullo, here are the convicts with their geese," people would say when they met them. "How did you train them?" "Here's something for the geese," another would add and give us alms. But in spite of their devotion they were all killed for some feast day.

On the other hand nothing would have induced the convicts to kill our goat, Vaska, if it had not been for a special circumstance. I don't know where he came from either, or who brought him into the prison, but one day a very charming little white kid made his appearance. In a few days we all grew fond of him and began to find entertainment and even consolation in him. They even found an excuse for keeping him by saying, "If we have a stable in the prison, we must have a goat." He did not, however, live in the stable, but at first in the kitchen and afterwards all over the prison. He was a very graceful, very mischievous creature. He ran up when he was called, jumped on benches and tables, butted at the convicts, and was always merry and amusing. One evening when his horns had grown fairly big, a Lezghian called Babay, who was sitting on the steps with a group of other convicts, took it into his head to butt at the goat; they were knocking their foreheads together for a long time—to play like this with the goat was a favourite pastime of the convicts—when suddenly Vaska skipped on to the topmost step, and as soon as Babay turned aside, the goat instantly reared on its hind legs and, bending his fore-legs inward, he butted with all his might at the back of Babay's head so that the man flew head over heels off the steps to the intense glee of all present, especially Babay himself. Everyone was awfully fond of Vaska, in fact.

When he began to be full grown it was decided after a long and earnest deliberation to perform a certain operation on him which our veterinary specialists were very skilful in, "or he will smell so goaty," said the convicts. After that Vaska grew fearfully fat. The convicts used to feed him, too, as though they were fattening him up. He grew at last into a fine and handsome goat of extraordinary size with very long horns. He waddled as he walked. He, too, used to follow us to work, to the diversion of the convicts and of everyone we met. Everyone knew the prison goat, Vaska. Sometimes if they were working on the bank of the river, for instance, the convicts would gather tender willow shoots and other leaves and pick flowers on the rampart to decorate Vaska with them; they would wreathe flowers and green shoots round his horns and hang garlands all over his body. Vaska would return to the prison always in front of the convicts, decked out, and they would follow him, and seem proud of him when they met anyone. This admiration for the goat reached such a pitch that some of our men, like children, suggested that they might gild Vaska's horns. But they only talked of doing this, it was never actually done. I remember, however, asking Akim Akimitch, who, after Isay Fomitch, was our best gilder, whether one could really gild goats' horns. At first he looked attentively at the goat and after serious consideration he replied that it was perhaps possible, but that it would not be lasting and would besides be utterly useless. With that the matter dropped. And Vaska might have lived for years in the prison and would perhaps have died of shortness of breath. But one day as he was returning home decked out with flowers at the head of the convicts, he was met by the major in his droshki. "Stop!" he roared; "whose goat is it?" It was explained to him. "What! a goat in the prison and without my permission! Sergeant!" The sergeant came forward and the order was promptly given that the goat should be immediately killed, that the skin should be sold in the market, and the money for it be put into the prison purse, and that the meat should be served out to the convicts in the soup. There was a great deal of talk and lamentation in the prison, but they did not dare to disobey. Vaska was slaughtered over the cesspool in the yard. One of the convicts bought the whole of the meat, paying a rouble and a half for it into the prison purse. With this money they bought rolls and the convict sold the meat in portions to the prisoners to be roasted. The meat turned out really to be exceptionally good.

We had for some time in the prison an eagle, one of the small eagles of the steppes. Someone brought him into the prison wounded and exhausted. All the prisoners crowded round him; he could not fly; his right wing hung down on the ground, one leg was dislocated. I remember how fiercely he glared at us, looking about him at the inquisitive crowd, and opened his crooked beak, prepared to sell his life dearly. When they had looked at him long enough and were beginning to disperse, he hopped limping on one leg and fluttering his uninjured wing to the furthest end of the prison yard, where he took refuge in a corner right under the fence. He remained with us for three months, and all that time would not come out of his corner. At first the convicts often went to look at him and used to set the dog at him. Sharik would fly at him furiously, but was evidently afraid to get too near. This greatly diverted the convicts. "Savage creature! He'll never give in!" they used to say. Later Sharik began cruelly ill-treating him. He got over his fear, and when they set him on the eagle he learnt to catch him by his injured wing. The eagle vigorously defended himself with his beak and, huddled in his corner, he looked fiercely and proudly like a wounded king at the inquisitive crowd who came to stare at him.

At last everyone was tired of him; everyone forgot him, abandoned him, yet every day there were pieces of fresh meat and a broken pot of water near him. So someone was looking after him. At first he would not eat, and ate nothing for several days; at last he began taking food, but he would never take it from anyone's hand or in the presence of people. It happened that I watched him more than once. Seeing no one and thinking that he was alone, he sometimes ventured to come a little way out of his corner and limped a distance of twelve paces along the fence, then he went back and then went out again, as though he were taking exercise. Seeing me he hastened back to his corner, limping and hopping, and throwing back his head, opening his beak, with his feathers ruffled, at once prepared for battle. None of my caresses could soften him; he pecked and struggled, would not take meat from me, and all the time I was near him he used to stare intently in my face with his savage, piercing eyes. Fierce and solitary he awaited death, mistrustful and hostile to all. At last the convicts seemed to remember him, and though no one had mentioned him, or done anything for him for two months, everyone seemed suddenly to feel sympathy for him. They said that they must take the eagle out. "Let him die if he must, but not in prison," they said.

"To be sure, he is a free, fierce bird; you can't get him used to prison," others agreed.

"It's not like us, it seems," added someone.

"That's a silly thing to say. He's a bird and we are men, aren't we?"

"The eagle is the king of the forests, brothers," began Skuratov, but this time they did not listen to him.

One day, after dinner, when the drum had just sounded for us to go to work, they took the eagle, holding his beak, for he began fighting savagely, and carried him out of the prison. We got to the rampart. The twelve men of the party were eagerly curious to see where the eagle would go. Strange to say, they all seemed pleased, as though they too had won a share of freedom.

"See, the cur, one does something for his good, and he keeps biting one," said the convict who was carrying him, looking at the fierce bird almost with affection.

"Let him go, Mikitka!"

"It's no use rigging up a jack-in-the-box for him, it seems. Give him freedom, freedom full and free!"

He threw the eagle from the rampart into the plain. It was a cold, gloomy day in late autumn, the wind was whistling over the bare plain and rustling in the yellow, withered, tussocky grass of the steppes. The eagle went off in a straight line, fluttering his injured wing, as though in haste to get away from us anywhere. With curiosity the convicts watched his head flitting through the grass.

"Look at him!" said one dreamily. "He doesn't look round!" added another. "He hasn't looked round once, lads, he just runs off!"

"Did you expect him to come back to say thank you?" observed a third.

"Ah, to be sure it's freedom. It's freedom he sniffs."

"You can't see him now, mates . . . ."

"What are you standing for? March!" shouted the guards, and we all trudged on to work in silence.

CHAPTER VII

THE COMPLAINT

IN BEGINNING THIS CHAPTER the editor of the late Alexandr Petrovitch Goryanchikov's notes feels it his duty to make the following statement to the reader:————

In the first chapter of "The House of the Dead" some words were said about a parricide belonging to the upper class. Among other things he was quoted as an instance of the callousness with which the convicts will sometimes speak of their crimes. It was stated, too, that the murderer did not admit his guilt at his trial, but that judging by accounts given by people who knew all the details of his story, the facts were so clear that it was impossible to have any doubt of his guilt. These people told the author of the notes that the criminal was a man of reckless behaviour, that he had got into debt, and had killed his father because he coveted the fortune he would inherit from him. But all the people in the town where this parricide had lived told the story in the same way. Of this last fact the editor of these notes has fairly trustworthy information. Finally, it was stated in these notes that the criminal was always in the best of spirits in prison; that he was a whimsical, frivolous fellow, extremely lacking in common sense, though by no means a fool, that the author had never noticed in him any sign of cruelty. And the words are added: "Of course I did not believe in that crime."

The other day the editor of the notes from "The House of the Dead" received information from Siberia that the criminal really was innocent and had suffered ten years in penal servitude for nothing; that his innocence had been established before a court, officially, that the real criminals had been found and had confessed, and that the luckless fellow had been already released from prison. The editor can feel no doubt of the truth of this news. There is nothing more to add. There is no need to enlarge on all the tragic significance of this fact, and to speak of the young life crushed under this terrible charge. The fact is too impressive, it speaks for itself.

We believe, too, that if such a fact can be possible, this possibility adds a fresh and striking feature to the description of "The House of the Dead," and puts a finishing touch to the picture.

Now we will continue.

I have already said that I did at last become accustomed to my position in prison. But this came to pass painfully and with difficulty and far too gradually. It took me almost a year, in fact, to reach this stage, and that was the hardest year of my life. And that is why the whole of it is imprinted on my memory for ever. I believe I remember every successive hour of that year. I said, also, that other convicts, too, could not get used to that life. I remember how in that first year I often wondered to myself what they were feeling, could they be contented? And I was much occupied with these questions. I have mentioned already that all the convicts lived in prison not as though they were at home there, but as though they were at a hotel, on a journey, at some temporary halt. Even men sentenced for their whole life were restless or miserable, and no doubt every one of them was dreaming of something almost impossible. This everlasting uneasiness, which showed itself unmistakably, though not in words, this strange impatient and intense hope, which sometimes found involuntary utterance, at times so wild as to be almost like delirium, and what was most striking of all, often persisted in men of apparently the greatest common sense—gave a special aspect and character to the place, so much so that it constituted perhaps its most typical characteristic. It made one feel, almost from the first moment, that there was nothing like this outside the prison walls. Here all were dreamers, and this was apparent at once. What gave poignancy to this feeling was the fact that this dreaminess gave the greater number of the prisoners a gloomy and sullen, almost abnormal, expression. The vast majority were taciturn and morose to the point of vindictiveness; they did not like displaying their hopes. Candour, simplicity were looked on with contempt. The more fantastical his hopes, and the more conscious the dreamer himself was of their fantastical character, the more obstinately and shyly he concealed them in his heart, but he could not renounce them. Who knows, some perhaps were inwardly ashamed of them. There is so much sober-mindedness and grasp of reality in the Russian character, and with it such inner mockery of self. Perhaps it was this continual hidden self-dissatisfaction which made these men so impatient with one another in the daily affairs of life, so irritable and sneering with one another, and if, for instance, some one of them rather simpler and more impatient than the rest were to make himself conspicuous by uttering aloud what was in the secret mind of all, and were to launch out into dreams and hopes, the others roughly put him down at once, suppressed him and ridiculed him; but I fancy that the harshest of his assailants were just those who perhaps outstripped him in their own hopes and dreams. Candid and simple people were, as I have said already, looked upon generally as the vulgarest fools, and they were treated with contempt. Every man was so ill-humoured and vain that he despised anyone good-natured and free from vanity. All but these naïve and simple chatterers, all the taciturn, that is, may be sharply divided into the ill-natured and the good-natured, the sullen and the serene. There were far more of the ill-natured and the sullen, and those of them who were naturally talkative were infallibly uneasy backbiters and slanderers. They meddled in everyone's affairs, though of their own hearts, their own private affairs, they showed no one a glimpse. That was not the thing, not correct. The good-natured—a very small group—were quiet, hid their imaginings in their hearts, and were of course more prone than the ill-natured to put faith and hope in them. Yet I fancy that there was another group of prisoners who had lost all hope. Such was the old dissenter from the Starodubovsky settlements; there were very few of these. The old man was externally calm (I have described him already), but from certain symptoms I judge that his inner misery was terrible. But he had his means of escape, his salvation— prayer, and the idea of martyrdom. The convict whom I have described already, who used to read the Bible, and who went out of his mind and threw a brick at the major, was probably one of the desperate class too, one of those who have lost their last hope, and as life is impossible without hope he found a means of escape in a voluntary and almost artificial martyrdom. He declared that he attacked the major without malice, simply to "accept suffering." And who knows what psychological process was taking place in his heart then! Without some goal and some effort to reach it no man can live. When he has lost all hope, all object in life, man often becomes a monster in his misery. The one object of the prisoners was freedom and to get out of prison.

But here I have been trying to classify all the prisoners, and that is hardly possible. Real life is infinite in its variety in comparison with even the cleverest abstract generalization, and it does not admit of sharp and sweeping distinctions. The tendency of real life is always towards greater and greater differentiation. We, too, had a life of our own of a sort, and it was not a mere official existence but a real inner life of our own.

But, as I have mentioned already, I did not, and indeed could not, penetrate to the inner depths of this life at the beginning of my time in prison, and so all its external incidents were a source of unutterable misery to me then. I sometimes was simply beginning to hate those men who were sufferers like myself. I even envied them for being, anyway, among their equals, their comrades, understanding one another; though in reality they were all as sick and weary as I was of this companionship enforced by stick and lash, of this compulsory association, and everyone was secretly looking towards something far away from all the rest. I repeat again, there were legitimate grounds for the envy which came upon me in moments of ill-humour. Those who declare that it is no harder for a gentleman, an educated man and all the rest of it, in our prisons and in Siberia than it is for any peasant are really quite wrong. I know I have heard of theories on the subject of late, I have read of them. There is something true and humane at the back of this idea—all are men, all are human beings. But the idea is too abstract. It overlooks too many practical aspects of the question, which cannot be grasped except by experience. I don't say this on the grounds that the gentleman, the man of education, may be supposed to be more refined and delicate in his feelings, that he is more developed. There is no standard by which to measure the soul and its development. Even education itself is no test. I am ready to be the first to testify that, in the midst of these utterly uneducated and down-trodden sufferers, I came across instances of the greatest spiritual refinement. Sometimes one would know a man for years in prison and despise him and think that he was not a human being but a brute. And suddenly a moment will come by chance when his soul will suddenly reveal itself in an involuntary outburst, and you see in it such wealth, such feeling, such heart, such a vivid understanding of its own suffering, and of the suffering of others, that your eyes are open and for the first moment you can't believe what you have seen and heard yourself. The contrary happens too; education is sometimes found side by side with such barbarity, such cynicism, that it revolts you, and in spite of the utmost good-nature and all previous theories on the subject, you can find no justification or apology.

I am not speaking of the change of habits, of manner of life, of diet, etc., though that is harder of course for a man of the wealthier class than for a peasant, who has often been hungry when free, and in prison at least has enough to eat. I am not going to argue about that. Let us assume that for a man of any strength of will all this is of little consequence compared with other discomforts, though in reality a change of habits is not a trifling matter nor of little consequence. But there are discomforts beside which all this is so trivial that one ceases to notice the filth of one's surroundings, the fetters, the close confinement, the insufficient and unclean food. The sleekest fine gentleman, the softest weakling will be able to eat black bread and soup with beetles in it, after working in the sweat of his brow, as he has never worked in freedom. To this one can get accustomed, as described in the humorous prison song which tells of a fine gentleman in prison:

> Cabbage and water they give me to eat,
> And I gobble it up as though it were sweet.

No; what is much more important than all this is that while two hours after his arrival an ordinary prisoner is on the same footing as all the rest, is *at home*, has the same rights in the community as the rest, is understood by everyone, understands everyone, knows everyone, and is looked on by everyone as a comrade, it is very different with the *gentleman*, the man of a different class. However straightforward, good-natured and clever he is, he will for years be hated and despised by all; he will not be understood, and what is more he will not be trusted. He is not a friend, and not a comrade, and though he may at last in the course of years attain such a position among them that they will no longer insult him, yet he will never be one of them, and will for ever be painfully conscious that he is solitary and remote from all. This remoteness sometimes comes to pass of itself unconsciously through no ill-natured feeling on the part of the convicts. He is not one of themselves, and that's all. Nothing is more terrible than living out of one's natural surroundings. A peasant transported from Taganrog to the port of Petropavlovsk at once finds the Russian peasants there exactly like himself, at once understands them, and gets on with them, and in a couple of hours they may settle down peaceably to live in the same hut or shanty. It is very different with gentlemen. They are divided from the peasants by an impassable gulf, and this only becomes fully apparent when the *gentleman* is by force of external circumstances completely deprived of his former privileges, and is transformed into a peasant. You may have to do with the peasants all your life, you may associate with them every day for forty years, officially for instance, in the regulation administrative forms, or even simply in a friendly way, as a benefactor or, in a certain sense, a father—you will never know them really. It will all be an optical illusion and nothing more. I know that all who read what I say will think that I am exaggerating. But I am convinced of its truth. I have reached the conviction, not from books, not from abstract theory, but from experience, and I have had plenty of time to verify it. Perhaps in time everyone will realize the truth of this.

Events, as ill-luck would have it, confirmed my observations from the first and had a morbid and unhinging influence on me. That first summer I wandered about the prison in almost complete loneliness, without a friend. As I have mentioned already, I was in such a state of mind that I could not even distinguish and appreciate those of the prisoners who were later on able to grow fond of me, though they never treated me as an equal. I had comrades too of my own class, but their comradeship did not ease my heart of its oppression. I hated the sight of everything and I had no means of escape from it. And here, for instance, is one of the incidents which from the beginning made me understand how completely I was an outsider, and how peculiar my position was in the prison.

One day that summer, early in July, on a bright hot working day at one o'clock, when usually we rested before our afternoon work, the prisoners all got up like one man and began forming in the yard. I had heard nothing about it till that minute. At that time I used to be so absorbed in myself that I scarcely noticed what was going on about me. Yet the prisoners had for the last three days been in a state of suppressed excitement. Perhaps this excitement had begun much earlier, as I reflected afterwards when I recalled snatches of talk, and at the same time the increased quarrelsomeness of the convicts and the moroseness and peculiar irritability that had been conspicuous in them of late. I had put it down to the hard work, the long wearisome summer days, the unconscious dreams of the forest and of freedom, and the brief nights, in which it was difficult to get enough sleep. Perhaps all this was working together now into one outbreak, but the pretext for this outbreak was the prison food. For some days past there had been loud complaints and indignation in the prison, and especially when we were gathered together in the kitchen at dinner or supper; they were discontented with the cooks and even tried to get a new one, but quickly dismissed him and went back to the old. In fact all were in an unsettled state of mind.

"They work us hard and they feed us on tripe," someone would growl in the kitchen.

"If you don't like it, order a blancmange," another would reply.

"I like soup made of tripe, lads," a third would put in, "it's nice."

"But if you never get anything else but tripe, is it nice?"

"Now, to be sure, it's time for meat," said a fourth; "we toil and toil at the brickyard; when one's work's done, one wants something to eat. And what is tripe?"

"And if it is not tripe, it's heart."

"Yes, there's that heart too. Tripe and heart, that's all they give us. Fine fare that is! Is that justice or is it not?"

"Yes, the food's bad."

"He's filling his pockets, I warrant."

"It's not your business."

"Whose then? It's my belly. If everybody would make a complaint we should get something done."

"A complaint?"

"Yes."

"It seems you didn't get flogged enough for that complaint. You image!"

"That's true," another who had hitherto been silent said grumpily. "It's easy talking. What are you going to say in your complaint? You'd better tell us that first, you blockhead!"

"All right, I'll tell you. If all would come, I'd speak with all. It's being poor, it is! Some of us eat their own food, and some never sit down but to prison fare."

"Ah, the sharp-eyed, envious fellow! His eyes smart to see others well off."

"Don't covet another man's pelf, but up and earn it for yourself!"

"I'll dispute that with you till my hair is grey. So you are a rich man, since you want to sit with your arms folded?"

"Eroshka is fat with a dog and a cat!"

"But truly, lads, why sit still? We've had enough of putting up with their fooling. They are skinning us. Why not go to them?"

"Why not? You want your food chewed, and put into your mouth, that's what you are used to. Because it's prison, that's why!"

"When simple folk fall out, the governor grows fat."

"Just so. Eight-eyes has grown fat. He's bought a pair of greys."

"Yes, and he is not fond of drinking, eh?"

"He was fighting the other day with the veterinary over cards. They were at it all night. Our friend was two hours at fisticuffs with him. Fedka said so."

"That's why we have stewed heart."

"Ah, you fools! It's not for us to put ourselves forward."

"But if we all go, then we shall see what defence he will make. We must insist on that."

"Defence! He'll give you a punch in the face and that will be all."

"And then court-martial us afterwards."

In short everyone was excited. At that time our food really was poor. And besides, all sorts of things came simultaneously—above all, the general mood of depression, the continual hidden misery. The convict is from his very nature fault-finding, mutinous; but the mutiny of all or even of a large number is rare, owing to the continual dissensions among them. Every one of them is aware of it; that's why they are much more given to violent language than to deeds. But this time the excitement did not pass off without action. They began collecting in groups about the prison wards, arguing; they recalled with oaths the whole of the major's term of office, ferreted out every detail. Some were particularly excited. Agitators and ringleaders always turn up at such times. The ringleaders on these occasions—that is, on the occasion of a complaint being made—are always remarkable men, and not only in prison, but in gangs of workmen, companies of soldiers and so on. They are of a special type and everywhere have something in common. They are spirited men, eager for justice, and in perfect simplicity and honesty persuaded of its inevitable, direct and, above all, immediate possibility. These men are no stupider than their fellows, in fact there are some very clever ones among them, but they are too ardent to be shrewd and calculating. If there are men who are capable of skilfully leading the masses and winning their cause, they belong to a different class of popular heroes and natural leaders of the people, a type extremely rare among us. But those agitators and ringleaders of whom I am speaking now almost always fail, and are sent to prison and penal servitude in consequence. Through their zeal they fail, but it is their zeal that gives them their influence over the masses. Men follow them readily. Their warmth and honest indignation have an effect on everyone and in the end the most hesitating give their adherence to them. Their blind confidence in success seduces even the most inveterate sceptics, although sometimes this confidence has such feeble, such childish foundations that one wonders, looking on, how they can have gained a following. The great thing is that they march in the front and go forward fearing nothing. They rush straight before them like bulls, with their heads down, often with no knowledge of the affair, no caution, none of that practical casuistry by means of which the most vulgar and degraded man will sometimes succeed, attain his object and save his skin. They inevitably come to grief themselves. In ordinary life these people are choleric, contemptuous, irritable and intolerant. Most often they are of very limited intelligence and that, indeed, partly makes their strength. What is most annoying in them is that, instead of going straight for their object, they often go off on a side-issue into trifles, and it is this that is their ruin. But the people can understand them and therein lies their strength. I must, however, say a few words to explain what is meant by a *complaint*.

There were some men in our prison who had been sent there for making a complaint. They were the men who were most excited now. Especially one called Martinov, who had been in the hussars, a hot-headed, restless and suspicious man, but honest and truthful. Another was Vassily Antonov, a man as it were coldly irritated, with an insolent expression and a haughty, sarcastic smile, extremely intelligent, however. He too was honest and truthful. But I cannot describe all of them, there were a great many. Petrov among others was continually flitting backwards and forwards listening to all the groups, saying little, but evidently excited, and he was the first to run out when they began to assemble in the yard.

The sergeant whose duty it was to keep order among us at once came out in a panic. The convicts, drawn up in the yard, asked him politely to tell the major that the prisoners wanted to speak to him in person and to ask him about one or two points. All the veterans followed the sergeant and drew themselves up on the other side facing the prisoners. The message given to the sergeant was an extraordinary one and filled him with horror. But he dared not refuse to take it at once to the major. To begin with, since the prisoners had already come to this, something worse might happen—all the prison officials were extraordinarily cowardly with regard to the convicts. In the second place, even if there were nothing wrong and they should all think better of it and disperse at once, even then it was the duty of the sergeant to report everything that happened to the major at once. Pale and trembling with fear, he hastily went without attempting to question the convicts or reason with them himself. He saw that they would not even talk to him now.

Knowing nothing about it, I, too, went out to stand with the others. I only learnt the details of the affair later. I thought that some inspection was going on, but not seeing the soldiers whose duty it was to carry out the inspection, I wondered and began looking about me. The men's faces were excited and irritated. Some were even pale. All looked anxious and silent, in anticipation of speaking to the major. I noticed that several looked at me with extraordinary amazement, but turned away in silence. It obviously seemed strange to them that I should have joined them. They evidently did not believe that I had come out to take part in the complaint, but soon afterwards all who were around me turned to me again. All looked at me inquiringly.

"What are you here for?" Vassily Antonov, who stood further off than the rest, asked me in a loud, rude voice. Till then he had always addressed me formally and treated me with politeness.

I looked at him in perplexity, still trying to understand what it all meant, and beginning to guess that something extraordinary was happening.

"Yes, what need have you to stand here? Go indoors," said a young convict of the military division, a quiet, good-natured fellow whom I knew nothing of. "It's nothing to do with you."

"But they are all forming up, I thought there was an inspection," I said.

"I say, so he has crawled out, too!" shouted another.

"Iron beak!" said another. "Fly-crushers!" said a third with ineffable contempt. This new nickname evoked general laughter.

"He sits with us in the kitchen as a favour," answered someone.

"They're in clover everywhere. This is prison, but they have rolls to eat and buy sucking-pig. You eat your own provisions, why are you poking in here?"

"This is not the place for you, Alexandr Petrovitch," said Kulikov, approaching me in a nonchalant way; he took me by the arm and led me out of the ranks.

He was pale, his black eyes were gleaming, and he was biting his lower lip. He was not awaiting the major with indifference. I particularly liked looking at Kulikov, by the way, on all such occasions, that is, on all occasions when he had to show what he was. He posed fearfully, but he did what had to be done. I believe he would have gone to the scaffold with a certain style and gallantry. At this moment, when everyone was being rude and familiar to me, he with evident intention redoubled his courtesy to me, and at the same time his words were peculiarly, as it were disdainfully, emphatic and admitted of no protest.

"This is our affair, Alexandr Petrovitch, and you've nothing to do with it. You go away and wait. All your friends are in the kitchen; you go there."

"Under the ninth beam, where Antipka nimble-heels lives!" someone put in.

Through the open window of the kitchen I did, in fact, see our Poles. I fancied, however, that there were a good many people there besides. Disconcerted, I went into the kitchen. I was pursued by laughter, oaths and cries of tyu-tyu-tyu (the sound which took the place of whistling in prison).

"He didn't like it! Tyu-tyu-tyu! At him!" I had never before been so insulted in the prison, and this time I felt it very bitterly. But I had

turned up at the wrong moment. In the entry to the kitchen I met T.,
a young man of strong will and generous heart, of no great education,
though he was a man of good birth. He was a great friend of B's. The
other convicts marked him out from the rest of us "gentlemen" and
had some affection for him. He was brave, manly and strong, and this
was somehow apparent in every gesture.

"What are you doing, Goryanchikov?" he shouted to me; "come
here!"

"But what's the matter?"

"They are presenting a complaint, don't you know? It won't do
them any good; who'll believe convicts? They'll try to find out the instigators, and if we are there they'll be sure to pitch on us first as responsible for the mutiny. Remember what we came here for. They
will simply be flogged and we shall be tried. The major hates us all,
and will be glad to ruin us. And by means of us he'll save himself."

"And the convicts would be glad to betray us," added M., as we
went into the kitchen.

"You may be sure they wouldn't spare us," T. assented.

There were a great many other people, some thirty, besides us
"gentlemen" in the kitchen. They had all remained behind, not wishing to take part in the complaint—some from cowardice, others from
a full conviction of the uselessness of any sort of complaint. Among
them was Akim Akimitch, who had a natural and inveterate hostility to
all such complaints, as destructive of morality and official routine. He
said nothing, but waited in perfect tranquillity for the end of the affair,
not troubling himself as to its result, and thoroughly convinced of the
inevitable triumph of discipline and the will of the authorities. Isay
Fomitch was there, too, looking much perplexed, and with drooping
nose listening greedily and apprehensively to our conversation. He
was in great anxiety. All the Poles of the peasant class were here, too,
with their compatriots of the privileged class. There were some other
timid souls, people who were always silent and dejected. They had not
dared to join the others, and were mournfully waiting to see how it
would end. There were also some morose and always sullen convicts
who were not of a timid character. They stayed behind from obstinacy
and a contemptuous conviction that it was all foolishness, and that
nothing but harm would come of it. But yet I fancy they felt somewhat awkward now; they did not look perfectly at their ease. Though

they knew they were perfectly right about the complaint, as they were proved to be in the sequel, yet they felt rather as though they had cut themselves off from their mates, as though they had betrayed their comrades to the major. Another man who was in the kitchen was Yolkin, the Siberian peasant condemned for false coinage who had carried off Kulikov's practice as a vet in the town. The Starodubovsky Old Believer was there, too. The cooks to a man had remained in the kitchen, probably convinced that they constituted part of the prison management, and consequently that it was not seemly for them to act in opposition to it.

"Almost all have gone out except these, though," I observed hesitatingly to M.

"What, is it true?" muttered B.

"We should have run a hundred times more risk than they do if we went out, and why should we? *Je haïs ces brigands.** And can you imagine for a moment that their complaint will have any effect? Why should we meddle in this foolishness?"

"Nothing will come of it," put in another convict, a stubborn and exasperated old man. Almazov, who was present, made haste to agree with him, saying:

"Except that fifty of them will get a flogging, nothing will come of it."

"The major has come!" shouted someone, and all rushed eagerly to the windows.

The major flew up, spiteful and infuriated, flushed and wearing spectacles. Mutely but resolutely he went up to the front row. On such occasions he was really bold and never lost his presence of mind. Besides, he was almost always half drunk. Even his greasy forage cap with the orange band on it and his dirty silver epaulettes had a sinister aspect at this moment. He was followed by Dyatlov, the clerk, a very important person, who in reality governed everyone in the prison, and even had an influence over the major; he was a sly man, very cunning, but not a bad fellow. The convicts liked him. He was followed by our sergeant, who had evidently just come in for a fearful wigging, and was expecting something ten times worse later

---

*I hate these bandits (French).

on. Behind him were three or four guards, not more. The convicts, who had been standing with their caps off ever since they had sent the sergeant to fetch the major, now all drew themselves up and pulled themselves together; every man of them shifted from one leg to the other, and then they all stood mute and rigid, waiting for the first word or rather for the first shout of the major.

It followed promptly; at his second word the major bawled at the top of his voice, almost squealed, in fact; he was in a violent fury. From the windows we could see him running along the front rank, rushing up to the men, questioning them. But it was too far off for us to hear his questions or the convicts' replies. We could only hear him shouting shrilly:

"Mutineers! . . . Beating! . . . Ringleaders! You are a ringleader? You are a ringleader?" he shouted, pouncing on somebody.

No answer was audible. But a minute later we saw a convict leave the general body and walk towards the guard-house. A minute later another followed him in the same direction, then a third.

"All under arrest! I'll teach you! Whom have you got there in the kitchen?" he squealed, seeing us at the open windows. "All come here! Drive them here at once!"

The clerk Dyatlov came to us in the kitchen. In the kitchen he was told that we had no complaint to make. He returned at once and reported to the major.

"Ah, they haven't!" he repeated two notes lower, obviously relieved. "No matter, send them all here!"

We went out. I felt rather ashamed of coming out. And indeed, we all walked with hanging heads.

"Ah, Prokofyev! Yolkin too. Is that you, Almazov? Stand here—stand here all together," the major said to us in a soft but hurried voice, looking at us amicably. "M., you are here, too . . . Make a list of them, Dyatlov! Dyatlov, make a list at once of those who are satisfied and those who are dissatisfied; every one of them, and bring the list to me. I'll put you all . . . under arrest. I'll teach you, you rascals!"

The list had an effect.

"We are satisfied!" a grating voice said suddenly from the crowd of the dissatisfied, but he spoke rather hesitatingly.

"Ah, you are satisfied! Who's satisfied? Those who are satisfied come forward."

"We are satisfied, we are satisfied," several voices chimed in.

"Satisfied? Men, you've been led astray. So there have been agitators working upon you. So much the worse for them!"

"Good God, what's happening!" said a voice in the crowd.

"Who's that who shouted?" roared the major, rushing in the direction from which the voice came. "Is that you, Rastorguyev? You shouted? To the guard-house!"

Rastorguyev, a tall, puffy-faced young fellow, stepped out and walked at once towards the guard-house. It was not he who had spoken, but as he had been pitched upon he went.

"You don't know when you are well off!" the major howled after him. "Ah, you fat-face! I'll find you all out! Those who are satisfied, step forward!"

"We are satisfied, your honour!" murmured some dozens of gloomy voices; the rest remained stubbornly silent. But that was enough for the major. It was evidently to his advantage to end the scene as quickly as possible, and to end it somehow pacifically.

"Ah, now all are satisfied!" he said hurriedly. "I saw that . . . I knew it. It's the work of agitators! There must be agitators among them!" he went on, addressing Dyatlov. "We must go into that more carefully. But now . . . now it's time for work. Beat the drum!"

He was present himself at the telling off of convicts to their different tasks. The convicts dispersed in mournful silence to their work, glad at any rate to be out of his sight as soon as possible. But after they had gone, the major at once went to the guard-house and punished the "ringleaders," not very cruelly, however. He hurried over it, in fact. One of them, we were told afterwards, begged his pardon, and was at once let off. It was evident that the major was not perfectly at his ease, and was perhaps even a little scared. A complaint is always a ticklish matter, and though the convicts' protest could hardly be called a complaint, because it was presented not to a higher authority, but to the major himself, yet it was awkward, it was not the right thing. What disconcerted him most was that almost all the prisoners had taken part in the protest. He must suppress it at all costs. They soon released the ringleaders. Next day the food was better, but the improvement did not last long. For some days afterwards the major visited the prison more frequently and found fault more frequently. Our sergeant went about looking anxious and perplexed, as though he could not get over his amazement. As for the convicts, they could not settle down for a long time afterwards, but they were not so much excited as before, they were in a state of dumb perplexity and bewilderment. Some of them were deeply despondent. Others expressed their discontent, but sparingly. Many in their exasperation jeered at themselves aloud, as though to punish themselves for having got up the protest.

"Put it in your pipe and smoke it," someone would say.

"We had our joke and now we must pay for it!" another would add.

"What mouse can bell the cat?" observed a third.

"There's no teaching us without the stick, we all know. It's a good thing he didn't flog us all."

"For the future think more and talk less and you'll do better!" someone would observe malignantly.

"Why, are you setting up to teach?"

"To be sure I am."

"And who are you to put yourself forward?"

"Why, I am a man so far, and who are you?"

"You are a dog's bone, that's what you are."

"That's what you are."

"There, there, shut up! What's the shindy about!" the others shouted at the disputants from all sides.

The same evening, that is, on the day of the complaint, on my return from work, I met Petrov behind the barracks. He was looking for me. Coming up to me he muttered something, two or three vague exclamations, but soon relapsed into absent-minded silence and walked mechanically beside me. All this affair was still painfully weighing on my heart, and I fancied that Petrov could explain something to me.

"Tell me, Petrov," said I, "are they angry with us?"

"Who angry?" he asked, as though waking up.

"The convicts angry with us—the gentlemen."

"Why should they be angry with you?"

"Because we did not take part in the complaint."

"But why should you make a complaint?" he asked, as though trying to understand me. "You buy your own food."

"Good heavens! But some of you who joined in it buy your own food, too. We ought to have done the same—as comrades."

"But . . . but how can you be our comrades?" he asked in perplexity.

I looked at him quickly; he did not understand me in the least, he did not know what I was driving at. But I understood him thoroughly at that instant. A thought that had been stirring vaguely within me and haunting me for a long time had at last become clear to me, and I suddenly understood what I had only imperfectly realised. I understood that they would never accept me as a comrade, however much I might be a convict, not if I were in for life, not if I were in the special division. But I remember most clearly Petrov's face at that minute. His question, "how can you be our comrade?" was full of such genuine simplicity, such simple-hearted perplexity. I wondered if there were any irony, any malicious mockery in the question. There was nothing of the sort: simply we were not their comrades and that was all. You go your way, and we go ours; you have your affairs, and we have ours.

And, indeed, I had expected that after the complaint they would simply torment us to death without mercy, and that life would be impossible for us. Nothing of the sort, we did not hear one word of reproach, not a hint of reproach; there was no increase of ill-feeling against us. They simply gibed at us a little on occasions, as they had done before—nothing else. They were not in the least angry either with the other convicts who had remained in the kitchen and not joined in the complaint; nor with those who had first shouted that they were satisfied. No one even referred to it. This last fact puzzled me especially.

CHAPTER VIII

COMRADES

I WAS, OF COURSE, most attracted to the men of my own sort, the "gentlemen" that is, especially at first. But of the three Russian convicts of that class who were in our prison (Akim Akimitch, the spy A., and the man who was believed to have killed his father) the only one I knew and talked to was Akim Akimitch. I must confess that I resorted to Akim Akimitch only, so to say, in despair, at moments of the most intense boredom and when there was no prospect of speaking to anyone else. In the last chapter I have tried to arrange all the convicts in classes, but now I recall Akim Akimitch, I think that one might add another class. It is true that he would be the only representative of it— that is, the class of the absolutely indifferent convicts. Absolutely indifferent convicts, those, that is, to whom it was a matter of indifference whether they lived in prison or in freedom, one would have supposed did not and could not exist, but I think Akim Akimitch was an example of one. He had established himself in prison, indeed, as though he meant to spend his life there; everything about him, his mattress, his pillows, his pots and pans, all were on a solid and permanent footing. There was nothing of a temporary, bivouacking character about him. He had many years still to be in prison, but I doubt whether he ever thought of leaving it. But if he were reconciled to his position, it was not from inclination, but from subordination, though, indeed, in his case it amounted to the same thing. He was a good-natured man, and he helped me, indeed, at first with advice and kind offices; but I confess, sometimes, especially at first, he produced in me an intense depression which still further increased my misery. Yet it was my misery drove me to talk to him. I longed sometimes for a living word, however bitter or impatient or spiteful; we might at least have railed at our destiny together. But he was silent, gumming his paper lamps, or he would tell me of the review in which he had taken part in such a year, and who was the commanding officer of the division and what his Christian name was, and whether he had been satisfied with the review, and how the signals for the gunners had been changed, and all in the same even, decorous voice like the dripping of water. He scarcely showed the slightest animation when he told me that he had been deemed worthy to receive the ribbon of St. Anne on his sword for the part he had taken in some action in the Caucasus. Only at that moment his voice became extraordinarily dignified and solemn; it dropped to a mysterious undertone when he pronounced the words "St. Anne," and for three minutes afterwards he became particularly silent and sedate. . . . During that first year I had stupid moments when I (and always quite suddenly) began, I don't know why, almost to hate Akim Akimitch, and I cursed the fate which had put me with my head next his on the common bed. Usually an hour later I reproached myself for the feeling. But this was only during my first year; later on I became quite reconciled to Akim Akimitch in my heart, and was ashamed of my foolishness. Outwardly, as far as I remember, we were always on good terms.

Besides these three Russians there were eight others, Polish prisoners, of the upper class in the prison while I was there. Some of them I got to know pretty well, and was glad of their friendship, but not all. The best of them were morbid, exceptional and intolerant to the last degree. With two of them I gave up talking altogether in the end. Only three of them were well educated: B., M., and Z., who had been a professor of mathematics, a nice, good-natured old man, very eccentric and not at all clever, I think, in spite of his education. M. and B. were men of a quite different type. I got on well with M. from the first; I respected him and never quarrelled with him, but I never could get fond of him or feel any affection for him. He was a profoundly mistrustful and embittered man with a wonderful power of self-control. But this very excess of self-control was what I did not like; one somehow felt that he would never open his heart to anyone. But perhaps I am mistaken. He was a man of strong and very noble character. His extreme and almost Jesuitical skill and circumspection in dealing with people betrayed his profound inner scepticism. Yet his was a soul tormented just by this duality—scepticism and a deep steadfast faith in some of his own hopes and convictions. But for all his skill in getting on with people, he was an irreconcilable enemy of B. and of the latter's friend T. B. was a man in ill-health, of consumptive tendency, nervous and irritable, but at bottom a very kind-hearted and even great-hearted man. His irritability sometimes reached the pitch of extreme intolerance and caprice. I could not put up with his temper, and in the end I gave up having anything to do with B., but I never ceased to love him; with M. I never quarrelled, but I never was fond of him. It happened that, through cutting off my relations with B., I had also to give up T., the young man of whom I have spoken in the last chapter when I described our "complaint." I was very sorry for that. Though T. was not an educated man, he was kind-hearted and manly, a splendid young fellow, in fact. He was so fond of B., had such a respect and reverence for him that if anyone were ever so little at variance with B. he at once looked upon him almost as an enemy. I believe in the end he was estranged even from M. on B.'s account, though he held out for a long time. But they were all morally sick, embittered, irritable and mistrustful. It was easy to understand; it was very hard for them, much worse than for us. They were far from their own country. Some of them were exiled for long periods, ten or twelve years, and what was worse they regarded everyone around them with intense prejudice, saw in the convicts nothing but their brutality, could not discern any good quality, anything human in them, and had indeed no wish to do so. And, as was very easy to understand also, they were led to this unfortunate point of view by the force of circumstance, by fate. There is no doubt that they were very miserable in prison. To the Circassians, to the Tatars and to Isay Fomitch they were cordial and friendly, but shunned the other convicts with abhorrence. Only the Starodubovsky Old Believer won their entire respect. It is remarkable, however, that all the while I was in prison none of the convicts ever taunted them with their nationality and their religion, or their ideas, as Russian peasants sometimes, though very rarely, do with foreigners, especially Germans. Though perhaps they do no more than laugh at the Germans; a German is always an extremely comic figure in the eyes of the Russian peasant. The convicts treated our foreign prisoners respectfully in prison, far more so than the Russian "gentlemen" prisoners indeed, and they never touched them. But the latter seemed unwilling to notice and consider this fact. I have spoken of T. It was he who, when they were walking from their first place of exile to our prison, carried B. in his arms almost the whole journey, when the latter, weak in health and constitution, broke

down before half the day's march was over. They had at first been exiled to U. There, so they said, they were well off, that is, much better
off than in our prison. But they got up a correspondence, of a perfectly harmless character however, with some other exiles in another
town, and for this reason it was considered necessary to exile these
three to our fortress, where they would be under the eye of a higher
official. Their third comrade was Z. Till they came, M. was the only
Pole in the prison. How miserable he must have been in his first year
there!

This Z. was the old man who was always saying his prayers, as I
have mentioned before. All our political prisoners were young, some
mere boys; only Z. was a man of over fifty. He was a man of unques-
tionable honesty, but rather strange. His comrades B. and T. disliked
him very much; they did not even speak to him; they used to say of
him that he was quarrelsome, obstinate and fussy. I don't know how
far they were right. In prison, as in all places where people are kept
together in a crowd against their will, I think people quarrel and even
hate one another more easily than in freedom. Many circumstances
combine to bring this about. But Z. certainly was a rather stupid and
perhaps disagreeable man. None of his other comrades were on good
terms with him. Though I never quarrelled with him, I did not get on
with him particularly well. I believe he knew his own subject, mathematics. I remember that he was always trying to explain to me in his
broken Russian some special astronomical system he had invented.
I was told that he had once published an account of it, but the learned
world had only laughed at him. I think he was a little cracked. For
whole days together he was on his knees saying his prayers, for which
all the convicts respected him to the day of his death. He died before
my eyes in our hospital after a severe illness. He won the convicts' respect, however, from the first moment in prison after the incident
with our major. On the journey from U. to our prison they had not
been shaved and they had grown beards, so when they were led
straight to the major he was furiously indignant at such a breach of
discipline, though they were in no way to blame for it.

"What do they look like!" he roared; "they are tramps, brigands!"

Z., who at that time knew very little Russian and thought they
were being asked who they were—tramps or brigands?—answered:

"We are not tramps, we are political prisoners."

"Wha—aat? You are insolent! Insolent!" roared the major. "To the guard-house! A hundred lashes, at once, this instant!"

The old man was flogged. He lay down under the lashes without a protest, bit his hand and endured the punishment without a cry, a moan, or a movement. Meanwhile B. and T. went into the prison, where M., already waiting for them at the gate, fell on their necks, though he had never seen them before. Agitated by the way the major had received them, they told M. all about Z. I remember how M. told me about it.

"I was beside myself," he said. "I did not know what was happening to me and shivered as though I were in a fever. I waited for Z. at the gate. He would have to come straight from the guard-house where the flogging took place." Suddenly the gate opened: Z. came out with a pale face and trembling white lips, and without looking at anyone passed through the convicts who were assembled in the yard and already knew that a 'gentleman' was being flogged; he went into the prison ward, straight to his place, and without saying a word knelt down and began to pray. The convicts were impressed and even touched. "When I saw that old grey-headed man," said M., "who had left a wife and children in his own country—when I saw him on his knees praying, after a shameful punishment, I rushed behind the prison, and for two hours I did not know what I was doing; I was frantic. . . ."

The convicts had a great respect for Z. from that time forward and they always treated him respectfully. What they particularly liked was that he had not cried out under punishment.

One must be fair, however: one cannot judge of the behaviour of the authorities in Siberia to prisoners of the educated class, whoever they may be, Poles or Russians, from this instance. This instance only shows that one may come across a bad man, and, of course, if that bad man is an independent senior officer somewhere, the fate of an exile whom that bad man particularly disliked would be very insecure. But one must admit that the highest authorities in Siberia, upon whom the tone and disposition of all the other commanding officers depend, are very scrupulous in regard to exiles of the upper class, and are even in some cases disposed to favour them in comparison with the other convicts of the peasant class. The reasons for this are clear: these higher authorities, to begin with, belong to the privileged class themselves;

secondly, it has happened in the past that some of the exiles of this class have refused to lie down to be flogged and have attacked the officers, which has led to terrible consequences; and, thirdly, I believe the chief explanation is that thirty-five years ago a great mass of exiles of the upper class were sent to Siberia all at once,[13] and these exiles had succeeded in the course of thirty years in establishing their character throughout Siberia, so that from an old traditional habit the government in my day could not help looking upon political prisoners as very different from ordinary convicts. The subordinate officers were accustomed to look upon them in the same way, taking their tone and attitude from the higher authorities, of course, and following their lead. But many of these commanding officers of inferior rank were stupid and secretly critical of the instructions given them, and they would have been very glad if they could have made their own arrangements without being checked. But this was not altogether permitted. I have good reason for this belief and I will give it. The second class of penal servitude in which I was serving—imprisonment in the fortress under military command—was incomparably more severe than the other two divisions, that is, servitude in the mines and in government works. It was not only harder for prisoners of the privileged class but for all the convicts, simply because the government and organization of this division was all military and not unlike that of the disciplinary battalions in Russia. Military government is harsher, the regulations are stricter, one is always in chains, always under guard, always behind bars and bolts; and this is not so much the case in the other two divisions. So at least all our convicts said, and there were some amongst them who knew what they were talking about. They would all gladly have passed into the first division, which is reckoned by the law to be the hardest, and often dreamed of the change. Of the disciplinary battalions in Russia, all who had been in them spoke with horror, declaring that in all Russia nothing was harder than the disciplinary battalions in the fortresses, and that Siberia was paradise compared with the life in them. So if, in such harsh conditions as in our prison under military rule, before the eyes of the Governor-General himself, and in spite of the possibility (such things sometimes occurred) of officious outsiders through spite or jealousy secretly reporting that certain political prisoners were favoured by officers of doubtful loyalty—if in such circumstances, I repeat, the political prisoners were looked upon somewhat differently from the other convicts, they must have been treated even more leniently in the first and third divisions. So I believe I can judge in this respect of all Siberia by the place where I was. All the tales and rumours that reached me on this subject from exiles of the first and third divisions confirmed my conclusion. In reality all of us, prisoners of the upper class, were treated by the authorities with more attention and circumspection in our prison. We certainly had no favour shown us in regard to work or other external conditions: we had the same work, the same fetters, the same bolts and bars—in fact, we had everything exactly like the other convicts. And indeed it was impossible to mitigate our lot. I know that in that town in *the recent but so remote past*[14] there were so many spies, so many intrigues, so many people laying traps for one another, that it was natural that the governing authorities should be afraid of being denounced. And what could be more terrible at that period than to be accused of showing favour to political prisoners? And so all were afraid, and we lived on an equal footing with all the convicts; but as regards corporal punishment there was a certain difference. It is true they would readily have flogged us if we had deserved it, that is, had committed a misdemeanour. That much was dictated by official duty and equality as regards corporal punishment. But they would not have flogged us at random on the impulse of the moment; and, of course, cases of such wanton treatment of the common convicts did occur, especially with some commanding officers of lower rank, who enjoyed domineering and intimidation. We knew that the governor of the prison was very indignant with the major when he knew the story of old Z., and impressed upon him the necessity of restraining himself in the future. So I was told by everyone. It was known also in prison that the Governor-General, too, though he trusted and to some extent liked our major as a man of some ability who did his duty, reprimanded him about that affair. And the major had made a note of it. He would dearly have liked, for example, to lay hands upon M., whom he hated from the tales A. told him, but he was never able to flog him, though he persecuted him and was on the look-out for a pretext and ready to pounce upon him. The whole town soon heard of the Z. affair, and public opinion condemned the major; many people reproved him, and some made themselves very unpleasant.

I remember at this moment my first encounter with the major. When we were at Tobolsk, the other political prisoner with whom

I entered the prison and myself, they frightened us by telling us of this man's ferocious character. Some old political exiles, who had been in Siberia for twenty-five years and who met us at Tobolsk with great sympathy and kept up relations with us all the time we were in the forwarding prison, warned us against our future commanding officer and promised to do what they could, through certain prominent persons, to protect us from his persecution. Three daughters of the Governor-General, who had come from Russia and were staying with their father, did, in fact, receive letters from them and spoke about us to their father. But what could he do? He merely told the major to be more careful. About three o'clock in the afternoon my comrade and I arrived in the town, and the guards took us at once to the major. We stood in the entry waiting for him. Meanwhile they sent for the prison sergeant. As soon as he appeared, the major, too, came out. His spiteful, purple, pimply face made a very depressing impression: it was as though a malicious spider had run out to pounce on some poor fly that had fallen into its web.

"What's your name?" he asked my comrade. He spoke rapidly, sharply, abruptly; he evidently wished to make an impression on us.

"So-and-so."

"You?" he went on, addressing me and glaring at me through his spectacles.

"So-and-so."

"Sergeant! To prison with them at once, shave them in the guard-house—half the head, as civilian prisoners; change their fetters tomorrow. What coats are those? Where did you get them?" he answered suddenly, his attention being caught by the grey overcoats with yellow circles on the back which had been given us at Tobolsk and which we were wearing in his illustrious presence. "That's a new uniform! It must be a new uniform. . . . A new pattern . . . from Petersburg," he added, making us turn round one after the other. "They've nothing with them?" he asked the escort.

"They've got their own clothes, your honour," said the gendarme, drawing himself up suddenly with a positive start. Everyone knew of the major, everyone had heard of him, everyone was frightened of him.

"Take away everything! Only give them back their underlinen, the white things; if there are any coloured things take them away; and sell all the rest by auction. The money for the prison funds. The convict has no property," he added, looking at us sternly. "Mind you behave yourselves! Don't let me hear of you! Or . . . cor—po—ral pu—nishment. For the least misdemeanour—the lash!"

This reception, which was unlike anything I was used to, made me almost ill the whole evening. And the impression was increased by what I saw in the prison; but I have already described my first hours in prison.

I have mentioned already that the authorities did not, and dared not, show us any favour or make our tasks lighter than those of the other convicts. But on one occasion they did try to do so: for three whole months B. and T. used to go to the engineer's office to do clerical work there. But this was done in strict secrecy, and was the engineering officer's doing. That is to say, all the other officials concerned knew of it, but they pretended not to. That happened when G. was commanding officer. Lieutenant-Colonel G. was a perfect godsend for the short time he was with us—not more than six months, if I mistake not, rather less perhaps. He made an extraordinary impression on the convicts before he left them to return to Russia. It was not simply that the convicts loved him; they adored him, if such a word may be used in this connexion. How he did it I don't know, but he gained their hearts from the first moment. "He is a father to us, a father! We've no need of a father!" the convicts were continually saying all the time he was at the head of the engineering department. I believe he was a terribly dissipated character. He was a little man with a bold, self-confident expression. But at the same time he was kind, almost tender, with the convicts, and he really did love them like a father. Why he was so fond of the convicts I can't say, but he could not see a convict without saying something kindly and good-humoured to him, without making a joke or laughing with him, and the best of it was there was no trace of the authoritative manner in it, nothing suggestive of condescending or purely official kindness. He was their comrade and completely one of themselves. But although he was instinctively democratic in manner and feeling, the convicts were never once guilty of disrespect or familiarity with him. On the contrary. But the convict's whole face lighted up when he met the lieutenant-colonel and, taking off his cap, he was all smiles when the latter came up to him. And if the officer spoke the convict felt as though he had received a present. There are popular people like this. He looked a manly fellow, he walked with an erect and gallant carriage. "He is an eagle," the convicts used to say of him. He could, of course, do nothing to mitigate their lot; he was only at the head of the engineering work, which, having been settled and laid down by law once for all, went on unchanged, whoever was in command. At most, if he chanced to come across a gang of convicts whose work was finished, he would let them go home before the drum sounded, instead of keeping them hanging about for nothing. But the convicts liked his confidence in them, the absence of petty fault-finding and irritability, the utter lack of anything insulting in speech or manner in his official relations with them. If he had lost a thousand roubles, and a convict had picked the money up, I do believe, if it were the worst thief in prison, he would have restored it. Yes, I am sure of that. With intense sympathy the convicts learnt that their "eagle" had a deadly quarrel with our hated major. It happened during the first month G. was there. Our major had at some time served with him in the past. After years of separation they met as friends and used to drink together. But their relations were suddenly cut short. They quarrelled and G. became his mortal enemy. There was a rumour that they had even fought on the occasion, which was by no means out of the question with our major: he often did fight. When the convicts heard of this their delight knew no bounds. "As though old Eight-eyes could get on with a man like him! He is an eagle, but the major a . . ." and here usually followed a word quite unfit for print. The prisoners were fearfully interested to know which had given the other a beating. If the rumours of the fight had turned out to be false (which was perhaps the case) I believe our convicts would have been very much annoyed. "You may be sure the colonel got the best of it," they used to say; "he's a plucky one, though he is small, and the major crawled under the bed to get away from him, they say."

But G. soon left us and the convicts sank into despondency again. Our engineering commanders were all good, however; three or four succeeded one another in my time. "But we shall never have another like him," the convicts used to say; "he was an eagle, an eagle and our champion." This G. was very fond of us political prisoners, and towards the end he used to make B. and me come to work in his office sometimes. After he went away this was put on a more regular footing. Some in the engineering department (especially one of them) were very sympathetic with us. We used to go there and copy papers, our handwriting began to improve even, when suddenly there came a peremptory order from the higher authorities that we were to be sent back to our former tasks: someone had already played the spy. It was a good thing, however; we had both begun to be fearfully sick of the office! Afterwards for two years B. and I went almost insepara- bly to the same tasks, most frequently to the workshops. We used to chat together, talk of our hopes and convictions. He was a splendid fellow; but his ideas were sometimes very strange and exceptional. There is a certain class of people, very intelligent indeed, who some- times have utterly paradoxical ideas. But they have suffered so much for them in their lives, they have paid such a heavy price for them, that it would be too painful, almost impossible, to give them up. B. listened to every criticism with pain and answered with bitterness. I daresay he was more right than I was in many things—I don't know; but at last we parted, and I was very sad about it: we had shared so many things together.

Meanwhile M. seemed to become more melancholy and gloomy every year. He was overwhelmed by depression. During my early days in prison he used to be more communicative, his feelings found a fuller and more frequent utterance. He had been two years in prison when I first came. At first he took interest in a great deal of what had happened in the world during those two years, of which he had no idea in prison; he questioned me, listened, was excited. But towards the end, as the years went on, he seemed to be more concentrated within and shut up in his own mind. The glowing embers were being covered up by ash. His exasperation grew more and more marked. "*Je haïs ces brigands,*" he often repeated to me, looking with hatred at the convicts, whom I had by then come to know better, and nothing I could say in their favour had any influence. He did not understand what I said, though he sometimes gave an absent-minded assent; but next day he would say again: "*Je haïs ces brigands.*" We used often to talk in French, by the way; and on this account a soldier in the engineers, called Dranishnikov, nicknamed us the "medicals"—I don't know from what connexion of ideas. M. only showed warmth when he spoke of his mother. "She is old, she is ill," he said to me; "she loves me more than anything in the world, and here I don't know whether she is alive or dead. To know that I had to run the gauntlet was enough for her. . . ." M. did not come of the privileged class, and before being sent to exile had received corporal punishment. He used to clench his teeth and look away when he recalled it. Towards the end he used more and more frequently to walk alone.

One morning, about midday, he was summoned by the governor. Our governor came out to him with a good-humoured smile.

"Well, M., what did you dream about last night?" he asked.

"I trembled," M. told us afterwards, "I felt as though I had been stabbed to the heart."

"I dreamt I had a letter from my mother," he answered.

"Better than that, better than that!" replied the governor. "You are free! Your mother has petitioned in your favour, and her petition has been granted. Here is her letter and here is the order relating to you. You will leave the prison at once."

He came back to us pale, unable to recover from the shock. We congratulated him. He pressed our hands with his cold and trembling hands. Many of the common convicts, too, congratulated him and were delighted at his good luck.

He was released and remained in our town as a "settler." Soon he was given a post. At first he often came to our prison, and when he could, told us all sorts of news. Politics was what interested him most.

Besides M., T., B. and Z., there were two quite young men who had been sent for brief terms, boys of little education, but honest, simple, and straightforward. A third, A-tchukovsky, was quite a simpleton, and there was nothing special about him. But a fourth, B-m, a middle-aged man, made a very disagreeable impression upon all of us. I don't know how he came to be one of the political prisoners, and, indeed, he denied all connexion with them himself. He had the coarse soul of a petty huckster, and the habits and principles of a shopkeeper who had grown rich by cheating over halfpence. He was entirely without education, and took no interest in anything but his trade. He was a painter, and a first-rate one—magnificent. Soon the authorities heard of his talent, and all the town began wanting B-m to paint their walls and ceilings. Within two years he had painted almost all the officials' houses. Their owners paid him out of their own pockets, and so he was not at all badly off. But the best of it was that his comrades, too, began to be sent to work with him. Two who went out with him continually learnt the trade, too, and one of them, T-zhevsky, became as good a painter as he was himself. Our major, who lived in a government house himself, sent for B-m in his turn, and told him to paint all the walls and ceilings. Then B-m did his utmost: even the Governor-General's house was not so well painted. It was a tumble-down, very mangy-looking, one-storey wooden house; but the interior was painted as though it were a palace, and the major was highly delighted . . . He rubbed his hands, and declared that now he really must get married: "with such a house one must have a wife," he added quite seriously. He was more and more pleased with B-m, and through him with the others who worked with him. The work lasted a whole month. In the course of that month the major quite altered his views of the political prisoners, and began to patronise them. It ended by his summoning Z. one day from the prison.

"Z.," said he, "I wronged you. I gave you a flogging for nothing. I know it. I regret it. Do you understand that? I, I, I—regret it!"

Z. replied that he did understand it.

"Do you understand that I, I, your commanding officer, have sent for you, to ask you your forgiveness; Do you feel that? What are you beside me? A worm! Less than a worm: you are a convict. And I, by the grace of God,* am a major. A major! Do you understand that?"

Z. answered that he understood that, too.

"Well, now I am making peace with you. But do you feel it, do you feel it fully, in all its fullness? Are you capable of understanding it? Only think: I, I, the major . . ." and so on.

Z. told me of the whole scene himself. So even this drunken, quarrelsome, and vicious man had some humane feeling. When one takes into consideration his ideas and lack of culture, such an action may almost be called magnanimous. But probably his drunken condition had a good deal to do with it.

His dreams were not realised; he did not get married, though he had fully made up his mind to do so by the time the decoration of his house was finished. Instead of being married he was arrested, and he was ordered to send in his resignation. At the trial all his old

---

*This expression was literally used in my time, not only by the major, but by many petty officers, especially those who had risen from the lower ranks (Dostoevsky's note).

sins were brought up against him. He had previously been a provost of the town . . . The blow fell on him unexpectedly. There was immense rejoicing in the prison at the news. It was a festive day, a day of triumph! They said that the major howled like an old woman and was dissolved in tears. But there was nothing to be done. He retired, sold his pair of greys, and then his whole property, and even sank into poverty. We came across him afterwards, a civilian wearing a shabby coat and a cap with a cockade in it. He looked viciously at the convicts. But all his prestige went with his uniform. In a uniform he was terrible, a deity. In civil dress he became absolutely a nonentity, and looked like a lackey. It's wonderful what the uniform does for men like that.

CHAPTER IX

AN ESCAPE

SOON AFTER OUR MAJOR was removed, there were fundamental changes in our prison. They gave up using the place as a prison for penal servitude convicts and founded instead a convict battalion, on the pattern of the Russian disciplinary battalions. This meant that no more convicts of the second class were brought to our prison. It began to be filled at this time only with convicts of the military division, men therefore not deprived of civil rights, soldiers like all other soldiers except that they were undergoing punishment in the prison for brief terms, six years at the utmost. At the expiration of their sentence they would go back to their battalions as privates, just as before. Those, however, who came back to the prison after a second offence were punished as before by a sentence of twenty years. There had been, indeed, even before this change a division of convicts of the military class, but they lived with us because there was no other place for them. Now the whole prison became a prison for this military section. The old convicts, genuine civil convicts, who had been deprived of all rights, had been branded, and shaved on one side of the head, remained, of course, in the prison till their full terms were completed. No new ones came, and those who remained gradually worked out their terms of servitude and went away, so that ten years later there could not have been a convict left in our prison. The special division was left, however, and to it from time to time were sent convicts of the military class who had committed serious crimes, and they were kept there till certain penal works were established in Siberia. So in reality life went on for us as before, the same conditions, the same food, and almost the same regulations; but the officers in command were different and more numerous. A staff officer was appointed, a commander of the battalion and four superior officers who were on duty in the prison in turns. The veterans, too, were abolished and twelve sergeants and a quartermaster were appointed.

The prisoners were divided into tens and corporals were appointed from the convicts themselves, nominally, of course, and Akim Akimitch at once became a corporal. All these new institutions and the whole prison, with its officials and convicts, were as before left under the control of the governor of the prison as the highest authority. That was all that happened.

The convicts were, of course, very much excited at first; they talked, guessed and tried to read the characters of their commanders, but when they saw that in reality everything went on as before, they calmed down and our life went on in its old way. But the great thing was that we were all saved from the old major; everyone seemed to breathe freely and to be more confident. They lost their panic-stricken air; all knew now that in case of need one could have things out with the authorities and that the innocent would not be punished for the guilty except by mistake. Vodka was sold just as before and on the same system, although instead of the veterans we had sergeants. These sergeants turned out to be for the most part a good sort of sensible men who understood their position. Some of them, however, at first showed an inclination to domineer, and, of course, in their inexperience thought they could treat the convicts like soldiers, but soon even these realised the position. Those who were too slow in understanding had it pointed out to them by the convicts. There were some sharp encounters; for instance, they would tempt a sergeant and make him drunk, and afterwards point out to him, in their own fashion, of course, that he had drunk with them, and consequently . . . It ended in the sergeants looking on unconcerned, or rather trying not to see, when vodka was brought in in bladders and sold. What is more, they went to the market as the veterans had done before and brought the convicts rolls, beef, and all the rest of it; that is, anything that was not too outrageous. Why all these changes were made, why convict battalions were formed, I don't know. It happened during my last years in prison. But I had two years to spend under these new regulations.

Shall I describe all that life, all my years in prison? I don't think so. If I were to describe in order, in succession, all that happened and all that I saw and experienced in those years, I might have written three times, four times as many chapters as I have. But such a description would necessarily become too monotonous. All the incidents would be too much in the same key, especially if, from the chapters already written, the reader has succeeded in forming a fairly satisfactory conception of prison life in the second division. I wanted to give a vivid and concrete picture of our prison and of all that I lived through in those years. Whether I have attained my object I don't know. And, indeed, it is not quite for me to judge of it. But I am convinced that I can end my story here. Besides, I am sometimes depressed by these memories myself. And I can hardly recollect everything. The later years have somehow been effaced from my memory. Many circumstances, I am quite sure, I have entirely forgotten. I remember that all those years, which were so much alike, passed drearily, miserably. I remember that those long wearisome days were monotonous, as drops of water trickling from the roof after rain. I remember that nothing but the passionate desire to rise up again, to be renewed, to begin a new life, gave me the strength to wait and to hope. And at last I mastered myself; I looked forward, and I reckoned off every day, and although a thousand remained, I took pleasure in ticking them off one by one. I saw the day off; I buried it, and I rejoiced at the coming of another day, because there were not a thousand left but nine hundred and ninety-nine days. I remember that all that time, though I had hundreds of companions, I was fearfully lonely, and at last I grew fond of that loneliness. In my spiritual solitude I reviewed all my past life, went over it all to the smallest detail, brooded over my past, judged myself sternly and relentlessly, and even sometimes blessed fate for sending me this solitude, without which I could not have judged myself like this, nor have reviewed my past life so sternly. And what hopes set my heart throbbing in those days! I believed, I resolved, I swore to myself that in my future life there should be none of the mistakes and lapses there had been in the past. I sketched out a programme for myself for the whole future, and I firmly resolved to keep to it. The blind faith that I should and could keep these resolutions rose up in my heart again. I looked forward eagerly to freedom, I prayed for it to come quickly; I longed to test myself again in fresh strife. At times I was overcome by nervous impatience. But it hurts me to recall now my spiritual condition at that time. Of course, all that concerns no one but me. But I have written all this because I think everyone will understand it, for the same thing must happen to everyone if he is sent to prison for a term of years in the flower of his youth and strength.

But why talk of it? I had better describe something else, that I may not end too abruptly.

It occurs to me that someone may ask, was it really impossible for anyone to escape from prison, and did no one escape in all those years? As I have said already, a prisoner who has spent two or three years in prison begins to attach a value to those years and cannot help coming to the conclusion that it is better to serve the rest of his time without trouble and risk and leave the prison finally in the legal way as a "settler." But this conclusion can only occur to a convict who has been sentenced to a brief term. The man with many years before him might well be ready to risk anything. But somehow this did not often happen in our prison. I don't know whether it was that they were very cowardly, whether the supervision was particularly strict and military, whether the situation of our town in the open steppes was in many ways unfavourable; it is hard to say. I imagine all these considerations had their influence. Certainly it was rather difficult to escape from us. And yet one such case did happen in my time; two convicts ventured on the attempt and those two were among the most important criminals.

After the major had gone, A. (the convict who had played the spy for him in the prison) was left quite friendless and unprotected. He was still young, but his character had grown stronger and steadier as he grew older. He was altogether a bold, resolute and even very intelligent man. Though he would have gone on spying and making his living in all sorts of underhand ways if he had been given his freedom, he would not have been caught so stupidly and imprudently as before and have paid so dearly for his folly. While he was in prison, he practised making false passports a little. I cannot speak with certainty about this, however. But I was told so by the convicts. It was said that he used to work in that line at the time when he frequented the major's kitchen and of course he picked up all he could there. In short he was capable of anything "to change his luck." I had an opportunity of reading his character and seeing to some extent into his mind; cynicism in him reached a pitch of revolting impudence and cold mockery, and it excited an invincible repugnance. I believe that, if he had had a great desire for a glass of vodka and if he could not have got it except by murdering someone, he would certainly have committed the murder, if he could only have done it in secret so that no one could discover it. In prison he learnt prudence. And this man caught the attention of Kulikov, a convict in the special division.

I have already spoken of Kulikov. He was a man no longer young, but passionate, vital, vigorous, with great and varied abilities. There was strength in him and he still had a longing for life. Such men feel the same thirst for life up to extreme old age. And if I had wondered why none of the convicts escaped from the prison, the first I should have thought of would have been Kulikov. But Kulikov made up his mind at last. Which of them had the most influence on the other— A. on Kulikov or Kulikov on A.—I do not know, but they were a match for one another and well suited for such an enterprise. They became friends. I fancy Kulikov reckoned on A.'s preparing the passports. A. was a "gentleman," had belonged to good society; that promised something different from the usual adventures, if only they could get to Russia. Who can tell how they came to an agreement and what hopes they had? But it is certain that they were hoping for something very different from the usual routine of tramping in Siberia. Kulikov was an actor by nature; he could play many and varied parts in life; he might hope for many things, at least for a great variety of things. Prison must weigh heavily on such men. They agreed to escape.

But it was impossible to escape without the help of a guard. They had to persuade a guard to join them. In one of the battalions stationed in the fortress there was a Pole, a man of energy, deserving perhaps of a better fate; he was middle-aged and serious, but he was a fine, spirited fellow. In his youth, soon after he had come as a soldier to Siberia, he had deserted from intense home-sickness. He was caught, punished and kept for two years in a disciplinary battalion. When he was sent back to serve as an ordinary soldier again, he thought better of it and began to be zealous and to do his best in his work. For distinguished service he was made a corporal. He was an ambitious, self-reliant man who knew his own value. He spoke and looked like a man who knows his own value. I met him several times during those years among our guards. The Poles too, had spoken of him to me. It seemed to me that his home-sickness had turned to a hidden, dumb, unchanging hatred. This man was capable of doing anything and Kulikov was right in choosing him as a comrade. His name was Koller.

They agreed and fixed on a day. It was in the hot days of June. The climate was fairly equable in our town; in the summer there was hot settled weather, and that just suited tramps. Of course they could not set off straight from the fortress; the whole town stands on rising ground open on all sides. There was no forest for a long distance round. They had to change into ordinary dress, and to do this they had first to get to the edge of the town, where there was a house that Kulikov had long frequented. I do not know whether his friends there were fully in the secret. One must suppose that they were, though the point was not fully established when the case was tried afterwards. That year in a secluded nook at the edge of the town a very prepossessing young woman, nicknamed Vanka-Tanka, who showed great promise and to some extent fulfilled it later on, was just beginning her career. Another nickname for her was Fire. I believe she, too, had some share in the escape. Kulikov had been spending lavishly upon her for a whole year.

Our heroes went out as usual into the prison yard in the morning and cleverly succeeded in being sent with Shilkin, a convict who made stoves and did plastering, to plaster the empty barracks, which the soldiers had left some time before to go into camp. A. and Kulikov went with Shilkin to act as porters. Koller turned up as one of the guards, and as two guards were required for three convicts, Koller, as an old soldier and a corporal, was readily entrusted with a young re-cruit that he might train him and teach him his duties. Our fugitives must have had great influence on Koller and he must have had great confidence in them, since after his lengthy and in latter years success-ful service, clever, prudent, sensible man as he was, he made up his mind to follow them.

They came to the barracks. It was six o'clock in the morning. There was no one there except them. After working for an hour, Kulikov and A. said to Shilkin that they were going to the workshop to see someone and to get some tool, which it seemed they had come with-out. They had to manage cleverly, that is, as naturally as possible, with Shilkin. He was a Moscow stove-maker, shrewd, clever, full of dodges, and sparing of his words. He was frail and wasted-looking. He ought to have been always wearing a waistcoat and a dressing-gown in the Moscow fashion, but fate had decreed otherwise, and after long wan-derings he was settled for good in our prison in the special division, that is, in the class of the most dangerous military criminals. How he had deserved such a fate I don't know, but I never noticed any sign of special dissatisfaction in him; he behaved peaceably and equably, only sometimes got as drunk as a cobbler, but even then he behaved decently. He was certainly not in the secret and his eyes were sharp. Kulikov, of course, winked to him signifying that they were going to get vodka, of which a store had been got ready in the workshop the day before. That touched Shilkin; he parted from them without any suspicion and remained alone with the recruit, while A., Kulikov and Koller set off for the edge of the town.

Half an hour passed; the absent men did not return and at last, on reflection, Shilkin began to have his doubts. He had seen a good deal in his day. He began to remember things. Kulikov had been in a peculiar humour, A. had seemed to whisper to him twice, anyway Kulikov had twice winked to him, he had seen that; now he remembered it all. There was something odd about Koller, too, as he went away with them; he had begun lecturing the recruit as to how he was to behave in his absence, and that was somehow not quite natural, in Koller, at least. In fact the more Shilkin thought about it, the more suspicious he became. Meanwhile time was getting on, they did not come back, and his uneasiness became extreme. He realized thoroughly his position and his own danger; the authorities might turn their suspicions upon him. They might think that he let his comrades go knowingly and had an understanding with them, and if he delayed to give notice of the disappearance of A. and Kulikov, there would seem to be more grounds for suspicion. There was no time to lose. At that point he recollected that Kulikov and A. had been particularly thick of late, had often been whispering, and had often been walking together behind the prison out of sight of everyone. He remembered that even at the time he had thought something about them. He looked searchingly at his guard; the latter was leaning on his gun, yawning and very innocently picking his nose. So Shilkin did not deign to communicate his suspicions to him, but simply told him that he must follow him to the engineer's workshop. He had to ask whether they had been there. But it appeared that no one had seen them there. Shilkin's last doubts were dissipated. "They might have simply gone to drink and have a spree at the edge of the town, as Kulikov sometimes did," thought Shilkin, "but no, that could hardly be it. They would have told him, they would not have thought it worth while to conceal that from him." Shilkin left his work and, without returning to the barracks, he went straight off to the prison.

It was almost nine o'clock when he presented himself before the chief sergeant and informed him of what had happened. The sergeant was aghast and at first was unwilling to believe it. Shilkin, of course, told him all this simply as a guess, a suspicion. The sergeant rushed off to the commanding officer, and the latter at once informed the governor of the prison. Within a quarter of an hour all the necessary steps had been taken. The Governor-General was informed. The criminals were important ones, and there might be serious trouble from Petersburg on their account. Correctly or not, A. was reckoned a political prisoner; Kulikov was in the special division, that is, a criminal of the first magnitude and a military one, too. There had never been an instance of a prisoner's escaping from the special division before. It was incidentally recalled that every convict of the special division should be escorted to work by two guards, or, at the least, have one each. This rule had not been observed. So it looked an unpleasant business. Messengers were sent to all the villages through all the surrounding country to announce the escape of the fugitives and to leave their description everywhere. Cossacks were sent out to overtake and catch them; neighbouring districts and provinces were written to. The authorities were in a great panic, in fact.

Meanwhile there was excitement of a different sort in prison. As the convicts came in from work, they learnt at once what had happened. The news flew round to all. Everyone received it with extraordinary secret joy. It set every heart throbbing. Besides breaking the monotony of prison life and upsetting the ant-hill, an escape, and such an escape, appealed to something akin in every heart and touched on long-forgotten chords; something like hope, daring, the possibility of "changing their luck" stirred in every soul. "Men have escaped, it seems, why then . . .?" And at this thought everyone plucked up his spirit and looked defiantly at his mates. At any rate, they all seemed suddenly proud and began looking condescendingly at the sergeants. Of course the authorities swooped down on the prison at once. The governor of the prison came himself. Our convicts were in high spirits, and they looked bold, even rather contemptuous, and had a sort of silent stern dignity, as though to say, "We know how to manage things." Of course they had foreseen at once that all the authorities would visit the prison. They foresaw, too, that there would be a search and got everything hidden in readiness for it. They knew that the authorities on such occasions are always wise after the event. And so it turned out; there was a great fuss, everything was turned upside down, everything was searched and nothing was found, of course. The convicts were sent out to their afternoon work and escorted by a larger number of guards. Towards evening the sentries looked into the prison every minute; the men were called over an extra time and mistakes in the counting were made twice as often as usual. This led to further confusion; all the men were sent out into the yard and counted over again. Then there was another counting over in the prison wards. There was a great deal of fuss.

But the convicts were not in the least disturbed. They all looked extremely independent and, as is always the case on such occasions, behaved with extraordinary decorum all that evening, as though to say, "There's nothing you can find fault with." The authorities, of course, wondered whether the fugitives had not left accomplices in prison and gave orders that the convicts should be watched and spied upon. But the convicts only laughed. "As though one would leave accomplices behind one in a job of that sort!" "A thing of that sort is done on the quiet and nohow else!" "And as though a man like Kulikov, a man like A., would leave traces in an affair like that! They've managed in a masterly way, every sign hidden; they're men who've seen a thing or two; they'd get through locked doors!"

In fact the glory of Kulikov and A. was vastly increased; everyone was proud of them. The convicts felt that their exploit would be handed down to the remotest generation of convicts, would outlive the prison.

"They're master-hands!" some would say.

"You see, it was thought there was no escaping from here. They've escaped, though," others added.

"Escaped!" a third would pronounce, looking round with an air of some authority. "But who is it has escaped? The likes of you, do you suppose?"

Another time the convict to whom this question referred would certainly have taken up the challenge and defended his honour, but now he was modestly silent, reflecting: "Yes, really, we are not all like Kulikov and A.; we must show what we can do before we talk."

"And why do we go on living here, after all, brother?" said a fourth, breaking the silence. He was sitting modestly at the kitchen window with his cheek propped on his hand. He spoke in a rather sing-song voice, full of sentimental but secretly complacent feeling. "What are we here for? We are not alive though we are living and we are not in our graves though we are dead. E-e-ch!"

"It's not a shoe, you can't cast it off. What's the use of saying 'e-e-ch'?"

"But you see, Kulikov . . ." a green youth, one of the impulsive sort, tried to interpose.

"Kulikov!" Another cut him short at once, cocking his eye contemptuously at the green youth. "Kulikov!"

This was as much as to say, "Are there many Kulikovs here?"

"And A. too, lads, he is a cute one, oh, he is a cute one!"

"Rather! He could turn even Kulikov round his finger! You won't catch him!"

"I wonder whether they've got far by now, lads? I should like to know."

At once there followed a discussion of whether they had gone far, and in what direction they had gone, and where it would have been best for them to go, and which district was nearer. There were people who knew the surrounding country; they were listened to with interest. They talked of the inhabitants of the neighbouring villages and decided that they were not people to reply upon. They were too near a town to be simple. They wouldn't help a convict, they'd catch him and hand him over.

"The peasants hereabouts are a spiteful set, mates, that they are!"

"There's no depending on them!"

"They're Siberians, the beggars. If they come across you, they'll kill you."

"Well, but our fellows . . ."

"To be sure, there's no saying which will get the best of it. Our men are not easy customers either."

"Well, we shall hear, if we live long enough."

"Why, do you think they'll catch them?"

"I don't believe they'll ever catch them!" another of the enthusiasts pronounces, banging the table with his fist.

"H'm! That's all a matter of luck."

"And I tell you what I think, lads," Skuratov breaks in: "if I were a tramp, they'd never catch me."

"You!"

There is laughter, though some pretend not to want to listen. But there is no stopping Skuratov.

"Not if I know it!" he goes on vigorously. "I often think about it and wonder at myself, lads. I believe I'd creep through any chink before they catch me."

"No fear! You'd get hungry and go to a peasant for bread."

General laughter.

"For bread? Nonsense!"

"But why are you wagging your tongue? Uncle Vasya and you killed the cow plague.* That's why you came here."

The laughter was louder than ever. The serious ones looked on with even greater indignation.

"That's nonsense!" shouted Skuratov. "That's a fib of Mikita's, and it's not about me, but Vaska, and they've mixed me up in it. I'm a Moscow man and I was brought up to tramping from a child. When the deacon was teaching me to read, he used to pull me by the ear and make me repeat, 'Lead me not into temptation in Thy infinite mercy,' and soon I used to repeat, 'lead me to the police-station in Thy infinite mercy,' and so on. So that's how I used to go on from my childhood up."

Everyone burst out laughing again. But that was all Skuratov wanted. He could not resist playing the fool. Soon the convicts left him and fell to serious conversation again. It was mainly the old men, authorities on such affairs, who gave their opinions. The younger and humbler prisoners looked on in silent enjoyment and craned their heads forward to listen. A great crowd gathered in the kitchen; there were, of course, no sergeants present. They would not have spoken freely before them.

Among those who were particularly delighted, I noticed a Tatar, called Mametka, a short man with high cheek-bones, an extremely comic figure. He could hardly speak Russian at all and could hardly

---

*That is, killed a man or woman, suspecting that he or she had put a spell on the cattle, causing their death. We had one such murderer amongst us (Dostoevsky's note).

understand anything of what was said, but he, too, was craning his head forward out of the crowd and listening, listening with relish.

"Well, Mametka, *yakshee?*"* Skuratov, abandoned by all and not knowing what to do with himself, fastened upon him.

"*Yakshee*, oh, *yakshee!*" Mametka muttered in great animation, nodding his ridiculous head to Skuratov. "*Yakshee!*"

"They won't catch them, *yok?*"

"*Yok, yok!*" and Mametka began babbling, gesticulating as well.

"So you lie, me not understand, eh?"

"Yes, yes, *yakshee*," Mametka assented, nodding.

"*Yakshee* to be sure!" and Skuratov, giving the Tatar's cap a tweak that sent it over his eyes, went out of the kitchen in the best of spirits, leaving Mametka somewhat perplexed.

For a whole week there was strict discipline in the prison, and search and pursuit were kept up vigorously in the neighbourhood. I don't know how, but the convicts got immediate and accurate information of the manœuvres of the police outside the prison. The first few days the news was all favourable to the fugitives; there was no sight or sound of them, every trace was lost. The convicts only laughed. All anxiety as to the fate of the runaways was over. "They won't find anything, they won't catch anyone," was repeated in prison with complacency.

"Nothing. They've gone like a shot."

"Good-bye, don't cry, back by-and-by." It was known in prison that all the peasants in the neighbourhood had been roused. All suspicious places, all the woods and ravines were being watched.

"Foolishness!" said the convicts, laughing. "They must have some friend they are staying with now."

"No doubt they have," said the others. "They are not fools; they would have got everything ready beforehand."

They went further than this in their suppositions; they began to say that the runaways were still perhaps in the outskirts of the town, living somewhere in a cellar till the excitement was over and their hair had grown, that they would stay there six months or a year and then go on.

Everyone, in fact, was inclined to romance. But, suddenly, eight days after the escape there was a rumour that a clue had been found.

---

*Tatar word.

This absurd rumour was, of course, rejected at once with contempt. But the same evening the rumour was confirmed. The convicts began to be uneasy. The next morning it was said in the town that they had been caught and were being brought back. In the afternoon further details were learnt; they had been caught about fifty miles away, at a certain village. At last a definite piece of news was received. A corporal, returning from the major, stated positively that they would be brought that evening straight to the guard-house. There was no possibility of doubt. It is hard to describe the effect this news had on the convicts. At first they all seemed angry, then they were depressed. Then attempts at irony were apparent. There were jeers, not now at the pursuers, but at the captives, at first from a few, then from almost all, except some earnest and resolute men who thought for themselves and who could not be turned by taunts. They looked with contempt at the shallowness of the majority and said nothing.

In fact, they now ran Kulikov and A. down, enjoyed running them down as much as they had crying them up before. It was as though the runaways had done them all some injury. The convicts, with a contemptuous air, repeated that the fugitives had been very hungry, that they had not been able to stand, and had gone to a village to ask for bread from the peasants. This is the lowest depth of ignominy for a tramp. These stories were not true, however. The fugitives had been tracked; they had hidden in the forest; the forest had been surrounded by a cordon. Seeing that they had no hope of escape, they had surrendered. There was nothing else left for them to do.

But when in the evening they really were brought back by the gendarmes, their arms and legs tied, all the convicts trooped out to the fence to see what would be done with them. They saw nothing, of course, except the carriages of the major and the governor outside the guard-house. The runaways were put in a cell apart, fettered, and next day brought up for trial. The contempt and the jeers of the convicts soon passed off. They learnt more fully the circumstances, they found out that there was nothing for them to do but surrender, and all began following the course of the proceedings sympathetically.

"They'll give them a thousand," said some of them.

"A thousand, indeed!" said the others. "They'll do for them. A. a thousand, perhaps, but Kulikov will be beaten to death, because he is in the special division."

They were mistaken, however. A. got off with five hundred blows; his previous good behaviour and the fact that it was his first offence were taken into account. Kulikov, I believe, received fifteen hundred, but the punishment was administered rather mercifully. Like sensible men, the fugitives implicated no one else at the trial, gave clear and exact answers; they said they had run straight away from the fortress without staying anywhere in the town. I felt sorriest of all for Koller; he had lost everything, his last hopes; his sentence was the worst of all, I believe two thousand "sticks," and he was sent away to another prison as a convict. Thanks to the doctors, A.'s punishment was light and humane, but he gave himself airs and talked loudly in the hospital of his being ready for anything, of his sticking at nothing now, and of doing something much more striking. Kulikov behaved as usual, that is, with dignity and decorum, and when he returned to prison after the punishment, he looked as though he had never left it. But the convicts looked at him differently; though Kulikov always and everywhere knew how to stand up for himself, the convicts had somehow inwardly ceased to respect him and began to treat him with more familiarity. In fact, from this time Kulikov's glory greatly declined. Success means so much to men.

CHAPTER X

HOW I LEFT PRISON

ALL THIS HAPPENED DURING my last year in prison. The last year was al-most as memorable as the first one, especially the last days in prison. But why go into detail! I only remember that that year, in spite of my impatience for the end of my time, I found life easier than during all my previous years in prison. In the first place I had by then in the prison a number of friends and well-wishers, who had quite made up their minds that I was a good man. Many of them were devoted to me and loved me sincerely. The "pioneer" almost shed tears when he saw me and my comrade off on the day we left the prison, and when, after leaving, we spent a month in the town, he came almost every day to see us, with no object except to have a look at us. There were some of the convicts, however, who remained morose and churlish to the end and seemed, God knows why, to grudge having to speak to me. It seemed as though there existed a kind of barrier between us.

I enjoyed more privileges towards the last than in the early years of my life in prison. I discovered among the officers serving in the town some acquaintances and even old schoolfellows of mine. I re-newed my acquaintance with them. Through their good offices I was able to obtain larger supplies of money, was able to write home and even to have books. It was some years since I had read a book, and it is difficult to describe the strange and agitating impression of the first book I read in the prison. I remember I began reading in the evening when the ward was locked up and I read all night long, till daybreak. It was a magazine. It was as though news had come to me from another world; my former life rose up before me full of light and colour, and I tried from what I read to conjecture how far I had dropped behind. Had a great deal happened while I had been away, what emotions were agitating people now, what questions were oc-cupying their minds? I pored over every word, tried to read between the lines and to find secret meanings and allusions to the past;

I looked for traces of what had agitated us in my time. And how sad it was for me to realize how remote I was from this new life, how cut off I was from it all. I should have to get used to everything afresh, to make acquaintance with the new generation again. I pounced with special eagerness on articles signed by men I had known and been intimate with. But there were new names too; there were new leaders, and I was in eager haste to make their acquaintance, and I was vexed that I had the prospect of so few books to read, and that it was so difficult to get hold of them. In old days, under our old major, it was positively dangerous to smuggle a book into prison. If there had been a search, there would immediately have been questions where the book had come from, where one had got it from. It would be surmised that one had acquaintances in the town. And what could I have answered to such inquiries? And therefore, living without books I had unconsciously become absorbed in myself, set myself problems, tried to solve them, worried over them sometimes. But there's no describing all that!

I had entered the prison in the winter and therefore I was to leave it and be free in the winter too, on the anniversary of my arrival. With what impatience I looked forward to the winter, with what enjoyment at the end of the summer I watched the leaves withering and the grass fading in the steppes. And now the summer had passed, the autumn wind was howling; at last the first flakes of snow fluttered down. At last the winter I had so long looked forward to had come! At times my heart began throbbing dumbly at the great thought of freedom. But, strange to say, as time went on and the end came nearer, the more and more patient I became. In the last few days I was really surprised and reproached myself. It seemed to me that I had become quite unconcerned and indifferent. Many of the convicts who met me in the yard in our leisure time would speak to me and congratulate me.

"You'll soon be going out to freedom, Alexandr Petrovitch, soon, soon. You'll leave us all alone, poor devils."

"And you, Martynov, will your time soon be up?" I would respond.

"Me! Oh, well, I have another seven years to pine away."

And he would sigh to himself, stand still and look lost in thought, as though staring into the future. . . . Yes, many joyfully and sincerely congratulated me. It seemed to me as though all of them began to be more cordial to me. They had evidently begun to think of me as no longer one of themselves; they were already taking leave of me. K-tchinsky, one of the educated Poles, a quiet and gentle young man, was, like me, fond of walking about the yard in his leisure time. He hoped by exercise and fresh air to preserve his health and to counteract the evil effect of the stifling nights in the prison ward.

"I am impatiently looking forward to your release," he said with a smile, meeting me one day as we walked. "When you leave the prison, I shall know that I have exactly a year before I leave."

I may mention here parenthetically that our dreams and our long divorce from the reality made us think of freedom as somehow freer than real freedom, that is, than it actually is. The convicts had an exaggerated idea of real freedom, and that is so natural, so characteristic of every convict. Any officer's servant was looked on by us almost as in his way a king, almost as the ideal of a free man compared with the convicts, simply because he was not shaven and went about unfettered and unguarded.

On the evening before the last day I walked in the dusk for the last time all round our prison by the fence. How many thousands of times I had walked along that fence during those years! Here behind the barracks during my first year in prison I used to pace up and down, alone, forlorn and dejected. I remember how I used to reckon then how many thousand days were before me. Good God, how long ago it was! Here in this corner our eagle had lived in captivity; here Petrov often used to meet me. Even now he was constantly at my side. He would run up and, as though guessing my thoughts, would walk in silence beside me, seeming as though he were secretly wondering. Mentally, I took leave of the blackened rough timbered walls of our prison. How unfriendly they had seemed to me then, in those first days! They, too, must have grown older by now, but I saw no difference in them. And how much youth lay uselessly buried within those walls, what mighty powers were wasted here in vain! After all, one must tell the whole truth; those men were exceptional men. Perhaps they were the most gifted, the strongest of our people. But their mighty energies were vainly wasted, wasted abnormally, unjustly, hopelessly. And who was to blame, whose fault was it?

That's just it, who was to blame?

Early next morning as soon as it began to get light, before the convicts went out to work, I walked through the prison wards to say good-bye to all the convicts. Many strong, horny hands were held out to me cordially. Some, but they were not many, shook hands quite like comrades. Others realized thoroughly that I should at once become quite a different sort of man from them. They knew that I had friends in the town, that I was going straight from the prison to "the gentry," and that I should sit down with them as their equal. They understood that and, although they said good-bye to me in a friendly and cordial way, they did not speak to me as to a comrade, but as to a gentleman. Some turned away from me and sullenly refused to respond to my greeting. Some even looked at me with a sort of hatred.

The drum beat and all went out to work, and I remained at home. Sushilov had got up almost before anyone that morning and was doing his utmost to get tea ready for me before he went. Poor Sushilov! He cried when I gave him my convict clothes, my shirts, my fetter-wrappers and some money. "It's not that that I want, not that," he said, with difficulty controlling his trembling lips. "It's dreadful losing you, Alexandr Petrovitch! What shall I do here without you!"

I said good-bye for the last time to Akim Akimitch, too.

"You'll be going soon, too," I said to him.

"I've long, very long to be here still," he muttered as he pressed my hand. I threw myself on his neck and we kissed.

Ten minutes after the convicts had gone out, we, too, left the prison, never to return. My comrade had entered prison with me and we left together. We had to go straight to the blacksmith's to have our fetters knocked off. But no guard followed us with a gun; we went accompanied only by a sergeant. Our fetters were removed by our convicts in the engineer's workshop. While they were doing my comrade, I waited and then I, too, went up to the anvil. The blacksmiths turned me round so that my back was towards them, lifted my leg up and laid it on the anvil. They bestirred themselves, tried to do their best, their most skilful.

"The rivet, the rivet, turn that first of all!" the senior commanded, "hold it, that's it, that's right. Hit it with the hammer now."

The fetters fell off. I picked them up. I wanted to hold them in my hand, to look at them for the last time. I seemed already to be wondering that they could have been on my legs a minute before.

"Well, with God's blessing, with God's blessing!" said the convicts in coarse, abrupt voices, in which, however, there was a note of pleasure.

Yes, with God's blessing! Freedom, new life, resurrection from the dead. . . . What a glorious moment!

POOR FOLK

A NOVEL

Ah, these story tellers! If only they would write anything useful, pleasant, soothing, but they will unearth all sorts of hidden things! . . . I would prohibit their writing! Why, it is beyond everything; you read . . . and you can't help thinking—and then all sorts of foolishness comes into your head; I would really prohibit their writing; I would simply prohibit it altogether.

PRINCE V. F. ODOEVSKY.[1]

My precious Varvara Alexyevna,

I was happy yesterday, immensely happy, impossibly happy, impossibly happy! For once in your life, you obstinate person, you obeyed me. At eight o'clock in the evening I woke up (you know, little mother, that I love a little nap of an hour or two when my work is over). I got out a candle, I got paper ready, was mending a pen when suddenly I chanced to raise my eyes—upon my word it set my heart dancing! So you understood what I wanted, what was my heart's desire! I saw a tiny corner of your window-curtain twitched back and caught against the pot of balsams, just exactly as I hinted that day. Then I fancied I caught a glimpse of your little face at the window, that you were looking at me from your little room, that you were thinking of me. And how vexed I was, my darling, that I could not make out your charming little face distinctly! There was a time when we, too, could see clearly, dearie. It is poor fun being old, my own! Nowadays everything seems sort of spotty before my eyes; if one works a little in the evening, writes something, one's eyes are so red and tearful in the morning that one is really ashamed before strangers. In my imagination, though, your smile was beaming, my little angel, your kind friendly little smile; and I had just the same sensation in my heart as when I kissed you, Varinka, do you remember, little angel? Do you know, my darling, I even fancied that you shook your little finger at me? Did you, you naughty girl? You must be sure to describe all that fully in your letter.

Come, what do you think of our little plan about your curtain, Varinka? It is delightful, isn't it? Whether I am sitting at work, or lying down for a nap, or waking up, I know that you are thinking about me over there, you are remembering me and that you are well and cheerful. You drop the curtain—it means "Good-bye, Makar Alexyevitch, it's bedtime!" You draw it up—"Good morning, Makar Alexyevitch,

307

how have you slept or are you quite well, Makar Alexyevitch? As for
me, thank God, I am well and all right!" You see, my darling, what a
clever idea; there is no need of letters! It's cunning, isn't it? And you
know it was my idea. What do you say to me now, Varvara Alexyevna?

I beg to inform you, Varvara Alexyevna, my dear, that I slept last
night excellently, contrary to my expectations, at which I am very
much pleased; though in new lodgings, after moving, it is always difficult to sleep; there is always some little thing amiss.

I got up this morning as gay as a lark! What a fine morning it was,
my darling! Our window was opened; the sun shone so brightly; the
birds were chirping; the air was full of the scents of spring and all nature seemed coming back to life—and everything else was to correspond; everything was right, to fit the spring. I even had rather pleasant
dreams to-day, and my dreams were all of you, Varinka. I compared you
with a bird of the air created for the delight of men and the adornment
of nature. Then I thought, Varinka, that we men, living in care and anxiety, must envy the careless and innocent happiness of the birds of the
air—and more of the same sort, like that; that is, I went on making
such far-fetched comparisons. I have a book, Varinka, and there is the
same thought in it, all very exactly described. I write this, my darling,
because one has all sorts of dreams, you know. And now it's spring-
time, so one's thoughts are always so pleasant; witty, amusing, and tender dreams visit one; everything is in a rosy light. That is why I have
written all this; though, indeed, I took it all out of the book. The author
there expresses the same desire in verse and writes:

"Why am I not a bird, a bird of prey!"

And so on, and so on. There are all sorts of thoughts in it, but never
mind them now!

Oh, where were you going this morning, Varvara Alexyevna? Before I had begun to get ready for the office, you flew out of your room
exactly like a bird of the air and crossed the yard, looking so gay. How
glad it made me to look at you! Ah, Varinka, Varinka!—You must not
be sad; tears are no help to sorrow; I know that, my dear, I know it
from experience. Now you are so comfortable and you are getting a
little stronger, too.

Well, how is your Fedora? Ah, what a good-natured woman she

is! You must write and tell me, Varinka, how you get on with her now and whether you are satisfied with everything. Fedora is rather a grumbler; but you must not mind that, Varinka. God bless her! She has such a good heart. I have written to you already about Teresa here—she, too, is a good-natured and trustworthy woman. And how uneasy I was about our letters! How were they to be delivered? And behold the Lord sent us Teresa to make us happy. She is a good-natured woman, mild and long-suffering. But our landlady is simply merciless. She squeezes her at work like a rag.

Well, what a hole I have got into, Varvara Alexyevna! It is a lodging! I used to live like a bird in the woods, as you know yourself—it was so quiet and still that if a fly flew across the room you could hear it. Here it is all noise, shouting, uproar! But of course you don't know how it is all arranged here. Imagine a long passage, absolutely dark and very dirty. On the right hand there is a blank wall, and on the left, doors and doors, like the rooms in a hotel, in a long row. Well, these are lodgings and there is one room in each; there are people living by twos and by threes in one room. It is no use expecting order—it is a regular Noah's ark! They seem good sort of people, though, all so well educated and learned. One is in the service, a well-read man (he is somewhere in the literary department): he talks about Homer and Brambeus[2] and authors of all sorts: he talks about everything; a very intelligent man! There are two officers who do nothing but play cards. There is a naval man; and an English teacher.

Wait a bit, I will divert you, my darling; I will describe them satirically in my next letter; that is, I will tell you what they are like in full detail. Our landlady is a very untidy little old woman, she goes about all day long in slippers and a dressing-gown, and all day long she is scolding at Teresa. I live in the kitchen, or rather, to be more accurate, there is a room near the kitchen (and our kitchen, I ought to tell you, is clean, light and very nice), a little room, a modest corner . . . or rather the kitchen is a big room of three windows so I have a partition running along the inside wall, so that it makes as it were another room, an extra lodging; it is roomy and comfortable, and there is a window and all—in fact, every convenience. Well, so that is my little corner. So don't you imagine, my darling, there is anything else about it, any mysterious significance in it; "here he is living in the kitchen!" you'll say. Well, if you like, I really am living in the kitchen, behind the partition, but that is nothing; I am quite private, apart from everyone, quiet and snug. I have put in a bed, a table, a chest of drawers and a couple of chairs, and I have hung up the ikon. It is true there are better lodgings—perhaps there may be much better, but convenience is the great thing; I have arranged it all for my own convenience, you know, and you must not imagine it is for anything else. Your little window is opposite, across the yard; and the yard is narrow, one catches glimpses of you passing—it is more cheerful for a poor, lonely fellow like me, and cheaper, too. The very cheapest room here with board costs thirty-five roubles in paper: beyond my means; but my lodging costs me seven roubles in paper and my board five in silver—that is, twenty-four and a half, and before I used to pay thirty and make it up by going without a great many things. I did not always have tea, but now I can spare enough for tea and sugar, too. And you know, my dear, one is ashamed as it were not to drink tea; here they are all well-to-do people so one feels ashamed. One drinks it, Varinka, for the sake of the other people, for the look of the thing; for myself I don't care, I am not particular. Think, too, of pocket-money—one must have a certain amount—then some sort of boots and clothes—is there much left? My salary is all I have. I am content and don't repine. It is sufficient. It has been sufficient for several years; there are extras, too.

Well, good-bye, my angel. I have bought a couple of pots of balsam and geranium—quite cheap—but perhaps you love mignonette? Well, there is mignonette, too, you write and tell me; be sure to write me everything as fully as possible, you know. Don't you imagine anything, though, or have any doubts about my having taken such a room, Varinka dear; no, it is my own convenience made me take it, and only the convenience of it tempted me. I am putting by money, you know, my darling, I am saving up: I have quite a lot of money. You must not think I am such a softy that a fly might knock me down with his wing. No, indeed, my own, I am not a fool, and I have as strong a will as a man of resolute and tranquil soul ought to have. Good-bye, my angel! I have scribbled you almost two sheets and I ought to have been at the office long ago. I kiss your fingers, my own, and remain

Your humble and faithful friend,

Makar Dyevushkin.

P.S.—One thing I beg you: answer me as fully as possible, my angel. I am sending you a pound of sweets with this, Varinka. You eat them up and may they do you good, and for God's sake do not worry about me and make a fuss. Well, good-bye then, my precious.

April 8.

DEAR SIR, MAKAR ALEXYEVITCH,

Do you know I shall have to quarrel with you outright at last. I swear to you, dear Makar Alexyevitch, that it really hurts me to take your presents. I know what they cost you, how you deny yourself, and deprive yourself of what is necessary. How many times have I told you that I need nothing, absolutely nothing; that I shall never be able to repay you for the kindnesses you have showered upon me? And why have you sent me these flowers? Well, the balsams I don't mind, but why the geranium? I have only to drop an incautious word, for instance, about that geranium, and you rush off and buy it. I am sure it must have been expensive? How charming the flowers are! Crimson, in little crosses. Where did you get such a pretty geranium? I have put it in the middle of the window in the most conspicuous place; I am putting a bench on the floor and arranging the rest of the flowers on the bench; you just wait until I get rich myself! Fedora is overjoyed; it's like paradise now, in our room—so clean, so bright!

Now, why those sweets? Upon my word, I guessed at once from your letter that there was something amiss with you—nature and spring and the sweet scents and the birds chirping. "What's this," I thought, "isn't it poetry?" Yes, indeed, your letter ought to have been in verse, that was all that was wanting, Makar Alexyevitch! There are the tender sentiments and dreams in roseate hues—everything in it! As for the curtain, I never thought of it; I suppose it got hitched up of itself when I moved the flower-pots, so there!

Ah, Makar Alexyevitch! Whatever you may say, however you may reckon over your income to deceive me, to prove that your money is all spent on yourself, you won't take me in and you won't hide anything from me. It is clear that you are depriving yourself of necessities for my sake. What possessed you, for instance, to take such a lodging? Why, you will be disturbed and worried; you are cramped for room, uncomfortable. You love solitude, and here, goodness knows what you have all about you! You might live a great deal better, judging from your salary. Fedora says you used to live ever so much better than you do now. Can you have spent all your life like this in solitude, in privation, without pleasure, without a friendly affectionate word, a lodger among strangers? Ah, dear friend, how sorry I am for you! Take care of your health, anyway, Makar Alexyevitch! You say your eyes are weak; so you must not write by candlelight; why write? Your devotion to your work must be known to your superiors without that.

Once more I entreat you not to spend so much money on me. I know that you love me, but you are not well off yourself. . . . I got up this morning feeling gay, too. I was so happy; Fedora had been at work a long time and had got work for me, too. I was so delighted; I only went out to buy silk and then I set to work. The whole morning I felt so lighthearted, I was so gay! But now it is all black thoughts and sadness again; my heart keeps aching.

Ah, what will become of me, what will be my fate! What is painful is that I am in such uncertainty, that I have no future to look forward to, that I cannot even guess what will become of me. It is dreadful to look back, too. There is such sorrow in the past, and my heart is torn in two at the very memory of it. All my life I shall be in suffering, thanks to the wicked people who have ruined me.

It is getting dark. Time for work. I should have liked to have written to you of lots of things but I have not the time, I must get to work. I must make haste. Of course letters are a good thing; they make it more cheerful, anyway. But why do you never come to see us yourself? Why is that, Makar Alexyevitch? Now we are so near, you know, and sometimes you surely can make time. Please do come! I have seen your Teresa. She looks such a sickly creature; I felt sorry for her and gave her twenty kopecks. Yes! I was almost forgetting: you must write to me all about your life and your surroundings as fully as possible. What sort of people are they about you and do you get on with them? I am longing to know all that. Mind you write to me! To-day I will hitch up the curtain on purpose. You should go to bed earlier; last night I saw your light till midnight. Well, good-bye. To-day I am miserable and bored and sad! It seems it is an unlucky day! Good-bye.

Yours,

VARVARA DOBROSELOV.

April 8.

DEAR MADAM, VARVARA ALEXYEVNA,

Yes, dear friend, yes, my own, it seems it was a bad day for poor luckless me! Yes; you mocked at an old man like me, Varvara Alexyevna! It was my fault, though, entirely my fault! I ought not in my old age, with scarcely any hair on my head, to have launched out into lyrical nonsense and fine phrases. . . . And I will say more, my dear: man is sometimes a strange creature, very strange. My goodness! he begins talking of something and is carried away directly! And what comes of it, what does it lead to? Why, absolutely nothing comes of it, and it leads to such nonsense that—Lord preserve me! I am not angry, Varinka dear, only I am very much vexed to remember it all, vexed that I wrote to you in such a foolish, high-flown way. And I went to the office to-day so cock-a-hoop; there was such radiance in my heart. For no rhyme or reason there was a regular holiday in my soul; I felt so gay. I took up my papers eagerly—but what did it all amount to! As soon as I looked about me, everything was as before, grey and dingy. Still the same ink-spots, the same tables and papers, and I, too, was just the same; as I always have been, so I was still—so what reason was there to mount upon Pegasus? And what was it all due to? The sun peeping out and the sky growing blue! Was that it? And how could I talk of the scents of spring? when you never know what there may be in our yard under the windows! I suppose I fancied all that in my foolishness. You know a man does sometimes make such mistakes in his own feelings and writes nonsense. That is due to nothing but foolish, excessive warmth of heart.

I did not walk but crawled home. For no particular reason my head had begun to ache; well that, to be sure, was one thing on the top of another. (I suppose I got a chill to my spine.) I was so delighted with the spring, like a fool, that I went out in a thin greatcoat. And you were mistaken in my feelings, my dear!

You took my outpouring of them quite in the wrong way. I was inspired by fatherly affection—nothing but a pure fatherly affection, Varvara Alexyevna. For I take the place of a father to you, in your sad fatherless and motherless state; I say this from my soul, from a pure heart, as a relation. After all, though, I am but a distant relation, as the

proverb says "only the seventh water on the jelly," still I am a relation
and now your nearest relation and protector; seeing that where you
had most right to look for protection and support you have met with
insult and treachery. As for verses, let me tell you, my love, it would
not be seemly for me in my old age to be making verses. Poetry
is nonsense! Why, boys are thrashed at school nowadays for making
poetry . . . so that is how it is, my dear. . . .

What are you writing to me, Varvara Alexyevna, about comfort,
about quiet and all sorts of things? I am not particular, my dear soul, I
am not exacting. I have never lived better than I am doing now; so why
should I be hard to please in my old age? I am well fed and clothed and
shod; and it is not for us to indulge our whims! We are not royalties!
My father was not of noble rank and his income was less than mine for
his whole family. I have not lived in the lap of luxury! However, if I
must tell the truth, everything was a good deal better in my old lodging; it was more roomy and convenient, dear friend. Of course my
present lodging is nice, even in some respects more cheerful, and more
varied if you like; I have nothing to say against that but yet I regret the
old one. We old, that is elderly people, get used to old things as though
to something akin to use. The room was a little one, you know; the
walls were . . . there, what is the use of talking! . . . the walls were like
all other walls, they don't matter, and yet remembering all my past
makes me depressed . . . it's a strange thing: it's painful, yet the memories are, as it were, pleasant. Even what was nasty, what I was vexed
with at the time, is, as it were, purified from nastiness in my memory
and presents itself in an attractive shape to my imagination. We lived
peacefully, Varinka, I and my old landlady who is dead. I remember my
old landlady with a sad feeling now. She was a good woman and did
not charge me much for my lodging. She used to knit all sorts of rugs
out of rags on needles a yard long. She used to do nothing else. We used
to share light and fuel, so we worked at one table. She had a grand-
daughter, Masha—I remember her quite a little thing. Now she must
be a girl of thirteen. She was such a mischievous little thing—very
merry, always kept us amused, and we lived together, the three of us.
Sometimes in the long winter evenings we would sit down to the
round table, drink a cup of tea and then set to work. And to keep Masha
amused and out of mischief the old lady used to begin to tell tales. And

what tales they were! A sensible intelligent man would listen to them
with pleasure, let alone a child. Why, I used to light my pipe and be so
interested that I forgot my work. And the child, our little mischief,
would be so grave, she would lean her rosy cheek on her little hand,
open her pretty little mouth and, if the story were the least bit terrible,
she would huddle up to the old woman. And we liked to look at her;
and did not notice how the candle wanted snuffing nor hear the wind
roaring and the storm raging outside.

We had a happy life, Varinka, and we lived together for almost
twenty years.

But how I have been prattling on! Perhaps you don't care for such
a subject, and it is not very cheering for me to remember it, especially
just now in the twilight. Teresa's busy about something, my head
aches and my back aches a little, too. And my thoughts are so queer,
they seem to be aching as well. I am sad to-day, Varinka!

What's this you write, my dear? How can I come and see you? My
darling, what would people say? Why, I should have to cross the yard,
our folks would notice it, would begin asking questions—there would
be gossip, there would be scandal, they would put a wrong construction
on it. No, my angel, I had better see you to-morrow at the evening service, that will be more sensible and more prudent for both of us. And
don't be vexed with me, my precious, for writing you such a letter;
reading it over I see it is all so incoherent. I am an old man, Varinka, and
not well-educated; I had no education in my youth and now I could get
nothing into my head if I began studying over again. I am aware,
Varinka, that I am no hand at writing, and I know without anyone else
pointing it out and laughing at me that if I were to try to write something more amusing I should only write nonsense.

I saw you at your window to-day, I saw you let down your blind.
Good-bye, good-bye, God keep you! Good-bye, Varvara Alexyevna.

Your disinterested friend,
MAKAR DYEVUSHKIN.

P.S.—I can't write satirical accounts of anyone now, my dear. I am
too old, Varvara Alexyevna, to be facetious, and I should make myself a
laughing-stock; as the proverb has it: "those who live in glass houses
should not throw stones."

April 9.

DEAR SIR, MAKAR ALEXYEVITCH,

Come, are not you ashamed, Makar Alexyevitch, my friend and benefactor, to be so depressed and naughty? Surely you are not offended! Oh, I am often too hasty, but I never thought that you would take my words for a biting jest. Believe me, I could never dare to jest at your age and your character. It has all happened through my thoughtlessness, or rather from my being horribly dull, and dullness may drive one to anything! I thought that you meant to make fun yourself in your letter. I felt dreadfully sad when I saw that you were displeased with me. No, my dear friend and benefactor, you are wrong if you ever suspect me of being unfriendly and ungrateful. In my heart I know how to appreciate all you have done for me, defending me from wicked people, from their persecution and hatred. I shall pray for you always, and if my prayer rises to God and heaven accepts it you will be happy.

I feel very unwell to-day. I am feverish and shivering by turns. Fedora is very anxious about me. There is no need for you to be ashamed to come and see us, Makar Alexyevitch; what business is it of other people's! We are acquaintances, and that is all about it. . . .

Good-bye, Makar Alexyevitch. I have nothing more to write now, and indeed I can't write; I am horribly unwell. I beg you once more not to be angry with me and to rest assured of the invariable respect and devotion,

With which I have the honour to remain,

Your most devoted and obedient servant,

VARVARA DOBROSELOV.

April 12.

DEAR MADAM, VARVARA ALEXYEVNA,

Oh, my honey, what is the matter with you! This is how you frighten me every time. I write to you in every letter to take care of yourself, to wrap yourself up, not to go out in bad weather, to be cautious in every way—and, my angel, you don't heed me. Ah, my darling, you are just like some child! Why, you are frail, frail as a little straw, I know that. If there is the least little wind, you fall ill. So you must be careful, look after yourself, avoid risks and not reduce your friends to grief and distress.

You express the desire, dear Varinka, to have a full account of my daily life and all my surroundings. I gladly hasten to carry out your wish, my dear. I will begin from the beginning, my love: it will be more orderly.

To begin with, the staircases to the front entrance are very passable in our house; especially the main staircase—it is clean, light, wide, all cast-iron and mahogany, but don't ask about the backstairs: winding like a screw, damp, dirty, with steps broken and the walls so greasy that your hand sticks when you lean against them. On every landing there are boxes, broken chairs and cupboards, rags hung out, windows broken, tubs stand about full of all sorts of dirt and litter, eggshells and the refuse of fish; there is a horrid smell . . . in fact it is not nice.

I have already described the arrangement of the rooms; it is convenient, there is no denying; that is true, but it is rather stuffy in them. I don't mean that there is a bad smell, but, if I may so express it, a rather decaying, acrid, sweetish smell. At first it makes an unfavourable impression, but that is of no consequence; one has only to be a couple of minutes among us and it passes off and you don't notice how it passes off for you begin to smell bad yourself, your clothes smell, your hands smell and everything smells—well, you get used to it. Siskins simply die with us. The naval man is just buying the fifth—they can't live in our air and that is the long and short of it. Our kitchen is big, roomy and light. In the mornings, it is true, it is rather stifling when they are cooking fish or meat and splashing and slopping water everywhere, but in the evening it is paradise. In our kitchen there is always old linen hanging on a line; and as my room is not far off, that is, is almost part of the kitchen, the smell of it does worry me a little; but no matter, in time one gets used to anything.

Very early in the morning the hubbub begins, people moving about, walking, knocking—everyone who has to is getting up, some to go to the office, others about their own business; they all begin drinking tea. The samovars for the most part belong to the landlady; there are few of them, so we all use them in turn, and if anyone goes with his teapot out of his turn, he catches it.

I, for instance, the first time made that mistake, and . . . but why describe it? I made the acquaintance of everyone at once. The naval man was the first I got to know; he is such an open fellow, told me everything: about his father and mother, about his sister married to an assessor in Tula, and about the town of Kronstadt. He promised to protect me and at once invited me to tea with him. I found him in the room where they usually play cards. There they gave me tea and were very insistent that I should play a game of chance with them. Whether they were laughing at me or not I don't know, but they were losing the whole night and they were still playing when I went away. Chalk, cards—and the room so full of smoke that it made my eyes smart. I did not play and they at once observed that I was talking of philosophy. After that no one said another word to me the whole time; but to tell the truth I was glad of it. I am not going to see them now; it's gambling with them, pure gambling. The clerk in the literary department has little gatherings in the evening, too. Well, there it is nice, quiet, harmless and delicate; everything is on a refined footing.

Well, Varinka, I will remark in passing that our landlady is a very horrid woman and a regular old hag. You've seen Teresa. You know what she is like, as thin as a plucked, dried-up chicken. There are two of them in the house, Teresa and Faldoni.[3] I don't know whether he has any other name, he always answers to that one and everyone calls him that. He is a red-haired, foul-tongued Finn, with only one eye and a snub nose: he is always swearing at Teresa, they almost fight.

On the whole life here is not exactly perfect at all times. . . .

If only all would go to sleep at once at night and be quiet—that never happens. They are for ever sitting somewhere playing, and sometimes things go on that one would be ashamed to describe. By now I have grown accustomed to it; but I wonder how people with families get along in such a Bedlam. There is a whole family of poor creatures living in one of our landlady's rooms, not in the same row with the other lodgings but on the other side, in a corner apart. They are quiet people! No one hears anything of them. They live in one little room dividing it with a screen. He is a clerk out of work, discharged from the service seven years ago for something. His name is Gorshkov—such a grey little man; he goes about in such greasy, such threadbare clothes that it is sad to see him; ever so much worse than mine. He is a pitiful, decrepit figure (we sometimes meet in the passage); his knees shake, his hands shake, his head shakes, from some illness I suppose, poor fellow. He is timid, afraid of everyone and sidles along edgeways; I am shy at times, but he is a great deal worse. His family consists of a wife and three children. The eldest, a boy, is just like his father, just as frail. The wife was once very good-looking, even now one can see it; she, poor thing, goes about in pitiful tatters. They are in debt to the landlady, I have heard, she is none too gracious to them. I have heard, too, that there is some unpleasant business hanging over Gorshkov in connection with which he lost his place. . . . Whether it is a lawsuit—whether he is to be tried, or prosecuted, or what, I can't tell you for certain. Poor they are, mercy on us! It is always still and quiet in their room as if no one were living there. There is no sound even of the children. And it never happens that the children frolic about and play, and that is a bad sign. One evening I happened to pass their door; it was unusually quiet in the house at the time; I heard a sobbing, then a whisper, then sobbing again as though they were crying but so quietly, so pitifully that it was heart-rending, and the thought of those poor creatures haunted me all night so that I could not get to sleep properly.

Well, good-bye, my precious little friend, Varinka. I have described everything to the best of my abilities. I have been thinking of nothing but you all day. My heart aches over you, my dear. I know, my love, you have no warm cloak. Ah! these Petersburg springs, these winds and rain mixed with snow—they'll be the death of me, Varinka! Such salubrious airs, Lord preserve us!

Don't scorn my description, my love. I have no style, Varinka, no style whatever. I only wish I had. I write just what comes into my head only to cheer you up with something. If only I had had some education it would have been a different matter, but how much education have I had? Not a ha'porth.

Always your faithful friend,
MAKAR DYEVUSHKIN.

April 25.

HONOURED SIR, MAKER ALEXYEVITCH,

I met my cousin Sasha to-day! It is horrible! She will be ruined too, poor thing! I heard, too, from other sources that Anna Fyodorovna is still making inquiries about me. It seems as though she will never leave off persecuting me. She says that she wants to *forgive me*, to forget all

the past and that she must come and see me. She says that you are no relation to me at all, that she is a nearer relation, that you have no right to
meddle in our family affairs and that it is shameful and shocking to live
on your charity and at your expense. . . . She says that I have forgotten
her hospitality, that she saved mother and me from starving to death,
perhaps, that she gave us food and drink, and for more than a year and
a half was put to expense on our account, and that besides all that she
forgave us a debt. Even mother she will not spare! and if only poor
mother knew how they have treated me! God sees it! . . . Anna Fyodorovna says that I was so silly that I did not know how to take advantage
of my luck, that she put me in the way of good luck, that she is not to
blame for anything else, and that I myself was not able or perhaps was
not anxious to defend my own honour. Who was to blame in that,
great God! She says that Mr. Bykov was perfectly right and that he
would not marry just anybody who . . . but why write it!

It is cruel to hear such falsehoods, Makar Alexyevitch! I can't tell
you what a state I am in now. I am trembling, crying, sobbing. I have
been two hours over writing this letter to you. I thought that at least
she recognised how wrongly she had treated me; and you see what
she is now!

For God's sake don't be alarmed, my friend, the one friend who
wishes me well! Fedora exaggerates everything, I am not ill. I only
caught cold a little yesterday when I went to the requiem service for
mother at Volkovo. Why did you not come with me? I begged you so
much to do so. Ah, my poor, poor mother, if she could rise from the
grave, if she could see how they have treated me!

V. D.

May 20.

MY DARLING VARINKA,

I send you a few grapes, my love; I am told they are good for a
convalescent and the doctor recommends them for quenching the
thirst—simply for thirst. You were longing the other day for a few
roses, my darling, so I am sending you some now. Have you any appetite, my love?—that is the most important thing.

Thank God, though, that it is all over and done with, and that our
troubles, too, will be soon at an end. We must give thanks to heaven!

As for books, I cannot get hold of them anywhere for the moment. I am told there is a good book here written in very fine language; they say it is good, I have not read it myself, but it is very much praised here. I have asked for it and they have promised to lend it me, only will you read it? You are so hard to please in that line; it is difficult to satisfy your taste, I know that already, my darling. No doubt you want poetry, inspiration, lyrics—well, I will get poems too, I will get anything; there is a manuscript book full of extracts here.

I am getting on very well. Please don't be uneasy about me, my dearie. What Fedora told you about me is all nonsense; you tell her that she told a lie, be sure to tell her so, the wicked gossip! . . . I have not sold my new uniform. And why should I . . . judge for yourself, why should I sell it? Here, I am told, I have forty roubles bonus coming to me, so why should I sell it? Don't you worry, my precious; she's suspicious, your Fedora, she's suspicious. We shall get on splendidly, my darling! Only you get well, my angel, for God's sake, get well. Don't grieve your old friend. Who told you I had grown thin? It is slander, slander again! I am well and hearty and getting so fat that I am quite ashamed. I am well fed and well content: the only thing is for you to get strong again!

Come, good-bye, my angel; I kiss your little fingers,

And remain, always,
Your faithful friend,
MAKAR DYEVUSHKIN.

P.S.—Ah, my love, what do you mean by writing like that again? . . . What nonsense you talk! Why, how can I come and see you so often, my precious? I ask you how can I? Perhaps snatching a chance after dark; but there, there's scarcely any night at all now,[4] at this season. As it was, my angel, I scarcely left you at all while you were ill, while you were unconscious; but really I don't know how I managed it all; and afterwards I gave up going to you for people had begun to be inquisitive and to ask questions. There had been gossip going about here, even apart from that. I rely upon Teresa; she is not one to talk; but think for yourself, my darling, what a to-do there will be when they find out everything about us. They will imagine something and what will they say then? So you must keep a brave heart, my darling, and wait until you are quite strong again; and then we will arrange a *rendezvous* somewhere out of doors.

June 1.

MY DEAR MAKAR ALEXYEVITCH,

I so long to do something nice that will please you in return for all the care and trouble you have taken about me, and all your love for me, that at last I have overcome my disinclination to rummage in my chest and find my diary, which I am sending to you now. I began it in the happy time of my life. You used often to question me with curiosity about my manner of life in the past, my mother, Pokrovskoe, my time with Anna Fyodorovna and my troubles in the recent past, and you were so impatiently anxious to read the manuscript in which I took the fancy, God knows why, to record some moments of my life that I have no doubt the parcel I am sending will be a pleasure to you. It made me sad to read it over. I feel that I am twice as old as when I wrote the last line in that diary. It was all written at different dates. Good-bye, Makar Alexyevitch! I feel horribly depressed now and often I am troubled with sleeplessness. Convalescence is a very dreary business!

V. D.

I

I WAS ONLY FOURTEEN when my father died. My childhood was the happiest time of my life. It began not here but far away in a province in the wilds. My father was the steward of Prince P.'s huge estate in the province of T——. We lived in one of the Prince's villages and led a quiet, obscure, happy life. . . . I was a playful little thing; I used to do nothing but run about the fields, the copses and the gardens, and no one troubled about me. My father was constantly busy about his work, my mother looked after the house; no one taught me anything, for which I was very glad. Sometimes at daybreak I would run away either to the pond or to the copse or to the hayfield or to the reapers—and it did not matter that the sun was baking, that I was running, I did not know where, away from the village, that I was scratched by the bushes, that I tore my dress. . . . I should be scolded afterwards at home, but I did not care for that.

And it seems to me that I should have been so happy if it had been my lot to have spent all my life in one place and never to have left the country. But I had to leave my native place while I was still a child. I was only twelve when we moved to Petersburg. Ah, how well I remember our sorrowful preparations! How I cried when I said good-bye to everything that was so dear to me. I remember that I threw myself on father's neck and besought him with tears to remain a little longer in the country. Father scolded me, mother wept; she said that we had to go, that we could not help it. Old Prince P—— was dead. His heirs had discharged father from his post. Father had some money in the hands of private persons in Petersburg. Hoping to improve his position he thought his presence here in person essential. All this I learnt from mother. We settled here on the Petersburg Side and lived in the same spot up to the time of father's death.

How hard it was for me to get used to our new life! We moved to Petersburg in the autumn. When we left the country it was a clear, warm, brilliant day; the work of the fields was over; huge stacks of wheat were piled up on the threshing-floors and flocks of birds were calling about the fields; everything was so bright and gay: here as we came into the town we found rain, damp autumn chilliness, muggy greyness, sleet and a crowd of new, unknown faces, unwelcoming, ill-humoured, angry! We settled in somehow. I remember we were all in such a fuss, so troubled and busy in arranging our new life. Father was never at home, mother had not a quiet minute—I was forgotten altogether. I felt sad getting up in the morning after the first night in our new abode—our windows looked out on a yellow fence. The street was always covered with mud. The passers-by were few and they were all muffled up, they were all so cold. And for whole days together it was terribly miserable and dreary at home. We had scarcely a relation or intimate acquaintance. Father was not on friendly terms with Anna Fyodorovna. (He was in her debt.) People came on business to us pretty often. Usually they quarrelled, shouted and made an uproar. After every visit father was ill-humoured and cross; he would walk up and down the room by the hour together, frowning and not saying a word to anyone. Mother was silent then and did not dare to speak to him. I used to sit in a corner over a book, still and quiet, not daring to stir.

Three months after we came to Petersburg I was sent to boarding-school. How sad I was at first with strangers! Everything was so cold, so unfriendly! The teachers had such loud voices, the girls laughed at me so and I was such a wild creature. It was so stern and exacting! The fixed hours for everything, the meals in common, the tedious teachers—all that at first fretted and harassed me. I could not even sleep there. I used to cry the whole night, the long, dreary, cold night. Sometimes when they were all repeating or learning their lessons in the evening I would sit over my French translation or vocabularies, not daring to move and dreaming all the while of our little home, of father, of mother, of our old nurse, of nurse's stories. . . . Oh, how I used to grieve! The most trifling thing in the house I would recall with pleasure. I would keep dreaming how nice it would be now at home! I should be sitting in our little room by the samovar with my own people; it would be so warm, so nice, so familiar. How, I used to think, I would hug mother now, how tightly, how warmly! One would think and think and begin crying softly from misery, choking back one's tears, and the vocabularies would never get into one's head. I could not learn my lessons for next day; all night I would

dream of the teacher, the mistress, the girls; all night I would be repeating my lessons in my sleep and would not know them next day.
They would make me kneel down and give me only one dish for dinner. I was so depressed and dejected. At first all the girls laughed at me
and teased me and tried to confuse me when I was saying my lessons,
pinched me when in rows we walked into dinner or tea, made complaints against me to the teacher for next to nothing. But how heavenly it was when nurse used to come for me on Saturday evening. I
used to hug the old darling in a frenzy of joy. She would put on my
things, and wrap me up, and could not keep pace with me, while
I would chatter and chatter and tell her everything. I would arrive
home gay and happy, would hug everyone as though I had been away
for ten years. There would be explanations, talks; descriptions would
begin. I would greet everyone, laugh, giggle, skip and run about.
Then there would be serious conversations with father about our studies, our teachers, French, Lomond's grammar,[5] and we were all so
pleased and happy. It makes me happy even now to remember those
minutes. I tried my very utmost to learn and please father. I saw he was
spending his last farthing on me and God knows what straits he was
in. Every day he grew more gloomy, more ill-humoured, more angry.
His character was quite changed, his business was unsuccessful, he
had a mass of debts. Mother was sometimes afraid to cry, afraid to say
a word for fear of making father angry. She was getting quite ill, was
getting thinner and thinner and had begun to have a bad cough.

When I came back from school I used to find such sad faces,
mother weeping stealthily, father angry. Then there would be scolding
and upbraiding. Father would begin saying that I was no joy, no comfort to them; that they were depriving themselves of everything for
my sake and I could not speak French yet; in fact all his failures, all his
misfortunes were vented on me and mother. And how could he worry
poor mother! It was heartrending to look at her; her cheeks were hollow, her eyes were sunken, there was a hectic flush in her face.

I used to come in for more scolding than anyone. It always began
with trifles, and goodness knows what it went on to. Often I did
not understand what it was about. Everything was a subject of
complaint! . . . French and my being a great dunce and that the mistress of our school was a careless, stupid woman; that she paid no attention to our morals, that father was still unable to find a job, that

Lomond's was a very poor grammar and that Zapolsky's was very much better,[6] that a lot of money had been thrown away on me, that I was an unfeeling, stony-hearted girl—in fact, though I, poor thing, was striving my utmost, repeating conversations and vocabularies, I was to blame for everything, I was responsible for everything! And this was not because father did not love me; he was devoted to mother and me, but it was just his character.

Anxieties, disappointments, failures worried my poor father to distraction; he became suspicious, bitter; often he was close upon despair, he began to neglect his health, caught cold and all at once fell ill. He did not suffer long, but died so suddenly, so unexpectedly that we were all beside ourselves with the shock for some days. Mother seemed stunned; I actually feared for her reason.

As soon as father was dead creditors seemed to spring up from everywhere and rushed upon us like a torrent. Everything we had we gave them. Our little house on Petersburg Side, which father had bought six months after moving to Petersburg, was sold too. I don't know how they settled the rest, but we were left without refuge, without sustenance. Mother was suffering from a wasting disease, we could not earn our bread, we had nothing to live on, ruin stared us in the face. I was then only just fourteen. It was at this point that Anna Fyodorovna visited us. She always said that she owned landed estates and that she was some sort of relation of ours. Mother said, too, that she was a relation, only a very distant one. While father was alive she never came to see us. She made her appearance now with tears in her eyes and said she felt great sympathy for us; she condoled with us on our loss and our poverty-stricken condition; added that it was father's own fault; that he had lived beyond his means, had borrowed right and left and that he had been too self-confident. She expressed a desire to be on more friendly terms with us, said we must let by-gones be by-gones; when mother declared she had never felt any hostility towards her, she shed tears, took mother to church and ordered a requiem service for the "dear man". (That was how she referred to father.) After that she was solemnly reconciled to mother.

After leading up to the subject in many lengthy preambles, Anna Fyodorovna first depicted in glaring colours our poverty-stricken and forlorn position, our helplessness and hopelessness, and then invited us, as she expressed it, to take refuge with her. Mother thanked her, but for a long time could not make up her mind to accept; but seeing that there was nothing else she could do and no help for it, she told Anna Fyodorovna at last that we would accept her offer with gratitude.

I remember as though it were to-day the morning on which we moved from the Petersburg Side to Vassilyevsky Ostrov. It was a clear, dry, frosty autumn morning. Mother was crying. I felt horribly sad; my heart was torn and ached with a terrible inexplicable misery . . . it was a terrible time. . . .

II

At first till we—that is mother and I—had grown used to our new home we both felt strange and miserable at Anna Fyodorovna's. Anna Fyodorovna lived in a house of her own in Sixth Row. There were only five living-rooms in the house. In three of them lived Anna Fyodorovna and my cousin Sasha, a child who was being brought up by her, an orphan, fatherless and motherless. Then we lived in one room, and in the last room, next to ours, there was a poor student called Pokrovsky who was lodging in the house.

Anna Fyodorovna lived very well, in a more wealthy style than one could have expected; but her fortune was mysterious and so were her pursuits. She was always in a bustle, was always full of business, she drove out and came back several times a day; but what she was doing, what she was in a fuss about and with what object she was busy I could never make out. She had a large and varied circle of acquaintances. Visitors were always calling upon her, and the queerest people, always on business of some sort and to see her for a minute. Mother always carried me off to my room as soon as the bell rang. Anna Fyodorovna was horribly vexed with mother for this and was continually repeating that we were too proud, that we were proud beyond our means, that we had nothing to be proud about, and she would go on like that for hours together. I did not understand these reproaches at the time and, in fact, it is only now that I have found out, or rather that I guess why mother could not make up her mind to live with Anna Fyodorovna. Anna Fyodorovna was a spiteful woman, she was continually tormenting us. To this day it is a mystery to me why it was she invited us to live with her. At first she was fairly nice to us, but afterwards she began to show her real character as soon as she saw we were utterly helpless and had nowhere else to go. Later on she became very affectionate to me, even rather coarsely affectionate and flattering, but at first I suffered in the same way as mother. Every minute she was upbraiding us, she did nothing but talk of her charitable deeds. She introduced us to outsiders as her poor relations—a helpless widow and orphan to whom in the kindness of her heart, out of Christian charity, she had given a home. At meals she watched every morsel we took, while if we did not eat, there would be a fuss again; she would say we were fastidious, that we should not be over-nice, that we should be thankful for what we had; that she doubted if we had had anything better in our own home. She was continually abusing father, saying that he wanted to be better than other people and much good that had done him; that he had left his wife and daughter penniless and that if they had not had a benevolent relation, a Christian soul with a feeling heart, then, God knows, they might have been rotting in the street and dying of hunger. What did she not say! It was not so much painful as disgusting to hear her.

Mother was continually crying; her health grew worse from day to day. She was visibly wasting, yet she and I worked from morning till night, taking in sewing, which Anna Fyodorovna very much disliked, she was continually saying that she was not going to have her house turned into a dressmaker's shop. But we had to have clothes; we had to lay by for unforeseen expenses; it was absolutely necessary to have money of our own. We saved on the off-chance, hoping we might be able in time to move elsewhere. But mother lost what little health was left her over work; she grew weaker every day. The disease sucked the life out of her like a worm and hurried her to the grave. I saw it all, I felt it all, I realised it all and suffered; it all went on before my eyes.

The days passed and each day was like the one before. We lived as quietly as if we were not in a town. Anna Fyodorovna calmed down by degrees as she began fully to recognise her power. Though, indeed, no one ever thought of contradicting her. We were separated from her rooms by the corridor, and Pokrovsky's room was, as I have mentioned before, next to ours. He used to teach Sasha French and German, history, geography—all the sciences, as Anna Fyodorovna said, and for this he had his board and lodging from her. Sasha was a very intelligent child, though playful and mischievous; she was thirteen. Anna Fyodorovna observed to mother that it would not be amiss if I were to have lessons, since my education had not been finished at the boarding-school, and for a whole year I shared Sasha's lessons with Pokrovsky. Pokrovsky was poor, very poor. His health had prevented him from continuing his studies and it was only from habit that he was called a student. He was so retiring, so quiet and so still that we heard no sound of him from our room. He was very queer-looking; he walked so awkwardly, bowed so awkwardly and spoke so queerly that at first I could not look at him without laughing. Sasha was continually mocking at him, especially when he was giving us our lessons. He was of an irritable temper, too, was constantly getting cross, was beside himself about every trifle, scolded us, complained of us, and often went off into his own room in anger without finishing the lesson. He used to sit for days together over his books. He had a great many books, and such rare and expensive books. He gave other lessons, too, for which he was paid, and as soon as ever he had money he would go and buy books.

In time I got to know him better and more intimately. He was a very kind and good young man, the best person it has been my lot to meet. Mother had a great respect for him. Afterwards he became the best of my friends—next to mother, of course.

At first, though I was such a big girl, I was as mischievous as Sasha. We used to rack our brains for hours together to find ways to tease him and exhaust his patience. His anger was extremely funny, and we used to find it awfully amusing. (I am ashamed even to think of it now.) Once we teased him almost to the point of tears and I distinctly heard him whisper, "Spiteful children." I was suddenly overcome with confusion; I felt ashamed and miserable and sorry for him. I remember that I blushed up to my ears and almost with tears in my eyes began begging him not to mind and not to be offended at our stupid mischief. But he closed the book and without finishing the lesson went off to his own room. I was torn with penitence all day long. The thought that we children had reduced him to tears by our cruelty was insufferable. So we had waited for his tears. So we had wanted them; so we had succeeded in driving him out of all patience; so we had forced him, a poor unfortunate man, to realise his hard lot.

I could not sleep all night for vexation, sorrow, repentance. They say repentance relieves the soul—on the contrary. There was an element of vanity mixed, I don't know how, with my sadness. I did not want him to look upon me as a child, I was fifteen then.

From that day I began worrying my imagination, creating thousands of plans to make Pokrovsky change his opinion about me. But I had become all of a sudden timid and shy; in my real position I could venture upon nothing and confined myself to dreams (and God knows what dreams!). I left off joining in Sasha's pranks; he left off being angry with us; but for my vanity that was little comfort.

Now I will say a few words about the strangest, most curious and most pathetic figure I have ever chanced to meet. I speak of him now, at this passage in my diary, because until that period I had hardly paid any attention to him. But now everything that concerned Pokrovsky had suddenly become interesting to me.

There used sometimes to come to the house a little old man, grey-headed, grubby, badly-dressed, clumsy, awkward, incredibly queer in fact. At the first glance at him one might imagine that he was, as it were, abashed by something—as it were, ashamed of himself. That is why he always seemed to be shrinking into himself, to be, as it were, cowering; he had such queer tricks and ways that one might almost have concluded he was not in his right mind. He would come to the house and stand at the glass door in the entry without daring to come in. If one of us passed by—Sasha or I or any one of the servants he knew to be rather kind to him—he would begin waving at once, beckoning, making gesticulations, and only when one nodded and called to him—a sign agreed upon that there was no outsider in the house and that he might come in when he liked—only then the old man stealthily opened the door with a smile of glee, and rubbing his hands with satisfaction, walked on tiptoe straight to Pokrovsky's room. This was Pokrovsky's father.

Later on, I learnt the whole story of this poor old man. He had once been in the service, was entirely without ability, and filled the very lowest and most insignificant post. When his first wife (our Pokrovsky's mother) died he took it into his head to marry a second time and married a girl of the working-class. Everything was turned topsy-turvy under the rule of his new wife. She let no one live in peace, she domineered over everyone. Our Pokrovsky was still a child, ten years old. His stepmother hated him, but fate was kind to the boy. A country gentleman called Bykov, who had known the elder Pokrovsky and at one time been his patron, took the child under his protection and sent him to school. He was interested in him because he had known his mother, who had been a protégée of Anna Fyodorovna's and had by her been married to Pokrovsky. Mr. Bykov, a very intimate friend of Anna Fyodorovna's, had generously given the girl a dowry of five thousand roubles on her marriage. Where that money went to I don't know.

That was the story Anna Fyodorovna told me; young Pokrovsky never liked speaking of his family circumstances. They say his mother was very pretty, and it seems strange to me that she should have been so unfortunately married to such an insignificant man. He was quite young when she died four years after their marriage.

From boarding-school young Pokrovsky went on to a high school and then to the university. Mr. Bykov, who very often came to Petersburg, did not confine his protection to that. Owing to the breakdown of his health Pokrovsky could not continue his studies at the university. Mr. Bykov introduced him to Anna Fyodorovna, commended him to her good offices and so young Pokrovsky was taken into the house and was given his board on condition of teaching Sasha everything that was necessary. Old Pokrovsky was driven by grief at his wife's cruelty to the worst of vices and was scarcely ever sober. His wife used to beat him, make him live in the kitchen, and brought things at last to such a pass that he was quite accustomed to being beaten and ill-treated and did not complain of it. He was not a very old man, but his mind had almost given way owing to his bad habits. The one sign he showed of generous and humane feeling was his boundless love for his son. It was said that young Pokrovsky was as like his dead mother as one drop of water is like another. Maybe it was the memory of his first good wife that stirred in the ruined old man's heart this infinite love for his son. The old man could speak of nothing but his son and always visited him twice a week. He did not dare to come oftener, for young Pokrovsky could not endure his father's visits. Of all his failings, undoubtedly the greatest and foremost was his disrespect to his father. The old man certainly was at times the most insufferable creature in the world. In the first place he was horribly inquisitive, secondly, by remarks and questions of the most trivial and senseless kind he interrupted his son's work every minute, and, lastly, he would sometimes come under the influence of drink. The son gradually trained the old man to overcome his vices, his curiosity and incessant chatter, and at last had brought things to such a point that the old man obeyed him in everything like an oracle and did not dare open his mouth without permission.

The poor old man could not sufficiently admire and marvel at his Petinka (as he called his son). When he came to see him he almost always had a timid, careworn air, most likely from uncertainty as to the reception his son would give him. He was usually a long time making up his mind to come in, and if I happened to be there he would spend twenty minutes questioning me: "How was Petinka? Was he quite well? What sort of mood was he in, and was he busy over anything important? What was he doing? Was he writing, or absorbed in reflection?" When I had sufficiently cheered and reassured him, the old man at last ventured to come in, and very, very quietly, very, very cautiously opened the door, first poked in his head, and if his son nodded to him and the old man saw he was not angry, he moved stealthily into the room, took off his overcoat and his hat, which was always crushed, full of holes and with a broken brim, hung them on a hook, did everything quietly, noiselessly; then cautiously sat down on a chair, never taking his eyes off his son, watching every movement and trying to guess what mood his "Petinka" was in. If his son seemed ever so little out of humour and the old man noticed it, he got up from his seat at once and explained, "I just looked in, Petinka, only for a minute. I have been on a long walk, I was passing and came in for a rest." And then, dumbly, submissively he would take his coat, his wretched hat, again he would stealthily open the door and go away, keeping a forced smile on his face to check the rush of disappointment in his heart and to hide it from his son.

But when the son made the father welcome, the old man was beside himself with joy. His face, his gestures, his movements all betrayed his pleasure. If his son began talking to him, the old man always rose a little from the chair and answered softly, deferentially, almost with reverence, always trying to use the choicest, that is, the most absurd expressions. But he was not blessed with the gift of words; he was always nervous and confused, so that he did not know what to do with his hands, what to do with himself, and kept whispering the answer to himself long afterwards as though trying to correct himself. If he did succeed in giving a good answer, the old man smoothed himself down, straightened his waistcoat, his tie, his coat and assumed an air of dignity. Sometimes he plucked up so much courage and grew so bold that he stealthily got up from his chair, went up to the bookshelf, took down some book and even began reading something on the spot, whatever the book might be. All this he did with an air of assumed unconcern and coolness, as though he could always do what he liked with his son's books, as though his son's graciousness was nothing out of the way.

But I once happened to see how frightened the poor fellow was when Pokrovsky asked him not to touch the books. He grew nervous and confused, put the book back upside down, then tried to right it, turned it round and put it in with the edges outside; smiled, flushed and did not know how to efface his crime. Pokrovsky by his persuasions did succeed in turning the old man a little from his evil propensities, and whenever the son saw his father sober three times running he would give him twenty-five kopecks, fifty kopecks, or more at parting. Sometimes he would buy his father a pair of boots, a tie or a waistcoat; then the old man was as proud as a cock in his new clothes.

Sometimes he used to come to us. He used to bring Sasha and me gingerbread cocks and apples and always talked to us of Petinka. He used to beg us to be attentive and obedient at lessons, used to tell us that Petinka was a good son, an exemplary son and, what was more, a learned son. Meanwhile he would wink at us so funnily with his left eye and make such amusing grimaces that we could not help smiling, and went into peals of laughter at him. Mother was very fond of him. But the old man hated Anna Fyodorovna, though he was stiller than water, humbler than grass in her presence.

Soon I left off having lessons with Pokrovsky. As before, he looked upon me as a child, a mischievous little girl on a level with Sasha. This hurt me very much, for I was trying my utmost to efface the impression of my behaviour in the past, but I was not noticed. That irritated me more and more. I scarcely ever spoke to Pokrovsky except at our lessons, and indeed I could not speak. I blushed and was confused, and afterwards shed tears of vexation in some corner.

I do not know how all this would have ended if a strange circumstance had not helped to bring us together. One evening when mother was sitting with Anna Fyodorovna I went stealthily into Pokrovsky's room. I knew he was not at home, and I really don't know what put it into my head to go into his room. Until that moment I had never peeped into it, though we had lived next door for over a year. This time my heart throbbed violently, so violently that it seemed it would leap out of my bosom. I looked around with peculiar curiosity. Pokrovsky's room was very poorly furnished: it was untidy. Papers were lying on the table and the chairs. Books and papers! A strange thought came to me, and at the same time an unpleasant feeling of vexation took possession of me. It seemed to me that my affection, my loving heart were little to him. He was learned while I was stupid, and knew nothing, had read nothing, not a single book . . . at that point I looked enviously at the long shelves which were almost breaking down under the weight of the books. I was overcome by anger, misery, a sort of fury. I longed and at once determined to read his books, every one of them, and as quickly as possible. I don't know, perhaps I thought that when I learned all he knew I should be more worthy of his friendship. I rushed to the first shelf; without stopping to think I seized the first dusty old volume; flushing and turning pale by turns, trembling with excitement and dread, I carried off the stolen book, resolved to read it at night—by the night-light while mother was asleep.

But what was my vexation when, returning to our room, I hurriedly opened the book and saw it was some old work in Latin. It was half decayed and worm-eaten. I went back without loss of time. Just as I was trying to put the book back in the shelf I heard a noise in the passage and approaching footsteps. I tried with nervous haste to be quick, but the insufferable book had been so tightly wedged in the shelf that when I took it out all the others had shifted and packed closer of themselves, so now there was no room for their former companion. I had not the strength to force the book in. I pushed the books with all my might, however. The rusty nail which supported the shelf, and which seemed to be waiting for that moment to break, broke. One end of the shelf fell down. The books dropped noisily on the floor in all directions. The door opened and Pokrovsky walked into the room.

I must observe that he could not bear anyone to meddle in his domain. Woe to anyone who touched his books! Imagine my horror when the books, little and big, of all sizes and shapes dashed off the shelf, flew dancing under the table, under the chairs, all over the room! I would have run, but it was too late. It is all over, I thought, it is all over. I am lost, I am done for! I am naughty and mischievous like a child of ten, I am a silly chit of a girl! I am a great fool!

Pokrovsky was dreadfully angry.

"Well, this is the last straw!" he shouted. "Are not you ashamed to be so mischievous? . . . Will you ever learn sense?" and he rushed to collect the books. "Don't, don't!" he shouted. "You would do better not to come where you are not invited."

A little softened, however, by my humble movement, he went on more quietly, in his usual lecturing tone, speaking as though he were still my teacher:

"Why, when will you learn to behave properly and begin to be sensible? You should look at yourself. You are not a little child. You are not a little girl. Why, you are fifteen!"

And at that point, probably to satisfy himself that I was not a little girl, he glanced at me and blushed up to his ears. I did not understand. I stood before him staring in amazement. He got up, came towards me with an embarrassed air, was horribly confused, said something, seemed to be apologising for something, perhaps for having only just noticed that I was such a big girl. At last I understood. I don't remember what happened to me then; I was overcome with confusion, lost my head, blushed even more crimson than Pokrovsky, hid my face in my hands and ran out of the room.

I did not know what to do, where to hide myself for shame. The mere fact that he had found me in his room was enough! For three whole days I could not look at him: I blushed until the tears came into my eyes. The most absurd ideas whirled through my brain. One of them—the maddest—was a plan to go to him, explain myself to him, confess everything to him, tell him all openly and assure him I had not behaved like a silly little girl but had acted with good intentions. I quite resolved to go but, thank God, my courage failed me. I can imagine what a mess I should have made of it! Even now I am ashamed to remember it all.

A few days later mother suddenly became dangerously ill. After two days in bed, on the third night, she was feverish and delirious. I did not sleep all one night, looking after mother, sitting by her bedside, bringing her drink and giving her medicine at certain hours. The second night I was utterly exhausted. At times I was overcome with sleep, my head went round and everything was green before my eyes. I was ready any minute to drop with fatigue, but mother's weak moans roused me, I started up, waked for an instant and then was overwhelmed with drowsiness again. I was in torment. I don't know, I cannot remember, but some horrible dream, some awful apparition haunted my over-wrought brain at the agonising moment of struggling between sleeping and waking. I woke up in terror. The room was dark; the night-light had burned out. Streaks of light suddenly filled the whole room, gleamed over the wall and disappeared. I was frightened, a sort of panic came over me. My imagination had been upset by a horrible dream, my heart was oppressed with misery. . . . I leapt up from my chair and unconsciously shrieked from an agonising, horribly oppressive feeling. At that moment the door opened and Pokrovsky walked into our room.

All I remember is that I came to myself in his arms. He carefully put me in a low chair, gave me a glass of water and showered questions on me. I don't remember what I answered.

"You are ill, you are very ill yourself," he said, taking my hand. "You are feverish, you will kill yourself. You do not think of your health; calm yourself, lie down, go to sleep. I will wake you in two hours time. Rest a little . . . lie down, lie down!" not letting me utter a word in objection. I was too tired to object; my eyes were closing with weakness. I lay down in a low chair, resolved to sleep only half an hour, and slept till morning. Pokrovsky only waked me when the time came to give mother her medicine.

The next evening when, after a brief rest in the daytime, I made ready to sit up by mother's bedside again, firmly resolved not to fall asleep this time, Pokrovsky at eleven o'clock knocked at our door. I opened it.

"It is dull for you, sitting alone," he said to me. "Here is a book; take it, it won't be so dull, anyway."

I took it; I don't remember what the book was like; I hardly glanced into it, though I did not sleep all night. A strange inward excitement would not let me sleep; I could not remain sitting still; several times I got up from the chair and walked about the room. A sort of inward content was suffused through my whole being. I was so glad of Pokrovsky's attention. I was proud of his anxiety and uneasiness about me. I spent the whole night, musing and dreaming. Pokrovsky did not come in again, and I knew he would not come, and I wondered about the following evening.

The next evening, when everyone in the house had gone to bed, Pokrovsky opened his door and began talking to me, standing in the doorway of his room. I do not remember now a single word of what we said to one another; I only remember that I was shy, confused, vexed with myself and looked forward impatiently to the end of the conversation, though I had been desiring it intensely, dreaming of it all day, and making up my questions and answers. . . . The first stage of our friendship began from that evening. All through mother's illness we spent several hours together every night. I got over my shyness by degrees, though after every conversation I found something in it to be vexed with myself about. Yet with secret joy and proud satisfaction I saw that for my sake he was beginning to forget his insufferable books.

By chance the conversation once turned in jest on his books having fallen off the shelf. It was a strange moment. I was, as it were, *too* open and candid. I was carried away by excitement and a strange enthusiasm, and I confessed everything to him. . . . Confessed that I longed to study, to know something, that it vexed me to be considered a little girl. . . . I repeat that I was in a very strange mood; my heart was soft, there were tears in my eyes—I concealed nothing and told him everything—everything—my affection for him, my desire to love him, to live with him, to comfort him, to console him. He looked at me somewhat strangely, with hesitation and perplexity, and did not say one word. I felt all at once horribly sore and miserable. It seemed to me that he did not understand me, that perhaps he was laughing at me. I suddenly burst out crying like a child, I could not restrain myself, and sobbed as though I were in a sort of fit. He took my hands, kissed them and pressed them to his heart; talked to me, comforted me; he was much touched. I do not remember what he said to me, only I kept on crying and laughing and crying again, blushing, and so joyful that I could not utter a word. In spite of my emotion, I noticed, however, that Pokrovsky still showed traces of embarrassment and constraint. It seemed as though he were overwhelmed with wonder at my enthusiasm, my delight, my sudden warm, ardent affection. Perhaps it only seemed strange to him at first; later on his hesitation vanished and he accepted my devotion to him, my friendly words, my attentions, with the same simple, direct feeling that I showed, and responded to it all with the same attentiveness, as affectionately and warmly as a sincere friend, a true brother. My heart felt so warm, so happy. . . . I was not reserved, I concealed nothing from him, he saw it all and grew every day more and more attached to me.

And really I do not remember what we used to talk about in those tormenting, and at the same time happy, hours when we met at night by the flickering light of a little lamp, and almost by my poor mother's beside. . . . We talked of everything that came into our minds, that broke from our hearts, that craved expression, and we were almost happy. . . . Oh, it was a sad and joyful time, both at once. . . . And it makes me both sad and joyful now to think of him. Memories are always tormenting, whether they are glad or bitter; it is so with me, anyway; but even the torment is sweet. And when the heart grows heavy, sick, weary and sad, then memories refresh and revive it, as the drops of dew on a moist evening after a hot day refresh and revive a poor sickly flower, parched by the midday heat.

Mother began to get better, but I still sat up by her bedside at night. Pokrovsky used to give me books; at first I read them to keep myself awake; then more attentively, and afterwards with eagerness. They opened all at once before me much that was new, unknown and unfamiliar. New thoughts, new impressions rushed in a perfect flood into my heart. And the more emotion, the more perplexity and effort it cost me to assimilate those new impressions, the dearer they were to me and the more sweetly they thrilled my soul. They crowded upon my heart all at once, giving it no rest. A strange chaos began to trouble my whole being. But that spiritual commotion could not upset my balance altogether. I was too dreamy and that saved me.

When mother's illness was over, our long talks and evening interviews were at an end; we succeeded sometimes in exchanging words, often trivial and of little consequence, but I was fond of giving everything its significance, its peculiar underlying value. My life was full, I was happy, calmly, quietly happy. So passed several weeks. . . .

One day old Pokrovsky came to see us. He talked to us for a long time, was exceptionally gay, cheerful and communicative, he laughed, made jokes after his fashion, and at last explained the mystery of his ecstatic condition, and told us that that day week would be Petinka's birthday and that for the occasion he should come and see his son; that he should put on a new waistcoat and that his wife had promised to buy him new boots. In fact, the old man was completely happy and chatted away of everything in his mind. His birthday! That birthday gave me no rest day or night. I made up my mind to give Pokrovsky something as a sign of my affection. But what? At last I thought of giving him books. I knew he wanted to have Pushkin's works in the latest, complete edition,[7] and I decided to buy Pushkin. I had thirty roubles of my own money earned by needlework. The money had been saved up to buy me a dress. I promptly sent old Matrona, our cook, to find out what the whole of Pushkin cost. Alas! The price of the eleven volumes, including the cost of binding, was at least sixty roubles. Where could I get the money? I thought and thought and did not know what to decide upon. I did not want to ask mother. Of course mother would have certainly helped me; but then everyone in the house would have known of our present; besides, the present would have become a token of gratitude in repayment for all that Pokrovsky had done for us during the past year. I wanted to give it alone and no one else to know of it. And for what he had done for me I wanted to be indebted to him for ever without any sort of repayment except my affection.

At last I found a way out of my difficulty.

I knew at the second-hand shops in the Gostiny Dvor one could sometimes, with a little bargaining, buy at half-price a book hardly the worse for wear and almost completely new. I resolved to visit the Gostiny Dvor. As it happened, next day some things had to be bought for us and also for Anna Fyodorovna. Mother was not very well, and Anna Fyodorovna, very luckily, was lazy, so that it fell to me to make these purchases and I set off with Matrona.

I was so fortunate as to find a Pushkin very quickly and one in a very fine binding. I began bargaining. At first they demanded a price higher than that in the bookseller's shops; but in the end, though not without trouble, and walking away several times, I brought the shopman to knocking down the price and asking no more than ten roubles in silver. How I enjoyed bargaining! . . . Poor Matrona could not make out what was the matter with me and what possessed me to buy so many books. But, oh, horror! My whole capital consisted of thirty roubles in paper, and the shopman would not consent to let the books go cheaper. At last I began beseeching him, begged and begged him and at last persuaded him. He gave way but only took off two and a half roubles and swore he only made that concession for my sake because I was such a nice young lady and he would not have done it for anyone else. I still had not enough by two and a half roubles. I was ready to cry with vexation. But the most unexpected circumstance came to my assistance in my distress.

Not far off at another bookstall I saw old Pokrovsky. Four or five second-hand dealers were clustering about him; they were bewildering him completely and he was at his wits' end. Each of them was proffering his wares and there was no end to the books they offered and he longed to buy. The poor old man stood in the midst of them, looking a disconsolate figure and did not know what to choose from what was offered him. I went up and asked him what he was doing here. The old man was delighted to see me; he was extremely fond of me, hardly less than of his Petinka, perhaps.

"Why, I'm buying books, Varvara Alexyevna," he answered. "I am buying books for Petinka. Here it will soon be his birthday and he is fond of books, so, you see, I am going to buy them for him. . . ."

The old man always expressed himself in a very funny way and now he was in the utmost confusion besides. Whatever he asked the price of, it was always a silver rouble, or two or three silver roubles; he had by now given up inquiring about the bigger books and only looked covetously at them, turning over the leaves, weighing them in his hands and putting them back again in their places.

"No, no, that's dear," he would say in an undertone, "but maybe there'll be something here."

And then he would begin turning over thin pamphlets, song-books, almanacs; these were all very cheap.

"But why do you want to buy those?" I asked him. "They are all awful rubbish."

"Oh, no," he answered. "No, you only look what good little books there are here. They are very, very good little books!"

And the last words he brought out in such a plaintive singsong that I fancied he was ready to cry with vexation at the good books being so dear, and in another moment a tear would drop from his pale cheeks on his red nose. I asked him whether he had plenty of money.

"Why, here," the poor fellow pulled out at once all his money wrapped up in a piece of greasy newspaper. "Here there's half a rouble, a twenty-kopeck piece and twenty kopecks in copper."

I carried him off at once to my second-hand bookseller.

"Here, these eleven volumes cost only thirty-two roubles and a half; I have thirty; put your two and a half to it and we will buy all these books and give them to him together."

The old man was beside himself with delight, he shook out all his money, and the bookseller piled all our purchased volumes upon him. The old man stuffed volumes in all his pockets, carried them in both hands and under his arms and bore them all off to his home, giving me his word to bring them all to me in secret next day.

Next day the old man came to see his son, spent about an hour with him as usual, then came in to us and sat down beside me with a very comical mysterious air. Rubbing his hands in proud delight at being in possession of a secret, he began with a smile by telling me that all the books had been conveyed here unnoticed and were standing in a corner in the kitchen under Matrona's protection. Then the conversation naturally passed to the day we were looking forward to; the old man talked at length of how we would give our present, and the more absorbed he became in the subject the more apparent it was to me that he had something in his heart of which he could not, dared not, speak, which, in fact, he was afraid to put into words. I waited and said nothing. The secret joy, the secret satisfaction which I had readily discerned at first in his strange gestures and grimaces and the winking of his left eye, disappeared. Every moment he grew more uneasy and disconsolate; at last he could not contain himself.

"Listen," he began timidly in an undertone.

"Listen, Varvara Alexyevna . . . do you know what, Varvara Alexyevna . . . ?" The old man was in terrible confusion. "When the day of his birthday comes, you know, you take ten books and give them yourself, that is from yourself, on your own account; I'll take only the eleventh, and I, too, will give it from myself, that is, apart, on my own account. So then, do you see—you will have something to give, and I shall have something to give; we shall both have something to give."

At this point the old man was overcome with confusion and relapsed into silence. I glanced at him; he was waiting for my verdict with timid expectation.

"But why do you want us not to give them together, Zahar Petrovitch?"

"Why, you see, Varvara Alexyevna, it's just . . . it's only, you know . . ."

In short, the old man faltered, flushed, got stuck in his sentence and could not proceed.

"You see," he explained at last, "Varvara Alexyevna, I indulge at times . . . that is, I want to tell you that I am almost always indulging, constantly indulging . . . I have a habit which is very bad . . . that is, you know, it's apt to be so cold outdoors and at times there are unpleasantnesses of all sorts, or something makes one sad, or something happens amiss and then I give way at once and begin to indulge and sometimes drink too much. Petrusha dislikes that very much. He gets angry with me, do you see, Varvara Alexyevna, scolds me and gives me lectures, so that I should have liked now to show him by my present that I am reforming and beginning to behave properly, that here I've saved up to buy the book, saved up for ever so long, for I scarcely ever have any money except it may happen Petrusha gives me something. He knows that. So here he will see how I have used my money and will know that I have done all that only for him."

I felt dreadfully sorry for the old man. I thought for a moment. The old man looked at me uneasily.

"Listen, Zahar Petrovitch," I said; "you give him them all."

"How all? Do you mean all the books?"

"Why, yes, all the books."

"And from myself?"

"Yes, from yourself."

"From myself alone? Do you mean on my own account?"

"Why yes, on your own account."

I believe I made my meaning very clear, but it was a long time before the old man could understand me.

"Why yes," he said, after pondering. "Yes! That would be very nice, but how about you, Varvara Alexyevna?"

"Oh, well, I shall give nothing."

"What!" cried the old man, almost alarmed. "So you don't want to give Petinka anything?"

The old man was dismayed; at that moment he was ready, I believe, to give up his project in order that I might be able to give his son something. He was a kind-hearted old fellow! I assured him that I should have been glad to give something, but did not want to deprive him of the pleasure.

"If your son is satisfied and you are glad," I added, "then I shall be glad, for I shall feel secretly in my heart as though I were really giving it myself."

With that the old man was completely satisfied. He spent another two hours with us, but could not sit still in his place and was continually getting up, fussing noisily about, playing with Sasha, stealthily kissing me, pinching my hand and making faces at Anna Fyodorovna on the sly. Anna Fyodorovna turned him out of the house at last. The old man was, in fact, in his delight, more excited than he had perhaps ever been before.

On the festive day he appeared exactly at eleven o'clock, coming straight from mass in a decently mended swallow-tail coat and actually wearing a new waistcoat and new boots. He had a bundle of books in each hand. We were all sitting drinking coffee in Anna Fyodorovna's drawing-room at the time (it was Sunday). The old man began by saying, I believe, that Pushkin was a very fine poet; then, with much hesitation and confusion, he passed suddenly to the necessity of one's behaving oneself properly, and that if a man does not behave properly then he will indulge; that bad habits are the ruin and destruction of a man; he even enumerated several fatal instances of intemperance, and wound up by saying that for some time past he had been completely reformed and his behaviour now was excellent and exemplary; that he had even, in the past, felt the justice of his son's exhortations, that he felt it all long ago and laid it to heart, but now he had begun to control himself in practice, too. In proof of which he presented him with the books bought with money which he had saved up during a long period of time.

I could not help laughing and crying as I listened to the poor old man; so he knew how to lie on occasion! The books were carried into Pokrovsky's room and arranged on the shelves. Pokrovsky at once guessed the truth. The old man was invited to dinner. We were all so merry that day; after dinner we played forfeits and cards; Sasha was in wild spirits and I was hardly less so. Pokrovsky was attentive to me and kept seeking an opportunity to speak to me alone, but I would not let him. It was the happiest day of all those four years of my life.

And now come sad, bitter memories, and I begin the story of my gloomy days. That is why, perhaps, my pen moves more slowly and seems to refuse to write more. That is why, perhaps, I have dwelt in memory with such eagerness and such love on the smallest details of my trivial existence in my happy days. Those days were so brief; they were followed by grief, black grief, and God only knows when it will end.

My troubles began with the illness and death of Pokrovsky.

He fell ill about two months after the last incidents I have described here. He spent those two months in unceasing efforts to secure some means of subsistence, for he still had no settled position. Like all consumptives he clung up to the very last moment to the hope of a very long life. A post as a teacher turned up for him, but he had a great distaste for that calling. He could not take a place in a government office on account of his health. Besides, he would have had to wait a long time for the first instalment of his salary. In short, Pokrovsky met with nothing but disappointment on all sides and this tried his temper. His health was suffering, but he paid no attention to it. Autumn was coming on, every day he went out in his thin little overcoat to try and get work, to beg and implore for a place, which was inwardly an agony to him; he used to get his feet wet and to be soaked through with the rain, and at last he took to his bed and never got up from it again. . . . He died in the middle of autumn at the end of October.

I scarcely left his room during the whole time of his illness, I nursed him and looked after him. Often I did not sleep for nights together. He was frequently delirious and rarely quite himself; he talked of goodness knows what, of his post, of his books, of me, of his father . . . and it was then I heard a great deal about his circumstances of which I had not known or even guessed before. When first he was ill, all of them looked at me somehow strangely; Anna Fyodorovna shook her head. But I looked them all straight in the face and they did not blame me any more for my sympathy for Pokrovsky—at least my mother did not.

Sometimes Pokrovsky knew me, but this was seldom. He was almost all the time unconscious. Sometimes for whole nights together he would carry on long, long conversations with someone in obscure, indistinct words and his hoarse voice resounded with a hollow echo in his narrow room as in a coffin; I used to feel terrified then. Especially on the last night he seemed in a frenzy; he suffered terribly, was in anguish; his moans wrung my heart. Everyone in the house was in alarm. Anna Fyodorovna kept praying that God would take him more quickly. They sent for the doctor. The doctor said that the patient would certainly die by the morning.

Old Pokrovsky spent the whole night in the passage at the door of his son's room; a rug of some sort was put down there for him. He kept coming into the room, it was dreadful to look at him. He was so crushed by sorrow that he seemed utterly senseless and without feeling. His head was shaking with terror. He was trembling all over and kept whispering something, talking about something to himself. It seemed to me he was going out of his mind.

Just before dawn the old man, worn out with mental suffering, fell asleep on his mat and slept like the dead. Between seven and eight his son began to die. I waked the father. Pokrovsky was fully conscious and said good-bye to us all. Strange! I could not cry, but my heart was torn to pieces.

But his last moments distressed and tortured me more than all. He kept asking for something at great length with his halting tongue and I could make out nothing from his words. My heart was lacerated! For a whole hour he was uneasy, kept grieving over something, trying to make some sign with his chill hands and then beginning pitifully to entreat me in his hoarse hollow voice; but his words were disconnected sounds and again I could make nothing of them. I brought everyone of the household to him, I gave him drink, but still he shook his head mournfully. At last! I guessed what he wanted. He was begging me to draw up the window curtain and open the shutters. No doubt he wanted to look for the last time at the day, at God's light, at the sunshine. I drew back the curtain, but the dawning day was sad and melancholy as the poor failing life of the dying man. There was no sun. The clouds covered the sky with a shroud of mist; it was rainy, overcast, mournful. A fine rain was pattering on the window-panes and washing them with little rivulets of cold dirty water; it was dark and dingy. The pale daylight scarcely penetrated into the room and hardly rivalled the flickering flame of the little lamp lighted before the ikon. The dying man glanced at me mournfully, mournfully and shook his head; a minute later he died.

Anna Fyodorovna herself made the arrangements for the funeral. A coffin of the cheapest kind was bought and a carter was hired. To defray these expenses Anna Fyodorovna seized all Pokrovsky's books and other belongings. The old man argued with her, made a noise, took away all the books he could from her, stuffed his pockets full of them, put them in his hat, wherever he could, went about with them all those three days, and did not part with them even when he had to go to church. During those three days he seemed as it were, stupefied, as though he did not know what he was doing, and he kept fussing about the coffin with a strange solicitude; at one moment he set straight the wreath on his dead son and at the next he lighted and took away candles. It was evident that his thoughts could not rest on anything. Neither mother nor Anna Fyodorovna was at the funeral service at the church. Mother was ill; Anna Fyodorovna had got ready to go, but she quarrelled with old Pokrovsky and stayed behind. I went alone with the old man. During the service a terror came upon me—as though a foreboding of the future. I could scarcely stand up in church.

At last the coffin was closed, nailed up, put in the cart and taken away. I followed it only to the end of the street. The man drove at a trot. The old man ran after him, weeping loudly, his lamentations quivering and broken by his haste. The poor old man lost his hat and did not stop to pick it up. His head was drenched by the rain and the wind was rising; the sleet lashed and stung his face. The old man seemed not to feel the cold and wet and ran wailing from one side of the cart to the other, the skirts of his old coat fluttering in the wind like wings. Books were sticking out from all his pockets; in his hands was a huge volume which he held tightly. The passers-by took off their caps and crossed themselves. Some stopped and stood gazing in wonder at the poor old man. The books kept falling out of his pockets into the mud. People stopped him and pointed to what he had lost, he picked them up and fell to racing after the coffin again. At the corner of the street an old beggar woman joined him to follow the coffin with him. The cart turned the corner at last and disappeared from my sight. I went home. I threw myself on mother's bosom in terrible distress. I pressed her tightly in my arms, I kissed her and burst into floods of tears, huddling up to her fearfully as though trying to keep in my arms my last friend and not to give her up to death . . . but death was already hovering over poor mother. . . .

June 11.

How grateful I am to you for our walk yesterday to the Island, Makar Alexyevitch! How fresh and lovely it is there, how leafy and green! It's so long since I saw green leaves—when I was ill I kept fancying that I had to die and that I certainly should die—judge what must have been my sensations yesterday, how I must have felt . . .

You must not be angry with me for having been so sad yesterday; I was very happy, very content, but in my very best moments I am always for some reason sad. As for my crying, that means nothing. I don't know myself why I am always crying. I feel ill and irritable; my sensations are due to illness. The pale cloudless sky, the sunset, the evening

stillness—all that—I don't know—but I was somehow in the mood
yesterday to take a dreary and miserable view of everything, so that my
heart was too full and needed the relief of tears. But why am I writing
all this to you? It is hard to make all that clear to one's own heart and
still harder to convey it to another. But you, perhaps, will understand
me. Sadness and laughter both at once! How kind you are really, Makar
Alexyevitch! You looked into my eyes yesterday as though to read in
them what I was feeling and were delighted with my rapture. Whether
it was a bush, an avenue, a piece of water—you were there standing
before me showing its beauties and peeping into my eyes as though
you were displaying your possessions to me. That proves that you have
a kind heart, Makar Alexyevitch. It's for that that I love you. Well, good-
bye. I'm ill again to-day; I got my feet wet yesterday and have caught
cold. Fedora is ailing, too, so now we are both on the sick list. Don't
forget me. Come as often as you can.

Your V. D.

June 12.

My darling Varvara Alexyevna,

Well, I had expected, my dear soul, that you would write me a
description of our yesterday's expedition in a regular poem, and you
have turned out nothing but one simple sheet. I say this because,
though you wrote me so little in your sheet, yet you did describe it
extraordinarily well and sweetly. The charms of nature, and the various
rural scenes and all the rest about your feeling—in short, you described it all very well. Now I have no talent for it. If I smudge a dozen
papers there's nothing to show for it; I can't describe anything. I have
tried.

You write to me, my own, that I am a kind-hearted, good-
natured man, incapable of injuring my neighbour, and able to understand the blessings of the Lord made manifest in nature, and you
bestow various praises on me, in fact. All that is true, my darling, all
that is perfectly true; I really am all that you say and I know it myself;
but when one reads what you write one's heart is touched in spite of
oneself and then all sorts of painful reflections come to one. Well, listen to me, Varinka dear, I will tell you something, my own.

I will begin with when I was only seventeen and went into the

service, and soon the thirtieth year of my career there will be here.
Well, I needn't say I have worn out many a uniform; I grew to man-
hood and to good sense and saw something of the world; I have lived,
I may say, I have lived in the world so that on one occasion they even
wanted to send up my name to receive a cross. Maybe you will not believe me, but I am really not lying. But there, my darling, in spite of
everything, I have been badly treated by malicious people! I tell you,
my own, that though I am an obscure person, a stupid person, perhaps, yet I have my feelings like anyone else. Do you know, Varinka,
what a spiteful man did to me? I am ashamed to say what he has done
to me; you will ask why did he do it? Why, because I am meek, because I am quiet, because I am good-natured! I did not suit their taste,
so that's what brought it upon me. At first it began with, "You are this
and that, Makar Alexyevitch," and then it came to saying, "It's no good
asking Makar Alexyevitch!" And then it ended by, "Of course, that is
Makar Alexyevitch!" You see, my precious, what a pass it came to; always Makar Alexyevitch to blame for everything; they managed to
make Makar Alexyevitch a by-word all over the department, and it was
not enough that they made me a by-word and almost a term of abuse,
they attacked my boots, my uniform, my hair, my figure; nothing was
to their taste, everything ought to be different! And all this has been
repeated every blessed day from time immemorial. I am used to it, for
I grow used to anything, because I am a meek man; but what is it all
for? What harm do I do to anyone? Have I stolen promotion from anyone, or what? Have I blackened anyone's reputation with his superiors? Have I asked for anything extra out of turn? Have I got up some
intrigue? Why, it's a sin for you to imagine such a thing, my dear soul!
As though I could do anything of that sort! You've only to look at me,
my own. Have I sufficient ability for intrigue and ambition? Then why
have such misfortunes come upon me? God forgive me. Here you
consider me a decent man, and you are ever so much better than any
of them, my darling. Why, what is the greatest virtue in a citizen? A day
or two ago, in private conversation, Yevstafy Ivanovitch said that the
most important virtue in a citizen was to earn money. He said in jest (I
know it was in jest) that morality consists in not being a burden to
anyone. Well, I'm not a burden to anyone. My crust of bread is my
own; it is true it is a plain crust of bread, at times a dry one; but there
it is, earned by my toil and put to lawful and irreproachable use. Why,

what can one do? I know very well, of course, that I don't do much by
copying; but all the same I am proud of working and earning my
bread in the sweat of my brow. Why, what if I am a copying clerk, after all? What harm is there in copying, after all? "He's a copying
clerk," they say, but what is there discreditable in that? My handwriting is good, distinct and pleasant to the eye, and his Excellency is satisfied with it. I have no gift of language, of course, I know myself that
I haven't the confounded thing; that's why I have not got on in the service, and why even now, my own, I am writing to you simply, art-
lessly, just as the thought comes into my heart. . . . I know all that; but
there, if everyone became an author, who would do the copying? I ask
you that question and I beg you to answer it, Varinka dear. So I see
now that I am necessary, that I am indispensable, and that it's no use to
worry a man with nonsense. Well, let me be a rat if you like, since they
see a resemblance! But the rat is necessary, but the rat is of service, but
the rat is depended upon, but the rat is given a reward, so that's the
sort of rat he is!

Enough about that subject though, my own! I did not intend to
talk about that at all, but I got a little heated. Besides, it's pleasant from
time to time to do oneself justice. Good-bye, my own, my darling, my
kind comforter! I will come, I will certainly come to see you, my
dearie, and meanwhile, don't be dull, I will bring you a book. Well,
good-bye, then, Varinka.

Your devoted well-wisher,
MAKAR DYEVUSHKIN.

June 20.

DEAR SIR, MAKAR ALEXYEVITCH,

I write a hurried line, I am in haste, I have to finish my work up
to time. You see, this is how it is: you can make a good bargain. Fedora
says that a friend of hers has a uniform, quite new, underclothes, a
waistcoat and cap, and all very cheap, they say; so you ought to buy
them. You see, you are not badly off now, you say you have money;
you say so yourself. Give over being so stingy, please. You know all
those things are necessary. Just look at yourself, what old clothes you
go about in. It's a disgrace! You're all in patches. You have no new
clothes; I know that, though you declare that you have. God knows

how you have managed to dispose of them. So do as I tell you, please buy these things. Do it for my sake; if you love me, do it.

You sent me some linen as a present; but upon my word, Makar Alexyevitch, you are ruining yourself. It's no joke what you've spent on me, it's awful to think how much money! How fond you are of throwing away your money! I don't want it; it's all absolutely unnecessary. I know—I am convinced—that you love me. It is really unnecessary to remind me of it with presents; and it worries me taking them from you; I know what they cost you. Once for all, leave off, do you hear? I beg you, I beseech you. You ask me, Makar Alexyevitch, to send you the continuation of my diary, you want me to finish it. I don't know how what I have written came to be written! But I haven't the strength now to talk of my past; I don't even want to think of it; I feel frightened of those memories. To talk of my poor mother leaving her poor child to those monsters, too, is more painful than anything. My heart throbs at the very thought of it: it is all still so fresh: I have not had time to think things over, still less to regain my calm, though it is all more than a year ago, now. But you know all that.

I've told you what Anna Fyodorovna thinks now; she blames me for ingratitude and repudiates all blame for her association with Mr. Bykov! She invites me to stay with her; she says that I am living on charity, that I am going to the bad. She says that if I go back to her she will undertake to set right everything with Mr. Bykov and compel him to make up for his behaviour to me. She says Mr. Bykov wants to give me a dowry. Bother them! I am happy here with you close by, with my kind Fedora whose devotion reminds me of my old nurse. Though you are only a distant relation you will protect me with your name. I don't know them. I shall forget them if I can. What more do they want of me? Fedora says that it is all talk, that they will leave me alone at last. God grant they may!

V. D.

June 21.

MY DARLING VARINKA,

I want to write, but I don't know how to begin. How strange it is, my precious, how we are living now. I say this because I have never spent my days in such joyfulness. Why, it is as though God had blessed me with a home and family of my own, my child, my pretty! But why are you making such a fuss about the four chemises I sent you? You needed them, you know—I found that out from Fedora. And it's a special happiness for me to satisfy your needs, Varinka, dear; it's my pleasure. You let me alone, my dear soul. Don't interfere with me and don't contradict me. I've never known anything like it, my darling. I've taken to going into society now. In the first place my life is twice as full; because you are living very near me and are a great comfort to me; and secondly, I have been invited to tea to-day by a lodger, a neighbour of mine, that clerk, Ratazyaev, who has the literary evenings. We meet this evening, we are going to read literature. So you see how we are getting on now, Varinka—you see! Well, good-bye. I've written all this for no apparent reason, simply to let you know of the affection I feel for you. You told Teresa to tell me, my love, that you want some silk for coloured embroidery. I will get you it, my darling, I will get the silk, I will get it. To-morrow I shall have the pleasure of satisfying you. I know where to buy it, too. And now I remain,

Your sincere friend,
MAKAR DYEVUSHKIN.

June 22.

DEAR MADAM, VARVARA ALEXYEVNA,

I must tell you, my own, that a very pitiful thing has happened in our flat, truly, truly, deserving of pity! Between four and five this morning Gorshkov's little boy died. I don't know what he died of. It seemed to be a sort of scarlatina, God only knows! I went to see these Gorshkovs. Oh, my dear soul, how poor they are! And what disorder! And no wonder; the whole family lives in one room, only divided by a screen for decency. There was a little coffin standing in the room already—a simple little coffin, but rather pretty; they bought it ready-made; the boy was nine years old, he was a promising boy, they say. But it was pitiful to look at them, Varinka! The mother did not cry, but she was so sad, so poor. And perhaps it will make it easier for them to have got one off their shoulders; but there are still two left, a baby, and a little girl, not much more than six. There's not much comfort really in seeing a child suffer, especially one's own little child, and having no means of helping him! The father was sitting in a greasy old dress suit on a broken chair. The tears were flowing from his eyes, but perhaps not from grief, but just the usual thing—his eyes are inflamed. He's such a strange fellow! He always turns red when you speak to him, gets confused and does not know what to answer. The little girl, their daughter, stood leaning against the coffin, such a poor little, sad, brooding child! And Varinka, my darling, I don't like it when children brood; it's painful to see! A doll made of rags was lying on the floor beside her; she did not play with it, she held her finger on her lips; she stood, without stirring. The landlady gave her a sweetmeat; she took it but did not eat it.

It was sad, Varinka, wasn't it?

MAKAR DYEVUSHKIN.

June 25.

DEAR MAKAR ALEXYEVITCH,

I am sending you back your book. A wretched, worthless little book not fit to touch! Where did you ferret out such a treasure? Joking apart, can you really like such a book, Makar Alexyevitch? I was promised the other day something to read. I will share it with you, if you like. And now good–bye. I really have not time to write more.

V. D.

June 26.

DEAR VARINKA,

The fact is that I really had not read that horrid book, my dear girl. It is true, I looked through it and saw it was nonsense, just written to be funny, to make people laugh; well, I thought, it really is amusing; maybe Varinka will like it, so I sent it you.

Now, Ratazyaev has promised to give me some real literature to read, so you will have some books, my darling. Ratazyaev knows, he's a connoisseur; he writes himself, ough, how he writes! His pen is so bold and he has a wonderful style, that is, there is no end to what there is in every word—in the most foolish ordinary vulgar word such as I might say sometimes to Faldoni or Teresa, even in such he has style. I go to his evenings. We smoke and he reads to us, he reads five hours at a stretch and we listen all the time. It's a perfect feast. Such charm, such flowers, simply flowers, you can gather a bouquet from each page! He is so affable, so kindly and friendly. Why, what am I beside him? What am I? Nothing. He is a man with a reputation, and what am I? I simply don't exist, yet he is cordial even to me. I am copying something for him. Only don't you imagine, Varinka, that there is something amiss in that, that he is friendly to me just because I am copying for him; don't you believe tittle-tattle, my dear girl, don't you believe worthless tittle-tattle. No, I am doing it of myself, of my own accord for his pleasure. I understand refinement of manners, my love; he is a kind, very kind man, and an incomparable writer.

Literature is a fine thing, Varinka, a very fine thing. I learnt that from them the day before yesterday. A profound thing, strengthening men's hearts, instructing them; there are all sorts of things written about that in their book. Very well written! Literature is a picture, that is, in a certain sense, a picture and a mirror: it's the passions, the expression, the subtlest criticism, edifying instruction and a document. I gathered all that from them. I tell you frankly, my darling, that one sits with them, one listens (one smokes a pipe like them, too, if you please), and when they begin to discuss and dispute about all sorts of matters, then I simply sit dumb; then, my dear soul, you and I can do nothing else but sit dumb. I am simply a blockhead, it seems. I am ashamed of myself, so that I try all the evening how to put in half a word in the general conversation, but there, as ill-luck would have it, I can't find that half word! And one is sorry for oneself, Varinka, that one is not this thing, nor that thing, that, as the saying is, "A man one is grown, but no mind of one's own." Why, what do I do in my free time now? I sleep like a fool! While instead of useless sleep I might have been busy in useful occupation; I might have sat down and written something that would have been of use to oneself and pleasant to others. Why, my dearie, you should only see what they get for it, God forgive them! Take Ratazyaev, for instance, what he gets. What is it for him to write a chapter? Why, sometimes he writes five in a day and he gets three hundred roubles a chapter. Some little anecdote, something curious—five hundred! take it or leave it, give it or be damned! Or another time, we'll put a thousand in our pocket! What do you say to that, Varvara Alexyevna? Why, he's got a little book of poems—such short poems—he's asking seven thousand, my dear girl, he's asking seven thousand; think of it! Why, it's real estate, it's house property! He says that they will give him five thousand, but he won't take it. I reasoned with him. I said, "Take five thousand for them, sir, and don't mind them. Why, five thousand's money!" "No," said he, "they'll give me seven, the swindlers!" He's a cunning fellow, really.

Well, my love, since we are talking of it I will copy a passage from the *Italian Passions* for you. That's the name of his book. Here, read it, Varinka, and judge for yourself. . . .

"Vladimir shuddered and his passion gurgled up furiously within him and his blood boiled. . . .

" 'Countess,' he cried. 'Countess! Do you know how awful is this passion, how boundless this madness? No, my dreams did not deceive me! I love, I love ecstatically, furiously, madly! All your husband's blood would not quench the frantic surging ecstasy of my soul! A trivial obstacle cannot check the all-destroying, hellish fire that harrows my exhausted breast. Oh, Zinaida, Zinaida!' . . .

" 'Vladimir,' whispered the countess, beside herself, leaning on his shoulder. . . .

" 'Zinaida!' cried the enraptured Smyelsky.

"His bosom exhaled a sigh. The fire flamed brightly on the altar of love and consumed the heart of the unhappy victims.

" 'Vladimir,' the countess whispered, intoxicated. Her bosom heaved, her cheeks glowed crimson, her eyes glowed. . . .

"A new, terrible union was accomplished!

*   *   *   *   *

"Half an hour later the old count went into his wife's boudoir.

" 'Well, my love, should we not order the samovar for our welcome guest?' he said, patting his wife on the cheek."

Well, I ask you, my dear soul, what do you think of it after that? It's true, it's a little free, there's no disputing that, but still it is fine. What is fine is fine! And now, if you will allow me, I will copy you another little bit from the novel *Yermak and Zuleika*.

You must imagine, my precious, that the Cossack, Yermak, the fierce and savage conqueror of Siberia, is in love with the daughter of Kutchum, the Tsar of Siberia, the Princess Zuleika, who has been taken captive by him. An episode straight from the times of Ivan the Terrible, as you see. Here is the conversation of Yermak and Zuleika.

" 'You love me, Zuleika! Oh, repeat it, repeat it!' . . .

" 'I love you, Yermak,' whispered Zuleika.

" 'Heaven and earth, I thank you! I am happy! . . . You have given me everything, everything, for which my turbulent soul has striven from my boyhood's years. So it was to this thou hast led me, my guiding star, so it was for this thou hast led me here, beyond the Belt of Stone! I will show to all the world my Zuleika, and men, the frantic monsters, will not dare to blame me! Ah, if they could understand the secret sufferings of her tender soul, if they could see a whole poem in a tear of my Zuleika! Oh, let me dry that tear with kisses, let me drink it up, that heavenly tear . . . unearthly one!'

" 'Yermak,' said Zuleika, 'the world is wicked, men are unjust! They will persecute us, they will condemn us, my sweet Yermak! What is the poor maiden, nurtured amid the snows of Siberia in her father's yurta to do in your cold, icy, soulless, selfish world? People will not understand me, my desired one, my beloved one.'

" 'Then will the Cossack's sabre rise up hissing about them.' "

And now, what do you say to Yermak, Varinka, when he finds out that his Zuleika has been murdered? . . . The blind old man, Kutchum, under cover of night steals into Yermak's tent in his absence and slays Zuleika, intending to deal a mortal blow at Yermak, who has robbed him of his sceptre and his crown.

" 'Sweet is it to me to rasp the iron against the stone,' shouted Yermak in wild frenzy, whetting his knife of Damascus steel upon the magic stone; 'I'll have their blood, their blood! I will hack them! hack them! hack them to pieces!!!' "

And, after all that, Yermak, unable to survive his Zuleika, throws himself into the Irtish, and so it all ends.

And this, for instance, a tiny fragment written in a jocose style, simply to make one laugh.

"Do you know Ivan Prokofyevitch Yellow-paunch? Why, the man who bit Prokofy Ivanovitch's leg. Ivan Prokofyevitch is a man of hasty temper, but, on the other hand, of rare virtues; Prokofy Ivanovitch, on the other hand, is extremely fond of a rarebit on toast. Why, when Pelagea Antonovna used to know him . . . Do you know Pelagea Antonovna? the woman who always wears her petticoat inside out."

That's humour, you know, Varinka, simply humour. He rocked with laughter when he read us that. He is a fellow, God forgive him! But though it's rather jocose and very playful, Varinka dear, it is quite innocent, without the slightest trace of free-thinking or liberal ideas. I must observe, my love, that Ratazyaev is a very well-behaved man and so an excellent author, not like other authors.

And, after all, an idea sometimes comes into one's head, you know. . . . What if I were to write something, what would happen then? Suppose that, for instance, apropos of nothing, there came into the world a book with the title—*Poems by Makar Dyevushkin?* What would my little angel say then? How does that strike you? What do you think of it? And I can tell you, my darling, that as soon as my book came out, I certainly should not dare to show myself in the Nevsky Prospect. Why, how should I feel when everyone would be saying, Here comes the author and poet, Dyevushkin? There's Dyevushkin himself, they would say! What should I do with my boots then? They are, I may mention in passing, my dear girl, almost always covered with patches, and the soles too, to tell the truth, sometimes break away in a very unseemly fashion. What should we do when everyone knew that the author Dyevushkin had patches on his boots! Some countess or duchess would hear of it, and what would she say, the darling? Perhaps she would not notice it; for I imagine countesses don't trouble themselves about boots, especially clerks' boots (for you know there are boots and boots), but they would tell her all about it, her friends would give me away. Ratazyaev, for instance, would be the first to give me away; he visits the Countess V.; he says that he goes to all her receptions, and he's quite at home there. He says she is such a darling, such a literary lady, he says. He's a rogue, that Ratazyaev!

But enough of that subject; I write all this for fun, my little angel, to amuse you. Good-bye, my darling, I have scribbled you a lot of nonsense, but that is just because I am in a very good humour to-day. We all dined together to-day at Ratazyaev's (they are rogues, Varinka dear), and brought out such a cordial. . . .

But there, why write to you about that! Only mind you don't imagine anything about me, Varinka. I don't mean anything by it. I will send you the books, I will certainly send them. . . . One of Paul de Kock's novels[8] is being passed round from one to another, but Paul de Kock will not do for you, my precious. . . . No, no! Paul de Kock won't do for you. They say of him, Varinka dear, that he rouses all the Petersburg critics to righteous indignation. I send you a pound of sweetmeats—I bought them on purpose for you. Do you hear, darling? think of me at every sweetmeat. Only don't nibble up the sugar-candy but only suck it, or you will get toothache. And perhaps you like candied peel?—write and tell me. Well, good-bye, good-bye. Christ be with you, my darling!

I remain ever,

Your most faithful friend,

MAKAR DYEVUSHKIN.

June 27.

DEAR SIR, MAKAR ALEXYEVITCH,

Fedora tells me that, if I like, certain people will be pleased to interest themselves in my position, and will get me a very good position as a governess in a family. What do you think about it, my friend—shall I go, or shall I not? Of course I should not then be a burden upon you, and the situation seems a good one; but, on the other hand, I feel somehow frightened at going into a strange house. They are people with an estate in the country. When they want to know all about me, when they begin asking questions, making inquiries—why, what should I say then?—besides, I am so shy and unsociable, I like to go on living in the corner I am used to. It's better somehow where one is used to being; even though one spends half one's time grieving, still it is better. Besides, it means leaving Petersburg; and God knows what my duties will be, either; perhaps they will simply make me look after the children, like a nurse. And they are such queer people, too; they've had three governesses already in two years. Do advise me, Makar Alexyevitch, whether to go or not. And why do you never come and see me? You hardly ever show your face, we scarcely ever meet except on Sundays at mass. What an unsociable person you are! You are as bad as I am! And you know I am almost a relation. You don't love me, Makar Alexyevitch, and I am sometimes very sad all alone. Sometimes, especially when it is getting dark, one sits all alone. Fedora goes off somewhere, one sits and sits and thinks—one remembers all the past, joyful and sad alike—it all passes before one's eyes, it all rises up as though out of a mist. Familiar faces appear (I am almost beginning to see them in reality)—I see mother most often of all . . . And what dreams I have! I feel that I am not at all well, I am so weak; to-day, for instance, when I got out of bed this morning, I turned giddy; and I have such a horrid cough, too! I feel, I know, that I shall soon die. Who will bury me? Who will follow my coffin! Who will grieve for me! . . . And perhaps I may have to die in a strange place, in a strange house! . . . My goodness! how sad life is, Makar Alexyevitch. Why do you keep feeding me on sweetmeats? I really don't know where you get so much money from? Ah, my friend, take care of your money, for God's sake, take care of it. Fedora is selling the cloth rug I have embroidered; she is getting fifty paper roubles for it. That's very good, I thought it would be less. I shall give Fedora three silver roubles, and shall get a new dress for myself, a plain one but warm. I shall make you a waistcoat, I shall make it myself, and I shall choose a good material.

Fedora got me a book, *Byelkin's Stories*,[9] which I will send you, if you care to read it. Only don't please keep it, or make it dirty, it belongs to someone else—it's one of Pushkin's works. Two years ago I read these stories with my mother. And it was so sad for me now to read them over again. If you have any books send them to me—only not if you get them from Ratazyaev. He will certainly lend you his books if he has ever published anything. How do you like his works, Makar Alexyevitch? Such nonsense . . . Well, good-bye! How I have been chattering! When I am sad I am glad to chatter about anything. It does me good; at once one feels better, especially if one expresses all that lies in one's heart. Good-bye. Good-bye, my friend!

Your

V. D.

June 28.

MY PRECIOUS VARVARA ALEXYEVNA,

Leave off worrying yourself, I wonder you are not ashamed. Come, give over, my angel! How is it such thoughts come into your mind? You are not ill, my love, you are not ill at all; you are blooming, you are really blooming; a little pale, but still blooming. And what do you mean by these dreams, these visions? For shame, my darling, give over; you must simply laugh at them. Why do I sleep well? Why is nothing wrong with me? You should look at me, my dear soul. I get along all right, I sleep quietly, I am as healthy and hearty as can be, a treat to look at. Give over, give over, darling, for shame. You must reform. I know your little ways, my dearie; as soon as any trouble comes, you begin fancying things and worrying about something. For

my sake give over, my darling. Go into a family?—Never! No, no, no,
and what notion is this of yours? What is this idea that has come over
you? And to leave Petersburg too. No, my darling, I won't allow it. I
will use every means in my power to oppose such a plan. I'll sell my
old coat and walk about the street in my shirt before you shall want
for anything. No, Varinka, no, I know you! It's folly, pure folly. And
there is no doubt that it is all Fedora's fault: she's evidently a stupid
woman, she puts all these ideas into your head. Don't you trust her,
my dear girl. You probably don't know everything yet, my love. . . .
She's a silly woman, discontented and nonsensical; she worried her
husband out of his life. Or perhaps she has vexed you in some way?
No, no, my precious, not for anything! And what would become of
me then, what would there be left for me to do? No, Varinka darling,
you put that out of your little head. What is there wanting in your life
with us? We can never rejoice enough over you, you love us, so do go
on living here quietly. Sew or read, or don't sew if you like—it does
not matter—only go on living with us or, only think yourself, why,
what would it be like without you? . . .

Here, I will get you some books and then maybe we'll go for a
walk somewhere again. Only you must give over, my dearie, you must
give over. Pull yourself together and don't be foolish over trifles! I'll
come and see you and very soon too. Only accept what I tell you
plainly and candidly about it; you are wrong, my darling, very wrong.
Of course, I am an ignorant man and I know myself that I am ignorant,
that I have hardly a ha'porth of education. But that's not what I am talking about, and I'm not what matters, but I will stand up for Ratazyaev,
say what you like. He writes well, very, very well, and I say it again, he
writes very well. I don't agree with you and I never can agree with you.
It's written in a flowery abrupt style, with figures of speech. There are
ideas of all sorts in it, it is very good! Perhaps you read it without feeling, Varinka; you were out of humour when you read it, vexed with Fedora, or something had gone wrong. No, you read it with feeling; best
when you are pleased and happy and in a pleasant humour, when, for
instance, you have got a sweetmeat in your mouth, that's when you
must read it. I don't dispute (who denies it?) that there are better writers than Ratazyaev, and very much better in fact, but they are good and
Ratazyaev is good too. He writes in his own special way, and does very
well to write. Well, good-bye, my precious, I can't write more; I must

make haste, I have work to do. Mind now, my love, my precious little dearie; calm yourself, and God will be with you, and I remain your faithful friend,

MAKER DYEVUSHKIN.

P.S.—Thanks for the book, my own; we will read Pushkin too, and this evening I shall be sure to come and see you.

MY DEAR MAKAR ALEXYEVITCH,

No, my friend, no, I ought not to go on living among you. On second thoughts I consider that I am doing very wrong to refuse such a good situation. I shall have at least my daily bread secure; I will do my best, I will win the affection of the strangers, I will even try to overcome my defects, if necessary. Of course it is painful and irksome to live with strangers, to try and win their good-will, to hide one's feelings, and suppress oneself, but Good will help me. I mustn't be a recluse all my life. I have had experiences like it before. I remember when I was a little thing and used to go to school. I used to be frolicking and skipping about all Sundays at home; sometimes mother would scold me—but nothing mattered, my heart was light and my soul was full of joy all the while. As evening approached an immense sadness would come over me—at nine o'clock I had to go back to school, and there it was all cold, strange, severe, the teachers were so cross on Mondays, one had such a pain at one's heart, one wanted to cry; one would go into a corner and cry all alone, hiding one's tears—they would say one was lazy; and I wasn't crying in the least because I had to do my lessons.

But, after all, I got used to it, and when I had to leave school I cried also when I said good-bye to my schoolfellows. And I am not doing right to go on being a burden to both of you. That thought is a torment to me. I tell you all this openly because I am accustomed to be open with you. Do you suppose I don't see how early Fedora gets up in the morning, and sets to work at her washing and works till late at night?—and old bones want rest. Do you suppose I don't see how you are ruining yourself over me, and spending every halfpenny? You are not a man of property, my friend! You tell me that you will sell your last rag before I shall want for anything. I believe you, my friend, I trust your kind heart, but you say that now. Now you have money you did not expect, you've received something extra, but later on? You know yourself, I am always ill; and I can't work like you, though I should be heartily glad to, and one does not always get work. What is left for me? To break my heart with grief looking at you two dear ones. In what way can I be of the slightest use to you? And why am I so necessary to you, my friend? What good have I done you? I am only devoted to you with my whole soul, I love you warmly, intensely, with my whole heart, but—my fate is a bitter one! I know how to love and I can love, but I can do nothing to repay you for your kindness. Don't dissuade me any more, think it over and tell me your final opinion. Meanwhile I remain your loving,

V. D.

July 1.

Nonsense, nonsense, Varinka, simply nonsense! Let you alone and there's no knowing what notion you will take into your little head. One thing's not right and another thing's not right. And I see now that it is all nonsense. And what more do you want, my dear girl? just tell me that! We love you, you love us, we're all contented and happy— what more do you want? And what will you do among strangers? I expect you don't know yet what strangers are like . . . You had better ask me and I will tell you what strangers are like. I know them, my darling, I know them very well, I've had to eat their bread. They are spiteful, Varinka, spiteful; so spiteful that you would have no heart left, they would torment it so with reproach, upbraiding and ill looks. You are snug and happy among us as though you were in a little nest; besides, we shall feel as though we had lost our head when you are gone; why, what can we do without you; what is an old man like me to do then? You are no use to us? No good to us? How no good? Come, my love, think yourself how much good you are! You are a great deal of good to me, Varinka. You have such a good influence . . . Here I am thinking about you now and I am happy . . . Sometimes I write you a letter and put all my feelings into it and get a full answer to everything back from you. I bought you a little wardrobe, got you a hat; some commission comes from you; I carry out the commission . . . How can you say, you are no use to me? And what should I be good for in my old age? Perhaps you have not thought of that, Varinka; that's just what

you had better think about, 'what will he be good for without me?' I
am used to you, my darling. Or else what will come of it? I shall go
straight to the Neva, and that will be the end of it. Yes, really, Varinka,
that will be the only thing left for me to do when you are gone. Ah,
Varinka, my darling. It seems you want me to be taken to Volkovo
Cemetery in a common cart; with only an old draggletail beggar-
woman to follow me to the grave; you want them to throw the earth
upon me and go away and leave me alone. It's too bad, too bad, my
dear! It's sinful really, upon my word it's a sin! I send you back your
book, Varinka, my darling, and if you ask my opinion about your book,
dear, I must say that never in my life have I read such a splendid book.
I wonder now, my darling, how I can have lived till now such an ignoramus, God forgive me! What have I been doing? What backwoods
have I been brought up in? Why, I know nothing, my dear girl; why, I
know absolutely nothing. I know nothing at all. I tell you, Varinka,
plainly—I'm a man of no education: I have read little hitherto—very
little, scarcely anything: I have read *The Picture of Man*, a clever work; I
have read *The boy who played funny tunes on the bells* and *The Cranes of Ibicus*;
that's all, and I never read anything else.[10] Now I have read *The Stationmaster*[11] in your book; let me tell you, my darling, it happens that one
goes on living, and one does not know that there is a book there at
one's side where one's whole life is set forth, as though it were reckoned upon one's fingers. And what one never so much as guessed before, when one begins reading such a book one remembers little by
little and guesses and discovers. And this is another reason why I like
your book: one sometimes reads a book, whatever it may be, and you
can't for the life of you understand it, it's so deep. I, for instance, am
stupid, I'm stupid by nature, so I can't read very serious books; but I
read this as though I had written it myself, as though I had taken my
own heart, just as it is, and turned it inside out before people and described it in detail, that's what it is like. And it's a simple subject, my
goodness, yet what a thing it is! Really it is just as I should have described it; why not describe it? You know I feel exactly the same as in
the book, and I have been at times in exactly the same positions as, for
instance, that Samson Vyrin, poor fellow. And how many Samson
Vyrins are going about amongst us, poor dears! And how clearly it is
all described! Tears almost started into my eyes when I read that the
poor sinner took to drink, became such a drunkard that he lost his

senses and slept the whole day under a sheepskin coat and drowned
his grief in punch, and wept piteously, wiping his eyes with the dirty
skirt of his coat when he thought of his lost lamb, his daughter Dun-
yasha. Yes, it's natural. You should read it, it's natural. It's living! I've seen
it myself; it's all about me; take Teresa, for instance—but why go so far?
Take our poor clerk, for instance—Why, he is perhaps just a Samson
Vyrin, only he has another surname, Gorshkov. It's the general lot,
Varinka dear, it might happen to you or to me. And the count who lives
on the Nevsky on the riverside, he would be just the same, it would
only seem different because everything there is done in their own way,
in style, yet he would be just the same, anything may happen, and the
same thing may happen to me. That's the truth of the matter, my darling, and yet you want to go away from us; it's a sin, Varinka, it may be
the end of me. You may be the ruin of yourself and me too, my own.
Oh, my little dearie, for God's sake put out of your little head all these
wilful ideas and don't torment me for nothing. How can you keep
yourself, my weak little unfledged bird? How can you save yourself
from ruin, protect yourself from villains? Give over, Varinka, think better of it; don't listen to nonsensical advice and persuasion, and read
your book again, read it with attention; that will do you good.

I talked of *The Stationmaster* to Ratazyaev. He told me that that was
all old-fashioned and that now books with pictures and descriptions
have all come in; I really did not quite understand what he said about
it. He ended by saying that Pushkin is fine and that he is a glory to
holy Russia, and he said a great deal more to me about him. Yes, it's
good, Varinka, very good; read it again with attention; follow my advice, and make an old man happy by your obedience. Then God Himself will reward you, my own, He will certainly reward you.

Your sincere friend,
MAKAR DYEVUSHKIN.

DEAR SIR, MAKAR DYEVUSHKIN,

Fedora brought me fifteen silver roubles to-day. How pleased she
was, poor thing, when I gave her three! I write to you in haste. I am
now cutting you out a waistcoat—it's charming material—yellow
with flowers on it. I send you a book: there are all sorts of stories in it;
I have read some of them, read the one called *The Cloak!*[12] You persuade
me to go to the theatre with you; wouldn't it be expensive? Perhaps
we could go to the gallery somewhere. It's a long while since I've been

to the theatre, in fact I can't remember when I went. Only I'm afraid whether such a treat would not cost too much? Fedora simply shakes her head. She says that you have begun to live beyond your means and I see how much you spend, on me alone! Mind, my friend, that you don't get into difficulties. Fedora tells me of rumours—that you have had a quarrel with your landlady for not paying your rent; I am very anxious about you. Well, good-bye, I'm in a hurry. It's a trifling matter, I'm altering a ribbon on a hat.

P.S.—You know, if we go to the theatre, I shall wear my new hat and my black mantle. Will that be all right?

July 7.

Dear Madam, Varvara Alexyevna,

. . . So I keep thinking about yesterday. Yes, my dear girl, even we have had our follies in the past. I fell in love with that actress, I fell head over ears in love with her, but that was nothing. The strangest thing was that I had scarcely seen her at all, and had only been at the theatre once, and yet for all that I fell in love. There lived next door to me five noisy young fellows. I got to know them, I could not help getting to know them, though I always kept at a respectable distance from them. But not to be behind them I agreed with them in everything. They talked to me about this actress. Every evening as soon as the theatre was opened, the whole company—they never had a halfpenny for necessities—the whole party set off to the theatre to the gallery and kept clapping and clapping, and calling, calling for that actress—they were simply frantic! And after that they would not let one sleep; they would talk about her all night without ceasing, everyone called her his Glasha, everyone of them was in love with her, they all had the same canary in their hearts. They worked me up: I was a helpless youngster then. I don't know how I came to go, but one evening I found myself in the fourth gallery with them. As for seeing, I could see nothing more than the corner of the curtain, but I heard everything. The actress certainly had a pretty voice—a musical voice like a nightingale, as sweet as honey; we all clapped our hands and shouted and shouted, we almost got into trouble, one was actually turned out. I went home.

I walked along as though I were drunk! I had nothing left in my pocket but one silver rouble, and it was a good ten days before I could get my salary. And what do you think, my love? Next day before going to the office I went to a French perfumer's and spent my whole fortune on perfume and scented soap—I really don't know why I bought all that. And I did not dine at home but spent the whole time walking up and down outside her window. She lived in Nevsky Prospect on the fourth storey. I went home for an hour or so, rested, and out into the Nevsky again, simply to pass by her windows. For six weeks I used to walk to and fro like that and hang about her; I was constantly hiring smart sledges and kept driving about so as to pass her window: I ruined myself completely, ran into debt, and then got over my passion, I got tired of it. So you see, my precious, what an actress can make of a respectable man! I was a youngster though, I was a youngster then! . . .

M. D.

July 8.

Dear Madam, Varvara Alexyevna,

I hasten to return you the book you lent me on the sixth of this month, and therewith I hasten to discuss the matter with you. It's wrong of you, my dear girl, it's wrong of you to put me to the necessity of it. Allow me to tell you, my good friend, every position in the lot of man is ordained by the Almighty. One man is ordained to wear the epaulettes of a general, while it is another's lot to serve as a titular councillor; it is for one to give commands, for another to obey without repining, in fear and humility. It is in accordance with man's capacities; one is fit for one thing and one for another, and their capacities are ordained by God himself. I have been nearly thirty years in the service; my record is irreproachable; I have been sober in my behaviour, and I have never had any irregularity put down to me. As a citizen I look upon myself in my own mind as having my faults, but my virtues, too. I am respected by my superiors, and His Excellency himself is satisfied with me; and though he has not so far shown me any special marks of favour, yet I know that he is satisfied. My handwriting is fairly legible and good, not too big and not too small, rather in the style of italics, but in any case satisfactory; there is no one among us except, perhaps,

Ivan Prokofyevitch who writes as well. I am old and my hair is grey; that's the only fault I know of in me. Of course, there is no one without his little failings. We're all sinners, even you are a sinner, my dear! But no serious offence, no impudence has ever been recorded against me, such as anything against the regulations, or any disturbance of public tranquillity; I have never been noticed for anything like that, such a thing has never happened—in fact, I almost got a decoration, but what's the use of talking! You ought to have known all that, my dear, and he ought to have known; if a man undertakes to write he ought to know all about it. No, I did not expect this from you, my dear girl, no, Varinka! You are the last person from whom I should have expected it.

What! So now you can't live quietly in your own little corner—whatever it may be like—not stirring up any mud, as the saying is, interfering with no one, knowing yourself, and fearing God, without people's interfering with you, without their prying into your little den and trying to see what sort of life you lead at home, whether for instance you have a good waistcoat, whether you have all you ought to have in the way of underclothes, whether you have boots and what they are lined with; what you eat, what you drink, what you write? And what even if I do sometimes walk on tiptoe to save my boots where the pavement's bad? Why write of another man that he sometimes goes short, that he has no tea to drink, as though everyone is always bound to drink tea—do I look into another man's mouth to see how he chews his crust, have I ever insulted anyone in that way? No, my dear, why insult people, when they are not interfering with you! Look here, Varvara Alexyevna, this is what it comes to: you work, and work regularly and devotedly; and your superiors respect you (however things may be, they do respect you), and here under your very nose, for no apparent reason, neither with your leave nor by your leave, somebody makes a caricature of you. Of course one does sometimes get something new—and is so pleased that one lies awake thinking about it, one is so pleased, one puts on new boots for instance, with such enjoyment; that is true: I have felt it because it is pleasant to see one's foot in a fine smart boot—that's truly described! But I am really surprised that Fyodor Fyodorovitch should have let such a book pass without notice and without defending himself. It is true that, though he is a high official, he is young and likes at times to make his voice heard. Why shouldn't he make his voice heard, why not give us a scolding if we need it? Scold to keep up the tone of the office, for instance—well, he must, to keep up the tone; you must teach men, you must give them a good talking to; for, between ourselves, Varinka, we clerks do nothing without a good talking to. Everyone is only on the look-out to get off somewhere, so as to say, I was sent here or there, and to avoid work and edge out of it. And as there are various grades in the service and as each grade requires a special sort of reprimand corresponding to the grade, it's natural that the tone of the reprimand should differ in the various grades—that's in the order of things—why, the whole world rests on that, my dear soul, on our all keeping up our authority with one another, on each one of us scolding the other. Without that precaution, the world could not go on and there would be no sort of order. I am really surprised that Fyodor Fyodorovitch let such an insult pass without attention. And why write such things? And what's the use of it? Why, will someone who reads it order me a cloak because of it; will he buy me new boots? No, Varinka, he will read it and ask for a contribution. One hides oneself sometimes, one hides oneself, one tries to conceal one's weak points, one's afraid to show one's nose at times anywhere because one is afraid of tittle-tattle, because they can work up a tale against you about anything in the world—anything. And here now all one's private and public life is being dragged into literature, it is all printed, read, laughed and gossiped about! Why, it will be impossible to show oneself in the street. It's all so plainly told, you know, that one might be recognised in one's walk. To be sure, it's as well that he does make up for it a little at the end, that he does soften it a bit, that after that passage when they throw the papers at his head, it does put in, for instance, that for all that he was a conscientious man, a good citizen, that he did not deserve such treatment from his fellow-clerks, that he respected his elders (his example might be followed, perhaps, in that), had no ill-will against anyone, believed in God and died (if he will have it that he died) regretted. But it would have been better not to let him die, poor fellow, but to make the coat be found, to make Fyodor Fyodorovitch—what am I saying? I mean, make that general, finding out his good qualities, question him in his office, promote him in his office, and give him a good increase in his salary, for then, you see, wickedness would have been punished, and virtue would have been triumphant, and his fellow-clerks would have got nothing by it. I should have done that, for instance, but as it is, what is there special about it, what is there good in it? It's just an insignificant example from vulgar, everyday life. And what induced you to send me such a book, my own? Why, it's a book of an evil tendency, Varinka, it's untrue to life, for there cannot have been such a clerk. No, I must make a complaint, Varinka. I must make a formal complaint.

Your very humble servant,
MAKAR DYEVUSHKIN.

July 27.

DEAR SIR, MAKAR ALEXYEVITCH,

Your latest doings and letters have frightened, shocked, and amazed me, and what Fedora tells me has explained it all. But what reason had you to be so desperate and to sink to such a depth as you have sunk to, Makar Alexyevitch? Your explanation has not satisfied me at all. Isn't it clear that I was right in trying to insist on taking the situation that was offered me? Besides, my last adventure has thoroughly frightened me. You say that it's your love for me that makes you keep in hiding from me. I saw that I was deeply indebted to you while you persuaded me that you were only spending your savings on me, which you said you had lying by in the bank in case of need. Now, when I learn that you had no such money at all, but, hearing by chance of my straitened position, and touched by it, you actually spent your salary, getting it in advance, and even sold your clothes when I was ill—now that I have discovered all this I am put in such an agonising position that I still don't know how to take it, and what to think about it. Oh, Makar Alexyevitch! You ought to have confined yourself to that first kind help inspired by sympathy and the feeling of kinship and not have wasted money afterwards on luxuries. You have been false to our friendship, Makar Alexyevitch, for you weren't open with me. And now, when I see that you were spending your last penny on finery, on sweetmeats, on excursions, on the theatre and on books— now I am paying dearly for all that in regret for my frivolity (for I took it all from you without troubling myself about you); and everything with which you tried to give me pleasure is now turned to grief for me, and has left nothing but useless regret. I have noticed your depression of late, and, although I was nervously apprehensive of some trouble, what has happened never entered my head. What! Could you lose heart so completely, Makar Alexyevitch! Why, what am I to think of you now, what will everyone who knows you say of you now? You, whom I always respected for your good heart, your discretion, and your good sense. You have suddenly given way to such a revolting vice, of which one saw no sign in you before. What were my feelings when Fedora told me you were found in the street in a state of inebriety, and were brought home to your lodgings by the police! I was petrified with amazement, though I did expect something extraordinary, as there had been no sign of you for four days. Have you thought, Makar Alexyevitch, what your chiefs at the office will say when they learn the true cause of your absence? You say that everyone laughs at you, that they all know of our friendship, and that your neighbours speak of me in their jokes, too. Don't pay any attention to that, Makar Alexyevitch, and for goodness' sake, calm yourself. I am alarmed about your affair with those officers, too; I have heard a vague account of it. Do explain what it all means. You write that you were afraid to tell me, that you were afraid to lose my affection by your confession, that you were in despair, not knowing how to help me in my illness, that you sold everything to keep me and prevent my going to hospital, that you got into debt as far as you possibly could, and have unpleasant scenes every day with your landlady—but you made a mistake in concealing all this from me. Now I know it all, however. You were reluctant to make me realise that I was the cause of your unhappy position, and now you have caused me twice as much grief by your behaviour. All this has shocked me, Makar Alexyevitch. Oh, my dear friend! misfortune is an infectious disease, the poor and unfortunate ought to avoid one another, for fear of making each other worse. I have brought you trouble such as you knew nothing of in your old humble and solitary existence. All this is distressing and killing me.

Write me now openly all that happened to you and how you came to behave like that. Set my mind at rest if possible. It isn't selfishness makes me write to you about my peace of mind, but my affection and love for you, which nothing will ever efface from my heart. Good-bye. I await your answer with impatience. You had a very poor idea of me, Makar Alexyevitch.

Your loving
VARVARA DOBROSELOV.

July 28.

MY PRECIOUS VARVARA ALEXYEVNA—

Well, as now everything is over and, little by little, things are beginning to be as they used to be, again let me tell you one thing, my good friend: you are worried by what people will think about me, to which I hasten to assure you, Varvara Alexyevna, that my reputation is dearer to me than anything. For which reason and with reference to my misfortunes and all those disorderly proceedings I beg to inform you that no one of the authorities at the office know anything about it or will know anything about it. So that they will all feel the same respect for me as before. The one thing I'm afraid of is gossip. At home our landlady did nothing but shout, and now that with the help of your ten roubles I have paid part of what I owe her she does nothing more than grumble; as for other people, they don't matter, one mustn't borrow money of them, that's all, and to conclude my explanations I tell you, Varvara Alexyevna, that your respect for me I esteem more highly than anything on earth, and I am comforted by it now in my temporary troubles. Thank God that the first blow and the first shock are over and that you have taken it as you have, and don't look on me as a false friend, or an egoist for keeping you here and deceiving you because I love you as my angel and could not bring myself to part from you. I've set to work again assiduously and have begun performing my duties well. Yevstafy Ivanovitch did just say a word when I passed him by yesterday. I will not conceal from you, Varinka, that I am overwhelmed by my debts and the awful condition of my wardrobe, but that again does not matter, and about that too, I entreat you, do not despair, my dear. Send me another half rouble. Varinka, that half rouble rends my heart too. So that's what it has come to now, that is how it is, old fool that I am; it's not I helping you, my angel, but you, my poor little orphan, helping me. Fedora did well to get the money. For the time I have no hopes of getting any, but if there should be any prospects I will write to you fully about it all. But gossip, gossip is what I am most uneasy about. I kiss your little hand and implore you to get well. I don't write more fully because I am in haste to get to the office. For I want by industry and assiduity to atone for all my shortcomings in the way of negligence in the office; a further account of all that happened and my adventures with the officers I put off till this evening.

Your respectful and loving
MAKAR DYEVUSHKIN.

July 28.

MY PRECIOUS VARINKA—

Ach, Varinka, Varinka! This time the sin is on your side and your conscience. You completely upset and perplexed me by your letter, and only now, when at my leisure I looked into the inmost recesses of my heart, I saw that I was right, perfectly right. I am not talking of my drinking (that's enough of it, my dear soul, that's enough) but about my loving you and that I was not at all unreasonable in loving you, not at all unreasonable. You know nothing about it, my darling; why, if only you knew why it all was, why I was bound to love you, you wouldn't talk like that. All your reasoning about it is only talk, and I am sure that in your heart you feel quite differently.

My precious, I don't even know myself and don't remember what happened between me and the officers. I must tell you, my angel, that up to that time I was in the most terrible perturbation. Only imagine! for a whole month I had been clinging to one thread, so to say. My position was most awful. I was concealing it from you, and concealing it at home too. But my landlady made a fuss and a clamour. I should not have minded that. The wretched woman might have clamoured but, for one thing, it was the disgrace and, for another, she had found out about our friendship—God knows how—and was making such talk about it all over the house that I was numb with horror and put wool in my ears, but the worst of it is that other people did not put wool in theirs, but pricked them up, on the contrary. Even now I don't know where to hide myself. . . .

Well, my angel, all this accumulation of misfortunes of all sorts overwhelmed me utterly. Suddenly I heard a strange thing from Fedora: that a worthless profligate had called upon you and had insulted you by dishonourable proposals; that he did insult you, insult you deeply, I can judge from myself, my darling, for I was deeply insulted myself. That crushed me, my angel, that overwhelmed me and made me lose my head completely. I ran out, Varinka dear, in unutterable

fury. I wanted to go straight to him, the reprobate. I did not know
what I meant to do. I won't have you insulted, my angel! Well, I was
sad! And at that time it was raining, sleet was falling, it was horribly
wretched! . . . I meant to turn back. . . . Then came my downfall. I
met Emelyan Ilyitch—he is a clerk, that is, was a clerk, but he is not a
clerk now because he was turned out of our office. I don't know what
he does now, he just hangs about there. Well, I went with him. Then—
but there, Varinka, will it amuse you to read about your friend's misfortunes, his troubles, and the story of the trials he has endured? Three
days later that Emelyan egged me on and I went to see him, that officer. I got his address from our porter. Since we are talking about it, my
dear, I noticed that young gallant long ago: I kept an eye upon him
when he lodged in our buildings. I see now that what I did was unseemly, because I was not myself when I was shown up to him. Truly,
Varinka, I don't remember anything about it, all I remember is that
there were a great many officers with him, else I was seeing double—
goodness knows. I don't remember what I said either, I only know
that I said a great deal in my honest indignation. But then they turned
me out, then they threw me downstairs—that is, not really threw me
downstairs, but turned me out. You know already, Varinka, how I returned: that's the whole story. Of course I lowered myself and my reputation has suffered, but, after all, no one knows of it but you, no
outsider knows of it, and so it is all as though it had never happened.
Perhaps that is so, Varinka, what do you think? The only thing is, I
know for a fact that last year Aksenty Osipovitch in the same way as-
saulted Pyotr Petrovitch but in secret, he did it in secret. He called him
into the porter's room—I saw it all through the crack in the door—and
there he settled the matter, as was fitting, but in a gentlemanly way,
for no one saw it except me, and I did not matter—that is, I did not
tell anyone. Well, after that Pyotr Petrovitch and Aksenty Osipovitch
were all right together. Pyotr Petrovitch, you know, is a man with self-
respect, so he told no one, so that now they even bow and shake hands.
I don't dispute, Varinka, I don't venture to dispute with you that I have
degraded myself terribly, and, what is worst of all, I have lowered myself in my own opinion, but no doubt it was destined from my birth,
no doubt it was my fate, and there's no escaping one's fate, you know.

Well, that is an exact account of my troubles and misfortunes,
Varinka, all of them, things such that reading of them is unprofitable.

I am very far from well, Varinka, and have lost all the playfulness of my feelings. Herewith I beg to testify to my devotion, love and respect. I remain, dear madam, Varvara Alexyevna,

Your humble servant,
MAKAR DYEVUSHKIN.

July 29.

MY DEAR MAKAR ALEXYEVITCH!

I have read your two letters, and positively groaned! Listen, my dear; you are either concealing something from me and have written to me only part of all your troubles, or . . . really, Makar Alexyevitch, there is a touch of incoherency about your letters still. . . . Come and see me, for goodness' sake, come to-day; and listen, come straight to dinner, you know I don't know how you are living, or how you have managed about your landlady. You write nothing about all that, and your silence seems intentional. So, good-bye, my friend; be sure and come to us to-day; and you would do better to come to us for dinner every day. Fedora cooks very nicely. Good-bye.

Your
VARVARA DOBROSELOV.

August 1.

MY DEAR VARVARA ALEXYEVNA—

You are glad, my dear girl, that God has sent you a chance to do one good turn for another and show your gratitude to me. I believe that, Varinka, and I believe in the goodness of your angelic heart, and I am not saying it to reproach you—only do not upbraid me for being a spendthrift in my old age. Well, if I have done wrong, there's no help for it; only to hear it from you, my dearie, is very bitter! Don't be angry with me for saying so, my heart's all one ache. Poor people are touchy—that's in the nature of things. I felt that even in the past. The poor man is exacting; he takes a different view of God's world, and looks askance at every passer-by and turns a troubled gaze about him and looks to every word, wondering whether people are not talking about him, whether they are saying that he is so ugly, speculating about what he would feel exactly, what he would be on this side and what he would be on that side, and everyone knows, Varinka, that a poor man is worse than a rag and can get no respect from anyone; whatever they may write, those scribblers, it will always be the same with the poor man as it has been. And why will it always be as it has been? Because to their thinking the poor man must be turned inside out, he must have no privacy, no pride whatever! Emelyan told me the other day that they got up a subscription for him and made a sort of official inspection over every sixpence; they thought that they were giving him his sixpences for nothing, but they were not; they were paid for them by showing him he was a poor man. Nowadays, my dear soul, benevolence is practised in a very queer way . . . and perhaps it always has been so, who knows! Either people don't know how to do it or they are first-rate hands at it—one of the two. Perhaps you did not know it, so there it is for you. On anything else we can say nothing, but on this subject we are authorities! And how is it a poor man knows all this and thinks of it all like this? Why?—from experience! Because he knows for instance, that there is a gentleman at his side, who is going somewhere to a restaurant and saying to himself, "What's this beggarly clerk going to eat to-day? I'm going to eat *sauté papillotte* while he is going to eat porridge without butter, maybe." And what business is it to him that I am going to eat porridge without butter? There are men, Varinka, there are men who think of nothing else. And they go about, the indecent caricaturists, and look whether one puts one's whole foot down on the pavement or walks on tiptoe; they notice that such a clerk, of such a department, a titular councillor, has his bare toes sticking out of his boot, that he has holes in his elbow—and then they sit down at home and describe it all and publish such rubbish . . . and what business is it of yours, sir, if my elbows are in holes? Yes, if you will excuse me the coarse expression, Varinka, I will tell you that the poor man has the same sort of modesty on that score as you, for instance, have maidenly modesty. Why, you wouldn't divest yourself of your clothing before everyone—forgive my coarse comparison. So, in the same way, the poor man does not like people to peep into his poor hole and wonder about his domestic arrangements. So what need was there to join in insulting me, Varinka, with the enemies who are attacking an honest man's honour and reputation?

And in the office to-day I sat like a hen, like a plucked sparrow, so that I almost turned with shame at myself. I was ashamed, Varinka!

And one is naturally timid, when one's elbows are seeing daylight
through one's sleeves, and one's buttons are hanging on threads. And,
as ill-luck would have it, all my things were in such disorder! You can't
help losing heart. Why! . . . Stepan Karlovitch himself began speaking
to me about my work to-day, he talked and talked away and added, as
though unawares, "Well, really, Makar Alexyevitch!" and did not say
what was in his mind, only I understood what it was for myself, and
blushed so that even the bald patch on my head was crimson. It was
really only a trifle, but still it made me uneasy, and aroused bitter reflections. If only they have heard nothing! Ah, God forbid that they
should hear about anything! I confess I do suspect one man. I suspect
him very much. Why, these villains stick at nothing, they will betray
me, they will give away one's whole private life for a halfpenny—
nothing is sacred to them.

I know now whose doing it is; it is Ratazyaev's doing. He knows
someone in our office, and most likely in the course of conversation
has told them the whole story with additions; or maybe he has told
the story in his own office, and it has crept out and crept into our office. In our lodging, they all know it down to the lowest, and point at
your window; I know that they do point. And when I went to dinner
with you yesterday, they all poked their heads out of window and the
landlady said: "Look," said she, "the devil has made friends with the
baby." And then she called you an unseemly name. But all that's nothing beside Ratazyaev's disgusting design to put you and me into his
writing and to describe us in a cunning satire; he spoke of this himself, and friendly fellow-lodgers have repeated it to me. I can think of
nothing else, my darling, and don't know what to decide to do. There
is no concealing the fact, we have provoked the wrath of God, little
angel. You meant to send me a book, my good friend, to relieve my
dullness; what is the use of a book, my love, what's the good of it? It's
arrant nonsense! The story is nonsense and it is written as nonsense,
just for idle people to read; trust me, my dear soul, trust the experience of my age. And what if they talk to you of some Shakespeare,
saying, "You see that Shakespeare wrote literature," well, then, Shakespeare is nonsense; it's all arrant nonsense and only written to jeer at
folk!

Yours,
MAKAR DYEVUSHKIN.

August 2.

DEAR MAKAR ALEXYEVITCH!

Don't worry about anything; please God it will all be set right. Fedora has got a lot of work both for herself and for me, and we have set to work very happily; perhaps we shall save the situation. She suspects that Anna Fyodorovna had some hand in this last unpleasant business; but now I don't care. I feel somehow particularly cheerful to-day. You want to borrow money—God forbid! You'll get into trouble afterwards when you need to pay it back. We had much better live more frugally; come to us more often, and don't take any notice of your landlady. As for your other enemies and ill-wishers, I am sure you are worrying yourself with needless suspicions, Makar Alexyevitch! Mind, I told you last time that your language was very exaggerated. Well, good-bye till we meet. I expect you without fail.

Your

V. D.

August 3.

MY ANGEL, VARVARA ALEXYEVNA,

I hasten to tell you, my little life, I have fresh hopes of something. But excuse me, my little daughter, you write, my angel, that I am not to borrow money. My darling, it is impossible to avoid it; here I am in a bad way, and what if anything were suddenly amiss with you! You are frail, you know; so that's why I say we must borrow. Well, so I will continue.

I beg to inform you, Varvara Alexyevna, that in the office I am sitting next to Emelyan Ivanovitch. That's not the Emelyan Ilyitch whom you know. He is, like me, a titular councillor, and he and I are almost the oldest veterans in the office. He is a good-natured soul, an unworldly soul; he's not given to talking and always sits like a regular bear. But he is a good clerk and has a good English handwriting and, to tell the whole truth, he writes as well as I do—he's a worthy man! I never was very intimate with him, but only just say good-morning and good-evening; or if I wanted the pen-knife, I would say, "Give me the pen-knife, Emelyan Ivanovitch"; in short, our intercourse was confined to our common necessities. Well so, he says to me to-day,

"Makar Alexyevitch, why are you so thoughtful?" I see the man wishes me kindly, so I told him—I said, "This is how it is, Emelyan Ivanovitch"—that is, I did not tell him everything, and indeed, God forbid! I never will tell the story because I haven't the heart to, but just told him something, that I was in straits for money, and so on. "You should borrow, my good soul," said Emelyan Ivanovitch: "you should borrow; from Pyotr Petrovitch you might borrow, he lends money at interest; I have borrowed and he asks a decent rate of interest, not exorbitant." Well, Varinka, my heart gave a leap. I thought and thought maybe the Lord will put it into the heart of Pyotr Petrovitch and in his benevolence he will lend me the money. Already I was reckoning to myself that I could pay the landlady and help you, and clear myself all round. Whereas now it is such a disgrace, one is afraid to be in one's own place, let alone the jeers of our grinning jackanapes. Bother them! And besides, his Excellency sometimes passes by our table: why, God forbid! he may cast a glance in my direction and notice I'm not decently dressed! And he makes a great point of neatness and tidiness. Maybe he would say nothing, but I should die of shame—that's how it would be. In consequence I screwed myself up and, putting my pride in my ragged pocket, I went up to Pyotr Petrovitch full of hope and at the same time more dead than alive with suspense. But, after all, Varinka, it all ended in foolishness! He was busy with something, talking with Fedosey Ivanovitch. I went up to him sideways and pulled him by the sleeve, saying, "Pyotr Petrovitch, I say, Pyotr Petrovitch!" He looked round, and I went on: saying, "this is how it is, thirty roubles," and so on. At first he did not understand me, and when I explained it all to him, he laughed, and said nothing. I said the same thing again. And he said to me, "Have you got a pledge?" And he buried himself in his writing and did not even glance at me. I was a little flustered. "No," I said, "Pyotr Petrovitch, I've no pledge," and I explained to him that when I got my salary I would pay him, would be sure to pay him, I should consider it my first duty. Then somebody called him. I waited for him, he came back and began mending a pen and did not seem to notice me, and I kept on with "Pyotr Petrovitch, can't you manage it somehow?" He said nothing and seemed not to hear me. I kept on standing there. Well, I thought I would try for the last time, and pulled him by the sleeve. He just muttered something, cleaned his pen, and began writing. I walked away. You see, my dear girl, they may be excellent people, but proud, very proud—but I don't mind! We are not fit company for them, Varinka! That is why I have written all this to you. Emelyan Ivanovitch laughed, too, and shook his head, but he cheered me up, the dear fellow—Emelyan Ivanovitch is a worthy man. He promised to introduce me to a man who lives in the Vybord Side, Varinka, and lends money at interest too; he is some sort of clerk of the fourteenth class. Emelyan Ivanovitch says he will be sure to lend it. Shall I go to him to-morrow, my angel, eh? What do you think? It is awful if I don't. My landlady is almost turning me out and won't consent to give me my dinner; besides, my boots are in a dreadful state, my dear; I've no buttons either and nothing else besides. And what if anyone in authority at the office notices such unseemliness; it will be awful, Varinka, simply awful!

MAKAR DYEVUSHKIN.

August 4.

DEAR MAKAR ALEXYEVITCH,

For God's sake, Makar Alexyevitch, borrow some money as soon as possible! I would not for anything have asked you for help as things are at present, but if you only knew what a position I am in. It's utterly impossible for us to remain in this lodging. A horribly unpleasant thing has happened here, and if only you knew how upset and agitated I am! Only imagine, my friend; this morning a stranger came into our lodging, an elderly, almost old man, wearing orders. I was amazed, not knowing what he wanted with us. Fedora had gone out to a shop at the time. He began asking me how I lived and what I did, and without waiting for an answer, told me that he was the uncle of that officer; that he was very angry with his nephew for his disgraceful behaviour, and for having given us a bad name all over the buildings; said that his nephew was a featherheaded scamp, and that he was ready to take me under his protection; advised me not to listen to young men, added that he sympathised with me like a father, that he felt a father's feeling for me and was ready to help me in any way. I blushed all over, not knowing what to think, but was in no haste to thank him. He took my hand by force, patted me on the cheek, told me I was very pretty and that he was delighted to find I had dimples in my cheeks (goodness knows what he said!) and at last tried to kiss me, saying that he was an old man (he was so loathsome). At that point Fedora came in. He was a little disconcerted and began saying again that he felt respect for me, for my discretion and good principles, and that he was very anxious that I should not treat him as a stranger. Then he drew Fedora aside and on some strange pretext wanted to give her a lot of money. Fedora, of course, would not take it. At last he got up to go, he repeated once more all his assurances, said that he would come and see me again and bring me some ear-rings (I believe he, too, was very much embarrassed); he advised me to change my lodgings and recommended me a very nice lodging which he had his eye on, and which would cost me nothing; he said that he liked me very much for being an honest and sensible girl, advised me to beware of profligate men, and finally told us that he knew Anna Fyodorovna and that Anna Fyodorovna had commissioned him to tell me that she would come and see me herself. Then I understood it all. I don't know what came over me; it was the first time in my life I had had such an experience; I flew into a fury, I put him to shame completely. Fedora helped me, and we almost turned him out of the flat. We've come to the conclusion that it is all Anna Fyodorovna's doing; how else could he have heard of us?

Now I appeal to you, Makar Alexyevitch, and entreat you to help us. For God's sake, don't desert me in this awful position. Please borrow, get hold of some money anyway; we've no money to move with and we mustn't stay here any longer; that's Fedora's advice. We need at least thirty-five roubles; I'll pay you back the money; I'll earn it. Fedora will get me some more work in a day or two, so that if they ask a high interest, never mind it, but agree to anything. I'll pay it all back, only for God's sake, don't abandon me. I can't bear worrying you now when you are in such circumstances . . . Good-bye, Makar Alexyevitch; think of me, and God grant you are successful.

Yours,

V. D.

August 4.

MY DARLING VARVARA ALEXYEVNA!

All these unexpected blows positively shatter me! Such terrible calamities destroy my spirit! These scoundrelly libertines and rascally old men will not only bring you, my angel, to a bed of sickness, they mean to be the death of me, too. And they will be, too, I swear they will. You know I am ready to die sooner than not help you! If I don't help you it will be the death of me, Varinka, the actual literal death of me, and if I do help you, you'll fly away from me like a bird out of its nest, to escape these owls, these birds of prey that were trying to peck her. That's what tortures me, my precious. And you too, Varinka, you are so cruel! How can you do it? You are tormented, you are insulted, you, my little bird, are in distress, and then you regret that you must worry me and promise to repay the debt, which means, to tell the truth, that with your delicate health you will kill yourself, in order to get the money for me in time. Why, only think, Varinka, what you are talking about. Why should you sew? Why should you work, worry your poor little head with anxiety, spoil your pretty eyes and destroy your health? Ah, Varinka, Varinka! You see, my darling, I am good for nothing, I know myself that I am good for nothing, but I'll manage to be good for something! I will overcome all obstacles. I will get outside work, I will copy all sorts of manuscripts for all sorts of literary men. I will go to them, I won't wait to be asked, I'll force them to give me work, for you know, my darling, they are on the look-out for good copyists, I know they look out for them, but I won't let you wear yourself out; I won't let you carry out such a disastrous intention. I will certainly borrow it, my angel, I'd sooner die than not borrow it. You write, my darling, that I am not to be afraid of a high rate of interest—and I won't be afraid of it, my dear soul, I won't be frightened. I won't be frightened of anything now. I will ask for forty roubles in paper, my dear; that's not much, you know, Varinka, what do you think? Will they trust me with forty roubles at the first word? That is, I mean to say, do you consider me capable of inspiring trust and confidence at first sight. Can they form a favourable impression of me from my physiognomy at first sight? Recall my appearance, my angel; am I capable of inspiring confidence? What do you think yourself? You know I feel such terror; it makes me quite ill, to tell the truth, quite ill. Of the forty roubles I set aside twenty-five for you, Varinka, two silver roubles will be for the landlady, and the rest I design for my own expenses. You see I ought to give the landlady more, I must, in fact; but if you think it all over, my dear girl, and reckon out all I need, then you'll see that it is impossible to give her more, consequently there's no use talking about it and no need to refer to it. For a silver rouble I shall buy a pair of boots—I really don't know whether I shall be able to appear at the office in the old ones; a new necktie would have been necessary, too, for I have had the old one a year, but since you've promised to make me, not only a tie, but a shirtfront cut out of your old apron, I shall think no more of a tie. So there we have boots and a tie. Now for buttons, my dear. You will agree, my darling, that I can't go on without buttons and almost half have dropped off. I tremble when I think that his Excellency may notice such untidiness and say something, and what he would say! I shouldn't hear what he would say, my darling, for I should die, die, die on the spot, simply go and die of shame at the very thought!—Ah, Varinka!—Well, after all these necessities, there will be three roubles left, so that would do to live on and get half a pound of tobacco, for I can't live without tobacco, my little angel, and this is the ninth day since I had my pipe in my mouth. To tell the truth, I should have bought it and said nothing to you, but I was ashamed. You are there in trouble depriving yourself of everything, and here am I enjoying luxuries of all sorts; so that's why I tell you about it to escape the stings of conscience. I frankly confess, Varinka, I am now in an extremely straitened position, that is, nothing like it has ever happened before. My landlady despises me, I get no sort of respect from anyone; my terrible lapses, my debts; and at the office, where I had anything but a good time, in the old days, at the hands of my fellow clerks—now, Varinka, it is beyond words. I hide everything, I carefully hide everything from everyone, and I edge into the office sideways, I hold aloof from all. It's only to you that I have the heart to confess it. . . . And what if they won't give me the money! No, we had better not think about that, Varinka, not depress our spirits beforehand with such thoughts. That's why I am writing this, to warn you not to think about it, and not to worry yourself with evil imaginations. Ah! my God! what will happen to you then! It's true that then you will not move from that lodging and I shall be with you then. But, no, I should not come back then, I should simply perish somewhere and be lost. Here I have been writing away to you and I ought to have been shaving; it makes one more presentable, and to be presentable always counts for something. Well, God help us, I will say my prayers, and then set off.

                                                                    M. Dyevushkin.

August 5.

My dear Makar Alexyevitch,

You really mustn't give way to despair. There's trouble enough without that.

I send you thirty kopecks in silver, I cannot manage more. Buy yourself what you need most, so as to get along somehow, until to-morrow. We have scarcely anything left ourselves, and I don't know what will happen to-morrow. It's sad, Makar Alexyevitch! Don't be sad, though, if you've not succeeded, there's no help for it. Fedora says that there is no harm done so far, that we can stay for the time in this lodging, that if we did move we shouldn't gain much by it, and that they can find us anywhere if they want to. Though I don't feel comfortable at staying here now. If it were not so sad I would have written you an account of something.

What a strange character you have, Makar Alexyevitch; you take everything too much to heart and so you will be always a very unhappy man. I read all your letters attentively and I see in every letter you are anxious and worried about me as you never are about yourself. Everyone says, of course, that you have a good heart, but I say that it is too good. I will give you some friendly advice, Makar Alexyevitch. I am grateful to you, very grateful for all that you have done for me, I feel it very much; so judge what it must be for me to see that even now, after all your misfortunes of which I have been the unconscious cause—that even now you are only living in my life, my joys, my sorrows, my feelings! If one takes all another person's troubles so to heart and sympathises so intensely with everything it is bound to make one very unhappy. To-day, when you came in to see me from the office I was frightened at the sight of you. You were so pale, so despairing, so frightened-looking; you did not look like yourself—and all because you were afraid to tell me of your failure, afraid of disappointing me, of frightening me, and when you saw I nearly laughed your heart was almost at ease. Makar Alexyevitch, don't grieve, don't despair, be more sensible, I beg you, I implore you. Come, you will see that everything will be all right. Everything will take a better turn: why, life will be a misery to you, for ever grieving and being miserable over other people's troubles. Good-bye, my dear friend. I beseech you not to think too much about it.

V. D.

August 5.

My darling Varinka,

Very well, my angel, very well! You have made up your mind that
it is no harm so far that I have not got the money. Well, very good, I
feel reassured, I am happy as regards you. I am delighted, in fact, that
you are not going to leave me in my old age but are going to stay in
your lodging. In fact, to tell you everything, my heart was brimming
over with joy when I saw that you wrote so nicely about me in your
letter and gave due credit to my feelings. I don't say this from pride,
but because I see how you love me when you are so anxious about my
heart. Well, what's the use of talking about my heart! The heart goes its
own way, but you hint, my precious, that I mustn't be downhearted.
Yes, my angel, maybe, and I say myself it is of no use being downhearted! but for all that, you tell me, my dear girl, what boots I am to
go to the office in to-morrow! That's the trouble, Varinka; and you
know such a thought destroys a man, destroys him utterly. And the
worst of it is, my own, that it is not for myself I am troubled, it is not
for myself I am distressed; as far as I am concerned I don't mind going
about without an overcoat and without boots in the hardest frost; I
don't care: I can stand anything, and put up with anything. I am a
humble man of no importance,—but what will people say? My enemies with their spiteful tongues, what will they say, when one goes
about without an overcoat? You know it is for the sake of other people
one wears an overcoat, yes, and boots, too, you put on, perhaps, on
their account. Boots, in such cases, Varinka darling, are necessary to
keep up one's dignity and good name: in boots with holes in them,
both dignity and good name are lost; trust the experience of my years,
my dear child, listen to an old man like me who knows the world and
what people are, and not to any scurrilous scribblers and satirists.

I have not yet told you in detail, my darling, how it all happened
to-day. I suffered so much, I endured in one morning more mental anguish than many a man endures in a year. This is how it was: first, I set
off very early in the morning, so as to find him and be in time for the
office afterwards. There was such a rain, such a sleet falling this morning! I wrapped myself up in my overcoat, my little dearie. I walked on
and on and I kept thinking: "Oh, Lord, forgive my transgressions and
grant the fulfilment of my desires!" Passing St. X's Church, I crossed

myself, repented of all my sins, and thought that it was wrong of me
to bargain with the Almighty. I was lost in my thoughts and did not
feel like looking at anything; so I walked without picking my way. The
streets were empty, and the few I met all seemed anxious and preoccupied, and no wonder: who would go out at such an early hour and
in such weather! A gang of workmen, grinning all over, met me, the
rough fellows shoved against me! A feeling of dread came over me, I
felt panic-stricken, to tell the truth I didn't like even to think about the
money—I felt I must just take my chance! Just at Voskressensky Bridge
the sole came off my boot, so I really don't know what I walked upon.
And then I met our office attendant, Yermolaev. He drew himself up
at attention and stood looking after me as though he would ask
for a drink. "Ech, a drink, brother," I thought; "not much chance of
a drink!" I was awfully tired. I stood still, rested a bit and pushed on farther; I looked about on purpose for something to fasten my attention
on, to distract my mind, to cheer me up, but no, I couldn't fix one
thought on anything and, besides, I was so muddy that I felt ashamed
of myself. At last I saw in the distance a yellow wooden house with an
upper storey in the style of a belvedere. "Well," thought I, "so that's it,
that's how Emelyan Ivanovitch described it—Markov's house." (It is
this Markov himself, Varinka, who lends money.) I scarcely knew what
I was doing, and I knew, of course, that it was Markov's house, but I
asked a policeman. "Whose house is that, brother?" said I. The policeman was a surly fellow, seemed loth to speak and cross with someone;
he filtered his words through his teeth, but he did say it was Markov's
house. These policemen are always so unfeeling, but what did the policeman matter?—well, it all made a bad and unpleasant impression, in
short, there was one thing on the top of another; one finds in everything something akin to one's own position, and it is always so. I took
three turns past the house, along the street, and the further I went, the
worse I felt. "No," I thought, "he won't give it me, nothing will induce him to give it me. I am a stranger and it's a ticklish business, and
I am not an attractive figure. Well," I thought, "leave it to Fate, if only
I do not regret it afterwards; they won't devour me for making the attempt," and I softly opened the gate, and then another misfortune
happened. A wretched, stupid yard dog fastened upon me. It was beside itself and barked its loudest!—and it's just such wretched, trivial
incidents that always madden a man, Varinka, and make him nervous

and destroy all the determination he has been fortifying himself with beforehand; so that I went into the house more dead than alive and walked straight into trouble again. Without seeing what was below me straight in the doorway, I went in, stumbled over a woman who was busy straining some milk from a pail into a jug, and spilt all the milk. The silly woman shrieked and made an outcry, saying, "Where are you shoving to, my man?" and made a deuce of a row. I may say, Varinka, it is always like this with me in such cases; it seems it is my fate, I always get mixed up in something. An old hag, the Finnish landlady, poked her head out at the noise. I went straight up to her. "Does Markov live here?" said I. "No," said she. She stood still and took a good look at me. "And what do you want with him?" I explained to her that Emelyan had told me this and that, and all the rest of it—said it was a matter of business. The old woman called her daughter, a barelegged girl in her teens. "Call your father; he's upstairs at the lodger's, most likely."

I went in. The room was all right, there were pictures on the wall—all portraits of generals, a sofa, round table, mignonette, and balsam—I wondered whether I had not better clear out and take myself off for good and all. And, oh dear, I did want to run away, Varinka. "I had better come to-morrow," I thought, "and the weather will be better and I will wait a little—to-day the milk's been spilt and the generals look so cross . . ." I was already at the door—but he came in—a greyheaded man with thievish eyes, in a greasy dressing-gown with a cord round his waist. He enquired how and why, and I told him that Emelyan Ivanovitch had told me this and that—"Forty roubles," I said, "is what I've come about"—and I couldn't finish. I saw from his eyes that the game was lost. "No," says he; "the fact is, I've no money; and have you brought anything to pledge as security?"

I began explaining that I had brought nothing to pledge, but that Emelyan Ivanovitch—I explained in fact, what was wanted. He heard it all. "No," said he; "what is Emelyan Ivanovitch! I've no money."

Well, I thought, "There it is, I knew—I had a foreboding of it." Well, Varinka, it would have been better really if the earth had opened under me. I felt chill all over, my feet went numb and a shiver ran down my back. I looked at him and he looked at me and almost said, Come, run along, brother, it is no use your staying here—so that if such a thing had happened in other circumstances, I should have been quite ashamed. "And what do you want money for?"—(do you know, he asked that, Varinka). I opened my mouth, if only not to stand there doing nothing, but he wouldn't listen. "No," he said, "I have no money, I would have lent it with pleasure," said he. Then I pressed him, telling him I only wanted a little, saying I would pay him back on the day fixed, that I would pay him back before the day fixed, that he could ask any interest he liked and that, by God! I would pay him back. At that instant, my darling, I thought of you, I thought of all your troubles and privations, I thought of your poor little half-rouble. "But no," says he, "the interest is no matter; if there had been a pledge now! Besides, I have no money. I have none, by God! or I'd oblige you with pleasure,"—he took God's name, too, the villian!

Well, I don't remember, my own, how I went out, how I walked along Vyborgsky Street; how I got to Voskressensky Bridge. I was fearfully tired, shivering, wet through, and only succeeded in reaching the office at ten o'clock. I wanted to brush the mud off, but Snyegirev, the porter, said I mustn't, I should spoil the brush, and "the brush is government property," said he. That's how they all go on now, my dear, these gentry treat me no better than a rag to wipe their boots on. Do you know what is killing me, Varinka? it's not the money that's killing me, but all these little daily cares, these whispers, smiles and jokes. His Excellency may by chance have to refer to me. Oh, my darling, my golden days are over. I read over all your letters to-day; it's sad, Varinka! Good-bye, my own! The Lord keep you.

M. DYEVUSHKIN.

P.S.—I meant to describe my troubles half in joke, Varinka, only it seems that it does not come off with me, joking. I wanted to satisfy you. I am coming to see you, my dear girl, I will be sure to come.

August 11.

VARVARA ALEXYEVNA, MY DARLING,

I am lost, we are both lost, both together irretrievably lost. My reputation, my dignity—all is destroyed! I am ruined and you are ruined, my darling. You are hopelessly ruined with me! It's my doing, I have brought you to ruin! I am persecuted, Varinka, I am despised, turned into a laughing-stock, and the landlady has simply begun to abuse me; she shouted and shouted at me, to-day; she rated and rated at me and treated me as though I were dirt. And in the evening, at Ratazyaev's, one of them began reading aloud the rough copy of a letter to you which I had accidentally dropped out of my pocket. My precious, what a joke they made of it! They called us all sorts of flattering names and roared with laughter, the traitors! I went to them and taxed Ratazyaev with his perfidy, told him he was a traitor! And Ratazyaev answered that I was a traitor myself, that I amused myself with making conquests among the fair sex. He said, "You take good care to keep it from us; you're a Lovelace,"[13] he said; and now they all call me Lovelace and I have no other name! Do you hear, my little angel, do you hear?—they know it all now, they know all about it, and they know about you, my own, and whatever you have, they know about it all! And that's not all. Even Faldoni is in it, he's following their lead; I sent him to-day to the sausage-shop to get me something; he wouldn't go. "I am busy," that was all he said! "But you know it's your duty," I said. "No, indeed," he said, "it's not my duty. Here, you don't pay my mistress her money, so I have no duty to you." I could not stand this insult from him, an illiterate peasant, and I said, "You fool," and he answered back, "Fool yourself." I thought he must have had a drop too much to be so rude, and I said: "You are drunk, you peasant!" and he answered: "Well, not at your expense, anyway, you've nothing to get drunk on yourself; you are begging for twenty kopecks from somebody yourself," and he even added: "Ugh! and a gentleman too!" There, my dear girl, that's what it has come to! One's ashamed to be alive, Varinka! As though one were some sort of outcast, worse than a tramp without a passport. An awful calamity! I am ruined, simply ruined! I am irretrievably ruined!

M.D.

August 13.

MY DEAR MAKAR ALEXYEVITCH,

It's nothing but one trouble after another upon us. I don't know myself what to do! What will happen to you now?—and I have very little to hope for either; I burnt my left hand this morning with an iron; I dropped it accidentally and bruised myself and burnt my hand at the same time. I can't work at all, and Fedora has been poorly for the last

three days. I am in painful anxiety. I send you thirty kopecks in silver; it
is almost all we have left, and God knows how I should have liked to
help you in your need. I am so vexed I could cry. Good-bye, my friend!
You would comfort me very much if you would come and see us to-
day.

V. D.

August 14.

MAKAR ALEXYEVITCH

What is the matter with you? It seems you have no fear of God!
You are simply driving me out of my mind. Aren't you ashamed? You
will be your own ruin; you should at least think of your good name!
You're a man of honour, of gentlemanly feelings, of self-respect; well,
when everyone finds out about you! Why, you will simply die of
shame! Have you no pity for your grey hairs? Have you no fear of God?
Fedora says she won't help you again, and I won't give you money either. What have you brought me to, Makar Alexyevitch? I suppose you
think that it is nothing to me, your behaving so badly? You don't know
what I have to put up with on your account! I can't even go down our
staircase; everyone looks at me and points at me, and says such awful
things; they say plainly that I have *taken up with a drunkard*. Think what it
is to hear that! When you are brought in all the lodgers point at you
with contempt: "Look," they say, "they've brought that clerk in." And
I'm ready to faint with shame over you. I swear I shall move from
here. I shall go somewhere as a housemaid or a laundrymaid, I shan't
stay here. I wrote to you to come and see me here but you did not
come. So are my tears and entreaties nothing to you, Makar Alexyevitch? And where do you get the money? For God's sake, do be careful. Why, you are ruining yourself, ruining yourself for nothing! And
it's a shame and a disgrace! The landlady would not let you in last
night, you spent the night in the porch. I know all about it. If only you
knew how miserable I was when I knew all about it. Come to see me;
you will be happy with us; we will read together; we will recall the
past. Fedora will tell us about her wanderings as a pilgrim. For my
sake, don't destroy yourself and me. Why, I only live for you, for your
sake I am staying with you. And this is how you are behaving now! Be
a fine man, steadfast in misfortune, remember that poverty is not a
vice. And why despair? It is all temporary! Please God, it will all be set

right, only you must restrain yourself now. I send you twenty kopecks. Buy yourself tobacco or anything you want, only for God's sake don't spend it on what's harmful. Come and see us, be sure to come. Perhaps you will be ashamed as you were before, but don't be ashamed; it's false shame. If only you would show genuine penitence. Trust in God. He will do all things for the best.

V. D.

August 19.

Varvara Alexyevna, Darling,

I am ashamed, little dearie, Varvara Alexyevna; I am quite ashamed. But, after all, what is there so particular about it, my dear? Why not rejoice the heart a little? Then I don't think about my sole, for one's sole is nonsense, and will always remain a simple, nasty, muddy sole. Yes, and boots are nonsense, too! The Greek sages used to go about without boots, so why should people like us pamper ourselves with such unworthy objects? Oh! my dearie, my dearie, you have found something to write about! You tell Fedora that she is a nonsensical, fidgety, fussy woman, and, what's more, she's a silly one, too, unutterably silly! As for my grey hairs, you are quite mistaken about that, my own, for I am by no means so old as you think. Emelyan sends you his regards. You write that you have been breaking your heart and crying; and I write to you that I am breaking my heart, too, and crying. In conclusion I wish you the best of health and prosperity, and as for me I am in the best of health and prosperity, too, and I remain, my angel, your friend,

Makar Dyevushkin.

August 21.

Honoured Madam and dear Friend, Varvara Alexyevna,

I feel that I am to blame, I feel that I have wronged you, and to my mind there's no benefit at all, dear friend, in my feeling it, whatever you may say. I felt all that even before my misconduct, but I lost heart and fell, knowing I was doing wrong. My dear, I am not a bad man and not cruel-hearted, and to torture your little heart, my little darling, one must be, more or less, like a bloodthirsty tiger. Well,

I have the heart of a lamb and, as you know, have no inclination towards bloodthirstiness; consequently, my angel, I am not altogether to blame in my misconduct, since neither my feelings nor my thoughts were to blame; and in fact, I don't know what was to blame; it's all so incomprehensible, my darling! you sent me thirty kopecks in silver, and then you sent me twenty kopecks. My heart ached looking at your poor little coins. You had burnt your hand, you would soon be going hungry yourself, and you write that I am to buy tobacco. Well, how could I behave in such a position? Was I without a pang of conscience to begin plundering you, poor little orphan, like a robber! Then I lost heart altogether, my darling—that is, at first I could not help feeling that I was good for nothing and that I was hardly better than the sole of my boot. And so I felt it was unseemly to consider myself of any consequence, and began to look upon myself as something unseemly and somewhat indecent. Well, and when I lost my self-respect and denied my good qualities and my dignity, then it was all up with me, it meant degradation, inevitable degradation! That is ordained by destiny and I'm not to blame for it.

I went out at first to get a little air, then it was one thing after another; nature was so tearful, the weather was cold and it was raining. Well, Emelyan turned up. He had pawned everything he had, Varinka, everything he had is gone: and when I met him he had not put a drop of the rosy to his lips for two whole days and nights, so that he was ready to pawn what you can't pawn, because such things are never taken in pawn. Well, Varinka, I gave way more from a feeling of humanity than my own inclination, that's how the sin came to pass, my dear! How we wept together! We spoke of you. He's very good-natured, he's a very good-natured fellow and a very feeling man. I feel all that myself, my dear girl, that is just why it all happens to me, that I feel it all very much. I know how much I owe to you, my darling. Getting to know you, I came first to know myself better and to love you; and before I knew you, my angel, I was solitary and as it were asleep, and scarcely alive. They said, the spiteful creatures, that even my appearance was unseemly and they were disgusted with me, and so I began to be disgusted with myself; they said I was stupid and I really thought that I was stupid. When you came to me, you lighted up my dark life, so that my heart and my soul were filled with light and I gained peace at heart, and knew that I was no worse than others; that the only thing is that I am not brilliant in any way, that I have no polish or style about me, but I am still a man, in heart and mind a man. Well now, feeling that I was persecuted and humiliated by destiny, I lost all faith in my own good qualities; and, shattered by calamities, I lost all heart. And now since you know all about it, my dear, I beg you with tears not to question me further about that matter, for my heart is breaking and it is very bitter for me and hard to bear.

Assuring you of my respect, I remain, your faithful

MAKAR DYEVUSHKIN.

September 3.

I did not finish my last letter, Maker Alexyevitch, because it was difficult for me to write. Sometimes I have moments when I am glad to be alone, to mourn, with none to share my grief, and such moments are becoming more and more frequent with me. In my recollections there is something inexplicable to me, which attacks me unaccountably and so intensely that for hours at a stretch I am insensible to all surrounding me and I forget everything—all the present. And there is no impression of my present life, whether pleasant or painful and sad, which would not remind me of something similar in my past, and most often in my childhood, my golden childhood! But I always feel oppressed after such moments. I am somehow weakened by them; my dreaminess exhausts me, and apart from that my health grows worse and worse. But to-day the fresh bright sunny morning, such as are rare in autumn here, revived me and I welcomed it joyfully. And so autumn is with us already! How I used to love the autumn in the country! I was a child then, but I had already felt a great deal. I loved the autumn evening better than the morning. I remember that there was a lake at the bottom of the hill a few yards from our house. That lake—I feel as though I could see it now—that lake was so broad, so smooth, as bright and clear as crystal! At times, if it were a still evening, the lake was calm; not a leaf would stir on the trees that grew on the bank, and the water would be as motionless as a mirror. It was so fresh, so cool! The dew would be falling on the grass, the lights begin twinkling in the cottages on the bank, and they would be driving the cattle home. Then I could creep out to look at my lake, and I would forget everything, looking at it. At the water's edge, the fishermen would have a faggot burning and the light would be reflected far, far, over the water. The sky was so cold and blue, with streaks of fiery red along the horizon, and the streaks kept growing paler and paler; the moon would rise; the air so resonant that if a frightened bird fluttered, or a reed stirred in the faint breeze, or a fish splashed in the water, everything could be heard. A white steam, thin and transparent, rises up over the blue water: the distance darkens; everything seems drowned in the mist, while close by it all stands out so sharply, as though cut by a chisel, the boat, the banks, the islands; the tub thrown away and forgotten floats in the water close to the bank, the willow branch hangs with its yellow leaves tangled in the reeds, a belated gull flies up, then dives into the cold water, flies up again and is lost in the mist—while I gaze and listen. How lovely, how marvellous it was to me! and I was a child, almost a baby. . . .

I was so fond of the autumn, the late autumn when they were carrying the harvest, finishing all the labours of the year, when the peasants began gathering together in their cottages in the evening, when they were all expecting winter. Then it kept growing darker. The yellow leaves strewed the paths at the edges of the bare forest while the forest grew bluer and darker—especially at evening when a damp mist fell and the trees glimmered in the mist like giants, like terrible misshapen phantoms. If one were late out for a walk, dropped behind the others, how one hurried on alone—it was dreadful! One trembled like a leaf and kept thinking that in another minute someone terrible would peep out from behind that hollow tree; meanwhile the wind would rush through the woods, roaring and whistling, howling so plaintively, tearing a crowd of leaves from a withered twig, whirling them in the air, and with wild, shrill cries the birds would fly after them in a great, noisy flock, so that the sky would be all covered and darkened with them. One feels frightened, and then, just as though one heard someone speaking—some voice—as though someone whispered: "Run, run, child, don't be late; it will be dreadful here soon; run, child!"—with a thrill of horror at one's heart one would run till one was out of breath. One would reach home, breathless; there it was all noise and gaiety; all of us children had some work given to us to do, shelling peas or shaking out poppy seeds. The damp wood crackles in the stove. Cheerfully mother looks after our cheerful work; our old nurse, Ulyana, tells us stories about old times or terrible tales of wizards and dead bodies. We children squeeze up to one

another with smiles on our lips. Then suddenly we are all silent . . .
Oh! a noise as though someone were knocking—it was nothing; it
was old Frolovna's spindle; how we laughed! Then at night we would
lie awake for hours, we had such fearful dreams. One would wake and
not dare to stir, and lie shivering under the quilt till daybreak. In the
morning one would get up, fresh as a flower. One would look out of
the window; all the country would be covered with frost, the thin
hoarfrost of autumn would be hanging on the bare boughs, the lake
would be covered with ice, thin as a leaf, a white mist would be rising
over it, the birds would be calling merrily, the sun would light up
everything with its brilliant rays and break the thin ice like glass. It
was so bright, so shining, so gay, the fire would be crackling in the
stove again, we would sit down round the samovar while our black
dog, Polkan, numb with cold from the night, would peep in at the
window with a friendly wag of his tail. A peasant would ride by the
window on his good horse to fetch wood from the forest. Everyone
was so gay, so happy! . . . There were masses and masses of corn
stored up in the threshing-barns; the huge, huge stacks covered with
straw shone golden in the sun, a comforting sight! And all are calm
and joyful. God has blessed us all with the harvest; they all know they
will have bread for the winter; the peasant knows that his wife and
children will have food to eat; and so there is no end to the singing of
the girls and their dances and games in the evening, and on the Saints'
days! All pray in the house of God with grateful tears! Oh! what a
golden, golden age was my childhood! . . .

Here I am crying like a child, carried away by my reminiscences.
I remembered it all so vividly, so vividly, all the past stood out so
brightly before me, and the present is so dim, so dark! . . . How will it
end, how will it all end? Do you know I have a sort of conviction, a
feeling of certainty, that I shall die this autumn. I am very, very ill. I often think about dying, but still I don't want to die like this, to lie in the
earth here. Perhaps I shall be laid up as I was in the spring; I've not
fully recovered from that illness yet. I am feeling very dreary just now.
Fedora has gone off somewhere for the whole day and I am sitting
alone. And for some time now I've been afraid of being left alone; I
always feel as though there were someone else in the room, that
someone is talking to me; especially when I begin dreaming about
something and suddenly wake up from my brooding, then I feel

frightened. That is why I've written you such a long letter; it goes off when I write. Good-bye; I finish my letter because I have neither time nor paper for more. Of the money from pawning my dress and my hat I have only one rouble in silver left. You have given the landlady two roubles in silver; that's very good. She will keep quiet now for a time.

You must improve your clothes somehow. Good-bye, I'm so tired; I don't know why I am growing so feeble. The least work exhausts me. If I do get work, how am I to work? It is that thought that's killing me.

V. D.

September 5.

My darling Varinka,

I have received a great number of impressions this morning, my angel. To begin with I had a headache all day. To freshen myself up a bit I went for a walk along Fontanka. It was such a damp, dark evening. By six o'clock it was getting dusk—that is what we are coming to now. It was not raining but there was mist equal to a good rain. There were broad, long stretches of storm-cloud across the sky. There were masses of people walking along the canal bank, and, as ill-luck would have it, the people had such horrible depressing faces, drunken peasants, snub-nosed Finnish women, in high boots with nothing on their heads, workmen, cab-drivers, people like me out on some errand, boys, a carpenter's apprentice in a striped dressing-gown, thin and wasted-looking, with his face bathed in smutty oil, and a lock in his hand; a discharged soldier seven feet high waiting for somebody to buy a pen-knife or a bronze ring from him. That was the sort of crowd. It seems it was an hour when no other sort of people could be about. Fontanka is a canal for traffic! Such a mass of barges that one wonders how there can be room for them all! On the bridges there are women sitting with wet gingerbread and rotten apples, and they all of them looked so muddy, so drenched. It's dreary walking along Fontanka! The wet granite under one's feet, with tall, black, sooty houses on both sides. Fog underfoot and fog overhead. How dark and melancholy it was this evening!

When I went back to Gorohovoy Street it was already getting dark and they had begun lighting the gas. I have not been in Gorohovoy

Street for quite a long while, I haven't happened to go there. It's a noisy street! What shops, what magnificent establishments; everything is simply shining and resplendent; materials, flowers under glass, hats of all sorts with ribbons. One would fancy they were all displayed as a show—but no: you know there are people who buy all those things and present them to their wives. It's a wealthy street! There are a great many German bakers in Gorohovoy Street, so they must be a very prosperous set of people, too. What numbers of carriages roll by every minute; I wonder the paving is not worn out! Such gorgeous equipages, windows shining like mirrors, silk and velvet inside, and aristocratic footmen wearing epaulettes and carrying a sword; I glanced into all the carriages, there were always ladies in them dressed up to the nines, perhaps countesses and princesses. No doubt it was the hour when they were all hastening to balls and assemblies. It would be interesting to get a closer view of princesses and ladies of rank in general; it must be very nice; I have never seen them; except just as to-day, a passing glance at their carriages. I thought of you then. Ah, my darling, my own! When I think of you my heart begins aching! Why are you so unlucky, my Varinka? You are every bit as good as any of them. You are good, lovely, well-educated—why has such a cruel fortune fallen to your lot? Why does it happen that a good man is left forlorn and forsaken, while happiness seems thrust upon another? I know, I know, my dear, that it's wrong to think that, that it is free-thinking; but to speak honestly, to speak the whole truth, why is it fate, like a raven, croaks good fortune for one still unborn, while another begins life in the orphan asylum? And you know it often happens that Ivan the fool is favoured by fortune. "You, Ivan the fool, rummage in the family money bags, eat, drink and be merry, while you, So-and-so, can lick your lips. That's all you are fit for, you, brother So-and-so!" It's a sin, my darling, it's a sin to think like that, but sometimes one cannot help sin creeping into one's heart. You ought to be driving in such a carriage, my own little dearie. Generals should be craving the favour of a glance from you—not the likes of us; you ought to be dressed in silk and gold, instead of a little old linen gown. You would not be a thin, delicate little thing, as you are now, but like a little sugar figure, fresh, plump and rosy. And then, I should be happy simply to look in at you from the street through the brightly lighted windows; simply to see your shadow. The thought that you were happy and gay, my pretty little bird, would be enough to make me gay, too. But as it is, it is not enough that spiteful people have ruined you, a worthless profligate wretch goes and insults you. Because his coat hangs smartly on him, because he stares at you from a golden eyeglass, the shameless fellow, he can do what he likes, and one must listen to what he says indulgently, however unseemly it is! Wait a bit—is it really so, my pretty gentlemen? And why is all this? Because you are an orphan, because you are defenceless, because you have no powerful friend to help and protect you. And what can one call people who are ready to insult an orphan? They are worthless beasts, not men; simply trash. They are mere ciphers and have no real existence, of that I am convinced. That's what they are like, these people! And to my thinking, my own, the hurdy-gurdy man I met to-day in Gorohovoy Street is more worthy of respect than they are. He goes about the whole day long, hoping to get some wretched spare farthing for food, but he is his own master, he does earn his own living. He won't ask for charity; but he works like a machine wound up to give pleasure. "Here," he says, "I do what I can to give pleasure." He's a beggar, he's a beggar, it is true, he's a beggar all the same, but he's an honourable beggar; he is cold and weary, but still he works; though it's in his own way, still he works. And there are many honest men, my darling, who, though they earn very little in proportion to the amount and usefulness of their work, yet they bow down to no one and buy their bread of no one. Here I am just like that hurdy-gurdy man—that is, not at all like him. But in my own sense, in an honourable and aristocratic sense, just as he does, to the best of my abilities, I work as I can. That's enough about me, it's neither here nor there.

I speak of that hurdy-gurdy, my darling, because it has happened that I have felt my poverty twice as much to-day. I stopped to look at the hurdy-gurdy man. I was in such a mood that I stopped to distract my thoughts. I was standing there, and also two cab-drivers, a woman of some sort, and a little girl, such a grubby little thing. The hurdy-gurdy man stopped before the windows of a house. I noticed a little boy about ten years old; he would have been pretty, but he looked so ill, so frail, with hardly anything but his shirt on and almost barefoot, with his mouth open; he was listening to the music—like a child! He watched the German's dolls dancing, while his own hands and feet were numb with cold; he shivered and nibbled the edge of his sleeve. I noticed that he had a bit of paper of some sort in his hands. A gentleman passed and flung the hurdy-gurdy man some small coin, which fell straight into the box in a little garden in which the toy Frenchman was dancing with the ladies. At the clink of the coin the boy started, looked round and evidently thought that I had given the money. He ran up to me, his little hands trembling, his little voice trembling, he held the paper out to me and said, "A letter." I opened the letter; well, it was the usual thing, saying: "Kind gentleman, a mother's dying with three children hungry, so help us now, and as I am dying I will pray for you, my benefactor, in the next world for not forgetting my babes now." Well, what of it?—one could see what it meant, an everyday matter, but what could I give him? Well, I gave him nothing, and how sorry I was! The boy was poor, blue with cold, perhaps hungry, too, and not lying, surely he was not lying, I know that for certain. But what is wrong is that these horrid mothers don't take care of their children and send them out half naked in the cold to beg. Maybe she's a weak-willed, silly woman; and there's no one, maybe, to do anything for her, so she simply sits with her legs tucked under her, maybe she's really ill. Well, anyway, she should apply in the proper quarter. Though, maybe, she's a cheat and sends a hungry, delicate child out on purpose to deceive people, and makes him ill. And what sort of training is it for a poor boy? It simply hardens his heart, he runs about begging, people pass and have no time for him. Their hearts are stony, their words are cruel. "Get away, go along, you are naughty!" that is what he hears from everyone, and the child's heart grows hard, and in vain the poor little frightened boy shivers with cold like a fledgling fallen out of a broken nest. His hands and feet are frozen, he gasps for breath. The next thing he is coughing, before long disease, like an unclean reptile, creeps into his bosom and death is standing over him in some dark corner, no help, no escape, and that's his life! That is what life is like sometimes! Oh, Varinka, it's wretched to hear "for Christ's sake," and to pass by and give nothing, telling him "God will provide." Sometimes "for Christ's sake" is all right (it's not always the same, you know, Varinka), sometimes it's a long, drawling, habitual, practised, regular beggar's whine; it's not so painful to refuse one like that; he's an old hand, a beggar by profession. He's accustomed to it, one thinks; he can cope with it and knows how to cope with it. Sometimes "for Christ's sake" sounds unaccustomed, rude, terrible—as to-day, when I was taking the letter from the boy, a man standing close to the fence, not begging from everyone, said to me: "Give us a half-penny, sir, for Christ's sake," and in such a harsh, jerky voice that I started with a horrible feeling and did not give him a halfpenny, I hadn't one. Rich people don't like the poor to complain aloud of their harsh lot, they say they disturb them, they are troublesome! Yes, in-deed, poverty is always troublesome; maybe their hungry groans hin-der the rich from sleeping!

To make a confession, my own, I began to describe all this to you partly to relieve my heart but chiefly to give you an example of the fine style of my composition, for you have no doubt noticed yourself, my dear girl, that of late my style has been forming, but such a de-pression came over me that I began to pity my feelings to the depth of my soul, and though I know, my dear, that one gets no good by self-pity, yet one must do oneself justice in some way, and often, my own, for no reason whatever, one literally annihilates oneself, makes oneself of no account, and not worth a straw. And perhaps that is why it hap-pens that I am panic-stricken and persecuted like that poor boy who asked me for alms. Now I will tell you, by way of instance and illus-tration, Varinka; listen: hurrying to the office early in the morning, my own, I sometimes look at the town, how it wakes, gets up, begins smoking, hurrying with life, resounding—sometimes you feel so small before such a sight that it is as though someone had given you a flip on your intrusive nose and you creep along your way noiseless as water, and humble as grass, and hold your peace! Now just look into it and see what is going on in those great, black, smutty buildings. Get to the bottom of that and then judge whether one was right to abuse oneself for no reason and to be reduced to undignified mortification. Note, Varinka, that I am speaking figuratively, not in a literal sense. But let us look what is going on in those houses. There, in some smoky corner, in some damp hole, which, through poverty, passes as a lodg-ing, some workman wakes up from his sleep; and all night he has been dreaming of boots, for instance, which he had accidentally slit the day before, as though a man ought to dream of such nonsense! But he's an artisan, he's a shoemaker; it's excusable for him to think of nothing but his own subject. His children are crying and his wife is hungry; and it's not only shoemakers who get up in the morning like that, my own—that would not matter, and would not be worth

writing about, but this is the point, Varinka: close by in the same
house, in a storey higher or lower, a wealthy man in his gilded apartments dreams at night, it may be, of those same boots, that is, boots in
a different manner, in a different sense, but still boots, for in the sense
I am using the word, Varinka, everyone of us is a bit of a shoemaker,
my darling; and that would not matter, only it's a pity there is no one
at that wealthy person's side, no man who could whisper in his ear:
"Come, give over thinking of such things, thinking of nothing but
yourself, living for nothing but yourself; your children are healthy,
your wife is not begging for food. Look about you, can't you see some
object more noble to worry about than your boots?" That's what I
wanted to say to you in a figurative way, Varinka. Perhaps it's too free a
thought, my own, but sometimes one has that thought, sometimes it
comes to one and one cannot help its bursting out from one's heart in
warm language. And so it seems there was no reason to make oneself
so cheap, and to be scared by mere noise and uproar. I will conclude
by saying, Varinka, that perhaps you think what I am saying is unjust,
or that I'm suffering from a fit of the spleen, or that I have copied this
out of some book. No, my dear girl, you must dismiss that idea, it is
not that; I abominate injustice, I am not suffering from spleen, and
I've not copied anything out of a book—so there.

I went home in a melancholy frame of mind; I sat down to the
table and heated my teapot to have a glass or two of tea. Suddenly I
saw coming towards me Gorshkov, our poor lodger. I had noticed in
the morning that he kept hanging about round the other lodgers, and
trying to approach me. And I may say, in passing, Varinka, that they live
ever so much worse than I do. Yes, indeed, he has a wife and children!
So that if I were in his place I don't know what I should do. Well, my
Gorshkov comes up to me, bows to me, a running tear as always on
his eyelashes, he scrapes with his foot and can't utter a word. I made
him sit down on a chair—it was a broken one, it is true, but there was
no other. I offered him some tea. He refused from politeness, refused
for a long time, but at last he took a glass. He would have drunk it
without sugar, began apologising again, when I tried to persuade him
that he must have sugar; he argued for a long time, kept refusing, but
at last put the very smallest lump of sugar in his glass, and began declaring that his tea was extremely sweet. Oh, to what degradation
poverty does reduce people! "Well, my good friend, what is it?" I said.

"Well, it is like this, Makar Alexyevitch, my benefactor," he said, "show the mercy of the Lord, come to the help of my unhappy family; my wife and children have nothing to eat; think what it is for me, their father," said he. I tried to speak, but he interrupted me. "I am afraid of everyone here, Makar Alexyevitch—that is, not exactly afraid but as it were ashamed with them; they are all proud and haughty people. I would not have troubled you, my benefactor, I know that you have been in difficulties yourself, I know you can't give me much, but do lend me a trifle, and I make bold to ask you," said he, "because I know your kind heart. I know that you are in need yourself, that you know what trouble is now, and so your heart feels compassion." He ended by saying, "Forgive my boldness and unmannerliness, Makar Alexyevitch." I answered him that I should be heartily glad, but that I had nothing, absolutely nothing. "Makar Alexyevitch, sir," said he, "I am not asking for much, but you see it is like this—(then he flushed crimson)—my wife, my children, hungry—if only a ten-kopeck piece." Well, it sent a twinge to my heart. Why, I thought, they are worse off than I, even. Twenty kopecks was all I had left, and I was reckoning on it. I meant to spend it next day on my most pressing needs.

"No, my dear fellow, I can't, it is like this," I said.

"Makar Alexyevitch, my dear soul, what you like," he said, "if it is only ten kopecks."

Well, I took my twenty kopecks out of my box, Varinka, and gave it him; it's a good deed anyway! Ah! poverty! I had a good talk with him: "Why, how is it, my good soul," I said, "that you are in such want and yet you rent a room for five silver roubles?" He explained to me that he had taken it six months before and paid for it six months in advance; and since then circumstances had been such that the poor fellow does not know which way to turn. He expected his case would be over by this time. It's an unpleasant business. You see, Varinka, he has to answer for something before the court, he is mixed up in a case with a merchant who swindled the government over a contract; the cheat was discovered and the merchant was arrested and he's managed to implicate Gorshkov, who had something to do with it, too. But in reality Gorshkov was only guilty of negligence, of injudiciousness and unpardonable disregard of the interests of government. The case has been going on for some years. Gorshkov has had to face all sorts of difficulties.

"I'm not guilty, not in the least guilty of the dishonesty attributed to me," said Gorshkov; "I am not guilty of swindling and robbery."

This case has thrown a slur on his character; he has been turned out of the service, and though he has not been found guilty of any legal crime, yet, till he has completely cleared himself he cannot recover from the merchant a considerable sum of money due to him which is now the subject of dispute before the courts. I believe him, but the court won't take his word for it; the case is all in such a coil and a tangle that it would take a hundred years to unravel it. As soon as they untie one knot the merchant brings forward another and then another. I feel the deepest sympathy for Gorshkov, my own, I am very sorry for him. The man's out of work, he won't be taken anywhere without a character; all they had saved has been spent on food, the case is complicated and, meanwhile, they have had to live, and meanwhile, apropos of nothing and most inappropriately, a baby has been born, and that is an expense; his son fell ill—expense; died—expense; his wife is ill; he's afflicted with some disease of long standing—in fact, he has suffered, he has suffered to the utmost; he says, however, that he is expecting a favourable conclusion to his business in a day or two and that there is no doubt of it now. I am sorry for him, I am sorry for him; I am very sorry for him, Varinka. I was kind to him, he's a poor lost, scared creature; he needs a friend so I was kind to him. Well, good-bye, my dear one, Christ be with you, keep well. My darling! when I think of you it's like laying a salve on my sore heart. And though I suffer for you, yet it eases my heart to suffer for you.

Your true friend,
Makar Dyevushkin.

September 9.

My darling, Varvara Alexyevna,

I am writing to you almost beside myself. I have been thoroughly upset by a terrible incident. My head is going round. Ah, my own, what a thing I have to tell you now! This we did not foresee. No, I don't believe that I did not foresee it; I did foresee it all. I had a presentiment of it in my heart. I even dreamed of something of the kind a day or two ago.

This is what happened! I will write to you regardless of style, just as God puts it into my heart. I went to the office to-day. I went in, I sat down, I began writing. And you must know, Varinka, that I was writing yesterday too. Well, this is how it was: Timofey Ivanovitch came up to me and was pleased to explain to me in person, "The document is wanted in a hurry," said he. "Copy it very clearly as quickly as possible and carefully, Makar Alexyevitch," he said; "it goes to be signed to-day." I must observe, my angel, that I was not myself yesterday, I could not bear the sight of anything; such a mood of sadness and depression had come over me! It was cold in my heart and dark in my soul, you were in my mind all the while, my little dearie. But I set to work to copy it; I copied it clearly, legibly, only—I really don't know how to explain it—whether the devil himself muddled me, or whether it was ordained by some secret decree of destiny, or simply it had to be—but I left out a whole line, goodness knows what sense it made, it simply made none at all. They were late with the document yesterday and only took it to his Excellency to be signed to-day. I turned up this morning at the usual hour as though nothing had happened and settled myself beside Emelyan Ivanovitch. I must observe, my own, that of late I have been more abashed and ill at ease than ever. Of late I have given up looking at anyone. If I hear so much as a chair creak I feel more dead than alive. That is just how it was to-day, I sat down like a hedgehog crouched up and shrinking into myself, so that Efim Akimovitch (there never was such a fellow for teasing) said in the hearing of all: "Why are you sitting like a picture of misery, Makar Alexyevitch?" And he made such a grimace that everyone sitting near him and me went off into roars of laughter, and at my expense of course. And they went on and on. I put my hands over my ears, and screwed up my eyes, I sat without stirring. That's what I always do; they leave off the sooner. Suddenly I heard a noise, a fuss and a bustle; I heard—did not my ears deceive me?—they were mentioning me, asking for me, calling Dyevushkin. My heart began shuddering within me, and I don't know myself why I was so frightened; I only know I was panic-stricken as I had never been before in my life. I sat rooted to my chair—as though there were nothing the matter, as though it were not I. But they began getting nearer and nearer. And at last, close to my ear, they were calling, "Dyevushkin, Dyevushkin! Where is Dyevushkin?" I raised my eyes: Yevstafy Ivanovitch stood before me; he said: "Makar Alexyevitch, make haste to his Excellency! You've made a mistake in that document!" That was all he said, but it was enough; enough had been said, hadn't it, Varinka? Half dead, frozen with terror, not knowing what I was doing, I went—why, I was more dead than alive. I was led through one room, through a second, through a third, to his Excellency's study. I was in his presence! I can give you no exact account of what my thoughts were then. I saw his Excellency standing up, they were all standing round him. I believe I did not bow, I forgot. I was so flustered that my lips were trembling, my legs were trembling. And I had reason to be, my dear girl! To begin with, I was ashamed; I glanced into the looking-glass on the right hand and what I saw there was enough to send one out of one's mind. And in the second place, I had always tried to behave as if there were no such person in the world. So that his Excellency could hardly have been aware of my existence. Perhaps he may have heard casually that there was a clerk called Dyevushkin in the office, but he had never gone into the matter more closely.

He began, angrily: "What were you about, sir? Where were your eyes? The copy was wanted; it was wanted in a hurry, and you spoil it."

At this point, his Excellency turned to Yevstafy Ivanovitch. I could only catch a word here and there: "Negligence! Carelessness! You will get us into difficulties!" I would have opened my mouth to say something. I wanted to beg for forgiveness, but I could not; I wanted to run away, but dared not attempt it, and then . . . then, Varinka, something happened so awful that I can hardly hold my pen, for shame, even now. A button—the devil take the button—which was hanging by a thread on my uniform—suddenly flew off, bounced on the floor (I must have caught hold of it accidentally) with a jingle, the damned thing, and rolled straight to his Excellency's feet, and that in the midst of a profound silence! And that was my only justification, my sole apology, my only answer, all that I had to say to his Excellency! What followed was awful. His Excellency's attention was at once turned to my appearance and my attire. I remembered what I had seen in the looking-glass; I flew to catch the button! Some idiocy possessed me! I bent down, I tried to pick up the button—it twirled and rolled, I couldn't pick it up—in fact, I distinguished myself by my agility. Then I felt that my last faculties were deserting me, that everything, everything was lost, my whole reputation was lost, my dignity as a man was lost, and then, apropos of nothing, I had the voices of Teresa and Faldoni ringing in my ears. At last I picked up the button, stood up and drew myself erect, and if I were a fool I might at least have stood quietly with my hands at my sides! But not a bit of it. I began fitting the button to the torn threads as though it might hang on, and I actually smiled, actually smiled. His Excellency turned away at first, then he glanced at me again—I heard him say to Yevstafy Ivanovitch: "How is this? . . . Look at him! . . . What is he? . . . What sort of man? . . ." Ah, my own, think of that! "What is he?" and, "what sort of man?" I had distinguished myself! I heard Yevstafy Ivanovitch say: "No note against him, no note against him for anything, behaviour excellent, salary in accordance with his grade . . ." "Well, assist him in some way, let him have something in advance," says his Excellency. . . . "But he has had an advance," he said; "he has had his salary in advance for such and such a time. He is apparently in difficulties, but his conduct is good, and there is no note, there never has been a note against him."

My angel, I was burning, burning in the fires of hell! I was dying. . . .

"Well," said his Excellency, "make haste and copy it again; Dyevushkin, come here, copy it over again without a mistake; and listen . . ." Here his Excellency turned to the others, gave them various instructions and they all went away. As soon as they had gone, his Excellency hurriedly took out his notebook and from it took a hundred-rouble note. "Here," said he, "take it as you like, so far as I can help you, take it . . ." and he thrust it into my hand. I trembled, my angel, my whole soul was quivering; I don't know what happened to me, I tried to seize his hand to kiss it, but he flushed crimson, my darling, and—here I am not departing one hair's breadth from the truth, my own—he took my unworthy hand and shook it, just took it and shook it, as though I had been his equal, as though I had been just such a General as himself. "You can go," he said; "whatever I can do for you . . . don't make mistakes, but there, no great harm done this time."

Now Varinka, this is what I have decided. I beg you and Fedora, and if I had any children I should bid them, to pray every day and all our lives for his Excellency as they would not pray for their own father! I will say more, my dear, and I say it solemnly—pay attention, Varinka—I swear that however cast down I was and afflicted in the bitterest days of our misfortunes, looking at you, at your poverty, and at myself, my degradation and my uselessness, in spite of all that, I swear that the hundred roubles is not as much to me as that his Excellency deigned to shake hands with me, a straw, a worthless drunkard! By that he has restored me to myself, by that action he has lifted up my spirit, has made my life sweeter for ever, and I am firmly persuaded that, however sinful I may be before the Almighty, yet my prayers for the happiness and prosperity of his Excellency will reach His Throne! . . .

My darling! I am dreadfully upset, dreadfully excited now, my heart is beating as though it would burst out of my breast, and I feel, as it were, weak all over.

I am sending you forty-five roubles; I am giving the landlady twenty and leaving thirty-five for myself. For twenty I can put my wardrobe in order, and I shall have fifteen left to go on with. But just now all the impressions of the morning have shaken my whole being, I am going to lie down. I am at peace, quite at peace, though; only there is an ache in my heart and deep down within me I feel my soul quivering, trembling, stirring.

I am coming to see you: but now I am simply drunk with all these sensations. . . . God sees all, my Varinka, my priceless darling!

Your worthy friend,

Makar Dyevushkin.

September 10.

My dear Makar Alexyevitch,

I am unutterably delighted at your happiness and fully appreciate the goodness of your chief, my friend. So now you will have a little respite from trouble! But, for God's sake, don't waste your money again. Live quietly and as frugally as possible, and from to-day begin to put by a little that misfortune may not find you unprepared again. For goodness' sake don't worry about us. Fedora and I will get along somehow. Why have you sent us so much money, Maker Alexyevitch? We don't need it at all. We are satisfied with what we have. It is true we shall soon want money for moving from this lodging, but Fedora is hoping to be repaid an old debt that has been owing for years. I will keep twenty roubles, however, in case of extreme necessity. The rest I send you back. Please take care of your money, Makar Alexyevitch. Good-bye. Be at peace now, keep well and happy. I would write more to you, but I feel dreadfully tired; yesterday I did not get up all day. You do well to promise to come. Do come and see me, please, Makar Alexyevitch.

V. D.

September 11.

MY DEAR VARVARA ALEXYEVNA,

I beseech you, my own, not to part from me now, now when I am quite happy and contented with everything. My darling! Don't listen to Fedora and I will do anything you like; I shall behave well if only from respect to his Excellency. I will behave well and carefully; we will write to each other happy letters again, we will confide in each other our thoughts, our joys, our cares, if we have any cares; we will live together in happiness and concord. We'll study literature . . . My angel! My whole fate has changed and everything has changed for the better. The landlady has become more amenable. Teresa is more sensible, even Faldoni has become prompter. I have made it up with Ratazyaev. In my joy I went to him of myself. He's really a good fellow, Varinka, and all the harm that was said of him was nonsense. I have discovered that it was all an abominable slander. He had no idea whatever of describing us. He read me a new work of his. And as for his calling me a Lovelace, that was not an insulting or abusive name; he explained it to me. The word is taken straight from a foreign source and means *a clever fellow*, and to express it more elegantly, in a literary fashion, it means a young man you must be on the lookout with, you see, and nothing of that sort. It was an innocent jest, my angel! I'm an ignoramus and in my foolishness I was offended. In fact, it is I who apologised to him now. . . . And the weather is so wonderful to-day, Varinka, so fine. It is true there was a slight frost this morning, as though it had been sifted through a sieve. It was nothing. It only made the air a little fresher. I went to buy some boots, and I bought some wonderful boots. I walked along the Nevsky. I read the *Bee*.[14] Why! I am forgetting to tell you the principal thing.

It was this, do you see.

This morning I talked to Emelyan Ivanovitch and to Axentey Mihalovitch about his Excellency. Yes, Varinka, I'm not the only one he has treated so graciously. I am not the only one he has befriended, and he is known to all the world for the goodness of his heart. His praises are sung in very many quarters, and tears of gratitude are shed. An orphan girl was brought up in his house. He gave her a dowry and married her to a man in a good position, to a clerk on special commissions, who was in attendance on his Excellency. He installed a son of a widow in some office, and has done a great many other acts of kindness. I thought it my duty at that point to add my mite and described his Excellency's action in the hearing of all; I told them all and concealed nothing. I put my pride in my pocket, as though pride or dignity mattered in a case like that. So I told it aloud—to do glory to the good deeds of his Excellency! I spoke enthusiastically, I spoke with warmth, I did not blush, on the contrary, I was proud that I had such a story to tell. I told them about everything (only I was judiciously silent about you, Varinka), about my landlady, about Faldoni, about Ratazyaev, about my boots and about Markov—I told them everything. Some of them laughed a little, in fact, they all laughed a little. Probably they found something funny in my appearance, or it may have been about my boots—yes, it must have been about my boots. They could not have done it with any bad intention. It was nothing, just youthfulness, or perhaps because they are well-to-do people, but they could not jeer at what I said with any bad, evil intention. That is, what I said about his Excellency—that they could not do. Could they, Varinka?

I still can't get over it, my darling. The whole incident has so overwhelmed me! Have you got any firewood? Don't catch cold, Varinka; you can so easily catch cold. Ah, my own precious, you crush me with your sad thoughts. I pray to God, how I pray to Him for you, my dearie! For instance, have you got woollen stockings, and other warm underclothing? Mind, my darling, if you need anything, for God's sake don't wound your old friend, come straight to me. Now our bad times are over. Don't be anxious about me. Everything is so bright, so happy in the future!

It was a sad time, Varinka! But there, no matter, it's past! Years will pass and we shall sigh for that time. I remember my young days. Why, I often hadn't a farthing! I was cold and hungry, but light-hearted, that was all. In the morning I would walk along the Nevsky, see a pretty little face and be happy all day. It was a splendid, splendid time, my darling! It is nice to be alive, Varinka! Especially in Petersburg. I repented with tears in my eyes yesterday, and prayed to the Lord God to forgive me all my sins in that sad time: my repining, my liberal ideas, my drinking and despair. I remembered you with emotion in my prayers. You were my only support, Varinka, you were my only comfort, you cheered me on my way with counsel and good advice. I can never forget that, dear one. I have kissed all your letters to-day, my darling! Well, good-bye, my precious. They say that somewhere near here there is a sale of clothing. So I will make inquiries a little. Good-bye, my angel. Good-bye!

Your deeply devoted,
MAKAR DYEVUSHKIN.

September 15.

DEAR MAKAR ALEXYEVITCH,

I feel dreadfully upset. Listen what has happened here. I foresee something momentous. Judge yourself, my precious friend; Mr. Bykov is in Petersburg, Fedora met him. He was driving, he ordered the cab to stop, went up to Fedora himself and began asking where she was living. At first she would not tell him. Then he said, laughing, that he knew who was living with her. (Evidently Anna Fyodorovna had told him all about it.) Then Fedora could not contain herself and began upbraiding him on the spot, in the street, reproaching him, telling him he was an immoral man and the cause of all my troubles. He answered, that one who has not a halfpenny is bound to have misfortunes. Fedora answered that I might have been able to earn my own living, that I might have been married or else have had some situation, but that now my happiness was wrecked for ever and that I was ill besides, and would not live long. To this he answered that I was still young, that I had still a lot of nonsense in my head and that my virtues were getting a little tarnished (his words). Fedora and I thought he did not know our lodging when suddenly, yesterday, just after I had gone out to buy some things in the Gostiny Dvor he walked into our room. I believe he did not want to find me at home. He questioned Fedora at length concerning our manner of life, examined everything we had; he looked at my work; at last asked, "Who is this clerk you have made friends with?" At that moment you walked across the yard; Fedora pointed to you; he glanced and laughed; Fedora begged him to

go away, told him that I was unwell, as it was, from grieving, and that
to see him in our room would be very distasteful to me. He was silent
for a while; said that he had just looked in with no object and tried to
give Fedora twenty-five roubles; she, of course, did not take it.

What can it mean? What has he come to see us for? I cannot understand where he has found out all about us! I am lost in conjecture.
Fedora says that Axinya, her sister-in-law, who comes to see us, is
friendly with Nastasya the laundress, and Nastasya's cousin is a porter
in the office in which a friend of Anna Fyodorovna's nephew is serving. So has not, perhaps, some ill-natured gossip crept round? But it is
very possible that Fedora is mistaken; we don't know what to think. Is
it possible he will come to us again! The mere thought of it terrifies
me! When Fedora told me all about it yesterday, I was so frightened
that I almost fainted with terror! What more does he want? I don't
want to know him now! What does he want with me, poor me? Oh! I
am in such terror now, I keep expecting Bykov to walk in every
minute. What will happen to me, what more has fate in store for me?
For Christ's sake, come and see me now, Makar Alexyevitch. Do come,
for God's sake, come.

September 18.

My darling Varvara Alexyevna!

To-day an unutterably sad, quite unaccountable and unexpected
event has occurred here. Our poor Gorshkov (I must tell you, Varinka)
has had his character completely cleared. The case was concluded
some time ago and to-day he went to hear the final judgment. The case
ended very happily for him. He was fully exonerated of any blame for
negligence and carelessness. The merchant was condemned to pay
him a considerable sum of money, so that his financial position was
vastly improved and no stain left on his honour and things were better all round—in fact, he won everything he could have desired.

He came home at three o'clock this afternoon. He did not look
like himself, his face was white as a sheet, his lips quivered and he
kept smiling—he embraced his wife and children. We all flocked to
congratulate him. He was greatly touched by our action, he bowed
in all directions, shook hands with all of us several times. It even
seemed to me as though he were taller and more erect, and no

longer had that running tear in his eye. He was in such excitement, poor fellow. He could not stand still for two minutes: he picked up anything he came across, then dropped it again; and kept continually smiling and bowing, sitting down, getting up and sitting down again. Goodness knows what he said: "My honour, my honour, my good name, my children," and that was how he kept talking! He even shed tears. Most of us were moved to tears, too; Ratazyaev clearly wanted to cheer him up, and said, "What is honour, old man, when one has nothing to eat? The money, the money's the thing, old man, thank God for that!" and thereupon he slapped him on the shoulder. It seemed to me that Gorshkov was offended—not that he openly showed dissatisfaction, but he looked rather strangely at Ratazyaev and took his hand off his shoulder. And that had never happened before, Varinka! But characters differ. Now I, for instance, should not have stood on my dignity, at a time of such joy; why, my own, sometimes one is too liberal with one's bows and almost cringing from nothing but excess of good-nature and soft-heartedness. . . . However, no matter about me!

"Yes," he said, "the money is a good thing too, thank God, thank God!" And then all the time we were with him he kept repeating, "Thank God, thank God."

His wife ordered a rather nicer and more ample dinner. Our landlady cooked for them herself. Our landlady is a good-natured woman in a way. And until dinner-time Gorshkov could not sit still in his seat. He went into the lodgers' rooms, without waiting to be invited. He just went in, smiled, sat down on the edge of a chair, said a word or two, or even said nothing, and went away again. At the naval man's he even took a hand at cards; they made up a game with him as fourth. He played a little, made a muddle of it, played three or four rounds and threw down the cards. "No," he said, "you see, I just looked in, I just looked in," and he went away from them. He met me in the passage, took both my hands, looked me straight in the face, but so strangely; then shook hands with me and walked away, and kept smiling, but with a strange, painful smile like a dead man. His wife was crying with joy; everything was cheerful as though it were a holiday. They soon had dinner. After dinner he said to his wife: "I tell you what, my love, I'll lie down a little," and he went to his bed. He called his little girl, put his hand on her head, and for a long time he was stroking the child's head. Then he turned to his wife again, "And what of Petinka? our Petya!" he said. "Petinka?" . . . His wife crossed herself and answered that he was dead. "Yes, yes, I know all about it. Petinka is now in the Kingdom of Heaven." His wife saw that he was not himself, that what had happened had completely upset him, and she said to him, "You ought to have a nap, my love." "Yes, very well, I will directly . . . just a little," then he turned away, lay still for a bit, then turned round, tried to say something. His wife could not make out what he said, and asked him, "What it is, my dear?" and he did not answer. She waited a little, "Well, he's asleep," she thought, and went into the landlady's for an hour. An hour later she came back, she saw her husband had not woken up and was not stirring. She thought he was asleep, and she sat down and began working at something. She said that for half an hour she was so lost in musing that she did not know what she was thinking about, all she can say is that she did not think of her husband. But suddenly she was roused by the feeling of uneasiness, and what struck her first of all was the death-like silence in the room. . . . She looked at the bed and saw that here husband was lying in the same position. She went up to him, pulled down the quilt and looked at him—and he was already cold— he was dead, my darling. Gorshkov was dead, he had died suddenly, as though he had been killed by a thunder-bolt. And why he died, God only knows. It was such a shock to me, Varinka, that I can't get over it now. One can't believe that a man could die so easily. He was such a poor, unlucky fellow, that Gorshkov! And what a fate, what a fate! His wife was in tears and panic-stricken. The little girl crept away into a corner. There is such a hubbub going on, they will hold a post-mortem and inquest . . . I can't tell you just what. But the pity of it, oh, the pity of it! It's sad to think that in reality one does not know the day or the hour . . . One dies so easily for no reason. . . .

Your
MAKAR DYEVUSHKIN.

September 19.

DEAR VARVARA ALEXYEVNA,

I hasten to inform you, my dear, that Ratazyaev has found me work with a writer. Someone came to him, and brought him such a fat manuscript—thank God, a lot of work. But it's so illegibly written that I don't know how to set to work on it: they want it in a hurry. It's all written in such a way that one does not understand it. . . . They have agreed to pay forty kopecks the sixteen pages. I write you all this, my own, because now I shall have extra money. And now, good-bye, my darling, I have come straight from work.

Your faithful friend,
MAKAR DYEVUSHKIN.

September 23.

MY DEAR FRIEND, MAKAR ALEXYEVITCH,

For three days I have not written you a word, and I have had a great many anxieties and worries.

The day before yesterday Bykov was here. I was alone, Fedora had gone off somewhere. I opened the door to him, and was so frightened when I saw him that I could not move. I felt that I turned pale. He walked in as he always does, with a loud laugh, took a chair and sat down. For a long while I could not recover myself. At last I sat down in the corner to my work. He even left off laughing. I believe my appearance impressed him. I have grown so thin of late, my eyes and my cheeks are hollow, I was as white as a sheet . . . it would really be hard for anyone to recognise me who had known me a year ago. He looked long and intently at me; then at last he began to be lively again, said something or other; I don't know what I answered, and he laughed again. He stayed a whole hour with me; talked to me a long time; asked me some questions. At last just before leaving, he took me by the hand and said (I write you it word for word): "Varvara Alexye-vitch, between ourselves, be it said, your relation and my intimate friend, Anna Fyodorovna, is a very nasty woman" (then he used an unseemly word about her). "She led your cousin astray, and ruined you. I behaved like a rascal in that case, too; but after all, it's a thing that happens every day." Then he laughed heartily. Then he observed that he was not great at fine speeches, and that most of what he had to explain, about which the obligations of gentlemanly feeling forebade him to be silent, he had told me already, and that in brief words he would come to the rest. Then he told me he was asking my hand in marriage, that he thought it his duty to restore my good name, that he was rich, that after the wedding he would take me away to his estates in the steppes, that he wanted to go coursing hares there; that he would never come back to Petersburg again, because it was horrid in Petersburg; that he had here in Petersburg—as he expressed it— a good-for-nothing nephew whom he had sworn to deprive of the estate, and it was just for that reason in the hope of having legitimate heirs that he sought my hand, that it was the chief cause of his courtship. Then he observed that I was living in a very poor way: and it was no wonder I was ill living in such a slum; predicted that I should certainly die if I stayed there another month; said that lodgings in Petersburg were horrid, and finally asked me if I wanted anything.

I was so overcome at his offer that, I don't know why, I began crying. He took my tears for gratitude and told me he had always been sure I was a good, feeling, and educated girl, but that he had not been able to make up his mind to take this step till he had found out about my present behaviour in full detail. Then he asked me about you, said that he had heard all about it, that you were a man of good principles, that he did not want to be indebted to you and asked whether five hundred roubles would be enough for all that you had done for me. When I explained to him that what you had done for me no money could repay, he said that it was all nonsense, that that was all romantic stuff out of novels, that I was young and read poetry, that novels were the ruin of young girls, that books were destructive of morality and that he could not bear books of any sort, he advised me to wait till I was his age and then talk about people. "Then," he added, "you will know what men are like." Then he said I was to think over his offer thoroughly, that he would very much dislike it if I were to take such an important step thoughtlessly; he added that thoughtlessness and impulsiveness were the ruin of inexperienced youth, but that he quite hoped for a favourable answer from me, but that in the opposite event, he should be forced to marry some Moscow shopkeeper's daughter, "because," he said, "I have sworn that good-for-nothing nephew shall not have the estate."

He forced five hundred roubles into my hands, as he said, "to buy sweetmeats". He said that in the country I should grow as round as a bun, that with him I should be living on the fat of the land, that he had a terrible number of things to see to now, that he was dragging about all day on business, and that he had just slipped in to see me between his engagements. Then he went away.

I thought for a long time, I pondered many things, I wore myself out thinking, my friend; at last I made up my mind. My friend, I shall marry him. I ought to accept his offer. If anyone can rescue me from my shame, restore my good name, and ward off poverty, privation and misfortune from me in the future, it is he and no one else. What more can one expect from the future, what more can one expect from fate? Fedora says I must not throw away my good fortune; she says, if this isn't good fortune, what is? Anyway, I can find no other course for me, my precious friend. What am I to do? I have ruined my health with work as it is; I can't go on working continually. Go into a family? I should pine away with depression, besides I should be of no use to anyone. I am of a sickly constitution, and so I shall always be a burden on other people. Of course I am not going into a paradise, but what am I to do, my friend, what am I to do? What choice have I?

I have not asked your advice. I wanted to think it over alone. The decision you have just read is unalterable, and I shall immediately inform Bykov of it, he is pressing me to answer quickly. He said that his business would not wait, that he must be off, and that he couldn't put it off for nonsense. God knows whether I shall be happy, my fate is in His holy, inscrutable power, but I have made up my mind. They say Bykov is a kind-hearted man: he will respect me; perhaps I, too, shall respect him. What more can one expect from such a marriage?

I will let you know about everything, Makar Alexyevitch. I am sure you will understand all my wretchedness. Do not try to dissuade me from my intention. Your efforts will be in vain. Weigh in your own mind all that has forced me to this step. I was very much distressed at first, but now I am calmer. What is before me, I don't know. What will be, will be; as God wills! . . .

Bykov has come, I leave this letter unfinished. I wanted to tell you a great deal more. Bykov is here already!

September 23.

MY DARLING VARVARA ALEXYEVNA,

I hasten to answer you, my dear; I hasten to tell you, my precious, that I am dumbfounded. It all seems so . . . Yesterday we buried Gorshkov. Yes, that is so, Varinka, that is so; Bykov has behaved honourably; only, you see, my own . . . so you have consented. Of course, everything is according to God's will; that is so, that certainly must be so—that is, it certainly must be God's will in this; and the providence of the Heavenly Creator is blessed, of course, and inscrutable, and it is fate too, and they are the same. Fedora sympathises with you too. Of course you will be happy now, my precious, you will live in comfort, my darling, my little dearie, little angel and light of my eyes—only Varinka, how can it be so soon? . . . Yes, business. . . . Mr. Bykov has business—of course, everyone has business, and he may have it too. . . . I saw him as he came out from you. He's a good-looking man, good-looking; a very good-looking man, in fact. Only there is something queer about it, the point is not whether he is a good-looking man. Indeed, I am not myself at all. Why, how are we to go on writing to one another? I . . . I shall be left alone. I am weighing everything, my angel, I am weighing everything as you write to me, I am weighing it all in my heart, the reasons. I had just finished copying the twentieth quire, and meanwhile these events have come upon us! Here you are going a journey, my darling, you will have to buy all sorts of things, shoes of all kinds, a dress, and I know just the shop in Gorohovoy Street; do you remember how I described it to you? But no! How can you, Varinka? what are you about? You can't go away now, it's quite impossible, utterly impossible. Why, you will have to buy a great many things and get a carriage. Besides, the weather is so awful now; look, the rain is coming down in bucketfuls, and such soaking rain, too, and what's more . . . what's more, you will be cold, my angel; your little heart will be cold! Why, you are afraid of anyone strange, and yet you go. And to whom am I left, all alone here? Yes! Here, Fedora says that there is great happiness in store for you . . . but you know she's a headstrong woman, she wants to be the death of me. Are you going to the evening service to-night, Varinka? I would go to have a look at you. It's true, perfectly true, my darling, that you are a well-educated, virtuous and feeling girl, only he had much better marry the shopkeeper's daughter! Don't you think so, my precious? He had better marry the shopkeeper's daughter! I will come to see you, Varinka, as soon as it gets dark, I shall just run in for an hour. It will get dark early to-day, then I shall run in. I shall certainly come to you for an hour this evening, my darling. Now you are expecting Bykov, but when he goes, then . . . Wait a bit, Varinka, I shall run across . . .

Makar Dyevushkin.

September 27.

MY DEAR FRIEND, MAKAR ALEXYEVITCH,

Mr. Bykov says I must have three dozen linen chemises. So I must make haste and find seamstresses to make two dozen, and we have very little time. Mr. Bykov is angry and says there is a great deal of bother over these rags. Our wedding is to be in five days, and we are to set off the day after the wedding. Mr. Bykov is in a hurry, he says we must not waste much time over nonsense. I am worn out with all this fuss and can hardly stand on my feet. There is a terrible lot to do, and perhaps it would have been better if all this had not happened. Another thing: we have not enough net or lace, so we ought to buy some more, for Mr. Bykov says he does not want his wife to go about like a cook, and that I simply must "wipe all the country ladies' noses for them". That was his own expression. So, Makar Alexyevitch, please apply to Madame Chiffon in Gorohovoy Street, and ask her first to send us some seamstresses, and secondly, to be so good as to come herself. I am ill to-day. It's so cold in our new lodging and the disorder is terrible. Mr. Bykov's aunt can scarcely breathe, she is so old. I am afraid she may die before we set off, but Mr. Bykov says that it is nothing, she'll wake up. Everything in the house is in the most awful confusion. Mr. Bykov is not living with us, so the servants are racing about in all directions, goodness knows where. Sometimes Fedora is the only one to wait on us, and Mr. Bykov's valet, who looks after everything, has disappeared no one knows where for the last three days. Mr. Bykov comes to see us every morning, and yesterday he beat the superintendent of the house, for which he got into trouble with the police. I have not even had anyone to take my letters to you. I am writing by post. Yes! I had almost forgotten the most important point. Tell Madame Chiffon to be sure and change the net, matching it with the pattern she had yesterday, and to come to me herself to show the new, and tell her, too, that I have changed my mind about the embroidery, that it must be done in crochet; and another thing, that the letters for the monogram on the handkerchiefs must be done in tambour stitch, do you hear? Tambour stitch and not satin stitch. Mind you don't forget that it is to be tambour stitch! Something else I had almost forgotten! For God's sake tell her also that the leaves on the pelerine are to be raised and that the tendrils and thorns are to be in appliqué; and, then,

the collar is to be edged with lace, or a deep frill. Please tell her, Makar
Alexvevitch.

Your
V. D.

P.S.—I am so ashamed of worrying you with all my errands. The
day before yesterday you were running about all the morning. But
what can I do! There's no sort of order in the house here, and I am not
well. So don't be vexed with me, Makar Alexyevitch. I'm so miserable.
Oh, how will it end, my friend, my dear, my kind Makar Alexyevitch?
I'm afraid to look into my future. I have a presentiment of something
and am living in a sort of delirium.

P.P.S.—For God's sake, my friend, don't forget anything of what I
have told you. I am so afraid you will make a mistake. Remember tambour, not satin stitch.

V. D.

September 27.

Dear Varvara Alexyevna,

I have carried out all your commissions carefully. Madame Chiffon
says that she had thought herself of doing them in tambour stitch; that
it is more correct, or something, I don't know, I didn't take it in properly. And you wrote about a frill, too, and she talked about the frill.
Only I have forgotten, my darling, what she told me about the frill. All
I remember is, that she said a great deal; such a horrid woman! What
on earth was it? But she will tell you about it herself. I have become
quite dissipated, Varinka, I have not even been to the office to-day. But
there's no need for you to be in despair about that, my own. I am ready
to go the round of all the shops for your peace of mind. You say you are
afraid to look into the future. But at seven o'clock this evening you will
know all about it. Madame Chiffon is coming to see you herself. So
don't be in despair; you must hope for the best, everything will turn
out for the best—so there. Well, now, I keep thinking about that cursed
frill—ugh! bother that frill! I should have run round to you, my angel,
I should have looked in, I should certainly have looked in; I have been
to the gates of your house, once or twice. But Bykov—that is, I mean,
Mr. Bykov—is always so cross, you see it doesn't . . . Well, what of it!

Makar Dyevushkin.

September 28.

MY DEAR MAKAR ALEXYEVITCH,

For God's sake, run at once to the jeweller's: tell him that he must not make the pearl and emerald ear-rings. Mr. Bykov says that it is too gorgeous, that it's too expensive. He is angry; he says, that as it is, it is costing him a pretty penny, and we are robbing him, and yesterday he said that if he had known beforehand and had any notion of the expense he would not have bound himself. He says that as soon as we are married we will set off at once, that we shall have no visitors and that I needn't hope for dancing and flirtation, and that the holidays are a long way off. That's how he talks. And, God knows, I don't want anything of that sort! Mr. Bykov ordered everything himself. I don't dare to answer him: he is so hasty. What will become of me?

V. D.

September 28.

MY DARLING VARVARA ALEXYEVNA,

I—that is, the jeweller said—very good; and I meant to say at first that I have been taken ill and cannot get up. Here now, at such an urgent, busy time I have caught a cold, the devil take it! I must tell you, to complete my misfortunes, his Excellency was pleased to be stern and was very angry with Emelyan Ivanovitch and scolded him, and he was quite worn out at last, poor man. You see, I tell you about everything. I wanted to write to you about something else, but I am afraid to trouble you. You see, I am a foolish, simple man, Varinka, I just write what comes, so that, maybe, you may—— But there, never mind!

Your

MAKAR DYEVUSHKIN.

September 29.

VARVARA ALEXYEVITCH, MY OWN,

I saw Fedora to-day, my darling, she says that you are to be married to-morrow, and that the day after you are setting off, and that Mr. Bykov is engaging horses already. I have told you about his Excellency already, my darling. Another thing—I have checked the bills from the shop in Gorohovoy; it is all correct, only the things are very dear. But why is Mr. Bykov angry with you? Well, may you be happy, Varinka! I am glad, yes, I shall be glad if you are happy. I should come to the church, my dear, but I've got lumbago. So I keep on about our letters; who will carry them for us, my precious? Yes! You have been a good friend to Fedora, my own! You have done a good deed, my dear, you have done quite right. It's a good deed! And God will bless you for every good deed. Good deeds never go unrewarded, and virtue will sooner or later be rewarded by the eternal justice of God. Varinka! I wanted to write to you a great deal; I could go on writing and writing every minute, every hour! I have one of your books still, *Byelkin's Stories*. I tell you what, Varinka, don't take it away, make me a present of it, my darling. It is not so much that I want to read it. But you know yourself, my darling, winter is coming on: the evenings will be long; it will be sad, and then I could read. I shall move from my lodgings, Varinka, into your old room and lodge with Fedora. I would not part from that honest woman for anything now; besides, she is such a hard-working woman. I looked at your empty room carefully yesterday. Your embroidery frame has remained untouched, just as it was with embroidery on it. I examined your needlework; there were all sorts of little scraps left there, you had begun winding thread on one of my letters. On the little table I found a piece of paper with the words "Dear Makar Alexyevitch, I hasten—" and that was all. Someone must have interrupted you at the most interesting place. In the corner behind the screen stands your little bed. . . . Oh, my darling!!! Well, good-bye, good-bye, send me some answer to this letter quickly.

MAKAR DYEVUSHKIN.

September 30.

MY PRECIOUS FRIEND, MAKAR ALEXYEVITCH,

Everything is over! My lot is cast; I don't know what it will be, but I am resigned to God's will. To-morrow we set off. I say good-bye to you for the last time, my precious one, my friend, my benefactor, my own! Don't grieve for me, live happily, think of me, and may God's blessing descend on us! I shall often remember you in my thoughts, in my prayers. So this time is over! I bring to my new life little consolation from the memories of the past; the more precious will be my memory of you, the more precious will your memory be to my heart. You are my one friend; you are the only one there who loved me. You know I have seen it all, I know how you love me! You were happy in a smile from me and a few words from my pen. Now you will have to get used to being without me. How will you do, left alone here? To whom am I leaving you my kind, precious, only friend! I leave you the book, the embroidery frame, the unfinished letter; when you look at those first words, you must read in your thoughts all that you would like to hear or read from me, all that I should have written to you; and what I could not write now! Think of your poor Varinka who loves you so truly. All your letters are at Fedora's in the top drawer of a chest. You write that you are ill and Mr. Bykov will not let me go out anywhere to-day. I will write to you, my friend, I promise; but, God alone knows what may happen. And so we are saying good-bye now for ever, my friend, my darling, my own, for ever. . . . Oh, if only I could embrace you now! Good-bye, my dear; good-bye, good-bye. Live happily, keep well. My prayers will be always for you. Oh! how sad I am, how weighed down in my heart. Mr. Bykov is calling me.

Your ever loving
V.

P.S.—My soul is so full, so full of tears now . . . tears are choking me, rending my heart. Good-bye. Oh, God, how sad I am!

Remember me, remember your poor Varinka.

VARINKA, MY DARLING, MY PRECIOUS,

You are being carried off, you are going. They had better have torn the heart out of my breast than take you from me! How could you do it? Here you are weeping and going away! Here I have just had a letter from you, all smudged with tears. So you don't want to go; so you are being taken away by force; so you are sorry for me; so you love me! And with whom will you be now? Your little heart will be sad, sick and cold out there. It will be sapped by misery, torn by grief. You will die out there, they will put you in the damp earth; there will be no one to weep for you there! Mr. Bykov will be always coursing hares. Oh, my darling, my darling! What have you brought yourself to? How could you make up your mind to such a step? What have you done, what have you done, what have you done to yourself? They'll drive you to your grave out there; they will be the death of you, my angel. You know you are as weak as a little feather, my own! And where was I, old fool, where were my eyes! I saw the child did not know what she was doing, the child was simply in a fever! I ought simply—— But no, fool, fool, I thought nothing and saw nothing, as though that were the right thing, as though it had nothing to do with me; and went running after frills and flounces too. . . . No, Varinka, I shall get up; tomorrow, maybe, I shall be better and then I shall get up! . . . I'll throw myself under the wheels, my precious, I won't let you go away! Oh, no, how can it be? By what right is all this done? I will go with you; I will run after your carriage if you won't take me, and will run my hardest as long as there is a breath left in my body. And do you know what it is like where you are going, my darling? Maybe you don't know—if so, ask me! There it is, the steppe, my own, the steppe, the bare steppe; why, it is as bare as my hand; there, there are hard-hearted peasant women and uneducated drunken peasants. There the leaves are falling off the trees now, there it is cold and rainy—and you are going there! Well, Mr. Bykov has something to do there: he will be with his hares; but what about you? Do you want to be a grand country lady, Varinka? But, my little cherub! you should just look at yourself. Do you look like a grand country lady? . . . Why, how can such a thing be, Varinka? To whom am I going to write letters, my darling? Yes! You must take that into consideration, my darling— you must ask yourself, to whom is he going to write letters? Whom am I to call my darling; whom am I to call by that loving name, where am I to find you afterwards, my angel? I shall die, Varinka, I shall certainly die; my heart will never survive such a calamity! I loved you like God's sunshine, I loved you like my own daughter, I loved everything in you, my darling, my own! And I lived only for you! I worked and copied papers, and walked and went about and put my thoughts down on paper, in friendly letters, all because you, my precious, were living here opposite, close by; perhaps you did not know it, but that was how it was. Yes, listen, Varinka; you only think, my sweet darling, how is it possible that you should go away from us? You can't go away, my own, it is impossible; it's simply utterly impossible! Why, it's raining, you are delicate, you will catch cold. Your carriage will be wet through;

it will certainly get wet through. It won't get beyond the city gates before it will break down; it will break down on purpose. They make these
carriages in Petersburg so badly: I know all those carriage makers; they
are only fit to turn out a little model, a plaything, not anything solid.
I'll take my oath they won't build it solid. I'll throw myself on my
knees before Mr. Bykov: I will explain to him, I will explain everything, and you, my precious, explain to him, make him see reason! Tell
him that you will stay and that you cannot go away! . . . Ah, why
didn't he marry a shopkeeper's daughter in Moscow? He might just as
well have married her! The shopkeeper's daughter would have suited
him much better, she would have suited him much better. I know
why! And I should have kept you here. What is he to you, my darling,
what is Bykov? How has he suddenly become so dear to you? Perhaps
it's because he is always buying you frills and flounces. But what are
frills and flounces? What good are frills and flounces? Why, it is nonsense, Varinka! Here it is a question of a man's life: and you know a
frill's a rag; it's a rag, Varinka, a frill is; why, I shall buy you frills myself, that's all the reward I get; I shall buy them for you, my darling,
I know a shop, that's all the reward you let me hope for, my cherub,
Varinka. Oh Lord! Lord! So, you are really going to the steppes with
Mr. Bykov, going away never to return! Ah, my darling! . . . No, you
must write to me again, you must write another letter about everything, and when you go away you must write to me from there, or
else, my heavenly angel, this will be the last letter and you know that
this cannot be, this cannot be the last letter! Why, how can it be, so
suddenly, actually the last? Oh no, I shall write and you will write. . . .
Besides, I am acquiring a literary style. . . . Oh, my own, what does
style matter, now? I don't know, now, what I am writing, I don't know
at all, I don't know and I don't read it over and I don't improve the
style. I write only to write, only to go on writing to you . . . my darling, my own, my Varinka. . . .

APPENDIX

THE PEASANT MAREY*

TRANSLATED BY KENNETH LANTZ

BUT READING ALL THESE professions de foi is a bore, I think, and so I'll tell you a story; actually, it's not even a story, but only a reminiscence of something that happened long ago and that, for some reason, I would very much like to recount here and now, as a conclusion to our treatise on the People. At the time I was only nine years old. . . . But no, I'd best begin with the time I was twenty-nine.

It was the second day of Easter Week. The air was warm, the sky was blue, the sun was high, warm, and bright, but there was only gloom in my heart. I was wandering behind the prison barracks, examining and counting off the pales in the sturdy prison stockade, but I had lost even the desire to count, although such was my habit. It was the second day of "marking the holiday" within the prison compound; the prisoners were not taken out to work; many were drunk; there were shouts of abuse, and quarrels were constantly breaking out in all corners. Disgraceful, hideous songs; card games in little nooks under the bunks; a few convicts, already beaten half to death by sentence of their comrades for their particular rowdiness, lay on bunks covered with sheepskin coats until such time as they might come to their senses; knives had already been drawn a few times—all this, in two days of holiday, had worn me out to the point of illness. Indeed, I never could endure the drunken carousals of peasants without being disgusted, and here, in this place, particularly. During these days even the prison staff did not look in; they made no searches, nor did they check for alcohol, for they realized that once a year they had to allow even these outcasts to have a spree; otherwise it might be even worse. At last, anger welled up in my heart. I ran across the Pole

*From Fyodor Dostoevsky, A Writer's Diary, Vol. 1, 1873–1876, translated by Kenneth Lantz (Evanston, IL: Northwestern University Press). Copyright © 1994 by Northwestern University Press. Reprinted by permission of the publisher.

M-cki, a political prisoner; he gave me a gloomy look, his eyes glittering and his lips trembling: "Je hais ces brigands!" he muttered, gritting his teeth, and passed me by. I returned to the barrack despite the fact that a quarter-hour before I had fled it half-demented when six healthy peasants had thrown themselves, as one man, on the drunken Tatar Gazin and had begun beating him to make him settle down; they beat him senselessly with such blows as might have killed a camel; but they knew that it was not easy to kill this Hercules and so they didn't hold back. And now when I returned to the barracks I noticed Gazin lying senseless on a bunk in the corner showing scarcely any signs of life; he was lying under a sheepskin coat, and everyone passed him by in silence: although they firmly hoped he would revive the next morning, still, "with a beating like that, God forbid, you could finish a man off." I made my way to my bunk opposite a window with an iron grating and lay down on my back, my hands behind my head, and closed my eyes. I liked to lie like that: a sleeping man was left alone, while at the same time one could daydream and think. But dreams did not come to me; my heart beat restlessly, and M-cki's words kept echoing in my ears: "Je hais ces brigands!" However, why describe my feelings? Even now at night I sometimes dream of that time, and none of my dreams are more agonizing. Perhaps you will also notice that until today I have scarcely ever spoken in print of my prison life; I wrote *Notes from the House of the Dead* fifteen years ago using an invented narrator, a criminal who supposedly had murdered his wife. (I might add, by the way, that many people supposed and are even now quite firmly convinced that I was sent to hard labor for the murder of my wife.)

Little by little I lost myself in reverie and imperceptibly sank into memories of the past. All through my four years in prison I continually thought of all my past days, and I think I relived the whole of my former life in my memories. These memories arose in my mind of themselves; rarely did I summon them up consciously. They would begin from a certain point, some little thing that was often barely perceptible, and then bit by bit they would grow into a finished picture, some strong and complete impression. I would analyze these impressions, adding new touches to things experienced long ago; and the main thing was that I would refine them, continually refine them, and in this consisted my entire entertainment. This time, for some reason, I suddenly recalled a moment of no apparent significance from my early childhood when I was only nine years old, a moment that I thought I had completely forgotten; but at that time I was particularly fond of memories of my very early childhood. I recalled one August at our home in the country: the day was clear and dry, but a bit chilly and windy; summer was on the wane, and soon I would have to go back to Moscow to spend the whole winter in boredom over my French lessons; and I was so sorry to have to leave the country. I passed by the granaries, made my way down into the gully, and climbed up into the Dell—that was what we called a thick patch of bushes that stretched from the far side of the gully to a grove of trees. And so I make my way deeper into the bushes and can hear that some thirty paces away a solitary peasant is plowing in the clearing. I know he's plowing up the steep side of a hill and his horse finds it heavy going; from time to time I hear his shout, "Gee-up!" I know almost all our peasants, but don't recognize the one who's plowing; and what difference does it make, anyway, since I'm quite absorbed in my own business. I also have an occupation: I'm breaking off a switch of walnut to lash frogs; walnut switches are so lovely and quite without flaws, so much better than birch ones. I'm also busy with bugs and beetles, collecting them; some are very pretty; I love the small, nimble, red-and-yellow lizards with the little black spots as well, but I'm afraid of snakes. I come across snakes far less often than lizards, however. There aren't many mushrooms here; you have to go into the birch wood for mushrooms, and that's what I have in mind. I liked nothing better than the forest with its mushrooms and wild berries, its insects, and its birds, hedgehogs, and squirrels, and with its damp aroma of rotting leaves that I loved so. And even now, as I write this, I can catch the fragrance from our stand of birches in the country: these impressions stay with you all your life. Suddenly, amid the deep silence, I clearly and distinctly heard a shout: "There's a wolf!" I screamed, and, beside myself with terror, crying at the top of my voice, I ran out into the field, straight at the plowing peasant.

It was our peasant Marey. I don't know if there is such a name, but everyone called him Marey. He was a man of about fifty, heavy-set, rather tall, with heavy streaks of gray in his bushy, dark-brown beard. I knew him but had scarcely ever had occasion to speak to him before.

He even stopped his little filly when he heard my cry, and when I rushed up to him and seized his plow with one hand and his sleeve with the other, he saw how terrified I was.

"It's a wolf!" I cried, completely out of breath.

Instinctively he jerked his head to look around, for an instant almost believing me.

"Where's the wolf?"

"I heard a shout. . . . Someone just shouted, 'Wolf' " . . . I babbled.

"What do you mean, lad? There's no wolf; you're just hearing things. Just take a look. What would a wolf be doing here?" he murmured, reassuring me. But I was all a-tremble and clung to his coat even more tightly; I suppose I was very pale as well. He looked at me with an uneasy smile, evidently concerned and alarmed for me.

"Why you took a real fright, you did!" he said, wagging his head. "Never mind, now, my dear. What a fine lad you are!"

He stretched out his hand and suddenly stroked my cheek.

"Never mind, now, there's nothing to be afraid of. Christ be with you. Cross yourself, lad." But I couldn't cross myself; the corners of my mouth were trembling, and I think this particularly struck him. He quietly stretched out a thick, earth-soiled finger with a black nail and gently touched it to my trembling lips.

"Now, now," he smiled at me with a broad, almost maternal smile. "Lord, what a dreadful fuss. Dear, dear, dear!"

At last I realized that there was no wolf and that I must have imagined hearing the cry of "Wolf." Still, it had been such a clear and distinct shout; two or three times before, however, I had imagined such cries (not only about wolves), and I was aware of that. (Later, when childhood passed, these hallucinations did as well.)

"Well, I'll be off now," I said, making it seem like a question and looking at him shyly.

"Off with you, then, and I'll keep an eye on you as you go. Can't let the wolf get you!" he added, still giving me a maternal smile. "Well, Christ be with you, off you go." He made the sign of the cross over me, and crossed himself. I set off, looking over my shoulder almost every ten steps. Marey continued to stand with his little filly, looking after me and nodding every time I looked around. I confess I felt a little ashamed at taking such a fright. But I went on, still with a good deal of fear of the wolf, until I had gone up the slope of the gully to the first threshing barn; and here the fear vanished entirely, and suddenly our dog Volchok came dashing out to meet me. With Volchok I felt totally reassured, and I turned toward Marey for the last time; I could no longer make out his face clearly, but I felt that he was still smiling kindly at me and nodding. I waved to him, and he returned my wave and urged on his little filly.

"Gee-up," came his distant shout once more, and his little filly once more started drawing the wooden plow.

This memory came to me all at once—I don't know why—but with amazing clarity of detail. Suddenly I roused myself and sat on the bunk; I recall that a quiet smile of reminiscence still played on my face. I kept on recollecting for yet another minute.

I remembered that when I had come home from Marey I told no one about my "adventure." And what kind of adventure was it anyway? I forgot about Marey very quickly as well. On the rare occasions when I met him later, I never struck up a conversation with him, either about the wolf or anything else, and now, suddenly, twenty years later, in Siberia, I remembered that encounter so vividly, right down to the last detail. That means it had settled unnoticed in my heart, all by itself with no will of mine, and had suddenly come back to me at a time when it was needed; I recalled the tender, maternal smile of a poor serf, the way he crossed me and shook his head: "Well you did take a fright now, didn't you, lad!" And I especially remember his thick finger, soiled with dirt, that he touched quietly and with shy tenderness to my trembling lips. Of course, anyone would try to reassure a child, but here in this solitary encounter something quite different had happened, and had I been his very own son he could not have looked at me with a glance that radiated more pure love, and who had prompted him to do that? He was our own serf, and I was his master's little boy; no one would learn of his kindness to me and reward him for it. Was he, maybe, especially fond of small children? There are much people. Our encounter was solitary, in an open field, and only God, perhaps, looking down saw what deep and enlightened human feeling and what delicate, almost feminine tenderness could fill the heart of a coarse, bestially ignorant Russian serf who at the time did not expect or even dream of his freedom. Now tell me, is this not what Konstantin Aksakov had in mind when he spoke of the advanced level of development of our Russian People?

And so when I climbed down from my bunk and looked around, I remember I suddenly felt I could regard these unfortunates in an entirely different way and that suddenly, through some sort of miracle, the former hatred and anger in my heart had vanished. I went off, peering intently into the faces of those I met. This disgraced peasant, with shaven head and brands on his cheek, drunk and roaring out his hoarse, drunken song—why he might also be that very same Marey; I cannot peer into his heart, after all. That same evening I met M-cki once again. The unfortunate man! He had no recollections of any Mareys and no other view of these people but "Je hais ces brigands!" No, the Poles had to bear more than we did in those days!

ENDNOTES

THE HOUSE OF THE DEAD

1. (p. 24) *"There, poor man, take a farthing, for Christ's sake!"*: According to the letters of Dostoevsky's wife, this is an autobiographical episode; a similar scene appears in *Crime and Punishment* (part 2, chapter 2).

2. (p. 34) *"One will be a Kantonist"*: Kantonists were soldiers' sons brought up in a military settlement and bound to serve in the army (Garnett's note).

3. (p. 69) *Gogol's Jew Yankel in "Taras Bulba"*: "Taras Bulba" (1835), by Russian writer Nikolay Gogol, is a story about the Cossack revolt against the Poles; Yankel, featured in chapters 10 and 11, is largely a negative stereotype of the Jewish people: He is avaricious, dirty, cowardly, willing to do practically anything for money, and so on.

4. (p. 79) *He was a monster; a moral Quasimodo*: Quasimodo is the central character in French writer Victor Hugo's very popular 1831 novel *Notre-Dame de Paris* (*The Hunchback of Notre Dame*); his name became synonymous with physical ugliness and deformity. Dostoevsky wrote a foreword to and published a Russian translation of the novel in the September 1862 issue of *Vremya* (*Time*).

5. (p. 80) *A. was a remarkable artist, almost on a level with Brüllov*: Karl Brüllov (1799–1852) was an artist well known in Russia for his portraits; he gained an international reputation in 1833, when *The Last Day of Pompeii* was exhibited in Italy.

6. (p. 86) *Some people maintain . . . that the purest love for one's neighbour is at the same time the greatest egoism*: This is a reference to the theory of "rational egoism," developed by Russian radical Nikolay Chernyshevsky; he introduced the theory in "The Anthropological Principle in Philosophy" (1860) and used it in his novel *What Is to Be Done?* (1863). Chernyshevsky was influenced by the work of German philosopher Ludwig Feuerbach (1804–1872) and other radical philosophers. Rational egoism essentially argues that an enlightened, reasonable man is fundamentally selfish, never acting against his own best interests, and that he wants to live in a beautiful, harmonious environment. To achieve harmony, it is in man's best interest to be kind and to take care of other people's needs; this way everyone gets what he wants—harmony and a utopia on Earth. However, this is possible only if everyone is enlightened **as** to their own best interests. Dostoevsky strongly disagreed with

431

this idea; his "Notes from Underground" (1864) is an argument against rational egoism.

7. (p. 104) *"I wanted to ask you about Napoleon. He is a relation of the one who was here in 1812, isn't he?"*: Napoléon III (Charles-Louis-Napoléon Bonaparte, 1808–1873) was the nephew of Napoléon I; he was elected president of the Second Republic of France in 1848 and in 1852 proclaimed himself emperor of France, a title he retained until the National Assembly deposed him in 1870.

8. (p. 105) *"Last year I read about the Countess La Vallière. . . . It's written by Dumas"*: Louise de la Vallière (1644–1710), a mistress of King Louis XIV of France, has been immortalized in various literary works: *Louise de la Vallière* (volume 2, or sometimes 3, of Alexandre Dumas's *The Vicomte de Bragelonne* [1848–1850], a continuation of *The Three Musketeers*); and the very popular *La Duchesse de La Vallière* (1804), by Madame Stéphanie-Félicité Genlis, published in Russian translation in 1805 and frequently reprinted.

9. (p. 192) *He was a tall man about thirty, big and fat, with red puffy cheeks, white teeth and with a loud laugh like Nozdryov's*: Nozdryov is a character in Nikolay Gogol's novel *Dead Souls* (1842). In chapter 4 of that novel Gogol writes: "Instantly Nozdryov burst into a laugh compassable only by a healthy man in whose head every tooth still remains as white as sugar. By this I mean the laugh of quivering cheeks, the laugh which causes a neighbour who is sleeping behind double doors three rooms away to leap from his bed."

10. (p. 193) *"the tradition is still fresh though it is hard to believe in it"*: This is a quote from Aleksandr Griboyedov's 1824 satiric play *Woe from Wit* (act 2, scene 2), one of the best-known plays in the Russian language; many of its lines have become proverbs.

11. (p. 201) *there were gentlemen who derived from the power of flogging their victims something that suggests the Marquis de Sade and the Marquise de Brinvilliers*: The Marquis de Sade, or Comte Donatien-Alphonse-François de Sade (1740–1814), was a French writer who argued that since both sexual perversion and criminality exist in nature, they are therefore natural; he was imprisoned frequently for various sexual offences. Sadism—sexual deviation in which cruelty is inflicted in order to attain a sexual release—is named after him. Marie-Madeleine-Marguérite d'Aubray Brinvilliers, or the Marquise de Brinvilliers (c.1630–1676), was a French society woman who poisoned her family and was suspected of perfecting her "potions" on the poor; according to popular accounts she enjoyed watching the suffering of her victims.

12. (p. 227) *with his passion for travelling he might have been another Robinson Crusoe*: Daniel Defoe's novel *The Life and Strange Surprizing Adventures of Robinson Crusoe* (1719), is supposedly based on the experiences of Scottish sailor Alexander Selkirk, who in 1704 requested to be put ashore on an uninhabited island and was rescued five years later.

13. (p. 277) *thirty-five years ago a great mass of exiles of the upper class were sent to Siberia all at once:* In December 1825 there was a mass uprising in Russia against Czar Nicholas I by army officers, most of them nobility, who had fought in the Napoleonic Wars and become influenced by Western democratic ideas. Known as Decembrists, these officers wanted to establish a representative government in Russia. Nicholas crushed the uprising on the first day of his reign, executing five of the leaders, imprisoning twenty-one, and exiling the remainder of the participants to Siberia.

14. (p. 278) *in the recent but so remote past:* Dostoevsky wrote this line for the purpose of passing the censorship. If he hadn't asserted that the atrocities he describes in his work occurred in the past, thus implying that things were now different, the work would have never have been allowed by the censor.

POOR FOLK

1. (p. 305) PRINCE V. F. ODOEVSKY: The epigraph is from the short story "The Living Corpse" (1844), by the Russian writer Vladimir Fiodorovich Odoevsky. Odoevsky was cofounder of the Lovers of Wisdom Society, and a noted writer.

2. (p. 309) *he talks about Homer and Brambeus:* The ancient Greek poet Homer is the reputed author of the epic poems the *Odyssey* and the *Iliad*. Baron Brambeus is a pseudonym of Russian writer Osip Ivanovich Senkovsky (1800–1858), editor of the very popular journal *Biblioteka dlia chteniia* (Library for Reading), whose literary reputation was not of the highest.

3. (p. 318) *There are two of them in the house, Teresa and Faldoni:* Teresa and Faldoni are lovers in Nicholas Germain Léonard's 1783 sentimental novel *Lettres de deux amans habitans de Lyon* (*Letters of Two Lovers Living in Lyon*), published in Russian in 1804. By the 1840s, when *Poor Folk* was published, they had become negative stereotypes of sentimentality.

4. (p. 321) *there's scarcely any night at all now:* In St. Petersburg the end of May is characterized by "white nights," when there are few hours of darkness.

5. (p. 325) *Lomond's grammar:* The reference is to an 1831 Moscow edition of "A Complete French Grammar . . ." by Lomond.

6. (p. 326) *Zapolsky's was very much better:* The reference is to an 1817 Moscow edition of the *New Textbook of the French Language*, edited by V. Zapolsky.

7. (p. 339) *Pushkin's works in the latest, complete edition:* Aleksandr Sergeyevich Pushkin (1799–1837) was Russia's first great writer; the edition referred to here is the eleven-volume St. Petersburg edition (1838–1841), the first posthumously published edition of Pushkin's complete works.

8. (p. 357) *One of Paul de Kock's novels:* Paul de Kock (1793–1871) was a French novelist whose work was considered frivolous and "naughty" by reactionary critics of the 1840s.

9. (p. 359) *Fedora got me a book, Byelkin's Stories:* The reference is to *Tales of Belkin* (1831), by Aleksandr Pushkin; three different editions (in 1831, 1834, and 1838) were published prior to the publication of *Poor Folk*.

10. (p. 363) *I have read* The Picture of Man, *a clever work; I have read* The boy who played funny tunes on the bells *and* The Cranes of Ibicus, *that's all, and I never read anything else:* These three works are meant as examples of passé literary tastes. *The Picture of Man, an Edifying Treatise on Aspects of Self-knowledge for All the Educated Classes* (1834), by Pushkin's former teacher, the psychologist and philosopher-idealist Aleksandr Galich, was most likely read to Dostoevsky as a child by his father during "family reading." "The Boy Who Played Funny Tunes on the Bells" is a reference to François-Guillaume Ducray-Duminil's 1809 novel *Le petit carillonneur* (*The Little Bell-ringer*), translated into Russian in 1810, about a destitute, miserable little boy traveling as a musician who finds his relatives and becomes a count. The 1797 poem "The Cranes of Ibicus" (also spelled Ibycus), by Friedrich Schiller, was translated into Russian in 1813.

11. (p. 363) *I have read* The Stationmaster: "The Stationmaster" is the title of one of Pushkin's Belkin tales (see note 9).

12. (p. 364) *I send you a book: there are all sorts of stories in it; I have read some of them, read the one called* The Cloak: The reference is to the third volume of Nikolay Gogol's *Works* (1843), which contains the first edition of his story "The Cloak" (better known as "The Overcoat"). The story's main character, a poor clerk named Akaky Akakievich, is similar to Dyevushkin. He scrimps and saves for a new overcoat and feels like a new man when he gets it; but the overcoat is soon stolen, and the hero dies. Nineteenth-century critics often discussed Akaky Akakievich and Makar Dyevushkin as the same "type": a poor man destroyed by society.

13. (p. 388) *"you're a Lovelace":* Lovelace is the name of the seducer in English novelist Samuel Richardson's sentimental novel *Clarissa Harlowe* (7 vols., 1747–1748); the book was extremely popular in Russia, where the name Lovelace became synonymous with a great seducer of women.

14. (p. 407) *I read the Bee:* The "reactionary" St. Petersburg newspaper the *Northern Bee* (1825–1864) was described by Gogol as "classic reading" for petty clerks in 1835 in his story "Notes of a Madman."

INSPIRED BY
THE HOUSE OF THE DEAD

MUSIC

Czech composer Leoš Janáček began work on an opera based on *The House of the Dead* in 1927, a year before his death. First staged posthumously in 1930, *From the House of the Dead* consists of vignettes about the broken lives of prisoners in Dostoevsky's novel. In the opera, the prisoners relate their crimes; Janáček contrasts their tormented stories with life-affirming metaphors of freedom: a released bird, a river, and rebirth at Easter. At the beginning of his score, Janáček penned the phrase "In every creature a spark of God," affirming his hope and ultimate faith in life.

Because *From the House of the Dead* was the composer's final work, and because Janáček's material—both textual and musical—seemed thin, the idea emerged that the opera was unfinished. The 1930 premiere of the work was therefore given an erroneous "correction" by Ota Zitek (the producer, who filled out some of the text and stage directions), along with Osvald Chlubna and Břetislav Bakala (pupils of Janáček, who reorchestrated the work). Together they created a finale that was more optimistic than Janáček's original. Not until 1964 was the original ending reinstated as an appendix to the score, and performances have employed this ending ever since. Attempts have been made as well to reinstate Janáček's original orchestrations—a perennial problem with performances of all his operas. Though his disciples attempted to finish and polish *From the House of the Dead*, it is often performed today almost exactly the way Janáček left it upon his death.

VISUAL ARTS

In October 1888, Vincent van Gogh wrote a letter to his sister Wilhelmina in which he mentions an article about Dostoevsky, whom he identifies as the author of *The House of the Dead*. Van Gogh tells his sister that the article has inspired him to complete his large-scale study of a fever clinic. Six months later van Gogh completed *Ward in the Hospital* in *Arles*. In the painting, a long room with bright lilac-green curtains and orange floorboards stretches into the distance; in the foreground, dark figures sit huddled around a black stove, while faceless nuns make the beds. The quiet despair of the patients mirrors the condition of the prisoners in Dostoevsky's camp—and reflects the depressed mental state of van Gogh himself.

While serving three years in a labor camp, Russian artist Leonid Lamm read Dostoevsky's *The House of the Dead* and began making sketches for a work based on the novel. In 1977, upon his release from prison, he began a series of lithographs that he titled *The House of the Dead*. Each of the twenty works corresponds to a chapter in Dostoevsky's novel. The lithographs are characterized by large black patches and unreal, round forms that represent the surreal nature of the camp. Bleak yet strangely energetic, the images connect the sufferings of two prisoners separated by more than one hundred years.

ONE DAY IN THE LIFE OF IVAN DENISOVICH

One of Russia's most gifted writers, Aleksandr Solzhenitsyn, followed in the spirit of Dostoevsky's *The House of the Dead* with the publication in 1962 of *One Day in the Life of Ivan Denisovich*, a fictionalized account of the Stalinist labor camps. Like Dostoevsky, Solzhenitsyn wrote from personal experience. In 1945, while serving as an artillery captain in the Red Army, he was arrested for criticizing Stalin, sentenced to eight years in a labor camp, and then sent into administrative exile. His citizenship was restored in 1956, three years after Stalin's death. *One Day in the Life of Ivan Denisovich* is a brutally honest depiction of camp life, in which men living in extreme conditions are faced with devastating moral dilemmas on an almost daily basis. The work, uncensored by Khrushchev's anti-Stalinist government, catapulted Solzhenitsyn into worldwide celebrity and paved the way for his masterpiece *The Gulag Archipelago* (1973–1975), an epic "history and geography" of the Soviet labor camps.

Solzhenitsyn's popularity at home waned quickly as he proved to be as critical of Khrushchev and the Soviets as he had been of Stalin. His popularity abroad remained strong, however, and he was awarded a Nobel Prize for Literature in 1970 (an honor he refused in order to be allowed to live in Russia). He was expelled from the Soviet Union in 1974, but in 1990 his Soviet citizenship was restored, and he moved back to his native country in 1994. In his Nobel lecture, Solzhenitsyn observed, "Literature transmits incontrovertible condensed experience . . . from generation to generation. In this way literature becomes the living memory of a nation."

COMMENTS & QUESTIONS

In this section, we aim to provide the reader with an array of perspectives on the text, as well as questions that challenge those perspectives. The commentary has been culled from sources as diverse as reviews contemporaneous with the works, letters written by the author, literary criticism of later generations, and appreciations written throughout the works' history. Following the commentary, a series of questions seeks to filter Fyodor Dostoevsky's The House of the Dead and Poor Folk through a variety of points of view and bring about a richer understanding of these enduring works.

COMMENTS

THE NATION

It is interesting, in connection with this translation of Dostoyevsky's famous story, 'Poor Folk,' to recall briefly the circumstances of its first reading. Dostoyevsky, a young man, twenty-three years of age, had completed his course in the Engineers' Institute, and had entered the Government service, like his fellow graduates. His dislike of this occupation led him, at the end of a year, to abandon it. He had no definite reason or plan of life, but was inspired to write 'Poor Folk.' His only literary acquaintance was Grigorovitch, who had published but one article at that time; and to him he gave his manuscript, that it might be shown to the poet Nekrasoff, who was making arrangements to print a periodical. Having given Grigorovitch his story, he spent the night with several friends rereading Gogol's 'Dead Souls.' It was the custom of the period for students to read and reread Gogol for the dozenth time whenever two or three chanced to meet of an evening. Returning home at four o'clock in the morning, in the brilliant daylight of a "white night" in June, Dostoyevsky sat down by his window, instead of going to bed, and was speedily summoned to the door by the ringing of the bell. Grigorovitch and Nekrasoff, unable to restrain their enthusiasm, had come to congratulate him on his work. Having begun with the idea that the perusal of ten pages would enable them to reach an opinion, they had been led on by interest and emotion to read the whole book aloud, and had taken turns as the voices of each failed. Nekrasoff's voice, they told him, had broken twice with uncontrollable feeling, as he read the description of the poor student's funeral. The next day Nekrasoff announced to the celebrated critic Byelinsky that "a new Gogol" had arisen. "Your Gogols spring up like mushrooms!" retorted Byelinsky; but by the evening, after reading the story, he was as much excited as Nekrasoff, and demanded that the new author be brought to him at once. 'Poor Folk' was published the next year, 1846.

—September 6, 1894

HENRY JAMES

Tolstoi and D[ostoieffsky] are fluid pudding, though not tasteless, because the amount of their own minds and souls in solution in the broth gives it savour and flavour, thanks to the strong, rank quality of their genius and their experience. But there are all sorts of things to be said of them, and in particular that we see how great a vice is their lack of composition, their defiance of economy and architecture, directly they are emulated and imitated; then, as subjects of emulation, models, they quite give themselves away. There is nothing so deplorable as a work of art with a leak in its interest; and there is no such leak of interest as through commonness of form.

—from a letter to Hugh Walpole (May 19, 1912)

PRINCE PYOTR ALEKSEYEVICH KROPOTKIN

The Memoirs from a Dead-House is the only production of Dostoyévkiy which can be recognized as truly artistic: its leading idea is beautiful, and the form is worked out in conformity with the idea; but in his later productions the author is so much oppressed by his ideas, all very vague, and grows so nervously excited over them that he cannot find the proper form.

—from Ideals and Realities in Russian Literature (1915)

NEW YORK TIMES BOOK REVIEW

In one sense, "The House of the Dead" is a less important work than "Crime and Punishment" or "The Brothers Karamazov"; in another sense it is even more important. For, though in itself rather a fragment of autobiography than a novel, relating as it does in terrible and dispassionate detail the story of four years' prison service in

Siberia, it does much to explain the obscurities and incongruities of the novels. We have most of us wondered at Dostoevsky's tender-hearted murderers, marveled how such bad people could possibly be so good and such good people so extraordinarily bad, and finally concluded that the Russian character must be very, very different from ours. In "The House of the Dead" we are brought down to bed rock, as it were; past the differences in the social strata, past even the fissures that divide race from race, down to the common humanity which, for some reason, reveals in misery, rather than in prosperity and happiness, its basic oneness. And having once realized the Russian character at its lowest terms as not intrinsically different from our own, we are able to build up again, in a way, to the strange, emotional, half-devil, half-angel souls that throng the pages of the novels, with a better understanding of them and a closer sympathy. To any reader who is inclined to make a study of Dostoevsky we should recommend a reading of "The House of the Dead" first of all, and a frequent reference back to it afterward, for in it is to be found the germ of all his later work.

—May 9, 1915

WILLIAM LYON PHELPS

To American readers for whom Dostoevski is yet but a name—and this would include a majority of American college professors,—I would suggest that they begin with "The House of the Dead." This is veridical history, in the diaphanous disguise of fiction; Dostoevski, as everyone does not but ought to know, spent nearly four years in a Siberian prison, where his daily companions were shameless criminals. This is the most normal book he ever wrote, just as Andreev's most cheerful novel is "The Seven Who Were Hanged." Fortunate indeed it was for us that so delicately minded and sensitively organized a man should have had to live with such folk; for his account of the environment has the double value that comes from experience and aloofness. If there were such a place as hell, and one could serve a limited term there, I had rather have, let us say, Nathaniel Hawthorne's account of it than Jack London's; that is, I should like to have someone tell me about it who I feel does not really belong there.

—from *Yale Review* (January 1916)

GEORGE W. THORN

The first and perhaps the deepest impression made by Dostoevsky's works is of the existence of intense and widespread suffering. In this respect his first book, Poor Folk, strikes the keynote of all his writing. In one of the letters which compose that story the pitiful "hero" tells of the poverty and suffering of some people lodging in the same house, and in the course of his letter he says: "One evening when I chanced to be passing the door of the room and all was quiet in the house, I heard through the door a sob, and then a whisper, and then another sob, as though somebody within were weeping with such subdued bitterness that it tore my heart to hear the sound." It is the sound of that sobbing with subdued bitterness behind the door that we always hear as we read Dostoevsky. Russia seems to be full of it. And yet, for the most part, there is no sign of rebellion; all is borne with pathetic resignation. Dievushkin, the poor clerk already referred to, believes that our lots in life are apportioned by the Almighty according to our desserts, and when doubts suggest themselves as to the justice of a scheme of things which allows such suffering as his he fears lest he should be guilty of "freethought." It is Dostoevsky's own attitude. Those who rebel against the suffering are the sceptics and atheists; his refuge was in the thought expressed to him by a young soldier when he was in prison awaiting trial. "Do you find it very tiring?" whispered this man through the peephole of his cell door, "Suffer in patience: Christ also suffered."

—from Contemporary Review (June 1918)

NEW YORK TIMES BOOK REVIEW

If Chekhov's picture of Russia is a cross-section under the microscope of the scientist, that of Dostoevsky is, as it were, a chunk of her bleeding, quivering flesh, torn off nearest the heart.

—February 16, 1919

QUESTIONS

1. People sometimes use the word "Dostoevskian" to describe a certain situation or sensibility. On the basis of The House of the Dead and Poor Folk, can you describe a situation or sensibility that seems particular to Dostoevsky?

2. Do you find Dostoevsky's Christianity intrusive, an imposed value of the author? Or does it seem inherent in the material, somehow there in what is depicted?

3. Do Dostoevsky's prisoners seem to you true to life, or do they seem distorted by Dostoevsky in certain directions and exaggerated in certain characteristics in order to make a point?

4. In Dostoevsky's fiction, guilt often drives characters to strange and destructive thoughts and actions. Describe the consequences of guilt in Poor Folk. Are the consequences credible? Are they just?

5. From what you have observed and read, would Dostoevsky's depiction of the poor, of an oppressed underclass, apply here and now? If Dostoevsky were writing today, who would his "poor folk" be?

FOR FURTHER READING

THE HOUSE OF THE DEAD

Dostoevsky, Fyodor. *A Writer's Diary*. Vol. 1, 1873–1876; vol. 2, 1877–1881. Translated by Kenneth Lantz. Evanston, IL: Northwestern University Press, 1993–1994. A collection of short works—autobiography, semifictional sketches, journalism, and a few short stories—that appeared under this title, which was first a column in a weekly periodical and later a journal written entirely by Dostoevsky.

Frank, Joseph. "Dostoevsky: *The House of the Dead*." *Sewanee Review* 74 (1966), pp. 779–803.

Frank, Joseph. *Dostoevsky: The Years of Ordeal, 1850–1859*. Princeton, NJ: Princeton University Press, 1983. Chapters 6–11 deal with *The House of the Dead* primarily from a biographical point of view.

————. *Dostoevsky: The Stir of Liberation, 1860–1865*. Princeton, NJ: Princeton University Press, 1986. Chapter 15 discusses *The House of the Dead* from a literary point of view.

Jackson, Robert Louis. *The Art of Dostoevsky: Deliriums and Nocturnes*. Princeton, NJ: Princeton University Press, 1981. Chapters 1–5 contain penetrating discussions of various aspects of *The House of the Dead*.

————. "The Triple Vision: 'The Peasant Marey.' " In *Critical Essays on Dostoevsky*, edited by Robin Feuer Miller. Boston: G. K. Hall, 1986, pp. 177–188.

Jones, John. *Dostoevsky*. Oxford: Oxford University Press, 1983. Chapter 4 deals with *The House of the Dead*.

Mochulsky, Konstantin. *Dostoevsky: His Life and Work*. Translated by Michael A. Minihan. Princeton, NJ: Princeton University Press, 1967. The best one-volume biography of Dostoevsky; chapter 9 is an excellent introduction to *The House of the Dead*.

Rosenshield, Gary. "Akulka: The Incarnation of the Ideal in Dostoevski's *Notes from the House of the Dead*." *Slavic and East European Journal* 31

(1987), pp. 10–19. Views this character as an image of Dostoevsky's Christian ideal.

―――. "Isai Fomich Bumshtein: The Representation of the Jew in
Dostoevsky's Major Fiction." *Russian Review* 43 (1984), pp. 261–276.
A careful analysis of Dostoevsky's handling of Jewish characters in
The House of the Dead and later works.

POOR FOLK

Belknap, Robert L. "The Didactic Plot: The Lesson about Suffering in
Poor Folk." In *Critical Essays on Dostoevsky*, edited by Robin Feuer Miller.
Boston: G. K. Hall, 1986, pp. 30–39. Stimulating analysis to show
that Dostoevsky did not always value suffering simply for its own
sake.

Fanger, Donald. *Dostoevsky and Romantic Realism: A Study of Dostoevsky in Relation to Balzac, Dickens, and Gogol.* Cambridge, MA: Harvard University
Press, 1965. A penetrating study of Dostoevsky's links with the Romantic tradition.

Frank, Joseph. *Dostoevsky: The Seeds of Revolt, 1821–1849.* Princeton, NJ:
Princeton University Press, 1976. Chapter 11 contains a lengthier
discussion of *Poor Folk* than is given in the introduction to this
volume.

Jones, John. *Dostoevsky.* Oxford: Oxford University Press, 1983. Jones
stresses the relation of *Poor Folk* to contemporary writers who dis-
orient the reader and downplays Dostoevsky's historical context.

Leatherbarrow, W. J. "The Rag with Ambition: The Problem of Self-
Will in Dostoevsky's *Bednye Lyudi* and *Dvoinik.*" *Modern Language Review*
68 (1973), pp. 607–618. Discussion of how the inner conflict in
Poor Folk foreshadows that of later characters.

Mochulsky, Konstantin. *Dostoevsky: His Life and Work.* Translated by
Michael A. Minihan. Princeton, NJ: Princeton University Press,
1967. Chapter 2 is an informative study of *Poor Folk.*

Neuhauser, Rudolf. "Re-Reading Poor Folk and The Double." *International Dostoevsky Society Bulletin* 6 (1976), pp. 29–32.

Terras, Victor. *The Young Dostoevsky (1846–1849): A Critical Study.* The Hague
and Paris: Mouton, 1969. Chapters 1–3. There is no special section
on *Poor Folk*, but the author informatively analyzes the work from
various points of view.